Signs of Fire

GW00691906

Jorge de Sena

SIGNS OF FIRE

translated by
JOHN BYRNE

CARCANET

in association with
CALOUSTE GULBENKIAN FOUNDATION
INSTITUTO CAMÕES
INSTITUTO PORTUGUÊS DO LIVRO E DAS
BIBLIOTECAS

Sinais de Fogo by Jorge de Sena
was first published by Edições Asa in Portugal in 1979
This translation first published in Great Britain in 1999
by Carcanet Press Ltd
Conavon Court, 12–16 Blackfriars Street
Manchester M3 5BQ

This translation © 1999 John Byrne

The right of John Byrne
to be identified as the translator of this work
has been asserted by him in accordance with the
Copyright, Designs and Patents Acts of 1988
All rights reserved

This book belongs to the series *From the Portuguese*
published in Great Britain by Carcanet Press
in association with the Calouste Gulbenkian Foundation (UK),
with support from Instituto Português do Livro
e das Bibliotecas and Instituto Camões,
and with the collaboration of The Portuguese Arts Trust

A CIP catalogue record for this book
is available from the British Library

ISBN 1 85754 385 8

The publisher acknowledges financial assistance
from the Arts Council of England

Set in 11/12pt Bembo
by XL Publishing Services, Lurley, Tiverton, Devon
Printed and bound in Great Britain
by Short Run Press, Exeter

I

Ramon Berenguer de Cabanelas y Puigmal was already a celebrated figure by the time our two classes were merged and we became classmates in the sixth year of grammar school. His calm, dreamy singularity; the air of mastery, the adult mystery which surrounded his small, athletic figure; his profound conviction that, since the twelfth or thirteenth century, Spain had owed his family the title of the counts of Barcelona, the preposterous questions, posed with the most assured, the most ingenuous air in the world – which made him the terror of any teacher who wasn't altogether sure of himself – together with his famous system of philosophy, which explained everything and allowed him, 'thanks to its control of energies of the brain', to miss classes (except in the most extreme cases): all this made him not so much an idol or a leader, but the most respected of beings, notwithstanding the mockery with which everybody pointed him out. Once, in a philosophy lesson (the teacher was some poor chap, a byword on account of the state of mental decline into which he had fallen, and to whom, one day, in the indisciplined pandemonium of these classes, we demonstrated the argument of Diogenes by sitting on all our briefcases and dragging them, to the four corners of the room), Don Ramon got up, objecting that all living things had souls, which, according to the rules of science, was a rule and not merely a controversial point of philosophical speculation. The silence was pregnant with repressed laughter. And the teacher, bending over his desk with his drooping, sallow moustaches, asked him: 'Which rules of science?'

And he, half opening his narrow lips in that way of his, by which one never knew whether he was smiling or pursing them in annoyance, said: 'Observation and experiment.'

'Very well then, and how have you managed to observe and experiment on the souls of animals?'

'How, sir? Personally.' There was a murmur of laughter; he remained quite calm.

'Personally?' repeated the teacher.

'Yes, sir: while photographing the death of a grasshopper.' There was more laughter.

'A grasshopper? And what was the purpose of the photograph?' asked the teacher as if aroused from his customary torpor.

'The photograph, sir, was taken by one of my brothers while I killed the grasshopper, but in such a way that its soul could be seen passing from its body. In it you can clearly see its soul going up to heaven.'

'The grasshopper's soul,' we all repeated, between fits of laughter, 'the grasshopper's soul.'

And he too, gazing over the tops of our heads, repeated: 'Yes, the soul of the grasshopper going up to heaven.'

The teacher laughed too in a way that we had never seen him do before: 'This is very good, Mr Puigmal, very good. Going up to heaven, eh? Ha, ha, ha. And how did it go up?'

'In a spiral, sir.' There was a babble of laughter.

He raised his hand to beg for silence; his face clouded over, he looked crestfallen. 'Excuse me, I am mistaken,' he said. Everyone was on tenterhooks in the silence which followed; surely, in a moment of high drama, he was going to own up to his joke. 'I was wrong, I made a mistake: it wasn't a spiral but a helix,' he said and sat down to the sound of uneasy laughter.

The teacher quite lost his temper: 'And where is this photo? Have you got it with you? You have? Very well, let me have it.'

Puigmal got up in a very dignified fashion: 'I do indeed have it, sir, but there is no law which obliges a scientist to reveal his researches while these are still going on.'

We looked from one to the other.

'There isn't, isn't there? I am in charge here. I. Do you hear? I.' We had never seen him like this.

'I cannot, I must not, because these experiments are not just mine but my brother's as well.'

'They aren't yours, eh? Of course they aren't yours; you are an impostor.'

'Sir, you are insulting me needlessly. But every scientist always expects to be a martyr in due course. I beg your permission to leave.'

By now you could have heard a pin drop.

'You beg my permission? You beg my permission? It is I who order you to get out; I'm telling you. Get out, take yourself hence!'

Ramon straightened his clothes, picked up his bag, moved along the rows of desks and when he reached the door turned round: 'Sir, you have done me an injustice. Together with my brother I have photographed the soul of a grasshopper. But that was merely by way of a document – because I saw it.' And opening the door gently, he left.

Some of us wanted to laugh; everyone was baffled. But that was nothing to our astonishment upon seeing that our teacher was crying: 'Woe, oh woe!... And if I had done the same with Alcinha, when she was dying, who knows, who knows...'

Alcinha was his daughter, as everyone knew, who had died young, in her teens, and about whom, in his worst moments, he sometimes rambled on in class. Fortunately the bell rang to put us out of our embarrassment. We ran out into the yard where Puigmal was walking up and down, his hands clasped behind his back. Opinions were divided: he had gone too far in the joke, he was serious, or he wasn't... We formed a circle around him. And Mesquita who was always chosen as the class representative, on account of his amorous adventures – he had a lover who was a married woman, nor was she the first, by any means – planted himself firmly in front of him and asked: 'Puigmal, this business of the grasshopper ... were you making it up just to take the mickey out of the poor chap?'

He raised his clear, impassive eyes in his square, expressionless face. 'I saw it,' he repeated.

'You saw it...' said Mesquita.

'I didn't see it exactly. But the soul of the grasshopper, yes that I saw.'

Mesquita raised his hand as if to say that what the other had done to old Torres he wasn't going to do to him; but then he lowered it again, perhaps thinking that one of Puigmal's talents was to fight and that he would be needlessly risking his authority in public.

'You swear that this story is true?' Mesquita said.

'Of course I swear it, in any way you wish. And it's what I will tell the rector if he calls me. But he won't call because Torres isn't going to tell him about me.'

The air of expectation petered out in the argument about whether the teacher would tell or not. Then the bell rang to call us to the next class, the last of the afternoon. Mesquita and I used to go home together, living close by as we did; I was a kind of recipient of the tales of his prowess. Puigmal, too, went in the same direction, though he lived much further from the school than us. There had never existed between him and us the kind of closeness which would allow us to walk all three together, perhaps because in the playground he used to put on airs, affecting an experienced superiority whenever Mesquita alluded, not boastfully but rather with a skilful reticence, to his amorous adventures. On that day the soul of the grasshopper brought us closer to him; our friendship dated from that moment.

From the first it was not an easy friendship; frankly I don't believe that it ever was. But we put up with his displeasure, the stuff about the counts of Barcelona, the soul of the grasshopper, the mystification, in exchange for a beguiling fellow-feeling which in the end, without our really being aware of it, shone out of him, in a mixture of childish joy and faintly ridiculous gravity, lighting up his square, vague features whenever he expatiated about whatever came into his head. We were already sufficiently mature in spirit to understand just how little of what he was saying had any solid base in fact, or was the product of the least scholarship. But, little by little, we discovered that neither was there the least falsehood in what he had worked out or dreamed up and – what comes to the same thing – that he was living in a world of his own, on which the ideas of others did not impinge and in which whatever he conjured up was just as valid as anything a Newton might come up with. And this certainty, which dispensed with the need to bother with demonstrations of the theorems, or to read any literary work (because whenever he got round to it, he was going to compose the definitive book which could not in any way be influenced beforehand by the style of anyone else), and which did not allow us any glimpse of his life (because a man, in order to be man, could only tell these things to his familiar spirit), if it was at first extremely irritating, it began to lose in time its artfulness and, with use, its power to wound us, something from which, we came to see, he derived an innocent pleasure. And so we no longer found odd the pedantic tone with which he would reveal, condescendingly, things which we, the two of us, had already studied.

We would study in turn in my house or in Mesquita's. Puigmal's house was like a sanctuary from which, with a fastidious reserve, he kept us away. Mesquita, through I don't know what kind of coincidence, knew his family: his father, mother and older brother. Sometimes, talking to me about them, he showed his inability to understand that reserve, which nothing in his experience seemed to justify. They were people like any other, friendly, kind even, who lived good lives; they had nothing to hide. And nothing would be more natural than that his friends would go to his house to study, in the same way that he came to our houses, but he always deflected any suggestions about such a one-sided sharing. And there was no way round such obduracy.

One day Puigmal missed school; the next day, too. On our way back from school in the afternoon Mesquita and I had the idea that he might be sick and that the best thing would be to phone to find out. In those days telephones were rare enough but both Mesquita and Puigmal had them.

'Perhaps we could go and see him,' I suggested.

Mesquita looked sideways at me and smiled; off we went.

We stopped in front of the building, on the Avenue; for its time, it was huge with an imposing, gloomy entrance.

Mesquita gazed at the windows in which the setting sun was reflected. 'What if he is angry with us?' he said. 'Wouldn't it be better to phone first, in any case?'

'Let's risk it,' I said. 'If he says he doesn't want anyone to visit him, when will we ever get another chance like this?'

We went in and up the stairs to the first floor where he lived; we hesitated in the dark, staring at the gilt bell on the door.

Now I was the one who held back. Mesquita rang the bell. The silence deepened around us in the shadows; the mustiness mingled with the smell of wax and the rush stair carpet. 'Shall we ring again?' I asked.

'Wait,' and we both glued our heads to the door. Not a sound. It seemed that nobody was at home. I rang and the bell echoed emptily. Nothing.

'Maybe nobody's there; perhaps they've all gone off to their country house,' suggested Mesquita. We knew about the country house that Ramon's father had just bought on the outskirts of Lisbon from various hints of his and, there in the dark, I could see again the images he had evoked: an old, low house, tucked away among the trees on the side of a hill, far from anywhere, with its abandoned cellars, stuffed with straw, creaking doors, the three or four lights above the table which barely served to chase away the damp shadows lingering in the corners of the room.

'Let's be off,' said Mesquita. 'They've all gone away. That's why he missed school.'

We had set off down the stairs as far as the landing when the light came on. We paused, turning back. The door half opened and Puigmal's head peeped out. 'What is it you want?' he said in that anxious, peevish voice of his.

'You've been absent for a couple of days ... we thought that you might be ill and we came to see you,' I replied.

'Hmm ... but I'm not ill,' and his head disappeared for a few moments while he looked inside before returning.

'Very well,' said Mesquita. 'If you're not ill we'll be on our way.'

'While you're here you might as well come up,' he said, opening the door.

We went up and in. The corridor was enormous, with doors along one side and another at the end. But it was a room on the left of the door into which he led us. It was a large room, curiously empty, with balcony windows out onto the avenue; there were two of those very high, antique desks up against the wall, the sort where one wrote standing up, in great ledgers. Following Puigmal, who had closed the door and gone ahead of us, we went into an adjoining room, which was also lit by a naked bulb hanging from the ceiling. He stopped behind a small desk close to the window and told us to sit down; he himself sat down, his hands joined and resting on the desk, like someone who had granted us an audience.

We sat down in chairs which were, except for a small armchair and a bookcase with glazed doors and yellow curtains, the only furniture in the small study other than his desk and chair. The same musty smell, mixed with wax and stair carpet, prevailed here too, as if it were a house which, after it had been swept and polished, had been closed up and uninhabited for a long time.

'Since you didn't show up at school for two days, yesterday and today, and you hadn't told us you were going to your country house,' said Mesquita, 'we thought you must be ill and came to see you.'

'You could have phoned.'

'I suppose we could,' said Mesquita; a strained silence ensued.

'My parents went to the farm, with the servants,' Puigmal explained finally, in solemn fashion, 'but my brother and I stayed here on account of school.'

Mesquita and I glanced at each other, puzzled.

'But we took advantage of the situation to do some experiments.'

I do believe that neither of us could contain a smile as we remembered the soul of the grasshopper. Puigmal saw and added: 'Not those; different experiments.'

'So where is your brother, then?' I asked, who had never met him but knew that he was a medical student.

'He's here in the house, just doing what he has to to finish an experiment.'

'Ah,' said Mesquita, who already knew the brother, 'So it's a medical experiment I suppose?'

'Not exactly. More precisely it's to do with anatomy, and physiology, too,' he said, smiling enigmatically, maliciously.

Mesquita's eyes lit up: 'Ah, so *that's* what you've been doing, then. And at home … alone?'

'*That* is a long story…' And Puigmal leaned back, indolently, in that way he had when he wanted to hint at another world of discreet pleasures.

'Tell us,' said I, hoping for another of those stories in which one could barely distinguish truth from fiction.

'It's quite simple,' he began. 'We really did stay behind on account of school. Our parents do go away from time to time; they do it so that we can fend for ourselves, on our own.' (The country house was a recent purchase and previously he had always spoken of his father as someone who travelled a great deal on business, always alone.) 'And in fact we coped quite well. Do you remember that I told you,' he said, turning to Mesquita, 'that story of our neighbours at the back? The two sisters who live in this block right here at the back?' (Mesquita nodded, but I recollected too a similar story about one of Mesquita's own great adventures: about how he had been the lover of some woman who lived in a building which backed onto his garden and how he had, at night while everyone was in bed, gone to her house, scaling the wall and going up the back staircase, all the while in his pyjamas, and how once the husband had come back unexpectedly from some trip and he had had to spend hours in the cold, completely naked, hidden in the stairwell, unable to jump back over the wall because the husband up above was keeping a lookout and shouting that he would kill the fellow whose pyjamas they were, that they weren't his, while his wife wailed that they were his, they truly were, and that she always slept with them when he was away … and that the whole neighbourhood could hear him…)

'Well, this is the story,' continued Puigmal. 'We could only carry on our affair by sending signals. And then yesterday and today, since we were alone in the house, they set off for a stroll around the block and then popped over here to study with us.'

'So they're in there now?' asked Mesquita. 'Shall we interrupt the lesson?'

'They are. But this afternoon's lesson must have already finished; it's well past the hour they should be at home. The worst of it is, with you here they must be afraid of coming out,' and so saying he got up and went into the next room, leaving us alone.

'Do you believe all this?' I asked.

'No,' replied Mesquita, 'but hold on for a moment while I see if I can catch him out.'

We both fell silent and it was not long before we heard in the corridor the sound of muffled steps, the murmur of voices and the opening and shutting of a door.

Ramon returned with his brother, who was the very spit and image of him, following close behind; the latter was like a replica, only larger and older (although the difference in ages between them was but one or two years). He introduced himself to me and greeted Mesquita, whom he already knew, effusively, after having, with a stiff formality which was almost Prussian, bowed briefly towards me.

We were all standing up: 'Well then,' said Mesquita, 'what with yesterday and today, you've had no respite from deflowering virgins.'

'Virgins?' repeated Ramon's brother, looking at us both, first one then the other.

'Were they not virgins?' he persisted. 'After all, it was just a matter of routine.'

'They were, and still are, virgins,' said Ramon.

'Ah, well, so you've been teaching them to play bisque, eh?' asked Mesquita. 'Or was it just a matter of a few hugs and kisses?'

'Neither one nor the other,' replied Ramon's brother dryly. 'We were merely conducting experiments on the elasticity of maidenheads.'

'But how interesting!' exclaimed Mesquita. 'Then you were but skirting the edge of the lake...'

'Strictly speaking, no,' said Ramon. 'We were trying out a new product, one from our own factory, which has this effect.'

Mesquita burst out laughing. 'What a terrific idea! The worst of it would be if the elasticity did not stretch to anything large!'

The two brothers were scandalised: 'It is perfectly adequate for normal sizes,' the elder retorted. 'Do you want to see?'

'The size? No, thank you. But this product, certainly.'

The student of medicine went out. 'You think this is just some story, don't you?' said Ramon, 'but you'll be astonished.'

The other returned and presented us with a little tin can which he opened. It contained a clear, perfumed cream. Mesquita took hold of the tin, held it to his eyes, to his nose and smeared some cream on his finger. 'This is vaseline, perfumed vaseline.'

'It is?' said the other. 'Observe.' And he went to the bookcase, fetched a small piece of silk paper, put it on top of the desk and, taking the tin from Mesquita, smeared it over part of the paper. Then, stretching out the paper tightly, he said: 'Put your finger through it.'

Mesquita stiffened his finger and pushed it hard against the paper which gave but did not break.

'You see?' said Ramon.

'This isn't silk paper,' said Mesquita.

'It certainly is silk paper, but this,' said Ramon's brother, brandishing the tin, 'is certainly not vaseline.'

Mesquita was intrigued: 'And how do you apply this stuff, for it to work?'

'With a finger; and you can apply some to yourself as well.'

'So you've been trying out this stuff with those girls?' I asked.

'Of course,' replied Ramon's brother. 'You realise that we couldn't do this with prostitutes.'

We all laughed together. Then the would-be doctor, glancing at his wrist watch, said: 'Do excuse me, I must be going.'

'You'll have to give me some of this stuff so that I can try it out for myself,' said Mesquita.

'You're welcome to this tin,' said the brother, leaving.

Ramon went back behind the desk while Mesquita closed the tin which he had just been sniffing and put it in his pocket.

We heard a knock at the door. 'Do sit down,' said Ramon, 'and stay a little longer.'

We sat down; I looked outside. Night had already fallen.

'Mesquita,' said I, 'I think it's about time we were going, too.'

He looked at his watch and nodded: 'It is indeed. Let's go; this has already made my day,' he said, winking at me.

'It's only half past six,' said Ramon, 'the nights still get dark quite early. But if you care to wait just ten more minutes you might see something you've never seen before.'

'Another cream like this? Or a portrait of the soul of the grasshopper?' asked Mesquita.

Ramon opened a drawer in the desk, pulled out a folder of papers, fiddled around in them and held up to us a photograph which I grabbed. It showed a penknife cutting off the head of a grasshopper, and above it, quite clearly, another grasshopper in flight. I passed the picture to Mesquita. 'These are two photos,' he said, 'one superimposed on top of the other.'

'That's right,' said Ramon, 'because they weren't taken at the same time. But they both show the same incident.'

'As far as the elastic cream you gave me goes, that's fair enough,' said Mesquita. 'But as for this story, no.'

'I'll tell you another. I'll only keep you another five or six minutes,' said Ramon, looking at his watch. 'Just think, my uncle died in this house, years ago. That was his bookcase.' We turned around to stare at the yellowing curtains behind the glass. 'Every afternoon, at the same time, when he returned from his stroll he went to the bookcase and took out a book. Now, there isn't a single book of his in the bookcase. But still, at the same time, the door of the bookcase opens and shuts. Do you want to see? In about four or five minutes.' I felt a cold shiver and looked at Mesquita. He sat with one leg tucked up beneath him, the other dangling insouciantly and his eyes lowered.

'The most curious thing is that my uncle,' said Ramon, 'was a free-thinker, who scoffed at everything and didn't believe in anything, much less in spirits. But the fact is that every day, even on Sundays, he comes to fetch a book from the bookcase. You'll see.'

We remained there, motionless, not saying a word, our eyes fixed on the bookcase.

'The time has almost passed,' said Ramon. 'Perhaps today he's not coming.'

There was a crack, and the door of the bookcase opened outwards, stopped and then slowly swung back.

I felt a chill and a fearful impulse to run away. 'Did you see it?' asked Ramon.

'How did you manage to pull this one off, you rascal?' exclaimed Mesquita. And getting up, he went to the bookcase which he opened, repeatedly opening and closing it to see how it worked. Then he squatted down and poked about on the bare floorboards, crawling over towards the desk, where he continued to examine the floor with his hands. Next he raised himself slightly and squinted at the lid of the desk, his eyes level with it. He got to his feet alongside Puigmal and grabbed him by the collar of his jacket. 'I don't believe this,' he went on. 'How did you manage to make the door open and shut?'

He, with a deft movement, freed himself from Mesquita's grasp and looked up. 'I didn't do anything. It wasn't I who opened and closed that door,' he said, his eyebrows arched.

'Who was it then?' I asked.

'My uncle. I've already told you,' replied Ramon.

Mesquita headed for the door: 'Come on, let's go before the house comes tumbling down and he tells us it was his grandmother who did it.'

Puigmal got up. 'I won't insist on your remaining any longer,' he said. 'It's already late. And as far as my grandmother, who is already dead, is concerned she moved to our country house the moment we bought it. Besides, it was to satisfy a dream of hers to have a country house, that my father bought it.'

'What about your grandfather?' asked Mesquita calmly. 'You've never mentioned him.'

'I've never talked about him because most people don't believe in these things. It was just that with your being here at the time when the bookcase door opened I had to tell you. We're talking about my paternal grandparents. My grandfather stayed in Barcelona.'

'Scheming to regain his title?' asked Mesquita.

'Precisely. He was never out of the provincial registry, always asking for deeds or conducting searches.'

'And what about you two, with all your family here in the house, even though you can't see them?' I asked. 'Are you ashamed to be conducting these experiments for elasticity in front of them? They could even be in the same room with you, couldn't they?'

'In the first place there is absolutely no need for shame since they have ceased to have those physical and moral constraints from which we suffer. And secondly, for as long as they are not summoned, the spirits remain dormant, requiring only the place where they have chosen to manifest themselves; in the case of my uncle, the door.'

We were in the corridor, next to the front door.

'Very well then, good night,' said Mesquita and we set off down the stairs.

When we reached the landing he called us and we stopped under the strong light illuminating the rich, wide staircase. Puigmal, throwing open the door, came out and quickly down the flight of stairs with athletic strides.

'Look, Mesquita, that stuff in the tin … it's not exactly what we said it was. It's a sample of a skin cream we were experimenting with. You can put it on; it might even do some good. And it makes things easier, of course.'

Mesquita took the tin out of his pocket; the metal shone. 'It would be better if you kept it,' he said. 'You might need it.'

'No, no, we won't. Keep it.'

'And your neighbours,' I asked, 'are they really your neighbours?'

'They are,' said Puigmal coming closer, 'but if you promise to keep it a secret I'll tell you the truth.' He paused dramatically. 'It wasn't they who were here just now, they were here much earlier. The fellows who were here, they were from Catalonia.'

'On account of this count business, I suppose?' said Mesquita.

'Yes. An uprising is imminent in Catalonia. But don't tell anyone because they are anarchists and quite capable of murdering the lot of us if the plot should fail because of our carelessness.'

'And are these anarchists going to install you as princes?' I asked.

'No, but at least our interests coincide in the matter of separatism.'

'And what if they proclaim a Catalan republic before you get there?'

'That is exactly the settlement we were discussing today.'

'What about your father?' asked Mesquita. 'Isn't he in on all this?'

'My father has abdicated in favour of my brother, which is why he left for the country yesterday.'

I couldn't hold back: 'He's gone into exile?'

He was unruffled: 'Exile? That wouldn't make any sense. He merely kept out of the way to facilitate the negotiations. Good night. I shall be back at school tomorrow.' And he climbed the stairs, went into the house and closed the door behind him.

We went out into the street and walked along for a long time in silence.

'They're stark, raving mad,' I said when we were already a long way from the house.

'Maybe,' replied Mesquita, taking from his pocket the tin which he had kept. We stopped under a street lamp, examining the object by its light. 'I'm going to have to ask my father to have it analysed.'

In addition to an astonishing collection of pornographic books his father also had a laboratory. But suddenly Mesquita changed his mind and hurled the tin into the gutter. 'The best thing is to get rid of this rubbish – we don't even know what it is.'

'But if your father analysed it then we would at least know, wouldn't we?'

'Know what?'

On reflection I realised he was right. What would we know? That it wasn't skin cream? It could be the unction essential to the conquest of the Catalan throne... Or even capable of bestowing elasticity on membranes, on organic material...

II

For a long time Mesquita and I never spoke to each other of our adventures on that day; and to Puigmal even less. However his behaviour had changed greatly and he curbed the worst of his affectations. I don't know whether it was for our sake but in school he had become almost invisible; it wasn't that he missed many classes, rather that he didn't get mixed up in things in that way of his, making things up as he went along, nor did he make it a point to show off his intellect; he had, too, given up putting on that air of false modesty with which, as we have seen, out in the schoolyard, he would take himself off, lost in thought and detached from the rest of us. He studied with us, as before; but in our houses he refrained from wasting our time with those ponderously argued enquiries of his, designed to demonstrate the obvious. He was the same old Puigmal still in that he refused to read books and listened to our discussions while gazing at the ceiling, apparently much abstracted, tucked up on the sofa, but attentive nevertheless, as if pondering some pertinent interruption, which he would sometimes make. It was then that we began again to observe his singular ways; having got used to them, we had forgotten just how odd they were.

The end of the school year, which would be our last at school, was fast approaching, together with our final exams. When we left school, however, we would not be going our separate ways because all three of us wanted to study at the Faculty of Science. In spite of all the fears with which our finals and, even more, the entrance exam to the Faculty filled us, we were already looking forward to the prospect of being undergraduates, with all the independence that this implied: lectures one didn't have to attend, subjects which, each year, would be more or less the ones we had chosen ... And it was not so much the idea of the career we wished to follow which inspired us but rather freedom, this famous, lofty freedom. One afternoon, in Mesquita's house, our conversation turned however to more concrete ideas of the future. And Puigmal, rambling on, declared that as far as he was concerned the Faculty of Science was no more than a short cut in his preparations to enter the Army College.

This declaration nearly caused us to jump out of our skins. A military career had never entered our thoughts and he had often even gone so far as to cultivate an ironic anti-military pose, saying that the army was a period of idleness subsidised by the state, a kind of illiteracy in uniform – as Mesquita could not refrain from reminding him.

'Of course it is,' he replied. 'I still think the same way. But when all is said and done it is just this which intrigues me. If the State is prepared to pay one for doing nothing, and if my profession merely obliges me to study nonsense, I'll have my free time to devote to other matters while my spirit will be free to concentrate on my researches.'

'But it isn't like that,' I said. 'Because the fellows you'll be living with, all the bull in the barrack room that will take up all your time, and because you'll always have to do as you're told, all that will be the end of you, it will make you just one more like everyone else.'

He smiled in superior fashion: 'No… By freely concentrating on one's spiritual energies, when one has great reserves of these energies and doesn't need to draw on them every day, in this way one can protect oneself from all this and even achieve a certain cachet.'

'A certain cachet? How?' asked Mesquita.

'It's very simple. Among your colleagues, because the superior man thinks about things which they don't understand. And among the world at large, because he is a soldier who thinks, and is therefore a superior sort of man: two kinds of cachet.'

'And even admitting that it could be so,' I observed, 'have you thought of all the tiresome stuff you'll have to put up with, spending the whole day ordering people around, left turn! right turn! that sort of thing.'

'I have. I don't think giving orders is going to be a bore; it might even be a pleasure. A squad of raw recruits, there at my command, and I, who can do with them whatever I want…'

'So in the end there was no uprising in Catalonia,' put in Mesquita. 'At any rate I didn't see anything in the paper. And it wasn't because I blabbed…'

'Not everything reaches the papers,' began Puigmal. 'Matters of high diplomacy are subject to Chancery rules of secrecy. But, to tell the truth, the uprising did come to naught. And we, for the time being, have put a stop to all political activity. As for the rest, it suits us to lie low for a while, so that my entry into the College won't be affected…'

It was my turn to butt in: 'So how can you be thinking of serving in the army, claiming to be Catalan, should the title of Count of Barcelona be restored to your family?'

He, however, had a reply for everything. 'What do you mean? The nobility in exile follow, in general, a military career, the one most compatible with their own traditions in the countries where they find themselves. But this in no way stops them from re-assuming their original nationality at the first opportunity. From the very first there have been many examples of this.'

Mesquita began to get hot under the collar: 'Look, Puigmal, let's have no more of your stories. You seemed to be getting better, but in fact this propensity of yours is getting even worse. If you now want to go to the Military College, there's got to be some reason for it, and not one of these tales you've been spinning. What I've always heard is that if anyone for one reason or another can't carry on with his higher education then he has to go to the army. Is that true or not?'

'It is and it isn't,' he replied without batting an eyelid. 'That might be the reason, but there might coincidentally be other reasons – which is my case.'

'Come on, you're just trying to convince yourself that you really like something which at bottom you haven't the slightest interest in,' replied Mesquita.

'No, sir. Nobody has ever convinced me of anything, so far, not even myself. If I am as I am it is because that's really how I am. I am not even master of my own self, nobody is; it is my spiritual energies which, depending on how I live, decide for me.'

Mesquita planted himself in front of him, hands in pockets, with the aggressive air he had on these great occasions: 'Where did you read all this stuff?'

'I never needed to read anything in order to know things. Sometimes it happens that I come across something which confirms my point of view,' he said, reaching down towards his coat pocket from which he took out a scrap of newspaper.

Mesquita snatched it from his hand and I got up to see. It was some little rag, badly printed on cheap paper, like those provincial papers which survive on the dutiful subscriptions of those who sometimes have to do with such things as births, or the comings and goings in the towns and villages where they are printed. But this was called *Voices from Beyond the Grave,* with the subtitle, 'The Monthly Scientific Bulletin of Spiritualism and the Metapsychic', being also the organ of the Portuguese branch of an international league of spiritualists.

'Do you belong to this organisation?' I asked.

'Me? That would be the last straw! No, I don't belong to it, nor would I ever belong to any organisation. My father and mother are members, but for them it's a kind of religion too, with Our Fathers and Hail Marys and everything else. I'm only interested in the scientific side of things.'

We smoothed out the paper and opened it; it only had four pages. On the third page however there was printed, indistinctly, an enlargement of a photo which we at once recognized. Above it the title ran: 'Animal metapsychics – the experiments of Professor Paulo Cabanellas of the Academy of Sciences, Zurich'.

'This professor – that's you and your brother?' asked Mesquita.

'That's us.'

'But this is a fraud.'

'How can it be a fraud? If my brother and I were to publish this under our own names, who would believe it? Apart from which the name is only partly a pseudonym. Cabanellas is one of our names. Our grandfather was called Pablo.'

'And what about the Academy of Sciences in Zurich? There's no such thing. Isn't that just a lie?' I went on. 'If the Academy exists, which it does, then it's not a lie.'

'But nobody called Paulo Cabanellas is a member of the Academy!' exclaimed Mesquita.

'This is something you can't ascertain without prior knowledge of the list of members. And who's going to check that? What is important is that our scientific message has been brought to public attention, and in a suitable fashion. Furthermore what the readers of this paper want is to be convinced. They don't bother themselves with these trifles.'

'But this is pure fraud,' I protested.

'I think that a fraud,' declared Ramon, 'is a lie aimed at people who don't want to be deceived. But if the matter is truthful and people are interested in it, the way in which they get to know about these things, if it's to their liking, then it isn't fraud. And that's what we've done.'

We stared at him as he got up and stretched out his hand for the paper.

'No, hold on, I want to read this,' said Mesquita. 'Who wrote it?'

Puigmal was the very picture of scientific modesty: 'I did.'

'And you didn't tell anybody?' I asked.

'Why should I? You are among those who laugh at these things ... and by the way: my father has been wondering why it is always I studying at your houses and never you in mine. Or rather it was my mother who was puzzled and spoke to me about it, and actually it is odd. I don't understand why you two never show up there. We must...'

'You never suggested it!' I said indignantly. 'You always kept us away! You never said a thing!'

'You never pursued the matter. It wasn't up to me to insist, and I never told you not to go there; in fact you went there without my saying so.'

'We went because we thought that you were ill,' grumbled Mesquita.

'But I wasn't ill and you used it as an excuse for going there.'

'Now that again!' exclaimed Mesquita. 'On top of everything else!'

'On top of everything else be damned. Perhaps you didn't realise that it was I who *called* you. Yes, indeed, *I.* I concentrated, I concentrated ... and you fetched up,' he said, opening his mouth wide in silent laughter so that his face became a rectangle.

'Very well, if it was you who called us,' I said, 'why are you annoyed with us for not going there? You could have called us before, and more often.'

'Of course I could, but since I am your friend I didn't want to influence you in any way at all.'

'But aren't you annoyed now because we don't show up there?' asked Mesquita.

'I didn't get annoyed. It was my mother and father who...'

'Enough! There's no end to it once we get talking to you. *Now*, you want people to come to your house. Very well. We'll be there tomorrow.'

'Fine, fine,' said Puigmal.

'But there's one thing I must warn you about beforehand,' said Mesquita. 'If you come to me tomorrow with any nonsense about elastic ointments, family ghosts or anything else, I'll make such a fuss as you'll remember all your life. Do we understand each other? Leave off your tricks with us for once.'

'But they're not tricks. My uncle...'

'Devil take your uncle. Do you think I didn't see the string fixed to the bookcase door?'

'You saw a string? OK, tell me one thing: if a string can pull the door open, how does it manage to close it again?'

'Well, another string, from behind, with someone pulling it behind the bookcase, from another room...'

'But you didn't see this string, did you?'

'No.'

'Well then...'

'Well, are you telling me that your late uncle only closes doors after you've opened them, is that it?'

'The one who opens the door is my uncle, too; but recently the door has been playing up and he needed help.'

'Right, you've been warned. Whenever we're there, you're not to help him.'

The following day we went to his house where the door was opened by a maid. We couldn't take our eyes off her as she went off down the corridor, her backside seeming to glow more and more the further she disappeared into the shadows. He soon came to the door of the large room to take us to the little study. But in the large room he introduced me to his father who was leaning up against one of the high desks; he was the exact image of Puigmal and his brother, or rather an intermediate model older – obviously – broader and with a bald patch. He was very amiable, greeting Mesquita effusively, asking after his father, and demonstrating in a somewhat short-sighted fashion (for he stuck his face too close to mine) his great satisfaction upon making the acquaintance of someone of whom Ramon had spoken so much. He concluded by insisting that we should feel completely at ease and that we should make ourselves comfortable in the next room. We settled down in the small study much as we had done the time before: Ramon sitting at the desk, with us in front of him in the armchairs.

Almost immediately, though, Mesquita jumped up, saying that he wanted to see the view from the windows. The view consisted of the tops of the trees growing along the middle of the avenue and, on the other side, a large building like the one in which we found ourselves. Mesquita asked him if he knew the neighbourhood well, who lived opposite, if there were any girls worth knowing. Ramon didn't know who lived in the houses in front, but further along – and he pointed – lived a lady, a friend of his mother, and her husband. They were only there though whenever one of them came down from Lisbon. For most of the time they lived in the Azores; in fact he was from the Azores, she was not. They were wealthy. I asked why, if they were never in Lisbon, they had such a house when they could easily stay in a hotel. Ramon declared that if they were wealthy they were perfectly justified in having as many houses as they wished. As for him, if he ever became rich, he would be happy to have several houses and to be a different person in each of them. Thus he would have as many lives as he had houses. Mesquita then asked him if he would have a different woman in each house. And I wondered to myself whether my own father was not a different person in each of the two or three houses that he had. Ramon thought not: unlike the sultans, he lacked what was needed to keep up with all these women. No. He, when he had his independence and his houses, couldn't put up with a woman in each one, he just wanted to enjoy being different people: in one he would be himself, in another a commercial traveller, in another a naval officer who spent most of his time cruising around the world, in another ... and so it went on. The mistresses of these fellows would belong to him and he would be responsible for them. What is more he always preferred the wives of others, that way it was much more convenient. Mesquita was quite shocked: how could he prefer them? What would he say when he himself was married if every man had the same idea? I reminded the latter that at least two of the women he had had were married, that he had gone into their homes and the homes of their husbands; indeed I brought up the episode of the back stairs.

'Ah,' said Mesquita, 'that's quite different. It was they who invited me in and I had no means of taking them anywhere else. And they all knew perfectly who I was. That's not the same as pretending to be a lot of other people, deceiving everybody. I never deceived anybody, not even the husbands whom I only knew by sight, because of my own doubts. They were the ones who deceived their husbands, and I might even say that one of them wanted to be deceived; the others would have to put up with her rather than him. Not to mention the fact ... that I had my work cut out.'

Puigmal and I were still laughing as he went on: 'You've no idea! Once I slept with her – and sleep isn't the word because I didn't close my eyes all night – and after so many, she was still asking for more and grabbing me there, and my poor little thing wasn't up to it any more, so I just leapt out of bed and legged it.'

'And then?' we asked.

'Then ... days later, I saw her in the street talking to some chap, and I saw her looking at me as if to say this one had more stamina than me. When I got home I phoned her, and that was exactly what she told me. I said that was a challenge I couldn't refuse. And I won.'

'How do you know you won? Did she tell you?'

'Get away with you; I don't fall for that nonsense. A challenge is a challenge. There we both were, first one then the other, one then the other, one then the other … and I won. When the other couldn't go on I gave her one more, just to show what I could do, as a gift. As for her, she couldn't even get up from the bed.'

'How come you've never told us this before?' I asked.

'I haven't? But Ramon never came with this theory of his about being different people. Because it's a very different matter having a lot of women, and the man sharing himself among them, from only having a few one after the other.'

Ramon did not agree. It was a lot safer, if you really wanted to win a woman over, to leave her hungry for more, hanging on, mistrustful, suspecting there were others in your life, than to have her so satisfied that she managed to convince herself she was the only one. From that moment on the man could only go down in her estimation.

'What estimation, what nonsense!' said Mesquita. 'My estimation is all here,' he said, pointing significantly.

'You mean,' I asked, 'that whoever has a lot of women, or wants to have them all at the same time, is afraid of not being able to hold onto one?'

'It's as clear as water.'

There was a knocking at the door and then it opened to admit a huge tray bearing a teapot, a tea service, cakes and jams, carried by the maid who had let us in, and a tall, thin lady who must have been Ramon's mother. We all rose to our feet and she greeted us with a sweet voice, mild and crystal clear, which matched her face, extremely fine, framed by a jet black ribbons, as in old portraits. Her sons did not resemble her in the least. But perhaps it was from her that they had that calm way of speaking, that all-enveloping easy-going way of theirs, and, at the same time, an unyielding pride which all the sweetness could not hide. Various pleasantries followed: from talking with her sons she had learned that we were good, sensible boys, very studious, that our mothers were extremely pleasant ladies – she asked to be remembered to them, too; she apologised for the intrusion but a nice cup of tea was always welcome, we couldn't be at our books all the time, we needed to rest, and after a cup of tea we could resume our studies with a will.

We should make ourselves at home, not stand on ceremony, the little honey cakes, which she had made, were particularly good, everyone liked them, and she hoped we did, too. The maid set out all the bits and pieces from the tray on the desk, while she continued talking and arranged everything to her own liking. The maid went out with the tray and the lady herself, after bidding us farewell with a wave of the hand, closed the door. We were speechless, ashamed of the conversation which she had interrupted and which had been our theme before she came in. But Ramon broke the silence, inviting us to have some tea which he himself poured and we soon set to, eating the cakes, smeared with jam, holding them delicately by the tips of our fingers, one after the other, at an incredible speed. Of that fastidious, supercilious way in which he took tea while at our houses nothing remained except the dexterity with which his fingers picked up the cakes.

From that time on we returned to his house regularly. The splendid tea never failed, nor Ramon's appetite. Nor were there any more 'tricks'. As for the rest, these were the days of examinations, first those at the grammar school, then the entrance test for the faculty, full of those strange feelings when one finds oneself in huge, strange halls, from which doors opened into vast, shadowy, domed corridors, along which milled a mass of boys and girls. We were separated from each other alphabetically, and we even got to know again a bit better some of our schoolfellows, who were, in that sea of suffering heads bent over their examination papers, like small islands that we recognised and with whom we exchanged smiles of encouragement and confidence. We were accepted by the faculty and so, finally, our holidays could begin. Ramon spent most of his at the country house, inviting me to spend some time there. But I, remembering that his grandmother 'lived' there – in reality, or in their imagination, which was the same thing as far as any possible effects were concerned – declined his much appreciated invitation and went to Figueira da Foz as usual, to spend the summer with an aunt and uncle of mine. Mesquita used to go every summer to Sesimbra, which I suppose was a family custom: neither he nor his parents, together with other close relatives and family, presumably could not imagine spending their summers anywhere else. We only got back together again in October in those domed corridors which we already felt we owned, although mistrustful of the looks bestowed on us by those who were no longer freshmen.

In the previous year, too, we had spent our holidays separately,
though this had merely been a short gap in the routine of the
grammar school; for years school holidays had amounted to no more
than that. No longer. Grammar school had come to an end and
with it a whole way of life, a network of duties. These holidays
were like a way of shedding an old skin for a new; in Figueira it
had felt exactly like that. My uncle, who spent every night, and all
the money he earned, in the casino, would sometimes take me with
him in previous years and I used to wander around until I had had
enough of it, through the ballroom, along the corridors, the
anterooms, since I was not allowed into the bar or the gaming
rooms. But these holidays were different. My uncle, insisting
categorically that I was now an 'undergraduate', and that an
undergraduate was, to all intents and purposes, a fully fledged adult,
had managed to extract from the management a pass which gave
me full access to the casino. So I, together with some friends I knew
from the beach and my cousin (this year also staying in my uncle's
house), roamed around the casino, full of ourselves, making sheep's
eyes at the apparitions behind the bar, with their angelic faces. I
even managed to fix myself up with one of them, who called me
'sonny' and took me back to her room for free. I had a blazing row
with my cousin because he, mad with envy (his bad luck was
legendary: he never got off with anyone he fancied), said that she
had paid me. This was something which we had chewed over at
length at school: the idea that one should be paid by a woman, that
one should receive money from a mistress in exchange for one's
services, seemed to us the height of masculine degradation. It was
clear that there were cases of men who owed their rise in society
to the fact that they had been the lovers of the wives of men of
influence. But, although this had not exactly been spelled out in
our discussions, even such cases did not seem quite so repellent as
'being paid for it': these men had not actually received any money
from the women... However, the business was none the less
unappetising, for it embraced certain self-interested aspects to do
with the business of giving oneself freely which, for us, constituted
the very essence of amorous virility. The opposite, though, did not
conflict with this notion. There was nothing more natural than that
a man should buy what he wanted. And if it is true that to have a
relationship with a 'serious' woman was the surest sign of one's
virility (and also of safety in so far as a 'serious' woman would not
be carrying a nasty disease), the truth is that 'going to whores' was,

quite apart from the risk of those diseases which were the price one paid for one's independence, a public and verifiable – on account of the questions about her later – demonstration of this virility and, at the same time, proof that a person had his own money; it mattered not whether he had earned it, or whether he was being given it by his parents, monthly, for this very purpose, by way of recognition by the family (the maiden aunts would shake their heads and smile surreptitiously, their eyes bright) that he was a man.

All this morality had on one occasion to be urgently reassessed when a maid servant in our house, who was the very image of dim-witted innocence, landed me with a disease which, in those days before sulphamides and antibiotics, was driving me crazy. But, at school, the difficulties I had in walking and the cotton wool which everyone could see when I changed for gym, were looked on with a mixture of terror and the greatest respect, something which largely made up for my suffering and fears. On account of this my cousin got a good hiding while I came away with a splendid black eye. At home we behaved as if nothing had happened, but on the beach, in the casino or in the street we didn't speak to each other. We made our peace at the end of the holidays when I let him have Odette (who, learning about the episode, did not even want to see him – 'I'm not so cheap, nor have I fallen so low, that I have to pay men') in exchange for the twenty escudos it needed to convince her to see him. Our mutual friends were the intermediaries in this diplomatic arrangement which in any case no longer meant anything as the summer season broke up with the advent of October.

III

Our lectures, far fewer than the huge blocks of lessons we had been used to at school, and spread out as they were through the day, allowed us or even imposed on us a kind of pointless slothfulness. Since we could come and go in the faculty as we wished and nobody ever asked where we were going, and we were – the three of us at least – far away from home, the feeling of freedom was absolute, so absolute in fact that we almost totally lost the habit of regular study. And it was true that everybody behaved thus. Only as the term tests approached did everybody disappear and shut themselves away in an orgy of swotting, interrupted only by an errand to one of the fellows who worked in the faculty, gross and greasy, who for a few coppers would provide us with sick notes so that we could take the exams at a second sitting. He even undertook the delivery of the applications and the certificates as well as reserving for us the dates we wanted. The other great novelty of the faculty was that there were girls, though at that time very few; between us and them there was no camaraderie. While I had started grammar school there had been a few girls in the last year; they were mythical beings of whom frightful things were said. In my last few years there the school had become mixed. Meanwhile, for the sake of the separation of the sexes and to provide for a population of female students, two all-girl grammar schools had been opened in Lisbon. And, in order for us to wonder at the numbers of girls who were studying (and would study?) just like us we had often as a group skipped classes and gone off on some trip to one of them. The girls ran away in groups, too, and we hadn't returned there since the police had been drafted in to stand on the corners and chase us away.

Now there they were in the faculty but it was difficult for us to think of them as our colleagues, these members of another human kind who, in the absence of sexuality, were mothers, aunts or sisters; and with a modicum of sexuality were acknowledged by us; and as fully sexual beings were all this and more, but destined for others. The sisters of one of our fellow students were famous on account of just this ambiguity, which was however shared by all our female cousins. In the parties he held in his house – a mansion on the avenue, surrounded by gardens – it all always ended up with our taking them or their friends off into the deepest recesses of the house to practise those activities – which merely skimmed the surface of things – in which they were experts. Concerning the house itself, the story went around of the very rich gentleman who, cautioning the boys who attended these gatherings of girls, suggested that they do what they had to without soiling the curtains on the windows.

Our female colleagues in the faculty were, however, very strange creatures indeed. Gradually they began to fall into three categories which in truth constituted the 'status' which they enjoyed according to the rules, already in existence, which we had begun to learn. Some of them, though very few (and they made quite a song and dance about it), turned out to be quite accessible, women who, nevertheless, acquired, in the corridors and in conversation, a discreet respectability which we found intimidating and which was, paradoxically, shared by another category, that of the extremely ugly and charmless, whom nobody thought of as female, in spite of their desperate efforts, or the efforts of some them, to be so regarded. A third group, also comprising very few, unfurled over the other two groups a cloak of such superiority that it made them seem like the ladies of some medieval court of love. They weren't by any means all beautiful, nor did anyone write poems to them or become their 'Knight-errant', but in respected circles their advice on the matter of dealing with problems was heeded and the contents of the lectures which they had missed were somehow provided for them. And sometimes tea was taken with them (and with some from the first category) in the 'General', which was the traditional name of a cake shop and tea-room in front of the school and which was part of the folklore of every family, through the tales of their parents and aunts and uncles. At that time, relations between us and our female colleagues were not at all natural: either the girls were deemed inaccessible by general consent, or they were comfortably desexualised by our own shyness. It would have been almost inconceivable that we should have gone out with them, while in fact they had boyfriends who did not attend the faculty and who came to pick them up at the gates and who strode unabashed down those corridors which were, in any case, open to the public.

There was no such thing as academic life. There was some kind of association, long since neglected, to which nobody ever went and whose leaders, whom we didn't even know, never did anything. Besides, we had grown unaccustomed to that sort of thing. At school the only sign of any collective action was, traditionally, a strike led by those in the final years, by dint of blows and kicks inflicted on the younger boys (who staged an invasion of the schoolyard for exactly this reason) on 11 November, Armistice Day, which wasn't a school holiday. Nobody gave any thought to the dead of the Great War, nor are we talking about any grand avowal of pacifism: it was merely a custom in which the older boys made the younger boys miss their lessons on that day, just as, years earlier, it had happened to them. None of us knew anything about politics: it was as if everything that we saw in the papers had happened centuries ago and thousands of miles away. Our families had no interest in politics either, except in terms of 'order', which they prayed the government would impose on the unruly country. We had not the slightest idea what this disorder was, nor of the order which the government would impose. The papers talked sometimes of the administrative and financial chaos of the past, while extolling the foresight of the government. The latter, according to the papers, was busy in setting up public works – stretches of road, public fountains, community centres all over the place – in connection with which the names of Afonso Henriques, Nun'Álvares, Vasco da Gama and other, lesser, heroes were always invoked. But transcendental questions like the budget and the public debt exceed by far the speculations of our middle and upper middle class families. 'Order' was the opposite of 'revolution'.

I myself remembered nothing of these past revolutions, which in our house had taken the form of a scandal involving a maid, in 1910, when on 5 October she had climbed out onto the veranda, full of enthusiasm, to greet with her cheers the revolutionaries marching past. My mother who was neither monarchist nor anything else, reimposed 'order' by booting her out, an act which I suppose the family regarded as courageous, the equal of some brave deed by our illustrious matrons such as D. Filipa de Vilhena. During my childhood 'revolutions' were still going on, linked inextricably for me with our having to spend three or four days confined to the innermost, darkest bedroom of the house, lying on the floor, 'in case of stray bullets', while my father and the neighbour from the floor below argued over which part of the city the shots were coming from: Penha da França, Graça, Ajuda, etc., without reaching any conclusion other than that my father, hearing some thunderous boom, started back inside and, answering the piercing cries of my mother, made for the darkened room.

Subsequently the revolutions were either stopped, in effect, or otherwise petered out silently elsewhere, shamed in addition by the severity of the newspapers' censure (which my father would read out loud, with much nodding of his head) and by groups of fishermen from Nazaré or washerwomen from the Minho who, decked out in their typical costumes would fetch up in the Terreiro do Paço, led by the chairmen of the parish council and the town band, to offer flowers to the saviours of order, who gathered at a window to acknowledge their gratitude while some of us, playing truant from school went along out of curiosity. But in general none of my family got involved in 'politics', an activity reserved for the kind of person not to be found within it: 'politicians' were all of them looked on with a kind of sardonic contempt, even if they belonged to the party responsible for the upholding of that much prized thing, 'order'. The family even disapproved of, and had spirited away like a secret disease, the telegram of congratulation which my uncle (in a moment of zeal following the latest revolution which we had spent underneath our beds) had sent to the government. It was only many years later that I found out that one of my mother's brothers, who had died young of tuberculosis, had been – if only through the reading of cheap translations – an 'anarchist'! My maternal grandmother never ever mentioned him and I believe she never quite made up her mind whether he had died seized in the lungs by the bacillus of Koch, or in the head, by that of Kropotkin.

Of course while still at school we talked about the 'Anschluss' as well as the invasion of Ethiopia. But the advent of Hitler, whose name was beginning to be more widely known, did not seem even in the news sections to constitute a threat to democratic countries but rather a disturbance of the 'order' established by the Allies after the Great War. As for Mussolini, he was widely praised officially, even though mostly on the quiet, on account of his authoritarian management of Italy's progress. Besides which, the invasion of Ethiopia wasn't really the same as the 'Anschluss'... Whatever might bring together people of the same language and race did not seem to us a matter for outsiders. The attack that was taking place against the Negus and the 'ras', the Abyssinian princes, was undoubtedly an act of aggression; these princes featured ingeniously and paradoxically in the news as a bunch of cannibals and savages who, at the same time, rejected the delights of progress in the name of an independence which dated from the time of Solomon and the

Queen of Sheba (and we all knew much more, in name, about
Ethiopia then Austria, especially since that country had figured
among the lists of names evoked by the kings of Portugal, a list we
had known by heart since primary school). The African campaigns,
it was plain, were not the same; they went according to the book.
It was not the Italians who had discovered Ethiopia in the way that
we had discovered everywhere, including Ethiopia. It was, in any
case, in just these versions of the historic past that everything was
measured; and, to such an extent were things remote from us, that
the republic had been proclaimed in Spain without any of us
noticing it. As far as I was concerned Spain was but a name like the
crowds of Spaniards who spent the summer in Figueira, filling the
streets and cafés with their bustle and noise. And, in my time, Spanish
girls had already been wiped out, as far as prostitution was
concerned, by the local competition. In Figueira they really didn't
feature much as whores because their compatriots immediately
began to think of sending them home, for the sake of the good
name of Spain, unless they were dancers in the casino who, with
their refined ways and the clattering heels of their dances, were the
very embodiment, in the admiring eyes of the Portuguese, of the
great art of the Hispanic nation. I once met one of these girls who
had been sent packing from Figueira, in the 'Pasapoga', a bar in
Madrid; every year she spent the summer with her family, thanks
to a patriotic sense of modesty.

Classes in the faculty, as I have already indicated, did nothing to
keep us together in the way that we had been before. Other than
practical classes, where we were kept busy, we only met in the
theoretical classes when for some reason we happened to turn up.
If our way of life broadened our horizons it was, at the same time,
restricted by a greater sense of solitude and a wider but indeterminate
choice of company. Thus we did not all three always study together,
Puigmal, Mesquita and I. I sometimes went to study with Mesquita
and there bumped into Puigmal, though I rarely went to his house
and Mesquita never. The latter had greatly extended the range of
his sexual activity, in which his greater freedom (the availability of
time which the girls' fathers had always granted them anyway) went
hand in hand with his equally increased frenzy. He had begun an
affair with a girl where they both spent hours on the phone to each
other. It was more than an affair, it was a courtship. And the more
ardent the courtship became the more his other involvements
flourished. I can never forget his wedding, a very solemn affair,

years later, with a whole gaggle of his old lovers there in the church, weeping their eyes out, some of them even congratulating him with hugs and kisses under the acquiescent and overbearing gaze of the one who was his wife and who knew all about his about his former conquests from Mesquita himself.

In the faculty Puigmal began to get up to his old tricks. Not in the lecture theatre where at the end of the room the teacher droned on without there being any chance of interrupting his erudite discourse; but in practical classes where, listening with much greater attention to the lecturer explaining what we had to do, he then changed the ratios in chemical analyses or fiddled around with the electrical wiring in physics, with extraordinary results so that, following heated discussions with assistants, it became necessary to summon the professor if he happened to be there. Initially, when the groups for practical work were formed, Mesquita and I made up one with him. But after a terrific row with the professor of physics in which the latter accused Puigmal of 'scientific perversion', and trembling with such fury (rolling up his trousers to show how the hairs on his legs were standing up stiff with shock) that he kicked our friend, our group was broken up in the next class by the wish of the same professor, who asked his assistants to convey his decision to us: Puigmal would in future only be able to damage the apparatus (as had happened) if he worked on his own... It was the same story in chemistry: the assistants (as it happened, an extremely fat assistant, who used to roll around, with papers always under her arm, among the high rack of test tubes) were demanding that Puigmal should not make up a group comprising more than one person... This ban, nevertheless, wounded him deeply: he was misunderstood, official science would not allow progress, all those in the teaching profession were incompetent donkeys and if it had not been for the Military College he would have given up such impossible studies. On the way home, a journey which during these moments of bitterness he made more frequently with us (and, for most of the time, with me, since, what with his phone calls – those in the course of his amour and others – as well as his visits to his intended and other appointments, Mesquita had his hands full), he would bemoan his lot. I warned him to give up the experiments since the faculty was merely the preparation he needed to enter Military College.

And as the year went on the more his bitterness turned into the sort of panic of which I had not thought him capable. If he did not pass in physics he knew that the College would not let him in conditionally and he would be lost. I didn't agree with such far-fetched ideas: it didn't seem to me that he was in any great danger, and if in fact he didn't pass he would have to spend one more year in the faculty, doing physics, and along with all the others, would join the Artillery. This way of thinking, though, didn't appeal to him. How could he devote himself freely to the invention of special weapons if he had to confine himself to the study of mere cannons and more cannons? His greatest dream was the preparation of the 'cloud of death', a vapour or gas which, after being spread around by conventional means (and of a density sufficient to resist being swept away by the wind), would ignite itself automatically, at his command. He just had to get into the College, and into the Infantry. And he ended up begging me to study with him, almost every day, as often as I could, so that he might pass. Which is what happened. If I stayed at home, then he would turn up there. If I went to Mesquita's, there he'd be. At other times he dragged me off to his place. I had to explain to him and repeat to him, out loud, the material we were studying. If he had to study on his own, he couldn't, but at least he listened to me closely, refusing point blank to go beyond his own notes or the printed notes provided by the lecturers. Whatever book from the faculty library which was needed to look more closely at some question became for him a barrier to his military career. When he thought that he already knew a subject in the way he ought to know it his studious lethargy disappeared as by magic. He became effusive, he demanded a break and standing by the window (when we were in his house) he would comment on the comings and goings around him. The two sisters who lived at the back, by now very serious young women, had married a couple of idiots and acted as if they no longer knew him. The lady that his mother used to know, the one from the Azores, was now in Lisbon, living with a nephew. And more of the same, pure, silly tittle-tattle, to which I listened patiently, happy to see him so well disposed. Tea was always served as usual on the afternoons I went there. His mother rarely favoured us with a show of her gentility and as for his brother, I hardly ever saw him. Only his father was there occasionally, talking to some other fellows when we passed through the study.

One afternoon when we got there, there was nobody in the study. The high desks stood out against the walls, with files piled high on top of them. But day by day the impression I got from it all, whether there was anybody there or not, was of a deserted stage which was being quietly covered by fine dust and a patina of dry mould. In the small study, which seemed to be solely for my friend's use (nobody ever came in to fetch anything), although he never actually took anything down from the notorious bookcase (which, whatever the time might be, regarded me with utter impassivity and the most impersonal innocence), we began our studies, or rather I began my imitation of a benevolent gramophone. One time I heard someone coming into the large study at the same moment that the front door was being closed. Low voices, one of them undoubtedly that of Mr Puigmal, were discussing something or other. I carried on with my recitation. But gradually, the voices began to grow louder, or at least one voice, which I did not recognise. This voice was speaking in some growing agitation which the other one was trying, soothingly to contain. I carried on as if there was nothing untoward while Ramon, seated at his desk, did the same. But the voices, even though we couldn't make out what they were saying, continued to grow louder so that it was impossible for my friend not to be disturbed by them, certainly much more than me. Suddenly Ramon got up and half-opened the door which was then slammed in his face. He didn't return to his chair but went to the window.

'Do you know who's out there?' he asked me, from beside the window.

I stuck out my bottom lip as if to say how should I know.

'That chap from the Azores, the rich guy, that my father used to know, the husband of the lady I was talking about. They used to live opposite us when they were in Lisbon. She's here, too, though I didn't know about it.'

I showed no sign of interest. What was unusual about all that? 'I always thought there was something odd about their life,' Puigmal carried on. 'She often comes to Lisbon, stays there for a month or so and goes off again, while he almost never comes. But what I always thought was the oddest thing was the way she lived. She must have an enormous family...'

'Why?' as the voices continued their argument, that of the other now tearful and pleading.

'Because there are so many of her nephews and nieces. Every now and then there's yet another one.'

'And what does it all mean?' (It was obvious that the speaker was weeping.)

'A lot. Because she's an old friend of my mother's and my father was always angry whenever she came to the house.' (Tears and supplications filled the adjoining room.)

'And her nephews and nieces never came with her. They are as much hers as I am.'

Then I heard Ramon's father say: 'Not so loud. This is disgraceful. There's someone here in the next room.'

'Do you understand? When she comes to Lisbon it's to gad about to her heart's desire. And to leave the others at home.'

Ramon's father was saying: 'You are crazy! You can't ask me something like that! That's just disgraceful! You must be mad! Get a grip of yourself!' And I remembered all of a sudden a woman who was a friend of my family, a widow, and who lived with her unmarried daughter, and never let her out of her sight for a moment lest she be assaulted at the front door by the baker, the milkman or even the callow shop assistants from the grocer's.

'This time, you'll see, he has found out.'

'And what's your father got to do with this?'

Then Ramon said, with an even greater air of mystery: 'My father owes him some great, some very great, favours. And my mother has a lot of influence over her. Perhaps he's come to ask him to step in.'

'To step in, but how?'

'I don't know. To tell her to be careful, or that they should separate. I don't really have much idea.'

The argument had died down somewhat but it was still going on. It seemed as though it had reached a state of equilibrium, in which it might yet continue for hours and hours. It was already getting too late for me, notwithstanding my curiosity about the fellow. I said it was time I was going. 'But how am I going to get out of here?' I asked, looking at a door beside the bookcase.

'Not that way,' said Ramon (and I recalled the time I had asked to go to the bathroom and the mystery of the doors which he had gone along shutting as, with him at my side, I made my way along the endless corridor to the bathroom down at the far end) as he went to knock on the dividing door.

The door opened somewhat and Mr Puigmal's head appeared in the gap. 'What is it?' he asked as stifled sighs could be heard behind him.

'My friend here needs to be on his way,' explained Ramon.

His father greeted me with a nod. 'You can leave now,' he said, and opened the door to allow me through.

I sped through the door, with a curt greeting and looking sideways at the fellow. Looking back it seemed to me that he was tall and well built but not fat, very well dressed, well groomed, with not a hair out of place; he was holding his glasses in one hand while he dabbed at his eyes with a handkerchief in the other, and I recall that he conveyed a sense of masculine elegance, not least from the fragrances he used. Probably some of these characteristics had suggested yet others to me which to tell the truth I hadn't had the time to ascertain properly. It was the only glimpse I would ever have of Mr Vilasboas.

IV

Days went by without my getting together with Puigmal. He hadn't got round to fixing up a study session with me but then, one night, he turned up at Mesquita's house where I happened to be. When our studies were neither urgent nor pressing Mesquita used to leave his friends in the room he used for studying (his house was huge, magnificent, with various rooms which were only opened up on the great feast days), and head for the phone into which he would murmur sweet nothings. To make these murmurings even more comfortable there was a couch beside the phone upon which if we needed him for any reason we would find him sprawled out sensually. If, however, our studies were really pressing then it was the telephone which he attached to a socket in the study while he, though more discreetly, and in a voice which at the other end of the line must have been inaudible, carried on his murmurings, turning aside from his studies, his gaze vacant and refulgent, or brandishing the receiver, joining in our discussions. This was all tremendously complicated, with long explanations over the phone whenever his fiancée thought something we had said among ourselves – which she had misunderstood – was intended for her, and with any areas of scientific uncertainty which we might have brought up being rebutted with many a sweet word – 'my girl', 'darling', 'my love', 'my angel' – aimed at us with the same devoted expression with which down the phone he expatiated on differentials and integers, blowing kisses all the while. That evening when Puigmal came along the confusion reached new heights of madness, what with me, the theory of mass, and the affair at each end of the phone line all going on together at the same time.

Waving goodbye to Mesquita who, all of a sudden, had fallen silent as he listened to some lengthy confession, Puigmal told me that he had dropped in at my house where they told him where I had gone. 'I know the whole story,' he added. 'It'll knock you out. It's quite a shock. She...'

'She? What's this story, then?' asked Mesquita, putting the phone down.

I butted in before Puigmal could say anything: 'Do you remember that time when we were in Puigmal's house and he was telling us about a lady who was a friend of his mother's and who lived just a few houses along, on the Avenue?'

'You mean that one from the Azores, their house was always closed up, and she sometimes came to Lisbon?' he reminded himself, explaining down the phone: 'It's Puigmal who's just got here and he's telling us this story about a neighbour, a friend of his mother's. The couple, they live in the Azores but she sometimes comes to Lisbon. No, I believe she comes alone, she prefers it that way' – he might just as well have been talking to us as down the phone – 'she can do what she likes. (Oh, Puigmal, does she deceive her husband? Yes, she deceives her husband. Hang on. What are they called?... Vilasboas... They're called Vilasboas... Do they have any children?... No, no children... Hm ... and ... what happened exactly? A few days ago Jorge was at Puigmal's place... They heard some great carry-on nearby... Yes... Puigmal's study is next to his father's... And when you went out you saw the Man himself, didn't you?... Jorge saw him, he did, he was ... hmm ... wiping his eyes... No, the conversation was with Puigmal's father ... so she was coming to Lisbon to deceive him at her leisure?... No, Puigmal says that his mother and father must have already suspected something because they sometimes used to row about it ... yes ... his father was the one who didn't trust her because he was already thoroughly browned off with her visits... Of course they were friends... Friends from childhood, Puigmal?... And they'd been to school together, too... So what did the fellow want? ... Just imagine it, my love, wait... Hmm ... She used to come to Lisbon to get fixed up with lovers... Hmm... Just think, young boys ... No, my girl, the very idea, I don't know the least thing about her, let me hear... It is, yes... She took them home with her until she'd had enough of them, and then went off back there... Yes, back to her husband. He pretended not to know... Ah, what a thing, eh?... Listen my girl, there's no knowing these things... But, Puigmal, she only got up to these things in Lisbon?... No?... He says that he said it was only in Lisbon... Who knows, perhaps over there she was a completely decent lady... No, Puigmal says that he also said that he was very fond of her... Yes, indeed, but he would rather she didn't show herself up over there in such a little place... What!?... Look, it seemed that this time she had taken the last of these chaps on the boat with her, she was crazy about him, so she took him with her... That's right ... A *ménage à trois*... Wait... No, he didn't like it ... written all over his face, no... So he booted the

fellow out, or rather, stuck him on the boat... Hmm... What?...
It was... No, no, she went after him... After the young chap, she
was crazy about him... You wouldn't follow me like that? ... You
wouldn't?... Ah, ah... He warned him never to come back. No,
he didn't just warn him, he forbade him ever to come back... She
went back to Lisbon... Wait, that's just it, he went after her, on
the next boat... He went to bring her back... From Puigmal's
house?... Puigmal, had she gone to your house?... No, she'd seen
them but she hadn't been to their house... It was... Vilasboas...
Who?... The husband, didn't I tell you he was called Vilasboas?...
She refused to go back home, however much he begged her ... I
don't know... Puigmal, did she want to leave her husband and stay
with the boy?... Yes, Puigmal says she didn't want to know about
anything else... Wait... Well, her husband kept on at her... No,
not like that ... it seems she didn't even want to talk to him... The
Vilasboas went to get Puigmal's father and asked him to be some
sort of go-between, yes, could you imagine me asking anyone to
be a go-between between us, my darling... Hmm ... my love...
He wanted Puigmal's father to put forward... Ah, ah, hold on a
tick ... you can't believe it ... to suggest to her that she should
return, return under any circumstances, with whomever she wished,
because he couldn't live without her... If you ever did this to me
... no ... no... Ah, what would I do? She's asking me what I would
do... Look, exactly what I did to that one I told you about... Ah,
ah, ah ... Puigmal, what about your father? ... His father refused...
Hmm... He threatened to execute some letters of credit which
Puigmal's father owed him... No, he didn't speak to her... And
where are they all now? In Lisbon or back there?... Puigmal doesn't
know... Maybe they are, maybe they aren't... Puigmal, are they
all three in the house?... Puigmal says he doesn't know... One of
his stories... No, he's quite angry, right here, now, can you hear?
He says it's true. It could well be... Oh, darling, you can never
tell... You know what he's like... Puigmal says he'll tell us the rest
of it when he finds out... Now, that should be worth seeing...
Doesn't say anything?... Hmm ... but this business of the unpaid
letters is pretty serious...' and he made a sign to Puigmal not to get
angry.

'We'll see... And when that's all over she'll be off after another...
Is my little babykins going Oh, Oh? Are you? And you're not afraid
about this stuff?... You won't go dwelling on such nonsense, will
you?... Yes, a bit of nonsense with your darling, of course... Yes,

of course... You can... That too... As long as you don't take advantage,' and his voice was lost in sweet nothings interspersed with kisses. When it was all over (and he was already putting the phone down when he picked it up again for more sweet nothings) and he finally replaced the phone, he said: 'What a story, eh? But I'd sort her out. If it were me I'd sort her out.'

'If it were you, you'd what?' I asked him.

'You bet...' and he stretched out, yawning and eyeing the telephone. 'If I were the husband I'd grab a gun and make the guy go at it till he was worn out. Or even until he was ashamed of her. And if I was the boy, well...' and he chuckled, 'if I were the boy I'd have hopped it down the back stairs, bollock naked and all.'

'And what about her, what would you do to her?' asked Puigmal.

'To her?' he repeated. 'Ah, I haven't even thought about it,' he said looking at the telephone, seemingly touched. 'I don't know, I really don't know what I'd do. Puigmal, make sure you let us know the rest of it, eh?'

Puigmal, however, never got round to telling us the rest of the story; I don't know whether it was because he avoided it or because we didn't pursue it. After the exams Mesquita and I still followed, with an interest which he made sure we shared, his progress towards the Army School. He passed. I soon found out, from his own lips. He called in at home, on his way back from the school, even before he had told his own parents. From his downcast bearing as he came in I thought that he hadn't made it. But how? He had passed the inspection, passed the written exams, had vaulted, amongst other things, the celebrated ditch...

'Well?'

'I made it.'

'Why the long face? Isn't it what you wanted?'

'It was.'

'Well, then?'

'Fine, but now it's all over.'

'All over; how come? You're in...'

'I'm in ... but how am I going to get out of there?'

'But you've just got in where you wanted to, you had nothing else in your head, and now you're thinking of how you can get out of it? You know how you get out of it? As a retired general, it's a life sentence.'

He sat down, lost in thought. 'I had such plans, I really did, but this is the end of them now.'

'Look, the truth is that you don't really want to go on with it any more, do you?' I said. 'At bottom, you don't really want it.'

'That's right,' he said, falling silent. Then suddenly: 'However, a military career has undeniable advantages, it certainly has. And can you imagine me in uniform? All the sweet little things hanging out of their windows to see me. Do you reckon a uniform would suit me?' he said, getting up and looking around.

'Uniforms always look good, to those who like them,' I said.

'Don't you think it would suit me?'

'Of course it would,' I said, looking at his athletic figure.

The following day I set off for Figueira da Foz on the morning train. I bought a newspaper. The front page was full of one thing: a Revolution had broken out in Spain, one that the paper, in capital letters, dubbed a National Revolution.

V

When I got to Figueira the station was a heaving mass of
Spaniards, with their bags and suitcases, all shouting, their children
howling, the women calling out to each other, the men waving
newspapers in the air, and a great crowd of people, all pressing up
against the booking office.

I didn't understand anything of what was going on and I did not
know how a revolution – a period which my family in times gone
by had spent in the darkness of the bedroom – could cause people
such alarm or cause them to want to return home so abruptly.
Revolutions were the work of soldiers and revolutionaries,
something for which they had prepared themselves specially, and
which were then crushed by the counter-attacks of the government,
for which the latter was acclaimed by crowds like the good folk
from the Minho. People who were spending the summer so far
away surely could not be revolutionaries. These sorts of people were
undoubtedly just like us, and if they neither had nor needed
darkened bedrooms, then they could very well calmly wait,
swimming in the sea under the Figueira sun, or in the cafés, or
around the tables in the casino, for the revolution to blow over. I
was thinking this over as, suitcase in my hand, I made my way to
my uncle's house. But then I recalled – either someone had told
me, or it happened in one of those obscure revolutions of my
childhood – that once my uncle had been staying at our home when
the revolution had broken out and that my aunt, who had not seen
him turn up, had thought that he had died. Those people, therefore,
could not have been with all the members of their family, some of
whom must have remained in Spain, while those here were fearful
of what might have happened to those back home – or to their
houses.

As far as I was concerned, a revolution was not the same as a war.
Some people and some regiments took to the streets, or there were
barracks which the street mob wanted to storm. But I remembered
the old engravings in the magazine, *Illustrated Portuguese News*, from
the Great War, showing Germans robbing the Belgians' houses,
and which I had leafed through as a child, looking for figures to cut
out; those people feared for their houses, naturally. But this seemed

incredible to me: a revolution in Spain wasn't a war, nor were there Germans breaking into everyone's houses in that way. Spaniards, however, were a terrible lot; who knows what they were capable of? I could already see my uncle's garden gate when something which I had read in the novels of Camilo (Castelo Branco) came into my head, something which had happened at the time of the French invasions and the liberal and various other revolutions – it might have been one of those. I pushed the door open and went in. The dog came to meet me, making a great fuss. I went round the house to the glass door which looked out over the garden. My aunt, her hair very blonde as usual, was sitting at a table, sewing. My uncle was standing up, waving his arms around. As soon as they saw me they came to the door, both of them, to hug me and ask after my parents (my mother was his sister) and my grandmother (his and my mother's mother). I told them my news and sat down. My uncle laid his hands on the table and asked about my exams, whether I had passed, about the 'General', the confectioners which he too had patronised when he was young while he was taking the first steps towards a military career, which the Great War (on account of the poison gas and what he went through in the German concentration camps) had cut short.

And then, abruptly, he said that that revolution was a terrible thing for Figueira, what with the Spaniards all leaving and even if the revolution didn't last long they'd never come back, the summer would be a disaster. My aunt simply nodded her head in agreement, sewing diligently all the while. I knew what she was thinking: my uncle lived on his small retirement pension (which, because of a falling out he'd had with the Ministry of War, had never been brought up to date), and on what he earned from the classes he gave in schools in the town. (They didn't pay him during the summer holidays.) In the summer he fleeced the Spaniards at a whole variety of games in the cafés (often I had seen him in the basement rooms, with his fine head of neatly combed black hair, now lightly speckled with grey, a cigarette which had gone out stuck in the corner of his mouth; he would be sitting at the table surrounded by rubberneckers, fascinated yet fearful of his skill and luck) where he would win enough to see him through the night at the roulette tables in the casino. It was only much later that I learned that the casino, independently of what he lost on his own account (for which they did not reimburse him), used to give him some chips for the tables so that he might stir up those around him a bit. He went on with his litany of complaint: already yesterday, at the very first news, the exodus had begun: the Aleixandres, the Pozas, the Murtells, they were all packing their bags.

'What about the station, eh? Full of them, I suppose?'

I confirmed his worst fears and launched into a lip-smacking description of the chaos.

'That's it, then,' he would say, 'and that isn't the worst of it. Woman, d'you know what's the worst? The worst is that even those who remain, afraid of the future, will simply hang on to their money, to see how it all pans out. Look, have you had lunch yet?'

'I had a snack on the train.'

'A snack? So, woman, you let my nephew, my nephew, you hear, the son of my sister is certainly my nephew, you let the boy starve? Go and rustle up some eggs. Do you want some eggs? You don't? Why don't you want some eggs? Of course you want some eggs. Woman,' he said, his thin, bent figure making his ungainly way through the room, his stick as usual on his arm, 'some eggs for my nephew. Eggs and ham – you'd prefer them with ham, wouldn't you?'

My aunt rang the bell and a maid appeared whom I didn't recognise from the previous year. While my aunt gave her orders to the girl, my uncle smacked the girl across her backside. 'You don't know this one, do you,' he said, winking at me. 'She's good, pretty good, you'll see how good she is.'

'Justino,' exclaimed my aunt, her voice crystal clear and good-humoured. 'Your uncle hasn't mended his ways, you see.'

'I haven't mended my ways? Is that so? That's because there isn't a woman worth mending them for.'

My aunt smiled and bent over her sewing again; she asked me if I wanted to have a wash. I said I did and went to the bathroom and then to unpack. What my uncle had said and my aunt had borne summed up the tragedy of their lives. They had had a son – and although they rarely talked about him, in their opinion he had been the most good-looking child, the most intelligent, the most lively and so on – who had died of meningitis many years ago. I had never even known him. He had fallen ill suddenly, or rather, what had seemed a common enough illness had suddenly got worse. My uncle would describe his cries, sharp and repeated at regular intervals, and the sheer terror with which the child had gripped his hands. And he would hold out his thin hand, long and bony, and still, despite his chewed fingernails and fingers stained with nicotine, very fine, in such a way that one could almost see the now invisible little hands still clutching his father's with the instinctive terror of death.

My aunt, not knowing what to do, had waited until the early hours for my uncle to come home. He had berated her stupidity, her shiftlessness and her lack of maternal feeling. Every Sunday morning my uncle would go to the cemetery where he would not allow anyone, least of all my aunt, to accompany him. In their dedication to that child who was their masterpiece they did not want another one and in this case my aunt accused my uncle of forcing her to have an abortion, to which my uncle retorted that it was not true and that it was her vanity which had dissuaded her from having any more children. I had gathered all this indirectly, from the jibes which they used to wound each other (something she rarely did), or through other, occasional, references. Years later, once the greatest intensity of the pain had passed – and the fear they had lest death would deprive them of any other children they might have – they once again ardently desired a child and my aunt became pregnant; the birth was premature, a catastrophe, so that she had to be operated on, with utterly final consequences.

From that on my uncle would say, more or less at random, that she wasn't 'worth' it, and took his revenge at home, visiting the servants' quarters at night. They slept, in any case, in separate rooms. I never understood though why my aunt didn't employ maids who were old and ugly so that at least that solution would please her somewhat. It was, for the rest, just as my uncle used to say, on those occasions when she showed an unhealthy jealousy: 'You're quite safe … there's no danger, is there? You can make a cuckold of me whenever you please.'

My aunt would reply, with her customary smile, that he was being old-fashioned and that there were lots of ways of avoiding the danger and that she would go to the chemist's to ask. He responded by saying that he wasn't at all old-fashioned, but that one only used these things with whores, that between lovers one didn't stop to say, 'Hold on, let me put this thing on first.' My aunt retorted that he was talking out of his arse; he turned to me – I happened to be there: 'You can see that your aunt doesn't talk out of her arse, can't you? You see, she knows. And then, afterwards, it's me who is the hoary old, reputed father,' he said, spitting out unmistakably the first syllable of the first adjective. I went back to the dining room, where the eggs were waiting for me on the newly laid table while my aunt carried on with her sewing.

'Your uncle has gone out, he said he was going to the station. If you want you can go and meet him after coffee.'

I ate while turning over in my mind a route which would allow me to see which of my friends from last year were here in Figueira; and as well I carried on answering my aunt's questions about my family which, between the lines of her questions, she gave me to understand were in her opinion just as daft as my uncle. Rarely did she leave the house. Sometimes she went to the cinema, whenever I (or another nephew there for the summer) felt like going with her. As far as I could tell, she didn't have much to do with anyone. Some afternoons she would put the lead on their great big Alsatian and go down to the beach, a long way off in the direction of Buarcos, where the wind skimmed lightly over the sands and the fishing boats, beached at the edge of the waters, seemed to float suspended, with the eyes on their prows open wide with surprise. My aunt would go along by the sea wall, the dog dragging her along, her golden hair shining in the setting sun. More than once, walking along with my friends I had seen her from afar but she was either lost in thought, or pretended that she couldn't pick me out among the passers-by at whom, to tell the truth, she wasn't really looking. Only once – the year before and almost at the end of my stay – had it been otherwise. She had unleashed the dog who was running at full speed along the beach, and the dog, upon seeing me, had run towards me and then started back to her. My aunt called it and then got hold of it. And then she bade me a smiling farewell with a wave of the hand; there was a youthfulness about her gesture that moved me and which I henceforth always noticed in her.

'Who's that?' asked one of my friends.

'His aunt,' answered another one.

'You won't be angry with me if I say something, will you?' said the first.

'No, what is it?'

'What a beautiful woman your aunt is,' he said.

And I looked at her again, remembering those features which I could see clearly from that distance. My aunt – and I had never really thought about it – must truly have been extremely lovely, but now, hidden within her, there was only a gracious, gentle girl.

'I don't find her beautiful,' I said.

'I'm sorry, I don't mean to be offensive,' said my friend, 'quite the contrary.' And the conversation had ended there.

I was having tea, my eyes on the golden hair of her head which was bent over her sewing, and asked if I might go out. 'Off you go; you boys, you never get tired. And after that journey of yours ... Hours... Go on, make the most of your holidays. Men aren't wanted in the house. Maria' – on account of my uncle's wishes all the maids who came in from 'outside' were called Maria, while the cooks were all Micaelas – 'has put your case in your room.' So I set off towards the Bairro Novo, the new part where the cafés were, already thinking about finding Odette.

The Bairro Novo, however, looked as though it had been swept by a gale force wind: the cafés were crowded as usual but the streets were empty of the usual swarm of people passing by. Groups of people were talking, but they were standing still; newspapers fluttered along the ground. And over everything hovered a violent tension, as if all those people were survivors of a hurricane. Although I didn't really know what was going on that was certainly how it felt to me. I ran to the boarding houses where my friends were wont to stay. Yes, two of them were spending the summer there, but they had gone out. I carried on to the boarding house, with a small palm tree either side of the gate, where Odette used to stay. This year she hadn't come, according to the landlady; she had stayed in Oporto, or had gone to Póvoa de Varzim, she'd been there once before. A woman who was sitting in a wicker chair near the little balcony and who had been looking hard at me, broke in: 'Odette? No...'

'She's in Oporto, some rich fellow's paying for her. I know...'

I left, downcast, but I took with me at least a small point of honour: the Odette who had been 'mine' for free was now being paid for by some rich fellow... It must have been because she was worth something, as I had thought. I went back to the streets of the Bairro Novo which as night fell began to acquire something of its former animation. But not greatly: suddenly at one of the tables in the street a scuffle broke out. Two men were fighting while others were about to join in to cries of 'communist' and 'fascist'. The tumult soon spread to other tables in the street. From among the groups standing around men broke away to join those fighting at the tables, while others fled, tripping over the flying tables and chairs. One man ran away, running, from amidst the scrum pursued by a handful of others who were in turn grabbed by those from another group. From the depths of another café streamed out a wave of people, all around me, and then suddenly at my side I saw Rodrigues, the friend of mine who had picked out my aunt at such distance and who had not been in the boarding house when I called. Rodrigues was fighting with some chap who had attacked him in the middle of the confusion and it was as if the rest did not even notice them. The throng of people streamed by us and with it the fellow who had been fighting with Rodrigues. He tripped up another who was running past and the fellow fell sprawling onto the ground. I seized Rodrigues by the arm, dragged him off to another street and we went into an empty café, with half a dozen other people and the waiters in their aprons at the door, peering out.

'What were you doing out there, knocking hell out of each other?' I asked. 'What have you got to do with all this?'

Rodrigues, so tall and lean, hitched up his trousers which were almost falling off him and tucked in his shirt. 'Nothing,' he said, 'but I took advantage of the situation to give a good hiding to these shitty Spaniards.'

His fury against Spaniards was proverbial, a fury nourished by his hatred of the Count of Trava, of the Castros of Dona Inês, of those who had been defeated at Aljubarrota and in the campaigns of the Restoration, and as well the claim to Olivença (still in Spanish hands), a fury with which, with loud cries, he would challenge any Spaniard, even a child, to dare to approach him. The holidays which he came to spend every year in Figueira were a martyrdom from which he derived a certain masochistic pleasure. And his great moment had arrived; his eyes glittered with sadistic satisfaction.

'That rabble... They come here to eat our food, soil our streets ... and now this uproar!' he said. 'And now you're here, eh?'

We sat down to talk. I knew that his life was somewhat complicated: his mother ran and was the owner of a large hotel near Buçaco; he had spent his school years in a boarding school in Figueira and had been studying in Coimbra for a couple of years now. His mother, a widow, did not want him around at home, or rather in the hotel since, without losing sight of the accounts or the key to the safe, she spent her life in a series of nocturnal adventures: with guests, waiters, the musicians who played during dinner, all in their turn, slept with her. During the day she was sternness personified; at night there were knocks on her door, someone had got the time or the day mixed up, or wasn't satisfied that he'd already had his turn. Rodrigues would recount all this, and there was bound to be some element of exaggeration, with that fury with which he said everything. His reputation in any case wasn't of the best. It was said that at college he got into some doubtful escapades and was much sought after by the pederasts to whose beds he would go. I had visited the college – I already knew the stories – where my uncle was a teacher. In truth the dormitories were quite strange: a series of wooden cubicles, in the middle of the room, with doors like you'd find in a hen-coop and a bed in each one. At bedtime the priests locked the students in. I asked how they could go to the lavatory at night and the servant who was accompanying my uncle and me to show us the college – it was during the holidays, obviously – smiled in superior fashion and opened the cupboard beside the bed, where, in a made-to-measure locker was stored a pot.

But those who were most interested in opening the doors had keys. The one who told me all this – a kid from Figueira who was part of our group and attended the school as a day boy – had added that for one of the prefects it was like the spice trade, selling keys and then confiscating them. Rodrigues would boast loudly of his virility and one of his great pleasures was to prove it in public, either by exposing himself (and we all laughingly agreed that he had much with which to intrigue the pederasts) or by paying a woman more for her to let the rest of us watch. And whenever we bumped into a young chap, extremely thin with wavy hair, who had been to the school, Rodrigues would follow him a bit, shouting obscenities at him which the other feigned not to hear; then he would return, red-faced, adjusting what he called his 'tackle' in his trousers and repeating the obscenities he had been using. Now, sitting across from me, he seemed possessed by the same kind of excitement. He had wasted a year in Coimbra, his mother would only let him have an allowance if he would study law, something he hated. I had heard all this two years earlier. He leant across the table towards me, his eyes moist, with bags under them and deep set in his pale olive features; his nostrils flaring at the end of his long nose while his lips were thick and discoloured, and his chin came to a point.

'Do you want to know why I'm so furious with the Spaniards, do you?' he asked and then paused while his eyes flashed. 'Because my father was Spanish, you hear?'

He had never spoken to me nor to anyone I knew about his father. To all of us he had always been the son of the lady who owned the hotel which he made into a legend, with its rambling corridors, carpets, the quintet playing at dinner.

'When did your father die? A long time ago?' I asked.

He sat back in his chair, his gaze fixed in the distance: 'I was ten when he died. But I already knew enough about life to realise that he was a shameless cuckold.'

I fell silent, not knowing what to say. He turned towards me.

'You don't have to make that face,' he said, smiling, as if to console me. 'It's true. Would you like a beer? I'll get it,' and he called the waiter.

Then as we were drinking he told me that during these holidays he had to take a decision on which the rest of his life would depend. If he didn't study law his mother would cut off his allowance. She wouldn't let him have anything so that he could study any other course. He wanted to read history, as I knew. Therefore he either carried on studying something he didn't want to or he let himself fail another year in which case he would have to fix something up for himself somehow. What did I think?

'Why don't you remain in Coimbra, working, giving private lessons, you know, and studying history as you want to? Then your mother will have to give you your allowance eventually since you are still studying.'

'You don't know her. And how am I supposed to work? Doing what? Giving lessons? You reckon that's easy in somewhere like Coimbra, with half the University giving private lessons to the other half?'

'Go to Lisbon, or Oporto.'

'I've already been thinking about going to Lisbon... With my "tackle" there I reckon I could earn a fortune. I've heard things...'

I looked away from him, remembering all the things that had been said about him. He understood, clenching his teeth and blinking tremulously. 'But that's just it, isn't it?' he hissed. 'At the college I had everything I wanted.'

I got up; he put some money on the table and followed me out. By the door he gripped my arm.

'I'm sorry,' he said, as I looked up at his face, which, from the height of his lean figure, bent down over me. 'But I have nobody. I have no family, no friends.' His voice quavered. He pulled himself up to his full height. 'Come on, let's see if that bunch of cuckolds has stopped shitting themselves with fear.'

The street where all the cafés were was practically deserted. The tables and chairs, neatly ranged and empty, formed an odd, white mass that I had never seen before. A couple of Republican guards, both fat and short, were walking towards us. 'That Spanish crowd,' asked Rodrigues as they passed us by. They've all run off then?'

'Some communists who were stirring things up have been arrested, yes sir,' replied one of them.

We carried on in silence towards his boarding house.

'Have dinner with me. Why don't you have dinner with me?'

'I only arrived today and I haven't told my aunt and uncle I wouldn't be dining with them,' I said.

'Oh, you only got here today? I thought you'd been here a while and that we hadn't got round to meeting yet.'

'Just ask them at the boarding house if I didn't come looking for you just now,' I said, sensing that demon in him, which we all tried to steer clear of and which was what we all felt when we were with him.

'Well then, dine with me. Yesterday I didn't have dinner at the boarding house so the landlady owes me one It doesn't matter about your aunt and uncle. Your uncle's a case; you did know he was my teacher of maths and drawing, didn't you? Have I told you about that time with the compasses? I have?'

Indeed he had; we had stopped in front of the boarding house. 'Zé Ramos is here, his sister, too,' he said having sung the praises of my aunt. 'Don't be angry about what I'm going to say,' continued Rodrigues. 'What I really need is a woman like your aunt. He mistreats her, I know; he even told us about it himself at the College. She doesn't deserve it. With a woman like her I would be all right. Have dinner with me, and then afterwards we can go back there and I'll show you what's new this year.'

'I'll dine with you but then I'll have to go straight back home,' I said.

We went into the room which for the benefit of the Spanish summer takeover had a sign with the word DINING ROOM written in that language. There were only four people, scattered among the tables, having dinner; we sat down and he started to stroke the tablecloth with the fork, quite forcefully.

'At school, once, I escaped from the dormitory one night and went to spy on your uncle's house... They didn't have that dog then... I think they don't realise that in fact they bought it on account of me... I climbed the tree to spy on your aunt, then I fell from the thing and started howling – not the first, obviously. All hell was let loose and I started to run away and leapt over the wall, but I could still hear your uncle calling her names, demanding to know who the fleeing lover was. It was me, perched up in the tree while she had no idea who I was. I never went back again.'

When we'd finished dinner we agreed to meet again the next day and I went off home.

VI

My aunt was sitting, as usual, at the table sewing; the dog, which had leapt up to greet me as I entered the avenue with the tall palm trees leading from the gate to the mansion, now came and laid down at her feet. In that house there were no set hours for anyone, above all during the holidays. She only asked me if I had had dinner and I replied that I had met a friend, Rodrigues – and I looked at her closely – and that he had insisted on my dining with him.

She looked back at me, wrinkling her brow in thought, holding up her needle. 'Rodrigues?' she wondered out loud. 'Isn't he from Buçaco; wasn't he a pupil of your uncle, in the college of S José? Your uncle was always talking about him; seems he was the very devil of a pupil there, used to leave the school at night.' She started to sew again. Then, smoothing out the cloth to see which bits still needed darning, she added: 'He used to tell everybody he was madly in love with me. It's quite common among students, isn't it, this business of saying they're in love with their teachers' wives?'

I said that I didn't know; in Lisbon we didn't know anything about our teachers' families.

'It must be something that only happens in the provinces, really. When your uncle heard about what the boy was saying he thought it was a hoot, called him an idiot; it was your uncle himself who told me about it all. I'd say it was the only time we ever managed to laugh about something like that, you know him and the strange ideas he gets. But it must have been because the boy had such a bad reputation and he didn't think of him as a threat.'

'Bad reputation?'

'Yes, didn't you know? Well, I don't know much about these matters in spite of the things your uncle says. Bad reputation, that's the expression they use. But they say that he wasn't kicked out of the College only because Rufininho had a crush on him, you know Rufininho, don't you?' Rufininho was the boy that Rodrigues had chased away, hurling abuse at him. 'And others, just as rich,' she continued, 'who all have crushes on him. If he had been expelled, then Rufininho and the others would have gone, too. And Rufininho's parents paid a great deal, and then some more, so that the fathers, in their benevolence, would keep Rufininho there.'

She fell silent again after saying so much about these indelicate matters, of which she spoke in a way naturally influenced to a great extent by my uncle's foul mouth and by the way in which he kept these topics to himself. Tiny butterflies were fluttering round the lamp. The dog pricked up its ears, got up, stretching mightily, and went to the door.

'It can't be your uncle; it's too early – unless the game isn't up to much today because of this revolution. Maria told me it was a stampede, everybody running away. Did you happen to bump into your uncle in the café?' she asked.

I said I hadn't and described the unruly scenes I'd witnessed. 'Isn't uncle coming back for dinner?' I enquired.

'No,' she said, smiling. 'But I'm not worried: your uncle doesn't give a fig for politics and this thing is the Spaniards' business; they're a cantankerous lot, anyway.'

That wasn't exactly my impression: they argued a lot, waved their arms about, too, but once that was over, they embraced or begged forgiveness, and addressed each other as 'sir'. But what had happened the previous day, that had been different.

The dog ambled back and settled down at her feet, with a snort, breathing deeply. 'Tejo, what is it?' she asked, bending over him. He shifted his tail and settled again. 'What's the matter with my Tejo?' He raised his head and then lowered it again. 'I don't know what's the matter with the dog today,' she said. 'He's restless; he knows there's something going on.'

'Perhaps it's the revolution,' I said. 'Do you think he could be Spanish?'

'You'll see if he isn't. Your uncle bought him one day before you started coming here from a Spaniard who he used to play with in the café. It was after we suspected there was someone prowling in our garden at night.'

Our lengthy silence was only broken by an occasional snort from the dog. I yawned discreetly.

'If you want to go to bed, don't stand on ceremony. You must be tired out. Anyway, I'm not going to wait up for your uncle.'

I bade her goodnight and went up to my room. The house had three floors: at the garden level there was the room where they ate, a large pantry, a kitchen, a laundry room and some other rooms. Above was an elegant floor to whose door one went up a staircase which opened out like a fan on either side from the street in front. Inside the floors were joined by a much smaller stairway. On this floor were the great rooms, unused by my aunt and uncle, except for the one in which they kept their library and to which they sometimes had recourse when they wanted a book. One went up to the bedrooms by stairs which led from a nook in the hall in a wide sweep; there were a lot of bedrooms, almost all of them closed up. Why did they want such a large house? Though they both accused each other of *folie de grandeur* the size of the house was never mentioned, as far as I ever heard anything, among the specifics of their recriminations. In my bedroom with its high ceiling I opened the window which looked out onto the side opposite the little basement entrance to the dining room. I leant out over the shadowy garden. It was a starry night and a slender moon seemed to hang motionless over the dark shadow of the belvedere which stood in that corner of the garden. To reach it one needed to make one's way through a thicket of bushes growing wild. The gardener who came to look after the garden once in a while only kept the other part of the garden clear and stocked with plants as if the avenue of palms, swept and pristine, was the dividing line between the undergrowth and a real garden.

It had been that way ever since my cousin died because my aunt used to go, with him in his pram, to the belvedere to sew. Perhaps it might even have been a sunstroke (for the stone belvedere, in the angle of the wall, had no roof) which, owing to my aunt's carelessness, had caused the illness which killed him. This was not, in any case, an article of faith for my uncle, but the belvedere and everything within it was given up to the nettles. Sometimes, in the late evening after dinner, I felt like going there, for the Tavarede road passed close by the wall; the road itself was white with a powder which burst from sacs growing in the walls which flanked it. Ox carts squeaked past and it was all very bucolic and peaceful. Once, when my uncle saw me going there he shot me a look of violent disapproval. He never said anything, though.

My uncle was very fond of me in that brusque, unpredictable way of his and only the fact that I never got the hang of that card game of his, nor of chess, brought me down in his estimation. This had risen considerably the previous year when, passing through the gaming room in the casino, he saw me fearfully chancing five thousand reis on the roulette wheel. He winked at me, stared falcon-like at the wheel and made me change the place of my chip. I lost. He gave me another five thousand and slapped me on the back. I won. However, I never had much money and I was always afraid of becoming addicted to gambling. At home the nearest we got to gambling was lotto, played with beans, on those rare occasions when the whole family got together. We didn't have even a pack of cards, and my family disapproved sternly of any trickery while we were putting our markers down, accusing each other of cheating and making references, to my mother's obvious disgust, to my uncle Justino's disgraceful way of life. But before I set off for Figueira, it was my mother who called me to one side as I was already half way through the door to whisper in my ear that gambling was a terrible thing and to warn me not to set foot in the casino. That place, for my mother, seemed to amount to nothing more than a lot of tables devoted to different forms of gambling; I always smiled to myself, ironically, at that ingenuousness which did not realise that within the casino there were other 'sins' into which one might fall… These, for her, did not even exist, for although she no longer treated me like a child, and showed a certain embarrassed shyness, she really had no idea what constituted the life of a man. She wept copiously over my father's infidelities, whenever she got to hear about them, which was not difficult. But this was like a cross, part of being married, which she put up with for better or worse, as the other women did, but which had no connection with masculine availability. When my parents talked about the antics of some young fellow or other, indirectly including me among their number, stressing that I was a grown man, she, in silent complicity, stubbornly refused to accept that these antics amounted to anything more than the odd game of lotto too many. Even when I had caught that disease which made me walk gingerly and soil my underpants she hadn't realised, not because she was being discreet but because she didn't want to know, and so doggedly insisted that I take tonics and stuff to stimulate my appetite.

I heard the dog bark and steps which scraped on the coarse sand along the avenue of palms; it would be my uncle coming home much sooner than usual. A tiny butterfly dared to fly around my head. I remembered the mosquitos and switched off the light, returning to the window. The silence was total within that noisy darkness. Cicadas and crickets were singing; something scratched on the sand again. Was my uncle going out again? I began to get undressed but I hadn't unpacked my pyjamas. I went to switch on the light but then I thought it would be better on account of the mosquitos to close the window first. I went to close it. I felt something was amiss. There was some movement in the belvedere – or was that only my impression? I stayed stock still, watching. There was nothing. I left the windows and wooden shutters ajar, put the light on, found my pyjamas and, putting them on, got into bed and switched off the light. I stretched out, yawning; I was exhausted.

The following day I went looking for José Ramos and his sister. I found them on the beach for I knew more or less the time when their parents would customarily rent a bathing hut. Mercedes was pretty and for me she stood out from her friends; with these we would play in the mornings by pushing them into the water, or, in the afternoons, stretched out on the sand under the vigilant eye of mummy we would endlessly try to knock over the target with sticks, which they would throw expertly, changing the rules all the while. To go for a walk with them was in those days out of the question. The most that they could do was to parade up and down of an evening on the promenade, in tight little groups, whose numbers made up for the lack of supervision on the part of the mothers and aunties. We, also in groups, would follow them or cross their path out of spite; even when one of the group was a brother of one of them we could not get close to them. On the contrary: this only made them even more remote.

When there were junior dances in the casino (to which, on such a night, the most obvious prostitutes were refused entry, and the ways to the gaming rooms were rigorously guarded) they came along, 'duly accompanied', for otherwise they could not come in. This rigour on the part of the management was greatly praised by the families, speaking to each other on the beach, from one bathing hut to the next. Sitting in their low sedan chairs, with their interminable knitting, the secrets of whose stitches they taught to one another, the ladies mulled over these questions and put one another discreetly in the picture about who we were, with an eye to their daughters' engagements. The pursuit of some of the boys, an insidious business, even went so far as to include brothers and cousins, or at least tried to ensure that their friendships, through someone 'with a position or with prospects' would lure the desired victim before the arena of the sedan chairs. Thus, forewarned, we never fell into the trap of playing quoits too close to the bathing huts, preferring the space under the canopies. These, taking the form of rows perpendicular to the bathing huts, constituted a kind of proletariat which was looked down on by the aristocracy of the huts. All those families who had a good conceit of themselves would hire a hut for the season. My aunt and uncle, who never even set foot on the beach, also had one, a fact which guaranteed me a certain 'standing' in the eyes of the good ladies. The canopies were for the hoi polloi who summered there and who, however much they might smile winningly never managed to get anything more out of the ladies of the huts than the merest nod of the head. It did them no good to try to manage to get close by means of their children. If any children from the huts strayed towards the canopies, maids were immediately dispatched to bring them back with the excuse that whoever went away might get lost.

The Spanish families had, generally speaking their own sections of the beach but even there the division between the canopies and the huts ruled. To be considered a 'pander' was among the gang of boys a most dishonourable matter, for a pander was someone who fostered the matrimonial intrigues of the families. I flirted with Mercedes more because her mother was watching me out of the corner of her eye than because of any interest she had awakened in me; and Zé, so that he wouldn't be accused of pandering, stayed away from us both. Rodrigues was treated ambivalently by the ladies: they knew that he was the heir to a grand hotel but it was said that he was shady character, that his mother might marry again at any time. But whenever he in his bathing costume approached the huts there was a hardly disguised frisson; and I had once heard two of the ladies comment that 'he was very well equipped'. The following day I had to go and look for Zé.

In the carpeted corridor a tree grew under whose shade my aunt, in her chemise was sewing. On one side and the other of the great corridor of the hotel there were doors to the hen-house which was full of boys crammed in there like hens. On top of the tree was Rodrigues in his bathing costume peeping down. From the hen-run the boys crowed and said things to my aunt such as my uncle used to say. At the end of the corridor was the street with the cafés, with tables arranged like in the General and Puigmal's mother serving tea. At the table were Mesquita, my uncle and I; my uncle had his back to the tree. Seeing Rodrigues at the top of the tree I did everything I could to distract my uncle so that he wouldn't turn round; Mesquita was on the phone talking to his fiancée, ignoring my uncle. Then Mercedes, dressed as if she were Odette, was lying on the bed, smoking, while Puigmal, in his uniform, was bending over her, telling her that his father had spoken to the chap. The latter, wearing thick glasses, was going out along the corridor and calling to Rodrigues. Near the tree was someone tall and young looking who wasn't wearing glasses and who looked like Rufininho. My uncle turned round, Mesquita put the phone down and two Republican Guards moved among the tables grabbing the men who were running away from the station ticket office, which was closed; it was situated in the shadowy belvedere in the garden. My uncle got up and ran in slow motion along the corridor, his stick clenched in his fist. I followed behind him. But then my uncle was at the top of the tree, shouting; it was not my aunt in the shade of the tree but Mesquita instead, naked and cowering.

My eyes sought my aunt, whom I couldn't see; instead I saw Rodrigues grappling with Rufininho while the rest of us surrounded the bed. However the one beneath Rodrigues was not Rufininho but a woman whom I had never seen; she was very blonde and seized my arm. 'I have nobody, I have nobody,' she was saying in Rodrigues' voice. Mercedes then led me behind a curtain, one of those from the windows of the casino, and began to unbutton my clothes. At that moment my uncle came along the corridor with two gentlemen I didn't know, and all the doors to the hen-houses flew open from which popped out the chamber pots. Fearful that my uncle might see me I pushed Mercedes' hands away. We were beside the water, up near Buarcos; it was night time and a group of men was jumping into a boat. Rodrigues came running along the beach, shouting, pursued by guards and policemen. The packet was putting off from the beach, moving steadily away. Then the blonde woman appeared by the water's edge, called out and plunged into the water, fully dressed and wearing shoes. I went down to the cabin where Puigmal was playing cards with my uncle and asked for the bathroom. Then I awoke in desperate need of a pee.

It was still night. I switched on the light and went out into the corridor; there was a light in the bathroom. I went back to my room and sat down on the bed to wait. I heard the bathroom door open and I got up to go again. A shape slipped stealthily into one of the empty rooms. I was utterly perplexed. But there was a light in my uncle's bedroom; someone had arrived in the meantime. Were those the steps I had heard in the garden? But whose were they? My aunt and uncle had told me nothing. I hesitated between going back to my room and knocking on my uncle's door. But in any case I went first to the bathroom for a pee. The flush brought to the surface of the lavatory a crumpled cigarette packet. My aunt didn't smoke, my uncle preferred to roll his own, I hadn't recently finished a packet ... I bent over to look. It was a packet of Spanish cigarettes.

So was a Spaniard the new guest, that shape which I had seen go into the other bedroom? I went back to my room, unable to make head nor tail of the matter, and went to bed. The following day I would find out.

VII

I woke early with the sun shining in through a gap in the shutters. At first I could remember nothing, merely savouring the prospect of the beach and my morning swim. But soon – as in a dream, vaguely remembered – I saw the cigarette packet. I pulled myself together and got dressed; I had the impression that there was nobody on my floor and that my aunt and uncle had already gone down. I ran down the large spiral staircase and down the narrow stairs. I went into the dining room. There, seated at a table were two men, one very young, with a moustache, the other older, fatter. I skidded to a halt. They both got up, with great ceremony. 'Good day,' they said in Spanish. 'Are you the nephew of Don Justino?' asked the fat one. Just then I noticed that my aunt and uncle were not there, although their table was set; I replied that I was, looking around at the same time. The older one said that my aunt and uncle were in the kitchen making coffee. I went to the kitchen where my uncle, dressed in his trousers but still wearing his pyjama top and slippers, as he always did of a morning, and with his stick in his hand (it seemed as though he even slept with it) was talking to my aunt who was heating the coffee on the stove.

'Have you met them already?' she asked.

'Who are they?'

My aunt did not move from the stove or look up. 'Another daft idea of your uncle's,' she said.

'Daft idea? Daft, eh?' he said. 'These fellows had nowhere to hide, they could have been arrested, so I offered them my house. What's daft about that?'

'Fair enough. But if the police come looking for them here I want to know how you'll wriggle out of that. Everything's a piece of cake for your uncle.'

'Be quiet, woman! No cop is going to come here. Put the coffee on the table. You,' he said, turning to me, 'be off to the beach and don't say a word to anyone. The maids didn't see them arrive; they came in from the Tavarede side' – those had been their shadows in the belvedere, without doubt – 'nobody knows they're here. Woman, you don't say a word to anybody at all, whoever they are. I can trust my nephew, he's my nephew and that's enough for me.'

My aunt picked up the coffee pot and went out of the kitchen.

'What about the maids? What if they talk?' I asked, although I thought the whole thing absurd.

He stood up straight, in high good humour and took out from his mouth the yellowing fag end and tapped the ash with his little finger. 'This uncle of yours here,' he said, 'in 1917 crossed Germany, from Austria to Holland without knowing more than three or four words of German.' His eyes were shining. 'It was a narrow escape. Do you think I'm crazy? The maids went away this morning; they're in Tavarede or somewhere, it's where they come from. And we're setting off first thing this morning for Coimbra because my mother-in-law is very ill. Anyway it's all done now. It all happened in a hell of rush.' And he lit a match close up to his cigarette, with his head inclined to one side.

'And the dog? Where did he go?' I said, entering into the spirit of the thing.

My uncle froze, the match burning his fingers; he cursed. 'The dog?' he repeated.

He put the cane hard down on the mosaic floor and, supported by both hands, rested his body on it. He blinked rapidly – a sign that he was lost in deep thought. 'Damn, I'd forgotten about the dog.'

'And me? Who only got here yesterday, where did I go?'

He raised his astonished eyes to me. 'Yes, you, where did you go?'

'You'd be the one to know, uncle.'

'Me? It's the devil, the very devil. Wait. But I can leave food for the dog for a quite a few days, can't I? Those girls are stupid, they won't think of that. And there's an even better reason why they didn't bother about the dog; they didn't think anything was amiss. They hate the dog, really, and they'd have been quite happy that we'd forgotten him.'

'And me?' I started to ask.

'You're the least of my worries. A boy, a man, you'd get by anywhere.' He straightened up again. 'Don't worry your head about it. When we start thinking about things too much they never turn out right. Let's have coffee.'

In the dining room the two men were already drinking coffee and eating bread and butter, laughing with their mouths full, in spite of the delicate way in which they held their bread aloft in their fingers. Their ability to adapt to things in carefree fashion seemed limitless. They stood up when we came in and sat down at the same time as my uncle; they did not start eating again until he had served himself. Once the polite silence had passed we all began to eat, noisily handing each other plates and things.

One of the Spaniards spoke in a mixture of Castilian Spanish and Portuguese. In a nutshell their story was as follows: for some days feelings had been running high within the Spanish colony, which was divided by what had happened in Spain. Each side demanded, in violent terms, the head of the other, believing the 'revolution' to be imminent. In spite of everything, though, the matter had gone no further than some falling out between neighbours, on the beach, in the cafés, hotels and boarding houses. Nobody believed that 'his' revolution would ever, even if it should blow up into something, demand more of him than that. On the previous evening, however, the contradictory and confused news bulletins on the radio – and it was the first time in my life that the radio had assumed such importance – made people think that the situation was extremely serious, with the military uprising spreading from Morocco to all the provinces and the people responding with violence in the streets and demanding weapons.

The revolution of the 'clergy', the older one had no doubt, was on the streets, against the 'Liberation of Spain', and was not merely, in traditional fashion, one more military coup to restore order. He stressed the word with heavy irony; 'that of the clergy and the generals, that of the bankers and aristocrats,' he added. The younger one criticised these generalisations: 'Those on the right' were many, but divided by deeply opposing views. There were the Carlists, the liberal monarchists, the Catholics who were republicans, and those who weren't, and the Falange. Some of them wanted the restoration of the monarchy, others not, For those who wanted it, however, the king was not the same. And there were other groups who wanted social reform, while others had made the revolution to prevent just such an eventuality. The older fellow acknowledged that this was true, but that 'our lot' were also many and even more divided. There were the anarchists, the communists, the socialists, the republicans – and he listed a series of initials standing for various parties which were all Greek to me. The struggle would be hard but swift; and the people would win at one fell swoop that which, with the Republic alone, without a revolution, would be much more difficult to achieve. That was the younger man's opinion.

The older man believed the opposite, saying that the politicians of the Republic were foxes, he knew them well, and that they had at bottom such a fear of the people, just like the generals and the priests and the bankers. And their falterings, their obsession with dealing with everything behind the scenes, would disgrace the revolution. The younger one retorted that between them the young people, the working class, the miners, had enough strength to win the day.

'What about weapons, have they got any weapons?' asked my uncle, lifting his chin to re-light his cigarette. They would get hold of them, they would attack the barracks (which began to have some resemblances to 'my' revolutions).

'All the barracks?' asked my uncle.

The younger got to his feet. 'You, Don Justino, do not know what is the Spain of the people,' he said in Spanish. 'We, those whom you know, will be the friends of the people, of the Spanish people.' And he fell into a patriotic-revolutionary meditation.

'Do you think it will drag on a long time?' asked my aunt. 'And what will our government do?'

The older man responded first, silencing my uncle with a gesture. It would be inappropriate to pronounce on anything that the Portuguese Government might do, but it was evident that official sympathies were with the rebellion, though hedged about by a certain caution, unsure of what might happen, such as the failure of the revolution, for example, which might jeopardise good neighbourly relations in the future.

The younger voiced an angry criticism. He begged our pardon, but this was not the moment for diplomatic evasions. The Portuguese radio was already at the service of the rebels, quite openly. It was said that trainloads of munitions were on their way. And what had happened yesterday left no room for doubt. What would be the fate of those who had been arrested yesterday? Would the same thing not be happening with the Spanish residents and holidaymakers?

The older remained silent; it was my uncle who broke the silence.

'You gentlemen are my guests for as long as necessary. If these scoundrels in the army which governs us do not know how to respect the laws of war, then I do.' And then in the same breath he added: 'What else could we expect from these people who do not even know how to pay a pension to a war invalid. Yes, indeed; I don't know if I have ever told you: my invalid pension – I am a genuine invalid, not like so many that I know, who are merely invalids because they can't shit, or have piles, who have never even set foot in the trenches – well, my pension has never been brought up to date. Today I am being paid what I was being paid twenty years ago. And do you know why? Do you know? Do you know why, woman? And you?' he said, gesturing to me with a nod of the head and waving the handle of his stick.

We all said as one that we did not know. He smiled in superior fashion. 'Not even my wife knows and if even if she did she still wouldn't understand.'

'Wasn't it because you never submitted your claim,' she asked, laughing, 'as you were supposed to.'

'My claim! My claim!' he cried, and tapping the side of his head he gestured his disdain to the Spaniards and to me. 'That was their excuse; it's a long story, a long story. I've already told you how I escaped from a concentration camp and crossed the whole of Germany, with a little German girl, haven't I?... Are you jealous, woman? She's jealous, you can be sure; and at that time, I didn't even know her. But let there be no doubt, you gentlemen are my guests; you will stay here, holed up quietly, and then we'll see.'

From my questions and those of my aunt, and from what the Spaniards told us, we established the following: during the preceding days, accusations had been hurled furiously within the Spanish colony. The Rightists wanted to persuade the Portuguese authorities that there existed an extensive plot on the part of the Spanish Republic to stir things up, plunge Portugal into chaos and drag her into an Iberian Communist Federation. It was clear that the Rightists' course of action had two ends in view: on the one hand to create in Portugal a strong current of opinion against the Republic and the social revolution which it had imposed (and which served the interests of those on the right in Portugal and in Spain too, since it would be an excuse to render ineffectual any reaction should Portugal become a base from which support was extended to the rebellion; and, under the aegis of which any demonstration in support of the Republic would be a sign of connivance with the enemies of Portuguese independence, to wipe out the last resistance to Portugal and the fascist countries coming closer together). And on the other hand, to prevent, by any possible means, the struggle against the rebellion becoming organised in such a way that, through the diplomatic immunity which of necessity protected it, the Rightist manœuvring – and it is clear that the Portuguese Government, or the greater part of it, was sympathetic to such manœuvring – might fail on account of any international repercussions. It was known that the Spanish Embassy in Lisbon was already surrounded, 'for its own protection' and that the ambassador was confined to his residence.

For the rest, General Sanjurjo, in exile in Portugal, was one of the centres of the conspiracy, a fact of which the Portuguese authorities could not have been unaware, since – and the Spaniards swore it was so – the authorities of the Republic even in Portugal kept a close eye upon these suspect activities and had more than once had to ask that this sort of thing (such as the free circulation of the conspirators, who met and came and went as they liked) be stopped. The two of them had been particularly marked out although they were not at the moment involved in political activity; not that there was much difference between them and those who had been arrested the day before, 'interned on account of subversive activities'. They were related to them, though distantly. Uninvolved as they were with immediate political action they still knew they were being watched. On the previous day, therefore, they had left their boarding houses with their families and had apparently taken one of the trains; these, it was known, were being stopped in Vilar Formoso on the frontier, which was already occupied by the rebels. There was no chance of getting to Madrid, according to what one could make out from the babble on the radio stations, and they would also be arrested at the frontier and then God knows what would happen to them: the rebels were trying to rule through terror, nobody was spared. They themselves boasted that they would give no quarter. Their families would not run the same dangers. And so there they were until the situation became clear.

I asked them how they had managed to get to my uncle's house if they had gone as far as to get into the train. Amidst all the confusion in the station what with everybody piling onto the trains, it had been a piece of cake. They laughed: all they had to do was get in one side and out the other – which is what they had done. Then my uncle related the rest. In the evening in the café, when the disturbances – which had been stirred up by the Fascists, the younger one stressed – had broken out they were playing poker with him and other friends. In the uproar they had nipped out the back and planned what to do. They had pretended to leave and at night they came to the belvedere and there they were. 'Now and for a few days,' concluded my uncle, 'while the revolution continues; and meanwhile, in peace here, we'll play a few hands of poker, special poker...'

My aunt and I exchanged a quick glance. The Spaniards fell silent, fiddling with their knives and forks. My uncle sensed the embarrassment. 'Beans, of course,' said my uncle. 'Woman, have we got enough beans in the house for all of us?'

There was a ripple of relieved laughter. My aunt assured us that she had quantities of beans, enough for lunch and dinner, with plenty left over for any other emergency.

I glanced at my watch: it was already too late to go to the beach. It would be better to miss swimming and go straight down to the coast road or look for my friends in their boarding houses. The younger of the two Spaniards noticed my hesitation and asked if my friends were waiting for me. As I was about to reply my uncle butted in: 'Nobody comes here for him, they really don't. The lads have never been in the habit of setting foot in here. With a wife like mine you can't be too careful...'

My aunt got up and went into the kitchen. The Spaniards and I sat with our gaze lowered. My uncle realised perfectly well what he had said but did not bother to correct himself. He rose and finished rolling and licking the cigarette in his hands, stuck his head on one side to light it, cupping his hands around it; he inhaled deeply and leant on his stick with both hands. 'The house is entirely at your disposal, sirs,' he said. 'Should you want books to read my nephew will show you the library.'

The three of us got up and I led them to the huge carpeted room, full of settees, armchairs, little tables with reading lamps, and the revolving bookcases, as tall as a person, groaning with books. The mainstays of the library were old editions from Chardron and, later, Lello: Eça de Queiroz, João Grave, Coelho Neto, Abel Botelho, the Lusitanian collection, the Rationalist Library, the Sermons of Padre Vieira, the New Forest of Padre Bernardes, Guerra Junqueiro and so on, together with a host of French novels, whose stitched yellow covers alternated with the reddish, leather bound backs of the rest. The prevailing tone of the room, however, was yellow, a kind of burnt yellow, in the carpet, of the upholstered seats, in the damascene wallpaper and even in the shades of the reading lamps and those on the many branches of the central crystal chandelier. Since the windows were always closed, the chandelier was switched on; it shed a dim, feeble light. And there was a musty smell, a clamminess, an air of quiet neglect which muffled our voices and which was inseparable for me from the burning excitement with which, years earlier, I had read those passages of erotic or naturalistic fervour which were to be found among those books, or the anti-clericalism of which others were redolent. As for Vieira and Bernardes, I had merely dipped into them and, losing interest, soon put them down. They both seemed to me, in their diverse ways, complete imbeciles. I span the bookcases around as they squeaked and wobbled on their axes. Behind me the two Spaniards said that I shouldn't put myself out and that they would stay there until lunchtime. I left them there and went down to the kitchen to have a few words with my aunt before I went out.

She was painstakingly preparing lunch and, with a girlish smile directed me to peer inside a pan from which she removed the lid: beans. 'It makes a change, having these people here, doesn't it?' she said, raising her large, greeny-blue eyes to me, eyes in which one of her tear glands had swollen and become red and ugly.

I nodded in agreement and said that they were staying in the library and that I was off down to the town.

'Off you go, then, off you go. Your uncle wants you to bring back some Spanish cigarettes for them from the Bairro Novo.'

In my mind I saw again the crumpled packet floating in the lavatory, and then I left. These little errands – this time on the Spaniards' behalf – were my summer responsibility. Either my aunt or my uncle would ask me to get this or that, but for the most part they forgot either to give me any money or to repay me. I enjoyed being of use to them, but what annoyed me was having to spend my own savings, money which I managed with a miser's caution. The morning was bright and warm; the palm trees rustled slightly as they swayed. At the gate, suddenly, I paused, peering around the neighbourhood; there was nobody to be seen, while the tar shimmered on the street which stretched out emptily before me.

VIII

I crossed the Bairro Novo; it was peaceful in the early morning with only the occasional customer sitting at the café tables enjoying the shade with a beer in front of them. They were, as one might expect, the paterfamilias who declined to fill their shoes with sand on the beach; fathers seldom went swimming, mothers and aunts likewise. Those rare specimens who did were not well regarded, according to the opinion of the inhabitants of the bathing huts. To expose one's naked flesh was the preserve of single people or the very young and by extension it was just about tolerated in the newly wed. Or else it was the badge of social inferiority, belonging to those from beneath the canopies (who, puffed up on their own little benches, slavishly followed the bathing huts in every detail); or of the ignorant countryfolk who, on Sundays, with their great wicker baskets full of food – this the ladies found quite shocking – invaded the beach to jump into the sea, shouting and running up and down, splashing water and scattering sand on their seedy bodies on which ancient, drooping bathing suits were overlain by knickers and by camisoles which clung to their flesh. For this reason the bathing huts remained empty on Sundays, all day, while the younger members of the families strolled along the sea wall without deigning to descend to the beach, or joined their parents in the cafés. On weekdays, towards the end of the day, the husbands – or at least a few of them – would put in an appearance to negotiate with great care the boardwalk leading down to the bathing huts. Their children had their own special, evening task which was to rearrange the planks of the boardwalk and clear them of the sand which their games and all their running around had thrown up onto it. The gentlemen, in their coats and ties and fanning themselves with their straw hats, would sit down in front of the bathing huts, among the ladies and their maids, greeting each other as if to suggest they hardly knew each other from the café tables and the casino to whose bar in the evening more or less all of them would sneak off. And they would sit gazing at the sea and the water's edge where sometimes engaged couples would stroll, hand in hand, silhouetted in the setting sun.

As I got nearer the beach, scanning it for the place where Zé

Ramos and Mercedes had their hut, I remembered that I had to buy cigarettes for the two Spaniards. Should I nip back? I decided it would be better to get them on my way back. I bumped into Carlos Macedo who was sitting on the edge of the sea wall; he had been part of our group the year before. He greeted me warmly and then strung together a spate of questions about my life at school during the last year before telling me about his own. That's just how he was, a terrible gossip, except for the times when he was tight-lipped, quiet as a mouse, for as long as it took him to prepare his next onslaught on unsuspecting ears, when he would unleash at the first opportune moment. However, I felt uneasy about all the gush he came out with; I thought he was probing about my uncle's house. Then while I was giving him vague answers to his questions (one didn't need to give precise replies because he never listened to them anyway) I recalled that he had been a day boy at Rodrigues' school, that it was he who had told me all about the place and that in some kind of way he had been a member of that group which worshipped my aunt. Rodrigues didn't like him at all, perhaps apprehensive that Macedo, with his famous memory, allied to his loquacity, would blab excessively. Because the former's sexual ostentation, the demonstrations of his virility – I noted now, looking at Macedo, who was small and nervous, dark-skinned and bearded (the ladies were as fascinated with his hairiness as they were with Rodrigues' 'equipment') – would be redoubled if Macedo happened to be with us and the occasion demanded it. Rodrigues, though, paid him some kind of special attention in his dealings with him; it was as if he wanted to buy his silence with these little courtesies which he showed to almost nobody else. Or else that good-looking little monkey (for Macedo was far from ugly, in the opinion of the girls who only regretted that he just shrugged his shoulders at them, or less) held some fascination for the tall, skinny, gaunt figure. Macedo was now in Oporto, studying medicine. There he had had Odette more than once; and when he had first come across her in the street, by chance, she had given him her services for free as a tribute to our group. I reckoned that it must have a tribute to me, but I said nothing. He asked me if I had already seen Rodrigues and Ramos and his sister. I replied that I had seen Rodrigues the day before but that as far as the others were concerned I had just now come looking for them.

'I'm waiting for them here,' he said. 'You got here yesterday, didn't you? And you waited until today? Why didn't you come for a swim? Did you arrive on the night train? No? Well, then, what kept you?'

'I was talking with my aunt and uncle.'

'Your uncle's getting worse, I don't know if you're aware of it. In the town everybody feels sorry for your aunt. What must she be going through! My brother says that in college nobody can stand him. Do you remember my brother?'

In my mind I recalled the figure of a painfully thin boy, quite different from his brother, who last year had insisted that he was really a man and had attached himself to our group though we tried to shake him off.

'You remember? Well, this year he's shot up, he's a man, he can knock around with us. My brother says that with your uncle in class, his pointer in one hand, chair in the other, the register all over the place, well, it's just bedlam. His jokes can't even work anymore. Some students complained about him and it is said the fathers called him in and said they would sack him if he went on like that. Do you think he paid any attention? On the contrary, he got worse. He grabbed poor Padre Augusto by the arm and dragged him off from class to class and made him tell him who were the ones who had complained. The father struggled and shouted but nobody ran to help because they were all too terrified of your uncle's stick. As for Padre Augusto, poor fellow – as if he were some rascal who deserved all that and more – well, he was going around, pointing to this one and that one and yet another one. Then your uncle called all the boys together, all this in front of the fathers, and declared that all those who had complained were to be expelled from the College, not because they had complained about him but because they weren't men, they were perverts who didn't have the guts to face up to him if they had anything to say about him. The boys were incandescent, the fathers, too.

'"Lieutenant, mind your language," said Father Augusto, wringing his hands.

'"Mind what?" roared your uncle at once. "Mind what? You, sirs, should be grateful to me for still being a teacher in this den of iniquity. The day I leave this place there will no longer be any men here. And you gentleman," he said, turning to the fathers, "have made a vow of chastity and these boys within a short time do not know whether their arse is their own or someone else's."

'At this Father Augusto fainted. Your uncle turned to the boys. "Do you want at least one man here or not?"'

'"We do! Long live the Lieutenant!" cried the mass of boys as one.

'But their humiliation didn't cease with that: the fathers no longer speak to him, but they didn't boot him out, although it is said that when he returns in October he'll be sent packing.'

'And what about those my uncle "expelled"?'

'Of course they carried on at the College. But you don't want to know what your uncle did to them. Lessons – no; registers – no; nothing but the written exercises that the classes have to do. The only words he said to them were: 'you, girlie, here, you, girlie, over there, Micaela, Maria, are you ladies not feeling well?' The worst thing is that it stuck, this vengeance of his, and now that's what everybody calls them. Micaela is my brother.'

Their father was the Captain of the Fiscal Guard; he had been stationed in Figueira for donkey's years. He had a drooping moustache, and that stiff, erect air of a retired general.

'Does your father know about all this?' I asked.

'Well, you know what it's like. Everybody is fond of your uncle, they pardon these outbursts of his. Then, the College is all right, it's the best, but it's got a bad name. At bottom everybody is having a good laugh and rubbing their hands in glee. What I say is that if my brother were one of those little tarts he'd have had it. My father even had him in and read him the riot act into the bargain.'

There was a sweet silence filled with the babble of the beach as it emptied. The sun was burning the pines.

'Have you really been waiting for Zé and Mercedes here?'

'Certainly, right here. They'll be along, I promise you. They won't let me down; I've got a message for them – an urgent message,' and he fixed me with his dark, shining eyes, waiting for me to take the bait. I said nothing and he got up and stretched, flexing his muscles as if he were some huge athlete. Next to me – I was still seated – he was just taller than my head.

'You've heard about the revolution in Spain, haven't you? You read the papers? And listen to the news?'

I said I'd heard about it and that I'd read the paper the day before; I yawned.

'Well, what do you think about it?' he said, staring at me.

'Think about what?'

'Come on, the revolution! Don't you know what happened yesterday? Don't you? No? Ah, you were here, at least? Then you must have seen the punch-up that the Fascists started in the Bairro

Novo; it was all in aid of capturing some Republicans that they had
their eyes on. The police took 'em off to Oporto this morning, by
car.'

I felt a cold shiver run down my back; I saw myself in a car with
my aunt and uncle and the two Spaniards, going to Oporto. I only
saw the car and the Clérigos Tower and the two iron bridges, for
I had never been to Oporto.

'It's a scandal. They got them and for what? And what are they
going to do with them? They say round here that they're going to
hand them over at the frontier. The chief of police told my father
that the order to take them to Oporto came from Lisbon, by phone,
so it must have been the Government. Have you heard the Radio
Club? It's enough to make you sick.'

I was puzzled for I had never known him to be interested in
politics, in any shape or form. 'But what's all this to do with you?'
I asked cautiously.

'To do with me? But can't you see that this revolution is directed
against us? Against freedom? That it's part of the whole Fascist
conspiracy?'

In the face of my silence he shut up and looked at me. 'When it
comes to it which side are you on?' he asked, knitting his brows.

'Me?'

'Yes, you?'

'I don't know.'

'You don't know? What do you mean, you don't know? Have
you been going around with your eyes closed?'

'No ... well, maybe... You could be right, perhaps I have been
going around with my eyes closed.'

'You really have, but it looks to me like you could be waking
up. You have to read these things I'm going to lend you. But where
the hell have this darned Ramos and his sister got to? Yes indeed,
old chap, if we win the revolution in Spain, there'll be a clean up
here too,' he said making a sweeping gesture.

'A clean up?'

'Of course. That will be the end of all this. And, if all these old
republicans think that they'll return to power, they've got another
think coming. There in Oporto our lads are working with a will.
Disciplined, obedient to the party's orders, recruiting ... but now
all hell is going to break loose. For all this is against us. Don't be
under any illusion; it will be just an excuse to send us to Tarrafal.
There in the boarding house everybody's on our side, they won't

give the show away. And you... will you give me your word of honour you won't breathe a word of this to anyone?'

'Certainly I will'

'The greatest care is hardly enough. I shouldn't have told you anything.'

'I won't say a word.'

'If I spoke to you it was because I always thought you were a serious fellow, someone I could trust. Now with Rodrigues...'

'What's up with Rodrigues?'

'Nothing, but I don't think I can trust him in these matters.'

I saw Rodrigues again, boiling over with anti-Spanish rage. 'The one thing he can't stand is Spaniards,' I said 'Do you know why?'

'Course I know... His father's Spanish and he let himself be cuckolded all over the place.'

'Did he tell you this?'

'He did; you too? But look, if he did tell you it's because he's your friend. You know he never mentioned this to anyone.'

'But everybody knew in the College, didn't they?'

'No. I knew because once he burst out crying and then he told me.'

'Crying?'

'Yes. One day during break, it was all a long time ago, someone started calling him a Galician; well, he set about the chap with blows, shouting out that he was Portuguese, that he'd been born in Portugal, his mother was Portuguese too, he didn't let on. Then when we'd dragged them apart I found myself next to him. He burst out crying and told me everything. It's an awful story, a typical example of the decadence of the capitalist world, of the moral breakdown of this shameful society we live in. His mother is a first class whore; she makes me sick. My father got to know his at the time when he used to go every year to take the waters. Whoever saw him, said my father, would never imagine that such a man, bowing in dignified fashion, so respectable, so well turned out, was the softest touch in all the world. Besides I'm convinced that my father went there for years on end not so much to take the waters as to sleep with her.'

I felt I wanted to give him something to think about. 'So your father also gave a hand to the decadence of the capitalist world?'

'I don't think so. It's one thing for someone to take advantage of his luck and another when he doesn't know when to stop.'

'Look, I know some fellow who is stinking rich, and who loves his wife so much that he'll put up with all the lovers she has.'

'It's the same thing. He must suppose that money gives him the right to keep his wife in spite of the fact that she's screwing everybody in sight. Rodrigues' father has got hotel society mixed up with a woman's bed. In Russia that just isn't possible: if a man wins a woman's heart and she agrees to sleep with him, that's fine; if she gets fed up with him or he with her, then they go their separate ways and that's it. And none of this has to do with their work. If my father has slept with Rodrigues' mother, and I don't know that he did, he did it because that's the way she wanted it. If the husband doesn't mind, it's a matter for her conscience and that of her husband.'

'And your father's, as well?'

His father had lost his wife when his youngest son was still very small. He hadn't remarried and an aunt – his sister – had come to take charge of the children. Captain Macedo's domestic set up was well known throughout Figueira for he used to stroll with two girls on his arm, in front of everybody, and of his sons, too, with the air of some chaste suitor, leaning solicitously with his drooping whiskers over the ladies of his choice. But everybody knew he was sleeping with them regularly, with the precision of a military timetable.

'As for my father, clearly not,' he replied.

'But how come? You can't mean that he didn't come between a husband and his wife, can you?'

'Look, here comes Ramos at last,' he said, waving to his friend who was coming towards us but without the sister who I had been waiting to meet, too.

Ramos was a tall, strong chap, light-haired and ruddy, and he embraced me effusively, but such behaviour, reserved for important occasions, had a dryness, a reserve, to it, like his infrequent utterances, which everybody attributed – to his intense irritation – to his teutonic ancestry. He always said, in his curt phrases and his measured, serious voice, that a German grandfather was an accident which could happen to anybody. His father (the teutonic grandfather was on his mother's side), whom my uncle had known, had been an officer in the army and had died in the Great War when he, Ramos, was only a few months old. And his personal drama, in later years, was precisely the fact that he had been brought up in an extremely Germanic atmosphere after the Germans had killed his father, a father for whom his mother had always retained obviously deep feelings. Mercedes was the daughter of this lady's second marriage, to a first cousin of her late husband; those apparent feelings had surely played some part in her marrying the cousin, for it was as if the two men shared the same soul. And without it affecting the feelings he had for his father, Zé Ramos had, nevertheless, a considerable filial attachment to his step-father.

'Your sister, where's your sister?' asked Macedo. 'Jorge here has been waiting here passing the time with me just to see her. He got here yesterday.'

'She went back to the boarding house. I'm sorry I'm late but I took her there.'

'It doesn't matter; time's not of the essence. We've been talking, especially about what happened yesterday. You know, they took the guys to Oporto first thing this morning, by car. The chief of police told my father they were going to take them.'

'And did they?' asked Ramos.

I didn't really know what he was going to say since he had insisted that they had already gone.

'They took them all right. I can swear to it because I asked one of the fiscal guards, a friend of mine, and he assured me that he'd seen them go.'

We had all known since we were children just how close he and his brother had been to the fiscal guard, former soldiers, immortalised in Figueira like his father. And, if their boast were to be believed, they were just as close to the smugglers as well.

'Well,' said Ramos.

'And what am I to do?' asked Macedo.

'For now, nothing,' said Ramos.

'You can speak freely,' added Macedo. 'Jorge is one of us.'

Zé looked me up and down as if he were looking at me for the first time. 'So you're one of us, eh? Do you know the risks you're running?'

'Look, Zé, I'm neither for you nor against you. I must admit I don't really know. I've only really started to think about it today.'

Suddenly, the two of them, the Spaniards in my uncle's house, the scuffles in the Bairro Novo, the news in the papers, all of these things seemed like a game for mad children, who thought they were something or other. What did I have to do with all that? It was as if, since yesterday, the world had moved on its axis, and with it, what was real. People were fighting each other in the street, others were being arrested without reason, my uncle was harbouring

Spaniards, these two were evidently mixed up in things I had never even dreamed of. And meanwhile, the beach was emptying, and we were virtually the only ones left, in front of a sea that the midday light bleached pure white, looking like it did every year.

'It's late,' I said. 'Let's be going home.'

We made our way in silence. As we crossed the street with the cafés Macedo pointed to one of them. 'That's where it all began,' he said.

'Was it?' repeated Ramos, stopping short.

'It was,' I replied. 'I saw it happen; I even bumped into Rodrigues in the middle of the whole thing.'

'What was he doing there?' asked Zé.

'Perhaps,' said Carlos Macedo, 'with that hatred he has for Spaniards he was just passing by and took advantage of the situation to give free rein to his instincts.'

'That's exactly how it looked to me,' I said.

Zé Ramos looked at me. 'How did you think he was?' he asked.

'Worse than ever.'

'Worse than ever, that's for sure. But that's not even a tenth of what he'll have to go through.'

'Go through?' I enquired.

'Until he destroys himself.'

I started to walk off again, mindful of the fact that I had to buy some cigarettes for the Spaniards, and also to get away from this conversation which was becoming too weighty for me.

'Where are you rushing off to?' asked Macedo.

'To get some cigarettes,' I said, going into the tobacconists.

When I came out Macedo asked me: 'So you smoke Spanish cigarettes, now, do you?'

I must have lost my nerve for I replied: 'Who? Me? Why?'

'Because I saw the Spanish cigarettes that you put in your pocket. Come on, let's have a look.'

'My uncle asked me to get him some.'

'But he's always rolled his own. What's going on?'

'I don't know. He asked me to get him this brand,' I said, taking one of the packets out of my pocket.

Zé Ramos looked at the packet. 'Look, Macedo,' he said, 'don't do anything. I'm going to ring Oporto and then I'll speak to you. Let's all three of us meet again this afternoon, eh? At four o'clock? See you soon.'

And we went our separate ways.

IX

When I got home there was nobody in the dining room nor any sign of the table having been set. The dog, however, had come to meet me and preceded me into the house; I followed it. The two Spaniards and my uncle were having lunch in one of the other empty rooms, sat round a very small table which could barely accommodate their shirt-sleeved arms. My uncle, still in his pyjama jacket, presided over lunch, talking animatedly. At his side stood my aunt with a tray in her hands; she smiled at me. 'Don Justino' shouted over the noise of plates, glasses and other movement, for me to sit down at an empty place, that they had moved into this room because of the danger of somebody fetching up without warning at the dining room door, that my aunt had cooked some beans for lunch because she wanted to use up the beans before they were taken for the little game of poker, and the beans had been very good, anyway. I sat down on the other spare chair which had clearly been put there for me. The Spaniards kindly gathered up the pots and plates and made a space for me to eat my beans. The general liveliness – largely due to the bottles which my uncle had unearthed from the dust of the larder (where every year I saw the stacks of bottles virginally covered with cobwebs) and which now littered the floor, their long, slender necks – contrasted with the unease which I had felt on my way up from the town; I resented it. I began to eat, so silently and circumspectly that my uncle noticed.

'What's the matter with you, lad?' he said. 'Do you think we won't win the war?'

'No, uncle,' I replied. 'It's just that I bumped into a couple of friends of mine and they saw me buying the cigarettes. I think they suspect something.'

The two Spaniards stopped short, one with his fork, the other with his glass halfway to his mouth, and stared at me. My uncle did the opposite: he plonked his arms on the table. My aunt was about to open her mouth but he beat her to it. 'Which friends?' he asked.

'Carlos Macedo and Zé Ramos.'

My uncle took a deep breath, glanced reassuringly at the Spaniards in turn; he explained that Carlos Macedo was the son of the chief of the Fiscal Guard, an old friend of his, and that Zé Ramos, like

Carlos, had been a student of his at the College. He knew them well; there was no danger from that quarter, they were both good boys.

'The worst thing is,' he added after a moment's thought, 'is that this Carlos is one of those who talks nineteen to the dozen. In class it's the very devil to shut him up. If he happens to meet somebody and he doesn't have anything else to talk about, he might let something slip.' He chewed thoughtfully on a mouthful. The others had stopped eating. He put one hand on his head and with the other loaded up his fork again. 'But Carlos won't say anything,' he said, 'not if I know the lad. A while back his father spoke to me about the boy and his ideas, he was a bit worried; he thought that being in Oporto had turned his head,' and he put down his fork to make a gesture of elucidation. 'He's got these progressive notions. Ah, yes, that's how it was. And Captain Macedo even told me it was all Zé Ramos' fault. So there we are. It's not worth getting upset about,' he concluded picking up one of the bottles from the floor and pouring the contents into the four glasses. Then, with his fork still hovering over the table he said. 'But you haven't said what happened to the cigarettes. Did you get them?'

I took the packets of cigarettes out of my pockets and laid them on the table; the Spaniards thanked me effusively and wanted to pay me. My uncle stopped them with a gesture which, though elegant, brooked no opposition, picked up the packets and, like someone giving out a medal or a diploma, handed them over to the Spaniards.

They were, however, both concerned about the lack of news since the previous day as there was no paper until the afternoon and no radio because my uncle did not possess one. They asked me if I had heard anything. I told them what Macedo had said: that the prisoners had been taken to Oporto at dawn. As far as what had been happening in Spain itself, I hadn't spoken to anyone so I knew nothing. They were uneasy; the euphoria of lunch, of wine and the beans, had disappeared completely; while I ate they discussed what they should do. If the others had been carted off to Oporto they had done the best thing by hiding until things became clearer, but, holed up and unable to contact anybody, they couldn't really judge what was happening, and – who knows? – they might be missing a golden opportunity to return to Spain and join their friends in Madrid, where they both lived.

The older, Don Juan de Dios de Medrano Y Arrabal, did not come from the capital but from the Asturias; the younger – I didn't know what the relationship between the two men was – was called Don Fernando de Azlarregui, and he was Basque. Don Juan had sent his wife and their children, a boy and a girl back to Madrid. But since the trains, it was widely reported, were not going beyond Vilar Formoso, he had advised them, should that turn out to be the case when they got to Alfarelos, not to continue on to Madrid via Vilar Formoso, but to take the down train to Lisbon and from there attempt to enter Spain through Badajoz. Don Fernando's wife, who was going with them, was to do the same. In Lisbon they had friends through whom they could keep in touch. They couldn't rely on the consul in Figueira; he and his staff were notoriously Fascists or Monarchists. Don Juan was too well known as the socialist leader in the Asturias, where he had played a leading role – so said the younger one – in the miners' revolt. It was for exactly this reason that he had been removed from politics in Madrid for having publicly opposed the military repression to which the Republican government had assented in order to appease the rightists. Don Fernando was an active agent in the movement of Basque separatists and belonged to the group of Catholics of Aguirre, one or other of whom was on the list of those who would end up in prison: during the brawl in the Bairro Novo one of the Fascists had shouted that the consul in Figueira had a list of all those in Figueira and that they would all be detained. All this combined to give me, as I finished off the beans, a tumultuous, troubled picture of Spain to be added to, in my mind, the marvellous Catalan separatism of which Puigmal used to speak. It was unthinkable for a Portuguese that the provinces of the Minho, the Beiras, the Alentejo or the Algarve should nourish such separatist ideas in relation to the Lisbon government of whatever stripe, while Puigmal's crazy enthusiasms did not constitute an adequate point of reference for me. Provinces which had belonged first to one country then to another were different, though even so my knowledge of history stretched no further than Alsace and Lorraine which, from conflict to conflict, were French or German. But that was different. Spain (which in my primary school lessons and then at grammar school had been Leon for D. Afonso Henriques, Castille for D. João, and since Phillip II and the Wars of Restoration as well, a dangerous monolith of a neighbour, an object of suspicion, whose formation I would see as somehow linked to Covadonga and to Eurico the presbyter) all of a sudden was transformed into something which was like a huge number of Portugals in 1640, all wanting to separate themselves off from the others, at the same time as everybody, on top of that, aspired to make a communist revolution.

But neither Don Juan nor Don Fernando (and I always thought it absurd, this proud way of addressing each other as Don when for me the word was redolent of those medals of kings which I had since primary school, with their vast 'synoptic panorama' of the History of Portugal, who never went without their nicknames: the Populator, the Eloquent, the African, etc.) were communists, or so they swore. The younger even professed to be a Catholic; being a Catholic was something else I didn't understand. In my family, whether on my father's or my mother's side, Catholicism meant the church where we were baptised or married, or the priest whom we called when someone was dying. The rest were provincial bigots or old maids with nothing else to do (and for exactly this reason my spinster aunts, so as not to draw attention to their state, did not go regularly to church). For a man to claim that he was Catholic, in the way that Don Fernando did, was incomprehensible and even ridiculous; nobody had ever done anything like that in front of me before. And what is more he was as furiously opposed to 'clerics' as Don Juan; if religion was the church and its priests, how could one be a Catholic and hate the priests so much? It was true that Don Fernando, from what I heard, made an exception for Basque priests, but it seemed to me that these men must have been from his point of view more Basque than priest. Subsequently everything was spoken of in terms of Fascist or Communist and even Zé Ramos or Macedo, who weren't Spanish or the children of Spaniards, or anything of the sort, also constructed their arguments along the same lines. I had understood that they were trying to analyse things logically; so that there were people, everywhere, who saw each other as in truth they were not. Communism was something belonging to Russia and of which one of our teachers had once spoken: and at that time the only thing which had stuck as far as I and my colleagues were concerned was something which he had gone out of his way to condemn: free love.

This free love business meant that women were in effect prostitutes, freely available, with any of whom one could sleep, without paying, without responsibilities, and without husbands who, at the top of the back stairs, waited with a gun in their hands to see us flee buck naked. What could be better? Which was exactly the comment which Mesquita, his hand in the air, had made to the teacher, having first asked him whether one wasn't forced to marry a girl after having deflowered her. The teacher – a young doctor, who we made blush with our shocking, malicious questions which he begged permission to answer in private but to which we noisily demanded answers there and then on the grounds that they concerned all of us, and whose subject was Hygiene – had got on his high horse and demanded indignantly whether this was the fate we wished upon our sisters. Puigmal, conspicuously, had asked permission to say that, with the odd exception, all women were naturally the sisters of some fellow or other and that, therefore, if all men were to respect every man's sisters, this would automatically prejudice only children or those girls who had no brothers. And then he launched into another question. If the sex of children depended on their fathers' right or left testicle – But who told you that? Who told you that? roared the doctor – there would be sound biological reason why these girls would be condemned to shame, on account of their fathers' testicles. The teacher then invoked the prohibition of incest: would we desire our sisters? We at once took great offence because that was not the subject under discussion: we were speaking, all of us, about other men's sisters. Mesquita then put a full stop to the question, affirming that, clearly, a man could respect the sister of a friend, as a friend; but that if he wanted a woman and if the woman permitted it, her relations were not in any way involved. The teacher of Hygiene retorted that we were monsters of depravity and that our parents could not have imagined what sort of creatures they were harbouring, animals capable of anything. Free love was a return to bestiality.

It was at that very moment that one of our schoolfellows, Vasconcelos, an extremely shy, withdrawn boy, asked a question that was to pass into legend: 'What about dogs?' All of us, the teacher and us, looked at him, thunderstruck. Fingering his book and with his eyes lowered he repeated the question: 'What about dogs?' The teacher asked if he was referring to the fact that, as far as sex was concerned, dogs had no conscience. 'Yes, that is what I wanted to say,' he said, without looking up. 'Dogs know no prohibitions of sex or incest so, if this free love were to have prohibitions relating to sex and incest, it would not be a return to bestiality but another way of looking at human relations. Over there,' he concluded, 'do men have ... relations with each other, freely? And with their sisters and mothers?'

'What on earth...?' The teacher was covered in confusion. 'Russians are men like us.'

'Well then, you cannot say that free love is a return to bestiality,' said Vasconcelos finally looking up to cast over the class a glance of malicious triumph, as if finally free after years of crippling shyness.

Later, during the break, we were discussing Communism: it was that abolition of property in all its forms, the State owned everything, it was the State which gave people what they needed while the people in turn had to work for the State in order to pay for those things. Our opinions were divided: those who were the sons of civil servants couldn't see any difference at all; those who were sons of doctors, lawyers, merchants, maintained that there was a difference in that a person could not earn what he wanted to. Which is where our arguments remained, becoming gradually more abstract, academic and remote.

The Spaniards rose from the table and my uncle asked me if I was going out after lunch to get a newspaper. He was going out, too, to bring back a surprise... A surprise... And what a surprise! We should see it. We all went up to our rooms; he paused suddenly on the steps above, causing us to fall over each other, to tell us once again what a great surprise it would be.

In my room, lying on the bed, weighed down by all I had eaten and drunk, I thought back over everything that had happened; I felt heavy with sleep. The light came through the cracks in the closed shutters; I took off my shoes and stretched out on the bed. It was oppressively hot and I got up, undressed completely as I liked to do and went to lie down again. I tossed and turned, gripping the bolster. Before anything else I had to deal with the matter of Odette; this very day; and I had to see Ramos' sister, At once I remembered too that I had to write home to tell them that I had arrived and with news of my aunt and uncle. It was a condition of my holidays. My family and they never wrote to each other; the fact that I never wrote either didn't count. For if I, on my holidays, didn't write to my parents, telling them that I'd arrived safely, that my aunt and uncle were fine, that the beach hadn't moved, that would have been unforgiveable. And I had to send seaside postcards as usual to the rest of our family, but once I had fulfilled this obligation I didn't have to write to anyone else again. But what about Maria Helena? I had to write to her. Before I had set off she had insisted that I write to her; I had protested that love letters were not my cup of tea. She had burst into tears, saying that I was only going on holiday so that I could ditch her and find other girls, to which I replied that I could perfectly well find other girls while writing to her every day as well. In the end we reached an agreement: I would write to her each week (which over three months was, I made her realise, a dozen letters for her to show her friends).

What was there to say? I had been thinking the matter over in the train. Could it be that I didn't really like her? or that I was, as she maintained, a desiccated sort of fellow, unable really to be fond of anybody, to lose myself in love (those were her words)? For me to love to distraction someone that I couldn't have sex with did not make sense. Privately I scorned Mesquita and all that passionate nonsense of his on the phone while I found it deeply distasteful to spend time dreaming, day and night, of the moment when the girls might finally be had when I couldn't have them anyway and when I hadn't the slightest intention of marrying them. Any idea of marriage was for me a remote possibility which, in my family, never entered in any moral sense into anyone's mind until that person had a 'situation' in life. What interested me was a tender, sweet intimacy, made more delicious through the excitement of contact and a frankness of talking which I never knew at home, and which I never gave to, or received from, the women with whom I occasionally had sex. But I always refused to make plans, of the type of 'When I'm yours I'll darn your socks', 'How would you like your house to be', 'Oh, I only want three children'; and I would even go so far as to say that these affairs finished as far as I was concerned on the day they started to ply me with these sentimental confidences.

Maria Helena, whom I had got to know going to the University, had accepted the express conditions that I laid down: she was never to speak to me of such tomfoolery, nor was she even to think about a time when we might marry. We started going out together, we went around together, I gave her long, knowing kisses on the stairway, I talked to her about anything and everything that came into my head, and that was it. She had accepted the situation but gradually our strolls and our conversations had started to acquire a melancholy tinge. I could see that she was making huge efforts not to take over my interior life, but I had been very browned off with the scene about the letters, with all its attendant tears and sighs. She had even managed to insinuate that I didn't love her because I never demanded anything more than kisses, and that I could only really love fallen women. I had protested and then held her and kissed her violently, to which she had given herself up, bent over backwards. I had lifted her skirt and lowered her knickers, pressing my hand against her down there, while she moaned her pleasure; I undid my trousers and squeezed myself between her tightly clenched legs. That's as far as it went, no more, and I wiped her clean with my handkerchief. But she was grateful for it, even for the shock I had given her when I had grabbed her on the stairs. And so we had parted with me promising to send her a letter every week.

Now, lying on the bed, I felt an enormous frustration. I would write to her as she had asked me to, addressing my letter to the tobacconist in the street next to where her house stood, and where I had met her that time when, passing by, I had gone in to buy cigarettes and she had been there leafing through some magazines. The owner of the place, a terrible old gossip, with curlers in her hair and her mouth daubed in the shape of a heart, looked after the romantic secrets of all the girls from round about. She accepted and sent messages, and in special instances such as someone going away on holiday, she acted as a letterbox. In my mind I began to compose a letter: I would say that I only wanted her for me, that I thought of nothing but the day on which I would have her, naked, on my bed, when I would penetrate her to the very core, and that I would screw the arse off her. No, no, I couldn't say that. I would say that her legs were like hot velvet, but that I wanted to feel another kind of velvet, one which was moist with blood and desire, that I would make her mine, with exquisite care, tenderness, violence, until she knew me not just by my hands, not just through the entry of my flesh, but through my movement, my weight, my... Where had I read all this stuff? What did I know? Had I ever had anyone beyond my own desire to possess someone? Even when they reached the final bit – and the first time this had happened to me I had had a fearful shock, believing that the maid, in my house, was having some kind of nervous seizure and that she would wake up the whole building, it was a shock which spoiled everything – I, though on the one hand proud to have aroused something which continued to be a most singular and unexpected mystery, on the other hand was troubled by this new dimension to my desires, as if the fact that a woman had allowed herself such deep and all-encompassing pleasure was a kind of unwelcome interference with my solitary satisfaction. I felt myself suddenly by the side of the bed and I looked at my cock with wonder. 'He' had never thought of anything but himself; I was a child, my friends were but children. It was as if none of us was any older than sixteen. And wasn't it a fact that almost every man went on in exactly the same way, that none ever really grew out of himself? And wasn't it the case that the whole world wanted us to carry on in that fashion? Wasn't it true that everybody was afraid to give himself because he was afraid to lose the little that he had? Wasn't it true, too, that everyone only lent himself like someone lending money at interest?

My cock affected to be uninterested, serenely innocent of what was going on. But did he not purchase his pleasure, without thinking of more remote pleasures? Did I not buy it for him, in cash, weighing it all up, with touching, with thoughts, with diligent attention as if he was someone quite apart from me? Suddenly 'he' began to throb and growl; it was as if he wanted to tell me that this was all true, that he went along with it and that he could do much more than I ever could... He was the future. Oh, not because he could make children; that was exactly what held him back. No, it was because he could give and get pleasure, he could be *my* freedom. Freedom from what, though? What I had was a rage because I hadn't actually *had* my girlfriend. Or was that not it? My freedom would be in being able to have her, without fearing that I might be bound to her, or just in not getting to the point of having her, in the absence of fear on my part or hers. Because, clearly, there on the stairs I couldn't have done more than I did; and if I had tried to do more she would certainly have fled... And on another occasion, who would there be to stop me being a little bit more careful and discreet, starting by deflowering her and finishing as I had finished before?

Then I remembered another situation I had known, and which had been a great topic of conversation among us for many years. Some chap had had sex with a maid at home, always with the utmost caution, without knowing that she was also inviting in one of the shop assistants from the grocer's. When she got pregnant she accused the poor chap of being the father of the child. If I allowed Maria Helena that freedom she could do the same to me. 'He', however, was a giver of pleasure and a liberator, but he could be bound to the one he had set free, the one who still had the freedom to choose whoever she wished to have bound. So, to prevent this happening several men would have to have sex with this woman, all with each others' knowledge. But how could a woman truly 'love' several men at the same time? And above all if she knew they all knew what the others were doing? Prostitutes had their favourites while we, too, prepared to go with this one or that one. This, though, wasn't love; it was habit, the liking for pretending that people weren't what they were, or for pretending that, in having sex, we also loved. So, was it only in marriage, then, that these two worlds met, the one which, through love, went no further than the thighs, and that in which, going beyond the thighs, there was no love? Did I know anyone who could show me that marriage was this harmonious union of the two worlds? My parents? My aunt and uncle? My friends' parents? The married lovers of my friends? That lady we had been told about by Puigmal? Where was their happiness? And weren't the families out there on the beach on the hunt as well? Wasn't it to get us married off? And did they ever ask themselves if the engaged couple really did love each other? Or if the girl would finally love the boy, simply because they plonked him down in front of her for her to get used to the idea that they would let her sleep with him whenever she wanted? And he? Would he not let himself love her because he finally came to see in her the person with whom he could – since she was his exclusively – sleep with all those who had had her and even those he had not had? It was then I felt a deep desire not for someone, but just to sleep with someone. So much was true: I had never spent the whole night with anyone. Never, not even in Figueira. And that was what I was going to do.

I got dressed and went downstairs. I would buy the postcards and on the following day write to everybody – or on another day. And I would buy the papers as my uncle had requested, and the cigarettes for the Spaniards. After dinner I would deal with my problem. I would love to see the faces that my aunt and uncle would make. Perhaps, though, they wouldn't make any at all.

X

At the tobacconist's – not the one where I had bought the cigarettes that morning – I bought some cigarettes and a few postcards to send to my family and then carried on to the spot where I had arranged to meet Macedo and Ramos. They weren't there; it was still early and so I went round to Ramos' boarding house. As I went in I was aware of an uneasy atmosphere among the guests who had gathered in the hall and the foyer; I felt that a similar atmosphere had been what had kept me from staying there while waiting for my friends in the agreed place. It seemed that in the end not so many Spaniards had fled as I had thought the previous day. On the other hand, though, the high spirits and the bustle of the groups, in the street, or in the hotel or boarding house, too, were still somewhat reserved, with everything expressed in silences or curt gestures finishing what was not expressed in words.

While I was waiting for Ramos I began to think that some of them were looking at me curiously, as if I were somebody who shouldn't be there or as if they suspected that I might be some clandestine messenger. Zé came down. 'Do you know what's happened?' he asked. He suggested it would be better if we went up to his room, where we found Macedo and another boy whom I didn't know; he was tall and skinny, with a very dark complexion, and was called Almeida. They had heard on the radio that morning that General Sanjurjo had been killed in Cascais in a plane crash. I had not the remotest idea who this general was and they were little better informed than me. The general had been in exile in Portugal and on the way back to Spain, to assume charge of the revolution, his plane had crashed and burst into flames. The plane itself was Spanish and had been sent to fetch him, but on taking off from the naval airfield, near Cascais, it had crashed into the trees in the nearby forest and broken up. For Macedo and Ramos the fact that the field belonged to the navy was proof of the Government's connivance. As it happened I knew the area, having once gone on a hike around there while on an excursion to the Boca do Inferno; it seemed to me that there was a country house there which, though supposed to belong to the navy, didn't really belong to the armed forces at all.

'OK,' said Macedo, 'a Spanish plane doesn't come right into this country, stop and pick up an important passenger like this chap without anybody knowing about it. Perhaps if it had been somewhere near the frontier it might have been possible, but when it had to cross the whole country, no.'

I agreed that this case was certainly different. But was that the reason why everybody was going around like this, unsettled and on edge, because of the death of this general? He said it was; there were those who thought that the revolution, leaderless, would unravel for lack of someone to hold it together. In each division of those who had risen up there was, without doubt, a general who had his eyes on the leadership. Would they come to an understanding among themselves?

I had some doubts, however, and I found myself explaining them to them. If the revolution was as big as they had said it was, and had broken out in so many places at the same time – or almost the same time, it wouldn't then depend on just one man but on many; it had also been very well organised. It wasn't something which would just break out spontaneously above all at a time when politics were so diverse and there were so many opposing forces. And, once these people had set something so widespread in motion it would take more than the death of one leader to derail it. Probably there hadn't been just one leader but many, all of them waiting to seize their opportunity when the shape of things had become clearer. The death of one of them would be a setback for the group which he represented, but the other groups might even benefit and such groups would not withdraw just because they had nobody at their head. Quite the contrary, for if they did withdraw and the revolution triumphed what would happen to them? And after this question, which followed the line of my reasoning, I shut up, aware of their silence as they fixed their eyes on me.

'Didn't I tell you?' said Macedo to Ramos. The latter was cleaning his fingernails, which he always kept scrupulously clean, even to the extent that on the beach he would scour them for the least grain of sand. 'Yes ... you're right,' he said. 'You are very well informed, aren't you?'

I denied it, saying that it was only since the previous day that I had been thinking about these things – which was true – and that perhaps for that very reason I could see things more clearly. But perhaps I had got it wrong; and I began to trace out arguments to the contrary. It might be the case that that movement was not so extensive as everybody believed, some because they wanted a revolution and dreamed that it would be a great victory, while others, in making such a big thing of it, would have the pretext they needed for another revolution, the communist revolution, the one they really wanted. If that were the case the death of the general could lead to the failure of the whole thing and the revolutionaries – if they didn't have the strength for a quick, decisive victory in every quarter – would not want to serve as a pretext for the triumph of the very thing against which they were struggling.

'But you said that one of these things, once begun, would not end up like this,' said the lad they called Almeid, who had not yet said anything. His voice was very slow and deep; looking at him I realised he was not a boy at all but a man of thirty, a lot older than the rest of us. Who could he be?

'I don't understand anything about these petty politics,' he continued. 'It's just a lot of nonsense for country bumpkins; nor do I want to know. What matters to me is the Republic; and they want to destroy the Republic in Spain first so that it will be easier for them to do the same here.'

The question I had asked myself was written in the glance I aimed at Macedo and Ramos; it was Macedo who spoke: 'Almeida is an officer in the fishing fleet; he's from Figueira.'

I was going to ask how it was that I had never seen him in previous years, when there was a knock at the door. It was Mercedes. I got up to greet her and in the agitation of seeing her – I was all smiles – I felt that after all it was for her that I had come here.

She, with her brown hair hanging down, her great big eyes, and her breasts rounded under her low, square cut blouse, smiled at me in friendly fashion; she leaning behind me to talk to the one whose view I was blocking out. 'Oh, Manuel,' she asked, 'are you coming on the walk with us to Tavarede?' I turned round to see if this Manuel she was addressing was the one they called Almeida. He replied that, yes, he would come and, getting up, went out with her.

The room was silent. 'Are you going on this walk to Tavarede?' I asked, trying to sound as natural as possible.

'They're the ones who are going, and some friends of my sister's as well,' replied Ramos. 'We're not going.'

'Who are these friends?' I asked. 'Do I know them?'

'My sister's going with Almeida, and the two Prates sisters – do you remember them? – two fat little things whom you know from

Lisbon, who were here last year, and the boyfriend of one of them and some other girls, and my parents as well because they've never been there before. They fixed it all up over lunch; they were counting on you too but we said that you were going to stay with us.'

This explanation of Ramos' left me unable to say anything. Only Almeida...

'Just who is this Almeida?'

'I've just told you,' said Macedo. 'He's something to do with cod-fishing. He's from these parts; I've known him for years, for ages.'

'I've never seen him before.'

'He couldn't always be here. Hang on. Nor could he have, what with spending the last few years always at sea, all the big expeditions. But this year he's staying behind.'

Silence reigned once again. 'He's going to marry my sister,' added Zé Ramos.

'Your sister?'

'Yes; what's wrong with that then?'

'But she's so young, your sister ... she's a lot younger than him, isn't she?'

'Not so much; he looks older than he is. He's only 26.'

'When are they getting married?'

They glanced at each other. 'They were thinking of getting married in the spring,' said Ramos.

'And they're no longer thinking of it?'

Ramos got up and went to the window which looked out onto a courtyard. 'If there's no hitch Almeida wants to get married next year before he goes to sea again,' he said.

'But now, with everything that's happening, I don't kn...' But Ramos cut him short in mid phrase and finished it for him: 'This is nothing to do with us; it's up to them.'

'Did he meet your sister in Oporto?'

'He did,' he said and he told me how it happened; it seemed that in the telling he felt relieved of some burden. 'This year he was in Oporto for a while to be treated by a doctor and he sought out Macedo so that he could stay in the same boarding house. And one day when we had fixed up to go to the cinema, to the matinée, I had to shoo away some chap who had sat down next to her and put his leg up against hers. In the interval Mercedes and I went to look for Macedo here and we found him talking to somebody who looked pretty much like the one we had just sent packing. And so it turned out. He was profuse in his apologies ... and he's ended up engaged to my sister. That's your Almeida; he's a pretty cool customer.'

'Well, that's a fine thing,' I said; I was going to add that a bit of footsie and a couple of brotherly smacks were one way of starting off on the road to matrimony; but I decided to say nothing.

'Are we going to stay here all afternoon, or shall we go out for a stroll?' asked Macedo.

'Let's go for a stroll,' I said, getting up.

'You two go,' said Ramos. 'I'm staying here.'

'What are you doing tonight?' I enquired.

'Nothing special; but don't count on me for anything.'

Macedo and I left; in the street he stopped. 'Look here,' he said, 'you seemed a bit choked with Mercedes' boyfriend. Did you come with some idea of making up to her?' And he looked directly at me.

'I don't know; honestly, I don't know. But none of us has ever been engaged to anyone. Here on the beach it seems to happen to some of the fellows, those older than us.'

'But did you come here intending to ask her to go out with you, or not?'

'I've already told you I don't know. But, yes, it's true I've been thinking about her a lot.'

'She used to have a soft spot for you, but these days she's only got eyes for Almeida. Forgive me for saying so, but she didn't even notice you. Not for any bad reason – we were talking about you at lunch. I don't know what it is about Almeida but it was always the same: with those swarthy, smooth looks of his the women fall for him like nobody's business. He just has to whistle. I think it's something to do with the fishing.'

'With fishing?'

'Yes, when they learn he goes off fishing for cod, and lives for six months of year without even seeing a woman, they're hooked. Maybe they're thinking of the head of steam he must get up in those balls of his. They dream about draining it all out of him; what they don't think about is having to spend the other six months looking out for boats.'

'It's a hard life, theirs,' I said.

'It is indeed, but they earn stacks of money. My brother wants to go off to sea. As soon as he's finished college he's going to Lisbon, to the Naval School. Not just for the money; he's always been crazy about the sea. I've been wanting to speak to you about it because we don't know anybody in Lisbon and you could keep an eye on him.'

'I could; I'd be happy to. He might even be able to stay in our house. When does he finish school?'

'Only next year, though I did want to speak to you about it now. Thanks, anyway,' and he raised his hand high to give me a friendly slap on the back.

'Shall we sit here?' I asked, spying some empty tables in the café.

'No, it gets on my nerves being in the middle of all this Spanish crowd. All these swaggering around here, they're all Fascists. It makes me sick to see them raising their arms with their cries of "Arriba España".'

'Is that what they do?'

'Ah ... you mean you haven't seen them? And it won't be long before it's the same thing here too.'

'Where, here?'

'Here, in Portugal, yes.'

I recalled the SAV which had been formed while I was at grammar school and to which boys from various classes belonged, though not mine. This 'School Action Vanguard' was a 'national syndicalist' organisation but only one boy in my class belonged to it; this was Coelho, a tall, broad-shouldered chap, softly spoken, with whom almost nobody had much to do. Not that he was a pain; he just seemed so much older than us, with that reserved way of his and his size. Once Mesquita had quarrelled with him because he had wanted to distribute some pamphlets in the class before the teacher arrived. Nobody showed the slightest interest so distributing pamphlets in that way seemed to us to be plain ridiculous, on a par with those notices in the street advertising a huge sale in the department store in the Chiado. Mesquita had declared that while he was there nobody was going to be distributing pamphlets. Coelho, very softly, asked him what he had against the SAV. Nothing, he said; he didn't even know what it was. Nor did he want to know. But politics in school, no. At the school gate, well, that was another matter.

When we were leaving school at the end of the afternoon there was Coelho at the school gate for the purpose of handing out his pamphlets; deliberately, watched over by Mesquita, so none of us had taken one. The following morning as Mesquita and I turned the corner of the school we saw a group of boys there, who blocked our way. They were members of the SAV from other classes. 'What are you doing, stopping the distribution of our pamphlets?' one of them demanded of Mesquita.

'In class, it's not on; out here, I don't care,' he replied. 'What do you lot want? Let me pass.'

The one who had challenged him took out a piece of paper from his pocket and crumpled it up into a ball. 'OK,' he said, 'you can go after you've swallowed this little pill and then you'll know who we are.' I looked around. There were ten of them and in threes they crowded round us in the middle. 'Well, since it isn't shit,' I heard Mesquita say, 'I'll swallow it. Are you sure it isn't shit? That your organisation isn't shit, either?' The others crowded in on him but hearing the other one, they stopped. 'Wait, he said he'd swallow it; let's see.'

'I'll swallow it. But first I want to know what the paper says,' said Mesquita.

'Let's thrash him,' said one of the others. 'That'll teach him to be so clever.'

'No,' said the one who had given him the paper. 'He has the right to know what he's swallowing.' And taking a sheet of paper from his pocket he showed it to Mesquita.

There were two gear wheels with teeth and an arrow joined a black point between them to the slogan: 'We are the grain of sand which will stop the infernal machine'; underneath in green letters was written SAV. It was the same as the posters which had appeared on various walls.

'But this is pure shit, it doesn't mean anything,' said Mesquita. 'And I don't eat shit.' And so saying he delivered a punch to the pit of the other's stomach.

A fight broke out. It didn't last long, for a policeman came running and they all fled. We set off for the school gates again, all the while glancing behind us to check whether the policeman, there on the corner, wasn't following us. Coelho was standing at the gates. 'If you'll excuse me,' he said, 'I had nothing to do with what happened; I do apologise.'

Mesquita looked him up and down. 'Don't mention it. And don't go handing out papers in class otherwise you will be the one to swallow them. And tell your bodyguards that I'm not afraid of them.'

Then something extraordinary happened: Coelho stood to attention and raising his arm, held it straight out. We were startled;

we didn't know what was going on. Then we turned round. It was Mr Pimenta, a history teacher, who had come in, and who returned the salute, but as if trying to disguise it, raising his arm without moving his elbow from his side. 'Not a word of this nonsense to anybody, you hear?' said Mesquita to me in class as we waited for our teacher to arrive. I had indeed forgotten completely about the incident for it had nothing to do with us at all.

Walking along with Macedo, though, I remembered it and some other facts as well. Regarding Mr Pimenta, who had never been my teacher, it was said that he was a monarchist, and never passed up the chance in class to speak about His Majesty. This Majesty was a vague entity as far as I was concerned, and I never understood, either, how he could do such a thing while he was a teacher of the Republic. He seemed even worse than Puigmal who had certain claims, at which we used to scoff, on a foreign country, while Mr Pimenta made his claims on his own country of which he was a servant. The monarchy had ended in 1910 and the deposed king had died and everybody had watched his funeral in Lisbon, where he had been brought from England. This Majesty of Mr Pimenta's was different: he was a grandson of Don Miguel, an absolutist, who had been banished a century ago. Don Miguel did not figure in the history books. While he had governed the king was D. Pedro IV; there was a monument to him in the Rossio.

'Look at that,' said Macedo, suddenly, by my side, 'look, it's your uncle.'

I looked where he was pointing. My uncle was crossing the street and clearing his way with great sweeps of his stick, smiling all the while. Behind him trotted a small boy with a large radio on his head As if he was canvassing for something, my uncle greeted all his acquaintances on all sides and, without stopping, turned about and pointed to the radio with his stick. People laughed and he, as if conducting an invisible orchestra, went on his way.

I ran towards him. Opening his mischievous eyes wide, he stopped, and with his stick tapped lightly on the machine. 'Now then, how about this for a surprise,' he said. 'What have you got to say about our surprise, then? Not bad, is it, eh?'

There was no doubt that the radio was big. I said that it was very fine, a very good make. 'Have you heard about the crash?' I asked in a low voice.

He said he had. He asked me if I had bought the cigarettes. I felt for them in my pocket.

'Give them here, I'll take them,' he said, and then standing close to me, all the while nodding and smiling a greeting to one of his acquaintances who had come up to admire the radio, he put them into his own pocket.

While he was still putting the packets of cigarettes away and talking to his friend I said abruptly 'Uncle, if you don't mind, I won't have dinner at home. I'll stay here.'

'Out on the spree, eh? Well, all these Spanish widows now, they'll need a shoulder to cry on. Stay out, by all means.'

And I continued to watch his hat, at a jaunty angle, and his stick waving in the air, and the radio moving from side to side as they disappeared into the crowd of heads.

I returned to where Macedo was standing. 'Your uncle's gone off then... To listen to news of the revolution, would you say?'

'I guess so. He was pretty excited about it.'

'Whose side is he on?'

'I don't think he's on anybody's.'

'That's just like him. With all that venom he had against the military, if he believes the Army is on the side of the rebels, then he'll be for the Republic. Those rows he used to have with my father were terrible, and in class he was always telling us how he had remained a lieutenant all his life. When my father defended the army he would retort that he too had been marking time with the rank of captain. But the funniest bit was him, did you know, insisting that we called him Lieutenant. He goes wild if anybody calls him "teacher" or "sir"; he replies immediately that if he's a sir then he's a horse's arse but in any case he's more competent than the dons of Coimbra. Mr Carvalho, who's a don at Coimbra, he tells him sometimes, half serious, half joking, that he has to take a course in maths. And your uncle went so far as to sign up, you know, but he soon got fed up and didn't do anything. You know one of Mr Carvalho's sons, the one who knocks around with us. This year he's stayed in Coimbra; his father won't let him come, he's got to resit his exams. It's the other one who's here.'

By this time I was only vaguely listening to him but he carried on rattling away. We were by the beach, going towards Buarcos. The sun was oppressive. 'Shall we go down to the huts?' I suggested.

'What for? Most of our lot aren't there. And anyway it's no longer early.'

On that side the beach was almost deserted and the strand curved away towards Cape Mondego, with its beached boats and one or

two outlined beneath the sand. Among the boats or seated on the
sea wall were the fishermen, mending their nets and tackle which
were spread out along the sand. To our right, on the other side of
the street, were low houses with women dressed in black at the
doors. We strolled idly across the sand as far as the water's edge; we
walked on across the wet sand. The boats were becoming fewer.
In the shade of one of them two people were lying. They were two
men and as we passed them I saw that they were peering out at a
body, naked except for trunks, stretched out close by another boat
further along.

The body had his back half turned to whoever was passing in
the damp sand, supporting his head on his left hand. The right hand,
hidden by the body was moving gently. A slight movement of the
body revealed that he had his penis cupped in his hand, which passed
over his shorts where they had been lowered in front. The two
men stirred. I was about to draw Macedo's attention to what I had
seen, but I had a strange feeling and so said nothing. At that moment
the body threw itself flat on the ground and hid his face in his hands,
a face that otherwise I would have seen if he had remained in the
same position as we went on past. But I stopped short; Macedo
went on talking. The two men raised their torsos, turned round
and sat up. One of them pulled out a cigarette and offered one to
the other. They stared at us long and hard from behind the cigarettes
that the first one had lit.

'Shall we go back?' I asked.

Macedo who had pulled up at my side, talking about this and
that all the while, seemed to wake up; that was when he saw the
two men. 'Do you know who they are? I know them from Oporto.
They're a couple of ... they must be here on the prowl – maybe
that guy lying over there,' he said. I shuddered. 'Everybody knows
about them in Oporto; they're friends of Rufininho's. He's in
Oporto taking Architecture. He's getting worse all the time,
mincing about and shrieking. There's a whole crowd of them there
but everybody knows who they are. Is it the same in Lisbon?'

I only knew of one who lived across the street from an aunt and
uncle of mine; he was a legend in our family. When he came to
the window, or went out, my cousins liked to spy on him. He was
bald, short and stout; he would appear at the window in some gaudy
outfit. In the street, however, he would walk down the steep slopes
very erect and only his hips swayed like a woman's.

'They all know each other, like some kind of freemasonry,'

Macedo was saying. 'Last year in Oporto I was coming out of the cinema at night with a colleague of mine and this chap started talking to us. He must have been about thirty-something, well groomed and turned out, wearing cologne. But he spoke with a very coarse voice. If you saw him you'd know something wasn't right. He trotted alongside us, asking where we lived, inviting us back to his place. Would we have a drink? We looked at each other and decided we would. You should have seen his house. He poured some expensive stuff, gin, whisky, you can imagine. We were sitting on a sofa and he came and sat between us. He'd put some music on this great big gramophone. And then he started with his hand, resting it on my leg. I got up and so did my friend. He backed away from us to the other side of the room and we followed him, to give him a good hiding. So he said he hadn't forced us to come to his house and that if we wanted we could leave at once.'

'What then?' I asked, glancing back. The boats concealed the shapes.

'We gave him a beating. He wasn't a soft touch, though, my dear chap, you can't believe the thrashing we gave him. When we got to the street we stared at each other in surprise. Who would have thought it, eh? It seems there are some who really are men, in spite of their preferences. He was one of that sort.'

'But what did he want?'

'Everything; he'd give everything, do everything.'

'How did you know?'

'He said so. When we were going after him, he told us. He told us to calm down, not to get mad, because he'd do the lot – meaning that he's no better than Rufininho.'

'And what about those over there?'

'They're just the same as well. Can you believe it, they even call each other by women's names; there's a café there in Oporto where they all meet. You only have to hear them. I've never heard them but that's what they tell me. And I've often seen Rufininho there with those two. Those chaps must be spying on some fisherman.'

'Of course,' I said.

We walked on; Macedo didn't say anything for a while. Then he spoke: 'Look, have you come across our stuff?'

'What stuff?'

'Our stuff – you know, those proscribed books.'

I knew that there was censorship of newspapers: there would even be a stamp saying 'Passed by the Censorship Commission'. A friend of one of my uncles – the one who'd sent the telegram to the Government – and who used to play bridge with him every week, was a member of the Commission. I'd never heard of proscribed books though, except for those dirty ones, badly printed, which were passed around under the desks at school.

'What books?'

'I'll lend you some; you'll soon see what I mean.'

'So how come these books are forbidden?'

'They just are: nobody can sell them, not even foreigners. And if the police catch you with one…'

'What do they do?'

'What do they do? Hmm… But you don't know anything! What have you been doing all this time?'

'Me?'

'Yes, you.'

I looked at him and raised my eyebrows. 'The same as most people, I suppose.'

He stopped and stood there at my side, looking downcast. He seemed even smaller than usual; his beard was like a blue shadow across his face. 'That's the way it is; that's what's so wrong about it. Everybody just goes on living, not bothering about anything else, not opening their eyes to the misery that there is. And even when there isn't misery, not seeing the exploitation of men by men, on which they live and through which they live.' He lifted his head towards me; his eyes were moist, something I found upsetting. 'Have you ever thought how those fishermen live? And the peasants in the country? And the workers? Have you ever thought?'

I had thought about them sometimes. But everything seemed to me to be part of some immutable law which kept us apart from those uneducated, unwashed folk who would continue to live as they had always lived. Everything seemed to me wrong in the world and much more so on that day. Or the world was, all of it, a gigantic error. But I hadn't thought about such things in the way that his shining, moist eyes spoke of them. 'I don't know,' I replied. 'Now that you ask it's as though I hadn't really thought about them. I don't know what to say to you.'

He raised a hand and as was his habit, slapped me on the back. 'You're a good lad; I always knew you were.'

I smiled, and he, as if enraptured, began to walk again. 'Do you want to have dinner with me?' I asked him, suddenly.

'When I'm here, and I'm only here for the holidays, my father prefers me to dine with him; he says it's a bad example for my brother. But when he eats out, that's another thing. Let's go by our house to find out. And I could bring my brother. But this time we go Dutch; everybody pays his bit, you hear? Let's go.'

He lived in the barracks, a big yellow building in front of the river, with a long row of balconies high up, above a huge wall on which were set a few narrow doors. He went up and I waited, gazing at the quays and on the other side of the river at the masts rising against the land. In the middle of the river a boat was stranded on a bar of sand; it was a trawler.

'My father has invited you to dine with us,' said Macedo, at the door. I was disappointed.

'Look, you know? I told my uncle I wasn't dining at home. I wanted to go out on the town, really paint the town red. That's why I asked you out. All that formality with your father and I've never eaten in your house. Honestly, I'm sorry but...'

'It doesn't matter. I'll tell him you can't. But I'll come with you. Let's meet at the casino, at ten o'clock, say, OK?' He leant against the wall. 'Frankly I wouldn't mind doing the same myself. Let's make a night of it. See you soon.'

I was on my own, as I had suddenly wished to be. I walked on as far as the small balcony, a series of steps and ornamental landings, by which one might go from beside the river to the beach by the mouth of the river, which was as far as the town extended. In a corner a couple disentwined themselves; he crossed his legs to hide the signs. They were people of modest means, they worked for somebody else, both of them. I went on to another terrace and they were hidden behind the corner of a cliff. I leant against the balustrade; it was made of concrete in the form of a tree. The sun had already set and only a reddish blotch marked where it had disappeared into the sea, which seemed like pewter, here and there in shadow. The beach stretched emptily as far as the cape and the boats in the distance were being pushed into the water by what seemed like groups of ants. The lighthouse beam flickered through 360 degrees so that it was impossible to see where it was coming from. Odd cries and calls floated indistinctly through the air which, at the water's edge and from the side of the river, seemed to form a thin mist which trembled. Down below the rocks were green with dark pools dotted among them.

I lit a cigarette; where would I have dinner? I didn't feel like eating; I wanted to get away somewhere. Where to? Why? Then suddenly a phrase came into my head: 'Signs of fire the souls take their leave, calm and quiet, from these cold ashes.' I looked around; where had that phrase come from? Who had said it to me? I tried to say the words again to myself: Signs of fire… But I had forgotten the rest. I made an effort to piece it together again: 'Signs of fire the men take their leave, worn out and afraid, when the night of death comes down cold over the sea.' No, that wasn't it; it wasn't. And what had it meant? Was it a poem? I went over it again in my mind: 'Signs of ash the men take their leave, launching the boats of this life upon the sea.' Once again the words were not the same, or maybe the same, almost, but in a different order. I pulled a piece of paper from my pocket and wrote: 'Signs of fire the men take their leave, launching the boats of this life upon the sea.' I read what I had written. What next? I looked out at the darkening sea; there were patches of light which spread over the heaving waters. The boats were ready to set sail and on some of them the lamps were lit. 'On the vast deeps…' On the vast deeps… That was absurd; what was I doing, writing verses? Why? I screwed up the piece of paper and hurled it away. But I hadn't crushed it tightly enough and the paper floated gently down until it came to rest on a rock. There it hovered and lay still and then, swirling abruptly, it fell down into the stones below and disappeared. The night was dark as I turned back to the town.

XI

The dimly lit, empty streets had a sad air about them. I found a small place to eat; the owner bowed to me from the long counter while in the other part behind stalls of painted black wood were the tables, only one of which was occupied. The waiter led me to one of them; the tablecloth was stained with spots of wine. He saw me glance at them so, bending low over the table, he smoothed out the tablecloth with great care, as if in removing the creases he would also remove the stains. Then he swept away the crumbs with the dirty napkin which he carried on his arm, and surveyed his work; then, with his hands resting on the front of his apron which was slung low and tight round his midriff, below the belt of his trousers, he asked me what I wanted.

'What's it to be then? We have boiled hake, fried mackerel, fish stew ... or I could do you a steak if that's what you want.'

'The hake, I think.'

He went to the counter and fetched a knife and fork and plates as well as a small bottle of wine and oil and vinegar in cruets. 'On the vast deeps which the oar's sweep measures out, the peaceful night slumbers.' They were lines of poetry, without doubt; but was there any reason for my composing them, or for them to be forming in my mind, on my own account? I had never read much by way of verse; nor did poetry hold much interest for me. In my family's life literature had never played any part and certainly nobody had ever been a writer. They read books, certainly, but only for entertainment and without remembering the writers' names. In my own house, even less than that for we didn't even have any books. Writing ... only in jest. One of my uncles used to write a little magazine every year but only as a way to cut a figure among the crowd on the beach with whom he spent the summer. To be a writer or anything like that of an artistic nature was even worse than being a politician; a writer, a painter, an actor had no place on the social scale while the word poet was used among the family to mean someone who hadn't a clue, gutless, a blithering idiot, when he wasn't going around owing money to all and sundry.

But I hadn't written some verses; it was just that some words, somehow, had come together in my head. No more than that. In any case it was a nonsense: men aren't signs of fire … and the sea, what was that about? And what did it mean to measure the vast deeps with the sweeps of one's oars? And the night slumbering over those deeps when the night, at night, covered everything? I smiled in relief and the waiter who was bringing my tray supposed that my geniality extended to him and the food and served me with bogus solicitude.

'The fish is absolutely wonderful. You'll see, sir. Perfection. The fish here, we cook it better than anyone else. We get people coming here specially to eat our hake.'

I looked at him and realised that he was very young, not much older than me, in spite of his weary air and the little pot belly that his sloppy apron only highlighted.

I sprinkled some olive oil over the potatoes. 'There aren't so many people around, they're getting fewer, aren't they?' I said.

'Getting fewer, why?'

'Well, with all the Spaniards leaving…'

'Are they leaving, then?'

'Yes. Don't you know?'

'Why? I don't know anything about it.'

My fork stopped halfway to my mouth. In a town of that size, which more or less survived on its summer income from the Spanish, that fellow didn't even know what was going on. He must have felt vaguely curious for he asked me: 'But why are they leaving?'

'On account of the revolution.'

'Ah, the revolution…' It seemed to me that his affability was some kind of act.

'The revolution in Spain,' I stressed.

'Yes … I've heard about it. But the Spanish don't eat here.'

'So it makes no difference to you then?'

'Well, it doesn't make any difference to the boss,' and he smiled, his teeth showing white.

'And to you?'

'To me neither. What difference would it make to me?' and he shrugged.

'You're perfectly happy here then?' I asked.

He hesitated.

'You're happy with your work here, are you?'

'I am, to be sure. It's not easy to get a job like this; and the boss is a good sort.'

'Are you from Figueira itself?'

'Me? No, sir. I'm from Soure.'

'And you come here to work?'

The man at the other table clapped his hands and he went to serve him. In the meantime I finished my meal and he returned and asked me if I wanted anything else and whether I had enjoyed my meal. Would I like a pudding? No, I didn't want anything else. I lit a cigarette and offered him one from the packet. He glanced at the owner who had been watching us and received a nod of the head. With his two figures delicately outstretched he took a cigarette and put it in his mouth; he bent down to take the box of matches I offered him and lit the cigarette and handed back the box, holding it rather as a lady of good breeding would hold a cup of tea. Then, holding the cigarette in the same way he took a deep draw on it, removed it from his mouth. 'A very fine smoke, indeed, sir,' he said holding it up for inspection in front of him. 'Yes, I'm from Soure. Are you a student in Coimbra, sir, or just travelling around?'

'Neither. I'm a student in Lisbon; I come from there.'

'I suppose you're here on holiday, then. Lisbon must be a fine city; I'd love to go there. I have a cousin in Lisbon – you might know him. He works in a little restaurant in the Poço do Borratém – I think that's what it's called, too. They say it's a great little place to eat. You must know it, sir.'

I thought that the restaurant must be no different from any other little bar; it might even be a lot worse ... in that part of town. No, I didn't know it, but, yes, it must be a fine place.

'It stays open all night, and...' and begging my permission, he sat down in front of me and leant across the table. 'The working girls, all of them from round there, they go and have supper there,' he whispered to me. 'My cousin fixes them up ... He writes to me. Out of friendship, to do the best he can for them. You know what I mean, sir?'

I winked at him. 'Just as you, if you went to Lisbon,' I said, 'would do your best for them, too?'

'Ah, there's none of that here. They're all fat pigs. My cousin says they wash themselves before and afterwards. It's true, isn't it? And in Coimbra they don't wash either, from what I've heard.'

'Have you ever been to Coimbra, then?'

'Once, when I was up from the country, but I didn't like it. If you don't mind my saying so,' and he took a long, deep drag of smoke, 'those students with their – hey, you, come here, and you, over there, hey, you, you peasant, come here, while everybody else has to call them young gentlemen, – yes, sir, no, sir, three bags full, sir. There's none of that stuff here, it's much better. It's like that in Lisbon, too, isn't it?'

'Lisbon's too big for that; nobody knows who's a student and who isn't.'

'They call my cousin Mr Joaquim, you see. And he's not old, he can't be much older than me. He says that one of them even washes it for him. Do you think that's true?'

So I, to keep him happy, told him about a prostitute I had known who specialised in other such variations: she used to wash us with great delicacy and then dry us in the same way, inspecting us close up to check that everything was perfectly clean; she used to put a glass on the bedside table into which she'd spit out everything when she'd finished, to drink or not, according to one's taste. We called her the Chinese girl.

He seemed lost in thought. 'A glass ... with a glass and all,' he said. He leant closer towards me. 'They've only done that to me once,' he confided, glancing sideways. 'It was in Coimbra, a student, and he gave me twenty thousand reis. I was only small and he got hold of me and dragged me off to some alley. I was terrified, I thought he wanted me to eat it. But you mustn't go thinking that I ... you wouldn't think that, eh?'

I assured him that I didn't. 'Really, I don't go for men,' he stressed, 'it was just that once. Did you think that I wasn't interested in the twenty thousand? I was though. My boss was a bad lot, he beat me and didn't pay me. I was interested enough, believe me, sir. But afterwards I was so afraid that I didn't even spend it; I've still got it. You might not believe me, but I have.'

He fell silent and then made as if to get up. 'I'm keeping you, sir,' he added. 'You've got your own life to lead.'

'No, I'm in no hurry,' I said.

'Well, then, if you're not in a hurry I'll tell you another thing. Back in the country my folk, my crowd there, we had a dog which, you know, licked you. It was so addicted to it, you'd hardly have sat down when it would come running with its tongue hanging out. Ah, but in Lisbon ... I'm saving every penny to go there.' He got up, looking as if he wanted to strike a bargain. 'Ten escudos,' he said, bending over me with a wicked smile. 'For ten escudos, sir, you've had boiled hake like no other.'

I paid and left a tip for which he thanked me with a discreet bow, accompanying me to the door. 'Whenever you wish, sir, we're at your service. And, look, the lunch is even better.'

I set off towards the casino; it was already past ten o'clock. From a corner a woman called me; she was frightful, old and toothless. Who knows, perhaps without teeth it might be better... Near the casino there was almost nobody about, though I could hear the music from the bar. I entered and went over to the gaming room to see if my uncle was there. He wasn't. I went to the bar which was dense with people and smoke; a raised arm beckoned me over. There at a table were Macedo and his brother, Rodrigues and two lads whom I knew from the previous year. They made a place for me and I sat down.

'We thought you weren't coming,' said Macedo.

'Where've you been all day?' asked Rodrigues. 'You didn't show up.'

I glanced at him. 'Here and there,' I replied. 'I'm sorry I didn't show up but we went for a walk on the beach in the afternoon.'

'In which direction?'

'I've already told him we went towards Buarcos,' Macedo butted in.

'But what time would it have been when you were round there?' persisted Rodrigues. 'In the afternoon I was swimming near the boats with some little thing I'd met and taken up there with me, but I didn't see you.'

'It must have been at a different time,' I said.

'You didn't see me then?'

'Come on, man,' said Macedo, 'When you're out with some girl we're not obliged to say we've seen you.'

Rodrigues stretched languidly in his chair like someone who was recalling some deep satisfaction. 'If only you knew ... behind that boat, I was going at it hammer and tongs, going like the clappers.' And he put his hands to his groin. 'I had a hard-on that was good for the whole night.'

'Keep it to yourself then,' said one of the others, who was called Oliveira and came from Coimbra.

'What do you mean, keep her? My exploits are public; don't you know I'm a man of the public? A man of the public,' he said, breaking into giggles, with a glass of beer in his hand. 'That's what happens when you've got tackle like mine. Something like that belongs to everyone, it's collective, isn't it Macedo? In Russia they'd make it public property...'

'I don't think so,' said Macedo, unruffled. 'The least that would happen to you would be that they'd cut it off.'

'Oh, yes? Might I know why? Don't they have any use for that sort of thing there?'

'They do, but they don't go around with it in their mouths all the time; they leave it nice and quiet between their legs until they need it.'

'Mine doesn't talk though – but if it could, it would tell you a thing or two...'

'It wouldn't tell us anything we don't already know.'

'And what do you know then?'

'The lot. Didn't you say you were a public man?' said Macedo, and the table roared with laughter. 'We know everything about public men – and what we don't know, they tell us.'

'They only tell us what suits them,' observed Macedo's brother.

We looked at him, olive skinned and his almost hairless face, and he blushed.

'Well, did you open your account with Dona Micaela, then?' said Rodrigues.

'Rodrigues, I'm not having any of this stupid nonsense,' cut in Macedo sharply. 'You leave off my brother and let this story drop. He's not a pansy and neither does he go down on anybody.'

'Are you insinuating that somebody here goes down on people?'

'I'm not insinuating anything. But you don't make that crack again.'

'Doesn't your brother know how to look after himself? Does he need big brother to help him?'

'Drop it!' said the other boy who hadn't spoken before. 'What a daft conversation! We're all friends and we're here to have a right good time. What we want is some women; with them we'll see if you can put your money where your mouth is and make your tongue do some real work.'

'If only you knew how good it is,' said Rodrigues, grinning. 'Does anybody know that story about the cardinal, and the definition he gives of it?'

We'd all heard it.

Rodrigues stared at Macedo's brother. 'But poor Luís doesn't know it, do you? No? The kids need to know these things. Two cardinals were discussing how one should define it and one of them said: "Your eminence, the best definition is a devout pilgrimage to the place of one's birth." That's a good one, isn't it? But the other cardinal wasn't too sure and so he asked: "Your eminence, why is it called devout?" And the first one said: "Your eminence, isn't it done kneeling down?"'

Macedo's brother smiled coldly. 'Does it have to be kneeling down? Can't you do on the bed?'

We laughed. 'That's one up to him, Rodrigues,' said Oliveira

'It is ... the kid knows his stuff. Macedo, your brother knows his stuff; I think he has a vocation.'

'For what?' asked Macedo.

'Well ... to stay on the bed, or standing up. He's one of those who doesn't kneel down. One after my own heart. Who wants him to kneel down in front of us, eh, Luís? I'd really like to see what you do.'

'If that's what you want.'

'If that's what I want? You can't imagine, my son. Only, I haven't brought my binoculars. And without my binoculars do you reckon there'd be anything to see?'

'I'll show you, whenever you feel like it,'

'Yes ... we could have a competition; maybe you'll get second prize. The prize for being the hairiest, that's what he'd win, your brother. And Oliveira there with those talents that I know all about from Coimbra...'

'You've heard about my talents?'

'I certainly have... You'd get the long distance prize. There's not a whore that could stand it; they could have lunch and dinner and you'd still be at it. You'd have to pay double.'

'No I wouldn't, but satisfaction guaranteed, I can tell you...' said Oliveira.

'Matos,' – he was the second of the two boys and was from Lamego but was studying in Coimbra, too – 'I don't know about him. I've nothing to go on, but we'll soon see.'

'What about me?' I enquired.

'You...' and he hesitated, 'you'd win the prize for getting it for free, that's your special thing.' He called the waiter and ordered beers all round. 'It's like this in love,' he continued. 'There are those who'd never get anything if they didn't pay for it. Others never leave off and get paid for it on top. And others, sometimes, get it for free. I'd like to know how they do it.'

'Maybe,' said Matos, 'it's because they treat their women well, because they treat them like people.'

'There aren't any people; nobody is people,' said Rodrigues. 'I'm not people, you certainly aren't, none of us here is. Just take a look around. Look at that bald fellow over there, dribbling over the woman with him: look at his slobbering lips, and his hands, can you see his hands? And her? When a woman has those creases in her neck then she'll have more than enough somewhere else; it would be like drawing back a pair of curtains. And the other woman, that skinny one back there; you couldn't get a regiment up hers.'

'All the better for you then,' said Macedo. 'You could pull her on like an old boot.'

'No, I like 'em tight so that I have to force my way in,' he said, draining his glass.

A few couples were dancing. He put his glass on the table. 'Have you ever seen anything dafter than dancing? There they are, rubbing each other up, pawing each other all over, and for what?' he asked.

'What's wrong with that?' said Oliveira.

'That's fine for you; you could stay there dancing a couple of hours, just working up to the real business.'

'Are we going to be stuck here all night?' asked Macedo's brother.

'Ah, so my laddo is in a hurry, is he? Be careful; rushing things, they sometimes turn out badly.'

'They do?'

'They do, especially with the girls. They go running off and then you're left with nothing. It's not like just putting your hand in your pocket.'

'I reckon it's time to get started. Let's make a little tour of the casino and see how many of the girls we can pick up. There are six of us so if we can get hold of three or four of them we can get a car and off we go,' said Macedo. 'We can fit six in my car and the rest can go in the other one.'

'Have you got a car now?' I asked.

'It's my father's but he's lent it me. We could go to Coimbra; our house is empty. My father's in Paris with my mother and my sister's gone to Lisbon. It's always better if we've a house to go to. Shall we go?'

'And who's going to drive the other car?' asked Macedo.

'Let's get a cheaper girl for him,' said Rodrigues.

'Why cheaper?'

'You can have a more expensive one if you want; or share yours and pay the difference. Is that the way it is in Russia?'

'There's no prostitution in Russia,' said Macedo.

'So how do you get hold of them there? My shirt is your shirt, comrade, is that it?'

'Come on, let's go,' said Oliveira. 'If we don't stop all this we could still be here tomorrow.'

'And he wouldn't have time to get started,' said Rodrigues who was already on his way to the bar.

It wasn't too easy to get hold of any girls, for they were suspicious of our proposals. To Coimbra? Where in Coimbra? The girls in the casino turned us down flat, pulled faces, wanted paying in advance. We managed to persuade five of them, payment up front, which one of them collected and left with a friend who didn't want to accompany us.

Macedo said he would get hold of another car and that we should wait in front of the casino. In the street, alongside Matos' car the girls argued and were still far from convinced. Rodrigues grabbed two of them whom he made get into the back of the car. 'They'd better shut up and keep quiet in there, or else I'll sit them on my knee, on this thing here,' he said, grabbing it with his hand, 'and by the time they get to Coimbra they'll be split up the middle.' And he jumped in between them.

Matos meanwhile was leaning against the car and talking to one of them. 'We can go in front,' he said, turning to us, 'and one of you can come with me while Oliveira stays with the others because he knows where my house is.'

I looked around at the others: Oliveira had to stay behind; should I leave Luís with him, waiting for his brother? The boy was looking at me as if to beg me not to leave him there. Either him or me. But then Rodrigues got out of the car and grabbed Macedo's brother by the arm. 'In there, get in the back and I'll go in front. Get stuck into both of them because later there'll only be five sevenths of a woman for each of us. The boy looked at him defiantly and got in. The two girls greeted him gaily enough. 'Hey, the kid's coming with us!' Rodrigues stuck his head in the car. 'Let's have some respect. This lad's no chicken; he's the cock of the north. You'll soon see what he can do.' And he pushed forward the seat so that he could talk to Macedo, and slamming the door behind him got in.

Matos walked round the car and sat down behind the wheel. 'I'll take it easy,' he said. 'You know how to get there, don't you, Oliveira?' And the car set off with Rodrigues and the girls shouting and screaming while the two who were left behind said goodbye to them with much merriment.

Oliveira and I hung around on the pavement, each with a girl hanging on our arm, who by good luck were the ones we had chosen. Still Macedo didn't come. 'This car, is the thing coming or not?' they asked. Mine, shaking her handbag with its long straps, asked 'And what if we went to the boarding house so we could go to bed without any bother?' and tickling under my chin.

At that moment I saw Macedo coming back on foot. We asked him where the car was. 'Where the devil are the others?' he demanded. 'Where've they gone? Where's my brother? I couldn't get the car I wanted. Wait here,' he said, disappearing into the casino.

'This is a fine thing,' said the smaller girl, hanging onto Oliveira 'No Coimbra, no nothing. Well, at least they've paid already – that's what matters. Let's go, but home instead – wouldn't that be a good idea? The others have already gone. That one inside is surplus to requirements. Why don't just the four of us go off. That's what they all deserve for leaving us here.'

'It doesn't cost anything to wait a bit,' said Oliveira. 'If we can't get a car sorted out then we still have time to go somewhere else.'

So we waited and eventually Macedo emerged from the casino together with another fellow whom I vaguely knew and who had a girl on his arm.

'Do you know Carvalho? He's got a car and he's coming with us.'

Carvalho was tall and broad. 'Four of you will have to go in the back,' he said. 'The girls can sit on your knee.'

We followed him to the car, parked in another street and Oliveira and I with our girls, got in the back while Macedo got in in front with the other girl in the middle. The car rolled easily away through the town and onto the road. Nobody spoke; it was warm and somnolent and our hands rested sleepily. The one who was half-seated on my lap nibbled my ear and as I kissed her I could see in front three heads silhouetted against the headlights. Then the middle head was resting on Macedo's shoulder and Carvalho inclined his head a little in their direction. We were going at some lick and the car sometimes almost took off, for a moment, landing gently so that we were thrown snugly against each other. And then almost without warning we pulled up with a great squealing of brakes.

XII

I looked over the heads and saw there in front a car stopped by the roadside; some people were milling around it – Rodrigues, Macedo's brother and two women. We – Carvalho, Macedo and I – got out of our car while the three women and Oliveira remained inside. Rodrigues and Luís, bottles in their hands, were chasing after the girls. What was going on? What on earth was going on? They were all drunk; they must have stocked up with drinks before leaving Figueira and they had already drunk enough in the casino. Rodrigues was shouting that there was a ruined convent nearby, up that path (and we saw a track leading off to the left from the road) and that he wanted to marry Luís to the two women. When he saw his brother, Luís stopped short, and then he began to say that the girls were afraid. They stood still, looking at us anxiously, believing that we had come to rescue them and trying to make out among the indistinct shapes the three others who were still in the car. Since they couldn't see them they must have assumed that it was three against six. Matos got out of the car and came towards us. Luís and Rodrigues grabbed the two women who began to shriek. To my surprise Macedo helped his brother to hold down his girl.

'Everyone back in the car,' said Macedo, 'I know the way. We can stay here even; there's an old chap up there who looks after the church.'

Macedo and his brother, with the help of Rodrigues, bundled the two women into the car and then jumped in himself. Matos got in too, put the car into reverse and moved it away from athwart the crossroads and set off up the yellowish incline. Carvalho and I went back to our car and followed them.

'Where are we going?' asked the girls.

'To the convent,' replied Carvalho, leaning back slightly to speak to them. 'Have you ever been in a convent?'

The path curved up and down until quite suddenly it opened onto a large square with a church at the far end, flanked by ruined buildings. Macedo began to sound his horn furiously and Carvalho at once did the same. Oliveira and Rodrigues got out and ran to hammer on the door. It didn't open but in the little window above an electric lamp appeared, lighting up the two of them and the cars. 'What do you want?' asked a querulous voice.

'The key,' shouted Rodrigues and Oliveira, a cry which we – including even the women who were gradually losing their fears and laughing – repeated in chorus.

The light was switched off and presently the door opened enough to let through a skinny old man, dressed in a nightshirt down to his feet.

'We'll have the marriage here,' said Rodrigues. 'Where's your sacristan?' he asked, using such foul language that it was clear that he meant that the 'sacristan' was sleeping with the old man. The latter barked back that he was alone and that we were to leave him in peace, take the key and leave him be. But Rodrigues and Oliveira shoved him to one side and went into his house while the old fellow hopped around us, in the glare of the headlights. The women pushed him, too, and roared with laughter. By now we had all got out of the cars. Oliveira and Rodrigues appeared at the door bringing with them a boy in a nightshirt just like that of the old man. The boy was trembling with fear and the women were lifting up his nightshirt while he in desperation, tried to pull it down again. Rodrigues tied up his shirt with his belt and he and Oliveira pushed the boy along in front of them. The two Macedo brothers took hold of the old man while Matos and the six women followed on at the back of the procession towards the church.

During this time the old man had not let go of the big key; now he opened the door for us. The church was as black as pitch and smelled musty and neglected. The women started to say they were afraid to enter. 'I'm not going in,' said one of them. 'I'm a religious person and you lot are committing a sacrilege.' She was the one between Carvalho and Oliveira. Then two of the others came out in her support, the two who had come in the other car. The three of them sat on the steps. 'No, this is going too far,' said the first one. 'God will punish us without warning; he won't spare us.' 'It's too risky,' said the other, at the same time. 'God will punish us.'

Rodrigues, without letting go of the boy, came back to the door with Oliveira. 'You're crazy,' he said. 'This church isn't being used. Ring the bell and in you go,' and he shook the old man whom the Macedos were still holding. 'Explain to these ladies that this church has already been desecrated.'

The old man cleared his throat. 'The ladies may go in. The church has been desecrated,' he said, tremulously.

Rodrigues gave him a slap. 'Tell them the story.'

'Story? Story?' he repeated.

In the end it was Matos who told us. 'Many years ago a crime was committed inside the church; the convent had already been abandoned. Two men killed the priest, with a gun, at the altar. He had dishonoured a girl from their family. It's even said that the priest still haunts this place, a soul in torment.'

The women crossed themselves. 'I don't want anything to do with tormented souls,' said one of them. 'Our Lady give me refuge. What if the priest should appear?'

'If he does,' said Rodrigues, 'the most he can do is to deflower you, which is what he liked to do. That being the case, none of you are in any danger.'

We all laughed, even the old fellow, despite himself. 'We can't see an inch in front of our noses,' said Matos. 'Have you got any lamps here in the house? You have? I'll go and get them.'

He went away and returned with two oil lamps, one in each hand. He went into the church; a loud noise made the women scream. 'What is it?' we called out. Macedo said it must have been a bench that he stepped on and knocked over. A match flared inside and one of the lamps stood at the edge of the altar while Macedo lit the other one, standing at the far end. We all went in. The church was enormous, empty except for a few scattered benches. Birds or bats fluttered about. When Rodrigues was looking up at the ceiling the boy untied himself from him and Oliveira and ran to the altar in front, heading for a door which stood on one side. But Matos, leaping up the altar steps, blocked his path, grabbed him and they fell in a heap. Meanwhile Rodrigues and Oliveira piled in on top of him, so that we, hanging back in a group, could only see a confused movement of bodies and strips of torn shirt. When they got up the boy was naked, rolling on the floor with his hands tied behind his back and his ankles bound, too. He whimpered. 'What are they going to do to him?' cried the old man. 'My God, what are they going to do?'

'Don't worry, nobody's going to cut your dick off,' said Oliveira.

'That depends,' said Rodrigues. 'If he's not going to need his tackle, we can cut it off...' He turned round to the old man who was being held by the Macedos and who was sitting on the floor choking back deep sobs. 'Does he need it, or do you go on top?'

The women laughed. He sighed but did not answer. 'Answer him; didn't you hear?'

'He does,' whispered the old man.

'Now we want to know whether he only likes old men,' said

Rodrigues, 'or women, too. Ladies, would you be kind enough to inspect.'

Three of them went towards the boy who was writhing on the ground; his eyes were staring, wide open, and for the moment, panting, he had stopped his groaning. The Macedos picked the old man up off the ground and we formed a circle around him.

'If you can't get it up,' said Rodrigues, bending over the boy, 'you've had it.'

The girls went to work with a will. The boy shook. And we laid bets: 'It's coming, now, it's coming; ah, no it's not.'

The old man shook himself free and kneeled down by the boy, weeping, while he held the boy's head and stroked it. The boy, furious, clenched his teeth and wrenched his head away from the old man.

'Untie his arms to make it easier for him,' said Carvalho.

Macedo bent down and undid the knots. While the girls were embracing him and rubbing themselves against him, the boy clutched at himself mechanically in such a state of anxiety that he clenched his teeth and screwed his eyes tight. Then a great cry of triumph greeted the momentary erection that he finally managed.

'You've saved your bacon,' said Rodrigues.

The boy, lying on the ground and sweating profusely, smiled foolishly.

'And now,' continued Rodrigues, 'as a sign of your gratitude and of your conversion to the secrets of *soixante neuf*, you are going to make a pilgrimage to the shrine of these ladies. Drawers down! Show him the holy place!'

From then on everything was a confusion of deep shadows which fell over the interior of the church; there was no telling who was who as the women ran around stark naked and everybody supped from the bottles which Macedo had fetched from the car, while the boy, his legs now free, joined in. At one point, disengaging myself from the girl in my arms, I glimpsed Rodrigues, naked from the waist down with a woman kneeling before him and clapping her hands. She was beating time to the movements of Luís and the boy, both on the ground on top of a woman. The boy finished first and then lay still, as if drained of life. Luís then got up. 'You've definitely got the second prize,' said Rodrigues, 'there's no doubt about it.' He put his hand on his shoulder. 'That was pretty good,' he added. 'You're quite a performer.' Luís stretched out, laughing.

Rodrigues peered across the church, making an inventory of the field of battle. He spied Oliveira in a corner and went up to the couple. 'Well, then, still only halfway through?'

'Halfway through?' said the woman from beneath 'He's already on his second go.'

Matos had got up and was leaning against the altar; Rodrigues made his way towards him. 'Well then, what's with you?' said Rodrigues.

'I got it over with quickly this time, and passed her on to Macedo,' he replied.

Rodrigues and I scanned the room looking for Macedo; he was close to the door, lying back next to his girl. 'You ready?' asked Rodrigues, his shadow huge against the wall.

Macedo, getting up, replied that he was and Rodrigues put his arm around his shoulders. 'Sorry if I offended you with all that stuff I said. But this is what we need, to hell with revolutions. Your brother conducted himself like a hero. And look there he's at it again.' And sure enough he was.

'What about the old fellow, where's he got to?' enquired Rodrigues loudly as he set off running out of the church with his shirt tails fluttering around him.

The naked boy, wrapped round one of the women, suddenly jumped up. 'I know where he'll be hiding,' he said with a wicked smile. 'Follow me.'

So, guided by the boy, prancing naked ahead of us, Rodrigues, Macedo, Matos, Carvalho and I, followed by the four women who had slipped on their shirts, we ran across the yard to the ruins where the boy skipped inside. Cries came from within; and then the old man emerged gripped by the boy who was raining blows on him. We dragged him into the church.

Rodrigues, with the help of the boy and Matos, shoved him towards the altar and then removed his shirt. The old man cowered on his knees and again they lifted him up.

'Here, your lords, ladies and gentlemen,' he began, 'we have the very image of human decadence. More bum or less bum, your lordships, if you get to his age, that's how you end up. With this drooping pelt, this body, falling apart, with these tears, with this dangling cock, with these empty balls, and attempting to enslave a youth such as this one to such a place, attempting to lure him into the dark hole which is this ruin, trying to suck him off with this foul mouth. Let us remember that everybody ends up like this; and let us give thanks to God and the Devil and pray that we die young, while we are still worth coveting, while are still attractive, while we still have some strength between our legs.' He knelt down in front of the old man. 'Father, bless me.'

The old man raised a trembling, uncertain hand.

'Now,' said Rodrigues, 'lay your blessing upon all here present.'

The old man straightened up and lifted his hand.

'And now,' continued Rodrigues, 'you will give everybody your farewell kiss.'

We all exchanged glances.

'If the ladies and gentlemen would be good enough to form a queue and present arms so that he might kiss it,' he announced. There was a murmur of protest.

'Remember,' said Rodrigues, 'that we are in the house of God – and that God punishes without warning and that in places such as this the blessing of the demon is required.'

Matos let go the old man while the boy continued to hold him and fell in behind Rodrigues who said: 'You first.'

The old man, released by the boy, fell to his knees. 'Not him,' he begged, 'not him.'

'Yes, him,' said Rodrigues and it was with him that the old man began.

As we came out, fastening up our trousers and the girls putting their clothes back on, the old man followed, complaining of his disgrace. The boy ran on in front towards the house where he went in. We came to a halt in silence, next to the cars; we seemed, all of us, to share an infinite weariness. Matos took a note from his pocket, as did Rodrigues; they held them out to the old man who was still bemoaning his fate. Suddenly, astonished by the value of the notes, he snatched them greedily. The headlights, now switched on, cast a strangely confusing light on the scene.

'Where's the boy?' asked one of our number.

'I'm here,' he shouted, emerging from the house and tucking his shirt into his trousers.

'This is for you,' said Rodrigues, holding out another note.

'Don't give him anything,' put in Macedo.

'I don't want anything,' said the boy. 'All I want is for you to take me with you. Take me away from here. I don't have anyone; he would catch me again. Take me away.'

'Where do you want to go?' asked Macedo.

'To the city,' he replied. 'Please take me.'

'I'll take him with me,' said the woman who had been with him.

'Hm,' said Rodrigues, 'that's you provided for; she wants to put you on the payroll; you don't know your own strength, do you, eh?'

Macedo's brother suggested a way out: 'Let him come with us,' he said. 'We can get him a job with my father.'

By now most of us had got into the cars, with Matos and Carvalho behind their steering wheels. It was then that the old fellow put his arms round the boy, weeping, asking him whether he really did want to abandon him, saying that neither of them had anyone else in the world and that we would leave him to his fate on the streets the moment we got back. The boy struggled to free himself from his embrace.

'You don't know the world,' insisted the old man, 'you don't know the town, you will be an outcast, you don't know how to work, what on earth will you do? And I, who was like a father to you, what will become of me without you? They will abandon you on the street. Do you know what the street is like? You'll be begging all over the town.'

They pushed him to the ground and tried to squeeze into one of the cars. The old man struggled to his feet – he seemed taller – and roared at us with his fist clenched. 'Damn the lot of you,' he screamed, 'may the pox rot you and kill you! May the earth open up and swallow you! Damn you for stealing him from me! Damn you! And you, when you're dying of hunger, when you haven't even enough strength to come crawling back here so that I can spit on you! And give you a kick in the balls and that thing you're so proud of! May he follow you, stick to you, till he rots in front of you! And then you'll sell yourself in the street and nobody will want you!' he shrieked, pummelling his own backside.

Rodrigues struck him violently so that he fell, bleeding from the nose. 'Go, go with them,' the old man raved on, 'go and may the devil take you!'

The boy knelt and grasped his head; he shot us a doleful, terrified glance. 'I'll stay…'

Rodrigues looked at them. 'OK, stay with the father that God gave you,' he said.

We got into the car and I could still see the image of the boy with the old man's head in his lap, waving us goodbye.

Dawn was breaking, a clear dawn, by the time we arrived in Figueira; some of us were silent, others dozing. The women asked us to buy them some coffee before we dropped them at the boarding houses where they lived. We went around, looking for some place open until we came across the one where I had earlier dined. Neither the boss nor the waiter was there. There was a fat woman serving coffee at the counter to some men. The women all sat down together in one of the stalls and we brought them cups of coffee and rolls with butter.

'Looks like they've had a good time,' said one of the men. 'The whole night, too.'

Matos was paying for the rolls and coffee. 'Are you jealous?' he asked.

'Me?' replied the fellow. 'Me, jealous of you and your worthless life? Rabble…'

In a flash we were beating the hell out of each other, the three of them against us. The prostitutes fled, shrieking. On the other side of the counter from which our cups had fallen the fat woman was screaming. 'Help, help! Herculano!' she shouted.

The owner, in his long drawers and shirt, appeared in the middle of us, as did the waiter, in his underpants. He immediately recognised me. 'Sir! Run away, run away!' he shouted in the confusion.

I didn't run away and in the end we overcame the three men who, still calling out insults and calling for the boss, left.

'Let's get out of here,' said Oliveira.

'Where shall we go?' asked Matos, who, with Carvalho, was discussing the price of the broken cups with the owner.

'Let's go to the beach,' said Rodrigues. 'We can have a dip over by Buarcos. We could all do with a good swim.'

The owner, still in his drawers, and the waiter, still in his underpants, insisted that we stay and have our coffee; quickly we swallowed the dark liquid, redolent of filthy dishcloths. The fat lady snorted at us insolently. 'Get out of here, you good-for-nothing,' she scolded the waiter, 'go and get dressed. How dare you walk around naked in front of me.'

At the door Rodrigues turned to her. 'If you, madam, think that a man in his underpants is naked,' he said, 'then come with us to the beach and you'll soon see.'

'Herculano, this man is behaving very improperly towards me,' she roared. But her husband, gripping his drawers with his hands, laughed after us as we were getting into the cars.

Now I was in Matos' car with Rodrigues and Luís. As we turned the corner a stone broke the rear window and barely missed my head. 'A bit of glass here or there,' said Matos, not slowing down, 'it's not much for the beating we gave them.'

The two cars came to a stop by the beach in front of where the boats usually lay and where there were now only a few, old and forlorn, stark against the dawning day. We got undressed and, leaving our clothes in the cars, ran towards the water in our underpants. At the water's edge, though, Rodrigues removed his and began to dance wildly, leaping around and waving them in the air like a flag in his upraised hand. 'Naked! Naked! Just like God brought us into this world!'

We all followed him except for Macedo whom, though he clutched his pants with both hands, we forcibly undressed. 'No, no, leave me be,' he cried. 'I'd had enough of your stupid antics!'

He remained sitting on the sand while the rest of us ran into the water, pushing and shoving each other in noisy horseplay and pretending to be ashamed of our nakedness. It was then that a beam of light shimmered across the dark waters almost as if it were a gust of wind. We turned round: the sun had quite suddenly broken through above the low houses and we were bathed from head to foot in its golden light. Quite still, we shaded our eyes with our hands to gaze at it in fascination while a light breeze stirred the sand around our ankles. Then we turned again, abstractedly, towards the sea which was now also glowing in the sun. Only the hollows of the waves were still a deep, dark blue, as they raced towards the beach, breaking in a golden foam.

Standing by my side, Rodrigues took my hand. I lowered my eyes, in distress and shock and tried to take my hand away. 'It's wonderful, isn't it?' he said. 'It's as if the world were beginning anew.' Then he held my hand tighter. 'Earlier today, you ... yesterday, you saw me here, didn't you?' he asked in a low voice.

I looked out over the sea. 'What do you want me to say?' I asked.

He let go of my hand and ran his own down his body as far as his thighs. 'They say that water washes everything away,' he murmured with his eyes closed.

Macedo, the down on his skin glowing in the sun, was at our sides. He must have heard everything. 'Almost everything,' he said, his voice low, too.

The others had fallen quiet and were all looking at us. And it was with a solemnity that matched our own that they followed us into the water which lay calmly all around us.

XIII

Morning had already broken by the time I got home. Only the kitchen door was open; my aunt was at the stove making coffee. 'Good morning,' she said, smiling. 'Have you had coffee?' I smiled back and sat down at the kitchen table without saying a word. She put a cup in front of me and then some bread and butter; she poured me some coffee and then sat down on a bench beside the table.

'Are you sad? Men are like that... They go out on the town to make themselves feel better and afterwards they just feel sad,' she said and looked at me with her clear, blue eyes.

'No, auntie, I'm not sad.'

'No? That must be because you're still young. Your uncle, when he goes off like that, he comes back worse than he went. You know that he bought that enormous radio yesterday so that the Spaniards could listen to the news? I want to know who's paying for it. They've put the thing in the study and they settle themselves up there of an evening until the small hours listening to the news from here and there and playing cards with your uncle. When they heard the news about the general they were all for taking the night train to Lisbon, but then they heard that the rebels were at the gates of Madrid and changed their minds. They say that if Madrid falls the revolution will have won and that if not there'll be civil war or even, who knows, war all over. Have you any idea? A world war because of Spain. You've never been to Spain, have you? I went there when we got married; we went on honeymoon to Madrid and San Sebastian, but I didn't like it. It's a dirty place, everybody badly turned out and all you can see from the windows of the express is just empty countryside. In Madrid we stayed some days in a very fine hotel on the Gran Via, but the beach in San Sebastian, it's no better than the one here in Figueira, I really don't think it is. And a world war for the sake of those people? Have you thought about it? And as for those two chaps here, I don't even understand them. They're just looking for some excuse not to go back: first they hide then they want to leave, then they don't. And all the while they're playing cards with your uncle.'

All of a sudden I could hear her no more; somebody was shaking me. I lifted my head and peered up at her leaning over me. 'The best thing is to go to bed; otherwise you'll fall asleep here in the kitchen.'

I got up, thick with sleep, went up to my room and fell across the bed. When I awoke I tried to make out the ceiling which seemed distant and indistinct. I sat up and took off my shoes and then I got up and undressed, slipped into my pyjamas and went to have a bath. From the corridor I could hear a clamour of voices and a constant crackle, over which there came a thin whining sound as they listened to the radio. The bath did me good but I felt even more light-headed than when I had first awoken. Either I couldn't remember anything or through my empty mind passed only vague, fleeting images or others which, alarmed, I tried to chase away. It was as if it had all happened ages ago, to other people, and I had been merely a spectator, and I didn't want to recall anything of that disgusting, mixed up spectacle. And suddenly I felt a piercing longing for last year in Lisbon, for my friends there, for Maria Helena. I just wanted to go back in time, to be strolling along the avenue with her on my arm. I went back to my room; I was hungry. It was four o'clock in the afternoon. I got dressed and went downstairs, to the library. The two Spaniards and my uncle were sitting at a green baize table, playing animatedly; at their side was another table full of glasses and bottles while the radio, planted imposingly on yet another table, crackled and hummed so that one could barely make out the frantic words of the speaker.

'Well then,' said my uncle in greeting, 'out on the razzle, a night to remember, eh? I wish I was your age again. If your mother were to find out that I'd let you out on the loose like that, she'd kill me. Or perhaps not. For someone who knows so much about life, she doesn't understand a thing. Between you and me, I don't know how your father ever got round to it with her.'

The two Spaniards had a pretty good idea of what he was saying and kept their eyes fixed on the cards without looking at me. As for me ... curiously I didn't feel the shock that I had expected.

'Our friends here,' continued my uncle, 'are waiting to see if that business in Spain sorts itself out, because if it doesn't, soon enough, it will be war and it won't be short either. And maybe there'll be war here, too. And now I'm going to have a laugh: I'm on the platform and you two are full of your manifesto' and with a roar of triumph he plonked down a hand of cards and gathered up all the beans (by now I was able to see) from the table. 'See how I earn my beans; it might be just beans now ... but it's all written down in here,' he crowed, showing me the piece of paper by his side.

'But when the reckoning comes this is all money. Our friends here, when this revolution is all over, they'll pay me for every bean.' He made another note in his book, counting up the beans with great care. 'You've already seen the radio, of course you have,' he said, shuffling the cards and quickly dealing them. 'It's one of the best, picks up everything. It looks like Spain has been split in two or maybe even three or four. Let's see what happens in Madrid.'

The two Spaniards tried to explain to me what was in the hands of the rebels and what wasn't, but my hazy knowledge of Spanish geography meant that I couldn't visualise what they were saying. In addition I could neither speak nor concentrate on account of my hunger. I nodded my head and bade them goodbye.

'That's right,' growled my uncle, 'be off with you. If you're not playing you only get in the way.'

I went down to the kitchen where my aunt had made me a hearty afternoon tea. 'Have you slept long enough?' she asked. 'Do you feel any better now?'

'I'm fine. Does uncle want anything from down in town?'

'I don't think so; he's arranged for someone from the tobacconist's to come up here with the newspapers and cigarettes.'

'That's one more coming in here,' I said.

'Another one, more or less, it doesn't make any difference. The boy from the grocer's, the butcher's lad, the fishmonger's wife, the lady with the vegetables, one more won't make any difference. And the Spaniards don't come down anyway; your uncle wouldn't let them.'

'Doesn't uncle go out any more? What if someone noticed?'

'He goes out; last night he was at the casino, and then when he came back he started playing with them.'

'At the casino? I didn't see him.'

'You didn't? Well it's a big place. I don't know why I put up with all this,' she said thoughtfully, her lips pursed. 'I could be nice and comfortable in my mother's house in Coimbra. She's always telling me to leave your uncle and come and live with her, and that whoever is closest to her will do well when it comes to the will. But I don't want my sisters – you know they've fallen out with my mother – I don't want them thinking that I'm taking advantage of the situation And then … you know … between the two of them, they're both crazy, your uncle and my mother, I don't know who would be worse.'

She continued talking, going over the reasons, logical and

otherwise, and I recalled the figure of this mother of hers, someone I had never seen yet knew through family lore, through what my uncles, each in his own way, would relate, through the stories which were told in my family, and even through what some of the lads from Coimbra said about her. Suddenly, while my aunt was talking, I could see myself in Puigmal's house, passing the chap who was weeping, and in Mesquita's house, too, watching him telling the story to his fiancée over the phone. Why had I not remembered then the story of my uncle's mother-in-law? It could only have been because I had placed school and holidays in separate, water-tight, compartments. Puigmal belonged to the world of school; my aunt's mother to that of holidays, in spite of all that was said about her at home over dinner.

Besides, the two cases were only the same up to a certain point; my uncle's mother-in-law was a widow while the other one was married; the latter didn't have any children while the former had four daughters and a terrible hatred of her sons-in-law. All the daughters had, one by one, run away from home to marry – except my aunt. For this reason she hadn't cut her off and had even gone along with her marriage. Why?

They both hunted down the young men they fancied; could it be that my aunt's mother detested her sons-in-law because she liked them as men, or for exactly the opposite reason? According to this theory, would she have liked my uncle, and then would she hate him for different reasons from those which made her hate the other sons-in-law? The truth is that my uncle paid her back in the same coin. And this made the fact that he had claimed that he had sent the maidservants away, alleging that they had had to go to Coimbra on account of her illness, utterly implausible. Whenever he brought her to mind (growling that he did not need the money, which she in any case gave no more of to this daughter than to the others, something my aunt never failed to stress), he loudly wished her dead. But perhaps this explanation was equally acceptable to him and to the maids as well. He was going to Coimbra to see his enemy die… My aunt's mother, a rich widow, had brought her daughters up in unheard-of luxury, in Oporto and Coimbra, and in other parts of the country where she had houses. She herself spent her life moving ceaselessly from house to house and only latterly had come to stay more often in Coimbra. And the gossips were saying that the Portuguese Athens, with its ever-changing student population provided a more favourable environment for the easy and diverse recruitment of young men. One – I don't remember whether it was Matos or Oliveira or one of the others – had been spreading some malicious stories about her. Rodrigues, backed up by other fellows from Figueira adopted by the college, had defended her out of his loyalty to my aunt.

I got up, my movement breaking into the flow of words with which my aunt accompanied the recently begun chore of peeling potatoes. 'Are you going out?' she enquired.

'Yes, auntie. And perhaps I won't have dinner – this tea…'

'Well, this is getting serious; you're not going to stay out tonight as well, are you?'

'I'm not meaning to; I'll be back in good time.'

I went off to the beach but as I approached the bathing huts I hesitated. The ladies must already know about what had happened the previous night, even if they hadn't got all the details. I retraced my steps. I had already gone back some way when I turned round again and went down, strolling in front of the huts. In front of several of them I was hailed with great politeness: they already knew I was there; were my studies going well? I answered them, all the while looking on ahead to the group, which I had glimpsed, containing Mercedes and her brother and some other boys and girls. Almeida, or whatever they called him here, was not among them. I greeted her parents and joined the group. Zé and the others, most of whom I did not know, looked at me uncertainly; I thought I detected a chill of disapproval in Ramos' eyes. The girls, especially Mercedes, were all smiles; it was evident that somebody had told them something and, paradoxically, in a mixture of fascination and fear, I, as a participant in that fantastic adventure, had risen quite a few degrees in their estimation. Though those events seemed far away, their significance had faded in my memory in such a way that all that remained was the palpable attraction those girls felt towards me. And probably I was the first of us to surface that day, bedecked with all the collective mystery of one hell of a night on the tiles.

'You didn't seem to know me yesterday,' I said, turning to Mercedes, who had made room for me at her side.

'Really, I didn't know you? And didn't I speak to you?' she said. 'But you seemed so wrapped up in your conversation that I didn't want to interrupt it with anything trivial.'

'Did you enjoy your walk?'

'Yes, it was lovely,' she replied and fell silent.

'It doesn't seem like you enjoyed yourself much.'

'Why do you say that?'

'You merely said your walk was lovely and no more...'

'What do you want me to say? Going on a walk to Tavarede isn't quite like going to China.'

'True, but there are things to see in Tavarede: the palace there is very beautiful. Did you manage to see it? Perhaps you didn't even notice it ... not having eyes for anything else...'

She smiled and straightened her long hair which framed her long, fine features, to which the slight incongruity of her full lips lent a special charm. 'You are very much mistaken; I didn't miss a thing,' she said, looking at me challengingly.

'Yes, of course. But these days you can't go looking around as you used to.'

'I can't? Why on earth not?'

I scooped up some sand and then let it trickle through my fingers; I looked at her without answering her question.

Our conversation wandered onto other, less important, matters. 'Jorge,' she said abruptly, 'I've got to talk to you.' She got up. 'Mother, I'm not feeling very well,' she said. 'I'm tired; I'm going back to the boarding house.'

Zé got up as well, at the same moment that I did. She signalled to him. 'You stay here,' she said. 'I've already asked Jorge to take me home.'

Such a thing was unheard of and I could feel the pairs of eyes fixed on us as we left the beach and went up on to the avenue, walking along side by side without a word. After quite a distance she stopped. 'Have you already heard that I'm going to marry Mário?' [sic] she said, looking up at me with her deep-set eyes.

'Mário? Ah, yes, Almeida; I heard about it yesterday.'

'But you know I'm going to marry him, don't you?'

'Yes.'

'What do you think?'

'Me? What is there to think? It's nothing to do with me. You're free to marry whoever you want.'

She stared out at the sea. 'Yes, in a way I am. But I thought you liked me.'

'What's that got to do with it? It's him you're going to marry.'

She turned to me: 'I do love him, you know.'

'Did you ask me to come with you just to tell me this?'

She put her hand on my arm. 'No. But it's such a very big undertaking ...'

'For you and him, yes.'

She said nothing and removed her hand. We carried on walking. 'Where is he?' I demanded.

'He went to Oporto; he has things to do there.'

Our steps led us on towards the narrow balconies at the edge of the beach; we climbed the steps, side by side, slowly and leant against the balustrade. The waves broke slowly and gently over the rocks, covering them with foam. 'Yesterday, when I saw you… Tell me, yes or no… Do you still like me?' she asked.

I felt a surge of tenderness for her. I put my arm around her waist; she did not demur. 'Yes, I do,' I murmured.

She turned and leant against me. 'Why didn't we go out with each other in earnest last summer?' she said.

'I don't know,' I said, stroking her hair. 'Perhaps we were just kids last year, and now we aren't.'

At the sound of footsteps and voices we sprang apart but when the group had passed I held her arms tightly and kissed her, at length, on her half open lips, and on her face, her neck until, breathless, I stepped back from her. But she looked at me and flung her arms around my neck; then it was she who kissed me in an embrace in which I enfolded her, pushing her body against the balustrade and crushing her breasts against my chest. But though I felt a burning desire which throbbed tightly between us, my arms strayed no further.

'And now?' she said, lowering her eyes as our bodies pulled apart.

I took her hands and kissed her fingers. 'And now?' she repeated.

I looked into her flickering eyes. 'And now what, my love?'

'What are we going to do?'

'Whatever you want.'

She took her hands away and put them on my face. 'But I don't know what I want,' she said as I saw her eyes bright with teardrops.

'You don't know? Do you want me to tell you?'

She nodded.

'You're going to get engaged to me. I want you to be mine.'

She moved away from me and, lifting her shoulders, stretched out her arms to the balustrade. 'It's so easy to say,' she said almost inaudibly. 'That's what Mário wanted too…'

I could hear Macedo's voice telling me how Almeida had made his play for her and I ground my teeth in rage. 'And you, whose do you want to be?'

I spat out the words so furiously that she turned away in fright, wide-eyed. Then more footsteps, voices and laughter behind us. She looked down at the ground. 'Yours,' was her response. Once more I held her and kissed her, this time sitting on a concrete bench in a corner while she gave herself up, her eyes closed, to my embrace. And then we sat, hand in hand, looking out at the sea, while I talked slowly, softly, making plans for our life together. She said nothing, merely squeezing my hand from time to time. Night was already falling. It was impossible to say now, looking at the sun, covered over as it was by dark clouds to which it lent a lining of red, whether it was still poised over the sea or whether it had already vanished into the waters. I remembered vaguely the lines I had written here on the previous evening and which I had thrown away on this very spot. I smiled to myself. 'It's getting late,' she said. 'Let's be going.'

We stood up and went on our way to the boarding house. I was still making plans: we would go to Oporto, I would finish my course, I would be with her all the time and then we would get married. She walked along by my side, silently, smiling at me from time to time. At the corner of the street where stood her boarding house I took her hands and held them long and tight in mine. 'Shall I see you tonight?' I asked.

'It would be better not to. Tomorrow morning on the beach,' she said as she took her hands away and made off towards the boarding house. There she turned, slender and delicate, her hair long and hanging loose, and smiled before going in.

I made my way towards my house. At the gate I put my hand in my pocket and found the picture postcards I had bought the previous day; they were all crumpled and torn, but they would still have to do. The dog leapt up playfully. A shady peace had fallen over the garden and frozen the branches of the palm tree into a grey stillness. I hardly heard my aunt saying that in the end I had got home just in time, for dinner was about to be served. I went up to my room. The tangle of bushes that stretched from the belvedere to the house was already in shadow and rustled gently. I could smell the fragrance of the fields, warm and with a salty tang, and I breathed in deeply and gratefully. I sat down at my table and began at once to write to my family; I could hardly see anything so I switched on the light; as I did so I remembered that I should write to Maria Helena. I would write a card ending it all. But ending what? I was not in any way committed to her and the difference between her and Mercedes was so vast – it was like going from a dark staircase out towards the wide sea beyond the balustrades. I wouldn't write:

it would all end in silence and she would never see me again. She didn't have the least importance for me. She was a girl who, barely knowing me, had almost given herself to me; and I hardly knew her either. I felt a dull ache. And Mercedes; did I know her any better? Almeida's fiancée, had she not given herself up to my arms and my kisses? When I hadn't even sought them? In the end it was because she loved me and I loved her. When she saw me she knew that it was me she loved. Once again I could hear Macedo and the foolish things he had said. Yes ... but it was me she loved. And I went down to dinner.

XIV

At dinner I ate little; my mind was elsewhere and I paid no attention to what was being said. The two Spaniards and my aunt and uncle seemed, like the table, to be floating in front of me, flaring into life and flickering briefly, surrounded by the murmur of distant conversation and the tinkling of cutlery.

My uncle addressed me loudly, making me jump: 'What's the matter with you, boy? Are you missing your home and Lisbon? Or are you pining for another night like last night?'

The Spaniards and my aunt smiled at me understandingly. 'You haven't touched a thing,' he repeated. 'Are you pining for something?'

'No, on the contrary, I'm not pining for anything.'

'What a happy man!' he said and went on to explain in great detail to the Spaniards that I felt no longing for anything or anyone.

There was sadness in the sympathy with which they both regarded me; Don Juan, the older one, speaking haltingly, explained that we, the Portuguese, were convinced that there was no exact equivalent in any other language to our word 'saudade' that word which meant so many things like longing and nostalgia, and that therefore no other people could feel what we denoted by that word. 'But these things belong to humanity,' he continued, fiddling with some breadcrumbs, 'there's nothing transcendent about them at all, or especially or specifically Portuguese. People feel a longing, as the Portuguese say, for what they have lost, or never had, or even for anything or person or place from which they are separated. It's just not true that other languages don't have words to express this feeling of "la soledad", of alone, solitary.'

'But "soledad" in Spanish...' exclaimed my uncle.

'In Castillian,' put in the younger one, the Basque.

'"Soledad" in Castilian is the same as "solidão" in Portuguese, and longing is something that one can feel inside one, even when there are lots of people around.'

Don Juan smiled. 'But, Don Justino,' he said, '"solidão" can also be felt among friends ... "La soledad"... You, sir, are doing everything you can to keep us busy, to entertain us, be with us; and I still,' and here he put his hand on his breast in an elegant gesture, 'feel it, far from my people and my country, for whose fate I fear so much.'

There was a pause. 'And even solitariness,' I said, 'is something we can feel, without reason, without knowing why. It's like a huge emptiness around us, or the absence of any meaning in the things which happen to us or which we see around us.'

My uncle looked at me. 'I didn't know you were a philosopher, boy, I didn't know you had it in you. Carry on, carry on.'

'There's nothing more to say; that's just the way I feel.'

'Because you,' said Don Fernando, the Basque, using the formal Spanish form of address, 'usted', 'because you are so young you haven't learnt to live with the awareness of the people to whom you belong. You are a victim of this society in which you live, a society which does not offer a young man like you anything which is truly worth becoming enthusiastic about.'

'And what about me!' exclaimed my uncle. 'Don't you think I feel what he says?'

'You, Don Justino, are...' and he hesitated.

'Yes, go on,' demanded my uncle.

'You are a man, a much older man, who has suffered great setbacks and who lacks a reason to live.'

My aunt looked at her husband while I waited for what would emerge from behind those keen eyes and the hands that shook as he lit the cigarette he had just finished rolling.

'That's true, I don't,' he said, gazing at the cloud of his own smoke. Then he said: 'At times in class I notice myself talking, explaining something, shouting, hitting a student – yes, I do belt them – and I ask myself what I'm doing here. Sometimes, playing cards, I'm holding them up in my hand or I'm following the roulette ball with my eyes, and I wonder what sense it all makes. The only thing that makes any sense, and that's only because it appeals to me, is a good woman. But, even with a good woman,' and he looked sideways, coldly, at my aunt, 'when it's over, I never know what I've been looking for in her, and I see all sorts of things wrong that I hadn't noticed before.'

It was Don Juan who broke the awkward silence. 'Because love is blind,' he said, 'and only after it has been satisfied can it see ... until the next time.'

My uncle was lost in melancholy musing. 'No, no it isn't,' he said. 'Love isn't blind; rather it is we that are blind. We look but we don't see; and when we do see the time has already passed. It amounts to the same thing, whether we had somebody we thought we wanted, or whether we didn't have anybody, for only when it's over do we understand what we wanted after all. And that's not even the worst of it: the worst thing is knowing later that the one we thought we loved was indifferent to us all along. You can see it in what happened to me. I couldn't follow the career I had always dreamed about, and I never really got used to the idea. But, if I had followed it, perhaps I would have got fed up with that too, for I have no real aptitude for the military life which was to be my career. I was a prisoner in Germany and ran away to Holland with a woman who gave me all the love she had. And I gave her all mine in return. And afterwards, when I left Holland to come back here, it was much less a matter of returning than of running away from her. And about this time I got to know this one here.' And he turned his head towards my aunt, and continued: 'Besides I already knew her. And I married her. And I loved her. But she always reminded me of the other one. Of the two of them, one I married either because she reminded me of the other and for that very reason, every time I looked at her, I began to think about escape, or I married her as a way of escaping from the other one, and I ended up in thrall to both of them, escaping neither. And there's yet another possibility: it is that I married this one out of vanity, proud to marry one of the daughters of Madame Simões, the wealthy and celebrated Madame Simões, because I wanted to show everybody that my life wasn't finished, that a career wasn't closed to me. For I was a war invalid. But what is certainly true is that, unsure as to whether I would ever have any future, I thought that I would marry money. Then my son was born ... I've told you about my son, haven't I?'

From the two Spaniards' doleful expressions it was obvious that, at some point between hands of poker, he had already told them the story, or perhaps even earlier than that. As for me I didn't dare to lift my eyes to look at my aunt. Then the older of the Spaniards interrupted the flow of my uncle's words. 'Don Justino,' he began in a dry severe voice, 'these things can happen to anyone, though this does not make the sorrow, to the one who suffers it, any the less intense. You cannot, however, spend the rest of your life weeping for the child who died. I, too, had a son who died in the same way but I have never spoken to you about him.'

'Because you, sir, were not tied to a woman who could not have children.' My aunt left the room.

'"Usted", Don Justino, have never forgiven your wife for this,' said Don Juan. 'But you have also given me to understand that you did not want to have any more children. And when later you came to want them again all the other things happened. One might think that it is the same thing which you said happens with love.'

'What?' said my uncle, staring at him, his brow furrowed.

'To know that the one we love deeply is indifferent to us.'

There was a moment's silence. 'Are you saying that I didn't want the son that I had?' demanded my uncle.

'I don't know,' replied the other cautiously but firmly, 'but perhaps you, sir, have not forgiven yourself for not wanting him, and so it is to punish yourself that you think about him so much and about how wonderful he was, blaming your wife for his death and for not being able to bear more children. Don Justino, I do not want to distress you, "usted", will forgive me for speaking like this, but I do think we must face the truth. And, if we do not have the courage to face up to it – because it would make us suffer greatly in the deepest part of ourselves – we must at least harbour a large doubt about the reasons which suit us, so that we do not inflict suffering on anyone else.'

'Do you believe, sir, that I am inflicting such suffering on my wife?' asked my uncle, his eyes blazing.

Don Juan raised his head; he looked like one of those bewhiskered tribunes of the history books. 'I do,' he said, gazing levelly at my uncle.

'But haven't you seen how she is? Do you really think that thing is capable of suffering?'

'Everyone, Don Justino, is capable of suffering. A frivolous person – and your wife is not frivolous – may suffer through his frivolities. A person with a large conscience, with a strong sense of honour, may suffer on account of that honour. A person who denies himself suffers at the hands of others. A selfish person suffers because all the others do not bend to his whims. Does it seem to you that any woman would feel happy if she is constantly being reminded of her inadequacy as a woman?'

'What inadequate woman? As for her she's free, she can do what she wants.'

'And does it seem to you that any woman would appreciate being constantly held responsible for the death of a child?'

'A woman who isn't a woman…'

'Even a woman like that would not like to be called such.'

Don Juan waited expectantly for my uncle's reply, a reply which never came. He rolled his cigarette, by now extinguished, from one corner of his mouth to the other and ran the fingers of his hand through his hair.

'Don Justino,' said Don Juan eventually, ' I ask you a favour, one more in addition to the great favours that we already owe you. It might be that this one will be, for you, even more difficult than any that you have already done for us. I beg you not to show such lack of respect for your wife in front of us.'

The other Spaniard did not move to back up his colleague's request; the mere fact that he remained quite still, not looking at my uncle, was enough.

My uncle turned me. 'You there,' he demanded, 'are you going to say anything on behalf of your aunt? Have you something to complain about, too?'

In spite of being fascinated by their conversation and above all by the way in which Don Juan had, by his powers of persuasion, controlled it, I couldn't help but feel somewhat detached, suffused by a tender, sweet clarity that made my whole body thrill as though Mercedes were there close by my side. But I pulled myself together. 'Uncle, if you would do your utmost to not hurt my aunt, especially in front of other people... She is such a good person...'

He let out an oath. 'Yes indeed,' he said, 'that's the worst of it, that's what's bad about it. Your aunt is so good, yes indeed, and it's not as if I'm easy to put up with. If she were a bad lot it would all be so much easier.'

It was the turn of the younger Spaniard to join in. 'Don Justino, sir, you are a gentleman,' he said, getting up. 'We don't need to say any more.'

'Yes, I am a gentleman, I am indeed. But I shall make no promises,' he said. Then he bawled out: 'Woman, woman!' But my aunt did not come.

The Spaniards exchanged glances and excused themselves on the grounds that it was time for the news and went off to closet themselves in the library. I was alone with my uncle; he got up and nodded towards the door. 'Do you know how much they owe me?' he said. 'Do you know how much I've won so far? How many beans they both owe me? Four thousand, seven hundred and thirty-five.'

At that moment the bell of the gate outside rang. We both started. The babble from the radio upstairs, together with the crackle and whine, stopped. My aunt came running from the kitchen and stopped halfway between the doors, uncertain, as uncertain as we were. The bell rang again, followed at once by the baying of the dog.

My uncle pulled himself up with the help of his stick. His brow was furrowed. 'Go on,' he ordered me, 'let's go and see who it is.'

He followed by my side along the dark avenue of palms. 'If it's the police,' he said in a low voice, 'you don't know anything. If it's a visitor, let them in and we'll receive them down here.' Down there in the dining room was where we always received everybody.

The dog was snorting and between the bars of the gate I could make out a shape, barely lit by the street lamp. It was José Ramos.

My uncle recognised him at once. 'Zé Ramos, what have you been up to? What brings you here?'

'Lieutenant, sir, forgive me for coming to your house, especially at this time, but I have urgently to speak to Jorge. I couldn't find him anywhere so I supposed he must be here. But I don't want to bother you.'

'No, no, come on in. It's a big house, there's room for lots of people.'

'Thank you but it's not worth coming in,' he said, turning to me. 'Can we go for a walk and have a chat. Can't you come?'

'I can.'

'Well, let's go. Good night, lieutenant, sir. Once again, I'm sorry.'

I went out and we walked together, not exchanging a word. I felt so strong that my very strength made me feel quite detached, especially by his side. He stopped abruptly.

'Do you mind explaining to me what all that was about today,' he demanded.

'Explaining what? Exactly what?'

'What went on with my sister. You don't have to come the gallant young knight or beat about the bush because she's told me everything. It's precisely why I came to look for you.'

'If she's told you everything, why do you need me to tell you?'

'What you have in mind, what all this means.'

'I have in mind ... look, I like her, I always did and she likes me and always did, too. That's all there is to it.'

'And now?'

'Now what? Now, I'm going out with your sister; and you have to agree that neither she nor I have to come running to you for permission.'

'I'm her brother; and she's engaged. You know perfectly well that she's engaged.'

'You're her brother and you're my friend – at least that's how I regard you, and I too was going to come and get hold of you to tell you just what you've come to find out. If I haven't ... I don't know ... I've been walking on air, I couldn't think of anything else.'

'But she's engaged. How could you just show up like that and spoil everything?'

'Zé ... no engagement is absolutely certain. If I'd been following your sister around, trying to wreck everything... But it's exactly because that's just what I didn't do that matters and which explains everything; it just happened.'

'Even so.'

I went on walking, wallowing in my happiness, without bothering to check whether he was following. 'But the fact that it happened like that,' I said, 'suddenly, proves two things: that it wasn't something sudden at all, and that your sister was making a big mistake. All of a sudden we both saw that we had always been thinking about the other and that really we were waiting for each other. But what was really sudden and meaningless was this ridiculous engagement.'

'Ridiculous?'

'Yes, because of what happened between your sister and me.'

He sighed. 'Every engagement, every marriage, is ridiculous, and the engaged couple too. But a pledge isn't.'

'Sure, but there's nothing to stop Mercedes telling her fiancé, tomorrow, that the engagement is off.'

'There's a lot to stop her.'

'Such as, for example.'

He lowered his voice. That she...'

I shivered. 'That she?'

'Yes, that she ... belongs to him.'

I struck him and bellowed out loud: 'You liar! You want to take her from me!'

'It's true,' he said impassively.

We stood stock still in silence.

'Why did you tell me this?' I murmured.

'Because it's true,' he said, and we continued on down the street in silence.

We came to a garden I didn't know; there were vague shapes on the benches. I sat down on an empty one while he remained standing. I rested my arms on my legs, clenching my fists.

'Zé ... this doesn't change a thing. I love your sister and she loves me. Didn't she tell you?'

'She did.'

'He doesn't have to marry her.'

'Will you?'

'I can't marry her yet. But I promise too – if that's what she wants. Does she know that you've come to talk to me?'

'Yes'

'Don't tell her you've told me anything.'

He sat down next to me. 'Look,' he began, 'I don't believe in any of these old ideas; I think they've the right to do what they want to do...'

'To do what?'

'It was in Oporto; after that, never again. I'm absolutely sure.'

'What were you going to say?'

'That I think one way and carry on in a different way. Why do you have to marry her?'

'And why does he have to marry her?'

'Because of my parents.'

'Do they know?'

'No; but if they did they wouldn't understand.'

'You're really saying they don't know, so they don't need to know. Zé ... please excuse my question. Was there, or will there be, any ... outcome?'

'No. Enough time has passed; it's OK. And, as far as he's concerned, after I talked to him, he hasn't touched her again.'

'Why? Doesn't he think like you?'

'More or less; but he's a loyal member of the party.'

'And that's why you prefer him to me?'

'Did I say I preferred him?'

'And that is why your sister...' and I sought wildly for some casual expression, some anodyne phrase. 'Ended up in his arms,' I blurted out. 'Or did he charm her, seduce her?'

'Something of the sort. Do you know how it happened?'

'I don't want to know,' I replied.

'Jorge,' he exclaimed suddenly, in a tight, almost inaudible voice, 'I beg you ... forget what happened ... we need him.'

'What has that to do with your sister? You...'

'No, no, you can't understand. Now, it can't be.'

'Why?'

'I can't tell you; I've already said too much.'

'I do have the right to know, though, don't I?'

He was troubled, wrestling with himself, no longer the cold, distant fellow I had known. 'It's my fault. I let him get close to her, knowing that women couldn't resist him. I let them get engaged to cover up something that could not have been more closely covered up than it was in any case. And now I can't even send you away with some false story or other. In the end my loyalty to my family, to my ideas, to my friends, is greater than what I owe to...'

I put my hand on his shoulder. 'What do you need him for?'

'To pilot the boat.'

'The boat? What boat?'

'The boat in which we're going to run away to Spain.'

'Who's going to run away?'

'You don't know them. Me, Macedo, some other colleagues, and some Spaniards who are hiding in Oporto and here.'

'Here in Figueira?'

'Yes, that's right.'

'Let me tell you something: there are two of them hiding up in my uncle's house.'

'I'd suspected as much.'

'Because of the cigarettes?'

'Not just that. It was also because your uncle went looking for one of our other chaps. It could only have been to make contact with him, and why would your uncle want to do that if somebody in hiding hadn't asked him to?'

'You're very well informed.'

'Not all that well,' he said, smiling a little vaguely.

'Those chaps in our house, though, they're not communists.'

'Right now that doesn't matter; what's more important is the unity of all anti-Fascists.'

'And what are you and Macedo and the others going to do in Spain?' I asked.

'Fight.'

'Half a dozen of you? How will that help matters?'

'It will help, for example, because our action will have repercussions,' he explained.

'But here in Portugal, who will even know about it?'

'Everybody: the republican radio will broadcast it and the international press, too, And it's a protest, it's like a protest on behalf of the Portuguese people, so that everybody knows they're not on the side of the rebels. Right now it's essential to oppose publicly the arrogance with which the Government supports them.'

'Has anybody ordered you to go and fight in Spain?'

'No. Actually I was one of those who suggested it.'

'When are you going?'

'Everything's ready; we just need to sort out a few things in Oporto. It's a great coup.'

'Are you setting off from here?'

'Yes.'

'To the north?'

'Yes, it's easier that way.'

'I suppose you can take those two chaps in our house with you?'

'Yes, of course. When it's time I'll let you know.'

'Can I tell them I've spoken to you?'

'Yes, you can.'

'What about the boat?' I asked. 'Will they have to pay anything?'

'It's already spoken for. We had, we're still having a whip-round, so if they can manage to give anything...'

'I'll talk to them about it.'

We got up from the bench; the garden was already deserted. Only on one bench was there a couple who seemed to be sleeping. We came eventually to a street which I recognised. 'Zé,' I said, 'I won't give up your sister for all the world. But she has to decide.'

'Decide what?'

'If she wants to string him along until you leave.'

'You can't leave a decision like that in her hands.'

'Why not? Only she can decide. I can't do any more than that. She won't be going with you, will she?'

'No, she'll stay here.'

'Has he come back yet?'

'Him? No, not yet. He'll be back tomorrow night.'

'OK, let's meet tomorrow morning on the beach.'

'Fine.'

'Good night,' I said, holding out my hand.

He hesitated for a moment and then grasped it.

'Good night,' he said.

XV

The following morning I got up early and went downstairs. Over coffee my uncle made it easier for me to broach the subject of the boat by asking what it was that Zé Ramos had been after so urgently. But the worried expressions of the two Spaniards and my uncle, too, when I told them, as far as it concerned them, of my conversation with my friend, gave me pause for thought in a way I hadn't felt before. In truth, merely the fact that he had realised that they were staying in the house did not justify the haste with which he had come looking for me so hastily, not to mention the strange matter of his not having discussed it with my uncle but rather had spirited me off to have a private conversation. I, though, was not prepared to give anything more away, and, just as the complicated web, made up of various factors which I wouldn't reveal made me see the story of the projected flight as improbable and fantastic, so my reluctance only made my own story seem not only improbable and fantastic, but also dubious; it was so dubious in fact that they received it with much less enthusiasm – or none at all – than I had expected or that they themselves would have felt under different circumstances. The night before, as I was trying to get off to sleep, and in a puzzled frame of mind which had only got worse after Zé Ramos and I had parted, I had avoided the situation altogether, and had separated the two things into completely different cases: my own with Mercedes, which was my affair; and the flight to Spain which was the Spaniards' affair.

Now, their misgivings and those of my uncle (who refused to believe that Zé Ramos – I hadn't mentioned Macedo, being unsure of the relationship between my uncle and his father – was intending to fight in Spain, or Almeida, something which, for their part, the Spaniards did accept, although the older one maintained that the struggle was purely a Spanish affair and that nobody should get mixed up in it beyond lending moral support), by calling into doubt the whole flight, awoke in reflex fashion similar uncertainties within me, not least concerning my situation with Mercedes. While they were talking the thing over (seeming to want to blame me for having broken the veil of secrecy without consulting them) I justified my own actions to myself, saying to myself that if I had been talking to my friends I still hadn't said anything to Mercedes – though in my beams, I had.

In the restless tossing and turning of that night I had been with her in the belvedere at the bottom of the garden, leaning out over the waves which broke over the rocks at the end of the beach, and near which a small sailing boat with Almeida at the helm, was being tossed back and forth at the mercy of those waves. As we talked Mercedes, still at my side, waved goodbye to the boat while Almeida waved and smiled back at her. Macedo, who was also in the boat (but not Zé, who did not figure in the dream at all), made obscene gestures to me, pointing to Almeida and shouting out that every woman was his. I shuddered lest Mercedes should overhear, but she did not even seem to see him and held me close, saying that she was mine and nobody else's. Every time that we embraced, everything dissolved, and then we were in a room in a hotel but the bed was my own, the one I was sleeping in. But as I was about to make her mine the lights came on and the room filled with people: all my friends, a jumbled mass of faces, and other faces, unknown, but perfectly distinct, who belonged to the 'party'. Almeida was not among them; Mercedes, though, got up and boxed Macedo round the ears. This scene played over a few times – or at least it seemed to me – until I fell asleep once and for all; when I awoke I was filled with the firm idea of speaking again to the Spaniards and to my uncle.

They were still talking. 'What should I say to Zé Ramos?' I said, breaking in on their conversation. 'I'm going to meet him now.'

They talked among themselves: Spain was truly split; the rebels had little by little captured the heights of the Guadarrama and were intensifying the siege of Madrid, though the capital still seemed to be holding out. Within a few days the situation would become clearer still. For its part, the government was intensifying the siege of Toledo. The desperation and false optimism with which the Portuguese Radio Club urged on the defenders of the Alcázar showed that the situation there was far from favouring the rebels. Giral's Ministry had armed the people without losing the support of the liberals and was in control of the territories which had remained loyal or where any incipient uprising had been put down. My uncle's contribution to the debate was a series of hostile asides in which, suddenly, I discerned a kind of resentment directed more against the fact that his involuntary guests might escape than towards either the occasion or the means. And to everybody's surprise it was my aunt, who had come up from the kitchen with fresh coffee, and who, putting the coffee pot on the table and smoothing out the tablecloth, suggested a solution.

I had to tell Zé Ramos something, didn't I? Even if the business of the boat were some kind of far-fetched madness, we were all still 'in the same boat' (she smiled at her pun). I should say that, yes indeed sir, we'd be happy to accept the offer and that we were awaiting instructions. There was no other way.

My uncle was staring at her. 'Woman,' he said, 'since when did you know anything about these matters?'

'Since they've been happening in my house,' she replied, and I remembered that I hadn't said anything about payment or asked them if they could contribute to the expenses, so I brought the matter up.

They didn't have much money. How much was needed?

Ramos hadn't told me, but in any case if everything was fixed they wouldn't be left behind on that account.

'I'll pay whatever's necessary,' said my uncle, 'but I don't think it's going to happen because I don't believe there's anything in it.'

'And where will you get the money from?' asked my aunt.

'From your purse and your mother's. If she's got enough to pay the whole lot of those fellows in the Academy in Coimbra to sleep with her...'

'Justino!'

'Justino be damned. That's just how it is. Get off with you to Coimbra and grab some money off your mother.'

'You know perfectly well she won't give it me. Only if I promise her categorically that I'm not coming back here.'

'Well, don't come back; send the money by post.'

The Spaniards protested that there was neither rhyme nor reason in his plan and that they couldn't possibly accept it. I got up from the table, saying it was already late for going to the beach and went out.

As I neared the beach the first person I saw, perversely, was Rodrigues. As usual, but this time even more persistently, he began to ask me where I'd been the previous evening because he hadn't seen me around.

'I slept through the morning and then I went to the beach. I didn't go out in the evening.'

'Didn't you?'

'No.'

'That was one hell of night, wasn't it?'

'Yes.'

'It looks like you're regretting it.'

'Me? Regretting what?'

He looked sidelong at me. 'Well … regretting something anyway. Macedo was mad with me because he took part in all that and his brother too. But that made the joke even better. I set the whole thing up beautifully, didn't I? Now you lot, all you nice, clean chaps, you can't even talk about me. The old man baptised us all with the kiss of peace.'

'It's not the same thing.'

'Isn't it? Of course it isn't, is it…'

'Look, Rodrigues, that's enough of that,' I said, looking straight at him. 'You know I saw you when you were exposing yourself to those guys on the beach.'

'Macedo didn't see though.'

'I can't think he did but only because I distracted him.'

'And for why? Why didn't you draw his attention to it and why didn't you both come over and catch me at it?'

'Because I'm your friend and I felt sorry for you and didn't want him to see you.'

'I don't want anybody's pity!' he shouted, adding peremptorily: 'What I was doing doesn't prove a thing. Anybody as well hung as me, and an exhibitionist like me, would do what I did if he were being spied on by a pair of perverts.'

'I don't know if they would; but that, together with what they say about you, would have been enough and more than enough to ruin you. I happen to believe you're a man and you don't want to be anything else.'

'Does anybody doubt it?'

'For the time being, no.'

'Not for the time being, not ever. It doesn't mean I'm not a man if some perverts put the word around and come looking for me. Or they pick up the scent when they pass me.'

'And if they pick up the scent isn't that because there's something about you? Why, when they look at you once do they get the idea they can continue looking at you?'

'Perhaps that's it,' he said, adopting a cynical pose. 'And so what?'

I wanted to put an end to the conversation once and for all. 'So what? That's up to you.'

His mood changed suddenly and, as he had done by the water's edge, he took my hand. 'But you won't tell anybody, will you?'

'No, I won't. But you must calm down and stop shouting your mouth off,' I said, removing my hand from his.

'Calm down?'

'Your life isn't my affair, but stop pretending that it's all some daring act that you're flinging in everybody's face.'

We had stopped by the sea wall and I was anxious to go down to the bathing huts. I asked him if he was coming down to the beach.

'Is it OK if I come with you?'

'OK? Don't be daft,' and we went down together.

I walked in front of the huts, exactly alongside that belonging to Ramos, followed by Rodrigues. Mercedes' mother was sitting there with another lady and with a desiccated smile – or so it seemed to me – she told us, waving her knitting needles, that they had all gone swimming. The neighbouring hut was empty but for some clothes hanging up inside; it was the Macedo's, so we got undressed there after lowering the awning. When we emerged in our bathing costumes Rodrigues paraded up and down for a while in front of the huts while I set off towards the sea. He doubled his stride and caught up with me.

'Did you see her?' he asked. 'Do you see how she was looking at me?'

'Who?'

'The other one. Do you know who she is?'

'No, I don't know her.'

'I do: she's Almeida's cousin, you know the naval officer who's going to marry Mercedes. She's from here, from Figueira. One time I was just about to... Anyway, one of these fine days, eh?'

We walked on to the water's edge and I, mistaking constantly the faces of those emerging from the waves, or the bodies which were running about in or sitting on the wet sand, could not pick out Mercedes. Nor any of the others: her brother, the Macedos, Oliveira, the other girls. Beside me Rodrigues rambled on about the adventure he didn't have with Almeida's cousin, though the fact that she was his cousin gave me a particular pleasure. 'Well, all that you have to do,' I said, still anxiously scanning the sea, 'is to chat the floosie up. And then get on top of her, though that might be more difficult. But...'

'That's not difficult for me,' he said, finishing my sentence. 'I had hardly got in when I shot off...'

At that moment I sensed somebody running towards us and turned to see Luís Macedo, all out of breath. 'We're all there at the back, behind Silva e Sousa's hut,' he panted.

We turned back and retraced our steps with him trotting along at our side like a gleeful little dog. Rodrigues chatted away affably to him in that supercilious way of his.

I could already make out the group with Mercedes among them and I quickened my steps, to see more closely those eyes which were fixed on me. We got there and I said hello to everybody all around without paying any special attention to Mercedes and, followed by Rodrigues, greeted the ladies sitting inside the hut; they were the mother and aunt of the Sousas, a pair of plain looking girls who were sticking close to the Ramos and the Macedos. The group made room for us and I said down by Zé with Mercedes on my right. Then came the two Silva e Sousas, between whom Rodrigues lay down, stretching out and resting on his elbow. Then, to complete the circle came Oliveira and Macedo. Luís was sitting on his haunches behind Rodrigues. They had all been swimming except for us; Mercedes' back and arms were covered with patches of sand. The two Sousas, disconcerted by the proximity of Rodrigues, clucked like hens, pretending that they were doing so because Luís had piped up again with some nonsense which he had begun before the others had sent him off to fetch us. Macedo, leaning against the pole, gazed out at the sea. I replied to the pleasantries of the ladies who were going through their usual match-making enquiries. But my hand, buried in the sand, found that of Mercedes who grasped it tightly. Suddenly, and as had not happened the day before, I wanted not just to take her in my arms, but to possess her entirely. So evidently did I desire her, not just as my fiancée, that I withdrew my hand, more swiftly than it was discreet to do. It was as though I felt it was a profanation of that desire, a kind of betrayal of it, because it was only now that I knew she was 'available' that I could want her in that way. Her eyes were questioning and I reassured, half-closing my own in a sign of love which also served to hide the guilt that I felt and that she might read in mine.

I leant towards Zé. 'I have spoken to them,' I said through my teeth. I said no more because he frowned at me, urgently bidding me be silent.

I couldn't keep my mind on the conversation. Rodrigues was making the two Sousas laugh, and their aunt and Luís with his jests.

Macedo scowled at his brother and at Rodrigues; Oliveira, close by, was explaining the jokes, as if to defuse them and thus Macedo's ill humour and so avert any outburst. Nevertheless it came: 'Luís, it's time we went home. Let's get dressed,' he said.

The boy lay down. 'You go,' he replied. 'It's still too early for me.'

His brother got up. 'We're going. It's time.'

'You can leave your little brother with us,' said Rodrigues. 'He won't get lost with all these people here. We'll all be taking care of him, won't we?' he asked around, and everybody, even the ladies, laughing, confirmed that he wouldn't get lost.

'Well then, you come with me,' said Macedo directly to Rodrigues. 'I want to talk to you.'

Rodrigues sat down and planted his hands on his knees. 'I've only just arrived and I haven't even had a dip. If it's only a few words, how about there behind the hut…'

Oliveira got up. 'Well, it's time for me to go,' he said, grabbing Macedo by the arm. 'Let the boy stay,' he added. 'I'll go with you.'

Macedo pulled himself free. In the midst of the shared awkwardness it was Ramos who spoke: 'Really, it would be better if you went on home,' he said. 'Let your brother stay, you can't be watching over him for ever. After all he's a man.'

All eyes were on Macedo who moved off obediently with Oliveira; it was then I felt Mercedes' hand in mine. I kept my head down, absorbed, contemplating her hand, small and slim, openly resting on mine. When I did look up again it was because I felt the gaze of the two ladies fixed on our entwined hands and on us. But neither Mercedes nor I took our hands away. The two ladies looked at each other knowingly. And Zé, moving away slightly, looked and then slowly got up. 'Jorge,' he asked, 'are you coming for a swim?'

'I'm coming, too,' said Rodrigues, getting up. 'Who's going for another swim?'

The two Sousa girls complained that they were already dry and weren't going to get wet again. Mercedes and I got to our feet and Luís as well. Ramos, though, stopped him. 'You stay here and keep the ladies company until we get back,' he said.

'We haven't got our clothes here, any of us,' Luís pointed out.

'Well done. You'd better go back to the hut to keep an eye on them,' said Ramos. 'Off you go.'

Luís hesitated and looked imploringly at Rodrigues, but the latter,

clearly mindful of the scene with Macedo, which however the two
ladies and the two younger girls would not have understood, didn't
rush to back him up.

We went down to the water, Ramos chatting to Rodrigues while
I walked silently at Mercedes' side. When the foam dashed around
our legs we both stopped at the very moment when the other two
ran headlong into the water.

'Well?' I asked, without looking at her.

'Zé asked me...'

'I'm not interested in what Zé asked you.'

'Only for a few days...' she said, giving me her hand; I held it
tight.

'For a few days you're going to carry on with him, isn't that it?'
I said, looking her in the eyes, wherein I read both shock and doubt.
Just then a beach ball hit her on the head and she staggered back as
two boys came hurtling after the ball now borne by the waves, and
bumped into me. Then we faced each other once again and the
fear and uncertainty had disappeared. 'What does it matter if it's
you that I love?' she asked reasonably.

'That's the very reason it does matter,' I replied.

This time the ball hit me and I turned round to see the two boys
laughing; they came running past, right by us, to get their ball. I
made as if to chase them and they sped off back to the beach.

'Let's walk in the other direction,' I said. 'And you want me to
go along with this engagement for as long as they remain here?' I
said, returning to the matter.

The ball hit me again on the back so I ran after it, picked it up
and hurled it into the sea.

'But what am I supposed to do?' she said; just then behind us
there came a great outcry of shouts and tears.

'What are you supposed to do?' I repeated, as the two boys came
near to me shouting so that everybody could hear. 'He threw our
ball out to sea,' they cried. 'That's him, that's the one who did it!'

Various people came up to join them including a fat gentleman,
his chest covered with white hairs and a jutting belly. 'What a
terrible thing to do, throwing the children's ball into the sea like
that!' he said. Meanwhile their maid had arrived and was trying to
console them – which only made them howl the more. 'Go and
fetch it,' she demanded, with the two boys clinging to her skirts,
'go and fetch it! Otherwise I'll call the beach superintendent!'

I plunged into the water, furious, and swam back with the ball, pushing it along in front of me. By the time I got back Mercedes had managed to turn the atmosphere around. 'These lads are devils,' said one lady who had a very white, feeble looking boy with her. 'I know! I know! I only need to be taking little Quinzinho here for a walk and they start to do this sort of thing!' The maid, too, was shaking the boys and admitted that they were a terrible handful.

We went off laughing; and Mercedes was still laughing when she spoke again. 'But what am I to do?' she asked.

The laughter which still played so absurdly on the corners of her mouth while her eyes were already brimming with tears, only served to infuriate me. 'Do what you want, but leave me in peace!' I said and stormed off towards the bathing huts.

Stunned at first by my fury, she came running after me. 'Jorge, don't leave me,' she cried.

I strode on, trying to make out the Macedo's hut where I had left my clothes. I wouldn't have found it if I hadn't seen Luís sitting on the sand, leaning against one of the poles of the awning and who waved to me.

'Go and get the others,' I told him, 'and then we can go.'

He hesitated, looking at us curiously. 'They didn't stick around here,' he said. 'I don't know where they are.'

'Go and look for them, Luís,' asked Mercedes.

He got up in no great haste and even when he was some distance away he still turned round to look at us suspiciously.

'What must he think of us?' she asked.

I pulled her inside the hut. 'Look, they can see us,' she said, resisting, but when, in response to her words, I looked at the hut next to ours I saw that the ladies were no longer there.

'Let them see, let everybody see,' I said pressing her strongly against me.

She wrenched herself away from me and stood, half bent, in a corner of the hut like a hunted animal. As I came towards her she let herself drop to the ground where she sat, looking tearfully up at me. 'What do you want me to do? I love you so much, oh how I love you!'

'I want you to be mine.'

'But I will be.'

'No, today.'

She lowered her head and slowly drew a line in the sand with her hand. 'All right.'

I squatted down beside and stroked her head which she had laid on my shoulder. 'At five o'clock I'll be waiting for you on the second corner there by the casino. There's a shop…'

'I know the one you mean,' she said.

I kissed her quickly. 'I'll wait a quarter of an hour for you.'

I got up first and helped her to her feet and then, as she turned it away from me I held her face in my hands. 'Look at me,' I said.

She glanced at me and then looked away again.

I smiled at her. 'A quarter of an hour, do you hear?'

She nodded.

As I was helping her to untie the flap so that she could fasten it up and get dressed the others arrived. Ramos grabbed his clothes and went off to the Macedo's hut where Rodrigues and Luís soon untied their flap. We didn't say a word as we got dressed. Mercedes was already dressed when I emerged but Zé, very particular about shaking the last grain of sand from his clothes, took the longest. The five of us left the beach together with Rodrigues making a song and dance about how it had been a long time since he had enjoyed a swim so much and insisting that Zé Ramos back him up in the matter. We entered the Bairro Novo where Luís went on his way; at the corner of the street to their boarding house the Ramos brothers said goodbye, too. Rodrigues asked me to have lunch with him, pressing me and saying it was late and that we could eat something there. I preferred to be alone and for that reason, too, I didn't even want to go home. But I couldn't be doing with him just then and so I resisted. In any case it wouldn't look too good if I treated my aunt's house like a boarding house, would it? We stopped in front of the door to a small restaurant. 'Your aunt …' he smiled. 'What a woman … I'm sorry; but if I could have a woman like that… Go on. Off you go, quickly,' he said, going into the restaurant. But in a moment he appeared again and called to me: 'Look, don't get involved with anybody else's woman, eh,' he said.

'Me?' I replied, surprised.

'Yes, you. You never know just how far they might be somebody else's, do you know what I mean?'

'No,' I said, going on my way.

XVI

It was half past one. A little further on I went into a teashop and ate two or three sweet rolls. The best thing would be to carry on home so that they wouldn't be worried, not knowing whether or not I had spoken to Zé Ramos. In truth I had hardly managed to speak to him, but by going home I could change and get ready. Get ready for what? To meet her: bridegrooms on the their wedding day bath carefully, apply all sorts of sweet smelling lotions, shave right down to the very last hair, to make themselves acceptable to the brides that they will shortly possess. Except that Mercedes was not my bride. And he, when he had her (once, how many times?) did he begin by preparing himself with all this care? If he had prepared himself that first time it was because it had all been calculated, like an assault, a seduction or an assignation with a lover. A furtive meeting, an adventure. And all these preparations then would have been part of the pretence, like a kind of mask, to cover up the lack of real love, or to hide behind perfumes and such the common, stinking nature of the place where the lovers had met. Or perhaps it had been a refined, expensive place, tarted up deliberately, like a whorehouse. I shuddered Where would I take her? She was not a mistress, she was Mercedes. And I couldn't do with her what the other had done. And I couldn't, in fact, for he had been the first and nobody could take that from him nor, indeed, from *her*. And it was clear that, at least in that moment, and in others following it, she had loved him, since if she hadn't, she wouldn't have agreed to marry him. How could she not agree? After what had happened he had to accept the responsibility. And it was only when she had seen me that she had realised that she had never loved him, that it was me she had always loved, me that she had been thinking about, though she hadn't realised it when she had given herself to him. That was the reason she had given in so promptly to my demands; in fact, she had given in very promptly. So very promptly. Too promptly? Yes.

After all, no sooner had she seen me than she had lured me to the end of the beach so that on the following day, without a moment's hesitation, she could reply with her 'very well' to my demands. But wasn't this a proof of love? Didn't it show just how much she had always loved me? Or did it just show that, now, everything had become easy for her and after the first one, why should there not be others? Or, on the contrary, since she had averted her eyes, had she been thinking that I had already lost my respect for her, knowing that she was no longer a virgin? But then she didn't know that I knew. It was unthinkable that her brother could have told her that he had told me everything. But perhaps she had thought, or imagined, or not so much clearly known even as sensed rather that, having lost her virginity, any other man would have some kind of sixth sense about these things? That there might be on her some kind of outward sign, on her face, on her body, in the clothes she wore, which betrayed her to anyone who knew something about women? But that was exactly what I had to do, in order to possess her, make her mine, to show her that there wasn't any such sign, to show that he had not marked her in any way. So far, anyway. And afterwards? The mere fact of my holding her in my arms would force her to tell me everything; she had to tell me before I could find out. Her confessing, however, her confessing to me, would mean that it was no longer 'their' secret, but would become *my* secret. And by being mine she would, in her turn, become more mine than anyone. He couldn't have loved her like I loved her, nor desired her like I desired her. To desire somebody like that it was first necessary to have an infinite respect for her, a respect that he hadn't shown. And did I have it? If I hadn't known what I did, would I have demanded what I had? It wasn't possible to think like that; the situation I was in wasn't the same: I had come on the scene only after the thing had happened.

Where could I take her? I tried to bring back to mind some of the possible places that I had known but instantly I felt an extreme revulsion at the very thought. To what level was I dragging her down, imagining her in those places? Seeing her naked in those beds? Seeing me naked with her within those walls? What did it matter? Yes, when all was said and done, the place didn't matter, though some place was an absolute necessity. The difference would be in the way we approached this place, in our attitudes of body and spirit. And what if somebody saw her? For at least the person who opened the door would see her. I could, though, go in first, sort everything out and let her in without anybody seeing her. And how would I take her there? Would she go no matter where I took her? What if she refused? If she used this as an excuse for not delivering what she had promised?

At that moment I remembered a little house in Buarcos, where I had gone once, which rented out rooms, and I saw the short woman, all in black, with a wrap-around skirt and a black kerchief on her head, opening the door carefully and disappearing down the flagged corridor. It had been an evening the last time I was there, with some girl I had picked up on the beach. It had been two years ago; would the woman in black still be there? Or the house? The best thing was to go there and arrange a time. So, having almost reached my uncle's house, I went off in another direction, taking a short cut through a jumble of ruined, low houses, all shut up. Would I recognise the house? Agonising, for that house suddenly seemed to me our only recourse, and I couldn't even remember any others; I trembled at the thought that I might not recognise her, or that she might have moved, or that the house, like the woman in black herself, didn't even exist. Had it really existed? Or was my memory playing tricks on me? I could see again the high, iron bed, the wooden shutters half closed, the three-legged washbasin in a corner, the water jugs on the wide, scrubbed floorboards; I even heard the hens clucking outside in the yard on to which the window gave. And what if I had to pay in advance? I didn't have enough money with me. The other time I hadn't had enough either but I had gone there with some girl that the woman in black had known. What if she, fearful of the police, and not knowing who I was, slammed the door in my face?

I stopped in front of a row of identical houses, with sash windows on either side of the doors. It was one of those; but which one? I looked around and saw that the street was empty. I picked out one of the houses and banged on the door with the little hand-shaped knocker. Nothing. I knocked again. Nothing. Again I banged on the door. In the next house a door opened slightly and a head with a black kerchief poked out. 'Are you looking for someone?' said a fluting voice. 'Nobody lives there.'

I moved towards her and the head withdrew, leaving only a tiny gap. 'I'm looking for a house here,' I said. 'I want to rent some rooms.'

The door opened some more and the head reappeared. 'Some rooms? What for?'

'Rooms...'

'Ah, rooms... Here they are; they're a hundred thousand reis a month.' (Should I give the currency in reis or escudos?)

'I don't want them for a month. I was wanting ... I was here once before.'

'I don't remember your name.'

'It was some time back, two years ... an afternoon ... I had a girl with me called...'

'Called?'

'Look, I can't remember.'

'So it's me who has to remember, is it?'

'I'm sorry but I really do need the room; at five o'clock. Please do me that favour. I'll pay; do you want me to pay now?'

She opened the door a little more to look me over carefully; she had a little tuft of hair beneath her chin. 'Not at five; come at half past. Knock on the door three times and then one more time,' she said and shut the door.

It was after half past two. I went on my way back home. There were still about two hours before I met Mercedes ... what if she didn't show up? I would be there at five on the dot; I would wait fifteen minutes and if she didn't come I would go away. And then? But she wouldn't let me down, I was absolutely sure she wouldn't. But if she did? There might be some problem. If she didn't show up this time, that would prove nothing. But if she didn't come today, the other fellow would return and everything would become more difficult, and she wouldn't be mine *in time*, even though she wanted to be. And she did want to be. But would she want to be in that way? Supposing she didn't deign to come with me to that house? She might refuse, though this wouldn't mean that she wouldn't give herself to me in some other place, at some other opportunity. If I were in the same hotel as her maybe she would let me come in one night, into her room. Was that how she had let him in? The fact that her brother had told there had been nothing between them since Oporto didn't mean a thing: he might not know, or he might be lying. But it could also be true and there really hadn't been anything between them. And so she had given in to my urging so quickly, not because she loved me, but because she liked to sleep with a man, and for the time being he wasn't sleeping with her; in which case she wouldn't fail to turn up. But what would be missing would be the real her, the one that in the end I would not get to possess, truly. It all depended so that if, in bed, I managed to be more than this for her, if I in effect succeeded in winning her heart, she would be mine, she would be that woman that I wanted for my own. She loved me. She had made her way into my arms, having been in his, having been ready to marry him, having been possessed by him. That she would give herself to me, as proof of her love, was what I had demanded. Under pressure from me she had given in. Would she come?

I went into the house where I came across my aunt talking in the kitchen to one of the maids. I was puzzled and merely said that I'd already had lunch and went up to the library where my uncle and the two Spaniards were sitting at the green baize table with their cards in their hands.

'The maid's downstairs, talking to auntie,' I said.

My uncle, his eyes fixed on the game, gestured to me to shut up, doubled his stake and the others showed their hands. As he swept up the pile of beans my uncle looked up at me and smiled. 'Yes, I know. She came to see if we had already returned, and, well, here we were.'

'What now, then?'

The two Spaniards shrugged their shoulders, resignedly. 'Now,' replied my uncle, 'I've spoken to her and told her that if she doesn't blab then she can have part of the stuff we're smuggling, once we've got it through.'

'What about the other one? Is she coming back, too?'

'Of course. I'm about to tell her. She'll get part of the stuff as well.'

'So now we're smugglers,' sighed the old chap, Don Juan, studying his cards; he seemed to have had the stuffing knocked out of him.

'I've spoken to Ramos,' I said.

Nobody showed the slightest interest. 'I've already spoken to Ramos,' I repeated.

'And what did he say?' my uncle finally managed to ask.

I felt terribly frustrated. In a way all my life was wrapped up in that matter, but they seemed happy to spend theirs here, just playing cards. 'When the time is right,' I said drily, 'he'll let us know.'

'Did he get round to talking about money?' asked my uncle; he didn't even hear me say no because with a whoop of triumph he showed his hand to the others and scooped up the beans victoriously.

I went up to my room; on the bed lay the postcards and the half-written letter. I sat down on the edge of the bed; I felt a weariness which drained me of all strength and thought. I lay down on my back, gazing at the ceiling. It was half past three. All along the length of the wire to the bedside lamp a fly was tenaciously pursuing another one, which jumped or took off to fly a few inches on ahead, escaping each time. Suddenly, waking with a start, I sat up on the bed and looked at my watch. It was ten past five.

I sprang up, dragged on my jacket in a fever of anxiety, checked the money in my pocket and sped downstairs. I ran across the kitchen and out onto the avenue of palm trees without even replying to my aunt who had called out to ask me where I was going in such haste. Seeing me running the dog bounded along, leaping up beside me. I rushed pell mell down the street, thinking of nothing, without even looking at my watch. I turned into the street where the casino was to get my bearings and stumbled against Macedo and Oliveira; I shoved them out of my way and ran on as far as the corner where I stopped, breathless, leaning against the wall. I had turned the corner so that they wouldn't see me. I looked around; there was no sign of Mercedes. Either she hadn't come or she had already left because of my lateness; it was already after twenty past five, nearer twenty-five past. I closed my eyes, overwhelmed by fatigue and bitter disappointment. And then I felt a hand on my arm and a voice said: 'Let's go.'

I opened my eyes and looked at her in gratitude. 'You've been running?' she enquired, smiling.

'Yes. I was delayed at home. I'm sorry. Where were you? At first I thought you hadn't come or hadn't waited for me.'

'I was in the shop.'

Then, all at once I remembered that we had to get moving as soon as possible, so that nobody saw us. What if Macedo and Oliveira were going in our direction? And we should not be late, either; what if the woman were to let the room once our time was up?

'Let's go quickly, follow me,' I said, diving into a narrow passage through the little streets in front of us. From time to time, breathing deeply, I shot a glance behind me. She was coming, to all appearances just strolling along unhurriedly. When I reached the corner from where the house was visible, I stopped. She came into sight and I pointed it out to her. I would knock, go in and wait for her inside.

'No, I'm coming in with you,' she said.

I looked at her. Although her face was perfectly serene the strain still showed. She gave me her hand. 'Come on.'

We went down the street together. I knocked three times and then once more. I didn't dare look up at the other houses. I knocked again. Nor did I dare look at Mercedes by my side. The door opened slightly and the face of the old lady peered out and then we were both inside in the dark corridor with the door shut behind us; she opened the door to a room whose windows gave out onto the street. Mercedes went into the room whose shadowy light was bright in comparison to the dark corridor. The old lady touched me on the arm. 'That'll be twenty thousand reis,' she said, 'but you can stay as long as you like.' She indicated the key on the inside of the door and, after taking the note that I put in her hand, closed the door. I turned the key and turned round; she was standing in front of the bed 'What did she say?' she asked me.

'That we could stay as long as we liked.'

I went up to her; she stood stock still, looking at me.

'You can go if you want,' I said.

'Oh, Jorge,' she sobbed, clinging tightly to me.

I kissed her tenderly on her face, on her mouth. She surrendered to my embrace and stroked my head, resting in her upraised arms. Then, suddenly, decisively, she pushed herself free. 'There's something you must know. I...'

I covered her mouth with my hand. 'No, don't say a word.'

XVII

Night had already fallen and it was dark when we crept out, furtively, and I went with her until the streets started to become brighter with their lights. She kissed me quickly, we squeezed each other's hands and I watched her disappear among the passers-by. The following day we would go there at the same time; in the morning I would go to the old lady's house to reserve a room. Nothing else mattered. We would meet every day, though on the beach I would try to avoid her if I could for we would be unable to hide the fact that we were lovers. And we could only get engaged, in the eyes of everyone, once the boat had left. She had given herself to me. And I myself had, unprompted, dropped my request that she break with Almeida at once. If he were to find out the break would be unavoidable and we would both suffer from whatever action he might decide to take. But that didn't matter. Before long she would go with me to Lisbon and we would get married. I didn't know and I didn't want to know how we would live. In my house. It could all be sorted out. There was no denying what had happened.

I avoided crossing the Bairro Novo and went on instead through the town, wrapped in an extraordinary sense of bliss, in the wonder that such profound happiness could be possible. I strolled along and it was as if, at the same time, I didn't even see the streets and people, that while the streets and people did exist, in my happiness, I didn't have to see them, though they felt the joyfulness which shone out from me. It had been so extraordinary and yet so simple. I had never imagined, not even in my wildest dreams, that love could bestow such plenitude. I had never felt, not even in moments of the greatest satisfaction, anything like that feeling of total control which was mine when I possessed her. And it had been, as I felt her tremble and moan with me, as if her virginity had been restored, precisely at the moment when and because I had possessed her. Confidence, pride, tenderness, fulfilment, the rout of weariness, as well as a newly reawakened desire which came just from thinking about her and not from thinking of what I had done with her: all this I felt and it was as if I was walking – no, dancing – on air, an utterly new feeling.

On those other occasions I had felt a little of the sort though I had never felt everything with such intensity, without going over everything that had happened, which anyway was still not clear in my mind. That was exactly what I didn't need to do now. No, it was more than that: it was what I wouldn't be able to do, as if it was part of my immense happiness, so that everything became part of me, dissolved into me, into my flesh, my blood, in the heart of my desire which, however, merely by not being able to go over it again, pulsed sweetly through my whole body. It was as if we, once in a while, after a new experience, were to find that we were still growing, that we were still in some sense children; and that there were within us infinite possibilities of plenitude. Even the sensation of hunger – which suddenly had begun to stir in me, and made me realise that I had hardly eaten all day – only added to my happiness. But it wasn't as if we ceased to be children that often, no. Nor was it a new experience. In the end it hadn't been a new experience; rather, it had been the same experience as always, but *like* new. And in that distinction lay the whole difference; in that lay what had made me feel so completely a man. And if it seemed to me that I had ceased to be a child it was because, every time something like this happened, it was as if a new level of awareness and feeling consigned to a distant and worthless memory everything that previously had been the same experience. Distant and worthless, though, not because they were useless but because they had been superseded. Even this more developed capacity I had for analysing what was happening in me in such a lucid fashion was new, and in spite of the fact that it was also a blind enthusiasm which took such delight in contemplating itself. My hunger, however, had not gone away and smiling to myself I went into a small tavern to have my dinner. Sitting at the table, eating and drinking, I realised that I was much less hungry than I had imagined and I leaned back in my chair, smoking, while my eyes barely registered the lights and dim shapes which moved around me.

We were stretched out naked in the bed, side by side; she, with her head resting on my breast, had insisted on telling me everything – everything I had not wanted to hear and which I did not let have any bearing on us. I ran my fingers through her hair as she whispered, her words almost stifled against my skin and her kisses reached for my mouth. And then she had raised herself a little: 'I have given you everything,' she had said. 'I can't give you more.'

I had kissed her avidly, tenderly, and we entwined again. 'You have me, all of me,' I had replied. And then she had given herself to me with such a force in the way she embraced me and held me that it was not me who possessed her but she who possessed me. I closed my eyes to savour the sheer joy and felt her hands on my back. The memory of it was almost sad and I wanted to leave the tavern and go towards her hotel.

I went past the door of the hotel and stopped a little further on. This was crazy; what if somebody bumped into me here, what would I tell them? But the craziness merely intensified the delight I felt just gazing at the hotel, knowing that she was there inside, thinking of me perhaps. What did I mean – perhaps thinking of me? I smiled to myself thinking that after all I was behaving like a fifteen-year-old, hopelessly in love, shy, with his eyes fixed on the windows of his unattainable lady. And I was in that state when I realised that Oliveira and Matos had seen me and were crossing the street towards me. I felt a strange mixture of apprehension and utter bliss.

'What are you doing here at this time?' asked Oliveira.

'Nothing much.'

'Well then, why don't you come along with us?'

'Where to?' I asked.

'This way,' replied Matos.

And off we strolled, chatting about this and that. 'This afternoon,' said Oliveira, 'you almost sent Macedo and me flying. Was it worth some fellow dying for?'

'Perhaps for a woman,' I replied. They laughed and while Oliveira was telling Matos what had happened I was already regretting bringing Mercedes into my jest. 'I had arranged to meet someone,' I added, 'and I fell asleep in the afternoon at home and only woke up when I was supposed to be there.'

Matos had a knack of telling jokes without looking at anyone. 'It's not advisable to go to bed before meeting someone,' he said, all seriousness. 'We should only go to bed once we're with them or afterwards, so that we don't fall asleep while we're still on the job.'

'Yes,' said Oliveira, 'but it depends. Once, quite by chance, I spent the whole night out on the tiles. In the morning because I'd missed a whole lot of classes I went straight to lectures; after lunch I looked at my watch and I thought to myself that I could still snatch a few hours sleep before my meeting. But I thought that if I did drop off to sleep not even the bells of the cathedral could wake me, let alone the alarm clock. I was trying to kill some time, strolling here and there, and at the appointed time I went into the house of my goddess who just happened to be some old boot of the first water. You know who she is,' he said in an aside to me and continued: 'She welcomed me with her usual grand airs, taking off all my clothes, wrapping me in a Japanese kimono, embroidered all over, which was part of the performance, and gave me a glass of port wine, which was also part of the ritual. As a precaution I had only drunk water at lunch. I thought I would only pick up the glass and not drink it. I only awoke sitting at the door of my student digs, wrapped up in the kimono, with my clothes in a bundle next to me. In a fury she had ordered her driver and her manservant to dump me there.'

'Was this in Coimbra, then?' I asked.

'Yes. Nobody knows the story; I was so angry that I never told anybody. The next day I parcelled up the kimono and went to her place; I knocked on the door and the manservant appeared, dressed in his fancy striped waistcoat. "What do you want, sir?" "Will you deliver this; your mistress may be missing it," I said, planting the thing in his paw.'

'But she never again dressed anyone else up in the kimono,' said Matos.

'How do you know?' demanded Oliveira.

'Because I had already heard people talking about the kimono, but when I was there it was rolled up into a ball and thrown down among the cushions.'

We burst out laughing, Oliveira and I. 'What would she have done with the kimono?' asked Matos. 'Wouldn't she have had another one? She must have had stacks of them.'

'Perhaps,' said Oliveira, laughing, 'she was afraid the kimonos could have had some soporific or anti-aphrodisiac effect; from what I heard she used to give people something in the wine. Did she give you a glass of port?'

'Yes, from a tall, slender, engraved crystal decanter; but she also drank some.'

'Of course she did; one wouldn't doubt it!' exclaimed Oliveira. Then he stopped suddenly. 'But, listen Matos,' he said abruptly, 'what an amazing woman for giving someone a good time, eh? I've never met anyone like her, not even paying for it, who knew the half of what she got up to. Once, with the money in my hand, I wanted to make a whore do the same, give it to her up the ... you know, and she raised the roof.'

In my happiness I had let the conversation carry on for some time; it amused me even, but that unspoken word, that woman who did not want to be made to do what the other lady used to do, shocked me to the core. Their words began to grate; after all I owed some respect to the lady and they to me.

'The one that she had – and has – her eye on,' said Oliveira, 'is Rodrigues. They say that she even sent her driver with messages and her car to his door; she'd either somehow divined or been told about his special gifts. But he wasn't having it. He even defends her when they say things about her, and, while we're on the subject, in Coimbra, especially, where everybody knows her, that is supremely ridiculous – and, with him, even more so. Everybody knows that he, whenever he let himself go, spent his nights in the house of that fellow Pousada who is to the perverts what she is to women. And that he gets paid for it. Well then, if he offers his services by way of consolation to Pousada there's no reason at all why he shouldn't offer his services to the poor old thing as well.'

'He has his reasons as far as that goes,' I said drily. They exchanged glances. 'I'm sorry,' said Matos. 'We had no intention of upsetting you or your family. Besides, she's not your grandmother; and it would be worse if we knew all this and talked about it and you knew that we talked about it but not in front of you. What I don't understand, though, is how your aunt, knowing all this, still goes there to see her. Because she does go; I've seen her. And there is no way she could not know what goes on. Here your uncle even tells everybody, at the top of his voice, even in classes he says that his mother-in-law sleeps with the whole Academy of Coimbra. Which isn't completely true because it seems to me that sleeping is the last thing you do in her house. But your aunt can't help but know that she has two or three a day.'

'She is her mother.'

'True enough, but he doesn't seem to pay much attention to that when he's with that crowd.'

We walked on in silence; I felt that if I stayed with them much longer my happiness would soon disappear and so, pleading weariness, I bade them farewell.

'Well you might,' observed Oliveira, 'running around like that. And then your exercises in applied gymnastics on top... Go and sleep in peace, enjoy your well-earned repose, safe in the knowledge that you won't wake up in a kimono at the door of your student house. And don't take it amiss, you hear?'

I ambled off towards my house.

Within me I felt a sadness which was somehow draining or

overshadowing the glow of my happiness. Not that that had abated one bit, but that sadness was surrounded by it in such a way that it entered slowly within it and I could almost see the dark streaks spreading through it; it was like watching the coffee in a glass form a dark mass which then spread out and mixed with the milk. It wasn't life's depravity which shocked and depressed me, nor that purity seemed to me to be a threatened, unreachable stronghold. One of the things which, precisely, I had been learning was that both coexisted in the most unusual ways and in the most unexpected situations. There were traces of deep purity in people and moments of total degradation; while so-called pure people were never so pure that degradation never touched them, as they liked to think. What pained and troubled me was not that, but that purity and degradation were so inextricably linked, depended so intimately one upon the other, that sometimes it was impossible to discern not only whether the motives for one were not logically those of the other, but also the extent to which one was not the other. And yet more, yet worse: to what point were we unable to recognise or distinguish them? In truth, much worse than one being or seeming to be the other was that, at any given moment or in any given situation, we could not know for certain which one we were dealing with.

It was clear that both were present in, and that both controlled, each one more or less, our motivations and their consequences. But not having a means of knowing *which* had the upper hand – that was what I was afraid of. And they were afraid, too – my friends, everybody I knew, they too were afraid. There was no other way to explain how, at the same time as they went along with or took part in some sordid business, they were able to laugh at these situations as if it wasn't they who had taken part. And in laughing like that, from the outside, they would condemn the illogicality of the behaviour of the other participants, as though the others had been on the *inside*. It was as if purity and depravity weren't really different worlds, but that people ended up making them like that: on the one hand, those who could do anything they liked without being touched by the evil; and, on the other, those, who by the merest gesture, were irremediably marked. However, those who were 'marked', as it were accepted their condition, took upon themselves a guilt which was not solely theirs, and in showing it thus gave it an external reality, while those who were 'untouched', relieved of any traces of guilt, were in no way affected by it, not even within themselves.

And in this way my fear was very different from theirs. For purity, for them, was a matter of not getting involved, of passing like a seagull close to the water, only diving out of the blue to catch a fish; while as far as I was concerned, to eat of one of these fish from time to time was no less than to have picked it out from the sea over which one was flying. But just how was I different from them? If I was one of the 'untouched', that in which I perceived a difference was exactly what made me the same as them: the belief that I was different, that I didn't belong to the world of the 'marked'. If, without knowing or even without anyone else knowing, I was one of the 'marked', it was also here that the difference I saw made me the same: the profound conviction that everyone, except me, had escaped unmarked from life's evil. And it was then, as I reached the gate of my uncle's house, that I realised what was implicit in this vision of the world that people had: everyone believed he was untouched even in the moment when he accepted his own guilt or that of the rest. But to accept guilt did not mean that people believed they were guilty, merely that they were behaving as others expected them to behave.

I paused by the gate. It wasn't quite that, because, on the contrary, the unmarked ones did the same in the end. They were the ones who would not involve themselves beyond what was considered customary even though they did much the same as all the others. And suddenly I felt that, beyond that identity by which everyone marked himself out differently from the others, one thing was happening, had happened in those few days in the accumulation of everything that poured down onto me: everything had been poured out higgledy-piggledy, without lines of demarcation and came to assume whatever value each one gave it; this, though, was everyone's own secret. I went into the house; the lights were on everywhere but there was nobody downstairs. I went up the narrow steps to the floor where the library was. The first person I saw was Zé Ramos.

XVIII

The two Spaniards and my uncle, who were all listening to him, looked at me; Zé smiled at me affably. 'So here you are,' I observed and was immediately struck by the obviousness of my remark which, however, did not so much register my surprise at coming across him there as an uneasy kind of sounding out what he knew about his sister and me. But at the same time his smile, though formal, managed to give my question a different meaning: it was as if there was a secret complicity between us, a relationship, which my possession of Mercedes that afternoon had sealed. But immediately I reacted against this interpretation as I listened to them talking. He was not in any way involved in what had happened between Mercedes and me; that matter concerned only the two of us. I couldn't allow the habitual, conventional forms of sociability to become a mask, to cover over with another face and to seize what had no other face nor name than my possession of her and her gift of herself to me. Even though I would marry her. I shuddered. But I was going to marry her, no matter what.

Then I heard Zé talking. '…there's no reason why you gentlemen,' he was saying, 'should have any hesitation about taking part in the escape, from a political point of view. I can guarantee that the Party accepts that the flight will take place although as an action it considers it premature. This means that the party does not assume any responsibility for it and that those taking part in it do so on their own account. If it does fail and the Portuguese police identify anyone involved in it as a communist the party will assert that this individual has never belonged to its cadres and that he is an agent provocateur. As far as you gentlemen are concerned this doesn't affect a thing; it will even clear you of any contacts which, for that matter, have been set up in Spain. Your alternatives are: to take the ship, to stay here or to appear in public again. The last possibility, given that you gentlemen are wanted men, precisely because you are in hiding, can only mean your being handed over to the rebels at the frontier. To stay here forever is impossible, all the more since the struggle is finely balanced. To escape in a boat going to the north of Spain is the only possibility. There is though another alternative, in effect, and which I haven't broached so far:

that is to try to reach the frontier in the Alentejo, at some point which hasn't yet been taken by the rebels and cross into Spain there. But our government has stepped up its vigilance in every respect all along the borderline. You could also, gentlemen, try your luck in Lisbon, embarking there for some other destination and in that case you would need false passports.

'Being here, as you are, and with a boat to hand, it seems to me you gentlemen have no real alternative. As I started to say, your case is by no means unique, and the message that I have brought from Don Marcelino Quiroga, whom you, sir' – and he motioned to Don Juan – 'have been endeavouring to contact, is in favour of flight. There remains another detail which I am authorised to set before you and that is the matter of money. The party makes it a matter of policy to offer its services only and does not contribute financially either directly or indirectly. Since this is a matter of showing support for your cause, which is our cause also, any contributions must stem from the generosity of those who wish to contribute. And the more the merrier. The boat is loaded and we have a pilot. We shall embark from a beach north of Cape Mondego within three or four days, perhaps sooner. You gentlemen must be ready to go immediately in the car which will come for you around about eleven o'clock at night. The thing will go ahead irrespective, with or without you gentlemen. The outstanding monies should be delivered to me before midday of the day after tomorrow. The amount is a million reis. I shall be waiting in my hotel.'

'Listen, Ramos,' asked my uncle, 'if it's going ahead with or without them why do you want a million reis?'

Ramos, in his role as impersonal emissary – in which I was seeing him for the first time, or, who knows, perhaps the second – remained unruffled, as though he had been expecting the objection. 'Because it's the best political guarantee they can have that any difference in cost is really not being paid by us.' He got up. 'I'm sorry to have to insist but I need to have a definite answer right now.'

The two Spaniards looked at each other. 'We shall go,' replied the Basque. 'As far as the money...'

'That can be got,' put in my uncle, and he went with me, in silence, to take Ramos to the gate. The dog, which was tied up, barked.

'Lieutenant, sir,' said Ramos at the gate, 'may I have your permission to say a few words in private to Jorge?'

He took my arm and moved a few paces away. 'Mercedes has spoken to me,' he said. 'Thank you.'

My uncle and I returned to the house; 'Where the devil are we going to get hold of the money?' he asked, brandishing his stick. 'This is blackmail ... don't you think it's blackmail?'

'He's a politician, uncle,' I said, 'and he's only repeating what he's been schooled to say. But it isn't blackmail.'

'He's got us between the devil and the deep blue sea; I don't mind if those two stay here for the rest of their lives but if they're going to have put themselves in hock to pay all that, when the devil are they going to pay me what they owe? I just don't have enough credit for such a sum. Ah, if only that damned old woman would just cough up. Not even your aunt could wring such a sum of money out of her.'

Then I had a shocking idea, so shocking that it made me chuckle to myself. 'Uncle, would you let me deal with this matter?'

'You? How?'

'I want you to ask auntie to write a letter to her mother asking for the money, with the greatest urgency, on account of a sudden calamity. I shall arrange for a bearer to go to Coimbra and come back with the money.'

'But she won't give it.'

'We can try,' I said, looking at him, my gaze somewhere between cold and mischievous. 'It all depends on the bearer,' I added.

His eyes lit up suddenly and he rushed into the house, calling out for his wife. He climbed the narrow steps and went towards the library, stopping on each step.

'What a great lark!' he said, between cries. 'The old baggage will pay for this. It depends on the bearer, eh?' and he roared with laughter, quite taken with the idea.

My aunt, in her dressing gown and with her hair hanging down and tied with a blue ribbon, was coming down the curve of the staircase. 'What's this racket at this time of night? Are you crazy, Justino? Do you have to call me like this?'

'Be quiet, woman! You're going to write a letter to your mother asking her for a million reis.'

'A million reis?'

'Yes, a million, for the boat in which they are going to escape.'

'You're out of your mind. Your uncle's gone crazy. Have you all gone crazy?'

'Nobody's crazy, woman. Your mother is going to pay.'

'My mother will never give so much money. You haven't got a hope.'

'No? Ah, ah … well, we have a hope, maybe more than a hope,' he said, nudging me. 'It depends on the bearer, hmm?'

'The bearer?' she demanded.

I looked down. 'I've got someone to take it, just to speed things up.'

'I'm not writing any letter,' said my aunt.

'No? You're not? You don't have to. We'll write it; all you have to do is copy it in that fine hand of yours.'

Without replying my aunt began to climb the stairs.

'Come down!' he shouted. 'Come here!'

She carried on up and my uncle made as if to follow her, consumed by anger; I restrained him. 'Let her go up and the devil take her,' he said, his eyes blazing. 'We'll see later whether she'll copy it or not,' he said.

In the library the two Spaniards were waiting for us; they were standing round, looking worried and anxious.

'Don Justino,' said Don Juan, 'What a commotion … and all this on our account.'

'On your account be damned,' said my uncle. 'On account of all these scoundrels, all these generals and priests and that rogue who came asking for money! Let's write the letter.'

He swept out of the room, across the corridor and into his study, the study that he never opened up except when he wanted to write letters – which he never did. Before following him in I explained briefly to the Spaniards that we were trying to get hold of the money and had asked my uncle's mother-in-law to help. They tried to refuse: it didn't make sense, what had my aunt's family to do with the business, that there was no way they wanted… My uncle appeared at the door. 'This is my business; it's not something for you gentlemen. Getting money out of my mother-in-law is a pleasure nobody shall deprive me of.'

They bowed, wished us good night and went up to their rooms. My uncle waved his stick in the air. 'Come on, there's no time to lose,' he said. 'The letter.'

The study, with its dark carpet, had high panels of chestnut halfway up the walls which were lined with 'grenat' damask wallpaper. Ranged along the wall were large high-backed chairs, black, with the seat and back in wicker and curved legs ending in claws above a ball. Two tall bookcases, with their yellow curtains behind the glass, occupied, one in front of the other, the two walls either side of the door. At the end, in the space between the two windows with their heavy, dark-red curtains, was a huge desk, black and bowed, with feet like those of the chairs but much smaller. Behind it stood a chair, resembling the others, in which my uncle had sat down, hooking his stick over the back, except that the back was higher, with a shield and carvings of fruit, which gleamed above his head.

He opened the drawer and took out some large sheets of white paper, placing them in front of him and tidying them up so that they once again formed a neat stack. Then he pulled the silver inkwell towards him so that he could reach it easily; the inkwell was made up of a lot of curves around a plaque on which was inscribed his name and the eternal gratitude of the students of 1930 in the College of São José. From among the curves emerged the little openings of the inkwells themselves which my uncle picked up to find that they were dry. He pushed the inkwell away again to where it had been before and, opening a door, and took out a pencil. 'This will do for the draft,' he said. From his coat pocket he took a fountain pen and laid it beside the paper. 'Your aunt can use it to copy with later,' he said. 'Right, the letter. You dictate and I'll write.'

'Me? Dictate?'

'Of course! Wasn't it your idea? And besides she knows the way I speak and I might forget myself and write something like "whore" on the letter. Then your aunt can copy it.'

'But she knows the way auntie writes,' I pointed out.

'So! So do you. The way your aunt speaks is the way she is. Come on. "My dear mother"... No, "Mummy" – she only calls her Mummy. And then? "I know you don't want to help us because Justino doesn't show proper respect for you." That's good, isn't it? "Justino doesn't show proper respect." Which is quite true. "But the anguish of a daughter who has always been true to you cannot mean nothing to my Mummy." Exactly; it's better to put that than "cannot mean nothing to you". Women don't use pronouns when they're writing to their mothers. "I am the victim of a terrible blackmail." That's pretty funny, isn't it? The worst thing though would be if the old girl, reading about the blackmail, took it to mean that your aunt had cuckolded me and wouldn't hand over the money, to make the blackmailer send me the proof of her adultery so that then I would leave her... No... Think of something better. You still haven't said anything after all. Come on, man, dictate something.'

I was standing up, looking over the top of the desk so that I could see what he was writing. 'Tell the truth, more or less,' I said.

'The truth? And what if the bearer reads the letter? And if she thinks of going and complaining to the police?'

'The bearer won't read the letter; and your mother-in-law won't want auntie mixed up in this business.'

'Hmm… Right then, say something,' he said, setting down the pen to light his cigarette with great care.

'You could put, uncle, that we have a refugee here but that the police are demanding a million not to blow his cover.'

'That won't hold water,' said a voice; it was my aunt at the door of the study.

My uncle lit his cigarette, drew on it lingeringly, studied the match and with his little finger flicked off a speck of ash.

'Come here, woman,' he said, pulling back the chair while still sitting in it, 'and sit here.'

She walked over to him, with the pompoms of her slippers just visible beneath her dressing gown; she stopped by the side of the great chair and leant over to see what he had written.

'It's fine where you've written "indifferent" but change it to "be indifferent to you", which sounds better. My mother is always angry with us when we don't write with that style which she paid so much money for us to learn.'

'Write it, woman, you write it.'

She sat down on his knee and began to write. I had never seen them thus. Having already moved away from the desk to let her pass I moved a little further away. My uncle noticed my movement. 'You've got your own life, eh? But your aunt sometimes doesn't mind sitting here on this old lad's lap.'

She was biting her tongue, which she stuck out from one corner of her mouth, and was writing away intently like a schoolgirl.

'Tomorrow,' I said, 'I'll get moving early so that I can take the letter in good time.'

'At what time?' enquired my aunt, without raising her head.

'Round about seven,' I replied, leaving the room.

I went upstairs slowly and into my room. On the table I happened to see the letter I had started and the postcards. It was as if an eternity had gone by since five o'clock. I picked up the postcards and the letter, tore them up and hurled the pieces out of the window. I didn't feel like finishing the letter or sending those cards. What I wanted to say, to whom could I say it? I leant against the window, gazing out upon the night. The more life seems to be ours, and really is ours, the more other people become caught up in it. And the more people do become caught up in it the more we have to say without having anyone to say it to. Because it was impossible to speak to anyone else about her without revealing how far there were others who were involved, even sometimes without knowing it. Therefore, perhaps, people talked so much, without really saying anything, to cover up just how much they knew, and to avoid revealing, even to themselves, the secrets which had been entrusted to them. Or they had put themselves in somebody else's hands, or those of a church, or a group, or to what they thought might be fate, so that they should not feel responsible for the immense weight of all those unknown lives. Or to love ... and with a shudder I realised that I had forgotten about Mercedes, forgotten her for some time, while I was busy weaving a web with her at the centre. I had forgotten – hadn't I, in truth? – under the weight of everything else, everything and everybody. And without any scruples. I had even stifled her, even her, within me without scruples. I leaned against the shutters of the open window. Or me in her, even? Or to the freedom which she had lost and which I had given back to her? Since, there was no doubt, I had freed her, and she herself had understood as much at the moment when she had said: 'I have given you everything: I have no more to give.' That is to say that in belonging to me completely, in giving herself to me completely, she had stripped herself of everything so that there was nothing which held her any more.

I went back inside and got undressed. My clothes were redolent of my being with her and on my skin there lingered a scent not just of her but also the scent of both of us together. I lay down naked on the bed. I breathed deeply, slowly. No, no I wouldn't have a bath before I went to sleep. I would remain like that, feeling her presence all around me, a presence which didn't just envelop me but was part of my breathing in and out, was the presence of her within me. I turned off the light and went to bed. In the darkness of my room her presence became palpable in images of her, momentary so that I didn't really see them, of her in my arms, but which, without my realising it, under her spell my eyes had kept in my memory. I could see her smiling, with her eyes closed, at the conclusive moment. I saw her with her eyes flickering, looking intently at me. I saw her, her head on one side, her hair hanging straight down. I saw her with her mouth slightly open, now with her teeth shining, now with her lips pursed. I saw her profile in shadow and against the light. And I saw too the face which I had felt, in the darkness, running my fingers over it. If it was passion that I felt, in this peace of seeing her without imagining her, I was possessed by passion. And not like a child dreaming of impossible adventures but like a man who recognised, in the love of the woman he had possessed, his own passion.

XIX

I didn't wake up immediately with the hammering on the door. I shivered as I stretched out in the cold morning air and then I heard a voice calling to me: 'It's seven o'clock.' I got up, went to the bathroom and then went down to the kitchen. From the door I could see the maids; my aunt was not in the kitchen but in the small dining room. She wished me good morning, smiling, and pointed to a white envelope on top of the table. 'There's the letter,' she said. 'Your bearer, when he goes for the money, I want him to bring back one and a half million.'

'One and a half?'

'Yes, one and a half. If we have to ask for something why don't we take advantage of the situation?' she said, raising her arm and tucking up her hair.

I gulped down my coffee, grabbed the letter. 'If I don't come back at one,' I said, leaving, 'I've gone straight on to the beach.'

The morning air was full of sun but with a cold edge to it that made the air seem transparent. In the empty streets I passed an occasional child with the maid behind on their way to the beach. A fisherman was coming along briskly, barefoot, his clothes dark, and carrying a fishing rod over his shoulder at the end of which dangled a fish whose weight bowed him down. At the entrance to the boarding house a servant, also barefoot and with his trousers rolled up, was sweeping the mosaic floor. His hair was grizzled and cut close to his scalp. I asked him if Rodrigues was there. Sr. Rodrigues? That tall young fellow who was always making those jokes?

'Ah, yes, sir. But it's very early, he'll still be abed, for sure. If he's sleeping at home,' he added. Then he looked at me sourly. 'You'd better go up, sir,' he said, 'and knock on his door. It's number seven.'

I went up, found the unlit corridor and knocked on the door. I had come prepared with the phrases I would use, but standing there in front of the door they all just seemed to me to be ridiculous. It would be all right; I'd find something to say. I heard some footsteps inside, the key turned in the door and then his face poked out, full of sleep and blinking.

'You? At this hour? Come in,' and he locked the door again behind me. He was only wearing his pyjama jacket. 'I was wondering who it was when I heard you knocking. I had only ordered coffee for nine o'clock.' He swept the pile of clothes off a chair. 'Sit down there,' he said and settled himself on the bed. It was so normal for him not to attempt to cover himself up that he sat there scratching his cock as he questioned me. 'What's been going on with you? You've never come looking for me so early; it must be something serious – although nobody ever talks about anything serious with me.'

'It is something serious, though, and only you can help.'

He looked at me intently, turned towards me and flopped back onto the pillow tucked under his arm on which he had been resting his head. 'What is it?'

'I need you to take a letter to Coimbra.'

'A letter? To Coimbra? And why does it have to be me?'

'It's a letter from my aunt.'

'From your aunt?' and with a sudden movement in which his feet became tangled in the sheet as he pulled it on top of him and covered himself up.

'Yes, it's a letter to her mother.'

He opened his eyes wide in silent astonishment and without uncovering himself sat up on the edge of the bed. 'But me?' he managed to whisper.

'You, and it's my aunt who's asking you to do it.'

He lowered his eyes to where his hands were hidden under the sheet. 'Does she remember me?'

'It's an urgent request for some money that she needs. I suppose you know what the old lady is like,' I said, and he looked at me, finding in the phrase another meaning which I had not intended. 'A skinflint who never gives a penny to her daughter. To telephone or send a telegram would be useless. To send a letter through the post, even if there were time, would also be useless. To send someone whom the old lady did not know would also...'

He interrupted me at the same time as he lay down again, staring at the ceiling. 'But she doesn't know me...'

'I think she does. Otherwise my aunt wouldn't be thinking of you.'

He was silent, not moving a muscle. Then he turned to me with his eyes glazed with tears. I wanted to run away. 'So I take the letter and come back with the money, is that it?'

I nodded.

'It's going to be a terrible business,' he said with a vague smile playing on his lips. 'Does anybody else know about this?'

'Only me and her. And you.'

'And me. But I don't know why, and I don't want to know. Can you swear it was your aunt who has asked me to do this?'

'I can.'

He got up off the bed, dragging the sheet with him and went to the window. Then he came over to me and was so close that I pulled back into my chair. He put his hand on my shoulder. 'Jorge,' he said, leaning over me, 'she ... of all people ... to ask me to do this.'

I looked down and remained there, with him in front of me, in his pyjama jacket with his lower belly ridiculously revealed below it.

He moved away and began to pick some clothes out of a drawer. He smiled a bitter smile and furrowed his brow, holding up underpants and shirts. 'I've got to choose my clothes with care, haven't I?' he said. 'I've got to make a good impression, otherwise she won't hand over the money. How much is it?'

'One and a half million.'

'What! One and a half million?' he exclaimed. 'Well, after all I'm worth a lot more than I thought.'

He made as if to go out.

'Wait a moment?' I said, 'don't set off right away. You'll have to meet me when you come back. When should I come back here?'

'I'll be back as quickly as possible.'

'After all ... these things take time, but if I go now I should be back tonight? or perhaps earlier.'

'I'll meet you at ten; does that seem OK? Right here.'

By now he was wearing his pyjama trousers with the jacket and carrying a towel and various items for his toilet in his hand. He hesitated a moment. 'What if the old girl isn't there?' he asked.

'According to the latest news I have, she'll be there.'

I took the letter from my pocket and handed it over to him. He took it carefully and looked at it closely. 'It's open,' he said, giving it back to me. 'Seal it.'

I licked the envelope and handed it back. He put it on top of the chest of drawers.

'Well, see you soon,' I said, opening the door.

He came out after me on the way to the bathroom. In the corridor he paused, wriggling his foot into his slipper. 'Listen...'

'What?'

The light coming through the door lit up his face, picking it out from the gloom of the corridor. I noticed the shadows under his eyes, and the tiny lines around them which aged him somewhat, just as the others at the corners of his mouth made his smile seem a little mechanical. 'What is it?' I repeated

'Nothing ... it's nothing,' he said moving off towards the end of the corridor.

I went down the steps and passed the fellow who was still cleaning the foyer, and went out into the street. Should I go home to tell them everything had been taken care of? I really didn't want to talk about the subject again, above all now. Should I go to the beach? I had promised Mercedes I wouldn't. But I wanted to see her. I arrived at the street full of cafés and sat down at a table. They were bound to pass that way. There were some people, very few, at the tables, most of them having their morning coffee. Behind me three Spaniards were talking together. The Communist Republic had had it. The fleet was now in Nationalist hands. The heights of the Guadarrama had all been taken. The army was already in the University City, at the gates of Madrid. The whole of Galicia had fallen. Italy and Germany were going to send help en masse. France and England had washed their hands of it, Russia too, for Stalin had better things to do at home than go haring off with a bunch of Spanish anarchists, damned tribe, they should all be shot. And the atrocities. They would pay for the atrocities they had already committed and had been committing since the Republic. In Barcelona alone they had murdered, with the most exquisite cruelty, two thousand priests and brothers after they had paraded them naked through the streets. And they had raped, in a public square, a terrible number of nuns, those virtuous brides of Our Lord. In Madrid lorries had gone from street to street, hunting out every respectable person, anyone of some standing, to be slaughtered and they, the communists, had forced women and children, little children even, to watch. Queipo de Lana, on the radio from Seville, had called that rabble by the names they deserved. In Madrid, on one day alone, they had shot Jacinto Benavente, the Quintero brothers, Ramiro de Maetzu and a whole lot of other glorious citizens of Spain.

'What absolute savagery!' exclaimed one of them, asking whether Benavente wasn't the well known writer of zarzuela. The other, who had been speaking earlier, said he wasn't, though he was a playwright, indeed he was, a writer of serious plays, who had even won the Nobel prize. Ah, the Nobel prize, said the other one – the one who had thought Benavente was the zarzuela fellow – indignantly; but then he wasn't so sure: was he a chemist then? The first man explained that there were Nobel prizes for just about everything, including literature. And then they were off, wondering how many of those prizes Spain had already won. They didn't know, but it was a terribly important prize which was only awarded to the greatest figures, those of recognised merit and universal fame. To murder a Spanish Nobel prize winner was the height of savagery, a betrayal of the country. Only the Republicans would be capable of such an act. One of the others declared that he was a Falangist and therefore a republican, and that he could not allow them to confuse the republic with communism. The Falange was in favour of a united republic which would bring together all the Iberian people under the guidance of a leader who would represent the spirit of the people. It was the only way, the one which all the peoples of Europe who had rediscovered the meaning of past glories were following: look at Germany, Italy, Portugal...

The other pointed out to him that Italy was a monarchy. Well then, what did it matter? Monarchy or republic, what mattered was the thinking of the leader, the *duce*, the *führer*. The third voice chimed in, asking who would be the leader in Spain: Mola? Queipo? Sanjurjo, the one who had died? José António, the prisoner of the Communists, who would never let him out alive? None of them. The leader would be General Franco, who was leading the African army. The other two laughed out loud. Franco? Was he crazy? Franco was indecisive; he had no policies whatsoever. Then the other began to give himself airs, adopted a certain tone of voice, as if he knew something, at the highest level of diplomatic intelligence. If there were monarchists and republicans, Falangists and 'requetés', who the devil, other than the generals could lead that lot? Only someone who wasn't one of any of them. Would he, though, be the man able to be the *duce* of Spain? A general! Now: only the Army and the Church were united in Spain, so who, except the Army, could unite the country? Did they think that the Portuguese, a people lower even than the Galicians, would accept the idea of a Spain 'from ocean to ocean'? Only if they were forced to. But England wouldn't allow it. Far that very reason, for that very reason; a strong, fascist Spain could not admit the presence of an opening in Portugal, an opening available to England. Germany and Italy would see to that. Sooner or later the matter would be settled, once and for all, with the so-called 'democracies' sent packing. 'Well then, Don Valentin,' quipped one of them, 'no longer will we need a passport to come to Figueira,' and the three of them laughed smugly. 'What slobs,' I thought, and I fell to imagining their faces when they learnt they had lost the war. They had to lose. 'Spain from ocean to ocean, eh?' That's all they wanted; so that Rodrigues, on his way to Coimbra, with the letter in his pocket, now seemed to me almost a martyr for the cause of national independence.

At that moment I saw Macedo and his brother passing by. I waved to them and they approached me. 'You're here a bit early,' he said. 'Are you coming to the beach?'

'Not for the moment.'

'Are you waiting for somebody?'

'No.'

'Well then, come on.'

I regretted having called them and said that I was fine where I was. 'Go on ahead,' said Macedo to his brother, 'I won't be long,' and he sat down at my table. He leant over towards me. 'Everything's fixed,' he whispered. 'You won't forget what I asked you to do for little brother down there in Lisbon, will you? And here, before you leave, if you could keep an eye on him, I'd be grateful. Don't let him go knocking around with Rodrigues.'

'Why not?'

'Didn't you see what he got us into the other day? To get us all mixed up in those things of his, to draw the boy into his web, and sure enough, Luís was drawn in. He only has eyes for him, for what he says, what he thinks. When I think of what went on there, and with the young one, I can't forgive him.'

'But he didn't force you to do anything,' I said.

'No, he didn't, but that's the cunning of the fellow. You don't know him like I do. He's quite capable of anything, only to get his own back on me.'

'On you? Why?'

'Because I always told him straight to his face. I've never been in with him.'

'So why don't you do the same now?'

'I've no time any more for all that; I don't even know what will become of me.'

'One more reason.'

'But I can't let him get the idea that, who knows, I might be talking to him for the last time.'

'No, of course you can't. Meanwhile there's always a way of saying things. He's not stupid, and I don't really think he's so bad. If you talk to him frankly – you don't have to make it seem like a final plea – maybe he'll listen to you. And then when he finally realises that it really was a last plea – and heaven help us all – the better he'd pay attention to what you said.'

'Do you think so?'

I studied him for a short while. Was he jealous of Rodrigues on account of the latter's power over his brother? Or was it really some sort of brotherly concern which was troubling him? Or... 'How long is it since you've had things out with him?' I asked.

'How long? What?' he asked, perplexed.

'In college when the Rufininhos were following him around all the time, you knew he was mixed up in these things, didn't you?'

'Yes, but those could just have been kids' stuff, the sort of dirty little things that I always detested, like any other decent chap. That's what I used to tell him, and he knows very well that I don't forget such things. That's why he's so furious with me.'

'And that's why you're furious with him, too.'

'Me?'

'Yes.'

He seemed baffled. 'You're the one who can talk to him,' he said.

'About what? About him not being a good example to your brother? I can. But about the fact that he hasn't made himself into your image and likeness? I can't, because I'm someone else.'

'This is all too complicated for me. I don't understand you.'

'All the better for you.'

'Are you having me on?'

'Not at all.'

Mercedes was walking by, between her brother and Almeida. I waved to them in a friendly fashion and she dawdled behind just a little to return my greeting more effectively. It was like a signal to me but she wasn't able to finish it because Macedo started off again.

'Aren't you coming down to the beach now?' he asked. 'I'm going with them.' He got up to go. 'You take care of my brother,' he repeated, his hands on the table. I nodded; he grasped my hand. 'You know?' he whispered, holding it tighter, 'it was me who fixed up the boat, with some smugglers I know. They're OK, but it wasn't that easy.'

It was my turn to grasp his hand. 'How much is all this costing?'

He hesitated a brief moment. 'A hell of a lot.'

'But how much?' He didn't reply.

'You got the boat and you don't know how much?' I said, enquiringly.

He averted his eyes and withdrew his hand. 'That's nothing for you to know.'

'You're very much mistaken. I want to know.'

He looked at me and then sat down again. 'These fellows here are listening to us.'

'They don't understand a thing; they're Spaniards.'

'But what do you want to know? Let's get out of here,' he said. He paid my bill and we went off together round the corner.

'Well?'

'To tell the truth, the boat didn't cost anything. The lads were all for the idea. They're going to steal the boat from their boss. But there's a whole lot of things we have to pay for.'

'Such as?'

'Provisions, weapons … lots of things.'

'That's all?'

'Don't you think that's enough?'

'No, I don't.'

'And we've got to take money with us. We can't go without money.'

'Everybody's doing it for free then?'

'What do you mean, for free?'

'You don't need the money for anyone. Is the pilot free?'

'The pilot's Almeida.'

'Yes, that's what I'm asking.'

'Of course he's doing it for free. What a thought! I've known Almeida for years; I've complete confidence in him and he's as keen on the idea as we are.'

'So it's all completely sewn up then?'

'Absolutely. It only depends on when they get here from Oporto.'

'They're coming from Oporto?'

'Yes, it's a terrific coup. You'll see.'

'Why aren't you doing all this in Oporto then? Why didn't you get a boat in Oporto?'

'Because we got it here. And to throw anyone off the scent.'

'That's fine then.'

'Are you coming to the beach now?'

'Not yet. You go.'

He took a few steps and then turned round. 'Can I trust you?'

'Do you doubt it?'

'Concerning my brother and what I asked you to do?'

'You can trust me.'

He shook my hand and went off. I set off for Buarcos to fix up a time for the afternoon. I told the old lady that unless she heard anything to the contrary to expect us at five o'clock. Then I went home.

I found my aunt seated at the table in the small dining room, sewing. She was surprised to see me back so early.

'What are you doing here?' she asked. 'Has the bearer gone?'

'He's agreed to go. He'll be on his way by now.'

'Your uncle's still asleep. They've gone upstairs to the library to listen to the radio. That's what they do when they're not playing cards with your uncle.'

Neither yesterday nor this morning had she asked me about the identity of the bearer, a bearer whom she must have known would have to be somebody very special. Was she completely incurious, did she really not understand, or was she just making out that she didn't understand? What could she and my uncle have put in the letter? She carried on sewing without giving any indication that she felt like talking. Finally, in the face of my silence, she spoke: 'The funniest thing about all this is that now we've written to ask for so much money and we've sent someone to Coimbra for that very reason, they don't want to go. They're thinking of going to Lisbon. I want to see your uncle's face when he gets up and they put him in the picture about these new plans of theirs.'

'They don't want to go?'

'As far as I understood it,' she said and then paused for a moment as her sewing demanded all her attention.

'How did the bearer go?' she asked. 'By train? or bus? or by car? When's he coming back?'

I replied that I didn't know how he'd gone, that I hadn't discussed the matter with him but that we would meet again at ten that night.

'Did you give him anything for his expenses?'

'No,' I said. 'He didn't even ask.'

She didn't look up from her sewing. 'Is he one of your friends?' she enquired.

'Yes.'

She put the cloth down on the table and looked closely at what she'd done and what remained to be sewn. 'I think it would be better if you spoke with them,' she said. 'And if they don't go, all the better: if I can do a lot with half a million then I can do even more with one and a half. Since they won't be here for ever...' And she looked up at me with her smiling, innocent's child's face. Without saying a word I rose and went on up to the library.

Don Juan was sitting in one of the big armchairs, smoking. The other had his ear glued to the crackling of the radio but he turned to me and together with Don Juan greeted me.

'My aunt said that you gentlemen are thinking of going to Lisbon. Is it true?'

They exchanged knowing glances. 'Yes, it is true,' said Don Juan. 'We've been thinking about the whole thing and we reckon it's a crazy, dangerous venture, and that, if we have to choose, maybe the lesser of the two evils is to try to cross the frontier in the Alentejo, going via Lisbon. In Lisbon, even holed up, we'd be less cut off than here.'

'So, this has only just occurred to you, has it?'

Don Juan looked pained, for my tone had been somewhat harsh; in the end it was the other one who replied: 'As things stand the boat wouldn't get through to the coast of Biscay: either the Portuguese or the rebel navy would intercept us, whereas on the southern frontier the Republican Government is still holding firm. Going in through the south I can subsequently get to my own land through France. And Don Juan wants to get to Madrid.'

'If you can get as far as the North, via France,' I pointed out, 'then Don Juan can, by the same route, reach Madrid.'

'And what about our families?' said Don Juan. 'If they haven't got into Spain they must be in Madrid with no news of us, as we have none of them.'

'But didn't you gentlemen hear Ramos say that you are wanted men. How can you be thinking of taking a train here and getting to Lisbon?'

'We could take a car to another station and then hire a car at some station, short of Lisbon, where the express stops.'

'And what are you going to do for money?' I enquired, 'if you'll excuse the question.'

'Your uncle would lend it to us,' replied Don Juan.

'And what about the money we've asked for?'

'Your uncle can give it to your friend if he so wishes,' said the other.

'But we asked for the money for your sake.'

'You,' said Don Juan in Spanish, 'are mistaken. It is for the journey, not for us, that your friend requires it.'

'Have you spoken to my uncle?'

'As soon as he comes down we'll speak to him.'

'What if he doesn't go along with your idea?'

The Basque was the first to reply: 'Your uncle cannot force us to accept another solution where our lives would be at risk,' he said.

'It's an escapade,' said Don Juan, his hands resting on his knees. 'An escapade...'

I left the room and went up to my uncle's bedroom door. 'Who is it?' 'Me, uncle.' 'What do you want?' 'To talk to you.' 'Come in.'

His bedroom, on what would be the second or third time I had ever gone in there since I had been coming to the house, was a complete tip. Fag ends, books and exercise books, dirty clothes, suits chucked on the floor, the wardrobe doors hanging open, other suits, which had slipped off their hangers, all piled up on the floor, in an evil-smelling heap, around the immaculate bed whose sheets my aunt changed, often more than once, every day, for sometimes when he took an afternoon nap he didn't even remove his shoes. Sitting on the bed, his knees forming a sharp point beneath the bedspread he asked whether our man was on his way.

'He is indeed, but now the Spaniards don't want to go.'

'They don't want to? Who told you that?'

'They themselves; they want to go to Lisbon, by train.'

'Are they crazy? We fix them up with this terrific escape and now they don't want to go? I go borrowing money from my mother-in-law on their behalf and they don't want to go? They've got to go. They'll go, they're on the their way.'

'But they're saying, uncle, that you can't make them set off on some escapade in which their lives are at risk.'

'Can't I indeed? Well, they don't know me. They'll go even if they have to go bound hand and foot. The only way they will leave this house will be by boat. What the devil are they thinking about? That we can fix up some fabulous, spectacular escape like this every day of the week? Where are they now? Hanging on every word of the radio? You take yourself off over there; I'm going to get up.'

In his trousers and shoes, still in his pyjama jacket, and with his stick on his arm, he paused halfway down the corridor. 'What time will the chap be back, the one who's taken the letter to my mother-in-law?' he asked. 'When he gets back he'll be another one of my mother-in-law's... You got hold of a lad who knows her from Coimbra, didn't you? Hmm. Wait a minute. If she doesn't send the money, which is a possibility, they are free to stay. If she does send it and they don't want to go we can say, when they come to pick them up, that they haven't got the money because we're under no obligation at all to cough up. Hmm... It's best to let things be for the moment until we know whether the money is coming or not. What time's the fellow coming back? At ten?... And they might even change their minds again. But such an ingenious escape, something which might even have international repercussions, an escape even more ingenious than when I made it to Holland ... that pains me. And if we don't stump up, who knows whether the whole shooting match might not fail at the eleventh hour? One and a half million is an awful lot of money and we'd have half a million for us – if it came – and that's not to be sneezed at. If the money comes I'll give you a cut. No, no ... you have it, of course I'll give you some, five hundred escudos, it's all yours.'

'What about the bearer's cut?' I asked.

'Eh? He's asked for a cut? Everybody wants a cut. His cut is what my mother-in-law pays him, in kind. Tell your aunt to have my breakfast sent up – but I don't want the old one bringing it up, otherwise I'll send the whole lot flying,' he said, returning to his room.

I went down to the ground floor and passed the message on to my aunt.

'It's almost lunch time,' she said. 'Your uncle likes to pretend he's still the cock of the walk and grab Maria.' Nevertheless she sent the younger maid, the one who didn't live in, to take him his breakfast. 'Have you spoken to him?' she asked. 'What did he say?'

'That it was better to wait to see whether we get the money or not.'

'We'll get it. We told her it was so that we could separate and your uncle leave me and set himself up in Oporto, because we couldn't stay here together after the scandal.'

'What scandal?'

'The fact that I've got myself a young fellow here at home,' she said, laughing, 'and I want to live with him.'

'Auntie, did you write that?'

'I did. Where my mother is concerned it's bound to work.'

'But it's down in black and white ... supposing she shows the letter to someone?'

'She won't. Who would she show it to? The next time I have a chance to go to Coimbra I'll get it back from her. The best bit is that she's bound to think the bearer is the young fellow.'

'Does the letter say that?'

'Well, not in so many words,' she said with an amused look on her face. 'But that's the way she'll take it.'

I smiled awkwardly at her and went upstairs.

Maria was tidying my room; with the broom leaning against the open door and a duster on the table, she was making my bed.

'Do you want me to come back later, sir,' she asked.

'No, you can carry on.'

I remained by the table watching her working away around the bed. When she bent down near me her breasts hung down roundly; from the back her dress stretched across her backside. I brushed against her. She didn't move away as she tucked in the sheets; then she went to tuck them in on the other side of the bed, from where she looked over at me. I turned around and casually, as if I wasn't interested, pushed the door to. The broom fell across the door and I had to fish it out. She carried on making the bed, bending down and I went up to her again and brushed against her. She neither moved away nor straightened up. I bent over her from behind and grabbed her breasts. She didn't move. I pushed her onto the bed while she silently struggled with me for the sake of appearances. She didn't let me enter her, though. And afterwards she picked up some article of my dirty clothes lying on the floor and wiped herself down and my trousers, too. She smoothed down her dress, opened the door and went out with the article in her hand. Then, having moistened it in the bathroom she came back and cleaned me up with great care, sitting on the bed. Finally she looked at my trousers and then up at me. 'You'll need to wash them,' she said and laughed. She was no beauty, with her thick lips and flat nose. I held her by the chin. 'Let me go.'

'Tonight?'

'No, you would only dishonour me, sir.'

'I won't dishonour you, I promise.'

'Promise we'll only fool around a bit.'

'I promise.'

'When you come back, sir, and everybody's asleep I'll come up. I've got to go now or they may suspect something,' she concluded and scooping up the dirty clothes and the duster from the table and the broom she left.

I got undressed, slipped on my pyjamas and went to take a long, leisurely bath. When I went down to lunch, having changed my trousers, there was nobody in the dining room. I crossed the garden and saw that Maria was watching me from the door of the kitchen. The dog leapt and barked at the end of its chain. I walked around the house. Rubbish, empty cardboard boxes, torn to pieces by the dog, newspapers, a mattress spewing out its stuffing, all variously covered the ground behind the building. And in the middle of all that, luxuriant and imposing, stood the great tree. I looked up towards its great, leafy branches which were almost touching the windows of the house. Hanging from them, here and there, were the tatters, black and rotten, of things which had been dropped or chucked out or just forgotten. The sun filtered through the leaves which trembled in the slight breeze which was not enough to disturb the rags. Birds, sheltering from the heat, were singing away in little, sudden cheeps, in its topmost branches. How could one climb such a tree? I walked around it but could not figure out a way. But there had to be some way. I felt some sense of dread which made walk away and go back to the house. Going in round the corner I paused and looked back at the tree. And, contrary to what I would have expected from such a distance, though it seemed to me less dirty and surrounded by rubbish, it did not seem to me to be so verdant; dark shadows were falling over it. From the kitchen door Maria called me to lunch. I squeezed past her, not bothering to hide the fact that I was rubbing against her, under the stern gaze of Micaela, the dark down on her upper lip bent over the dishes. Maria affected surprise. 'Would you believe it! The young devil! Away with you!'

I, in the doorway to the corridor, turned away laughing. Micaela nodded to me condescendingly and stared severely at the other.

XX

Lunch went off silently with nobody, neither my aunt and uncle, nor the Spaniards, nor I wanting to show what was really on our minds as a group: namely, the Spaniards' escape. The furtive glances, the odd phrase, above all the exaggeratedly relaxed air of my aunt and uncle and the long, silent intervals conspired to make things even more strained. Maria served us at the table, coming and going with a motion that was both graceful – as far as her body was concerned – and yet heavy on her feet; she did not once look at me. Restless and uncertain, I even began to wonder whether the matter of her visit to my room wasn't one cause of the awkward silence which reigned. But though the doubt remained, my uneasiness melted away because my aunt and uncle were not terribly strict in these matters… And I smiled to myself, wondering what Maria meant by saying I would dishonour her. Perhaps, as far as she was concerned, the dishonour or danger consisted in the continuation in bed of our amorous adventures. For, clearly, someone like her, half country girl, half town girl, who was not a minor, would have already had plenty of opportunities to lift up her skirts for any Tom, Dick or Harry, given the ease with which she had lifted them for me. Nor was it to be supposed that the resistance she had put up, since the moment was not the most convenient for leisurely preparation and subsequent satisfaction, would always have prevailed. Obviously she was no longer a virgin; she had resisted me so as not to bring disgrace on the house and because the situation wasn't the most propitious. Perhaps too she believed in the superstition that full and prolonged penetration was a pre-condition of becoming pregnant: sleeping with a man in the same bed – therein lay the danger.

Suddenly I was troubled by two simultaneous but divergent thoughts: that the maid wasn't a virgin and that Mercedes might become pregnant. In my sudden passion, in the joy of possessing her I hadn't given it a thought. The silence at table meant that I could easily pursue my train of thought which, however, owed little to logic but was, rather, a confining obsession; the same silence enabled me also to leave the table as soon as lunch was nearing its end and go up to my room. But I was really afraid that Mercedes might get pregnant … and all at once my fear was redoubled: it was that she might get pregnant and that I might be capable, even loving her as I did, of regretting it. But I could love her and want her so much, want to marry her without it meaning that we wanted, or that life would allow us, to have children. And if she should have a child of mine before we got married, or if because of this I was obliged to marry her, she would perforce feel tied to me, seeing that I was the father of her child. Tied in this way to each other, wouldn't there be circumstances surrounding our love which, by forcing us into it in that way, could only – who knows – poison and diminish it? In the world in which we lived, however, such conditions could have a hold over us, whether we liked it or not, and if I had feared that these would bind me, didn't that mean that everything that I had been pondering, in truth, amounted to the desire not to be tied by them to Mercedes? If I was afraid of being bound to her, what kind of love was this love of mine? The desire to possess her forever and longer, my tenderness for her, was so strong that I didn't even stop to think that I hardly knew her, hardly knew what sort of person she really was; was this not love? And how could I, caught between having possessed her for the first time and about to possess her once more in a renewal of those magical hours, on only our second time together, have rubbed myself up against the maid and wanted her so violently that I had taken my pleasure in such a dubious, juvenile fashion? How, so few hours after holding in my arms the one who was not only my betrothed, the woman I loved above all else, but also my lover, could I have got hold of that coarse female, failing only to finish the job off properly because she put up a bit of a fight? And did I still want her to be a virgin just so that I could have the pleasure of deflowering her?

All the girlfriends I had had, the whores I had known, now, when I tried to recall them, took on Mercedes' features. But not this girl. Was it because she was nearer to me, the occasion of a brief satisfaction while the others were far away, no longer close to me and I no longer had the slightest interest in them at that moment? Or because, given the idea that she might be a virgin, she didn't belong to the past like the others, nor to the present, like Mercedes. As for Mercedes, however, when I had her it was as if she had been a virgin: the purity, the daring modesty, the sad caresses with which she gave herself to me, were as if, in my arms, she had rediscovered through me her virginity – the virginity which another had taken from her. And if, in her love for me, the other had been a memory who had taken on my features, and above all, in the intimate recall of her flesh, my cock, it was not on that account that I could overlook the fact, not that I had not been the first, but that in her and in the sensation I felt in my loins, there was not that physical resistance which had to be torn open – even when the woman gives herself up to us, passionately, without any resistance – except the supreme hesitation which was the very stuff of a great love. That was how Mercedes had given herself to me; I was sure she hadn't given herself to him like that, but merely in a moment of physical madness before a man who was in the habit of dazzling and possessing, and who knows, deflowering women. And that which he didn't have, that instinctive sense of loving and respecting, she had found in me, had sought in me, as a way to punish him. But what sort of respect had I shown in my brutal urging which could only be the outcome of my knowing that she had been another's? And what was I looking for in hoping that the maid might be a virgin? The physical virginity that Mercedes had not had, and the physical violence of which 'the other' had robbed me?

I was horrified at the idea that this maid of my uncle's, with her thick lips and flattened nose, and the lingering odour of parts unwashed, could, on account of someone else, be not so much a temporary satisfaction (which all the others had seemed to me to have been, and which she, in parallel with a woman, who was not just an image of desire but a lover desired because possessed, could not be) as the real face of my basic, animal frustration at not having had, for myself, Mercedes' virginity. But, remembering my love, and Mercedes' body, which I had contemplated, laid on the bed, before and afterwards, I saw that it was exactly this which made my love so much deeper. I had not had her in order to violate her but to win her back. And everything in love which belongs to the bloody, basic animal in us made me look for another person in whom this would be recognisable, but at a level on which my love for Mercedes, and my desire for her, could not and could never want to be. And it was this which made me want them, both of them so ardently. And if they both got pregnant? If it was the maid it would be one of those absurd situations which could destroy Mercedes' confidence in me. And if it was Mercedes? I had to take precautions. Would she, though, want me to? Isn't a love which needs precautions an insult? I shuddered to think that, for love, I would use the same things that I used to use with whores so that I wouldn't get some shameful, filthy infection. I was horribly perplexed and depressed. Would she come to the same conclusion? Wouldn't she be eternally insulted? Hadn't we, though, on the previous day behaved like irresponsible children? As for her, what precautions had she taken; had she taken them in time; what in fact could she take? Despairingly, I realised my complete ignorance, as well as hers, in these matters.

And not just ignorance. Who could we turn to? If something happened, there was one way, the one everybody had always used. And the dangers? When I was a child my mother sometimes visited a midwife (though it was only much later that I realised what she was, remembering the plate on the door and that fat lady, with her brusque, almost masculine way of doing things), while I used to wait in an anteroom, sitting on an upholstered chair, with some friend or other of my mother or one of my aunts. My mother had been at death's door, bleeding profusely while I played at length with the empty phials of some medicine – haemo something or other – which she had to take almost hourly; I had used them as guns. But my mother had had recourse to those measures in secret, protected by her family. In her and my family who would do such a thing for Mercedes? She might even die. The fact that she might die precisely as a result of that love of ours appalled me.

I could see before my very eyes the bloody cloths which the maids, tiptoeing silently, retrieved from her room, discreetly, and which I went to inspect in the basket of dirty linen. I flung myself down on the bed, my hand over my eyes. Why wasn't life just so much simpler and easier? Above all when for some, for all its dangers, it was? What reason demanded that Mercedes and I might have to pay such a high price, the price of her own life? And I didn't want to lose her, it was inconceivable, I couldn't accept that I might lose her with the blood pouring out of her, blood that had been mingled with mine. This might also happen, however, with Maria, whom I did not love but whom I desired furiously, though somehow repelled by her, too, which made her more attractive to me, should she be a virgin and I were to deflower her. Or even if she weren't, for one thing was not conditional on the other, except in that duality in which love was not needed. And the fact that it was not necessary, in truth, made me see how everything to do with love and flesh are at the same time independent of each other, and yet complement each other, without it even being necessary for the people to be the same, nor us the same for them. But that's how they are while life goes on; but they can't be so when life stops. That Mercedes might be taken from me was a terrible realisation that had only just struck me; and if she were to be taken there were no other arms which might console me. But if I did lose her, for what other reason might it be except death? What if all of a sudden she left me, cut herself off from me? What arms could then console me? Could I somehow accept her loss? Could I carry on as I had before I had possessed her, knowing that I loved her so much, and possess her in other women? What Maria, however beautiful she might be, however refined, could make up for her? Knowing that Mercedes' face and body existed independently of me, and not just for me, could other faces and other bodies become her for a brief moment? But nothing could take me away from Mercedes now that she belonged to me; nor should I contemplate any other possibility but that I had had her, I had her, I was going to have her, I would have her. For that I would sacrifice everything and everybody. And the sacrifice had already begun.

I felt something touch one of my hands and saw Maria by the side of the bed with a silly grin on her face. I got up.

'Are you crazy?' I said in a low voice. 'Now? Hadn't we fixed everything up for tonight?'

Without replying she got hold of me, feeling me. I shook her. She paused her hands half outstretched, uncomprehending.

'It's only a bit of fooling around,' she said.

'Fooling around, what on earth for?' I replied. 'Later, when it's the time.'

I realised that what she wanted, or was in the habit of doing, was to 'make them come' to minimise the risk later.

'Later,' I repeated, 'didn't we agree, later. Now be off with you,' I said, as at the same time as I wished I didn't even know she existed, and the image of Mercedes, profaned, came between me and that monster. Nevertheless, I took her in my arms.

'Are you afraid of sleeping with a man?' I asked. 'Have you never slept with one? Never...' I left the sentence unfinished.

She understood, though, and shook her head.

'Do you really want me to believe that?' I asked.

She looked up at me, offended. 'What sort of person do you think I am?' she demanded.

I did not reply directly. 'A woman who likes men and whom men like, too.'

'But you don't love me, sir,' she said. 'I know exactly what you want, though.'

I took her head in my hands. 'That's exactly what I want, too, you're right.'

She looked away. 'I know that well enough; it's what they all want.'

'You should start now, somebody's got to be the first.'

'So that's all you want, sir, then you'll go away and I won't matter a fig to you.'

'And then I'll go away and you won't matter a fig to me,' I said, mocking the truth she had told. Perhaps without even noticing my remark she put her body up against mine and I stroked her hair and face.

'You want to, don't you?' I said, and as I steered her down on to the bed she resisted a little.

'At least you aren't deceiving me,' she said, and then she let herself go, panting. With my hands roaming all over her I aroused her even more, but I wasn't going to have her now, not now, nor would I let her do to me what she had done that morning. I lifted her up, wild and shaking as she was. 'Not now, I've got to go out for a little while. When you come tonight you'll see.'

She leant against the door. I pushed her out and putting my lips together kissed her violently. At the same time that I felt an enormous relief on account of Mercedes' love, the love I was about to enjoy, all my body was boiling over, telling me exasperatedly that I should have taken advantage of the situation. And my love for Mercedes did not stop me worrying, deep inside me, lest Maria did not turn up that night. I would wait for her and if she did not come I would go down and fetch her, even at the risk of a scandal. That risk, though, if I had to go and get her, would certainly break any last resistance to which she might be clinging. Nor would I need to drag her back to my bed; the place didn't matter, I would take her into the garden, to the belvedere, for example. Yes, indeed, the belvedere; or underneath the tree.

But what if she returned now? I felt so uneasy that I got ready and left the house in a hurry. Before meeting Mercedes I had to go the chemist's. The image of the chemist's, as I realised as well at that moment, had been, as much as that of Mercedes, hovering between me and that woman who had offered herself to me at such an unpropitious hour.

It was still early but after I had left the chemist's I could hardly wait to see Mercedes; at the same time I feared I might bump into someone, which would complicate matters even more. My only thought was to run to the little house and there in the room, alone, give myself over to the delicious agony of waiting for her. But because it was still early I kept the same, even, pace. Meanwhile, the frustration that I had felt since I had rejected the maid had turned into a heart-pounding need to see Mercedes, to see her and feel her. But what if she didn't show up? If she didn't come? I reached the corner of the street still tormented by that anxiety that everything in me sought to beat back. There was still more than half an hour to wait till five; there was nobody to be seen. And if the room weren't free − where could I wait for her? I passed in front of the house without stopping and then strolled around in some of the nearby streets. Children and cats − there didn't seem to be any in the other street − were idling around, while the fishermen's wives chatted with each other at the doors of their houses and some men, leaning against the walls, eyed me mistrustfully. I went down as far as the edge of the beach, walking around aimlessly, my mind fixed on going back to the house. Which I did. As I turned the corner the door opened on to the still, deserted street and a boy whom I vaguely knew by sight came out; he spotted me on the corner and slunk off up the street without a backward glance. I stayed exactly where I was and it wasn't long before another figure in turn came out of the door. It was Rufininho who, spying me, came ambling down the street and passed close by me but without looking at me. So in the same house where he would bring his conquests I would be with Mercedes, who knows, perhaps even in the same bed. It was as if all life's squalor had been heaped up over her and over our love. I just wanted to wait until she arrived and then bear her off somewhere far away, so far that nobody would see us, nobody would touch us, that nothing had been used before by anyone else, whoever they might be. But where? I knew of no other place (and the place which I did not know was not even at the end of the world, but a bedroom in which we both would be), and everywhere had already been used. In every one of them someone had slept or laid themselves down there, whores, adulterers, pimps, pederasts, lesbians, old and young, healthy ones, unhealthy ones, out of addiction, or despair, or love.

Even when we had a room in my own house for me and for Mercedes, which would be really mine, could I really ask myself, expecting an answer, who had lived there, what they had done within those walls, before my parents and I had lived there? Only by having a house built from scratch, with new furniture, everything

new, made expressly for us, could we be sure that things would not
carry the marks of other hands, of other bodies. But even that
wouldn't be the case because somebody would have to make these
things and would their hands be clean enough? And what about
me, at this very moment: had I washed my hands after having
touched that other one? I looked at them. I would go in and wash
them in a basin where the water had flowed for others, and clean
them on a towel which, though newly washed, was one which had
been used by others. Water washes everything we had said,
Rodrigues and I, by the water's edge, on that morning which now
seemed so long ago. And time, too, was like water, but with that
qualification of Macedo's, 'almost all'. But that 'almost' was, at once,
the life that was left to us as life and the stain upon it like a nasty
taste in our mouths. On us and on everything that had been used.
For, if the sea had washed away the sins of Rodrigues I had ordered
him to commit the one sin he had not yet committed so that I
might possess my Mercedes more surely; and it wasn't even certain
that his sacrifice was necessary for me to be there, able to be there,
waiting for Mercedes, to have her, for her to be mine, in the same
way that, in the same house, Rufininho enjoyed those one-off little
adventures of his. I knocked on the door.

The old woman opened the door, her mouth curved into an
ingratiating smile which seemed to be part of the general dispatch
with which she made way for me to come in and close the door
behind me. I looked sideways at the half open bedroom door, but
she intercepted me at once and pulled it to.

'Not there, I haven't been in to tidy it up yet,' she said. 'If you
don't mind, sir, waiting a little while in there, follow me,' and she
passed in front of me.

At the end of the small corridor, at the door of the room where
I had been that time before, and which was on the corner with the
kitchen, I spied a shape which turned away towards the garden. I
paused.

'Not in that one,' I said. 'What about this one here. Is that all
right?'

'Yes, that's all right, but the other room is better and I'll tidy it
up in a tick, while you wait here, sir. That,' she said, smiling again,
'is for one of my regular customers.'

I opened the door of the room at the end. 'No…' I replied. 'I'll
wait here and we'll stay here.'

She shrugged.

'As you wish, sir,' she said, but after I had shut the door she knocked and opened it slightly. 'When your young lady arrives I'll bring her down here,' she said. My almost imperceptible reaction must have registered with her. 'But, sir, if you would rather wait in the room at the front,' she added, 'you could open the door to her yourself.'

I couldn't make up my mind between the room which had been ours but had also been used by Rufininho, and the other room where I had once been with a whore. And so I followed her down to the other room at the front, only now noticing the immaculately clean towels she had over her arm. The room didn't look as though it had been used except for the pot which had been moved next to the washbasin and a bundle of towels, carefully folded and placed on the floor next to the pot; the bedclothes and pillows, too, were heaped up on the bed and there was a vaguely sour, even excremental, odour in the air which made me shudder. The old woman solicitously opened the windows and closed the shutters again, put back the bedspread and smoothed it out, shaking the pillows, from which she stripped the pillowcases, replacing them with clean ones from the wardrobe with the mirror on it; she placed the towels on the basin, pushed the pot under the bed, shot me a smile, and scooped up from the floor the heap of used, folded towels, tucking them under her arm.

'It's all tidy now, sir,' she said, stopping by the door. 'If you want …'

I replied dryly that I would stay there for the moment, waiting, and that then I would want to go back to the other room. She didn't think much of the idea.

'Excuse me, sir, but there is no chance of you having the two rooms. You and your girl, you're not the only ones coming here at this time. Didn't you see the lady waiting in the kitchen? If her chap turns up before your girl, they'll use the room at the end, won't they? So you'll have to stay here, sir. If you'd got here any later you'd have had this one, wouldn't you? It's because you saw the boys leaving, isn't it?' she said, glancing into the room again, with her hands folded over her stomach. 'But he's one of my best customers, he's a good lad who's helped me through a lot of bad times, and he only brings decent people here, people with a bit of class, he respects this place of mine. He knows too that if he started bringing any old riff-raff from the streets in here I'd slam the door in his face. This, I'd like you to know, sir, is a respectable house.

Don't think that any old tart can set foot in here, only those with some sense, the decent ones. And what people get up or don't get up to once they're behind those doors, as long as they're decent people, well, that's their business. My house is a clean house and these things they don't leave any trace. My late husband, may God keep him,' she said, crossing herself, 'was always saying to me that these things, they don't leave a mark of any kind. And it's true, isn't it? And then you, sir, after you've been here because there's nowhere else where you can be with your girl and feel free with her, if you'd had anywhere else, you wouldn't come here. And if that's the case with you, it's the same with everybody else. They all come here because it's proper house, a safe house, and because they need my co-operation; and I need to earn my living because this house is all my husband, bless him, left me. And it hurts when you can't help those who need help. Do you want me, sir, because all you can think about is those others, to close my doors to those who need me most, those who, more than anyone, help me to live? Yes indeed, sir, those boys were here in this very room, this one which that lad Rufininho always uses. If you don't want to use the same bed, sir, because you think there's something catching about these things, then go on down to the other one. But don't try to meddle in other people's lives. Which is to be, here or there? But you can't hang about here in the middle of the house for, if your girl doesn't want to be seen, or can't afford to be, then it's exactly the same for everybody else; they don't want you to see them either. It's only young Rufininho who doesn't give a hoot for these things, though of course the others don't want to be seen with him. Here or down there?'

I fished a note out of my pocket and stuck it in her hand. 'I'll stay here,' I replied. She went to close the windows and then the shutters.

'When your girl arrives, sir,' she said with an evil smile as she left the room, 'you'll forget everything else. Feel free to stay as long as you want. This room is yours.'

I remained there on my own, waiting. I was going to sit down on the bed when I heard someone knocking at the door. I peeped through the window and at the same time as I heard the old woman's footsteps I made out the figure of a man, close to the door, which then opened to let him in. The footsteps went on into the house and I heard the door of the other room close, tentatively, with some effort. The house fell silent again. I went back to sit on the bed and pondered how, in a room like that, Mercedes and I were at the mercy of things and of other people, and of ourselves, except for the shelter of our love. Precisely in such a house and such a room, where love was the most incidental thing in the world, a desire which needed nothing more than that someone be available to satisfy it, what we needed was that it should be strong, pure, all absorbing, and at the same time a surrender, unconditional, of the deepest wellsprings of ourselves. What we should desire and should have was something which we could share no matter where. And I wanted her so much. But in love, desire and possession were different things: and it was as if, all around me, everything seemed inimicable, so that my love should demand something more, more than could be given, and as well a kind of lazy complicity, which our love had to accept before it could be fulfilled.

The awful staggering, nightmare of these days would not be slow in passing. Nothing would stop me having Mercedes publicly, marrying her, no matter what happened. And I felt an exquisite pain: the necessity, even the miserable necessity of keeping our love hidden had been, in a way, the guarantee of its purity, of its integrity, of its grandeur, even. Should it become public, scandalously, or calmly legalised (and what conditions, in all truth, did we have for either of these solutions?), that would be what I would take from it, not the fascination of a secret adventure, an idea which I believed was unworthy, but the heart of something which was ours alone, which we did not share, for better or for worse, with anyone else.

The very shame of that house, of the old woman's attitude, somewhere between hostility and complicity, was a guarantee of our isolation as a couple, which had been true of our first meeting there and would be the most intimate spirit of our love. Neither of us would ever say to the other just how much the other had emerged as something which made whole what we already had or as someone who even shunned, quite deliberately, what we believed, paradoxically, we thought or felt. And neither of us could appeal to those things which eventually surround us, neither to those who knew us but were not aware of our love, nor to those who, in exchange for money, let us have a room where we could undress and lie down in bed. There, however, dreadful things could have happened, not very long ago; they passed rapidly before my eyes in my horrified imagination. And nothing terrible had taken place in that other room between me and the woman who had brought me to that house and who was, after all, the one to whom, indirectly,

Mercedes and I owed our passion and our possession of each other. I could almost see, without recalling her, that woman sitting on the edge of the bed, pulling on her shirt and stockings, guarding herself with a modesty which the day before, a smiling Mercedes had not shown. I shook with a horror which only the relief that it had not been in this room managed to dispel. True love, desperately true love, was − I suddenly realised, at the same moment that I strove to bring back the same image of Mercedes − possessed of an immodesty for which no experience could ever prepare us. The least gesture of loving abandonment is shocking to one who has never loved as I loved. No, no, it wasn't because I had already possessed her that Mercedes exhibited herself naked, carelessly, with an immodesty which the others had never shown, and which had made them, after making love, cover up their most intimate parts with extreme discretion. Because she had loved me purely, because she had given herself to me, all of her, even her most secret flesh, was natural to our eyes. Nor had I covered myself up before her, as I had in front of the others, who had given themselves to me as if they were pretending they did not know how one entered them, or came all over them without entering them.

But if she had been so natural with me, out of her pure love for me, it was also because my love and my physical possession had been stripped by another of so much imagined mystery, as well as the terror, and the fear of neither giving nor receiving pleasure which exists in a woman who has never surrendered herself before. And if I had gone about in front of her as I had, not from some showy, debauched exhibitionism, nor the false respect of mutual satiety, it was also because she, with her complete ease, though it had shocked me, had freed me from the buried fear of not being up to the standard she had expected of me, not of what it might be in dreams of physical love, but in the reality of what it could truly be. I smiled to myself cynically, thinking how much I owed to that idiot Almeida, who had had her first, just, in that way and for that reason, to lose her.

With a start I looked at my watch: she was almost twenty minutes late. Could she not come? Or had what had happened yesterday not meant much to her? What excuse had she given the previous day for getting back so late? And what had she dreamed up for today that might be credible? She had her parents, her brother, Almeida too, and those who met her in the street and she had to explain to everybody, or find a way of not having to explain, so that she could

slip away at the end of the afternoon, only to show up hours later
when it was already night, with her eyes tired and shining, which
only the absent-minded could fail to notice. Who knows whether
it hadn't all gone wrong today; who knows whether, our meeting
yesterday having escaped detection – luck had been on our side –
we had already been found out today, before we could seal all the
more deeply our mutual commitment in the same way? And then
what would become of us? How would we meet again? We would
have to run away. Where to? Where would we get the money?
And what if she didn't want to run away? But she would, she would
not hesitate. Rather than think that, even I was afraid of running
away, moved to my very soul by a passion for her, so overwhelming,
so sudden, like a tiny fire that I had lit and which all of a sudden,
fanned by extraordinary circumstances, had flared up into a huge
blaze. For she had not simply given herself to me from one day to
the next; without my even knowing it she had but consummated
with me that which, since she had known me, she had dreamt of
consummating. I had been, in the end, the other who had possessed
her; for these men, the Almeidas of this world, who conquered
every woman, passed from one to another, could not even call their
sex their own; it was always someone other, that did not touch
these women, and who in them – these men – and on their behalf
possessed these women.

Leaning against the window I kept an anxious watch out on to
the street through the crack in the shutters. A shape passed close by
but I didn't have enough time to make it out. For a few seconds I
waited expectantly but my hopes were dashed by the noise of a key
opening the door. The door closed and soft footsteps echoed
through the house – someone had a key, or someone who lived
with the old woman, a relative perhaps. They were a man's footsteps.
Maybe Mercedes was already waiting at the corner for the fellow
to pass by and disappear inside. If that were the case she wouldn't
be long. I was in a fever of suspense, waiting for her to come. But
she didn't come. I kept glancing at my watch, amazed that even so,
under my constant gaze, it still ticked on. I couldn't keep my mind
on any single thing, nor could my head even think straight. Only
the horrible thought that she might not come, that we would never
see each other again, that she might be lost to me; and the frenzied
desire, sweeping in waves through my body, to hold her, to kiss
her, to possess her. It was not as if her body were dazzlingly before
me; quite the opposite, I could not see her. Rather it was as if I was

within that body that I desired so much, and the pulsing of blood in my temples, in my sex, was that of her flesh in its hardness.

Thus it was that only after I had heard some footsteps approaching the door did I hear more clearly the hesitant knocking on the door which had already begun moments ago. I went to the bedroom door and saw Mercedes leaning against the door which was already closed behind her. Breathless, grave, she let herself fall limply into my arms, surrendering to the kisses with which I bore her to the bed. She held me in turn, so tightly that I could not undress her. Her eyes were shut tight and, speechless, she did not answer my questions, and only little by little, in response to the caresses which today relaxed her as much as yesterday they had made her tense, could I undress her so that she could open herself utterly to me, as if the need to hold me were even greater than her desire, so great that, dispensing with the preliminaries, made the desire itself its own fulfilment. But that fulfilment was so very different from anything I was expecting. She gave herself up to me and possessed me so attentively, in every detail, her concentration such that she closed her eyes tightly and dug her fingernails deep into my back, not wanting me to move off her, not even to begin again. It was as if every sense were alert, awake, and at the same far away, in a distance of someone who sought a space in which, within herself, within her eyes, she could keep the memory of every moment which her body felt and of which she could, zealously, take complete possession. I raised myself until I was on top of her and could see her face; it was strained, shining with a strangely tormented satisfaction which seemed, in the trembling of her lips and her nostrils, as though it were a kind of aching sorrow. I covered those features of hers with kisses and, as I kissed her, I lost sight of them; and losing sight of them I felt them beneath my lips, finding in them new ways by which I might soothe that spasm of sorrow.

When we lay side by side, first on our backs and then facing each other, our hands straying over each other in quiet caresses, her eyes regarded me without expression. Caress followed caress on my face; I began to feel that she was speaking to me through those hands, that through them she was giving back to her eyes the expressiveness they had lost. Something on my skin, an instinctive shrinking back that I neither felt nor was aware of, had told her that I had understood her wordless message of anguish. But I was somewhere far from there, far from that curious situation into which the joyousness of our satisfaction had brought us, if by the side of the object of our happiness we feel that it is ours to do with what we want. I had understood what I felt through her hands and my skin registered my unease. But I myself, there at bottom, was like an amused spectator, happily present at some event staged in his honour. It was with some surprise even that I felt myself emerging from the twilight depths of happiness, summoned by those signs which were addressed to me. But I still hadn't surfaced, there was something in me which resisted the idea, as she ran her finger all along my chin and spoke.

'I shouldn't have come,' she said. I turned onto my back and gazed at the ceiling, my hand resting on her belly.

'Why not?'

She did not reply at once and I began to sink back into a drowsiness which was both a return to that state of happiness and my protection against what was waking in her.

'Do you think it was easy to get away?' she asked. 'Do you think I can just disappear like that for hours on end? Do you think nobody notices?'

'Who's noticed then?'

She did not reply.

'So what. If somebody does find out, so much the better.'

She was silent, gazing at the ceiling as well, and I believe that our gazes met under the same dark stain on the green painted wood, a dirty, faded green. The stain shimmered, spread out, then narrowed again and finally became thicker and darker again. I closed my eyes.

'Jorge ... I can't come tomorrow.'

I turned towards her. 'Why not?' I demanded.

She did not reply and remained staring at the ceiling.

'Is it tomorrow they set off?'

She still said nothing and I gripped her belly tighter and repeated my question.

'I don't know.'

'You don't know?'

'Don't ask. You can't imagine how happy I am with you, not thinking of anything or anyone, not speaking of anything or anyone. I only wish...' she hesitated and turned towards me.

Then later, as if nothing had happened she finished what she had been saying: '...I only wish that nothing had ever happened, that we could be just as we were when we met each other for the first time.'

I stroked her skin. 'I wish that, too,' I said. 'But, my love, it's a mistake to think that: if nothing had happened we wouldn't be here, the two of us, in each other's arms, belonging to each other. Neither you nor I would know in all truth just how much we loved each other, how the love we feel could be so strong.'

'I'll never forget you, never,' she whispered.

I bent over her. 'I'm not going to let you, darling. Why should you forget? I'll always be with you and you with me; we'll always be within each other.'

She embraced me with great tenderness, kissing me lightly, sweetly. 'You don't understand, darling, you don't. It's so difficult to explain... When you insisted so strongly, when you wanted to make me yours... Yes...'

'Did I upset you?' I asked.

'No, I wanted it, too, ever since I first kissed you,' she said, looking away, laughing. 'That's what makes it worse,' she added.

I knelt on the bed beside her; she was sitting on the edge. 'Worse? Why?'

She stood up. 'Come on, we must be going.'

I sprang up by her side, holding her. 'It's still early. And tomorrow, can't you make it then? No? And the day after?'

She dressed slowly, as if I were not there. She combed her hair in the mirror. I started to get dressed, too.

'And the day after tomorrow?' I asked again.

'How can I know? We'll see.'

As I smoothed the jacket I had just slipped on I stuck my hands in my pockets as usual. I shuddered.

'Have you lost something?' she enquired, staring at me.

'No, nothing.'

'Well then, what's wrong?'

'Nothing, nothing.'

'What did you find in your pocket that made you go so pale?' she insisted.

'Nothing.'

'Let me see.'

'There's nothing to see.'

'Show me,' she demanded, putting her hand out towards my pocket.

'There's nothing to show you.'

'Is it something I shouldn't see?'

'Yes.'

'And what sort of things are they that I shouldn't see?'

I took the things I had bought at the chemist's from my pocket. 'Things like this, for example.'

She drew her hand back and lowered her eyes. In my confusion I began to put them back, not looking at her; and then I was taken by surprise by the long embrace with which she enfolded me and all of a sudden sought my lips. Still clinging together, with her face close to mine she said: 'Thank you for forgetting to use it.'

'But you know what this thing is? He used one, didn't he?'

She pulled away from me, her eyes lowered. 'You have no right to ask me that,' she said. 'But since you ask I can tell you he never used one. Goodbye,' she said with her hand on the door key.

I held her, begging her to forgive me, to pardon me; I told her I was crazy about her but at first she did not return my embrace but then she held me tightly and kissed me greedily.

'You don't need to ask my forgiveness for anything,' she said. 'I love you so much.' And she went out.

I stayed motionless by the door, for how long I don't know.

'Well then,' said the voice of the old lady, bringing me back to my senses. 'Well then, was everything OK? Are you pleased? Are you both coming back tomorrow? At the same time?'

'Not tomorrow. I'll let you know,' was all I could say to her in passing as I dashed off after Mercedes.

I ran up the street and round the corner. I couldn't see her. I ran from street to street, tracing the route I thought she would have taken; I felt as if I was being lured by some scent of hers. I had to talk to her; above all I had to see her. But why had she run away? How had she disappeared so completely? She seemed to have vanished. And meanwhile something was calling me through those streets, running on ahead of me, as if someone had abducted her and she was desperately crying out for me. It wasn't me she was running away from, no; and I had started to run after her even before I had felt myself drawn by that force, that voice which was calling me. I stopped on a corner, and then on another, uncertain, and so it went on. I had to talk to her and see her, now, before she got to the hotel. If she went in there before I could speak to her… A panic drove me on, lest I didn't get there in time. In time for what? I had offended her, hurt her, I was going to lose her. But before anything else she had said that she wasn't coming tomorrow. Yes, before anything else, but I wasn't going to lose her on account of that. 'You don't have to ask my forgiveness for anything. I love you so much.'

In one of the most crowded streets I thought I could pick her out. Pushing people out of my way I came closer; then I lost sight of her and then I saw her again, and by stretching out my hand between two passers-by I managed to grasp her arm. She turned round in surprise; it wasn't her. I carried on as far as the entrance to the hotel. She was at the reception desk, picking up the key. After the initial shock of seeing me at her side she immediately recovered her composure, smiling in a friendly fashion.

'Why did you run away?' I asked.

She shook her head, still wearing the same counterfeit friendly smile. 'I didn't run away. It was late. I'll see you tomorrow,' she said holding out her hand delicately. 'But no, not tomorrow,' she corrected herself, 'later.'

I gripped her hand but she pulled it free and made for the stairs. On the landing, where she couldn't be seen from the desk, she stopped for a moment and waved me a furtive goodbye. It was then that I noticed that, standing before me and next to me, the whole time, her eyes had been glazed with tears.

I went out into the street and only then realised that night had already fallen. It was after nine. I would go and grab something to eat and then go home. Home? What about Rodrigues? Perhaps he had already returned. Of course he had. Even more surely by ten o'clock. I went into a café, had a drink and a sandwich and went off in search of Rodrigues.

XXI

At the boarding house where Rodrigues was staying the same fellow who had been there in the morning was on the door, still with the same air of cynical mischief; he told me I could go up and that *he* was waiting for me in his room. Leaning against the doorjamb he turned on his shoulder and repeated with relish the final phrase after I had passed close to him; he made no effort to pull back or even move as I made my way past. There was a light in the room; I knocked.

'Come in,' shouted Rodrigues.

He was absolutely naked, stretched out on his back on the bed with his hands folded behind his head; he did not move when he spoke. 'Ah, it's you,' he said. 'The money's over there.'

I picked up a white envelope; though it was open, I did not count the money.

'Count it. There's only one million escudos. They came inside a note which I got her to write explaining why she didn't send more; as an emissary I'm only worth a million. Isn't that what she says?'

I counted the money and looked at the note.

'But in my coat pocket there's another half a million she gave me and which I earned with the sweat of my brow, not to mention other parts. Take that, too.'

'But it's yours.'

'No, it's not mine; it belongs to your aunt. I don't need it.'

I rifled through the pockets of a coat hanging on the back of a chair and found the notes.

'Count it. Is it all there?'

I didn't reply.

'You deliver the letter with the one million and the note, and then the other half million: as a gift from me, you understand?'

I nodded.

'Do you know what I regret? Do you? That I didn't cuckold your uncle. I must have thought that she was no different from any of the others. I was an idiot, a child, an innocent at large. If I had done what I wanted to do she would have found a love which she never got from your uncle and would have had no need to go around deceiving me, yes, really deceiving me, for she should have known that there was someone who adored her and whom she cast aside so that he even gets involved in some wrretched business like this. And then it's the boy here who has to sell himself just so that Her Excellency can come out of this all pure and smelling of roses.'

'She's not mixed up in any of this.'

'Is she? Do you think she is? Do you think I'm daft? Don't you think I read her letter? I didn't want to, but that old woman is a devil. She read the thing to me, she made me listen to her. And do you know what the letter said? Do you? That I, the bearer, was the man of your aunt's dreams, and the man, too, who was after the money. So the old crone thought that she had won on both counts: she had got me stitched up and got this rascal off her daughter's back while she could be slavering up and down over some rascal that she'd had her eye on. Aren't you laughing? Don't you think it's a hoot?'

He got up and shook me. 'You're not laughing. Don't you think it's funny? Have you ever heard anything funnier?'

'No.'

'Neither have I,' he said, sitting down dejectedly. 'Neither have I.'

I hadn't the words to tell him. Even if I were to tell him what was behind it all – how much I had wanted that journey to take place so that it could take Almeida with it to perdition, how much my aunt had lied to get the money out of her mother, even if I were to add that all of us – Mercedes, me, her brother, the others, my aunt and uncle, all of them seemed, before him, a bunch of irresponsible children – I could not in any way make up for the evil of having picked him for that mission, nor the fact that my choice coincided with the incredible letter of which he had been the bearer.

'Did you read the letter yourself, or did she just read it to you?' I asked him. 'Did you just imagine it? Or was the old crone making it all up as she read it to you?'

He threw himself down again along the bed. 'It doesn't matter.' He rolled over. 'Don't you understand that it really doesn't matter?' he asked angrily. 'Don't you see what happened? What happened to me?'

He held out his left hand to me on which, all of a sudden, I saw the sparkle of a handsome diamond ring.

'By giving you the half a million I haven't lost everything; there's more where that came from. Can you see it? It's a fine one, isn't it? It must be worth two hundred thousand escudos. Do you know whom it belonged to? Your aunt's father. Can you imagine what I had to listen to? Can you imagine her delight when she saw me? Can you imagine, on top of all this, how happy she was because, as well as having me ... and the wild things she was telling me, dribbling with delight from the corners of her mouth ... and as well as having me, she was stealing me from her own daughter? And whenever I want I just have to knock on her door. She'd never paid so much, never given so much money to anybody, that's what she said. That I could have anything I wanted, I only had to ask. I would be her favourite son, she would be a mother to me. That monster. And she even looks like my mother, damn her. It suited everybody. But that's the end of it.'

He stood up on the bed, holding his cock with both hands and shaking it about. 'But now, are you watching? It's all over. I'm free. Now I can sell myself, whole and entire. Give the whole lot, everything,' and he danced around, sticking out his backside and pulling his buttocks apart with his hands.

'Are you crazy?' I asked.

He paused, bending over me with a demented look which soon dissolved into tears. 'Yes, I am. Tell me, who isn't?'

He flung himself on the bed. 'I thought that the evil was something in me, a rage which filled me, a misery which enveloped everybody,' he sobbed. 'But now I know that it isn't. It isn't within me, nor does it fill me nor enfold anybody else. It doesn't exist. Are you listening to me? It doesn't exist. And if it doesn't exist how can I worship the one, whoever it is, who can save me? There's nothing to be saved, nobody to be saved, nobody who can save anybody else. They just don't exist.'

'So what does exist then?'

'Everything that doesn't matter. Only what doesn't matter exists.'

He turned to me. 'Do you know what I'm going to do? You don't? I'm going to Lisbon.'

I forced myself to laugh if only to try to lighten the atmosphere a little. 'So at the end of all that drama the epilogue is that you're going to Lisbon?'

He lifted up his eyes to me. 'You don't you think much of the idea then?'

'It's something you've thought about before,' I replied, sitting down on the chair.

'I have, but this time it's different. I'm going to have a visiting card made, with my name, and all my measurements, and these words:

"All services, both active and passive, for both sexes and all ages. Price to be agreed depending on requirements". What do you think?'

'I think you ought to have a price list.'

'A price list, hmm?'

'Yes, to save you the chore of discussing the price each time there's a special case, because, if you think about it, they're all special cases. So either you work for a fixed price, no matter what the service or, better, you have price list.'

'You don't think I'm serious, do you?'

'Yes, I do. But not this stuff you're saying, no.'

'Don't you believe that I'm capable of suffering?'

'Yes, I do. I even think that you must be the one who suffers the most of all the people I know.'

'And what wrong have I done to deserve this, won't you tell me? You're my friend, aren't you?'

'Yes.'

'Do you know that I don't trust anyone but you?'

'Why?'

'Look, it could be that as far as these things in my life are concerned you're on the outside, you're just someone who comes for holidays, someone who knows me as I am and not as I have been. All the others belong to my family or that damned hotel or those who were with me at school. They all think they know me either because they once caught me mixed up in it or they know that someone else caught me. I only want you to tell me one thing: whatever I become, however I end up, you won't stop being my friend, will you?'

'No.'

'You swear?'

'Yes.'

'Do you want me to tell you something? I really like you.'

I shuddered.

'You see, you got a shock. In spite of being my friend you thought that I was going to make you some kind of declaration of love, didn't you? But it's just the opposite: I've never made a declaration of love to anyone. I've never felt, and I suppose I never will, love for anyone, nor admiration either. All I feel is rage; and the only person towards whom I don't feel this rage is you. I'm not mad at you, therefore I'm your friend. I think that even if you betrayed me I'd be able to forgive you and even say thank you very much into the bargain.'

'Well, it's what you're going to have to do.'

He got up with a start. 'Why?' he demanded.

'Because I've already betrayed you.'

'You?'

'Yes. It was me who had the idea to send you to Coimbra.'

He sat down on the edge of the bed gently wringing his hands. 'Is that really true? Was it you?' he asked without lifting his head.

'Yes, it was me.'

He remained in the same posture, making the same gestures. Then he lifted his face; his eyes were moist and a smile played across his lips. 'Life's a funny thing, isn't it?'

'That depends,' I replied.

'The woman I love, the only person I've ever loved, and my only friend, not that I've had any others, they both get together, one with the other, to do this... I've got this all wrong, there's no doubt about it.'

'Got it wrong, what do you mean?'

'No, it's not what you're thinking. It's just that as well as the fact that she's never had anything like the love which I offered her, you've never had anything like the friendship which I have for you. It's something which only concerns me, just me.'

He began to get dressed. 'Do you know why I'm not wearing any clothes?' he asked me. 'She told her chauffeur to take me back by car. When I got back it seemed as though I could still feel her mouth all over me. I had a bath even though I'd already had one in her house when it was all over. She herself gave me it. But I thought that I'd never be able to get dressed again, that I would stay lying there, naked, for the rest of my life. My whole skin was burning; I suppose it will burn for ever. But now I can get dressed. When all is said and done that's going to be my fate, getting dressed and undressed at any old hour. Have you had dinner?'

'Yes.'

'So where are you going?'

'Home.'

'To take the money, I suppose?'

'Of course.'

'Don't forget to do everything that I told you to.'

'That's OK.'

'Are you coming back afterwards?'

'No.'

He stopped in the middle of the room. 'Shall we see each other tomorrow?'

'I suppose so,' I said.

Smiling, he held out his hand to me. 'Put it there.'

I shook it. He gripped mine. 'If you are truly my friend you'll see just how much friendship costs. From now on you'll see. You'll have to pay me back plenty for all this. Wait there, I'm going out, too.'

We went down the steps together and crossed the vestibule where two ladies and a man were sitting. The fellow was still on the door and stepped out of the way with a surly 'good night'. Rodrigues turned round and stared at him, scowling menacingly. 'What sort of greeting is that?' he demanded.

The man shrugged mockingly. 'Greeting?… I merely wished you good night.'

'Well, let's hear it again.'

'Good night,' the man said again.

He seized him by the shoulders. 'Again.'

'Good night…'

'That's it, you've got it. My friend here is a man who merits a certain respect, I'd like you to know. While I,' he said, turning to the vestibule, 'if I were at the service of someone who was paying me, or even someone who wasn't, I would manage to give them a civil good night, and more, together with some fine phrases and whatever else was necessary.' And he let him go, pushing him back inside.

He caught up with me as I had gone on ahead and walked with me for a while. 'I can be whatever they like but they'll have to respect me. Rabble … well, you be about your business and I'll get on with mine. So we'll meet tomorrow? Yes? In the morning, on the beach? We could have lunch together. If we don't meet up on the beach let's get together in the café where we were before,' he said and off he went.

I headed home, with a weariness that was partly a disgust with myself and partly with the others, troubled on account of Mercedes, full of pity for Rodrigues, in an inconsolable agony that redoubled every time I felt the envelope in my pocket. I couldn't think straight. Everything seemed senseless, random. But at the same time everything was linked and interwoven with its own logic, rather like the contagion of some infectious disease. It was as if a poison, a fever, a malignant virus had invaded my life and that of all the people around me, without anyone being able to locate the source of the infection. Everyone's life seemed to be infecting the lives of everyone else, but I couldn't even begin to say where it had all sprung from, or how long it had been soiling everything and everybody, spreading like some huge stain. It seemed to me, on the other hand, that, without wanting it, merely by means of one action, something inadvertent, inconsequential, I had set in motion around me – and continued to do so – a series of catastrophes, which in their turn had unleashed yet others.

But my action in dragging Rodrigues into that business had been neither inadvertent nor inconsequential. What I had demanded from Mercedes had been neither inadvertent nor inconsequential. If my inability to keep quiet about the Spaniards in my uncle's house had been inadvertent, it had surely not been inconsequential. The one who had suggested the orgy, though it was not intended to be such a monstrous affair, was me. The one who had got his hands on the maid, though Mercedes was already his, had been me too. And I recalled, with repugnance and detachment (as well as with anger at that very repugnance and detachment), that I had invited the maid up to my room that very night. After everything else, her too … and she would also end up embroiled in the plot which had already ensnared … how many people? Myself, Mercedes, Rodrigues, Almeida, Mercedes' brother, the two Macedos, the two Spaniards, my aunt and uncle, and who knows how many more besides; at least a dozen people. But was I really the one who had unleashed all that? Wasn't it Mercedes who had come to me, quite openly? Hadn't Almeida been there before me? Hadn't Ramos and the rest organised the flight by boat before they knew about the Spaniards? Hadn't it been my uncle who had taken the Spaniards into his house? Hadn't my aunt, together with him, written the letter that Rodrigues would take to the old woman? And she was, even without my ever having seen her, yet one more person embroiled in this ever spreading business. And there were others.

I hadn't done these things, though, or I had only done some of them. To be precise, I had fetched up in Figueira and a series of facts and people, in the air, so to speak, waiting for the first one to pass by, had fallen together in a heap through the action of the person who, by mere chance, had some common point of contact with all of them. They were like a piece of material which somehow gets snagged on some passer-by, who then drags the whole thing along behind him; if everything was getting mixed up together like strands of material that didn't make it some kind of cape which I had thrown over my own shoulders. I was on holiday; we were all on holiday, except life itself which wasn't on holiday. But that wasn't quite it. There were those who were on holiday, others who weren't. However, both the events and the people involved, although they somehow sustained each other beyond their own particular spheres, still conducted themselves with the air of the very same unique, profound reality of which they were the momentary, provisional faces.

But wasn't it, though, just the opposite? Wasn't it the case that a common affliction had given them these faces, or given rise to the mutual attraction which brought them all flocking together in their confusion? Or did it come about just because I, I alone, was both witness to, and actor in, these various parallel series of events? But the position of the others – or of some of them at least – wasn't much different; only the events weren't wholly the same for them as they had been for me. If there were things that I knew and others didn't, then there were also things where I was in the dark. But just what was it I wasn't in the dark about? Did I know what had really gone on between Mercedes and Almeida, or between her and her brother? Had I read the letter which my aunt had written? Did I know anything about what Zé Ramos had agreed with the others? Even if I did know there were three ways in which I might know, like everybody else: because somebody had told me; because I had been present or because I had taken part in it. When I hadn't taken part in something, but had heard about it from what they told me or had seen what they did in front of me, could that really be the truth? Were they aware of all these things in the same way that I was aware of them? In that case they would know nothing or almost nothing and would merely be behaving as if they did know. The meaning which I might bestow on what I had seen or heard could not be, would not be, the same meaning which they might give it; and this meaning of theirs could not, in turn, be the one which things held for the others.

What I was beginning to discern was terrible, much more terrible than Rodrigues' discovery, the one he had made in front of me, of the nature of evil, the discovery that it did not exist. Events did not have a *cause*, people did not have *motives*; these events, those people, were given a causality *a posteriori*. And when we, voluntarily or involuntarily, made something happen, we didn't do so by the exercise of our will, nor impelled by some kind of fate. It was only the notion of causality itself which had created the dilemma of autonomy or fate. Where there is no cause nor motive, there is no necessary relation between the action which occasions it and the process thereby set in motion. If a person's past conditions him or her to act in one way or another, according to circumstances, it conditions that person equally to act in precisely the opposite way. And events, in the way in which they are linked, can just as much be understood in the order in which they have occurred as the other way round. It was just that this possible dual understanding was equally a figment of my imagination; but, since my imagination preceded the events themselves which it was creating or interpreting, these would emerge, in the haphazard way in which they did emerge (and which depended on so many other things which I didn't know and would never know), as my *responsibility*. There being neither causes or motives for anything, everything would happen as if each one of us were the one exclusively responsible for things for which he or she did not have the least responsibility. And that was the meaning of life. Henceforth I, even at the cost to others, could make of my life what I felt like as long as I accepted as part of that choice such consequences as might, out of the blue, be heaped on me.

At the same moment I ceased to understand whatever it was. Muddled and confused, I came to the conclusion that understanding and not-understanding were much the same thing. Not-understanding was to understand clearly that one didn't understand, in the same way that to understand was the not-understanding of what one understood: a game of words. And the mistake – for it was suddenly clear to me that it was a mistake – was to seek to understand, of necessity through words, what did not belong to the order of words. Words served us to communicate with each other, didn't they? But if they were used to communicate by those who were not even aware of their non-existent motives, they couldn't be used to explain a single thing, but only to communicate things whose only explanation was that they could or even could not be put into words. Therefore that experience of life which grows out of understanding our relations with others and with ourselves is exactly what cannot be put into words; otherwise it loses its very condition of existence, which is to make sure that we, ourselves and the rest, are all in step. Therefore our knowledge of others depends as much on what they do not actually do, or do not say when they speak. It depends precisely on what we surely cannot know and on what they themselves often do not know. Hence, in the end, words serve two opposing ends at the same time: to envisage what is probable; and to suggest the silence of the possible. There could not be formulas to contain people in themselves, except when people, fearing the loss of the security of causes, invent them and attribute to themselves motivations which they did not have or were not exactly what they imagined they were. Thus there would be no difference between imbeciles and those who could see clearly, between an honest man and a rogue. Or only one difference: that of wanting to see clearly or of wanting to be true. What was left was therefore very little: an imperfect capacity to see clearly and a faith which had no sure object.

When I arrived at the gates of the house I noticed that I had strayed far not just in my thoughts but also on the way, as if the unravelling of what I had discovered coincided with the time I needed to find my way back, the envelope in my pocket, to confront yet another unpredictable series of events. Behind the gate the dog leapt at me through the bars; I opened and closed it carefully so as not to let the dog out. The kitchen door had been left open, obviously so that I could enter, though there was nobody in the kitchen. The radio was bellowing away in the library. I went up to my aunt's room where the light was still on: I knocked. A voice asked if it was me and bade me come in.

She was in her dressing gown, seated at her dressing table; she looked up from doing her nails, her face smiling and guileless. 'Has the money arrived?'

I passed her the letter, from which she took out the banknotes and her mother's note. She read it. 'Only one million?' she asked, laughing.

'The other half million's here,' I said and handed it over. 'They were given to the bearer who has in turn given them to you.'

'To me?'

'Yes.'

'That's extremely kind of him.'

'I think so, too,' I said.

She worked away at the corner of a fingernail with her little scissors: 'As for your uncle, it would serve him right if this were all true.'

I said nothing.

'And, if it's written down, that's it. Too bad for him.' She picked up the little polishing cloth.

'What have I been all these years, my boy... You know what I've been? An ass. Yes, sir, an ass. For I could have had all the men

I ever wanted, I could have been loved and worshipped like no woman ever was. And at least once, with one of them, I could have been happy; but I've spent my life being faithful to your uncle, who is the only man who has never been faithful to me, who didn't even respect me.'

'But he's your husband; and he's never left you.'

'Yes, he is indeed my husband. Do you think that's enough? And he's never left me because he never found anyone who would be his slave like I've been.' She paused, absorbed in polishing her nails. 'The most extraordinary thing is that my mother is to blame for all,' she added.

'Your mother?'

'Yes. If she weren't as she is and if I, ever since I was a child, hadn't seen those men coming and going in and out of her life like passengers on a tram − even though the comparison isn't quite accurate, because on the trams the passengers pay rather than the contrary − I wouldn't have done as I have. She's been at it with all and sundry. But she has already done − and is still doing − all that I could have done and she hasn't left, nor will she leave, anyone or anything for me.'

She got up, lifting up her arms to arrange her hair. 'But your aunt isn't so old yet. From a distance she still looks good.'

'Everybody looks good, from a distance or even close up to those who love to see them,' I said.

'Close up, in the dark, as your uncle says.' She picked up the million reis. 'Take this to your uncle. I'll keep the rest and the note. After all is said and done, they're mine, aren't they?'

'You know best, auntie,' I said and went out holding the banknotes.

I went down the stairs and into the library. The three of them were sitting at the table, playing, while the radio crackled behind them. My uncle lifted his head from the cards. 'Well then, has the money arrived?'

The others didn't move. 'Here it is,' I said, handing it over.

'What the devil's this? Only one million? What about the rest? Did the old witch only send a million? It looks like she guessed something was amiss; she's the very devil, the devil personified, there's no doubt about it.'

'The other half a million was sent, too, but separately. Your mother-in-law gave it to the bearer and he passed it on to auntie.'

Fitting the actions to his words he said: 'The old crone gave it to the bearer and he passed it on to your aunt and your auntie is going to give it to me and I…' He held his hand aloft and gave a chuckle. 'It's almost like some kind of chain letter. What about your commission? Who's going to pay you? Or have you been paid already?'

'Nobody's paid me anything; I don't want anything.'

'Come now! You get all that money going round in a single day and you won't accept any commission? You don't have any choice.'

'Leave it till later,' I said.

'Later … and they all lived happily ever after. Very well then. Everything has been sorted out,' he said, addressing the Spaniards. 'You gentlemen now have enough money to set sail. Tomorrow morning my nephew here will hand it over and so that there's no possibility of a swindle,' he said, using a Spanish expression, 'will ask for a receipt which I shall keep. As a loan for a week, like a gambling debt, because this whole thing could be a fairy story and there might not be a boat at all, or it might not turn up. If it is just a fairy story I'll complain to the police.'

'And what if we don't go?' asked Don Juan, rifling through his cards.

'Ah…' said my uncle. 'I've heard something of the sort. It's a very sad state of affairs; I don't even want to think about it.'

'Sad? Why sad, Don Justino?' asked the other Spaniard.

'Because it's a coward's way out, of someone who should have thought of it earlier. But since you gentlemen are not cowards I know that you will go ahead as planned.'

They were silent.

'Because, if they didn't go ahead, and decided, just as an example, to leave this house and take the train to Lisbon…'

'What would happen?' asked Don Juan, looking hard at him.

'What would happen? They'd be arrested by the police.'

'It's a risk we would run.'

'It's a risk I'm not going to let you run.'

'Do you mean to say that we are being kept prisoner in your house?' demanded the patriotic Basque, as Don Juan held him by the arm.

'More or less. You only get out of here if you take the boat – if there is a boat. The best thing you can do is to pray to all the saints that there isn't. For, if there should not be a boat then you can go wherever you wish. It is perfectly clear that I got into this affair from pure altruism, since, if anything goes wrong, I'll come out of

it a million reis better off, won't I? And if you gentlemen do go…'
but he did not complete the sentence.

The two Spaniards rose. 'Don Justino …' began Don Juan.

'Don Justino, nothing. I am a lieutenant and here in Portugal
nobody has been a "Don" since 1910. It's late … you must be tired.
Very well. Good night.'

They were on their way through the door. 'One thing,' he said,
'one more thing. I suggest to you my friends that you do not try
to escape from here. As you know, the dog is somewhat evil-
natured. But worse by far than the dog is the fact that I have taken
my own precautions.'

'Precautions … lieutenant?' repeated Don Juan.

'Yes, indeed… But you are not going to ask me to tell you what
they might be, are you?'

'The worst thing that could happen to us is to be arrested by the
police.'

'That is your opinion, sir,' replied my uncle. 'But there is worse,
far worse.'

Don Juan smiled, restraining the other. 'You (in Spanish) are not
going to kill us, are you?'

'Me? The very idea! Do you not know, sir, that story of the chap
who was arrested after he had emptied a hail of bullets into his
enemy? When they captured him he looked down at his hand and
said: "So that's what you are, eh? You do this sort of thing to me…"'

'Well, if you, sir, do not let us leave,' said Don Fernando
haughtily, 'we shall stay here in your house.'

'Oh no you won't. One way or another you won't stay here.
But for the time being neither will you leave,' and he got up, holding
out his arms, his stick hanging from one of them. 'You won't leave
until the time when those men arrive. You will give me your word
of honour that you will wait until then. Or you are not men. Tell
them yourselves that you are not going. Or do you not have the
balls for that?'

They were struck dumb by the coarseness of his remark and it
seemed to me that they were torn between hurling themselves upon
him or rushing out of the door. It was Don Juan, drawing himself
up to his full height who finally spoke. 'You are right, lieutenant,'
he said drily. 'We shall wait until we can speak to them.'

'I give you my word that I shall wait,' added the other. 'But you
must know that I am not afraid. Prudence is one thing, madness
another.'

'Without madness nothing would get done,' replied my uncle. 'The whole thing is madness; it is something we are caught up in and your country as well.'

After they had gone out he turned to me. 'What's this about not wanting any commission? But hang on, I have to give something to the maids.'

The reference to the maids awoke in me an anguish which pulled me in different directions: I had forgotten, at least in the forefront of my thoughts, that the maid would be waiting for everybody to go to bed before she came up to my room. And, on the one hand, I no longer wanted her (I was weary from the day and fearful of more complications and repelled by her as well), while on the other some sudden rage made me want her to come up, a virgin in whom I could defile all the stupidity of the world.

But my uncle did not seem inclined to go up; rather, he was ready to talk He rolled his little cigarette, remaking and licking it in his own special way and then lit it with the same slow deliberation. Then he switched off the radio which had been whining and crackling away all the while. In the empty silence which filled the air and in which the whole of the 'library' suddenly assumed a misty, distant hue, redolent of disuse, I waited for him to speak. 'Did you see those dolts?' he began. 'They worm their way into my house, owe me a pile of money at cards, along comes a way of escaping which can't fail we get into some frightful scheme to raise the money to pay for their escape, we actually get hold of the money and now they don't want to go... But they'll go, believe you me, they'll go. Because they won't dare set foot outside of here and the instant they get into the car which comes to fetch them they won't have the guts to go back.'

'Don't you think they're right, though?' I asked.

'Right? What's right and what isn't, can you tell me that? Obviously it's a risky business and it might even be that they don't relish the thought of going by boat because they might get sick. Me, when I went to France, in the boat which took our lot, I was throwing up like a hake. But with all those soldier boys all throwing up everywhere, vomiting on the straw on which we slept in the holds, and pissing on top of the vomit, who wouldn't have thrown up? When I came back ... but I came back from Holland, on the train. And in Greta's aeroplane ... did you know she was called Greta, the one who kidnapped me? What a hell of a name, that's what I used to tell her. In the aeroplane, the funny bit of my escape was that I got sick too. I don't think that there was any part of the German countryside over which we passed which I didn't throw up on. But look,' he said changing the subject abruptly, 'what sort of trouble have you got yourself into?'

'Me?'

'Yes, you. Don't you think I can't see it in your face?'

'The same trouble we're all in.'

'Don't fob me off with your nonsense; that's not what I'm talking about.'

'What then?'

'What's written on your face, in your eyes... Do you think that when a lad like you is in it up to his neck, up to his ears, in some bother, we can't see it in his face?'

'So what does it matter?'

He laughed and sat down on one of the armchairs. 'It doesn't... Only that people at your age get everything mixed up and when you least expect it, or reckon that you're in love and then find out you're not, when there's no way out, or when you take advantage of a situation, when you're not really involved at all, and you end up in love and by then it's far too late.'

'In any case...'

'There's no way out, is that what you're trying to say? You're very much mistaken; of course there is. It's the sort of mistake you make at your age.'

I was still standing, there in front of him, letting the conversation take its own course and at the same time putting off my business with Maria, so that my desire for her became more urgent, more intense. 'So what's the way out then?' I asked.

'The way out, my dear chap, is to know when it's time to say goodbye to all of it.'

'But that's what we all do when we don't want somebody any longer and we've already had enough of her physically.'

'And when we think we love somebody?' he asked, taking a deep pull on his cigarette.

'In that case it doesn't matter,' I replied. 'Is there any difference between loving somebody and thinking we love her?'

'Yes, there is. Look, man: when you feel that terrible fury at being trapped by somebody and every waking hour you want to be quit of her, and the more you do to be free of her the more you end up being close to her; then you love her. But it's when you feel that you're head over heels in love and you can't think of anything else, when you're convinced you love somebody, then you don't.'

'Just the opposite of what everybody says? And what everybody feels?'

'But what do you want people to say? What they really feel?'

It all seemed to me quite unreal, not so much that philosophy, but the fact that my uncle should be philosophising about these ideas, whether truthfully or not I didn't know, but certainly with a perspicacity which I found disturbing. Or could it be that his perspicacity had nothing perspicacious about it and was simply the sort of rambling you got from adults who had lived a bit? What was perspicacious about saying what everybody said, or even the opposite?

'Well, it's time to go to bed,' said my uncle, getting up. 'Tomorrow morning you'll give the money to Ramos, won't you? Take it now; but don't go out without the receipt which I'll have to draw up, you hear?'

But what I heard instead was a maddening howl of the dog, a howl accompanied by a snarling as if he were trying to attack somebody who in turn was fending him off. We looked at each other and ran out into the corridor towards the staircase from where, up above, the two Spaniards, in their pyjamas were looking down. Down below I could make out the white shapes of the two maids in their skirts. My uncle went up to his room and came down with a pistol in his hand, almost jaunty, with his cane swinging on his left arm. The two Spaniards followed him down. In the kitchen where I joined them he switched on the garden light, a lamp on a corner of the house at the back. He ordered the Spaniards to stay in the kitchen where, as I arrived, I could see at a glance that they were part of a confused group with the two maids (with Maria looking at me). When we went out the dog had already stopped barking; it was lying there, some way past the corner, with blood pouring from its throat, which had been cut. Somebody had got in and killed it. Absolute silence reigned. My uncle searched the bottom of the garden. I didn't join him but instead looked up at the huge tree. The lamp cast shadows which seemed to make the darkness all the more impenetrable, except for a vague, greenish patch of light over the surface, as if it were some cardboard scenery running parallel to the front wall of the house. My aunt was silhouetted in the light from her window. I moved so that she could see me clearly. 'Have you seen anybody, auntie?'

'No, I just heard the dog barking,' she said, leaning out. 'What is it?'

'Somebody has got in and killed the dog,' I said, pointing to it. She leaned out further. 'How awful! What now?'

My uncle had returned. 'Go over to the other corner while I search over there by the belvedere,' he said. 'If you see anything running away, shout.'

I did as I was told and as I passed in front of the lit kitchen four shapes were crammed into the doorway; I told the Spaniards to hide inside. In the darkness I could make out the outline of my uncle and I could hear his steps rustling in the undergrowth. Time was passing slowly, it seemed like an age before he came back. 'There's nobody here, but somebody must have got in, got in and killed the dog. Unless…'

'He's already fled…' I interrupted.

He didn't reply and went round the outside of the house again, close to the tree. The rubbish around the tree seemed to hang in the fine dust of the penumbra which illuminated it. My uncle looked up at the window where my aunt remained, motionless. And then, suddenly he pointed his pistol at the tree. 'Whoever's up there, come down,' he hissed from between his clenched teeth, 'or I'll shoot.'

There was a long silence then from the tree came a voice, shaking with rage yet with a resolve born of desperation: 'Shoot and kill me then, you son of a whore. I'm not coming down.'

My uncle raised his arm higher.

'Kill me,' said the voice, 'Get me out of here if you can.'

I toyed with the idea of taking my uncle by surprise and grabbing his arm but that might have caused him to shoot.

'Kill me,' said the voice again, 'come on, kill me, shoot, get me down from here.'

My uncle slowly lowered his arm. 'You can stay there for the rest of your life,' he said, adding the foulest insult which must have wounded Rodrigues to the very depths of his soul. My aunt remained motionless at the window. Then he turned to me. 'Drag the dog over to the long grass by the belvedere. Go along the other side.'

I did as I was told and when I returned he was standing calmly by the kitchen door, while everyone else had disappeared. 'Wait for him there,' he said. 'Then let him out.' Then he went back inside the house.

The window had by now been closed and the tree was no longer illuminated by its light. 'Come down,' I called from the bottom of the tree.

He didn't answer; not a single thing stirred within the tree. I was about to call to him again when he spoke. 'Switch off that light.'

I went to the kitchen and switched it off. In the darkness I found him already down on the ground, finding his feet, tall, bending over to wriggle first one foot then the other into the beach shoes he had left by the tree. We said not a word to each other and then he vanished into the shadows.

I went into the house, closing the kitchen door behind me. As I went upstairs I switched off each light as I passed; there was nobody about. In the top corridor there were no lights in any of the rooms. It was as if he had taken ages to slip on his shoes, though he had in fact seemed to me to be very swift. I switched on my own light and started to undress for bed, my mind a blank. I put the light out and lay down on the bed. The door creaked; I lay still, roused abruptly from my drowsiness. In the uncertain light of the room I made out Maria, standing at the foot of the bed and bending over towards me. I half raised myself and clouted her. She grunted with surprise and pain. But as she retreated towards the door I grabbed her and toppled her down onto the bed, sticking my hand over her mouth. She writhed on top of me. Virgin she was not, not at all. I withdrew from her, my sense of betrayal extinguishing the violent desire I had felt.

'Be off with you,' I said.

She went and I fell asleep; I slept like a log.

XXII

The following day when I went downstairs for breakfast I found them in the dining room, all acting as if nothing had happened, while Maria served at table. In fact, as all those crazy goings on piled one on top of the other, I had lost all sense of time and I had ceased to worry whether things were true or I had just dreamed them. That was what I was most aware of, in my surprise at that feigned air of normality, when that surprise was not justified by the heavy atmosphere of confused forgetfulness of which my head was full. They carried on chatting, all smiles, as the coffee pot did the rounds, together with the bread, the butter, the jam, the little biscuits, passing from hand to hand. Only for one moment did everything suddenly freeze: 'Don't go without my receipt,' my uncle reminded me, but soon the conversation flowed again. I neither took part in it nor followed it: I seemed to be elsewhere, as though drifting far away, having absolutely nothing to do with what was going on around me.

All of a sudden I fell out of my reverie as my uncle hurled a piece of bread across the room. 'No, not that!' he exclaimed, 'Not that! What has Portugal to do with you gentlemen? Union? A Federation of Iberian Republics? Is that all you want? Portugal has existed for centuries within its own frontiers. It's not like the other kingdoms of Spain, which never knew for certain where they were. If Spain didn't have the Pyrenees and the sea around it, it would never have existed. What matters for you is that there is a Portuguese frontier, one marked out there for you, otherwise you Spaniards would never know where you were. But that way at least you know you're not Portuguese.' He turned to me for support. 'Are you listening to these people? Some of them want a Spain running from ocean to ocean, which is exactly the sort of nonsense I heard yesterday on the radio, while others want a Spain from land to land ... and all this while Spain itself is split into two, and they're all slaughtering each other. What a people, eh?' he said turning back to them. 'And you dare say such things in my house? Perhaps you think it's some kind of special honour to be Spanish, and that we're only waiting for England to give us permission to become Spaniards too, eh?'

'But, Don Justino…' began Don Juan.

'Haven't I already told you, sir, that I am a lieutenant, not a "Don". Don't come Spanishifying me with your titles.'

'But, lieutenant,' continued Don Juan, 'What our friend said was not that at all. He didn't say that Spain would absorb Portugal; that's what the rebels and the Fascists want. He said that Spain consists of a federation of states into which Portugal would enter on the same footing as Galicia, Catalonia, the Basque country. It's the only reasonable way…'

'Reasonable be damned! From being on an equal footing with Spain we would then pass on to the same footing as one of the provinces, isn't that so? That's like getting off a horse and jumping on a donkey!'

'Patience,' urged the other. 'That's not the question at all. It is because Spain rules some nations which should be independent.'

'But they're not, and what has Portugal got to do with the problems of these nations? Why can't they do as we did? We were under the heel too but we threw it off with our own efforts and won our freedom again.'

'Freedom…' laughed Don Juan. 'Do you call this freedom, the way you live now?'

'No sir, I don't call the way we live now freedom; but why should I even think about exchanging it for some absurd federation?'

'In order to make possible the social revolution which this country needs. Do you believe that if Portugal belonged to an Iberian federation the powers could stand in the way of her political evolution?'

'They wouldn't need to. You gentlemen have already taken that upon yourselves.'

'I regret that it's not possible to talk politics with you, sir.'

'This kind of politics, no. Well, I've got to write the receipt,' he said, getting up from the table. I followed him to his study where, with some ceremony and after several drafts, he drew up a receipt which he then gave me. 'You don't hand over the money to Ramos,' he said, 'before he signs this paper, do you hear? Look, one more thing,' he said as if struck by a sudden flash of inspiration, running his fingers through his hair. 'Go and get Macedo first, eh? Give him the money and get the receipt from him. It will be safer.'

I had been thinking vaguely during the previous conversation how extraordinary it was that, if they had been thinking in that way about an Iberian Federation, the row with my uncle hadn't erupted earlier. Or were they going over an argument they'd had before? In any case it was comical how I had got so worked up about those fellows in the café, blaming Fascism for those schemes of theirs, which these fellows, their opponents, also cherished. Or were they really the same thing? My uncle repeated his bright idea: 'Are you listening to what I'm saying?' he asked.

'Yes, uncle,' I said, which was when it dawned on me that he was talking about Carlos Macedo. 'But why Macedo?' I demanded, not having mentioned him when I first discussed the matter with my uncle. Had I really not mentioned him? I was no longer certain of anything.

'Macedo, yes, sir. To anyone who knows him, he's incapable of hiding the least thing. As it happens I met him yesterday and I've no doubt he's mixed up in all this. It's the father I feel sorry for... One son is running away from him to Spain, or is mixed up in some frightful business or other, while the other is going to Lisbon, for Dona Micaela is going to Lisbon, that's settled – to the Nautical School if I'm not mistaken. His brother even told me he was going to ask you to help the boy down there.'

'He's already asked me if Luís could stay in our house; I don't know whether my parents would like the idea.'

'That can be sorted out; I'll write to your father. Anyway make sure you hand over the money to Macedo, you hear? That's by far the best way.'

I shuddered to think that another person was now involved, involuntarily, in this business, a hostage to events. 'Where am I going to get hold of Macedo?' I objected. 'I haven't arranged to see him. Ramos is the one who's waiting for me, until midday.'

'Till midday be damned! Do you think I believe that? That was some fairytale of his to force you to come up with the money he needed within a certain time. You can bet he'll still be there after midday and he'll be there, in a muck sweat until you turn up with the money. And sure enough you can turn up all right, but without the money. Let them sort it out between them later.'

I set off for Macedo's house with a heavy heart; I knocked on his door but neither he nor his brother were there. They had gone to the beach. Should I go looking for them on the beach, or would only Luís be there, having left the house at the same time as his brother? What if I went to the boarding house where the Ramos brothers were staying? Perhaps Macedo might have dropped in there? Perhaps he was there already. And, even at the risk of confronting Ramos and Almeida, perhaps I might meet Mercedes. A wave of tenderness and longing swept over me, engulfing the unease I felt about her; it was like a silence within which all the other facts, other voices, other people, echoed randomly. It was she I wanted to meet, nobody else. She should be on the beach. When I got to the huts they were empty and the neighbours hadn't yet seen either the Ramos brothers or Mercedes and her brother. I went back up to the Bairro Novo, straight to their boarding house. The fellow on the door confirmed that they hadn't come down, they had visitors and that I could go up.

I went up, my knees knocking; shaking, I hesitated in front of the bedroom doors. That one must be hers. I knocked, my knuckles barely making a sound on the door. At the noise I glanced left and right, expecting one of the doors on either side to open suddenly. The key turned in the lock and I could see her in the narrow crack which opened up. 'You?' She seemed more beautiful than ever, with her wide-open eyes, and her half-combed hair. I pushed her inside and closed the door behind me.

'Are you crazy?' she said, but flung herself into my arms nevertheless; she seemed so vulnerable in the long nightdress she was still wearing.

Quickly she freed herself and went to lock the door. 'This is madness,' she said. 'What do you want? You should go, go quickly; somebody might knock or call me.'

I held her tightly. 'Why haven't you been down to the beach yet?' I asked in a whisper. 'Why are you still here at this time?'

She leant her head on my shoulder and passed her hand across my breast. 'There's nobody to go with,' she replied. 'Nobody went to the beach this morning.'

I lifted her head in my hands to look directly into her moist eyes. 'What's happened? Have we been found out?'

She shook her head and smiled. 'I went to the dressmaker at Buarcos the day before yesterday, and yesterday too, with one of the Silva girls. Don't get upset. What I told her was that I was going for a walk with my fiancé.' She paused then added, resting her head on my breast: 'The lies we tell for love, eh?'

She lifted her head and wrapped her arms around my neck. 'Kiss me again and then go.'

Her kiss was like some harrowing goodbye. On her lips which trembled on mine, on her tongue which moved with mine, on her whole body, tight against mine, there was a kind of incongruous chill which frightened me. 'Later,' I asked, moving my mouth away, 'are you coming?'

I felt the 'I can't' which she murmured, with her lips and tongue against mine, within my mouth rather than heard it.

'Why can't out?' I demanded.

'Because they're coming today. Is that what you want to know?'

There was a knock at the door. We kept quiet, holding each other. A voice called out 'Mercedes'. It was Almeida. 'What is it, Manuel?' she asked.

'Aren't you ready yet?' and I kissed her hair as she replied: 'Not yet.'

'Can't I come in?' he said in a low voice, close up to the door.

'No,' she replied and I held her face in my hands, looking imploringly into her troubled, clouded eyes.

'I've got to go now; I'll only be back this afternoon,' he said, as I kissed her eyes.

'At what time?' she asked in a low voice. I put my face tight against hers.

'Round about three,' he said. 'Can't I kiss you?'

Furious with me, she drew away and went to unlock the door. I grabbed her wrists but she managed to turn the key in the lock. I hid behind the door but I couldn't close my eyes to block out the sight of his arms around her, and the kiss I couldn't see.

'I'll come for you at three,' I heard him say, and she closed the door which he had pushed open as he embraced her. I heard Macedo's voice making some crack about Almeida's way with the women. When she closed the door, whispering something to him that I couldn't make out, we stood there again in silence, facing each other. 'Go now,' she said finally.

I went out. I stopped halfway through the door. 'Where are you going at three?' I enquired. 'I don't know, wherever he takes me.'

'Do you know what you are?'

She covered my mouth with her hand. 'Don't say a thing. I'm not; you know I'm not. Tomorrow I'll run away with you,' and she reached up her mouth to me.

I took my hanky out of my pocket. 'Wipe your mouth first,' I said, holding it out to her.

Her expression, tense and rueful, pierced me to the heart. But she took my hanky, wiped her lips and kissed me lightly. Then with tears in her eyes she gave me it back. I remained looking at her, and looking, too, at the hanky, white against my upraised hand.

'Keep the hanky,' said a voice at my side. It was Ramos.

She turned back into her room and shut the door. I put the hanky in my pocket. 'Have I come too early?'

'Much too early. Come here into my room.'

I went into his room; Macedo was already there. I spoke to him first. 'My uncle has got the money, I have it with me.' They looked at each other. 'But he wants you to sign a receipt.'

'Me? But wasn't it Ramos who spoke to him?'

'Yes, but this is what he's asked me to do.'

'What sort of receipt does he want? Have you brought that as well?' asked Ramos.

'Yes, I have,' I said, showing it to them. 'He drew it up.'

He read it carefully and passed it to Macedo. 'I don't think this is important. You can sign it. All the more since...' he said, his clear eyes fixing me, 'since I am leaving a letter for Captain Macedo, assuming personal responsibility for Carlos' part in all this. Sign the receipt,' he ordered Macedo.

He signed it and handed it to me. I took it and put it away; then I pulled the money from my pocket. 'Here are the million reis.'

Ramos took the notes, checked the amount and handed them to Macedo. 'Put it with the other money. The rest will be here by three. Then you can hand over half the agreed price; only half.'

'When will you be setting off?' I asked.

'We still don't know for sure,' Ramos replied before Macedo could speak. 'Perhaps tomorrow, though they need to be ready for any eventuality today, after eleven o'clock tonight. Those chaps in your house, tell them exactly that.'

'How did your uncle know I was involved?' asked Macedo. 'Did you tell him something?'

'No, I told him nothing. But he guessed something the last time he talked to you.'

He looked crestfallen but then raised an imploring look to Ramos. 'I don't know what this is all about. I've never said a thing; everybody knows I don't blab.'

Ramos smiled a wintry smile. 'For that reason it's better if we set off as soon as possible.' He sat down on the bed. 'If it's not too indiscreet can I ask how you got hold of so much money?' he said. 'To be frank with you, I'd hoped you'd pull it off, so to speak, but even so I really didn't expect you'd get the lot.'

'It's a long story; too long to tell now. But there's one thing I must warn you about: the Spaniards have now decided they don't want to go. My uncle completely lost his rag with them; he's dead keen on the idea. They want to go to Lisbon so that they can get into a part of Spain which is still in government hands through the Alentejo. My uncle almost threatened to kill them, or hand them over to the cops if they left the house and he made them promise that they would have to tell you to your face if they still refused to go. To see if they had the guts to do it.'

'But I'm not going to show my face there. It's not me that's going to get them.'

'Nor me,' said Macedo.

'So who is it? How are we to know it's not a set-up?'

'That's just what I'm going to sort out with you now,' replied Zé Ramos. 'Somebody you know – one of our group – will come to your house, with a car. But don't say anything, because I might be in the car as well. In any case, and it's no lie, they're saying that yesterday, in Oporto and here, they arrested a whole lot of people; and in Lisbon, too, it seems.'

'Spaniards?'

'Spaniards and Portuguese.'

'You're in great danger, then?'

'Yes, a lot. One of those captured in Oporto was one of our men, one of those involved in fixing up the boat.'

'What if he talks?'

'He won't; he's not like that. But one never knows.'

'I have the feeling,' said Macedo, 'that if they leant on me to speak, then I wouldn't.'

'Wouldn't it be better to bring the departure forward?' I enquired.

Just as they were exchanging glances, Ramos spoke: 'It's a possibility. Macedo,' he added, 'I need to talk in private to Jorge here.'

'Me too, but not in private,' said the other. 'It'll only take a moment.' He turned to me. 'Can you come to our house this afternoon? My father would like to talk to you about my brother.'

'At what time?'

'About three; I have to go out afterwards.'

'Couldn't it be a bit later?'

'If you want. How about six?'

'I'll be there.'

He said goodbye and left. Ramos got up, locked the door and turned to face me. 'What are you trying to do?' he demanded.

'About what?'

'Not what, whom. With my sister.'

I didn't reply but, crossing my legs, I studied my shoe intently.

'Yesterday and the day before you were with her all afternoon.'

'Did she tell you that? Did she tell you she'll be with Almeida all afternoon today?'

'I wouldn't be talking to you about this if I thought I'd have another opportunity. But I won't have one. Yes, she did tell me. This morning. I already suspected something. What I can't forgive, although it might just be one of my little quirks, is your taking her where you did.'

'Where would you like me to have taken her then? To the beach? To some field?'

He was clearly making great efforts to control himself; the muscles in his face twitching and then suddenly freezing.

'She is responsible for her own actions, isn't she?' I continued. 'In that case, it seems to me that the place doesn't matter. And she was with me alone; nobody saw her. Didn't she tell you that?'

'And what do you think you'll do?'

'Right now, I don't know.'

'If you hadn't come on the scene none of this would have happened.'

'Of course not. But neither would she have married this Almeida fellow who has found such a heroic way of wriggling out of his promise of marriage.'

'He's not wriggling out of it.'

'No? Well, why didn't they get married before the escape?'

'There wasn't enough time.'

'Exactly the same for me; I didn't have the time to spare, either.'

'You've all the time in the world in front of you. You could have waited.'

'Waited for what? For her to fall into his arms again – that is if she ever fell out of them!'

He made as if to strike me, but pulled back. I didn't move a muscle, utterly convinced as I was that he wouldn't do anything; I was sure he wanted to save something of the relationship which he sensed was crumbling within me. 'I'm absolutely certain that's not true,' he said between clenched teeth.

'I don't know how you can be; and I'm just as sure that even if it was, it isn't any longer. I heard them arrange to meet this afternoon for that very purpose.'

'How did you hear that?'

'Because I was inside her room when he came to say goodbye,' I replied, feeling that in telling him I had betrayed a deeply intimate secret, something of our own self-respect.

'Were you inside?'

'Just for a few moments when I got there. I had to speak to her; I wanted to know why she had told me yesterday that she couldn't meet me today. And after all she hadn't spoken to you at that time.'

'But she was with you instead, in the same bed,' he said, sitting on the edge of the bed, as he buried his face in his hands.

'For that very reason. And the mere fact of your being so busy and on the eve of the departure, too, that's no reason, since you can't drop the pretence you've been keeping up all this time, the pretence that it's just a normal summer holiday? You're not going to get the whole family together to say goodbye, are you?'

'Don't you understand,' he said, raising his livid face to me, 'that you've made her lose any respect she had for herself?'

'A woman giving herself up to the man she loves, or loving the man to whom she gives herself – that doesn't seem to me to be betraying that respect. Above all according to your standards.'

'It isn't; but breaking your word is.'

'What word? Her commitment to marry Almeida, the man who deflowered her?'

'Her previous commitment not to give herself again to anyone, not even to him.'

'Who did she promise this to? To you?'

'No, to herself.'

'But she didn't just give herself to anyone, rather to someone who really loved her. Otherwise she wouldn't have given herself. Sometimes we realise that it was a mistake to give our word, no, not a mistake but a promise made heedless of everything else. That was what happened to us when we met and if you hadn't told me what you did about what had happened to her I wouldn't have demanded what I did. Because it was me who demanded it, me. And she agreed and went with me.'

'You mean that she only gave in at your urging.'

'But I couldn't have made her do my bidding if I hadn't loved her and she wouldn't have given in if she hadn't loved me more than a whole raft of promises.'

'Do you know what she told me?'

'No.'

'That if, out of love for you she had broken her own word and also the commitment she gave to Almeida, she no longer has the right to refuse him when he leaves for good.'

It was what I had feared all along, what I had not allowed myself to admit. I realised this was not truly news to me and that, from the first, I had felt that dilemma. But if that dilemma did exist it was because her love for me was not so strong that it overwhelmed all the other considerations which were tearing her apart. I was seized by a loathing for her, I wanted an end to it all, I wanted to be rid of her; but in that very moment the fear of losing her assailed me, the terror of losing that love of hers which meant everything to me. Let the devil take whatever he wished, all the apprehensions, all the jealousy, all the words spent on her account. I wanted her no matter what the price. But instead I put on a show of defiance. 'And what do you think of it all?' I asked.

'I think it's their problem,' he said, lowering his eyes.

'And mine, isn't it my problem, too?'

'Yes, yours too.'

'And yours, and this whole thing's as well, don't you think? Isn't it the case that you're afraid that Almeida, if she betrays him, will betray you all at the last minute?'

'What do you want me to do?' he asked after a short pause.

'I want you to stop them from making a mistake, from making a mistake that could destroy her, because, if she goes with him today and she doesn't come to me, that's the end of it. And neither you nor he will be here to save her, if it comes to that.'

'Save her from what?'

'From losing the respect and love of the only person she's got and to whom she is bound. The only person left. Me.'

'Are you asking me to go telling tales on my sister to you?'

'No. We are talking like men who haven't hidden anything from a woman who is, forgive me, the lover of one and the brother of the other. But I don't want your sister as my lover; I want her to be my wife and I can't accept that, after having been mine, and before she becomes my wife, she should be somebody else's. If she doesn't understand that you have to stop her.'

'How?'

'I don't know how you lead your life; you're the one who knows what you can do. As for me, I'll be here at the door at three o'clock.'

'What if I don't do anything?'

'If you don't do anything and if I can't do anything … I don't know ... but I won't consider myself bound to your sister, although I still love her just as much.'

'How can you... When this afternoon they go out...'

'Whatever happens then will depend on the circumstances.'

I got up and went towards the door; he followed me. 'Look, Ramos, if I don't see you again,' I said, standing by the open door, 'I hope everything goes well.' And I reached out my hand to him.

He took it. 'I would very much like you to...'

'Yes?'

'You to...'

The Teutonic bearing, very upright, which he, involuntarily or reluctantly, assumed on formal occasions, dissolved and he gripped my hand tighter. 'Without you what will happen to Mercedes?'

'She has her parents.'

'Parents ... at times like these what use are parents to us?'

I was taken aback, remembering the closeness that was evident between him and his parents, although Mercedes' father was only his stepfather. But I remembered, too, that his father was, within the family, like a spiritual stepfather to her, and to him as well, in the way that those who don't have parents fool themselves into believing they might one day have them. I realised this in a split second and returned his handshake, gripping his hand as tightly as he had mine; I said no more except to wish him '*bon voyage*', without looking at him.

In the street I wasn't sure where I should be heading. I realised, though, that my uncle was so crazy that if I was late in turning up with the receipt he was quite capable of believing that I had run off with the money. Hadn't he read in my face that I was deep in some trouble or other? And in truth that was what I should have done: run off with that money of which I had been, through Mercedes, doubly the intermediary. At that moment when I had been in her room I should have confronted her, I should have tried to convince her to run away with me. And yet, somehow belatedly as far as the opportunity was concerned, and anticipating what I, having already got rid of the money, was now thinking of, she had glimpsed the real possibility of our running away with that same money. I had only said 'tomorrow', when the money would already be gone, and, perhaps, she would also be gone as far as I was concerned. That is the way we grasp life: in terms of what it had been and what it might be. And if ever we by some chance got it right it was because we hadn't got round to doing the very thing through which that understanding had become possible. It was only when I no longer had the money in my hand that the thought of running away crossed my mind. Was that because I was honest, and because she wasn't 'mine'? But did that money belong to 'somebody'? Was it because in truth I didn't really want to run away with her, and so I had an excuse, as far as the flight was concerned, now that I no longer had the means to accomplish it?

But what would we need the money for? To go off somewhere, to set ourselves up there, wherever it might be? Did I not need, even there in Figueira, some money to pay for a place where we could sleep together? Without money even that was out of the question. Either that or we, bound by habit to money, didn't know what to do without it. Everything could be bought or sold, and there were extremely ingenious ways of buying and selling that which would be shameful if they were obtained or bought with money. To what extent had we, I, Mercedes, Ramos, Rodrigues, my aunt and uncle, Almeida, the two Spaniards, the Macedo brothers, the one who had allowed the use of his boat, and my uncle's mother-in-law, all of us, been bought or sold in the same measure that we had been buying and selling? To the extent that we could not know clearly how such an extremely complicated chain of interlocking relationships, of which some of the major actors themselves were unaware, had been formed. But this train of thought was an attempt to banish certain images which were filling my spirit with dread: Mercedes, at the door of her bedroom, in her nightdress, looking at me and wiping her lips with my hanky, Almeida's arms on her back and around her waist; Rodrigues at the foot of the tree, steadying himself on one leg as he slipped into his shoes; the two Spaniards staring at my uncle as he forced them on towards that venture; my aunt, motionless, silhouetted in the window; an old hag with the same features as the woman who owned the house and of that whore who had made a beeline for me on the night of the bacchanal, slavering over a body which was Rodrigues; Matos, Oliveira, and a great square, lit by car headlights, in which a boy was kneeling by the side of an old man, stretched out by the edge of the waves on which the morning sun glinted, while a group of us, all naked, plunged into the waters. From all the images and the others which followed, some stood out, more absorbing because they engulfed all the others: that of Mercedes bending over my bed, with me striking out at her with my white hanky; and that of Rodrigues (as if he were my uncle, or Macedo, or Ramos, or Almeida). With him and in him I had desecrated that sense of a distant, pure adoration that I could not have in Mercedes; and in Mercedes I had possessed everything which partook simultaneously of that sense and as well of a body which I desired passionately on account of the fact that others had already possessed it. It was as if I had taken on Almeida's cock and he had stripped me of the rest.

But in truth none of this mattered. What mattered was that I should have Mercedes entirely to myself. There was no doubt that I would give up everything and everybody for that; I would welcome her into my arms even if she were coming to me from Almeida's embrace. Passion, I realised was this: at once a desperate desire for complete, exclusive possession and an acknowledgement, somewhere between desperation and bliss, that everybody identified with us. That very moment when, in our passion, we felt supremely ourselves was when everybody else was ourselves within us. But if that was how it was, if, in the complete knowledge of ourselves through our passion, we identified much less, in reality, with the object of that passion than with everybody else, who, through that object, partook of its reality – was part of it even – then the passion would annihilate itself, or we ourselves would annihilate ourselves, and everyone else, within it.

I felt a kind of vertigo; immediately I realised we ourselves invented this passion. Mercedes was becoming, in my life, a 'femme fatale', but the one who had created her in that image, and the fatal quality which overwhelmed and distorted everything, was I myself. If I were to lose her I would look for her in every woman; if I finally won her I would lose her within me. When I had bent the image of me to fit the image that she had accepted in others, and in exchange had imposed on her something more or less than my own person and my own body, I had given up any right to have her as a person, since she could not be a person within an image, any more than I could possess my own image. But who would not be, in the love of others, all the images of those that that person had ever dreamed of? Who was ever himself in the images of others? Really, was not the ideal woman or ideal man what we were looking for in others; but we even idealised ourselves, we were idealised, and given the imaginary reality of those who, if they were dreamed of, had not been possessed, or, if they had indeed been possessed, had not been dreamed of. This process of idealisation had nothing to do with purity or innocence or spontaneity; it was, on the contrary, a sum, an accumulation, a confused mixture of all the sordid matter which we did not dare dream of, in and through others, and in ourselves alongside them, even at the moment when, in an embrace, a kiss, a fool, having somebody, even though we weren't at all interested, we transformed ourselves or were transformed into what we had not even managed to be, personally and in the imagination of the one to whom we had given ourselves. We were in that case no more than a string of alien moments, alien experiences, to which we submitted ourselves, overwhelmed, so that we might be ourselves in somebody else. And, with all this doleful knowledge, which only overshadowed my determination not to let go of Mercedes, whatever the price I had to pay, I went on into the house.

XXIII

At lunch I handed the receipt over to my uncle; he scrutinised it carefully as though making sure that it was the same one that he had written. I passed on, too, the message from Ramos, that the departure was imminent and that they should be ready to go when the car, whose driver I would recognise, came, even if Ramos himself wasn't in it. Everybody seemed much less forthcoming, so that the atmosphere was quite unlike the carefree one which had prevailed at breakfast. But I wasn't prepared to let other people's worries affect me any longer; when all was said and done I had enough on my plate with my own, which were, in any case, inextricably mixed up in all this. I escaped as quickly as I could, without saying anything else, and went up to my room. But almost immediately it occurred to me that Mercedes and Almeida might leave earlier than originally agreed and I rushed out into the street, virtually running, and headed for the Bairro Novo. What should I do? Should I go in or wait at the boarding house door? Should I wait around some distance away, where nobody could see me from the door? Would they come out together, or first one, followed by the other? Should I accost Mercedes directly or should I follow them? What would be the best, most decisive course of action? But what if they didn't come out? But in the boarding house there would be no chance of anything like that for they would be forced to be discreet there; the most they could do would be what they had already done that morning. Clearly, they would go out; if they didn't it would mean that nothing had happened. And later? They might delay things until I had grown tired of waiting and then go out. Was I going to stand guard out there all afternoon? One never knew: Ramos might be in league with them, or they in league with each other against Ramos and me.

Was what I was feeling jealousy? If I suspected her of complete duplicity – and I had every reason to – it was jealousy. But was it really? Or was I taking advantage of jealousy and wounded *amour-propre* to avoid my responsibilities towards a girl whom I had not scrupled – because I knew she belonged to another – to make mine? But she had been the one who had given herself to me; when she had hauled me off to the terrace at the end of the beach, making

me the one who was in her everything that I and many others had
been (the man whom she really loved), and that she was, in me,
the woman who was desired in all the rest. I had not won her heart
at that moment, nor afterwards when I had made her give me what
she had already given to the other. If she had come to me she had
come of her own accord; I had not gone to fetch her, nor drag her
along by the arm. Or I had not taken her with me the second time.
What had happened, surely, was that she had realised, seeing me,
that in truth she didn't care for the other, or didn't care for him as
much as she had imagined, or that she had wished that her first lover
had been me rather than him. But she had given in to my urging,
who knows, because seeing me had awakened in her the desire for
an intimacy from which she had refrained since she had first been
intimate with him; and from that memory, her thwarted pleasure
had been transformed into the prospect where now she could get
it from someone who had been but indirectly, in the imagination,
one of the potential agents of the pleasure which she had not felt
at that time.

I could not, however, doubt her love for me; I just could not.
Everything that had taken place between us on those two afternoons
on which she had been mine would not have taken place in such
a way if I had been merely the instrument of a displaced desire or
of some dirty little adventure. She had been mine in every way;
mine to a degree in which possession was mutual, and if I, being
inside her, my arms around her, covering her body with my own,
had held her body down with my own weight and strength, she,
in responding to my embrace and accepting my flesh inside her,
had involved me completely in her. When lovers are said to be
entwined, that's exactly what the expression means: a penetration
that is a reciprocal involvement, a bond which we had tied with
our own flesh, and not one in which one binds the other but one
in which we are each bound to the other.

Yes, certainly it was jealousy that I felt, a very special jealousy,
however, special in the way that our situation had become special.
For it was less a fury that she was at risk of belonging to him whom
I had replaced in her than the despair of feeling that I hadn't replaced
him so completely that he might vanish into thin air like smoke.
Yes, despair, more than any possible shared possession, more than
being equalled, or on a par with, in our rights, in the imagination
which would grant the possession. In the passion which had
overtaken me I understood that it was this parity, this confrontation,

which was the source of my humiliation. It wasn't a physical humiliation, appearing to be unable, physically, to eradicate him, once I had obtained her assent and an entry, and yet another entry, which was sufficient to safeguard my physical pride. But what was humiliating me was what had humiliated our love itself, which was not so powerful as to allow the deception which we had been forced to adopt. Behind that door I had behaved like a fugitive lover hiding from the husband who has arrived at an inopportune moment, so that he, had I revealed myself at her side, would have been forced to recognise that he was, not so much a furtive lover as a rejected husband or a lover finally cast aside. In not revealing myself I had not compromised her dignity in front of him, nor the plan in which, whether we knew it or not, so many lives were reciprocally linked. But I had, before myself and before her, too, compromised the dignity of the love that was ours. It was a love which not only accepted that it had to hide itself away from others: in this we would not have, even if there had been no 'other', much choice (although it had happened like that precisely because of the existence of this other one); it also accepted the need for deception (and who had been precisely the agent from which it, like love, and like possession, had received the freedom which sanctioned it). And a love which thus accepts the need to deceive the one on whom it depends is a love which is in thrall to deception, which consents to deceive its very self. I didn't love her any the less, nor desire her less; on the contrary, I wanted her more than ever. But I loved her like someone in love with the idea of catastrophe, and she, when the other was no longer there to deceive, would love in me the catastrophe that the other one had not been. She would deceive me, too, without even wanting to or realising it, with the empty space that I had left, behind a door which had concealed me, when the door would close on our intimacy, and we would be alone with our bodies; or, worse still, with the fact that we had forgotten just how much, with a door between us, or a hanky proffered to clean her lips, we had both suffered and how we had been cut to the core, to where even the thrill of physical possession does not reach, however all-embracing it might be, unless there be not, in these distant channels of memory, the traces of an offence, within which love debates and moves, prisoner of the little pricks which tear it and which it ignores so that it can live with itself – in order to resist, in order to be accepted as love. But I wanted Mercedes. I saw Almeida going towards the boarding house door and I crossed the street towards him so that when he did see me and recognise me I would be already in front of him, blocking his way. He gave a start and then recognised me; then after greeting me he looked around him instinctively to see if he was being tailed or whether anybody was expecting him.

'Can I have a word with you?' I asked, addressing him formally.

'Right now?'

'Yes, now.'

There we were, facing each other, as if he were expecting me to speak right there. He was, too. 'We can talk here in the entrance,' I said and he went towards the foyer.

We sat down. 'I am your fiancée's lover,' I said without further ado.

He got up abruptly and then fell back into his chair, looking at me like some half-wit, unable to believe what he had heard. I watched him (and I felt a great, cold calmness, or only the trembling, attentive anxiety of a small boy pulling the wings off flies) and saw the fine, smooth skin of his strained face, the confident eyes of the lady-killer, bright and a little weary, blinking uncertainly, the long, broad hands which were still upraised, holding the sides of the chair into which he had fallen.

'I am Mercedes' lover,' I said again. 'She is mine, she belongs to me. Leave her alone. You're not going to marry her,' I said, getting up and standing in front of him. 'You had all the time you needed to marry her. Now she's mine. Mine. Just ask her where she was yesterday and the day before yesterday, in the afternoon.' He tried to get up but it didn't need much force to make him sit down again. 'You have no claim on her; what happened between you is over. You are going to disappear from her life because today or tomorrow you are leaving and you don't know if you'll return. She doesn't love you, she doesn't want you. Let her go for good.'

He suddenly sprang from his chair and aimed a blow at me; when I recovered from my surprise he was running up the stairs to the bedrooms. I ran up after him with a guest and a waiter at my heels. He stopped in the corridor and saw them. He stared at me furiously. 'Shit … scum…' he hissed, banging on the door of Ramos' room.

I turned to the two who were coming after me. 'It's nothing,' I said. 'Leave us alone.'

But they grabbed me and tried to drag me off downstairs. Ramos poked his head out of the door and saw Almeida there and the scene at the end of the corridor.

'Let that gentleman go,' he ordered. Uncertain, they released me. 'Would you be kind enough to go back downstairs,' he added, 'this is a private matter.' They hesitated before going down.

'Is it true?' Almeida asked him.

Ramos lowered his gaze. 'Yes, it is.'

'Did you know about it?'

'Yes, I did; I found out yesterday.'

'Why didn't you tell me?'

'Because I didn't want you to have to deal with such a rotten thing practically on the eve of our departure.'

'Do you find it acceptable?'

'Acceptable or not, it happened.'

It all seemed to happen in a flash; they were like actors rehearsing a dialogue in a play, still quite matter of fact, without much expression. It is a truism that something like that never comes out properly in real life, like a play which hasn't been rehearsed, or when one actor doesn't know his lines and brings everybody else down to his level. On some impulse I knocked on Mercedes' door. She emerged, though, from her parents' bedroom.

When I saw her behind them, as they half turned towards her, and myself before all three of them, I felt an exquisite pain encompassing the futility of the whole thing, an emptiness which made my head spin, and they, there in the vague light of the corridor, almost disappearing like ghosts, leaving me in a dreadful, serene solitude. She made as if to come towards me and they began automatically to move out of her way to let her pass. The pain I felt, spreading throughout my whole body (much more than merely in my grievous imagination), increased and deepened into a sudden pounding which contrasted with the peace which, along with the pain, flowed through me side by side wherever she happened go. I didn't move a muscle. I believe that even if I had tried I wouldn't have been able to. Mercedes looked at me for a long time but only after she had looked again at the other two. I looked at her unblinking, deeply, intently, conscious that within me I felt no passion at all, rather an emptiness which horrified me, all the more so because of the passion concentrated in my gaze. Then, turning my back on her, I went towards the stairs and slowly descended them. I don't know whether or not I felt their eyes fixed on my back; even less do I know whether she called me by my name. Perhaps, going down the steps, I wanted, in spite of the cold void I felt within me, to hear her call me. I want to believe, though, that there was a call and I did hear it. But I went out into the street with the same slow step with which I carried on walking away from them.

In the street it seemed to me that the brightness of the sun was much more intense than could simply be explained by my coming out of the shadows into the light. A naked morning clarity picked out the surfaces and the shadows starkly just as it also flattened everything into two dimensions. Few people ventured out of the shade and they went around as if carrying an aura of silence with them. I stopped on the corner, trying to make out if it was just me not being able to see clearly around me, whether it was this which was making me lose my sense of material reality. Above the indistinct concert of voices I could hear a distant echo; I had never realised before that one could hear the sea from there. To be precise, I had only ever assumed that one couldn't hear it. I carried on towards the beach, where few of the bathing huts had been erected and their struts and crosspieces, like the struts of the canopies waiting to be fitted together, stood out tiny and black, like spent matches strewn over the whiteness of a sheet. Out there the sea was white, too, broken by sudden, dark streaks. Gradually, borne along by the airy distance which seemed to be accompanying me, I reached the terraces at the end of the beach and made my way along them, one by one. As my gaze rested on the mouth of the river I was seized by an agony: which was the terrace – I couldn't recognise any of them – where I had been with Mercedes? I had passed it without knowing which one it was. I retraced my steps, slowly, as my feet were weighed down with weariness. But my memory refused utterly to recall where I had been with her. My response was to go up and down in desperation from one terrace to the other. Was it this one? Or those rails? On that bench? Against that wall? On the other? Or yet another? It was as if there were so many of them, all alike. I sat down on one of the benches and leaned my head against the wall. The blinding white around me made me close my eyes; it was only much later that I moved from that spot.

XXIV

When I awoke from what one could not really call sleep, the white of the day had turned a murky, tinny colour and the horizon across the sea was a black mass in which the sea and the sky were separated by a silvery line. I leant over the balustrade, watching the motion of the dull, greasy water and went down to the beach which was deserted as if summer had already ended. I wandered along the sea wall, my eyes absently fixed on a virtual image of my own footsteps. I wasn't thinking of anything or anyone. A complete emptiness, a great peace, at the same time vacant and a little tremulous, overcame me. The beach on my left ran away behind me in a slow, swaying motion in which abandoned boats bobbed and the odd figure stood out black and tiny. Then the beach disappeared and I was walking among houses with closed windows which would suddenly open and then close again. A yellow dog suddenly appeared on a corner and stopped to eye me suspiciously. As I passed by it snarled. I turned the corner and stopped at the door of the house; I knocked. The dog came and sat down behind me. The door opened and the old woman's head poked out. Hearing her speak with a voice that seemed to come from within her pointed chin, I realised where I was and that there was nothing I wanted or expected there. There was surprise in her voice and affability also, a saccharine affability. I hadn't told her, what was I doing there? Anyway, I was to come in, come in, wait a moment, everything could be sorted out. I don't know how but I found myself in the kitchen, sitting on a bench; and on the other side of the deal table a boy with dark features was looking at me intently while he ate slices of smoked sausage and bread. The bread, the sausage and the knife he was using, all danced from the table into his hands and his hands to the table as they conveyed the pieces, all together, to his mouth and he crammed them into his mouth, chewing all the while. Long black locks tumbled down from his head, and his eyes, as if they did not belong in that face which was so intent on its food, continued to stare at me, now calmly, now with a slight air of understanding which began to disturb me as soon as I noticed his eyes fixed on me repugnantly.

The old woman asked if I wanted anything to eat and apologised for his being such a lout, eating without offering me anything. He grinned and shrugged but then reached out his hands, bread in one, sausage in the other. I said I didn't want anything. He shrugged again and resumed his eating, ostentatiously, without looking at me as if I had just vanished, while I, unsure of what I was doing there, had the feeling that I wasn't really there.

'Don't hang about,' said the old woman, bringing me back to where I was, 'the gentleman can have a room already and wait there. Don't pay any attention to this good-for-nothing. I don't even know why I open the door to him and let him eat. If it wasn't for the good offices of my nephew I'd be on my uppers...'

He winked at me, stopped eating and pushed the knife and the food away from him.

'You poor thing,' he said, 'you don't know why you open the door to me and let me eat. It's the business I bring you, isn't it, Auntie Mariana?' And he stretched out obscenely on the bench, bending forward and then leaning back against the wall.

'Only the best,' stretching again, 'when I'm not here on duty, waiting for the customers who're counting on me, eh, Auntie Mariana?'

'Shut up, you devil! What kind of a house is this gentleman going to think my house is? If it wasn't for my nephew...'

'Now, now... If this gentleman comes here he knows perfectly well what kind of a house this is... And this story about your nephew already stinks to high heaven. Does the gentleman know who your nephew is? I'm your nephew.'

The old lady, with her hands resting on the table, bent over me, as if trying to put herself between me and what he was saying.

'Don't believe this layabout, sir. I curse the moment I let him into this house for the first time. My nephew is a respectable young man.'

'I'm a respectable young man. Don't you think I'm a respectable young man, sir?'

I didn't say anything.

'Be off with you, damn you,' said the old woman. 'You've nothing to do with this place. Thank goodness we'll be seeing the back of you today; you might get killed which is what you deserve.'

'Oh, Auntie Mariana, you know very well that nobody has ever seen my back. It's me who's seen the backs of so many people' – and he laughed – 'and as far as getting killed is concerned' – and he hesitated suddenly – 'as for that, life is short enough and nothing ventured, nothing gained.'

The old lady who was standing next to the chimney wiped away a tear with the corner of her apron. He put his arms around her.

'Go on, that's enough; you're just worried about me. If you're afraid, buy a dog.'

She began to weep uncontrollably. 'I'd rather you were dead than mixed up in all this... No... No... If I lose you I've nobody else... Ah... Ah... Don't leave me... But be off now and may God go with you and make you a man...' And she freed herself from him and sat down sighing at the edge of the chimney beside a small heater which had gone out.

'He's already done that,' said the boy standing in front of her with his back to me. 'I don't need tears, I just need some wine to swill down the bread and sausage I've eaten. Come on, get me a glass of wine.'

'A glass?' she demanded, raising her head to him. 'There's no wine in this house.'

'Go and get the bottle you've hidden under the bed, go on. And then the gentleman can have a drop, too.'

'I haven't got any bottle,' she murmured, lowering her head.

'Of course you have. Under the bed. For when you want to let your hair down, have a glass or two. Go and get it.'

She got up, resting her hands on her knees, extremely feeble.

'It's only for when I don't feel too good.'

'Sure it is. And now, what with all this commotion you're not feeling too good. Go and get the wine.'

She went out, sighing and gulping sharply for breath.

The boy turned to me: 'Are you waiting for your girl, sir?' he asked, his hands in his pockets.

I looked at him without replying and at the same moment I felt a sharp pang of frustration through my whole body.

'Don't take it amiss, sir, but she's a bonny little thing, your girl. She's class, you can see that at once. I know where she lives.' And he rocked back on his heels.

The old woman returned with the bottle, sighing no longer. She took two glasses from the cupboard and set them on the table beside the bottle.

'Get yourself a glass, too, there's nothing to be ashamed of,' said the boy.

'I don't want any.'

'For someone who doesn't want any there's quite a lot here,' he said and poured the wine into the two glasses, holding out one to me and picking up the other. 'Drink it, it's one of the best. Well, here's health,' and he drained it.

I sat there with my glass in my hand. Suddenly I raised it. 'Here's to your journey,' I said.

He, his empty glass still in his hand, looked at me slowly. 'Sure ... but who told you I was going anywhere?' he added.

'You did, and your aunt, as well.'

'It was us as told you?'

'Yes.'

'You listening, aunt? So people are talking about the trip then? I don't think you heard aright, sir.'

'No, I hear things very well.'

He came close to me. 'You didn't hear nothing, sir... If you heard anything, sir, or said anything about it... '

I pushed him lightly away from me.

'So, what will happen?'

'Take no notice of him, sir,' the old woman interrupted, 'he's just a poor devil, he wouldn't harm a flea…'

'Oh wouldn't I … the girl's parents might just get to know what's happening…'

The door of the bedroom opened and the door onto the street, too, so that the old woman hesitated between going out to the corridor and leaving us alone. Her hesitation left enough time for some light footsteps to approach the kitchen door; from an indistinct shape came a wavering, fluting voice: 'Goodbye, Auntie Mariana. Oh…' It was Rufininho leaning in the doorway.

'I'm sorry if I'm disturbing you,' he said, looking at us one by one. His gaze rested on me particularly. 'Are you waiting for anybody?'

'Not for you,' I said, pushing him to one side.

'I can believe you… Oh, Alberto, are you going to let him treat me like this?'

I could see that the boy, even with his back to me, was put out by Rufininho's intervention. I was going out into the corridor followed by the old woman when there came a burst of sharp laughter from the kitchen.

'Wait, sir,' said the old woman to me at the door, holding me back. 'Don't take any notice… What if the girl comes?'

'She's not coming,' I said.

'Not coming? So what do you want here, sir?'

'I want her to come,' I said, looking at her, and I went out to the street.

I wandered slowly through the narrow streets to the Bairro Novo. When would this ball of string which was endlessly involving more people in the events surrounding my life stop unravelling? Did all those people who crossed my path, cross it because they were already mixed up in things, or were they mixed up in things because they'd strayed into the chain of events, each one of which gave rise to others which, in turn, were linked to some previous events or perhaps to all of them? Weren't there others who stood outside all this? Would all my life be of necessity made up of people who were involved or those I had involved in it; or in things that weren't even part of it? Would I always have to be liable to the invasion of people and things which belonged to something which was part of it only through some mere chance? When would this dance end, a dance in which couples entered and left only to form other couples from among the same people? Or brought with them newcomers whom I didn't know yet were part of it even before they knew me? If I were to cross the street and ask the old fellow sitting over there by his door for a light, would he too be involved and would he recognise me?

Figueira was such a small place where all the threads of a skein crossed each other. But I wasn't from Figueira. It had to be one of two things: either a Figueira always crystallised around any person, as soon as that person began to act on his own account (which immediately involved him in the affairs of others), or chance was making me into some sort of catalyst who couldn't take a single step, or see anyone, or speak to anyone without unleashing a range of reactions merely by his presence, reactions which awaited only this presence for them to take place. Not, though, any old reaction, but only those which, of all those which might occur in the most unforeseen combinations, contained elements common to the reactions in which the catalyst had already had a hand. Was this happening through the select powers of this catalyst which was me, or would the same thing happen with anyone else whom chance might launch into the heart of those volatile compounds? This same doubt led me back to the thought that when a place was as small as it was, or however big it was, it closed in around someone, as if the scale of people was what determined whether Figueira chose to close in around someone. In truth, I had caused everything to happen that had happened to me or had discovered that it was happening; everything had flowed from conditions and circumstances which had preceded me. People hadn't been born at the moment I or anyone else needed them; and the need which they fulfilled had depended strictly on what they had been and done up until then. But did they continue to be the same as before? Was I the same person who had arrived in Figueira to spend my holidays? What had really happened? Did people change because accidental circumstances changed them, or did these accidents merely permit them to behave as they really were, something they could not previously have done.

At a given moment might this happen to everybody, or would it be the case that, out of the whole lot, the range of possibilities was focused on a mere half dozen, or even several dozen people, who, quite suddenly, entered a frenetic dance to the sound of an orchestra comprising not just them? How many of these dances were there each time, though? One, into which a group entered, or a number of them, which each dancer saw as his turn to dance with everybody? If that were so, then in any of the cases there would always be contiguous groups, and yet others contiguous to these, multiplying as far as the horizon; and not only as far as the horizon in space, but as far as that in time also. My friends and acquaintances, their friends and acquaintances, and so on in succession, in a proliferation which embraced the whole of humanity, would make up both successive and simultaneous groups. Yet what would happen on their account would result just as much from the entry of a new dancer or catalyst, who would bring with him all the virtual realities of the past and future, just as these virtual realities would so to speak be picked up on contact with the group and become that which the group itself gave rise to. It was as if everybody in the world were at once alone and yet in bad company: in bad company because no event could be foreseen, other than through some glass darkly, and then after the process was already underway, bearing us off in some new direction, it would be no less of an alien past which had become ours through our participation in it. Ours, but how?

I halted, feeling once again the sharp stab of pain at the base of my head, and at the base of my sex as if it were part of my head. I had had Mercedes and lost her. But had I lost her in having her, or had I had her because before that she was lost to me? Had I genuinely once thought of marrying her? Did I want to possess her through love and through feeling her love for me, or because I had seen her, with all the preconceptions of the world in which I lived, as available? And she, giving herself to me, loving me in fact, had she wanted to destroy in herself the very love she had for me, the love she didn't know she had? Or did she know? Or was she capable of loving two men at the same time, loving them both intensely, though not in the same way?

And then it was that I understood, or imagined I was beginning to understand something terrible: we were living, without noticing it until the decisive moment (which perhaps we ourselves provoked *in order to know*), in various tiny Figueiras. Some lay latent deep within us, others were more on the surface (and, for anyone who as yet had no experience of life, the ones on the surface were the only one, quite simple and limited). In each of them it is possible to be in love with a person, for reasons specific to that little world; it is even possible to give ourselves totally to this person. But then suddenly we change our tiny world. And in this other one we can once again give ourselves to another person, with the same or even greater passion. But these two tiny worlds, within us and outside of us, being different, coexist in space and time, although with a different set of persons. And, without ceasing to be different worlds, they come abruptly together, or the people, in them and in us, change worlds all of a sudden, because the excessive contiguity which we grant them allows (or forces) them to move. In the moment when this happens (and sometimes when other little worlds in which we were living without realising it, or without being really aware of it, become apparent), being faithful to one world is to betray the other; or it is so even in the very world to which it applies because the cause or person or object, through whom the betrayal takes place, has moved precisely from one world to the other, and has reached what would be fidelity if this world to which he has come were the other to which he belonged. When this happens we have already lost what we have gained and have only gained that which we have already lost.

Yet, I wondered, if that's the way it is, would there be anything we didn't lose except what we hadn't gained? What sense would love have then? Did I not love Mercedes? Or had I not loved her? Or was I going only to love her now, always looking over my shoulder? I did love her, I loved her so much, I had never loved anybody like that, and I would never love anybody in the same way or so much as I had loved her so swiftly yet so intensely in those few days. Love was something which had nothing really to do with all that I had understood or thought I had understood, or in effect feared to understand. Or had it, insofar as it sought to be, in us, the negation of that total mobility in which everything dissolved and came together again. Love was, in us the desperate attempt to eliminate from the possible outcomes the other world which existed alongside the one in which for that instant we might wish to inhabit. And it could only be, after all, a kind of fetter, welded to our feet, with which we bound ourselves to a world which would disappear (in order to preserve it), without our being able to hold onto it, and only managing to delay our passage from one world to another to which this love did not belong, and managing to overturn, in the other world, the order and the peace which this order would provide.

It wasn't the case that we might possess a person totally, and that she might not give herself to us totally. This totality only applied in the world where it was; in another it was incomplete or didn't make sense. No world, however, of these tiny, latent or surface worlds, which coexisted in us, was what our consciousness or being said it was. They were all made up of various consciousnesses or beings. And our possible consciousness from among the living beings was fleetingly made up of little bits of these sets that we formed. Love, like a passion for politics, like indifference even, or wickedness, all these were an attempt to merge consciousnesses without having to leave them; and therefore they lived on beyond the death which injured them, so that each time, having changed our world, all the reasons for being were lost in relation to the original terms. I might be able to have Mercedes again; I might even want to have her. I might be able to love her more each time. She might be able to want me as she had never wanted anyone. She might feel she wanted to give herself to me totally. She might be able to love me more and more, even loving, in another place of things and awareness, another person. Our union might be more intimate, more complete, deeper than it had ever been. And yet, in the moment in which this might happen, might continue to happen, even, our love would not exist, dead already before it could become the great love which it was ready to be.

I lifted my eyes, not only within me, but from the street itself and saw Mercedes before me. My first impression was of unreality, absurdity, that she was just an apparition that my own ideas had created and summoned up, that she wasn't really there. But it was her; she spoke:

'Where have you been?'

'Here and there.'

'Where are you going?'

'Macedo's house.'

'Why didn't you wait for me?'

'What for?'

I continued walking with her now by my side. She reached for my hand and grasped it.

'Why do people wait for each other?' she asked, her hand still in mine.

'I don't know.'

'You don't know, or you don't want to know?'

'It doesn't make any difference.'

'You're wrong. Have you thought that what one wants could be the same as what the other person wants?'

'The same as what the other person wants, how?' I said, suddenly fearing that I had fallen into a dialogue that I felt I didn't relish.

'Sometimes we want what the other wants and at other times we want them to want what we want.'

'Did you ever want what I wanted to be what you wanted?'

'Yes, always. All the more since I have been yours,' and she held my hand more tightly.

'But it didn't amount to much, did it?... Or was I to blame?'

'Only you, darling.'

I snatched my hand away violently: 'On top of everything else?'

'On top of what?' she asked, her eyes moist and full of astonishment.

'Of everything else that's happened today.'

'But everything that happened today, my love, it was you who caused it.'

'Me? So it was me too who embraced you when I was behind the door?'

'But you chose to be behind the door.'

'Are you trying to say I shouldn't have hidden there? Or that I shouldn't even have been there? Or that, subsequently, I shouldn't have turned up to stop you giving yourself by way of farewell to a man to whom you no longer belonged?' I said, feeling the uselessness of what I was saying, the complete lack of sense of all this, put in that way.

'You don't understand anything,' she said, her eyes downcast.

'What don't I understand?'

'All of it.'

'All what? What's all this about you that I don't understand? What more is there to understand?'

She was silent for a moment.

'Don't you want to love me?' she said after a moment.

'In what way?'

'So you do, then?'

It was my turn to lower my eyes.

'I don't know.'

'And when will you know?'

'Why? Are you in a hurry? Can't you wait? Is there someone else awaiting his turn and might I miss my chance between tonight when one's out of the way and tomorrow when the absent one will be me?'

She looked at me, her eyes cold and furious, raised her hand and struck me.

'Are you satisfied?'

'Are you?'

'Goodbye,' and I set off, quickening my pace, leaving her with her hand still in the air.

She ran a little, quickening her pace also until she was at my side.

'You won't be free of me.'

'I know very well I won't.'

'I'm sorry, I didn't mean that.'

'There's a great deal you didn't mean to do or say but you did it and said it.'

She gripped my arm abruptly; I tried to shake her off but she forced me to stop.

'But not to be yours.'

'Are you sure?'

'Yes, completely sure.'

'But it was me who made you.'

'Yes, but I did everything to make it possible, didn't I?'

'So why am I to blame?'

'Why are you asking so many questions?'

'Didn't you say the blame was mine alone?'

'What does that matter? Have you got tired of me so soon?'

'There wouldn't be anything odd about that. Don't you think that there are a lot of us mixed up in this? After all when I go to bed with you I don't know for sure how many others are with us in the same bed.'

'Are you crazy?'

'Haven't I enough reasons to be?'

'And me? Do you ever by chance spare me a thought?'

'I don't think of anything else but you.'

'Do you really want me to leave you?'

'That's up to you. Only you know.'

'Me?'

'Or we two, if you prefer. But it doesn't look as though we'll ever make our minds up. Perhaps we've got into the habit of having other people between us. Go and get your war council together and put it to the vote.'

'You know very well that my war council is leaving tonight if that's what you're trying to insinuate. Tomorrow I'll only have you.'

'You've still got them today, though.'

'Jorge, I don't have anybody.'

'What am I supposed to say?'

'You've got me, all of me.'

'Have I?'

'Yes, and for all time, whether you want it or not. That's why I said you'll never be free of me.'

'So then, that must be why I've gone along with all this, eh?'

'But it doesn't seem like that's got us very far, Jorge,' she said, smiling sadly, 'or why would we be arguing interminably like this? If you want to finish, we'll finish. If you want to spend your life arguing with me, we've got our whole lives for that.'

'It was you who followed me. I didn't ask you to.'

'You did. You don't do anything else but call me. And you can't imagine how unbearable it is.'

'Don't say anything, just go away, don't listen to me.'

'Listen to one thing: I could have given myself to you without loving you. And I could have afterwards, even though you bowled me over as you did, carried on though I didn't love you, continued in the same way, giving myself to you. Understand once and for all. I could even have thought that I loved you before, and then discovered that I didn't and continued to give myself to you for the pleasure you could give me, and give me not just by being a man, but by being, even beyond that, you. Understand this.'

'I do understand.'

'Then understand, too, that I loved you, and that I went on to love you more. And that this has nothing to do with any other person, or no longer has. And that it no longer has anything to do with the rage that I feel at you forcing me do something even though I wanted it and making me be yours like some woman you'd met who was just dying for it.'

'Rage?'

'Yes, rage. Enormous rage. So enormous I can't bear to see you.'

'Close your eyes then.'

'That's what I did every time you had me. And what I had to do every time I wanted to remember you and be in your arms. And when I want you to remember me and be sad because you've lost me.'

'Telepathy, eh?'

'Call it what you will.'

We stood facing each other threateningly.

'Therefore,' I said slowly, 'I've lost you because I had you and I had you by having lost you?'

'That's more or less it.'

'And also therefore, having lost you, I didn't lose you, and, having had you, I didn't have you?'

'But you can have me whenever you like.'

'In between the others?'

She looked at me defiantly.

'No. Just because I love you, the others can come between us.'

'Is that what you'll say to all of them?'

'If you leave me, yes, because I'll be needing them, so that I don't forget you. But that doesn't mean it's true or indeed that I can't bear life without you and that thinking about you isn't enough for me. After being yours in the way I was, a person can't just give it up.'

'That's what happened with me. Is that the explanation you gave to the other one?'

'You're doing everything to hurt me and all you're doing is hurting yourself. I didn't have any explanations to give about all this. And they're explanations which I will only give to you, to tell the truth. You know that's how it is. Or do you want to reduce it all to nothing?'

'I want it all to be nothing.'

'Is this the end?'

'Maybe it's just the beginning.'

We had stopped in front of Captain Macedo's door.

'Will you give me a kiss?' she asked.

We went in as far as the entrance into the shadow which covered the long staircase in darkness. I held her and kissed for a long time. It was what I wanted, to kiss her like that, without reasons or consequences, forever. Yet a kiss does not last forever, just as possession does not last forever, even though we remain within or on top of the body we have just possessed.

It was what she was thinking, too, her eyes fixed on mine for when our lips parted she said: 'I would like to stay like this forever, like this in your arms, like this with your mouth on mine, not saying a word, like this beyond everything except you. The moment we begin to talk, or when we're apart other things and other people come between us.'

'Or even we ourselves,' I said, stroking her tenderly, and she began to kiss me again, holding my head in that way she had.

Then she freed herself from my embrace.

'I shall always be yours,' she said, going out of the door, 'whenever you want, whatever happens. Don't ever forget that.'

And she was gone.

XXV

I lingered for a few moments in the entrance before beginning to climb the steep, stone stairs which led without landings right up to the Macedos' house; I had never been there before and it was only when I stopped outside the door that I remembered why they had invited me there. What would I tell them in fact? That I was going to say no, that I had really thought hard about the situation, that I would really like to be of some support to Luís in Lisbon, that I would be completely at his disposal whenever I was needed, but that I didn't want the responsibility of his living with us; and that anyway I didn't know how my parents would respond to the idea, and that in the last analysis everything depended on them, that my parents were people who, at the same time, talked a great deal about their duties and had so much work to do, with all the attendant worries and responsibilities, so that they didn't accept any… In this case they knew neither Luís nor the captain and if there was anything which frightened them it was people they didn't know, anything which might not belong to that world which they discreetly thought of as their own. The suggestion was in any case absurd; and I didn't want any greater involvement with people or things which, whatever they were, might drag out these infernal days through which I had been living. Let those days and the people who belonged to them remain in the Figueira they had made. So far, yes, I'd been mixed up in, but from now on if they wished to move down to Lisbon, to plonk down there these Figueiras of theirs, let them leave me out of it. The very idea suddenly brought to mind the image of Rodrigues crouched under the great tree in my uncle's garden before he was ignominiously sent packing; I hadn't seen him again since then. How much was I to blame for that? But had I had the time to look for him, to find out what state he was in, having been in such a state of despair even before that? It was out of the question to go and look for him today; tomorrow though it would the first thing I would do. I knocked at the door.

Standing behind the maid who opened the door was the aunt I had already met. Dry and stiff as a ramrod, she led me into a study which looked like some office in a barracks, so bare was it and such was the impersonal character of the furniture and décor; and yet it was a barracks office to which, in order to preserve some notion of conventional domesticity, as well as the grenades and little military models on the desk and drawers, had been added a large number of doilies with their crocheted edges hanging down disconsolately. She asked me to wait a little because the 'Captain' still hadn't arrived; she added that Luís was at home and would come at once. But in saying this she sat down and started to talk, offering me a chair. She was talking about my uncle, praising him, though somewhat off-handedly and with a good dose of sermonising (she referred to his gambling and salty language), when Luís came in. By her side he seemed more of a man and, realising I had always taken him for a boy, I paid more attention to him. Yet at the same time as his aunt was talking I noticed, too, how he had taken on the air of an adult, the recollection of the events in the abandoned church flitted across my mind and I had the feeling, from the vague smile that hovered on his lips, that Luís had read what I was thinking as I looked at him. Was that smile of his one of randy, adolescent connivance? Or was it, on the contrary, a shy, juvenile attempt to establish some kind of masculine fraternity in the face of that prating woman? Or was it, in another way, an uncertain and incongruous attempt to build through me a bridge to the Lisbon he so desired?

It was just this that his aunt was talking about and I could detect in those words of hers a certain bitterness towards the idea of a life at sea to which the boy stubbornly clung. She even hinted at just how far he had gone to find a course which could be found nowhere except Lisbon. The smile reappeared on Luís' lips and I couldn't help but smile too when she started to talk, though not in so many words, of Lisbon as some kind of Babylon. To me Babylon was that Figueira which she thought was the height of provincial peace, a great place in which to bring up a young boy. I happened to say that, no matter what higher course he might attend, there was no university in Figueira and a move to Lisbon, Oporto or Coimbra was inevitable. It was then I understood that as far as she was concerned there was no such thing as a higher course and that the only worthwhile career was that of arms, on dry land or at sea, according to whether one was talking about the Army or the Navy (for here the Air Force was not part of any army, but the fantasy of madmen). Now, given that these military courses in Lisbon involved living in barracks, the boys would be subject to an iron discipline which she believed was indispensable to a man's education. Luís, who had remained almost silent until then, burst out into a diatribe against the military and boarding schools in general. She cut him short harshly, declaring that what was wrong with them (meaning the two nephews) was precisely that they had never gone to a boarding school, and worst of all was that they had attended a boarding school without having been boarders themselves. In that way they had been exposed to the bad influence of the boarders with their moaning – they always moaned about the very thing that was best for them – without reaping the benefits of discipline.

I said that as far as I knew her nephews were fine boys and I didn't see why she seemed so worried about a discipline they didn't seem to lack. Luís' face lit up with satisfaction when she replied brusquely that we, boys or men, were all the same. It even seemed, if we were to believe what she was saying, that armies and their discipline had been a feminine invention, originally the mark of certain chosen Amazons among whom, at least in the mists of her own memory, she numbered herself. At bottom, this daughter of soldiers, perhaps a granddaughter of soldiers, sister of Captain Macedo, he of the military moustaches, could not forgive her nephews for wanting to follow careers which she found less manly. For her the masculine sex was neither whole nor authentic unless it was covered by a uniform. And the impression all this gave me was exactly the opposite of the image which she had of herself and which she was putting forward. For the boys the Army could only mean the ridiculous, sedentary life of their father which they associated with that loose fraternity of the elderly customs officers he commanded, who themselves were pretty thick with the smugglers and fishermen – which is what the smugglers also were or pretended to be. It could never be their purpose in life since it held no kind of fascination for them, except for the very fact that, despite her theories (which she no doubt preached at all times until they'd had as much as they could take), it was not the army. And probably she herself was getting her revenge for the fact that her brother had remained a provincial captain all his life rather than some distinguished general resplendent in his decorations.

'Your father and the captain's, was he a general?' I asked her all of a sudden.

She halted in mid flow and looked at me uneasily as if I had uttered some impertinence which had taken her unawares. And, looking down at her lap and at the same time fiddling with the pendant which hung down on her skinny breast from a gold chain she replied: 'Our father, God rest his soul, retired as a colonel.'

'Ah, colonel, that's quite something,' I said.

Her eyes gleamed. 'Much more than a lieutenant,' she said, without doubt trying to get at me by alluding to my uncle.

'A great deal more; even a captain is more than a lieutenant,' I commented, leaving her puzzled. 'Isn't Captain Macedo the commander of the Praça?'

'Praça?' she repeated.

'Yes, Praça. There at home we usually talked about my great grandfather as the "commandant of the Praça" because he was the most senior officer in his home town. Isn't the Captain the commander of the Praça in Figueira?' And I laughed to myself at the little Lisbon pun whereby the captain had been promoted to the commander of Lisbon's most famous market, the 'Praça', or 'Square'. Her head still lowered she replied that she didn't know whether he was while I saw the captain's moustaches passing for all the world like some great general through the heaps of cabbages and caged fowl. Luís was exultant, not because he got my pun, but because my sarcasm was so obvious. I realised that he detested his aunt and father equally; or at that moment he hated the latter insofar as he supported the former. This probably caused her to exhibit her hostility quite openly towards me and in which there figured a certain envy of the fact that I was from Lisbon. Such hostility made me inclined to dismiss any suggestion of a compromise in the matter for which I had gone there. Luís felt it, too, and at once intervened to stop her for now she had started to attack me with poisonous words to which I, satisfied with the response I had provoked, did not bother to listen.

'Aunt, you know very well that I want to go to the Nautical School and be an officer in the merchant navy,' he declared. 'And if you don't let me go, I'll run away and go anyway.'

I shuddered; it was as if at his words everybody and the war in Spain had come into the room, and Mercedes, too, and she was taking possession of my shaking body. That very day his brother was taking a similar step, but one so great that it could lead him to death, to prison, to who knows what.

'Be quiet,' she said, imposing her authority. 'Enough of your impertinence. Run away where? And with whose money?'

From that confused mass of people had emerged my aunt and uncles, Rodrigues, my uncle's mother-in-law, the old woman's nephew from the house of assignation, the old woman, Rufininho, a whole pandemonium.

'These boys,' she was saying, 'you should know, sir, I've been a mother to them, and all that they want is to run away from me. While their father, instead of being the father they needed, let them do what they wanted, and was more like a big brother to them, and now even he, deep down, wants them out of here so that he won't need me any more and can do what he likes.' And she began to sniffle pitifully.

That sniffling, in one who gave the impression of being a sergeant in civvies, was extremely incongruous, all the more so because it was not tears to which her grief gave rise but rather a kind of streaming cold in her head and nose. In addition she had never been close enough to me to be able to make scenes like these. It was as if I was carrying some virus which attacked people, making them assume such odd attitudes; or perhaps better, behave in keeping not with their own world but with what, without their knowing, this world had in common, through me, with other, equally stricken and crisis-ridden worlds. Faced with that spectacle from which her nephew averted his eyes in embarrassment, and with the room full of the people of my imagination who moved in time to her sniffling, I asked myself whether it was really a virus I was carrying around or whether everything was dancing, perhaps in obedience to some hidden, discordant music, which was that of the whole world through me, in that I, as I emerged from the sleep of childhood and adolescence, had discovered that life was not that conscious state that I had discovered as I felt and saw myself more and more as a man, but the intrusion of silent figures into a play which previously we imagined we could stage ourselves.

At that moment Macedo entered and I understood that the civil war, to which he and the others who were so eager to go, had not been, nor would be, anything but the terrible demonstration that everybody depended on everybody else, above all to kill and to die; and that it was not I carrying the virus but life which had reached the point where, from then on, it could not be lived other than as a fatal, malign disease, in which people used each other in order to satisfy their illusion that it was not they who were being used. I felt all this more than I could decipher for myself, and it happened very quickly although it continued in my head all the while, notwithstanding the change of scene which my friend's arrival had caused.

For there was no doubt that his entry had caused a complete change. The aunt swallowed her sobbing; Luís reverted to his role as the younger brother; and I smiled affably at the new arrival with the air of one who was making a pleasant visit to some old friends to mull over the state of the weather. Macedo apologised for his late arrival, adding that his father would not be much longer and bade me accompany him and his brother inside until their father came. The aunt stayed behind, reduced to a piece of furniture or one of the doilies which I supposed she had draped over the gleaming brass of the decorative grenades. Only much later did I learn that, on the contrary, she detested those doilies, both on account of their being so pathetically inadequate for the bellicose atmosphere which she cherished in the study and because they were votive relics of the dead sister-in-law whom she believed had, just as the doilies had for the grenades, insinuated herself into the very marrow of her nephews, coming between them and the bewitching beauty of burnished militarism.

They took me to their own study where there were tables, chairs, books, beachballs, fishing rods, and, on top of a wardrobe, model boats which I examined closely, asking if they belonged to Luís. He said they did and doubtless to escape the atmosphere that we both brought with us of his aunt's conversation whose stifling influence we still felt, busied himself in showing them to me, one by one, with clear relief at the opportunity as well as a genuine childish satisfaction in his collection. It was the fishermen who with infinite patience had made those little boats, adding the flimsy rigging (often more than the reduced scale demanded) and painting them with minute care. Behind us I could feel the older brother readying himself to ask me something. Eventually he did so.

'Did my aunt say much to you? Did she give you the full range of her grumbles? Did she bemoan the fact that everybody wants to leave and nobody wants to go to the Army school? Do you know that my grandfather never made it higher than sergeant? I suppose she told you he was a colonel? It's a lie. He was a sergeant, just as she has been all her life. My father reached the rank of captain and we were supposed to make it to colonel, and that's what she can never let us forget, the fact that we were meant to go one better, for it didn't even have to be the same person, if at least it happened from generation to generation.'

'So you're really going to make her jump for joy,' I said.

He laughed a little bitterly, and changed the subject. He gave me the impression that Luís knew what was going on, but that the matter hadn't been 'officially' discussed between them and that therefore everything which would transpire, without a word between them, as if he knew nothing. This being the case I didn't let on.

'Our aunt started off with that stuff of hers and I had to tell her that if they didn't let me go to the Nautical School in Lisbon I'd run away.'

'That's enough of this nonsense. If you want to take the course you will. If you have to go to Lisbon, you shall. Father isn't against the idea, just as he didn't oppose my going to Oporto when I could have gone to Coimbra which is nearer. The only thing is that we don't know anybody in Lisbon.'

'Nobody's going to eat me in Lisbon,' replied Luís.

'That depends. It's always better when we're in some strange place that we have someone we can rely on in case of necessity.'

That their exchange was very well rehearsed was evident in the calm way they talked. It was a formality they both went through each time the subject came up, though the pros and cons had already been thoroughly discussed and they both equally accepted them. The older, reflecting that nobody should be left on his own, feared the possibility of malign influences on his brother, while the younger, in his role of one who didn't need anyone to protect him from such things, reckoned he was sufficiently strong to resist any 'malign influences', which in any case as an officer he refused to countenance.

'I know perfectly well that father will allow you to go,' said Macedo, 'and that he won't stand in the way of a course on which you've set your heart. But he will be much easier in his mind, and I, too, obviously, if you are with someone we know and to whom you can turn if ever you need to. That's always much better than if you get help by chance, or if someone turns up who offers help but only wants to lead you astray.'

'You can't get that out of your head, can you?' said Luís. 'You seem afraid someone's going to try to deprive me of my virginity.'

'There are many ways of depriving someone of his virginity and one of them is to convince him that there's nothing wrong in doing those things we shouldn't do, given that we do them because we feel like it or, even worse, because these things don't matter, or anything else, and we can do it for a laugh, and because it doesn't mean anything as far as we're concerned, neither that nor anything else.'

'Yet, the other day, who was it who was putting forward just this same argument? Who was it who persuaded you to take part in that affair in the church?' asked Luís.

'Nobody persuaded me,' replied Macedo. "But for that very reason we shouldn't take part in things which, though we know how they start, we don't know how they end up.'

'There's nothing, though, which we know for sure how it will end up,' I said. 'Look, do you know how the Spanish Civil War is going to turn out? Does the way it will end depend on you?'

'That's different. In something like that we are helping to defend something which is worth more than us and any evil that they do to us or we do to them has only to do with this particular task that we've undertaken. And the way it turns out doesn't depend personally on any one of us. What matters is dedication and example. And even if none of this amounts to anything, at least we know that we're linked to something which is greater than us.'

'But if you reckon that the outcome doesn't depend on you and that you have no power to influence anything, how do you know you're contributing to something greater than you?' I demanded.

'Anything which isn't merely my own is greater than me; and it guarantees the integrity of my ideas and my dedication.'

'So does it, if you see that way, guarantee your personal integrity? Couldn't it just be the case that, when all is said and done, it's your contribution which is precisely what matters to you most?'

He glanced at his brother before replying.

'My personal integrity – or anybody's – is only not vouched for if I remain closed within myself and in the lives of only those whom I know and mix with – if I'm on my own.'

'Yet,' I said, 'if you're so afraid of being on your own, or of anyone else being on his own, why is it that in some things you're worried about people falling into bad company and, in others, you reckon that your salvation doesn't depend on such company?'

'When did I say that?' he exclaimed.

'That's how I understood it,' I replied.

'But it's not like that. On my own I run every kind of risk; with somebody else I can judge better what I should do or not do.'

'And if you're mixed up in bad company?'

'I can't be in bad company, though, if I'm with those who think the same way as I do.'

'And so you won't be in bad company either, then, if you let yourself be dragged off by someone into a life which you yourself, in all conscience, might think is wrong and which threatens your integrity. For the rest' – and I shot a knowing glance at Luís – 'is it ever the case, other than in exceptional circumstances, that anyone is dragged into something which, at bottom, he doesn't want to do, with all his usual defences in disarray?'

'No.'

'No, meaning what?'

'That evil is something outside of us against which we fight.'

'And it isn't anything within us that we have to defend ourselves against?'

'That's another kind of evil.'

'How so?'

'Because evil isn't some abstract entity which becomes incarnate in us.'

'So then it doesn't become incarnate either in the other one whose evil influence you really fear, in certain cases.'

'Can't you see, though, that evil doesn't exist? That all there are are circumstances which could lead us to commit evil acts which might destroy what we are?' he said, almost bellowing.

'But how can the actions be evil if evil doesn't exist? And how can they destroy someone if, given there is no evil, integrity doesn't exist either?'

'Integrity does exist and is the desire to be, above all else, better than we are.'

'Even at the cost of others' integrity? Luís,' I asked, turning towards him, 'can you go and see whether your father's arrived yet; I want to have a word in private with your brother.'

He hesitated before going out. As soon as he had gone out of the door I began to speak.

'Do you know who got the money to pay for the boat in which you're off to save the Spanish Republic?' I asked Macedo. 'You don't? It was Rodrigues. Do you know how? By selling himself to my aunt's mother-in-law, the one who'd been after his body for a long while. And do you know how all this was achieved? I asked him to take a letter written by my aunt to the old woman, in which she asked her to help her out with some money because she was being blackmailed. And have you any idea who wrote the letter? My aunt and uncle. And did you know that Rodrigues had always had a crush on my aunt and that he wept when I told him that it was she who had wanted him to take the letter to Coimbra? Do you know that he went and for one last time perched in the tree in my uncle's garden, just as he used to do as a young boy, so that he could gaze at her in defiance of my uncle? Do you know that he got caught and my uncle threw him out like a dog? And do you know why I did this? Because I was Mercedes' lover and I didn't want anything to stop Almeida leaving here, such as you not having enough money for the boat. And do you know that Almeida wasn't just engaged to Mercedes, but that he had been her lover in Oporto? Do you know that I took Mercedes to a house in Buarcos, more than once? Do you know that Rufininho too goes to this house – which you probably know – with his boyfriends? Do you know that the nephew of the woman who owns the house, and is one of the crew of your boat and one of your friends, the smugglers, is one of Rufininho's boyfriends? Do you know... ?'

'Shut up,' he pleaded, his face in his hands which rested on the table.

'I'm not going to shut up. Do you know that Ramos knew all about my relationship with Mercedes? And that he asked me to put off our meetings until your departure lest Almeida go crazy and refuse to pilot the boat? Do you know that the two Spaniards in my uncle's house didn't want to go? And that my uncle threatened them with the police and made them go? And that I was also terrified lest their refusal, or the fact that we couldn't sort out the money on account of their reluctance to go, might mean that the journey didn't go ahead?'

'I knew a lot of these things,' he murmured.

'Well, if you knew, where does that leave your famous integrity in the midst of all this? Who's the pure one in all this? Which one of us? Didn't we all sell ourselves off to each other in the most filthy and wretched fashion?'

'I didn't know Rodrigues was mixed up in this.'

'But it is to the fact that he prostituted something that was the purest part of him, deep down inside him, that you owe the money which will enable you to take part in this something which is greater than you.'

'There's nothing pure about him, nothing. It's all a lie. It's just some kind of show he's putting on to justify himself.'

'And everything you do isn't done to justify yourself? Is there anything we don't do for that very reason? Or to get what we want?'

'Or for revenge on somebody or something, Jorge. I beg you, above all to look after Luís. If you don't, Rodrigues will take it out on him. Now, more than ever. When he knows what the money is being used for, with that rage he has against all Spaniards, he'll make it his business to ruin my brother in revenge.'

'Revenge, why?'

'Revenge against me. Don't you remember my telling you – I'm sure I did, didn't I? – about how he told me all about his life? But he didn't just tell me that. Swear you won't tell anyone else what I'm going to tell you?'

'Yes, I swear.'

'My brother above all? OK. Can you imagine what that boy means to me? I sense in him a strength, a security, an assurance of being which is wonderful. It's as if he were my son, a son like I want my own son to be. He's a man like I would like to be. It was on account of him that I let myself get mixed up in all those filthy goings-on that Rodrigues staged for him and me. So that he wouldn't do, or wouldn't think of doing anything without me. For, if I had refused, in front of so many people, or attempted to back out of it, he could have taken against me, saying I was scared, and all would have been lost. Or he could have felt he'd missed out on something, not having been there or taken part in it, do you see?' And he fell silent.

I waited for him to go on, but he didn't. Then, after a long pause he picked up the thread again.

'What a grubby affair life is... So many people and so much dirty business in all this. The worst thing is that when we come across some tangled mess like this we don't know which is dirtier, the people or the things.'

I felt sorry for him.

'Things are made by people and it's only people who are dirty. Or is it not really the dirt that you're afraid of?'

'I'm terribly afraid, you can't imagine,' he said, and then added suddenly: 'It's what happened with me and with Rodrigues. At first in college we were great friends; in that shameless set up we kept ourselves aloof from it all. Once Rodrigues told me that what he wanted was to spend his whole life without touching anybody, not even himself, by the side of a friend like me – a friendship between men for life and until death. But at the same time he was very proud of the curiosity and attraction which that physique of his aroused. He was a terrible exhibitionist, playing around, and I fell out with him about it. He told me that I was jealous of the others and to show him that I wasn't and that my friendship was above any jealousy or any evil desire, it was me who urged him to take advantage of the others like Rufininho who was a little nancy boy, terribly spoiled, though not what he is now.'

'And then?'

'Then Rodrigues accused me of preserving my purity at his expense.'

'But you had never dreamt of getting mixed up in such things.'

'Never, I swear it. Nor he. The fact was, I was just afraid that the other boys would think ill of our friendship.'

'And he?'

'He always used to say that two friends have nothing to fear from anyone, nor from what they think.'

'But if it was really you who pushed him into it, what reason could he have for being so mad at you, and why should you be, as you are, so full of fury?'

'The thing was, once, I felt he was getting the taste for it and I told on him. And they caught him at it.'

'I don't think that's enough reason. After all, these things would happen in college anyway, and I always thought you didn't attach much importance to them if anyone was caught on the job. Telling on him, that's more serious, I grant you, but was it for that that he's still mad at you, at least in your version?'

'No. I'd already threatened to do it more than once. I did what I did because he challenged me to do it.'

'And that's what you can't forgive.'

'I don't know.'

'And what he can't forgive you.'

'What?'

'Come on, you know. But it doesn't seem to me sufficient reason for him to take it out on your brother. Your brother might just have inherited that fascination which he held over you.'

'He has, in fact.'

'I can't fight against this with the same weapons.'

'You can, with other weapons. Luís has a lot of time for you and, anyway, he's convinced that you are the *sine qua non*, the one condition on which my father will let him go to Lisbon.'

I got up.

'Your father should be here by now. I want to say one thing to you. I'm utterly fed up with everything and everybody, just like you, perhaps more. I'm not going to be responsible for your brother. He's a man, let him look after himself. I've had enough up to now of getting my life mixed up in that of other people and of them in mine. Forgive me for asking... Have you ever been in love with anyone? Never? But I, in the middle of all this, am in love with Mercedes. It's not just a fling; and I don't know how it's going to end up. We're here talking and I don't even know if I'll see her again. Don't ask me to commit myself in any way as far as your brother is concerned. Without committing myself in any way, I'll do what I can, no more.'

'He would be able to stay in your house, though.'

'My parents don't understand what it means to have guests, or even receive visits from people they haven't known since before they were born. Don't count on it. What I can do, since I'm going to Lisbon, is fix up somewhere for him to stay, and then introduce him at home. As I'm no longer the little boy that my parents brought up, they might adopt him, if they take to him, and accept him. That's all. Let's see if your father's here yet.'

He got up as well and followed me.

'What do you think of Ramos?' I asked, stopping by the door.

'Ramos? In what respect?'

'Every respect.'

'In some ways he's…'

'What you would like to be?'

He lowered his head and did not reply.

Captain Macedo was in the study with Luís and greeted me with great affability, adding that my uncle had already talked to him about me.

'Here at home my boys have also talked about you many times,' he said thoughtfully, stroking his moustaches, 'but it's one thing for an uncle or the lads to talk about someone they like and quite another to see that person for ourselves. It's extremely important to see a person,' he added, looking at me in silence, with the air of a commander weighing up the character of some volunteer whose qualities he does not really know much about and who is about to embark on a mission of particular gravity. I passed the examination.

'It seems to me you are a fine lad.'

I smiled.

'Don't laugh. Aren't you a fine young lad?'

'I think so.'

'The way a fellow declares that he's a good lad is very important; that way you can tell whether you can trust him.'

'But why do you need to trust me, Captain?'

He was taken aback, shot a glance at his sons and stroked his moustaches.

'It's…' and then asked abruptly. 'Don't you have any naval officers in the family?'

'There must be the odd one.'

'Must be? You mean you don't know?'

'Well, I've never been much interested in such things.'

'Hmm ... Luís here wants to be an officer in the Merchant Navy.'

'It's a fine career,' I said.

'Do you think so?'

'Undoubtedly, and anyway it's what he wants to be, isn't it?'

'Well then, don't you think he's up to it?'

'It doesn't matter, does it? The most important thing is for him to be what he wants to be.'

I felt Luís breathe a sigh of relief.

'He has to go to Lisbon,' I continued, 'unless he takes a ship here to learn things the hard way first, or whatever you call it.'

'But I don't want him to be an officer in the cod fisheries; I want him to command packet steamers. You can earn stacks of money cod fishing but it's a smelly old business, and hard, too, months and months without setting foot on shore. Have you seen that Almeida chap whom I've known since I was a kid. Do you know him?'

'I can't really place him.'

'Don't you know him? He's about to get married to the sister of one of my sons' friends. Excellent young man, excellent young man, that's what I'd call him, no disrespect to you, sir.'

'Well, thanks very much.'

I wondered why I was being so disagreeable to that man.

'Almeida's spent his life in the cod fisheries, earned a lot of money, and what does he do with it?'

'I don't know.'

'You don't? I do. He blows it on having a good time while he's waiting for the next expedition. Is that any kind of life? The only person he respects is his mother. His mother is a good woman, always was. Now my lads have no mother, which is why I don't want Luís, my Luís here, in any kind of boat. Only on packets.'

'There are cargo ships, and more.'

'Nor are there as many as our country needs. We need to have a strong merchant marine.'

'So your son won't lack opportunities, then.'

'Exactly my thinking. Will you dine with us, sir?'

'No thanks; they'll be waiting for me at home.'

'Your uncle expecting someone? That's a new one on me.'

'It depends on circumstances. Will you excuse me sir?'

He did not know what to say, looking from me to his sons and back again, searching for some clue. I gave it to him.

'If I can be of any use to your son in Lisbon, I'm entirely at your service.'

'Ah ... thank you so much, so much. Come whenever you like. You really don't want to dine with us?'

'Another time,' I said, bidding him farewell.

At the door the aunt appeared.

'Has he entrusted the other son to you then?

'Indeed yes, madam.'

'May it serve them right, the ingrates.' And she turned back up the corridor.

I took Macedo's hand; I held on to it for a few moments.

'I'm sorry if I hurt you. I hope it goes well.'

I smiled as I clapped Luís round the shoulders. By the time I reached home dark night had fallen.

XXVI

It seemed an eternity since I had last been there and I had to make a real effort to recall how I had run out of the house so that I could be at the door of the boarding house by three – had it really been at three? – that same day. And, as they say, there was still no end to it all. What was going to happen that coming night? What else could still happen? For there were many things were still waiting to happen: they were coming for the Spaniards; would those two go with them or not? And then? Would they all leave in the boat together? How? And what about those who stayed behind, me among them? An image of Mercedes came into my head, but it was like a vague, fleeting vision which left behind it only some gloomy vestige. The hall was empty and as I crossed it I heard a clap of thunder which made the whole house shake. In the vestibule, where the little passage to the kitchen, the stairs to the top of the house and the corridor to the other parts of the ground floor all met, I almost collided with Maria who was coming by carrying a tray. She was taken aback more by the noise of the thunder and by the surprise of our sudden encounter than by the rapid movement of my hand as I placed it on her backside and felt a sense of release arising as much from my action as from the thunder, whose brooding tension I had been conscious of all day.

They were all sitting round the table when I entered the little room in the wake of that backside that I had been fondling like a naughty little boy. My uncle greeted me rather too heartily, bidding me sit down and eat. His heartiness, which stemmed mostly from the bottles piled up on the floor beside him, did not add to whatever it was I was feeling, but rather made me hear more clearly the rain which whipped through the leaves of the trees and onto the gravel in the garden, and rattled against the windows of the house, like a fusillade rolling deafeningly down the stairs to where we were all gathered. Hearing the rain and a crack of thunder once more – and suddenly I remembered that on the way back and at the gate of the house too I had heard other distant rumblings without really registering the fact – and seeing the two Spaniards eating made me fear lest the whole thing went wrong, something to which the storm might well contribute. A moment later, with my soup spoon left hanging in mid air, I realised that I didn't give a damn whether the whole venture came to naught or not. Any involvement – if I had had any – had vanished, or had been replaced by other motives, in which any hope I had of possessing Mercedes no longer depended on anything or anyone else, but solely on me and her – on our wanting it and on our having the opportunity. My uncle was talking, my aunt too, but I scarcely heard them. Looking at the Spaniards again – who gave me the distinct impression that they weren't listening to them either – I saw that their faces betrayed a blissful relief at the outbreak of that tremendous downpour (although they did not know what day or just what time it was, as I in some way knew), which it seemed that my uncle, in his euphoria, had not yet heard. I felt within me a kind of revulsion, though I could not make out whether it was a consequence of the fact that I wanted them to be involved in a venture of which they were an integral part and in which I was no longer interested; or whether, on the contrary, I was really still interested in it, in spite of what, at that same moment, I was thinking.

When dinner had finished I realised that my uncle had undoubtedly heard the rain and thunder begin and that hearing the storm had merely increased his sense of satisfaction: there had been rain when he escaped from Germany, a great deal of rain at that.

'It was on just such a night,' he was saying, 'that I ran away from the hospital with Freya. And right until we reached Holland it carried on raining, sometimes pouring down, or a fine drizzle, the sort that seeps and soaks into everything, or that rain that isn't either rain or mist – every kind of rain. Me, when I feel the rain on my face, it's as if I were escaping again. Freedom, as far as I'm concerned, is a matter of the rain, I reckon. Without rain there's no freedom,' he chuckled, pouring himself more wine and for the others, too, who said nothing. For them at that moment the rain represented freedom, too, but in a completely different way: so safe did they feel under that roof on which the rain beat down and which the thunder shook that they allowed themselves to smile indulgently at the talk of flight, coming from the lips of the man who had made them prisoners in order that they should flee.

'I became a prisoner on that April day,' continued my uncle, 'when they all sold us down the river ... above all those poor wretches like me, who had been abandoned at the front, utterly exhausted, months earlier. And it's obvious that the German attack didn't just land on us by chance. They knew that nobody had been

sent to replace us, and that neither our arms nor our supplies had
been topped up. They would have known this from their spies in
Lisbon, though it wouldn't have needed much by way of espionage
to find out, because it was public knowledge, notoriously so, that
Sidónio's government had been elected to take us out of the war,
one way or another.'

Don Juan stopped him to ask who Sidónio was, because he
couldn't recall much about him.

'Sidónio,' explained my uncle, 'was a chap who'd been military
attaché in Berlin and had staged a revolution based upon the fear
which most people had of a long drawn-out war; monarchist
propaganda and that of the opponents of the ruling parties – they
who had prompted our entry into the war – portrayed our
involvement as a political manœuvre on the part of the government
to remain in power and control the country. It's clear that all that
type of person supported him; and most of them, now, are behind
the present government, that is when they are not actually part of
it. All of them, those who stayed behind making a commotion in
the streets of downtown Lisbon, down by the Terreiro do Paço,
all those types who didn't take into account my years of service,
who believed that I had run away and hadn't returned to the service
again. Me! Me, who was one of those who suffered that fiasco at
the front, with my unit, when the English left us high and dry,
because our defeat suited them to a T, so that we would pull out
of a war which they hadn't wanted us to enter, and where we'd
gone to defend those colonies which they had already secretly
divided up with the Germans; and when the Germans attacked us
after we had been sufficiently softened up by the neglect of the
Portuguese government, this dictatorship of Sidónio's, with all those
women around him, all dying for it, because he was a big he-man,
and they only had eyes – and any other bits – for him, and with a
whole crowd of fellows all fawning over him, too. That's what I'm
telling you.

'When he was assassinated,' he continued, 'there were those who
were weeping over his body; and as for his funeral, it was the most
extraordinary event, so they tell me – because I only got back to
Portugal afterwards – with thousands weeping and bombs going off
and people running around like headless chickens. What a day and
night that was, the Germans on top of us, us who had spent three
months in the trenches with no relief at all. It was disaster, a fearful
disaster, it's all in the books, but they, those responsible for it, those

who had wanted the war and those who were behind that disaster, all of them celebrated our defeat as if it had been a great victory... There's this great military parade and they come and put flowers on the monument to the war dead, in the Avenida da Liberdade ... I reckon the flowers are also for those poor devils who, in all that muddle, I was forced to kill. Yes, sir, me. Half our company had already been killed when we were taken prisoner by the Germans. I can still see, as the grenades exploded all over the place, those poor chaps down the trench – it wasn't really a trench at all – and the survivors by the light of the rockets, their bayonets pointing at me, wanting to run away and me not letting them because if they had tried they would only have died even sooner. If they had jumped out of the holes – because the way back to the second line had been cut – it would have been even worse, they would have just been mown down. They were great friends of mine, but fear, panic, drives men crazy. And they wanted to kill me so that they could run away. So then I pulled out my pistol and shot the two of them there and then, before they could kill me; it was for their own good. All the rest just cowered down on the ground while I felt myself leaning up against what remained of the side of the trench, able only to look at the pistol in my hand and at the two of them stretched out there, one on top of the other. And the bombardment suddenly ceased and we realised full well that was their strategy of attack.

'Nobody moved, though; how many of them could even stand? That's how we were when the Germans jumped down into the trench, landing on top of my men, one of them even impaling himself on a raised bayonet. They started slaughtering men indiscriminately as though they were ripping apart dead dogs. I fired my pistol at them and then, groggy as I was from all the gas I had inhaled, from everything, I only came round to find myself in a cart with a whole lot of others whom the Germans were carrying back through their rearguard. We were all officers and the others were either in the same state as I was or else severely wounded. Along the road, on one side or the other, marched lines of prisoners; they did not look at us. They took us to a campaign hospital where they divided us up: the wounded on the one hand, the healthy ones on the other. It was there that we recognised some of our colleagues, whom we knew from being in the war together or from the Army School.

'I was sent to a concentration camp in the south of Germany

where there were officers of every stripe and quality. We ate what the pigs ate: potato peelings, onion skins, pigswill; we starved with the cold in wooden huts, and, on top of everything else, we Portuguese were ill-treated by the English who were held alongside us and who had better food, although it wasn't so good as that of the Germans who were guarding us. These treated us like dogs, demanding to know whether we weren't niggers, and one of the standing jokes in the camp was for the English to answer back that's just what we were. While we, in turn, got back at the English by asking about their skirts, pretending we thought they were all Scottish, because I don't know if you know what had happened in the trenches, in our bit, when a Scot, in his fancy kilt, wandered by mistake into the midst of our rabble... He wasn't able to sit down for a whole week; shut up, woman, that's life.

'Weak as I was, I couldn't bear any more and I fell ill with dysentery, with pneumonia, with everything going and more, damn it. When I was no longer aware of what was going on, stuck all day and night in my bunk, delirious all the time, shitting myself too, a Red Cross doctor showed up and managed to have me transferred to a hospital for officers where I remained for days, hovering between life and death. Neither the nurses nor the orderlies treating me could make out a word I said; nor could I understand anything they said to me. But they were very good to me. See how things are: if I had died on the battlefield nobody would have cared tuppence, but there, because I'd gone there quite by chance, they even treated me as though I were a German. Until one day...'

He broke off and smiled to himself, one elbow on the table, his chin resting on his hand, while his stick hung from his other arm and he ran his fingers through his hair.

'Until one day, one day, Freya — Freya or Frieda, I can't remember exactly — appeared. I suppose I can't remember because at first when she came and seemed like an angel to me, I didn't know what her name was. She did seem like an angel; or from the height of her, an archangel. She truly was; she flew.'

There was pause during which we could hear the rain drumming on the house. The thunder, though, seemed to have stopped.

'She was blonde, blonde, so blonde,' my uncle began again, 'and a flyer. A brother of hers was ill in the same hospital, she spoke French and she used to go through the ward greeting all the officers there. I was the sole Portuguese there and she came to see how I was. And she saw, I swear that she saw ... From then on she came

and brought me little home-made rolls which she chucked onto
my bed with that way she had, like a soldier in civvies. But that
was only on the surface, so that nobody would know that she was
really an angel in disguise. I used to say to her in French:
"Mademoiselle, you are an angel. I did not know that there were
such angels in Germany," and she would laugh out loud and reply,
also in French: "Me, I used to think that the Portuguese were a lot
of monkeys. Are you a real Portuguese?" And I would reply: "And
if I am? Come on then and have a closer look." And she would
laugh and say: "Ah, no, there are some very dangerous monkeys
about." And I replied: "But I'm not a monkey, Mademoiselle, I
am a Portuguese." "They say that's worse," she replied. And I asked:
"Worse than what, Mademoiselle? We do things just like the all
the rest except that we are the real experts, and we do them better
than anyone else in the world. Even the Germans are as nothing
alongside us." And she roared with laughter.'

'When I got up,' he continued, 'and went to sit in the sun,
swathed in blankets in that cruel cold, she came sometimes to sit
beside me and even introduced me to her brother who was a flyer,
too, and had only one leg after his aeroplane had come down and
burst into flames. She flew because she liked it but he, above all,
was an officer. This brother showed his displeasure quite clearly on
his face. Later, when I was already much better and could stroll
around in the sun, she would accompany me out into the gardens.
And it was pitiful to see the roundabout ways her brother went in
his wheelchair just so he could spy on us from afar. What I wanted,
what I couldn't stop thinking about, was to sleep with her, and her
poor brother knew exactly what I was up to and had more than
enough reasons to keep an eye on me. She looked after him with
great tenderness, clearly in the same lofty, upright, rather dry way
in which she came to love me. And, although he was pretty angry
with me and with her, and followed us all around in his wheelchair
so as not to let us out of his sight, and had that long, disapproving
face of his whenever we were near him, he never actually said
anything. We decided to run away to Holland. It was her idea, not
mine. I only wanted to sleep with her and it hadn't entered my
head to try to escape from there. As far as I was concerned the war
was over and as for the rest I realised, even there in the hospital
reading it in the faces around me and between the lines of the news
that they translated for me, that the war couldn't last much longer
and that Germany had had it. But I had had enough, fearful of the

prospect of having to go back to the concentration camp, of starving like I'd done before, of suffering what I had already suffered. From the moment she came to me with that idea I was crazy for her and for the idea of flight, both of which came to much the same thing. One night she brought me a uniform belonging to her brother and I put it on in the garden and we walked off together. She took me back to the little place where she was staying and what a night of love that was … my God!'

'Justino!' exclaimed my aunt.

'Be quiet, woman! This is not women's talk. If you're not happy with it, you can go somewhere else. But, to tell the truth, it wasn't easy… In everything in life you've got to keep on top of things and for months I hadn't seen a woman like that before me, for all the months on end in the trenches, all the months in the field, in the hospital … and how long had it been since I seen a woman before me like that, so clean, so decent, so pretty, so willing? It was near the end of September and I had been taken prisoner in April. Yes, there had been the odd quickie in the hospital with one or two of the nurses, but hurried and unsatisfactory. Shut up, woman, don't butt in on me. So there I was in front of her, yearning, and then in bed, blissful, completely helpless, unable to do anything. She even had to undress me.'

'Justino, do you need to go into all the details?' demanded my aunt.

'Shut up, woman! You can't skip bits of a story or nobody would get it. Afterwards I slept like a log. I was only aware of it when I awoke next morning to find her bending over me like some wonderful guardian angel, watching me sleep. That room was so comfortable that it seemed that the war was already over and that all we had to do was just be there, the two of us. And then I remembered that I had run away, we two were running away, and that someone might knock at the door and that from one moment to the next it would be all up with me. I grabbed her and gave her one before she could even cry out. I was ashamed, even,' and he stopped talking, pensive.

'We left the place,' he went on, 'and got into her car; we drove along the roads and there were soldiers everywhere, saluting right and left. I can never forget that on the same afternoon, crossing a forest, an incredible place, unbelievable, like something out of a fairy tale, with huge trees, and ferns growing up to your chest, we stopped the car and lay down in the midst of all that vegetation, green and brown and yellow and red, and the sun filtering through the high branches. How beautiful it all was … but a beauty which was broken by a forest guard,' he said, turning to me and my aunt, 'a tall fellow, with a moustache like that of Captain Macedo' – and all of a sudden I remembered that 'they' would be hammering at the door, that is if the rain hadn't ruined their plans, and at once I was puzzled by the absence of rain in my uncle's story, which he had said was so full of rain – 'who questioned us formally, humming and hawing in panic, until I got up and started fastening up my clothes and he could see my uniform. It was then that I saw it myself. From within the car Freya whispered to me: "Don't you know you are a colonel?" and I gestured grandly to the guard to stand at ease, for he had remained standing to attention by the car.

'Days later we arrived at her house, her parents' house, which was shut, with only the servants, an old couple taking care of the place and who were greatly surprised to see me. But she ordered them not to say a word to anybody and so they treated her as if she was a little girl and I was one of her toys. Her parents were in Berlin, had been since the beginning of the war. Later she took me to a hangar behind the house – the house was like a palace, full of chandeliers and statues and tables the size of football fields – and showed me her little plane. From there to Holland was just a hop in that plane; I had never been in a plane in my life, knowing only those which flew over us in the trenches. And I've never been in one since. That night, after dinner, I went up to a bedroom, all gilt, with a bed under a canopy and a feather mattress in which one could drown. And when she came to me, by the light of a wood fire, in a long nightdress dragging on the polished floor, we drowned in the mattress once again. In the morning it was chucking it down; how could we fly in all that? But we did and we made it. I was as sick as a dog. The rain soaked me to the bone and the roast turkey, too, wrapped in a towel, its legs sticking out, which I was carrying on my lap. Then the rain eased up and became just an icy drizzle; and then a mist which wasn't quite rain or any other thing either, but which, through the gaps in the clouds, let me see a dark river, its banks crowded with villages and towns with pointed towers, the tips of which came so close to us that it made my flesh creep. The turkey which the old couple had put in my lap was just a mess of my vomit but I didn't know what I could do about it, until the moment when we were passing over a field with some people in it I hurled the thing at them. They all set off running, believing it to be a bomb. A turkey bomb. Have you ever thought what the effect would be of a roast turkey falling out of the sky?' and he laughed, breaking off his story.

'It wasn't long after I had chucked it out,' he continued again, 'that another aeroplane appeared out of the mist. I felt a knot in my stomach, a knot which soon became a prayer to God. We must have been crossing the frontier with Holland when that damned thing came along to screw things up! I saw the iron crosses on its wings; it was a German fighter plane. We were lost. I tapped Frieda on the back, fearful that she hadn't seen it. But she gestured to me to keep calm, and, sitting there in front of me, carried on flying the plane as if it were nothing. But to me, with the mist now opening up, now closing in around us, it seemed as though the one plane was a multitude and that we were being pursued by a whole squadron. It even came closer and flew alongside us. My pilotess was signalling behind her and pointing towards me; then I understood. I put on the cap which had fallen down beneath my seat and while I held it on with one arm I pointed to my stripes with the other. The other pilot gave me a salute which almost made him lose control of his plane and then left us in peace. This might seem like some tall story but it's completely true; and the best bit is still to come.

'We started our descent and I glimpsed some fields with windmills and cows, which told me that we were in Holland; there were lots of canals as well. I started to shake, believing that in the midst of those canals, like silver ribbons, and the windmills and cows there would be no space for us to land. We landed on a flat field and were taxiing across it when the plane span round and pitched us into the water. I waved my arms about in panic; I was in the water up to my waist. A bit further ahead there was Freya, also in water up to her waist, laughing her head off. And there we were, the two of us, sitting on the canal bank, laughing like mad and kissing each other. In trousers, in her flying suit, and with only her blonde hair tumbling down over her shoulders it must have seemed that I was kissing a pilot who hadn't had his hair cut for a long time. Some peasants appeared, armed with cattle prods and whips, who were pretty much like the Dutch you see in pictures, what with their wooden clogs and the women with their little white lace caps.

'Frieda spoke to them and they took us to the police station in the village. From there we were taken to Rotterdam; we weren't banged up because she knew somebody in the German embassy there. But before that came the best part of the whole story. As soon as we arrived in Rotterdam we were kept in a hotel. That very same night we woke up in a terrible fright: there were two men in our room. Can you guess who they were? Two Englishmen in disguise, who seemed to think, insisted even, that I was who knows what German colonel whom they had been awaiting so that they could open negotiations for the surrender of Germany! We had, Freya and I, a real struggle to convince them that I was neither a colonel nor German, but merely a Portuguese lieutenant who had run away to Holland with her. When we finally got through to them, they turned nasty and threatened us with I don't know what if we breathed a word to anyone. I never did. But the fact is that in the middle of all that nonsense it was as if I had kicked off the peace negotiations between England and Germany, there on my honeymoon in Holland. For it was a honeymoon, in every respect. We strolled around, slept, ate in restaurants, visited museums and did nothing else. I told Frieda that it couldn't last, that I couldn't live my life at her expense, seeing that I hadn't two pennies to rub together, obviously and that the Portuguese legation didn't want to know about me and that, what with this honeymoon business, I hadn't even time to look for work. In any case what could I do in Holland, apart from what I was doing with her? I believe that, despite all the shame I felt, it was the happiest time of my life. Then came the peace; Freya only wanted things to get back to normal so that I could go back to Germany with her. And I told her that it was impossible, that I loved her very much but that there was no rhyme nor reason to my returning with her to Germany.

'And then she burst into tears and it was strange to see a Valkyre like her in tears, and she said it didn't matter, we would remain in Holland and get our papers sorted out so that we could get married. And then one day I vanished from her sight, out of her life completely. I got the idea into my head and went to the Portuguese legation and made a bit of a song and dance and got myself repatriated. As far as Frieda was concerned I never heard of her again. And when I arrived here they screwed up my life for me. They said that I was a war invalid and had to retire; and they never gave me what I was entitled to. And on top of all that I married this blonde woman here, who isn't called Freya, or Frieda, and she can't fly either and all she can do is drive little nancy boys daft so they climb trees to spy on her.'

My aunt got up and left the room and the narrative subsided into an embarrassed silence because the two Spaniards did not understand the allusion at whose meaning they could only have guessed. The rain, which I had forgotten about, continued to fall, now only lightly, but without any sign that it might ease off or stop altogether. In the midst of this we heard quite clearly, its tones crystal clear in the night, as though sluiced clean by the rainwaters, the sound of the doorbell.

The Spaniards and I looked at each other, uncertainly. My uncle got up, triumphantly. 'My dear sirs, the time has come. Here they are, come to get you. At this time it can only be them, can't it it?'

'I'll go and see who it is,' I said and went out into the rain; I saw at the end of the avenue of palms, a car stopped in front of the gate. My heart was beating furiously as I drew closer. And in the rain, picked out brightly by the lamp on the corner, I saw standing there, his suitcase on the ground, one of my cousins, the one who I had fallen out with back in Figueira. I felt let down, angry. Couldn't he find some other day, some other time, to turn up? And what was he doing in Figueira?

'Open the gate,' he shouted and waved the taxi away. I opened the gate and we ran up the avenue while he told me that he still hadn't had any news from me in Lisbon, that it didn't seem possible. Then the bell rang again.

My cousin stopped. As I turned back towards the gate I saw someone whom I couldn't make out in the rain. Just for a brief moment I hesitated, wondering what to do about my cousin. If he were to return to the gate, or even just remain where he was, he would see who had arrived; if he went into the house so suddenly my uncle wouldn't have the time to hide the Spaniards from his sight. Which would be worse?

'Go inside,' I said, making my decision. 'I'll go and see who it is.' He ran towards the light which came from the side door of the ground floor. At the gate I found Carvalho with his car, and seeing that there were people inside it I peered in and made out Ramos in the front seat; he waved a hand at me.

'Those chaps, are they coming or not?' demanded Carvalho. 'We've no time to lose: we've another hour's drive along some bad roads.'

'I'm not sure,' I replied. 'I'll have to go and tell them you're here; unfortunately my cousin has just fetched up this very moment; you all know him, don't you? When he rang my uncle thought it was you. I'll be right back.'

I ran to the house and at once came across the two Spaniards, my uncle and my cousin, all together in the entrance hall. My uncle was leaning on his stick.

'This one is my nephew, too' he was saying, 'the son of one of my brothers. Of course I can't be entirely sure that he's my nephew as I can be of that other one, who's the son of one of my sisters. But there's nothing to fear; my nephew – well, it as if he were me. Who is it? Is it them already?'

I said that it was, glancing at my cousin who was completely at a loss to know what was going on, looking from one to the other, without understanding a thing.

'These gentlemen have been guests in my house,' said my uncle, addressing him directly, 'and they're off on their way now.' He turned to them. 'You're off on your trip now, aren't you? And a fine trip, too,' he said, putting his hands on their backs and pushing them gently towards the door. They didn't even have their cases with them, the ones with which, as I passed their rooms, I had seen them arrive. But between the surprise at my cousin's arrival and the car waiting in the road, they did not resist my uncle's gentle but firm pressure.

'Jorge,' he called out as he followed them out of the door, 'come and say goodbye to our friends. Ramiro, go up and see your aunt.'

I followed the group going along the avenue of palms, as it were just a pleasant stroll, while my uncle kept his hands on their backs; the evening was now calm and bright. By the gate Don Juan stopped and said that they had forgotten their bags. My uncle, his cane bobbing up and down on his arm, threw up his hands.

'Don Juan,' he said, 'what on earth do you need bags for? I was captured in Flanders, taken to a concentration camp, then to hospital, I ran away from the hospital to Holland, stayed there a while, and then returned to Portugal, all without suitcases. Bags just bog us down. And when we die we've got to leave them behind anyway.'

However, Don Juan and the other Spaniard dug in their heels; they wanted to have their bags. So than my uncle began to argue with them while at the same time he recognised Carvalho and began to talk to him in a very natural fashion.

'How's your father then, lad, with all that science of his? Is he in Coimbra? These gentlemen here are crazy; they're off to some beach somewhere, by the sea, all set up, and they're thinking about taking suitcases. This car is your father's, eh, lad? Big trouble if they catch you with it, eh? Bags, what on earth for? Now, let the thing drop. Or do you really think I want to keep those cases of yours? Is that what you think? Are you going straight there or are you picking someone else up? No? They're all here?' he asked, bending down to peer inside the car. 'Well then, all that money came in handy then, eh?' he said on seeing Ramos. He turned to Carvalho: 'That fellow there is another Spaniard, isn't he?'

'What about the cases then?' he said to the other two. 'Take the damn things, take what you want so that you can just leave them on the beach and put the whole thing in jeopardy. Jorge, go and get our friends' cases, if you don't mind. Since when have we seen anyone making his getaway with a suitcase in his hand? You wouldn't want to take even a toothbrush. Off you go,' he said to me again.

The younger Spaniard span round: 'You're right, sir, We don't need anything. Many thanks for everything. Goodbye.'

'Lieutenant,' said Don Juan, backing up Don Fernando, 'you'll take care of everything, won't you? Many, many thanks.'

My uncle relented and embraced them effusively: 'God – or the devil – go with you, whichever one of them is up there. I hope all goes just as you wish. Safe journey.'

They got into the car, Carvalho settled in behind the wheel and they set off. The rain was still falling, but my uncle stepped out from the gateway, whose tall posts always provided a little shelter, into the middle of the road and, lank and dishevelled, raised his stick in a farewell gesture.

'Poor fellows,' he said, coming up to me and putting his hand on my shoulder, 'if your cousin hadn't fetched up suddenly like that they wouldn't have been caught on the hop and they wouldn't have gone. But they've gone, anyway, and now it's all over.'

In the rain he quickened his pace, leaning on me and his stick. 'I'm already old; I seem to have got even older with all this nonsense,' he said, bent over. At the door to the little room he shook the water from him and ran his fingers through his hair. 'Do you know how many thousand beans they owe me?' he asked, smiling. 'You can't imagine. But I've got it all written down and signed by them, yes, sir. And they are honourable men; if they come through this lot, they'll pay up.'

He headed off towards the kitchen. 'Come on, let's have a nice warm cup of coffee before we turn in. Where's your cousin going to sleep? Well, your aunt can sort that out. You know something?

I think that cousin of yours is a terrible pain; but now that Ramos and Macedo have gone, and with Rodrigues sent packing, he might be some company for you. Or don't you need company?... How's this great affair of yours? Come on, I know it's a grand affair, it's written all over your face, I only have to look at you. Do you know what I'd do if I were you?' and he looked at me, holding his cup in his hand.

'No, uncle.'

'I'd go and jump on Maria; but since she sleeps in the other one's room I'd call her up to mine.'

'Is that really what you'd do, uncle?'

'That's what I think, lad. When you've been doing what we have these last few days and you end up sending those fellows off to their deaths, there's nothing like a good bunk up with some big rough thing. I'm even going to have a go with your aunt – if she'll have me, of course. Good night.'

'Good night,' I replied, following him up the stairs.

He stopped on the step ahead. 'I've already told you what to do. Go and call Maria; she sleeps like a log and she won't come unless you go and wake her yourself.'

'Do you think that they'll manage to get away, uncle?' I asked.

'Get away, yes, I think so. These smugglers are used to nights like this; it's a stroke of luck, really. But actually get there ... well, that's another matter. It's a long journey and the Portuguese navy will be working with the Spanish ships who are loyal to the revolution, keeping watch on the coast with them. But, with luck, anything's possible, and these boats are used to the Biscay run.'

'How will we find out?'

'Well, one gets to know everything, sooner or later.'

That was exactly what worried me, where life itself was concerned.

XXVII

The next day the morning sun rose hot and bright; the day was perfect for the beach but for the humidity, which, arising from the earth, soaked by the previous night's rain, was carried on the cool, trailing wind, drunk with the moisture drawn up by the sun. The gravel in the garden sparkled. Although I hadn't followed my uncle's advice, and had slept badly, my sleep troubled by cars and boats in the darkness, in the midst of towering waves and empty dunes onto which the rain beat down, I got up and put on my clothes with a sense of joyful rebirth, as if I had not only awakened from a restorative sleep – which had not been the case – but also from one of great peace after some jumbled nightmare. Everything now seemed to me just some old story, vaguely recalled, concerning whose unknown outcome I harboured but a gambler's idle curiosity, without anxiety or urgency.

It was as if nothing – bearing everything in mind – depended on the outcome; and whether it had succeeded in every respect, or had fallen through, or had ended in disaster (since the possibility couldn't be ruled out), wouldn't change the situation. Even if they hadn't set off, or the worst had befallen them, the people and everything connected to them seemed to belong to a cycle which had reached an end, to a past which did not extend into this new day, this present day of sun. The consideration that, had everything gone well, those people most directly, if not completely, tied to me or me to them (in some way or other, clearly) – Mercedes, Rodrigues, Luís – would not exactly have gone away *but stayed*, not even this consideration could affect my sunny morning outlook. Their links to me depended so much on everything that had happened and had resulted in the flight, failed or not, of the previous night, that I observed them mentally from the same distance as I had the others.

I smiled to myself at these great, melancholy dramas which in the end only touched me from afar. My holidays were at last about to begin and I came to regard not unkindly even the unexpected presence of my cousin, who had contributed so decisively at the crucial moment to the outcome. It was then that it seemed to me that I deplored the ease with which everything had taken place, at the end and at the outset, even feeling somewhat frustrated as far as my dramatic expectations were concerned. Looking back it was as if I, more than anybody, had suffered enough, or as if what had happened had not been sufficiently tragic or melodramatic to account for so much suffering. Seen clearly, those events had had something even ridiculous or petty about them. Was it true that nothing turns out the way our presumption of suffering would like it to? And that life does not match our sentimental taste for the spectacular and important? Or that, after the event, we cease to see things in their true measure, which can only depend strictly on the emotions of the moment? Or not that we can't see them, but that in order that events and people do not loom over us for any longer than we can bear, or for longer than time itself can bear, we *reduce them*, through a kind of craven spite, to a smaller scale than that which they really have; and, in reducing them, apply some kind of distancing mechanism, so that things and people, once we have lived through them, are no longer perturbed? And isn't this kind of reduction an artifice by which things and people we have known are reduced to the level of those we haven't known? Doesn't it serve to put what really did happen on the same footing as that which could have happened but never did? Isn't it a knack we have, to bestow a hypothetical or virtual character on reality, when some part we have played in it weighs too heavily upon us?

And when, therefore, one feels a frustration, as I did, because these events had not assumed any more than the qualities common to other events which lacked the same transcendental quality, what does it mean: real frustration, mirroring the fact that we demand of people and things more than they can give (and precisely because we ourselves shirk from contributing in our own way to these transcendental aspects); or the feeling of guilt, inherent in the fact that, subsequently – and depending on how malleable our spirit – we had reduced to nothing or to something negligible those people and things caught up alongside us? This awakened in me an urgent curiosity about the rest of the events, although this curiosity was merely an idle dabbling, merely a game. But was it just a sport, or a defence against the fact that we aren't interested in the consequences of our own acts when we are not actually present, or doing something, playing some effective part? I wasn't interested, or pretended not to be more than perfunctorily interested, in whatever events I had no part or had not witnessed, though I had been a decisive actor. It was a kind of revenge through which those things and those people we manipulated slip through our hands; or through which these hands, and our own eyes, and our own machinations, don't end up where they, people and things, do end up. Those people, though there were some who were still part of my life (were they still?), had, at some point, left it, in a car, on a rainy night, which would have seemed a delusion had it happened the evening before. And it was this fact which, at bottom, I couldn't forgive them, notwithstanding the enormous sense of relief which it gave me.

In any case, these things and people had not been determined by me, or at least not solely by me. It was even impossible – hopelessly impossible, I felt – to know for certain each one's part, the part which each one had played in his own right, and the part which everyone had played in everyone else's part. Life was the most promiscuous thing in the world; it was as if someone were to sleep at the same time with many others without ever knowing for sure which one he had slept with. The only possible recourse was to choose a few partners arbitrarily and make sure that neither us nor them slept with anyone else. Perhaps that way they might end up only sleeping with us. It is that choice which is decisive, in so far as it forces a reciprocal choice on the others. But equally decisive, or at least what had a similarly limiting effect and which bound us in the same way, was an intermittent non-promiscuity, through which, from time to time, we would reveal to ourselves that we are dependent, want to be imprisoned even, without the reciprocal guarantee of a similar wish. That was the case as far as Mercedes was concerned: I had bound her to me, it would seem forever, but not exclusively to me in that I had demanded of her, in a fatal moment, what she would have gladly given me at the right time. Certainty of opportunity was what we had never had; and when by chance we did have it, through some coincidence which we was lost on us and which we only later recognised, then neither did we have the opportunity of certainty.

There were three things I needed to know: whether the escape had been successful; whether, following the flight, Mercedes was still mine, and in what way; and whether Rodrigues had used the events that I had unleashed as a pretext to destroy himself and the others. It was as if, though, these things now no longer depended, through me, each·upon the others, but were three new threads of possibilities which, even if they were strung together, would do no more than carve me up, in parallel, among themselves, if I did not refuse them. The flight, in truth, no longer concerned me, successful or no. And why should the lives of the other two, or that of Luís, whose brother had entrusted him to my care, concern me? I could perfectly well refuse to bring with me from the past, even the recent past, any responsibility; I could feel sorry for one, look the other in the face, and sleep with Mercedes, without this implying anything on my part. They were each some kind of survivor of what had been a shipwreck; or, rather, they had been among those who had stayed on the quayside and who, after all the business of tears and waving hankies, had put their hankies in their pockets and gone off home. Why should we all have to get in the same car, or I in one of their cars? Why should I want to know anything, except by complete chance, should it arise, of the fate of any of them? And even if this chance did present itself, in what way was I supposed to let them be any more than simply this? When all was said and done all of them were just friends from the summer; I hardly knew them. They had never set foot in my house, they hadn't been my colleagues in any way, they had never knocked around with me in Lisbon. What bad it all to do with me? Nothing. But it was exactly that nothing that was everything, as I understood it. Having nothing at all in common except the circumstances which linked us was the real, mutual bond. Much greater, much deeper than that which bound me to my family, to my day-to-day friends, to everything which forever had its habitual, well marked, place in my life. All this is not our life but the veil behind which we shelter to avoid its attacks. Our life is these very attacks, coming from without, at the hands of chance, and which, in revealing to us that we are not 'ourselves' (along with everything else which, around us, gives us this unifying security), obliges us to realise that we are 'all of us', 'we as many', according to the occasion and the circumstances. I wasn't just an I, but an I-Mercedes, I-Rodrigues, I-Macedos, I and all those who were not a past beyond time or events. And when I returned home, to my friends, I would see that all of them, in Lisbon, would only be 'I' in so far as they ceased to be 'myself', this vague awareness that there was an intermediate step between infantile non-existence (where there are no others) and real existence (where there are only others and we are only one of them in relation to them). This was true for everyone and was the real meaning of that adventure which would still have happened without me, undoubtedly, but wouldn't have affected the people involved in the same way, since my part in it had made them different from what they would have been without the confessions I had extracted from them. They had all said, or not said, certain things (and not others, according to their pleasure); and in speaking and acting had been transformed. Into what? Into nothing, into less than they imagined, into something other than the illusion that they themselves were those selves. Everything that had happened – dragging all of them into a cruel and present reality – meant that nobody could continue calmly to be, in all innocence or not, what he or she had been until then. This was what the Spanish Civil War had done.

My motives, those of my aunt and uncle, those of Ramos and Mercedes, of Almeida, everybody's, were utterly secondary; these motives had all coincided in a general way which the war had precipitated into two distinct modes: as repercussions; and as something on which things hinged decisively. None of their lives could continue in any kind of rotten peace. Nor would it be a clean peace; it was a war with everything that that implied by way of decay and dirt. My war, like that of those who had already set off (if indeed they had) was beginning now. Against whom? And on whose behalf? This did not seem at all clear to me, but without doubting my right, and that of the others, *to project myself onto them and through them*, reciprocally. But against whom? Against the need to be, purely and simply, an ideal, fictitious union. And what had that to do with that war which had thrust Mercedes into my arms, and made Rodrigues face up to himself, and which, for many others, there, so far from everything and in the middle of some crazed plan of political action, had done the same. For even the life of my aunt and uncle could not be the one they had lived for so long. Would it be worse? Or better? Different, for sure, although to all appearances it would carry on as the farce it always had been. And so things changed, without changing; they continued to be the same, and they weren't the same. Analysing it more carefully, two factors had precipitated the events in which I had taken part: my uncle had harboured two fugitive Spaniards in his house; and Ramos, with the others, had decided to mount a spectacular escape to Spain. It was not pity based on a political conviction but rather a mix of complex emotions (to play with them and fleece them, as he always did with the Spanish on their summer holidays, as well as an animus against the present order) which had motivated my uncle. And what lay behind the actions of Ramos, Macedo and Almeida? Simply a political passion, the conviction they were doing what they had to? Not solely. But also not just the personal motivations which they would have for such an action or by being that which brought them to it. I understood that what people are does not explain their actions, although their actions may be explicable by them; in the same way that a war or an ideal do not work within us merely through the involvement they demand of us, but also by being the convulsion which unleashes certain events.

What had happened – all of it – was inconceivable; it was so in terms of what, in previous years' summers, had always been supervised by certain people, certain families and hedged about by the strictest conventions. Was it then the case that, by mere coincidence, we, the younger element, had reached that adult age at which other things, at least behind drawn curtains, were now possible? Or was the opposite true? Had everything begun to crumble thanks to circumstances, allowing us a freedom which previously we would not have enjoyed, even at our age? To give oneself to a girl, a group of boys running away for whatever reason, people betraying each other – there was nothing new there in any case. So what was new about what I had experienced and what I had begun to understand? Beyond this diverse idea I now had of personality, of my own and of others, there was a certainty that the world was no longer something outside of us that could be imposed on us. It was, on the contrary, that which we imposed, one on the other, at every moment, in a sequence of events, whether close to us or far away. Therefore, in this sleepy, provincial town, where people spent their summers, where the most scandalous things were the casino and a few whores, and where a group of boys harboured, at the bottom of their hearts, a grudge against life and the school which they attended, where my uncle was a teacher, what had happened had been possible, not just the horrors implicit in this as in everything, but a debacle which had dragged us through a welter of horrors. A welter? Of horrors? In the end, neither one nor the other; or rather the loss of the meaning of horror, in the widespread acceptance that everything was possible, was probable, and at the same time the refusal to accept that what we had been doing and were continuing to do were even possible or probable – betraying each other, to the exact extent to which we project ourselves into the other.

I felt a violent curiosity; I wanted to know what had happened. But who could I find who would know? Those who had stayed behind would know nothing. Carvalho, perhaps, because he would have been there when they left. But how could I get hold of him? I couldn't go to the boarding house to get Ramos or to the Macedos' house. I decided to go to the beach; but who was I hoping to meet? I went downstairs.

I found nobody there. What had become of my aunt and uncle? And my cousin? What explanation would they have given him? I needed to know. I went to the kitchen where the two maids greeted me with smiles; they would surely have had their 'commission' from the smugglers by now. Maria, in particular, didn't show any signs of remembering what had happened between us; she was all smiles. I drank some coffee and asked after my aunt and uncle. They were still upstairs. And what of my cousin who had arrived the previous evening? He'd had his breakfast and gone out early. I went upstairs again and knocked on my uncle's door. There was no reply, where could he be? Then I recalled what he had said the night before; and as if in answer to a call I hadn't yet made, but undoubtedly because she had heard me knocking, the door to my aunt's bedroom opened and she appeared, in his dressing gown but with her hair already combed. Like the maids, she too was all smiles.

'So it's you; what do you want?'

'I want to know what you told Ramiro.'

'Ramiro? Which Ramiro?'

'Your nephew who came here yesterday.'

'Ramiro came here yesterday? That's a good one; your uncle never said a word.'

'Well, would you be kind enough to ask him what explanation he gave him to account for the Spaniards being here and for them leaving without their suitcases? In case he asks me. Didn't he come up to have a word with you last night when he arrived?'

'No,' she said, closing the door in my face. Then the door opened again and just her head peeped out. 'Your uncle says that he didn't give any explanation at all other than what you heard. And that it's better not to say anything more about it. Your uncle has taken care of the cases. He did it the moment he came up; they're in his room As far as your cousin...'

'He was in the bathroom,' shouted my uncle from within the room, 'and I sent him directly to bed, in one of the empty rooms. Come here, woman!' and she disappeared back inside.

It was clear that there was a general tacit agreement not only to wipe the slate clean of the events and consign them to the past as if they had never happened, so that life could return to its everyday normality, but also, more than this, to recreate, over those events and at their expense, a greater happiness than before, something which was perfectly symbolised in that morning nuptial, with my uncle still in bed with my aunt, on whom, like a king, he had deigned to bestow his body, while she emerged rejuvenated and groomed, shooing me away from the door like some tiresome spectre.

Would the same thing be happening with all the others? Was I more tied than all the others to a past which dated from last night? Was I like some hangover from a past which, along with the disappearance of all the others, had vanished from the lives of those who had remained behind and did not want to know more than what had been done at their expense? And why was I some kind of hangover? Why was I more of a hangover than the others who were still there? Perhaps because, in the whole thing, I had been the link between them and what had happened, between them and their own actions; and because in that way it was only my presence which prevented them from returning to an everyday 'normality', which, though, could never be identical to the previous one, however much they wished it to be. I was the one who knew everything, although in fact I didn't; at least I knew more than anyone else. And knowing what I did I was thus in all that business the image of the one who, in it all, had gone further than them and in going further, had made them responsible.

Perhaps this was carrying it a bit too far, though, and my being an *agent* rather than a link was enough to disrupt the urge for reintegration in the series of commonplace events which, though they might seem uncommon, never went beyond one's intimate knowledge or the ken of one's habitual friends and for this very reason, could not be perceived as out of the ordinary. This feeling of being *de trop*, suddenly, made my blood run terribly cold, causing me a great, undefined fear; previously I had never been anything more or less than the others (and frequently much less than many of them). They had shut me out. But from what? From everything or just from that business? Or, on the contrary, would it be me who cut myself off by not accepting the rules of the game that 'it was all over and done with'?

I had to see Mercedes there and then. In fact I was already out on the street and on my way to the beach. And what was I going to do there? I felt that I couldn't go to the boarding house after the scenes that had taken place there even though my presence there would not endanger the fugitives, or – and I shuddered – I would not give myself away to the police even if they had got wind of what had happened and were keeping watch on all of us. I turned round to see if I was being followed. I wasn't – unless it was by a woman coming down the street with a bag of vegetables in her hand. That made me laugh. In any case the disappearance of those who had gone could not already be known. The fact that a boat had set off would not, in itself, be a matter for suspicion; and Macedo, Ramos and Almeida could have put it about that they were off on some night jaunt from which they hadn't yet returned; and there would be no obvious link between them and the boat as far as anyone else was concerned. That was probably how things stood for the time being. And who knows, if it subsequently changed in a series of barely perceptible ways, whether this 'jaunt' with its hasty departure, with its sudden interruption of the summer routine – for people sometimes set off suddenly, seemingly without rhyme or reason – whether the effect of the final transformation might not be to deprive the adventure of the repercussions of which they had been dreaming. If everybody busied themselves in eliminating the fact from their lives (and the participants along with it), the risk they would run would be enormous.

The beach, although somewhat short of atmosphere and already redolent of the end of summer and of the empty feeling which followed the departure of the Spanish contingent, was still bright and lively. And these high spirits, indifferent to what had torn my life and that of so many others, in two and which everyone was now busy ignoring or patching up, far from reconciling me to things, gave me, as I watched and heard rather than saw the noisy gestures of those who were running around and playing in the sand, a sense of shock, of agony, of revulsion, not so much against these people but against myself. What had happened was 'something', meant 'something', had changed 'something'. It could not be suppressed or ignored; it must not be. Above all, it must not be. But who would see to it that it was not ignored, and how, without distorting the real reason why these things had happened; that duty was to make the events known in themselves and not through what people, for good or bad, for better or worse, had given of themselves and others for a goal to which many of them were not truly committed or of which they did not even know they were a part. It was exactly this idea of 'a pledge' which went through my mind and made me shudder, remembering the pawnshop, with the people, like objects, wrapped up and stored on shelves, the vases, the folded sheets, the knick-knacks – anything which could be pawned. This was what was happening: people and their acts, wrapped up and labelled, on the shelves in miserable little shops under the layers of dust; others going out of the shop, carrying in their purse the ticket, which they meant to lose or perhaps keep as the vague recollection of some object lost to them because they failed, through an act of calculated neglect, to pay off the arrears in time.

But what had happened was something important, comprising lots of events and many people. It was important. Would it still be? What was it that was important? What did it mean to be important? The value which we or circumstances gave to it? Or an importance which, within certain limits, is the same and is important for others as well? Had that wind which, so to speak, had in its contagion swept us together, blown only over our lives, or was it blowing equally over everybody's? In another way, might it not have blown at all? How many, like me, would not affect a complete ignorance of what had happened? Nevertheless, what I had affected was not the same as that of my aunt and uncle. I was hiding the events from the ken of those who weren't ready to recognise them; they were hiding them from themselves. I had won and lost a great love; while they... Had they perhaps, by contrast, regained a lost love, which would explain why they adopted a position which was the reverse of mine? Even in this inverted sense I found the comparison repellent; I found this second honeymoon of my aunt and uncle unworthy and shameful. What had been between Mercedes and me, with everything that I had done, and that which perhaps I shouldn't have done, and with everything that she had misunderstood about me and the others (and I hadn't?), it didn't just amount to *that*, but to a great love.

I stopped, filled with dismay, already by the line of huts, asking myself how it was that I was thinking of my love for Mercedes and hers for me as something already *in the past*. Of our love. But was it really a great love? Had it been? Was it? Would it be? That ineffable emptiness, within which so many contradictory feelings of attraction and repulsion were being tossed around, was that a great love? In truth I hated and desired Mercedes avidly. No. I loved her deeply, and I did not desire her except as a means of forgetting, in those arms of hers, that I loved her. So much; so sorrowfully; so jealously; so proudly; so ashamed of continuing to love and desire her. I had to have her once again, today even, however it might be. I had to see what was the true condition of our love, now that all the others were out of our way. Had they really gone? And what if, on reaching 'their' tent, I should find them all sitting on the sand, perfectly happy, playing a kind of skittles with the children? This thought made me slow down to a pace so leisurely that it was hard to maintain. It was as if the nervous haste with which I had pressed on so that I could check that they weren't there had filled my shoes with lead. And then I realised that on my way to the beach and to the row of huts I had deliberately gone the long way round, some distance from where I knew for sure their huts were to be found; it was as if my passing slowly in front of the other huts were some kind of greater guarantee that they had all in fact disappeared. I was angry with myself, in the same way that I was angry with the indifference and ignorance of the others. I wanted them to succeed, I didn't want it to be meaningless, this adventure which had involved all of us with each other. But it wasn't just for this reason that I was afraid that they might not have got away, but rather for a reason identical to that which the 'others' used in order to forget or overlook what had happened: I too was suppressing them and wanted them out of my way, gone, independently of what had happened or not happened.

But in the huts, in 'ours', there was nobody to be found; only some clothes hanging up in the Macedos' hut. I went in and saw three pairs of men's trousers: those of Luís, Rodrigues and perhaps my cousin's whose presence I only now remembered. The agreement which I had, in some fashion, made with the older Macedo not to allow Rodrigues to get his hooks into Luís, came into my mind as I was getting undressed and hanging my clothes up beside his. That was the least of it; it even seemed a bit ridiculous. More serious right now was the possibility that Luís might open up to Rodrigues, or the latter might make him, in his cunning way and with that instinct he had for the secrets of others, drop some kind of clue. There was a real danger, once he had put it all together, that he might become so driven by rage (and he had on his own account plenty of reasons for that) and commit some inadvertently spiteful act which would place everything and everybody in jeopardy. On the other hand, my cousin had seen the two Spaniards and had seen them leave, but he didn't know just how critically this might be linked to other facts and other people. And if Rodrigues' skilful probing were to take place in front of him he might also inadvertently furnish Rodrigues with yet more extensive evidence about the events I had involved him in; and so the discovery that the way in which my aunt and I had used him was even more gratuitous than he had supposed, could hurl him into a rage or into a mad despair far worse than whatever state he might be in at the moment. I should not have abandoned Rodrigues; I should have gone and found him after that doleful late supper in my uncle's house. And not because I wanted to forestall him, nor out of friendship; but out of pity, and from the sense of obligation which I felt, too, that I should not abandon someone whom I had betrayed even beyond the point that I had admitted to him. At the first opportunity, and precisely to stop him getting to know these things at second hand, I had to tell him the whole truth about the matter. And, who knows whether, on learning it, he might not respond favourably and not feel, there at the bottom of his necessary illusions, that he had not entirely lost the image of my aunt? An image which might live on in him as that impassive profile, outlined in the light of the window… And even more, realising just how far the Macedos had indirectly taken advantage of him, in their Spanish adventure, it was possible that instead of seeking vengeance through Luís, and spurred on by new, urgent, reasons, he might on the contrary seek to distance himself from the company of one who also had a hand in his betrayal.

For my plan to succeed, I needed to implicate Luís, laying the blame on him rather more than was strictly the case; I needed to find out, discreetly, whether the three of them had talked that morning, and then to talk separately with Luís and Rodrigues. As far as my cousin was concerned it would be better, should he not have said anything, to keep him in the dark and, by talking to him subsequently, lead him to believe that his memory of what happened could only be explained away by what he, like me, knew about those stunts of which my uncle was capable. Nothing could be easier than to overlook my uncle's stunts if they were perceived as such; and there could be nothing easier, either, than to talk about them in that fashion if my uncle himself were to join in such an innocent conversation.

Sitting in the sand, in the sunshine, leaning back against one of the struts of the hut, I turned all this over in my mind as I tried to make out whether any or all of them were approaching. All at once I felt like taking a dip, going into the sea and diving among those shimmering, intensely blue waves, but if I moved from that spot I ran the risk of missing them altogether. And Luís was, at that moment, the best source of my finding out what had transpired. No. The best and safest source was Mercedes herself; I had to find her as quickly as possible: talk to her, and eventually – only eventually and if she herself suggested it – take her to Buarcos. Now that Almeida was not there, how would she behave? For his disappearance was much more decisive for her than for me. Without him I was myself; and I was everything that he had not been, or what was not of what he had been. He had ceased to be the point of reference; that was something which I had consummated, in which I had replaced him. But – and I hardly dared consider the possibility – it could turn out in precisely the opposite fashion: what if he had taken me with him, if in her thoughts and desires, I had gone away in *him*? Really, did not the way in which she had talked to me, the way she had spoken so painfully of a brief period set aside for me, and which, everlastingly, would not be any the less irregular, in some prefigure this very thing? Or not?

Puzzling over this point and other melancholy notions, I was none too pleased – like someone interrupted in the middle of some very personal business – to see them coming towards the hut; they were waving to me in a carefree fashion and perhaps it was this very carefree air of Luís and Rodrigues that irritated me. Neither of them had the right, as far as both I and they were concerned, on that morning, to wave to me like that, even with my cousin at their side. But their gesture, after the initial irritation, had in fact a calming effect on me; if they were waving to me like that it was because nothing untoward had happened between them, and it was only then that I realised that perhaps my worries had been disproportionate since what Luís knew about the events must have been very little. There was no reason to believe that, apart from what he might have inferred, he was aware of the clandestine political activities of his brother. And he wouldn't be such an idiot, if he guessed that they really were clandestine, as to be anything other than circumspect about them. For that reason it was Rodrigues' gaze which held my attention most closely.

They sat down by me and my aversion towards that cousin of mine soon became evident. Even though I was unable to talk about anything with any of them in front of others, the very fact of his presence there became more irritating than anything I had ever felt before. By the side of the other two he was more *de trop* than ever. Feeling the eyes of Rodrigues upon me, notwithstanding the fact that he covered everything up in smiles and little jokes, I turned on my cousin: where the hell had he got to the previous night, why had he turned up so unexpectedly, why had he been in such a hurry to get out of the house that morning? My bitterness was quite clear, and he was so unused to it, that he reacted by replying that our aunt and uncle's house was as much mine as his, and that he too was entitled to spend the summer there like me. This reply reminded me of the decisive role which he, unwittingly, by arriving at precisely the most inopportune moment, had played in the departure of the Spaniards and in the success – success, what was I talking about? – of our carefully laid plans. He probably thought he had got the better of me with his quick riposte, and the fact that I was grateful to him for the very thing with which I had upbraided him made me feel like laughing; suddenly mindful of my debt to him I didn't answer him harshly, just because of that very gratitude which transformed him, paradoxically, into a figure of fun. For my part this lifted the cloud which had hung over things and our conversation turned to light-hearted, more trivial matters. Then, abruptly, Rodrigues spoke.

'I'm going to Coimbra this afternoon, by car,' he said, looking at me closely and deliberately. 'They phoned very early and the car's coming to fetch me. Do you think I should go?'

'It's up to you,' I replied, while the other two exchanged glances instinctively, suspecting that it might be something which neither of them knew anything about.

'I'm thinking of asking someone to come with me, to share the burden,' continued Rodrigues.

'Can't you manage her on your own?' I asked.

'I could, I can. But...' and he laughed in the direction of the other two, 'but I'm not the sort to keep things just to myself. If I share something with someone else it seems to be mine even more. Is there anyone you could suggest?'

'Look...' I said slowly, 'why not take Rufininho.'

The others laughed uneasily, or at least it seemed so to me.

'I'd already thought of that,' he replied coldly.

'Well, if you've already thought about it you don't need suggestions from anyone else, do you?'

'That's true. The worst thing would be if he died of fright when he saw the old woman heading for him,' he said and turned to the other two. 'We're talking about a rich old lady who likes her boys well hung; it's not what you might be thinking about. As it happens Rufininho isn't exactly lacking in that department, it's just that it doesn't work except on its own account, or as a reaction.'

'As a reaction?' asked Luís.

'Yes,' explained Rodrigues solemnly. 'When somebody hits Rufininho with a stick on the backside, his tackle rises up in front.'

'Well, there's the solution,' I said in the midst of general ribaldry. 'You can use him as a kind of intermediary.'

'He's already done that, much more than you think,' observed Rodrigues. 'Just a few days ago, I bumped into him quite by chance; I got to know a whole lot of things.'

My face must have turned livid, recognising the allusion he had made about the passion we might cherish for someone else's woman, remembering Rufininho's sharp voice talking to the old woman's nephew in Buarcos. There was no doubt that he knew all about my relationship with Mercedes. Did he know about the escape and anyone who was involved in it? That was what I wanted to find out.

'A whole lot of things? What sort of things?' I enquired, sure that he would not venture more than was needed for me to understand. It was better, too, on account of my cousin, that I didn't back off.

'A whole lot of things.'

'Such as?' and I felt Luís' eyes fixed anxiously on me.

'Well, well, you've known that all along; far more than me; I can't believe any of that tittle-tattle coming from a little pansy like Rufininho.'

He had backed off, the directness of my attack forcing him to hold back.

'So it's something about me, then?' I persisted, while Luís was torn between relief and a renewed disquiet.

'Exactly. Whoever takes a woman to one of those houses risks being seen by Rufininho. When it comes to it, those who need a room can't choose between men and the likes of Rufininho, can they? What matters is that the customer coughs up.'

'Are you meaning to say that Rufininho saw me? I know that already.'

'The woman,' he said, emphasising the word in loathsome fashion, 'he didn't see her. In spite of his tittle-tattle, and the fact that he enjoys the telling of it all, Rufininho doesn't make any of it up. The one who saw her and identified her was one of his boyfriends.'

I heard the voice of the old woman's nephew as he tried to blackmail me. 'Do you really know who his boyfriends are?' I asked.

His eyes blazed. 'No. But when he talks to me about some lad he knows it's bound to be one of them, because he doesn't know

any other kind. That's how it was with me,' he added, in response
to the puzzlement he felt in us and in himself. 'Everyone knows it
was me who … deflowered him! That's why he was always so
grateful to me, looked up to me,' he said and then laughed, as if to
say there wasn't a word of truth in it and that he was only joking.

'Look what sort of people I've become mixed up with since I've
been here!' commented my cousin, half laughing, half disgusted,
making me aware of the desire to please, the complicity, the
collective shame, the awful degradation, which was all mixed up
with the noble motives of some, and of the passionate opportunism
of the others, in 'our group'. It was something that I had known
and felt all along, but it was a very different matter when it was
pointed out by someone outside the group; and more serious, too,
because it showed me clearly what we were, just what we were
becoming, with hardly any sense of shock, at least according to
conventional standards, about anything at all. Because for us
everything was becoming something else, and degradation was, in
exactly the same way as virtue and love, something which sustained
that situation as well. But it was Luís who broke in unexpectedly
before I had time to reply.

'In what respect are you any better than the others?' he demanded,
leaving me in some doubt as to whose side he was really on, and
alerting me to the fascination which Rodrigues exercised over him.

My cousin, Ramiro, was openly scandalised.

'Better? This has nothing to do with better or worse. I never
went around with any Rufininho, I was never involved in anything
like that, and I wouldn't talk about it in front of anyone else even
if I had been. Nor could I hold my head up, like you, after hearing
what Rodrigues has just said. There's a limit to everything; I can
see that since last year you've all grown up a lot. The best thing for
me would be to get out of here before somebody starts feeling up
my backside in the street.'

Before he had time to say anything more Rodrigues and Luís set
about him, hitting him violently while I noticed the people under
the neighbouring awnings looked on smiling, thinking it was merely
some rough lads' game. I remained there impassively watching them
administer their punishment in which they almost smothered his
face in the sand, and which ended with him sobbing and Rodrigues
mounted obscenely on him – at which the neighbours made a great
show of staring out to sea.

'You bastard,' shouted Rodrigues through clenched teeth, 'this is to teach you some respect for me, so that you know what I'll do to you if you don't look what you're saying.' Then he got up while Luís let go the boy's wrists. The latter got up, too, furious and shamefaced. 'You there, you, you'd let them do this to me, eh?' he jeered, wiping the sand – and the rage – from his eyes and mouth.

I didn't reply, the whole thing seemed merely comically absurd, like some scene played out by men who had slipped back into adolescence, or, as was the case with Rodrigues and Luís, had never left it or never would.

Although a split between them suited me and everybody else for that matter because it kept Ramiro away from them, their behaviour made me feel more drawn to my cousin; at that moment Luís thrust his clothes into his hands.

'Get out of this hut and never set foot here again,' he said.

'Now then ... that's enough of this madness. There's no need for such a row,' I said, the words coming out feeble and inept. My cousin must have thought so, too, for he went off muttering resentfully, cursing the whole lot of us. 'Now, back at home, I'll be the one to catch it,' I said after he had disappeared among the huts.

'What an obnoxious, stupid prig that cousin of yours is,' said Rodrigues, shaking himself and untying the flap in front of the hut so that he could fasten it and get dressed. 'I could never stand him. Do you remember that story with Odette, last year?'

I did, longing now for that time which now seemed to me inconceivably far away, disconnected utterly from the present. At that time we were still boys, with all the things that hadn't yet happened assuming an immense importance for us. Now it was the things which were happening which didn't seem to be important. Sitting out there, in the same place, leaning against the strut, I watched them through the openings as the wind billowed the sheet which had fallen down and was only secured at the bottom; they were taking off their swimming trunks and putting on their clothes. Rodrigues addressed me from within. 'Listen, I really am going to Coimbra, it's no fairytale. Are you still going to hang around here on the beach?'

'Yes.'

'You'd have some fun if you came with me.'

'Are you crazy?'

'You know perfectly well I am, and I don't want to be anything else.'

'I hope it suits you.'

They came out together, lifting up the awning of the hut. 'I think I'll ask Luís here to come with me,' said Rodrigues, tying up the strings.

Luís laughed. 'But what's it all about?' he asked.

'Some old woman I have there in Coimbra. If I bring her a young lad like you she'll go crazy.'

'Where's your brother got to?' I asked abruptly. 'Why isn't he here on the beach today?'

Luís opened his eyes wide, stuttered and changed colour. Unexpectedly, it was Rodrigues who answered my question.

'Don't you know? Those pure souls went out on the razzle again, just like the other night, with their cars and all. But we weren't invited – we three were specifically not invited. But I caught them red-handed when Ramos and Macedo bumped into Matos and Carvalho last night. Luís says that come morning they still hadn't got back.'

Who was he fibbing to? To me? To Luís? Or had he really not put two and two together? Or did he really not know what to make of what he'd learned from Rufininho? Or had Rufininho not told him about the imminent departure in which the nephew of the woman who owned the house was involved as well? And how could it have been that they managed to get rid of him if it was true that he had met them at the very moment in which they were setting off on their adventure? Before anything else I needed to speak to Luís and with Mercedes, too. But how was I to prise those two apart? They were about to go, bidding me farewell after I had said goodbye, insisting that I was staying behind.

'What time is the car coming to get you?' I asked Rodrigues.

'At two.'

'You don't have much time left to have lunch and get ready, all kitted out and smelling sweetly.'

'Smelling sweetly? Ah … you don't know her, do you? What she likes most about me is my smell. She sniffs me as if I were a rose. But it would be some revenge if I were to take Dona Micaela here.'

I reacted instinctively to the epithet, despite myself, as if, really and as his brother had wanted, I had fully assumed my role and taken Luís under my wing.

'Put a sock in that business once and for all. Otherwise one of these days when you least expect it Dona Micaela will climb on top of you and you'll find out what it feels like, what you did to Rufininho.'

'I know: when it doesn't hurt them, I don't enjoy it either,' replied Rodrigues.

'I forbid you to fool around with these matters,' I said, looking at him sternly. 'There's a huge difference between all us lads talking about all these things, jokingly, and you, playing around and talking about it. There're those who talk about it but they don't do anything …'

'And I'm playing around with it for real, is that it? But the big mistake,' – and he crouched in front of me – 'is that I'm not playing. I'm serious. I'm going to live my life seriously. Don't you think I have the right?' he demanded, the bitterness clear in his voice.

'Yes, you have; but it all depends on the kind of seriousness. What kind of story is this about it being a fine revenge to take Luís with you?' I asked, without pausing.

Luís hovered, unsure of whether to sit down. Rodrigues, realising it, made him sit. 'Squat down here, lad,' and in his voice I recognised with some astonishment, the timbre and expression of my uncle, 'so that I can talk about something that will interest you. Now then, wouldn't it be some revenge if I were to deliver her mother to the fellow whom he humiliated, treating him as he were some nancy boy?'

'Whose mother?' asked Luís.

'My aunt's,' I said.

'Your … aunt's!' Luís stammered.

'Yes, indeed,' said Rodrigues, 'that's the old woman I have in Coimbra.'

All these thoughts of revenge, which were all mixed up within him, had in some paradox of virility turned into a rehabilitation of Luís. But what sort of revenge? Wasn't Carlos Macedo mixed up in it all too? And in glorifying Luís wasn't he also mixed up in debasing him? Who was he glorifying and debasing in all that business, if not himself? And everything and everybody along with him? But what was there that was not degrading about all those things we had done? How could we cast the first stone at him? But…

The speed with which all this crossed my mind was less rapid than the surprise which seized Luís, followed immediately by the transformation of this horrified surprise which I read in his open-mouthed features, for, while I was thinking, and before I had time to order my thoughts into some coherent speech, he had already begun to speak.

'It would be a great joke,' he said, his eyes shining. 'I'm sorry,

Jorge, but it would really be a great joke if I were to go; not least because your uncle is always going on about his mother-in-law.'

My protests were plentiful enough, but at bottom I was no more than going through the motions because I, too, had been wounded by the unscrupulous behaviour of my aunt and uncle and the perfunctoriness with which they had claimed to have forgotten about their actions.

'Luís, don't even let the idea enter your head,' I said. 'Are you listening to me?'

'But what harm is there in his going?' asked Rodrigues, 'especially since so many of those we know have already been her lovers? Going with the old woman could even do you good; it's like going not just with your mother, but your granny, too.'

'Well then,' I said, 'it's time you went your own way, or off to your old woman. Luís, hang on a minute, I want to talk to you.'

'Are you going to give him a lesson in morality? Explain to him that...'

'I'm not going to explain anything. I just want to talk to him, that's all.'

Rodrigues got up. 'So you're sending me away so that you can keep Dona Micaela under your wing?' he said, his tone of voice clearly intending to provoke me and Luís, too.

'I'm asking you to leave for your own good, and so that you don't slight someone who can pay for you to go to Lisbon.'

'Sure...' and he moved away. He soon turned back. 'Couldn't we have lunch together,' he said, 'come along this way... If you stayed with me, I wouldn't go. All my life my mother's been paying for me, and does this old woman have to pay for me now, as well? Does everybody exist just to pay me? Is there nobody who'll let me do something for them for free?'

'But you want them to pay you, don't you?'

'I do. On the day they give me nothing, or I don't ask for anything, I've had it. I'll fall out of the tree, for sure. You see, I wanted everything in this world, cocks especially, to be free. You know how they have those mussels all threaded onto a stick, with a peppery sauce. I would like to be that stick.'

'Something that people just throw away.'

'Just so, that's true. They eat the mussels and then chuck me away. Look, Luís, I...'

'What is it?' said Luís, raising his downcast eyes to him.

'Nothing, nothing; but don't run away with the idea that I'm always like this.'

'Like what?'

'Like this, some kind of sucker. So long,' he said, and was gone.

'Did they get away?' I asked with Rodrigues hardly gone. 'Did everything go to plan?'

'I don't know whether it went to plan or not because my brother didn't tell me anything clearly. But they did get away because he still hadn't come back by the morning and nobody came to alert my father. They fled to Spain by boat, didn't they? And they embarked just north of the cape, didn't they? On the beach they met up with the ones who were running away from Oporto, didn't they?'

'Those who were running away from Oporto?'

'Yes; I know as much because I overheard my brother talking to Zé Ramos. Those who were held in Oporto were running away and coming here to meet them. The date and time of them meeting up depended on this escape, I believe.'

Suddenly I recalled some vague words of his, and the trips to Oporto. So there was that, too. This venture went much further, was more daring and complicated than I had imagined.

'Is that all you know?' I asked.

'Yes. It was my brother who fixed us up with the boat, through some lad in Buarcos who used to sell us contraband stuff.' If Almeida were to go for it, everything would look much more dubious, I thought.

'What's he look like, this lad?' I demanded, and Luís' description was so close to that of the nephew of the old lady in Buarcos that I could not contain myself. 'Do you know who this chap is? He's the same one who saw me in his aunt's house.'

'One of those who go around with Rufininho, yes, I knew that. And I know which house it is, too.

'Have you ever been there?'

'No...' he said, colouring. 'I'm going to tell you something... Before the other day I never...'

'Never?'

'Never, at least not all the way, not like I wanted to, no.'

'Well, it wasn't the best start, was it? In front of so many people.'

He seemed surprised, his face very animated. 'Wasn't it? I thought it was terrific.'

'Terrific, eh? To have a woman or two? In front of everybody?

And that dirty tomfoolery, with the old man and the boy? What was terrific about that?'

'Everything. Just think ... me, a mere boy, in the middle of all that, with all you fellows, men already. And the old chap on his knees in front of everybody, in a church. It had everything.'

'Everything, how come?'

What had been for us some filthy madness (or, for Rodrigues, everybody indulging in those vices of his) had been, for Luís, a triumphant experience. I realised just how much barely suppressed rebellion there was within that tall, slender, calm boy, someone so quiet that my uncle had taunted him with the name Dona Micaela.

'And my brother, who's been preaching at me all my life,' he continued, confirming what I was thinking, 'wasn't he there, too? And all for my benefit.'

'Your benefit?'

'Of course. Wasn't it just to try me out and to humiliate my brother that Rodrigues set the whole thing up?'

'I don't think that's anything to be proud of,' I replied.

'Proud of, no; but when I saw the old man in front of me... it was as if the whole world were kneeling there before me.'

'And what would you be wanting with the whole world down on its knees in front of you?'

He looked at me painstakingly, unable to find either reasons or the words to express them. Finally he spoke: 'Because I'm sick of being pushed around: by my father – who doesn't even spare me a thought; by my aunt – who isn't my mother; by my brother – who's always going on about purity; by my teachers – who can only insult me; by my school fellows – who want me to be this or that, by...'

'You seem to have a terrible fear of things, and even of yourself, don't you?'

'I'm not afraid of anything.'

'You are, and of everything; if you weren't, you wouldn't have been so impressed by what happened.'

'Who isn't afraid of everything? You're not afraid? Rodrigues? My brother, isn't he afraid? And Ramos?'

'It's hard to say, Luís. For instance, right now your brother and Ramos are putting their lives on the line.'

'We all are, aren't we?'

'It's not the same thing. It's one thing to play with your life knowing you'll come out of it alive. The other, and it's a lot different, is to risk death.'

'Do you really think they might die?'

'Jesus wept! Think about it. We don't know whether the cops, on the heels of the Oporto escapees ... whether they really got away; if they didn't, the police will have slaughtered them. But even if they did embark they could have been shipwrecked; it's a long, dangerous journey, you know; Or they could have been attacked and sunk by a warship; or they could have been captured and shot by the Spanish. And if they arrive in one piece they could die in the war. Because it really is a war, do you understand that? And you think it doesn't amount to much?' I demanded, thinking to myself, as I listed the dangers, that I too hadn't been fully aware of just how great they were.

'I hadn't realised all that,' replied Luís, visibly impressed. 'It was just some mad stunt; I blame Ramos because he was the one who was ordering everyone around. But it'll be something worth shouting about if they pull it off.'

'Even if they don't manage to, it could still be something to shout about. It all depends on the circumstances,' I said, getting up and putting my clothes on over my bathing costume which I hadn't got wet. 'If you hear of anything else, let me know at once.'

'Let's go,' I said when I was ready.

He had been lost in thought. 'I only stuck around to have a word with you,' I said to him.

'Are you sure? Or was it to get me away from Rodrigues? Wasn't that the job my brother entrusted you with? And which my father unwittingly endorsed?'

'No; I stayed behind to find out something about what had happened. And as far as my "job", as you call it, is concerned, my feeling is that it's entirely up to you. You are the one who can profit from the situation if that's what you want; but don't forget that, whether you do or not, your going to Lisbon depends entirely on me; and it might depend even more once your father finds out that your brother has disappeared, and for some time, if not forever.'

'Will Carlos be away long?' he asked, like a child enquiring after someone who has vanished over the horizon.

'If he goes... Look... Even if the war doesn't last long and whether the Spanish Government wins or not, your brother might not return, while we have this government of ours here. If he did return it would just be to rot in gaol.'

'How is it that he can't come back?... But if they win the war and this government falls, then you'll see.'

'So you want your brother back quickly, then, eh? Aren't you happy to be shut of him?'

We were going along side by side up the street. 'That's different,' he said stopping.

'Very different,' I said, and we carried on in silence, with him accompanying me on my way (which I realised when I saw that he didn't seem to know where he was going), and going further out of his own. I stopped on a corner.

'Look, Luís, go on home,' I told him. 'And if you find anything out, we'll meet up round the end of the afternoon, in the café, that one over there. As long as we don't know anything, we can't move from here, understand?' I said, giving him a hard, deliberate stare.

He merely lowered his head. 'What time?' he asked.

'Any time between five and six,' I replied and we parted with a cold 'so long'.

What was I going to do now? Find Rodrigues, tell him everything, stop him going off on that absurd adventure with the old harpy? I couldn't, not before I had found out what had happened. Look for Mercedes? And it hurt me anew to think that I had forgotten her again. What if I phoned from somewhere beforehand?

I went into a shop and asked if I could use the phone. At the boarding house, they went to call her; she was such a long time that I was wondering if she was there or not, whether she wanted to speak to me or not, whether something serious had happened to stop her coming to the phone. With great reluctance I was about to replace the receiver and had almost put it back on the hook when I heard her voice: 'Who's there?'

'It's me, Jorge.'

'Ah, it's you, is it... What do you want?'

'To see you again.'

'Right now?'

'If it's possible.'

'I can't, right now.'

'You can't? Why not?'

'Not now. Call me later and I'll explain why.'

'Has something terrible happened?'

'No ... no... but phone me later,' she said and added in a whisper: 'Don't come here.'

'Why? Because of what happened in the corridor and the foyer last time I was there?'

'That too.'

'And what else?'

'Let me be, let me be…'

'Let you be, how can I? Don't you want me to talk to you again? Don't you want to see me again?'

'I'm only asking you to call me later,' she whispered in a worn-out, mournful voice.

'Do you love me?'

'I do. Very much. And you?' and because there was an almost imperceptible and brief hesitation in my voice, as I replied that I loved her so much, she fell silent at the other end of the line. 'Call me. I want you to…' she said after some moments.

'What do you want?' I asked, at the same time as, suddenly, I wanted not to possess her but to love her and court her ardently and tenderly, walking with her, hand in hand, on the beach, in the calm of the setting sun as it enfolded our footsteps in its intimate silence. 'What do you want?' I asked again.

'I've already told you.'

'I didn't hear. I was thinking of you, not listening to you. What did you say?'

'Nothing … nothing… Phone me.'

'Give me a kiss.'

There was short silence.

'I've done that,' she said. 'Oh, Jorge, Jorge … if only you knew …' and she hung up.

I went out into the street, my head reeling. Did I love her, after all, or not? Did I want her or not? What did I want her for?

That final question was going round and round inside my head; I couldn't get rid of it. What did I want her for? For my girlfriend – which she could no longer be, and because, too, since girls had been the occasion of our 'dirty little games', had the adolescent phase of chaste boy and girl friendships equally been consigned to the past? For my wife? For my lover? Could I love her and want her for no more than a lover? Could I have her and have her again, and still love and respect her? Or would I begin to treat her just as an object and not as a person? And, she, what did want of me? The idea of marrying her now seemed out of the question as far as she was concerned. And as for me? No, I didn't want to marry her, nor anybody else, or her, least of all. That really was the truth. And the truth was a little bit stranger still: I didn't want to marry her in order to have her; I didn't want to marry anyone in order to love that person. It was clear (at least it was clear to me) that she loved me and desired me. But she didn't want to cling to me, or, better, have me clinging to her. What there was, had been and would be between us depended on many people, on a lot of things which had happened, too many people, too many happenings, for our lives not to be at once closely bound and very separate. The blows we had inflicted on ourselves, with that story of a love snatched in the intervals, were much deeper than I had hitherto felt. Or the blows had hit so deep, precisely because our love, secretly, was like an open door, a house open to the public, a bed where many people had slept, all together.

It was the same thing, too, secretly, at the bottom of our own selves, and not because so many people knew about it, or even the fact that they knew. It had been born, or had grown, or we had possessed each other because there were so many people; and these people, although somewhere outside our life, had left a vacuum within it where, at any time, anybody else might come in, to do exactly as the first one had done. Therefore she continued to want me. And therefore I didn't want (I truly didn't want) to marry her. Not to marry her; or perhaps never marry. Perhaps she would. And, with me still single and her married, I would have her (or she would have me) as often as one of us wanted it. Because, marry whom she may, the man she met would always have enough of me in him for her to be unfaithful to me with him and not unfaithful to him with me. And for the rest, what state was I in to get married? Could we get along as lovers, more or less, for some years, getting married when I was earning enough to keep us? What sort of marriage would that be? One of those where the man ends up marrying when he's old and she is, too, with their maids who, as well as darning his socks and cooking their lunch, share their bed, too? Nor could I even picture Mercedes in any domestic setting: merely to try to imagine her doing things around the house made my flesh creep. Every domestic image I had seemed irredeemably grubby to my mind: my mother, my aunts, my friends' mothers. Grubby, not because they were truly dirty, but precisely because these people had agreed to start where the maids, whom they despised and who did all the dirty work, had left off.

Mercedes was, for me, such a painful, such an absolute love that I hadn't even realised just how great she was. And I couldn't see myself, lying in bed beside her, after eating the dinner which she had supervised. She didn't live in such a commonplace world. She lived, certainly, in a world full of things, people, ideas, events, all of them terrible, in which the noble and the sordid were impossible to prise apart, in which one could hardly tell which was which (an elegant way of convincing oneself, with some relief, that not everything was sordid). Even though the commonplace perhaps was not so, and there was nothing more commonplace, in spite of the way in which, unexpectedly, those days had given me such an incredibly vivid picture of life, than the fact that this very thing seemed to me – and was – so dreadful. But, even so, even with all this, or even in spite of all this, she, Mercedes, was different, a flower of many colours, a body with its own strange tang, a being who, even in betraying me, set a standard beside which all the rest of humanity would seem insignificant. There were things about her which I hated: her lips, the way she folded her hands; the way she hesitated, trying to express some thought whose convolutions escaped me. The way she enjoyed closing her legs tightly on my cock, or of releasing them again when she was driving me crazy. The way she had of looking beyond me. The concentrated passion with which she took me into her as if I was merely some kind of instrument. But, and I was finding all this out, what I hated was exactly what satisfied me most, was what bound me most to her, was what made her the first woman that I, in not knowing her, truly knew her, the last one I would know, for no other could be anything to me but a part of her.

This was what love was. It was love, truly love. But – and I smiled to myself – how difficult and irksome it was! Above all, it wasn't anything planned, just something that had happened by chance! At that I shuddered. We were but a chance happening, our meetings would be a matter of chance, our knowledge, our experience, of each other would always be a matter of chance, forever a random, contradictory sum of disconnected bits and pieces. A sum which would never amount to anything, to any final outcome, except merely a dream-like existence from which we would awake, sometimes, in each others' arms (and, who knows, in someone else's arms, too). Our life would not be – I couldn't even say 'our life', for this wasn't one, but two lives which we had, each one of us on his or her own account – an unclouded reality, with intervals of blissful dream, in which, in each other's arms, inside each other's bodies, we might attain for each other what each one could not attain for himself or herself. It would be just the opposite: everything that we might have, we would dissipate, from time to time, on these occasions, in each other's arms. We wouldn't be any use to each other. We could even – and this would be more certain – harm each other: we would see ourselves, each in the other, as in a mirror. And each time we saw each other like that, in these occasional meetings, we would only see ourselves to our own detriment. But we wouldn't have, it was true, other faces except those in which, reciprocally, we mirrored ourselves, and in which we could see that, on each occasion, we were further away from what we could have been, and, on each occasion, nearer, in the meantime what we were. Could this be love, could I call it love? Love – this onslaught, now and then, on the small part of us which we had preserved of ourselves, one against the other? Love – this shame in which we lived as though under some wretched spell, stripped of both integrity and dignity?

By now I was close to my uncle's gate and the thought of integrity and dignity made me laugh. Whose were these fine notions? What were they worth? What price did they command? There was only one way out for me: to run away from there, go back to Lisbon as quickly as possible, before I ceased to believe that there were others in the world beyond those around me and in whose lives I had become so entangled. But wasn't this really just the way life was? This awareness that there wasn't anybody else except all those who lived in the space around us? No, no, it wasn't. Or it was only, would only be so, to the extent that this 'space around us' might expand for ever, until it embraced the whole world, even if they were non-concentric circles and the widest ones not did not entirely enfold the lesser ones. These parts common to all the different circles were the coincidences which touched us all. And the secret resided in the fact that no circle was ever still, and that the coincidences were always changing, so much so that they could never repeat themselves. Did I not then want to see Mercedes again? What did the others matter to me? Was it because of them that I wanted to see her? Or was it because she had been so evasive when I phoned her? But wasn't I the one who hadn't listened to her when she had so clearly offered herself to me? What had really happened? It was clear, though, that it was nothing terrible, for she herself had assured me of that. What was the reason then for her low whispers on the phone? Had there been somebody standing nearby? And, if it wasn't because of those unpleasant scenes between Almeida and me which ruled out my going for her, what else could it be?

XXVIII

As I was going into the house I came across my cousin in the dining room.

'Are you proud of the way you behaved this morning?' he demanded, looking at me askance. 'Why did you stay out of it, without doing anything?'

'You lumped me in with them with your insults, and you still think I should have leapt to your defence? If you say something like that then you've got to accept the consequences.'

Ramiro was studying law; he was short, thick-set and stout, always set himself up as some tribune of the people. The hiding he got and the fact that Rodrigues had mounted him would have been the ultimate humiliation for him. For him and for anyone. But I was enjoying myself, seeing his face burning with an irritation which gave his ruddy cheeks and lantern jaw a silky glow. And as his chin quivered it was as if the ironic hand of Odette, over whom we had sometimes quarrelled, was chucking him under it with her whore's tenderness.

'I promise you that I'm going to get together half a dozen chaps who'll teach Rodrigues a lesson. He'll see.'

'Are you going to act out that story about the Chinaman with him?'

'What Chinaman?'

'Don't you know that one about the colonial administrator who, when he asked which women were available there in the little village to which he had been posted, was told that there weren't any woman, just the Chinaman? The problem was, it needed six men to hold him down?'

'Very funny.'

'Well, I think so.'

'I'd like to see whether Rodrigues thinks so afterwards.'

'Who knows if you won't be doing him a favour? He might end up thinking so.'

'You're utterly depraved. The Government is quite right to say that the time for a clean-up is here. Salazar, now, he's going to put things straight.'

'Ah, so you're all for the clean-up?'

'Yes, I am. And I can tell, too, that you're on the side of the rabble.'

'Well then, what are you doing here in Figueira, at the very moment when the Government needs you to be sweeping the streets? Probably, down there in Lisbon, there's a broom just waiting for you. And I'm not on the side of any rabble, by the way.'

'I've the same right as you to be here.'

'Sure you have; but you shouldn't abuse it by acting like some crazy idiot.'

'When auntie and uncle come down for lunch I'll let you know who's crazy here.'

'Are you going running to them to complain? I bet you've already pissed in your pants.'

'No, I haven't. But you'll see how I shit on that lot when they mess me about.'

'Since you only got here yesterday you haven't had that many people to shit on yet.'

'One morning is enough for me to learn a lot of things.'

'Such as?'

'When they come down you'll soon find out.'

'About me?'

'More or less.'

'I'm already quaking in my boots.'

'Carry on, then; you'll be quaking for real soon enough.'

'The worst thing for you will be if they already know what you're going to tell them.'

'Maybe they don't know.'

'Maybe not. But will it be something that interests them? For they're not all that interested in other people's lives, nor, quite frankly, in their own.'

That was a subtlety way beyond the bombast which, in him, sometimes passed for wit. And I myself, to my surprise, read in his face, just as I had changed the way in which I understood others, that he was on the point of putting this understanding into words, and of hearing them. I smiled, but only to myself rather than to him, with something of a childish, self-satisfied superiority, which wasn't lost on him. 'Smile, smile away...' he said. And then in French he added: 'He who laughs last laughs best.'

His little bit of French got right up my nose: 'It's only idiots who quote French,' I said.

My aunt and uncle entered the dining room, followed by Maria with the soup tureen. They seemed more like newly weds coming down into the great hall of the hotel where they were spending their honeymoon than someone whose own house it was. They took their places, exchanging affectionate glances which didn't go so far, other than as a brief acknowledgement, to include either of us. My aunt served the soup while my uncle picked up his napkin – and, oddly, he hesitated between putting it on his lap or tucking it around his scrawny neck – and dipped his spoon into the soup.

'Well then, Ramiro,' he demanded, 'is everything all right down there in Lisbon?'

'The family is fine. And there's a great deal going on down there; everybody is full of approval for the Government's firm stand over the matter of the war in Spain.'

My uncle set down his spoon and ran his fingers forward through his hair. 'Everybody?' he asked, looking fixedly at Ramiro. 'Who are these people who are so full of approval? Only those guttersnipes in the army who are carrying on the war with their inanities on the radio.'

I smiled, glancing at the non-plussed Ramiro; he wasn't one to disagree openly with those to whom, for whatever reason, he was beholden. With his nose poised over the soup he prepared his little lawyer's volte-face: 'Oh, those … nobody takes them seriously. But, truly, many people are all for it,' he said lifting up his head, his demeanour suitably modified.

'And you? Are you all for it?' asked my uncle, breaking off a piece of bread.

'Very much. I believe it is the only just position to take.'

'I never knew you had such strong political convictions. Have you already got some job in mind?' asked my uncle, crumbling his bread into the soup.

'A job? Goodness, uncle! But it is very fitting that everybody should be required to declare his beliefs, for whoever is not for us is against us.'

'Us? Who, exactly?'

'We, the patriots, we who don't want the country handed over to Communism. You would not believe, uncle, the network of those people; it's a huge conspiracy.'

'I would, I would. So, whoever is not for us is against us then?'

'Exactly.'

'Woman,' roared my uncle, 'Take this filthy soup away! It's full of crumbs. Woman!' (and my aunt shot an accusing look at Ramiro while Maria hastily snatched the bowl away). 'Your nephew is a wretch. Against us, eh? Listen, you halfwit, did you come here to Figueira to swim in the sea or did you come here to my house to scoff my soup and preach your asinine notions as well.'

'Oh, Justino…' began my aunt.

'Be quiet, woman, don't be an idiot. Only an idiot like you could have a nephew like this.'

'But don't you know these are yours!'

'Mine? They're only mine when they aren't talking through their backsides. When they do, they're yours. Woman!…'

Ramiro decided to take the initiative and change the angle of attack: 'And when they make a hash of things they're not yours, either?' he asked.

My uncle looked at him and exchanged a glance with me. 'When they make a hash of things *they're mine*, too,' he said. 'Every man makes a hash of some things. It's only those fellows who just dribble and slobber who aren't men.'

'Justino, you can't say things like that,' said my aunt, butting in.

'I can and I will. Don't you know by now? Have you never made a hash of anything?' he demanded, accusingly, of Ramiro, pointing with his spoon.

'Not so far as I know. But…'

'But what?'

'There are those who have.'

'Leave off making signs with your eyes towards your cousin,' exclaimed my uncle. 'What nonsense has he been up to, that bothers you so much? Deflowered a virgin, is that it? Taken her to some joint somewhere, is that it? And got mixed up with her and doesn't know how to extricate himself, is that it? Do you think that, just off the train yesterday, you can tell us things we don't already know? And wipe that expression off your face, like St Anthony at the garden gate, you halfwit. Now, go and eat soap. Woman, what's happened to my soup?'

I was torn between delight at this little tussle with Ramiro and unease at the fact that my secret was no longer a secret, as well as sickened that it wasn't me who had deflowered Mercedes, that they had assigned to me a pleasure the lack of which maddened me. But how had Ramiro found out? From Rodrigues, unquestionably. And my uncle, how had he got to know everything? Was the matter public knowledge? The fear that I felt made me uncertain as to its real meaning: was it disgust at my – and Mercedes' – intimate affairs being bruited around, or was it the fear that this public knowledge might land me with responsibilities which I didn't want to take on, nor, at that time, could take on? But, if I didn't want to, or couldn't, what sort of love was this of mine? For shouldn't I, in truth, be thinking in terms of responsibilities, not even whether to accept them or refuse them, but in terms of love alone? That was what was going through my mind, while I did not raise my eyes to anyone, during the strained silence which followed my uncle's outburst.

My uncle put his spoon down on the empty bowl (having drunk the soup which my aunt had served him again). 'Jorge...' he said, 'I want to talk to you after lunch.'

'Very well, uncle.'

'I...' stammered Ramiro, 'I... I'm sorry, uncle, I didn't mean any harm.'

'I believe you, my lad, I believe you. When animals bite they do it without meaning any harm. It's in their nature to bite; or kick out. Now that you've kicked out, have your lunch in peace. So there are all those approving souls in Lisbon then? Well, here too. It's quite clear that the moment they start recruiting you'll be the first to join up, isn't that so?'

'Me?' said Ramiro in amazement.

'When people are all for a war, then they join up for it, didn't you know?' said my uncle grinning, as he mashed his potatoes into the meat stew. 'In the great wars it doesn't matter if the people aren't exactly in favour, because they get called up anyway and the Government will take care of any enthusiasm. I, for example, who was a soldier, never needed enthusiasm. Any enthusiasm on my part was merely a professional matter. But a civil war is the enthusiast's delight. If I were you, I'd join up; and if there's no chance of that I'd run off to Spain.'

My aunt and I exchanged hasty, embarrassed glances.

'But there is so much to fight against here in...' began Ramiro.

'Fine, fine,' said my uncle. 'But don't get worked up about it; I'm not making you hand your little body over to the manifesto. But don't come quoting the *Diário de Notícias* at me.'

'How you have changed, uncle,' said Ramiro, 'what with this new interest in politics.'

'Me?' said my uncle. 'I've never been interested, nor am I now, you're very much mistaken. Politics is for politicians. But there are some things which everybody has a duty to understand.'

'That's what I believe, too,' said Ramiro.

'That's as maybe,' replied my uncle. 'We all think that way, but it's things themselves that can't remain the same.'

'The fundamental things, though, are always the same,' said Ramiro, ponderously. 'Don't you agree, uncle?'

'In these times ... how does it seem to you, Jorge?'

'Eh?'

'Do you believe that the fundamental things are the same for everybody?'

'It depends.'

'Eating, sleeping, having a good scratch,' said my uncle, 'these are all the same for everybody. But then ...'

'Then?' repeated Ramiro, obligingly.

My uncle fell into a silent study, gathering his thoughts; he looked at Ramiro. 'Then, lad, that's it,' he said. 'As the saying goes, the cows died and the bulls were left. And the most important thing is not to be a cow.' Ramiro essayed a joke: 'All the bulls are cows, once they die.'

'Yes...' said my uncle, 'and it's this very thing which marks out a man, for as far as having horns is concerned you can't tell one cuckold from another. Justino!' he added, fondling my aunt's hand. 'Have you seen what it is to have an attentive husband? Before one even took the bait, I saved her the bother of telling me off. Or should I keep quiet about it?' He turned to us: 'Perhaps not, for as far as the horns are concerned your aunt is less sensitive. With time, people can get used to anything.'

My aunt drew her hand away and made as if to get up.

'Stay where you are, woman,' he said, taking her hand again, 'it's not good form to leave the table before your nephews have finished' – only Ramiro was still eating – 'and it's not even worth it for something which is the most trivial thing in the world. Is there anyone in this world who hasn't cuckolded someone or been cuckolded himself? We never even know whether the horns are ours or someone else's.'

My uncle got up and motioned me to follow him. At the door he turned round. 'Look, Ramiro,' he said, 'go off for a dip in the sea, eat and sleep in our house, keep your aunt company since Jorge hasn't time to do it, and as far as Lisbon politics are concerned, keep your trap shut. This is Figueira da Foz, do you hear?'

He went up to his study, seated himself on the throne, studiously rolled a cigarette and only looked at me when, with his head cocked, he had lit it. He must have been waiting for me to speak first but I remained silent.

'What nonsense is this that you're mixed up in which that slimy little cousin of yours is bursting to tell me about?' he finally demanded. 'What on earth did you do to make him so furious with you?'

'This morning when I got to the beach I found him there with Rodrigues and Luís Macedo. Rodrigues, as usual, was spouting all that dirty rubbish of his and then Ramiro started insulting all of us and so Rodrigues and Luís gave him a hiding and I didn't try to stop them.'

'Hmm ... and what about the story he was dying to tell? That'll be the day when I pay any attention to gossip, and in front of your aunt, the little schemer, the little Dona Micaela!'

The beating given Ramiro by Luís had evidently meant that the title had been passed on, as though it were some kind of boxing championship in reverse; I laughed to myself at this promotion of Ramiro to the title of Dona Micaela, which fitted to a T his chubby, rubicund figure.

'But what's really going on?' my uncle persisted. 'There's no question there's more to it than that.'

Could it be that he really knew nothing or almost nothing, and he'd only been making these clever little assumptions just to shut Ramiro up?

For that reason I merely said: 'I never deflowered any virgin.'

'You didn't? So she wasn't a virgin then?'

'She? Who?'

'Whoever she is! I don't know and I don't even want to know. But are you mixed up in some sort of shady goings on?'

'No, uncle, not in that sense. There's someone I love and I took her to one of those houses, you know, and I ended up going back again with her. And I don't want to let her go.'

'Are you sure?'

'Yes.'

'Do you know what you have to do? No? Take the next train back to Lisbon. She's not from Lisbon, is she? She can't go chasing down there after you, can she?'

'But why should I have to run away from her? Why shouldn't I make the most of the situation while it lasts?' I said, my heart aching at having to speak in this way.

'Of course you should; you have to, even. It's a man's duty to take advantage of such opportunities, so that he doesn't weep subsequently in his bed which is only warm when he's not alone. But,' and he paused to think, 'if she's older than you, make the most of it, because there's no danger, it's something every boy goes through, for they all need at some time to feel they're older and more manly than they really are. But if you're the same age, get out or you're lost.'

'Lost, in what way?'

'Ah, so she is your age then … just as I'd thought. Get out, lad, get out. Or you'll end up falling for the one thing a man shouldn't fall for. Don't you know what it is? The hole between her legs. There's a lot of it about and it's there for us to give and take pleasure in. That's all. Falling for someone is another matter. You'll take my advice tonight? You won't; why not?'

'No.'

'Can't you see?'

'I'm not going to because she doesn't attract me.'

'What do you mean, she doesn't attract you? There's a woman who opens her legs on the spot and she's not ugly and a man isn't interested in her? Fairytales… And you don't want the other one right now; that's just where the danger lies.'

'It isn't that, uncle'

'Why isn't it?'

How could I explain it to him?

'You can't compare one with another,' I said.

'You can't? Aren't they both at your beck and call? Or can't you manage two of them?'

'Of course I can.'

'Or are you thinking that you soil your girl if you stick it in her after the other one? Water washes everything away.'

I pictured myself at the edge of the water, in the dawn, with Rodrigues and Carlos Macedo. 'Almost everything,' I said.

'Yes … you're quite right … it would be an awful bother.' I looked at him in surprise as he followed this new chain of thought. 'Yes … and you couldn't be sure you wouldn't catch some disease through Micaela and then… Look,' he said suddenly, as if alarmed by some new idea, 'but you must have been a real idiot to… Of course you were, it's obvious you were. That's always the case. Look, what if she gets pregnant…?'

'You know about these midwife things, uncle…'

He smiled indulgently at the bitterness he observed in my voice.

'That's so,' he replied, 'and more than you might think. Nobody gets away with being a teacher of boys, like I have been for so many years without... And I can tell you there are a lot more difficult labours.'

I remembered Rodrigues. 'It's just that sometimes the child dies,' I observed.

He opened his eyes wide, arching his eyebrows in theatrical surprise. 'Oh, Jorge ... when it's a boy, the child always dies.'

Momentarily I was absorbed in thought; I felt for him deeply. 'If I need anything I'll talk to you,' I said, after a moment.

'That's just what I want to hear,' he said, getting up from his throne behind the desk; he walked round it and laid a hand on my shoulder. 'You know something? One day you'll look back with longing at these strange days; you'll see how it is. In time people end up being nostalgic about everything,' and he smiled.

'Life's a shameless business,' he added.

'You know, uncle,' I began, 'it looks like they got away.'

He took his hand off my shoulder. 'They? Who?'

'They.'

'That's all behind us now, we won't talk about again. It's over and done with. Did you find anything out?'

'Not yet, though Luís told me there's no sign of his brother. When I find out I'll tell you.'

'You can; but I'm not interested. Goodbye,' he said and waited for me to leave before solemnly closing the study door behind me.

XXIX

Shortly afterwards I left the house to phone Mercedes. I went along the road, looking for a shop from where I could call; but I knew very well that, in truth, I was doing my very best to get close to her physically, so much so that the two or three places with phones that I passed didn't seem to me to be at all suitable, though perhaps they were no less so than the one, down by the Bairro Novo, from where I phoned her.

She answered quickly, to my surprise and consternation (for at the same time I was looking forward to the perverse pleasure, which I had been missing, of her taking her time, of savouring the enjoyment of knowing that she was there close to the phone, doing nothing but waiting for my voice).

'Is that you?'

'Yes. Well, were you waiting for me?'

'I was. If you want...'

'Where shall we meet?'

'There... Do you think we can?'

'What time? I'll get there first.'

'At five.'

'Any news?'

'I'll tell you later.'

'Darling...' and there was a silence at her end, as if she had closed her eyes to let my voice sink in more completely.

'Goodbye for now,' she said finally and hung up.

It was half past two. I could go and find Rodrigues, to get some explanation about who had sent him to say things to my cousin, for he must already have said a lot more than he had admitted in front of me, or Ramiro would not otherwise have spoken with such menacing assurance. In the final reckoning, to say that Rufininho had seen me with a woman in that joint was not sufficient for what my cousin had been trying to suggest. Or could it have been Luís? But how? I headed towards Rodrigues' boarding house, not sure whether I would still find him, if that story about the car which the old woman was sending to pick him up was true. Two hours had already gone by.

From afar, though, I could see him at the door, with a

nervous air of expectation. I approached him.

'Ah! So finally you've decided to come with me, eh?' he said at once. 'You're lucky the car's late; they must be putting me to the test, to see whether I'd wait or not. But I'm here all right, as you can see.'

'Rodrigues, can you tell me what you said about me to Ramiro?'

'About you?'

'Don't beat about the bush.'

'Nothing.'

'Nothing, other than what you said in front of me?'

'Is that why you've come?'

'It is, and because he's going around pretending he knows something big, and only you could have told him. He even tried it on with my uncle to get his own back for the beating.'

'I didn't tell him anything. I only said that now, you wouldn't be quarrelling with him over anyone like Odette, and that he could relax and take his pick of all the whores now.'

'And does he know who the girl is?'

'Yes, he does.'

'Who told him that? You or Luís? He only arrived last night and this morning he was with you two.'

'But everybody knows.'

'Right now it doesn't matter to me who knows, or how. What I want to know is how he found out.'

'I didn't tell him; nor, in front of me, did Luís.'

'Can you swear to that?'

'Well ... not exactly. But I can swear that he asked if it was true and I told him it was.'

'Have you got anything to back you up? If he's not my friend, nor yours either, why did you need to be so open with him?'

He smiled cynically, jiggling his hands in his trouser pockets and leaning against the door jamb. 'I always feel the need to be open with somebody... Only later do I realise that I've picked the wrong person...'

'How does he know? How is it that everybody knows? Who are they, all these people in the know?'

'Seeing that you really want to know the lot... Look, Rufininho saw you... And that chap of his there, too, saw her quite plainly, and had the idea of blackmailing you both, because he followed you and found out who she was. Rufininho went looking for me, so that I could warn you not to go there again.'

'When was all this?'

'Last night. And I told Rufininho that if anything happened, he'd pay for it with his skin.'

'And that's when everybody got to know about it, so much so that this morning Ramiro, who only got here yesterday, has already got wind of it, too? Do you reckon it's possible?'

'The damned car, it's not coming ... the old woman has stood me up... Eh? Yes, it doesn't seem possible, really... Do you think that your cousin bumped into Rufininho and he told him?'

'Ramiro doesn't talk to Rufininho. None of us talk to Rufininho, not even you.'

'Of course not, not even me. I've never talked to him. Even when he ... well ... then I speak even less.'

'For shame!'

'Don't forget that it was through your intervention or through what you swore to that I lost all shame.'

'But how on earth did Ramiro find all this out?'

'Ask him.'

'I don't trust him enough to do that.'

'Well then...'

'You know more than you're prepared to admit.'

'And you? Don't you also know something you don't want to tell me?'

At that moment a huge, black car, covered in dust, pulled up in front of us. Within there was an old woman who leaned out of the just opened window and directed a brazen smile, full of malice, at Rodrigues; the smile was directed at me, too, and had a slow, leisurely insolence, fixed contemptuously on us, a smile such as one sees in the eyes of the rich when, in front of some shop window they disdainfully weigh up all the things they know they can afford to buy. But in her gaze, which I bore equally fixedly and with some curiosity, there was also a watery, voracious light, and a flicker of unease and insecurity in the darting, wavering movements of her pupils. Her dark blonde hair hung in curls around a face heavily powdered with white, in which her lips were tight and thin within the wider, red smear of lipstick. Her hand, with its long fingers and the pink oblongs of her nails, rested on the open window; there were two or three rings on each finger, all heavy with huge stones. She must once have been much more beautiful than my aunt had ever been, but it was as if my aunt, instead of that air of absent-minded purity which hovered over her features and gestures, had tricked herself out as some carnival harpie, or as Teodora de Bizâncio after she had worn out successive generations of stableboys and carried in her unwashed face the taste of cock cheese from unclean foreskins. Her tongue, which flickered between her half open lips, seemed forked, more frayed than viperous. She was a fascinating creature, so intensely perfumed and of such repugnance that even the car and the uniformed chauffeur, who had alighted to open the door for Rodrigues, seemed to partake of it too. When Rodrigues got in the car, climbing over her to sit on the other side, she put her hand on the curve of his waist, like someone stroking an ill-tempered pet dog. And when he had sat down, and barely turned to me with an expression full of anxious embarrassment, she put her other hand on his thigh, at the same time smiling a benign goodbye at me which suggested, in an almost professional fashion, that that thigh now in her possession, could just as well be, on some other occasion, mine.

The car shot off and as I turned a little to look after it I could still see in the face of the clerk at the boarding house, standing dumbfounded by the door, the respectful awe which the rings and the car and the curls had produced in him. And with a smile of complicity, which also embraced the new heights to which Rodrigues had ascended (and me, indirectly) his awe turned into a kind of envious servility.

'That's some car... We could get a whole lot of us in that...' he said.

I turned away and in my imagination I could still see, sparkling, the old woman's teeth, which, though she hadn't opened her mouth, must have been white and pointed, flecked all over with green, like those of a vampire. In my mind her mouth opened up, dark, ruby, damp with white fibres, tepid, sucking in breath, and, in the teeth sharp as razor clams, behind the front ones (sharp, curved) there were stuck between them, like bits of bread, bloody, spongy pieces of the cocks she had bitten off after she had caressed them with her ring-heavy fingers. The car itself seemed like her mouth: it was lined with flesh; or the mouth itself, for its part, revealed a lining of fabric, opening on hinges onto the bodywork, which, black, was her white-pigmented face. Going into the car Rodrigues had been like the child in a human sacrifice, flung headlong into the burning belly of gods who feasted on human flesh. The car door, as it slammed behind him, was like the knife which gelded him. And the one who had sold him into all that was me. Shuddering at the horror of it all, craving the soft tenderness of Mercedes' breast, I made my way to the house of the other old woman.

Suddenly Rufininho's warning, the one Rodrigues had passed on to me, made me stop in my tracks. But I immediately recalled that if they had set off then the lad had gone with them, taking his planned blackmail with him. And only afterwards did I remember that, because everybody (who exactly?) knew about us, then the blackmail had no force. But who were all these people in the know? Maybe Mercedes could tell me. I knocked on the door.

The old woman took her time opening the door; and when she eventually did come, after I saw her first peep out at me through the window, she did not open it enough to let me through.

'What do you want, sir?'

'A room at five o'clock.'

'There isn't one at five. Go somewhere else,' she said, her face bright with malice.

'I've already fixed it up.'

'Well, unfix it, then.'

'Are you going to let me come in, or do you want me to tell the police what I know?'

She looked at me, clearly uneasy.

'Tell them what?' she asked, before countering: 'And do you want me to tell them that you've brought respectable girls to my house, ruining them for your own dirty pleasure?'

I stuck my foot in the door; just as she tried violently to close the door, hurting me terribly in the process. 'Just drop all that nonsense,' I said, when the worst pain had passed. 'Open the door. Your nephew set off last night, didn't he? I knew all about it; I already knew when I ran into him here.'

She opened the door at once. 'I've been betrayed, betrayed,' she sighed. 'These fellows can't even respect my house,' and she shut the door behind me.

I followed her to the kitchen, where she sat down at the table, her head bowed, without saying a word.

'I know that your nephew, among others, stole a boat,' I began, 'and that they fled with it last night.'

'They didn't steal anything; they borrowed the boat.'

'But it was for a long trip from which they might not even return.'

'What do you mean, not return? They will return, god willing. And the boat's not going for any further than it regularly does.'

'Is your nephew among those who're bringing it back?' I demanded.

'He swore to me he would.'

'What's this story that he was trying to blackmail me? I know all about that? too. He tried it on the other day, you know. Is that something you do often here? You have people in and then you go after them, eh? Do you think that it would work with me? It's no secret that I come here? you know.'

'He's a scoundrel that boy, a good-for-nothing wretch, a cross I have to bear. Whenever he can he's up to some mischief. One day he'll fetch up here dead, what a disgrace...' and by the way in which she slurred her words I realised she was drunk, and that, so far, she had had just enough sense and speech to keep me at bay. There were two bottles by the side of the chimney.

'But you'll get some of what he gets out of it, won't you?'

'He gives all the money he earns; I don't really know why. He's such a good boy, sometimes,' and she burst into tears. 'Such a good boy! He says they're just a rabble and they have the money to pay for their vices.'

'And his vices, who pays for them?'

'He doesn't have any vices. Only the devil within him.'

'And when he shuts himself up in a bedroom with Rufininho or one of Rufininho's friends, who are his customers and the lad's, too, you don't call that vice?'

'No, sir, I don't. They're the wicked ones, they're the ones who've led him off the straight and narrow. He takes their money, though, even from Rufininho, who's looked after us so much, he always takes his. If he didn't take it that would be vice. Rufininho is so kind, poor chap. He likes my boy so much, he's always telling him they should go to Lisbon together. But my boy laughs in his face and makes him pay the going rate.'

'The going rate?'

'Yes, sir, the price he's fixed for Rufininho,' and she raised to me her face which was so much like that of the other old woman, as if her vices were those of the other. Her lips drooped down with deep lines at the corners. With a great effort she half opened her eyes. The lines on her face were deeply marked, not just with old age but also with black grime. If she ever wished to clean herself up one day she would need to scrape out the lines, one by one, with the specially sharpened nail of her little finger. Her purple stained tongue hung slackly and with her head lolling on one side with the effort of getting up, she looked like someone who'd just been hung. In fact her life had been a kind of hanging. I shuddered to think how much like all of us.

'The room is clean and made up, excuse me, sir. I was so worried, I didn't know what I was saying. I trapped your foot, I'm sorry. I didn't hurt you, did I? Do you know where they went, sir?'

'No.'

'But you said you knew.'

'I said I knew that they had gone, but not where. You are the one who knows where they've gone because you told me the boat was going no further than it had already been.'

'I don't know ... I don't know. It usually goes to Vigo, or even Corunna, that's what I've heard. Sometimes further, to the open sea up there.'

'Well, then, they must have gone as far as the open sea up there.'

She did not reply. Then she spoke: 'Sir ... if your girl should need anything ... talk to me, don't go looking for anyone else.'

'Need what?'

'Well...' and she made an effort to smile. 'Sometimes, when people aren't too careful, things happen ... many women come looking for me... and it's all done so cleanly.'

'But it's you who ...'

'Well ... if it's a cheap job it's me ... but when you can pay a bit more I have someone − self-taught, she is − who has a knack for these things,' she said. 'You haven't come here,' she added with a sudden voluble passion, 'to have babies, have you? You and your girl come here to enjoy yourselves, because you're just kids, because you love each other, because you love ... you do love each other, don't you?'

I nodded.

'And do you want her to be left with a baby in her arms? Does she want to be left with your kid in her belly? Because you, you men, think it's only a matter of sticking it in, poking it about and taking it out, and the worst bit is what you leave in there. And the girls never remember that bit, when they're in the thick of it, having a good time,' she said, her eyes glittering. 'It's just having a good time, isn't it? A good time...' and she paused, remembering the good times with voluptuous relish, her eyes empty and wide open. 'A good time which turns out bad,' she concluded finally, her face set hard.

'Why does it turn out bad?' I asked.

'Hmm, you mean you don't know ? Everything that begins well ends badly, and everything that begins badly ends well. That's the way it is. You get your girls, everything's going along fine, everything in the garden's rosy, it's all a delight, isn't it? And then her belly starts to swell, and then another wretch is born into this world of Christ. And you tell me, sir, for what?'

'I don't know.'

'What do we come into this world for? Go on, what for? I know, I know. To suffer; so that we all suffer, all of us. And do you know why? Because we just enjoy ourselves without thinking. And then later there they are. If we thought about it, we wouldn't be born.'

'Nor would we have children.'

'Nor would we have children, that's very well put, sir. And if they dared to show their faces, we'd get rid of them.' Her eyes blazed with furious glee. 'Get rid of 'em, wash 'em down the drain. The drain, eh?' and she laughed abruptly. 'The drain … the drain …' she repeated, 'down the drain.'

A cold shiver ran down my spine as I thought that I too could have gone down the drain, tipped from a bucket (like those other babies that my parents had not wanted). My reaction was to think vengefully how good it would have been if − in retrospect − we had known in good time whom to dispatch in that fashion. That old woman, for example. And what if such a thing had happened to Mercedes, too? But then she would no longer be Mercedes but some disgusting foetus. And I heard a knocking at the door, in a fluster of happiness, as if I, Mercedes, the world, only that knocking, were all emerging from some filthy drain into each other's arms.

'Go on, open up, it's her,' said the old woman, 'I'm not expecting anyone else today, not at this time. Don't forget,' she added as I was already in the corridor, 'I'm here at your service, whatever you need.' And she sniggered and then tripped over, which at least made me smile.

I opened the door a bit and there was Mercedes; she came in, kissed me greedily on the lips and slipped into the room where we had been previously.

Inside the room she turned to me. 'You know that I am lost, don't you?' she said. 'My parents know everything − they even know that I'm here with you now.'

'Does that bother you? If you're here with me, why should it bother us that everybody knows about us?'

She nestled close to me, rubbing her stomach against mine, kissing me and holding my head in her hands. 'It only bothers me because they might want to stop us meeting each other; they might want to make you marry me.'

'And then?'

'I don't want you to be forced to do anything. I don't want to be forced to do anything. I only want to be able to carry on seeing you.'

I helped her to get undressed, she undressed me; our mouths never parted for an instant. Naked, standing up, we faced each other and she put her hands on my shoulders. 'I want to be yours, freely yours. If at any time I want you, even though I have the best men in the world, and the worst, and I call you and you don't come ... do you know what I would do?'

I drew her to me but she stepped back. With the tips of her breasts rubbing against my chest and her hands reaching down to grasp my erect cock I hardly heard her speak.

'I'd kill myself,' she said.

XXX

We lay stretched out side by side; Mercedes' hand was stroking me softly up and down my chest, my stomach, my waist, while I traced the line of the furrow up the middle of her back with the hand which half held her over me.

'Did they get away?' I asked.

As soon as I had asked I knew it wasn't the question I wanted to ask.

'Yes, they did,' she replied, carrying on with her caresses.

'Are you absolutely sure?' And since that was also a question I did not want to ask, I felt that it really didn't matter to me whether they had set off, because, for me, as for the others, it was as if they had gone.

'I'm absolutely sure.'

'How do you know?' It was like a game of questions and answers.

'Because Carvalho, as we had arranged, called me when he got back from taking them.'

'Called you?'

'Yes, me.'

'To tell you what?'

'Nothing. If he called me it meant everything had gone according to plan.'

'But it was very late. Did you stay up waiting?'

'Yes.

'Didn't your parents suspect anything?'

'No; they know now, though.'

Instead of asking her how they had found out her words reminded me of another kind of discovery.

'And how did they find out about us?'

'Because, last night, before they set off, Almeida told them.'

'Bastard.'

She stopped caressing me, just as I had done. 'No, he isn't. He said that, in spite of what had happened between you and me, he would still marry me.'

'Of course he is. If he went...'

She raised herself so that she could look me straight in the eye. 'Jorge... He didn't go...'

I sat up abruptly. 'He didn't go?'

'No,' and she adjusted her hair with an automatic movement. 'At the last moment he didn't go, precisely because of what he had said.'

'And you?'

'I said that I wouldn't marry him, nor you.'

'And he?'

'He? What?'

'Where is he?'

'He must have gone today.'

'Where to?'

'I don't know and I don't care.'

'You don't care?'

'Do you know what he did yesterday? Made a scandal in the casino, in front of a crowd of people, shouting out loud at the top of his voice that I was a...'

'Don't. What a shit...'

'No, he isn't. He was right. That's what I am.'

'Don't say that.'

'Why not? Does it bother you? Isn't that what you've made me?'

I grabbed her arms, squeezing them. 'If you don't shut up...'

'What will you do? Hit me?'

I let my hands drop. We were sitting side by side on the edge of the bed.

'If you don't shut up, that is really what you are,' I said, in a dull voice.

Then there I was, unable to look at her, unable to make any kind of gesture, unable to put an idea or even two words together. For an age, like that. Until, without understanding or even wanting to understand, I saw her roll over and kneel before me, and putting her arms around my haunches, bury her head in my loins. Bending her head, and her hair spilling over my lap I felt at the same time her mouth, gently nibbling on me. I tried to pull her up but she resisted. Then falling backwards, I pulled her towards me and made her turn until I could hold her hips, my eyes unseeing under her loins as she had gripped my hips too. Later, as our mouths met again neither of us knew any longer which part of us was our own and which the other's.

Then, our arms around each other, in the gathering night which was filling the room, spreading like a black mist from its dark corners, sparing only the whiteness of our bodies, we told each other, in a jumble of details and speaking of things which the other one did not always understand clearly but still grasped at a deeper level. She told me about those scenes at which she had not been present: her brother, Almeida, her parents, it was as if they were there, calm and contemptible, sitting at our side. The same thing happened with my aunt and uncle, the Macedo brothers, Rodrigues, my uncle's mother-in-law. None of them were more than bit players in the story of our love. And our love itself, far-off, satiated, was no more than a bit player in its own story, and we felt none of its pain.

We got up, washed and dressed.

'Tomorrow my parents are leaving,' she said. 'They know about the escape to Spain, too.'

At first I didn't understand. 'They're off? Where are they going?'

'We're going home.'

'Home?'

'You too?'

'Where do you want me to go? Do you want me to stay? But how?'

'Stay with me.'

'Where?'

'You see how I am what he said I was,' she said in answer to my despairing silence. 'You don't even have anywhere you can take me...'

'Don't say that,' I said, motionless beside her. 'I've nowhere to take you because I have nowhere I can call mine.'

'Nor I.'

'Neither of us has anything but the other.'

'And each of us is too much in the other's life,' she said slowly.

I embraced her and kissed her. 'No ... no ... that's not so,' I replied.

'It's true, though. Do you want me to show you?'

'No, I don't want you to.'

She covered my eyes with her hands. 'You can't see, but listen anyway,' she said tenderly. 'Can I go to your uncle's house? No. Can I go with you to Lisbon? No. Can I live here in this room? No. Can you pay for a room for me somewhere? No.'

'But we could work and live together.'

'Work? At what? Only if it was this thing we do together ... Oh, my love, how I wish it wasn't like this... I can only ruin your life ... You know? We met each other too young, or too late. And you only ventured to have me as you did because someone else had

had me before you. And I gave myself to you, whom I loved, only because the other had made me his and yours too. Before, we would not have loved as we did love, would we? And now it's too late to start from the beginning again; we never had a beginning, my love. The only thing we can do is not let there be an end to our love. Anything more that we do for it, that we sacrifice for it, can only end it sooner, or end the life which allows us to have it.'

'How can you say all this, how can you even think it, so calmly?'

'But I'm not calm, darling, not at all. Quite the contrary.'

'And do you think our love can stand all this? That it will last forever if we are not always, at all times, close to one another?'

'If it doesn't last, even with all those other people around, it's because it isn't the love we think it is.'

'And do you think the others will put up with all this?'

'They don't need to know.'

'But if they don't know, how can we hold up our heads honestly in front of them?'

'I don't owe anything like that to anyone, except to you and to myself. Yet you're already thinking you might marry someone else, have children and from time to time, in spite of everyone else, be with me, be what you are to me.'

'I'm not.'

'I believe you. But you don't need me.'

'I need you all the time, at every moment of the day.'

'But I'm not with you all the time, at every hour of the day, only for these hours, these moments. I know your body, like no other woman has ever known it, and I belong to you completely, as if I were some woman that you paid for.'

'No.'

'Yes... You pay me with your love, not just with your flesh, or with your thoughts. When you're inside me you don't think of anything, anything at all, do you? Not even of me? Not even of yourself? Your love – what I feel love should be – is this. You could never give me more than you do.'

'Do you think I don't give you enough, that I'm not able to give you any more?'

'No; I've explained myself badly, I'm sorry, darling. What I want to say is that for me this is as far as it's possible to go, it's more than everything.' She gave me a fleeting, hasty kiss. 'We must go.'

We went out into the dark, gloomy corridor and I opened the door for her. I gripped her hand.

'What now?' I said.

'I'll write to you later.'

'You promise?'

'Yes.'

The old lady emerged from the darkness and stood next to me. 'She's never coming back? She's off, is she? But you'll be back, sir, eh? Come back any time; the house is yours,' and she took the note that I slipped into her palm.

I was already going down the street, anxious to follow and catch up with Mercedes, when the old woman called me back. I stopped and turned round. She was making affectionate gestures towards me, her lips pursed, casting a shadow on her face in the light of the lamps in the street. I took a few steps towards her.

'Forgive me for asking, sir ... but since it looks like the young lady isn't coming back ... if you know anything about them ... any news ... you understand ... will you tell me? Come any time you wish ... come as you please, with whoever you feel like... and if you have any problems, pay me when you can...'

I had already reached the corner, running, when her final words, those ones I had heard, came into my mind again. What was she insinuating? That I should be sure to come to her if Mercedes got pregnant? Or that I should continue to use her house for other liaisons once that with Mercedes was finished? Perhaps she wanted to hint at both things which, originating from the fact that I had rented a bed there, would for her amount to much the same thing. And what she would want, too, would be not to lose contact with one of the people who might be able, indirectly, to bring her news of her nephew.

I didn't have to run too much to catch up with Mercedes. Even the distance I had run was enough for me to overtake her without seeing her, for she had stopped and was leaning against a wall. It was she who called to me as I went past.

She was crying; I wiped away her tears. Absurdly, I asked her what was the matter, as though, like an idiot, I could comfort her. My question, like one we would ask a child who is crying for a reason we know perfectly well, made her smile, just as a child, too, smiles at our little game of pretending not to know what the child knows we know. And for that moment, the power over us which our question has granted the child, at the same time takes away the weight of its pain; or, if it does not take it away, relegates it to the realm of all that is insignificant and ridiculous.

She took my hand. 'Shall we go back? Do you want to? Shall we stay there?'

We went back. The old woman showed no surprise as she opened the door, as if to go back was the most natural thing in the world. Perhaps it was just that, being so used to one couple following on another, she could no longer tell whether we were the same ones or not. She offered us dinner. I was about to turn her down categorically when Mercedes declared that she was hungry and that, yes, indeed, she would be much obliged. We sat down at the kitchen table while the old lady ate from the plate in her hand, standing up, the same fish soup as she served us; she sprinkled wine over hers and looked at us with a tender expression in her eyes.

'You're like two little doves,' she said, while I, torn between my own hunger and my irritation at Mercedes' appetite – I had never seen her eat at table – hardly ate or spoke. I was even lost for words, shocked by the feminine intimacy which had sprung up between the two of them, with smiles and understanding glances, directed towards me and which annoyed me. The old woman said that young people like us needed to eat heartily, and there was nothing like love to stimulate the appetite nor anything like a full belly to provoke love.

'When you're hungry, you can't do anything properly, not even that,' she concluded portentously, which made Mercedes laugh openly and freely, something which infuriated me. Her teeth, white in her smile, shone so much that it made me feel how physically I had given myself to that body, with its teeth, like a bowl of fish soup, greasy and fluid.

A series of knocks on the door obliged us to flee to 'our' room where the muddle of sheets and towels gave our return, contrary to what might be expected, less a sense of renewed pleasure than of contact with some sordid business which was not of our doing but of some chance previous occupants of the room. I understood that what had happened before us was always like something strange and sordid, a kind of devastation and mess, to which we ourselves contributed, which we imposed on the 'others', those we had preceded, who might be our very selves. The disgust we feel at others' dirt and disorder is no different than if 'they' were or had been ourselves. But this disgust, turning us into the others, just accentuates – and accentuated – the pleasure of coming together again in crumpled sheets, as if the freedom of returning, despite everything and everyone, whatever the consequences, would not be fully realised, whatever the disorder, if it were not the same disorder of our own lovemaking. The dirty towels, the dirty water, everything which made the room a den of vice which a good tidy-up only momentarily disguised, all this was, after all, the measure of our desires.

Holding Mercedes close to me, once more sprawling naked on the bed, our love had in any case an air of free play, of vital exuberance, like children rolling around in the sand on the beach. Not only in life, as in bed, we had banished any common shame, that last drop of reserve, by which hands, mouths, genitals, are still kept according to adult conventions as parts apart. And so we were children rolling around in our own muck, though we were neither children nor was it muck. Our own scents of all those secretions which hands and mouth and nose touched, the scents which we lapped up, all repugnance forgotten, though without the audacious madness with which that afternoon we had broken through the last taboos, these scents, all mixed together, hung over us. It was just this which stripped from it any disgust: only what comes from one as 'one' is disgusting. And we were not even like children who discover to their astonishment the existence of other children; we were children, one in the other, penetrating each other much further than ever life, lived among others, but without ever penetrating each other, allows children or adults to do. It wasn't, though, the hot smell of our own selves which excited us, which made us despair because our tongues were not long enough to kiss each other. Our overflowing stemmed from the calm, anxious security of possessing each other without possession, of the possibility of being not so much a conquest as a handing over, less an advance in which the extension of the body is limited by the walls of flesh than a recission of ourselves through the surrender of our power to impose our physical limits on the other.

When we had relaxed and I was enjoying the pleasure of feeling myself against her hard stomach, her pulsing sex, I thought of nothing. My thought was the feeling that her skin made on my hands while I idly, gently moved them up and down. It was her breathing, almost imperceptible but sweetly warm; sitting up a little I saw that she had fallen asleep in my arms. She was sleeping, so quietly, so serenely, so deeply, that it was as if she were dead. And I shuddered, remembering that she had said she would kill herself if I ever refused her my love; but gazing at her eyes, her lashes immobile, her mouth lightly half open, the damp sweat on the end of her nose, her rounded breasts, the dark triangle on her belly, how could I ever cease to love her? Could I ever refuse to give myself to her? No. In the silence of the room, the house, the street I heard footsteps in the corridor and a door opening and closing. They went away, their pleasure concluded. They wouldn't see each other again because this time of theirs together been a fiasco, or perhaps it was just some chance meeting, and they would avert their eyes when they passed in the street, until there might be another chance meeting, or, in their hunger, in the illusions of memory, they might have forgotten the first failure or wanted to transform it into some sweet triumphant recollection.

Or they might be addicted to this sort of thing, greedily battening on each other, as often as they could get away to that place, frustrated substitutes which each one, within the closed eyes of the other, represented. Nobody could be lovers like we were. Nobody was, nobody could be, unless everything was repeated exactly as it happened to us. And what lives repeated themselves unless ours was among them? My tenderness redoubled, I ran my eyes over her body bit by bit (keenly, but lightly lest my gaze wake her from that sleep in which she was wholly mine), a body which my scrutiny made me realise was not so much Mercedes' as my own body given form in another. Not the ideal other half for which one looks; not the woman through which, in ourselves, we are men; and much less the man made woman outside of us. All this, imprecisely apprehended in the intensity with which I scrutinised her, was not her, nor my, relation with her, with that body. But I myself, like a love which materialises, like a reality which assumes space and shape, like sex which loses its isolation as an instrument in order to acquire the independence of an autonomous, unforeseen isolation, in which sex is not a part which structures and dominates a body, a link around which life revolves, but a centre within which it lingers, a whole in which it is concentrated, like a living – not a lived – thing. In that way I felt the extent to which it is not by being things, or being treated as such, that we cease to exist freely, or merely to exist, just like that. And especially when we do not rise to the dignity which things have, in order to lose the momentary, fleeting fragility of which we are made.

That body was not Mercedes but a thing which I was as well, because we had freed it from everything in order to be it. Love was not a spiritual entity which assumed bodily form; then it would be false, a poor imitation of its own being in itself. What love was, what love could only be, to be truly love, was that act of reification in a body not just desired, not just possessed, not simply recognised in every detail and devoured by a gaze which completes the unsatisfied possession, but realised, recreated not through one's eyes and one's dreams, but through one's own gestures and acts of love. That thing, that debased thing, could be like the human desire which it visits on itself to console it. Human, only human, it would be so, if we had remained beyond what we did not know in it. But the dignity of the form, of existence, of creation, of the thing which does not need to perfect itself with souls or airy thoughts of the imitation of love, this her body, lying there by my side, had achieved. It was and it was not her. Not because she had dissolved herself and the body like hers (and like her) too, but because my caresses had made of it so, had shaped it so, without making of it a false image which amounted to, in one body, other bodies desired since time immemorial. Exactly what transformed it into a truly real thing was that no body, no image, had contributed to its making. Everything had been shut out by it, in it, and for it. Even Mercedes; even me. Absolutely everything. And it was at that moment that I understood why I could not love her and I fell asleep peacefully at her side, aware that I was falling asleep.

While I slept, in a deep restful sleep which released me from the knowledge of what I had just been thinking, I could still feel Mercedes' head on my arm, and smell, too, the scent of her sex on my now idle fingers. As though my eyes were open I was present at the dream I saw myself dreaming. Mercedes got up, got dressed, kissed me on the forehead and left silently, but as she was leaving her body gleamed bright and naked in the doorway. The old lady came in, followed by her nephew, he in turn by Carlos Macedo, he by Rufininho, and he by Rodrigues, then my uncle's mother-in-law, she by my aunt, and she once again by Rodrigues, followed by Luís Macedo, and he by the boy from the church, the boy by Carvalho; and he in turn by my uncle's mother-in-law, she by my uncle, he by my cousin, Ramiro. The latter was followed by Odette, she by Helena, and Helena by Almeida, who was followed by José Ramos, he by my uncle's maid, she by my friend Mesquita's girlfriend, the one on the phone, she by Mesquita himself, he by the woman from the island who was a friend of Ramon's mother, she by Ramon's mother, then Ramon, then Don Juan de Diós, who was followed by the shape I had seen within the car, the shape by Don Fernando, he by the Macedos' aunt, she by Captain

Macedo, he by my father, my mother, all followed finally by myself.

And then after me came my aunts and uncles, sailors, fishermen, soldiers and policemen, and a blonde figure in the form of a beach with boats. The room spilled over with people, and they all began slowly, in spite of the lack of space which meant they were all jostling each other, to take their clothes off with great deliberation, all the while smiling at each other. With extreme care they folded their clothes and then piled them up in a corner of the room where they began to move around and twist all on their own and changed, little by little, into legs and arms and hair. To the extent that they were all naked, none had a body, and I could see behind them the furniture belonging to the room. This was, at the same time, my uncle's house on the outside, the dormitory of the college I had visited inside, and also a beach by night, with lamps as signs in the night. At this moment two cars pulled up alongside the beach and from within them emerged into the room, in spite of the fact that they were already there, Carvalho, Ramos, Carlos Macedo, the old woman's nephew and Almeida. The latter, pulling out a pistol, fired silent shots into the cars' tyres, which immediately deflated. Then another car arrived on the scene from which the Spaniards got out, together with other characters in uniform. The casino bar was lit up in the middle of the beach, and the beach was now the square in front of the church; here though there were none of all those people, except me, sitting in the restaurant, eating the boiled fish which the waiter had brought me. The owner, extremely fat and wearing only his underpants, was going along by the cubicle doors in the college dormitory. Then suddenly many of them had sacks in their hands with which they ripped the bed sheets and from the rents there flowed blood which drenched the sand on the beach, the boiled fish, and the stair carpet in Mercedes' boarding house. It was then that Mercedes returned and that I saw Ramon's father's friend weeping in the room next to the office where we used to study. My uncle's maid opened her legs and one could see her belly inside, like a newly swept, polished corridor.

Suddenly they all disappeared; I heard shots which, however, were silent, and a fourth car came on the scene and squealed to a halt at the foot of the bed. In it were Rodrigues and my uncle's mother-in-law. Mercedes climbed into it and the car sank slowly into the sea. Then, by the water's edge José Ramos lay dead. As I bent over him I heard Almeida, in the middle of the bar in the casino, calling Mercedes names, José Ramos, smiling, winked at me and fell soundly asleep, immersed in a light greenish, sea-scented darkness, which reeked of fish soup and through which some figures still were passing. Then I half opened my eyes, feeling a terrible pain while the taste of the fish soup rose in my gullet. Mercedes was sleeping by my side, in the livid light which was the dawn filtering through the window. A chill seized me and I pulled the sheet up over Mercedes. I got up slowly, absolutely dying for a piss, as if I hadn't been for days. I picked up the bucket in my hands and as I was about to piss with my back to Mercedes, I realised that I wouldn't be able to do it with my back to her, because I could see her body in my mind and because at the same time I had no shame before her. I turned back to her and, seeing her, I had my piss. She rolled over onto her back and sighed. And I, getting back into bed, uncovered her, regarded her body and her legs, which had been so far from me in the dream, and poised myself over her, supported on my feet and hands, touching her only with my cock. She stirred, groaned and wriggled, and then opened her frightened, impassioned eyes.

'I dreamed you had had me by force,' she said after I was inside her.

Then – and it was all very quick – she got up and sat on the bucket and had a piss, laughing at me. She sat on the bed, stretching in leisurely fashion and then let herself topple onto my body.

'How could you dream that I had had you like that?' I asked, remembering my own vivid dream.

'Exactly as you did the first time,' she replied.

On another occasion I would have thought that I was still dreaming; but not now. She was the intact body of our love. It would always be me who, taking her by force, made that body more a body than ever. What the other had torn was another body. And I gazed at the sheet with which we had covered ourselves and which was seamless as if it had only been torn in dreams.

She got up and began to get dressed. As she was combing her hair I thought that, truly, I could not love her. She was my love. Nothing remained to me of that with which I had caused her so much pain. I closed my eyes peacefully, certain that I would always have her in that way, just as she wanted always to be mine.

We left without making any noise; there was no sign of the old lady. The sun rose over our heads and over the roofs of the single-storey houses. The pungent smell of the sea almost singed our nostrils. We went along, hand in hand, indifferent to the fact that

that would be the last time we would be together for the time being and for who knew how long. We went down step by step towards the beach. The sea which we glimpsed when we were not exchanging fleeting glances with each other, was perfectly calm; on the empty beach there was, along the whole length of the strand, a group of people who looked like fishermen bent over their nets. We approached them. Between the bare legs we could make out an oblong, dark shape, like a huge fish, which was the focus of attraction and wonder of those people who were milling around it. As we got closer we could see that the movement was not so great as it had seemed and there was even in the movements of the group a kind of solemn deliberation. It was not a fish; it was a man's body. It was not dark; rather, it was very light.

I grabbed hold of Mercedes.

'Let's be off,' I said.

With her teeth clenched and her eyes fixed in fascination on the body she shook herself violently loose from me.

'No, let me see,' she said and almost ran towards the group. The whole expanse seemed to be quicksand which grabbed at my legs, dragging me down into it. The semi-naked body, lying on its back, was horribly swollen, covered with blue-black marks from fish bites and the first signs of greenish decay on the deadly white skin.

It was José Ramos, and the group spread out mechanically to allow us to come closer and see him better.

XXXI

Mercedes stepped back, her eyes fixed on him and her hands to her mouth, while the men in the group said that it was no sight for a woman, and what was a woman doing walking on the beach at dawn like that. I grabbed her round the shoulders and dragged her away.

'It was him, wasn't it?' she asked me, stopping, her gaze vacant.

'Yes, it was.'

'I was expecting it.'

'Why?'

'It wasn't an accident, I'm absolutely sure it wasn't. He killed himself, or allowed himself to die. For our sake.'

'Don't be such an idiot.'

She sat down by the quayside, weeping. 'I'm not an idiot. He knew that we had sold each other out, and that, when all was said and done, it hadn't been worth it.'

'Don't say that.'

'But it's true. Because, really, everything was going according to plan and the other wasn't needed at all.' In spite of her tears there was a chill about our conversation which horrified me.

'And he killed himself or allowed himself to die by way of revenge on us,' she continued.

'Revenge on us?'

'Yes. You can't imagine the horror he had of any man coming near me, the hate he felt ... for Manuel ... and for you.'

'But it's quite natural for him to hate men whom, for other reasons, he couldn't oblige to pay ... for the evil that they had done to you and were doing to you.'

'It's not like that; you're mistaken. Or not just that. He was, in spite of the fact he seemed to be free of any prejudices, extremely narrow-minded; it was as if he considered the whole world was wrong because it wasn't some little haven of purity. You know how he began to lead this life of his, into which he used to try to drag in all those close to him? It was when the Germans started all this Nazi business and he began to feel more and more German. The most difficult thing for him was that we had the same mother and two different fathers, in spite of the fact that at home it didn't make any difference whatsoever.'

I listened to her, still watching the faraway group, and my horror grew at the idea that we were sitting there talking as if José Ramos' body had been buried long ago, and that it was not the centre of that group of inquisitive vultures.

'You can't have any idea of the efforts he put into organising this trip, even against the wishes of the party. He wanted something which would make a big impact, and would bind everybody to it once and for all. But if Almeida didn't go and you stayed behind, he couldn't stop one thing, nor run away from the other. Do you know what his fiancée told me once?'

'He had a fiancée?'

'Yes. She said that he used to terrify her, so intense, so hard, was the way he looked at her and spoke when he was having her. Do you know one of the reasons why he killed himself?'

'Because of his despair at being unable to stop thinking about you and me, because we were in the end more important than anything he wanted to do,' I said, not really thinking of what I was saying.

She opened her eyes wide. 'Yes, you guessed it.'

'Let's get away from here,' I said, getting up.

She stood up by the edge of the sea wall, gazing at the distant group. 'If only you knew how much I loved my brother...'

'I do know,' I said, taking her arm.

'And now he's dead, I can't bear to see him again. That's no longer him.'

'You're wrong,' I said, as we walked along, 'that is him.'

'No.'

'Yes, it's him. But he didn't take his revenge on us. It wasn't he who brought the body there. It wasn't he who led us to the beach so that we would find him there. He only had revenge on himself; anything else that happened was pure chance,' I added, remembering how I had seen him dead in my dream.

'Chance, you say ... chance is the most horrible thing there is.'

'Precisely because it doesn't seem like chance.'

We walked on in silence for a while.

'And now? What are we going to do now?' she demanded.

'Nothing. He's dead, was washed up on the beach. We didn't see him.'

'We didn't see him?'

'No. You go to your boarding house, to your room, lie down and go to sleep, that's all. Don't play the game of chance. Leave him to his own devices.'

'He? Who?'

'Your brother – or chance. It's all the same.'

'And you think I can?' Her face seemed haggard with age.

'You can, because it's me who's telling you to do it.'

'But you don't tell me what to do.'

'I didn't used to. But I am now. For the first and last time.'

She paused, put her hands over her mouth, her eyes full of tears. 'Oh, Jorge, forgive me ... but I'm so happy ... it's awful ... so happy ... I'm alone, alone, alone...'

We were at the door to the boarding house; the door was still closed.

'Goodbye,' she said, before knocking. 'Till forever ... now it's till forever. We won.'

I held her tight and kissed her. 'Yes, we did win.'

She went in and I made off immediately. A few streets further on I stopped. 'What did we win?' I cried out aloud, and answered myself in the same breath that what mattered was to have won, irrespective of knowing what it was. The death of José Ramos was an absurdity full of meanings, or a meaning full of absurdities. But it wasn't real, I didn't feel that it was. We had seen the corpse, we had talked over the death of him who was now that body, we had parted, freer than ever because of that body (and, while it lingered on the beach, Mercedes had become more to me than life, and so far away and yet so close like it, become the body of what love is), but this death had no reality whatsoever. Because it was unexpected? And was it? Because it was didn't make any sense? And did it not? Because it was so incongruous? But was it? It wasn't real because death has no reality. It is an anomaly, so astonishing every time it happens that it loses all reality. At the very moment when it is real for the one who dies, it ceases to be so, for whoever dies, dies; and for everyone else it has no reality in itself, only the emptiness to which it gives rise, or the opposition which it causes. Or not even that.

José, dying because he had wanted to die, or because he had happened to die perhaps exactly as he had wished, had not even left us an emptiness, nor opposed us in any way. And wasn't it odd that it was in the end this simple nothing which had manipulated so many of our lives, so many of us? No, it wasn't. Either because he had manipulated us, in a desperate effort to rise above the nothing he was; or, manipulating the lives of others becomes nothing to us, the more so the more we make the lives of others our own. Because life ... and I went into a little bar for a coffee. Drinking it and spreading butter on the bread, I thought that life was just that: bread which we swallow, a weight in our stomach, together with the coffee which makes it lie less heavy. And the warmth in the stomach afterwards. And the burps after drinking the coffee. I asked the owner of the bar if I could use the lavatory; it was filthy. Life was also a matter of not being able to put our feet in someone else's shit; I stepped back. But it was also the stabbing ache in the stomach which there was no escaping and which would not let me leave that place. The walls which the lamp on the ceiling illuminated were covered with pencil scrawls. The door against which I was leaning had messages carved into it: Down with the Government, various obscenities, Long live the Republic, the landlord was a cuckold, drawings of men and women, or men and men, in the most diverse positions, boasts of what someone – whose name was spelled out – had done to someone else, various bits of advice in verse such as 'Don't go singing while you shit, or your turds'll have a dancing fit', improbably large pricks and balls, statements of sexual preference, portraits (even self portraits labelled 'this is me'), not to mention little tricks like the pencil line which wound around the walls and ended with an insult to whoever had followed it with his eyes. Those walls were, like the lavatory where I was sitting, a lavatory of life. Heads emptied themselves in there just as bodies did into the basin. Suddenly I saw in front of me, as if it were floating in a bowl of soup, the decomposing, decomposing body of José Ramos. And leaning forward I was sick all over the floor, awash with piss and full of dirty bits of paper.

Then I remained at length, dazed, leaning forward over the sickening odours of the little cubicle, the reality of which thus assailed my nostrils. When I opened my eyes the madness and pain had passed and, together with them, dissolved in the acrid stench which had penetrated the whole of my being, the wavering image of Zé Ramos. I got up, wiped myself and made myself presentable, and thanking the owner of the bar I slipped out into the street and headed off, on that clear morning, towards my uncle's house. Inside my head, around the resplendent body of Mercedes, flitted the drawings and mottoes of those walls.

I pushed at the closed gate; I went slowly along the palm avenue, hearing the gravel grate beneath my feet. At the door of the kitchen was the elder of the maids, looking at me out of the corner of her eye and shaking her head ... I went up to my room, took off my disgusting, grubby clothes, slipped into my pyjamas and went into

the bathroom. I took my pyjamas off and turned on the hot water
to fill the bath. A long, lazy bath, hot enough, wherein I could float
… No, I don't want all that water to float in, just enough to cover
me, full of suds. Sitting on the side of the bathtub, I looked down
at my body. Then I went to the cupboard, the one with the mirror
inside. It was a long time since I had looked at myself, not since I
was a child looking in the mirror in the bathroom in my own house,
observing myself in different poses. But I couldn't manage to do
more than glance at myself and I soon shut the door. Everything
that I saw, which was my whole form, would decay. The only thing
which would last longer would be what one could not see, that
framework, with all its joints and articulations, which supported the
being which I was.

And my senses, and my cock, everything which felt, and gave
life, everything capable of pleasure, all that could come together to
prolong desire, all that would rapidly vanish. First it would be
stinking corruption, then a sticky mess, finally a heap of dust
indistinguishable from any other dust. That through which we were,
felt, knew, existed, which made us into an all-conquering body,
would end with us, would not survive us; the only thing which
would endure longer was the frame, unable even to stand up on its
own. I saw again the skeleton we used to have at school, hanging
from an iron spike, like someone who had been hanged, and with
its bones fixed to one another by little wires. And that was life: the
duration of that fleshed out set of bones, through which our
consciousness, our faculties, this 'I' of ours existed. I understood
that my horror didn't make sense: we were flesh, our genitals,
through what we were, we could not be anything else but flesh,
delicate, fragile flesh, like life itself.

I got into the bath and washed myself down diligently, with great
care, as if I was carrying out a sacred ritual… There was no crease
that I didn't scrub repeatedly, sweetly, voluptuously. Then I lay,
stretched out in the water, delightfully somnolent, beyond time and
being. I was awoken by a movement on the door handle, followed
by a knocking. I said that I would be out in a trice, I wouldn't be
long. I dried myself, put on my pyjamas and opened the door. There
was nobody in the corridor. I went back to my room, closed the
windows and lay down on the bed. I felt utterly relaxed, a great
lassitude came over me, a vast, deep sense of repose such as the
vague clarity of the room – which made the ceiling seem so high
– rather than the darkness somehow suggested to me. I couldn't

manage to call anyone to mind. But I didn't feel alone. I was alone, I didn't remember anything or anyone, the feeling of repose was complete, I didn't feel alone. Lying on my back I gazed at the high ceiling; and then there began to rise, within me, a kind of sobbing. Turning onto my side, huddled up, I realised that the sobbing was a cry which shook me, which little by little ceased to shake me, which became like a peaceful flow of tears which transported me smoothly into a gentle sleep.

When I woke up it seemed to me as if I had been sleeping for hours on end. I felt at the same time both empty and heavy, though in fine fettle. The weight which I felt in my head, however, came from the emptiness itself which I also felt alongside it. It was as if the relief of not remembering anything or anybody weighed on me; and as if, in contrary fashion, this weight which had neither names nor shapes gave me a feeling of agreeable emptiness. But the very sensation of nameless emptiness, like the well-being which filled me (like that of someone who has slept at length after an overwhelming weariness), drew from that weight a kind of uneasiness, a fluid awareness of a guilty selfishness. Stretching out, extending my body, this awareness grew somewhat, as if, to avoid it, I would have to stay completely still without moving a muscle, without making any gesture which might be reminiscent of those which my memory, in the interests of my peace of mind, had suppressed. But, in its waxing I recognised, too, its evasions though I wasn't able to identify them; and there came, too, a surge of that detached, incurious security which was making me free. And, little by little, cautious gesture by cautious gesture, I began to see that, if I didn't dive headlong into the motions it was making, I would be able to get up and carry on my life, without recalling anything. Or at least without anything assuming on, presumptuously, an importance which my present state of mind would shirk from bestowing on it. What time was it? A few minutes after eleven; perhaps I had not even slept for an hour. But that awareness refused to confirm just how much, even approximately, I had slept. To confirm it would be to recognise that I had slept very little and must therefore be exhausted; and it would be, too, in recalling the time I had gone to bed, to recognise the chain of facts which had brought me there, and had caused me, in their wake, to sleep so little.

It was in this state that, once I was ready, I went downstairs to find my aunt in the dining room, talking over the day's tasks with the maids.

'Your uncle's in the garden,' she said on seeing me. 'But have some breakfast first.'

I thanked her, saying I didn't really want anything, and went out into the garden. I walked round the house without finding my uncle; finally I saw him up in the belvedere. I crossed the thickets and suddenly started running to get away from a horrible smell which brought everything back to me. I could only think automatically as I ran – by now under the gaze of my uncle who had seen me – that it was a dead dog.

'What's all this running for?' demanded my uncle. 'You get back so late and now you're running?'

I said nothing, merely smiling briefly. I sat down on one of the stone benches. He came towards me, leaning on his stick for support.

'Well then, happy, pleased with yourself?' he asked, standing in front of me and bending over me.

I lifted my wondering gaze to him. 'Happy and pleased with myself?'

'Yes ... wasn't a whole night sufficient for you to say your goodbyes?'

'How do you know?'

'Hmm ... because her father came looking for me last night; he wanted me to go with him to break in on you, wherever you were, some house in Buarcos. Fortunately he didn't know for sure where it was, and so I was able to convince him that if it was all up with her, as he claimed, it didn't make any difference whether you slept in peace one more night with her or not. Of course, sleeping in peace is only a manner of speaking. And they must have gone this morning. They'll have gone by now,' and he fell silent, staring at me, waiting for me to say something. I said nothing, though, and he carried on again: 'It's your luck that the other rascal had stirred things up already, and the poor father, knew perfectly well that he couldn't make you do anything without causing an even greater scandal.'

'The other rascal?'

'Yes, the *other one*. Because he was the first and you were the second. Or don't you think so?'

I had seized on that expression, in order not to acknowledge that, probably, they would not have set off, because... But perhaps she...

'I don't think so,' I merely said. 'In any case, it doesn't mean anything.'

'I can't think it does, either. What I think is that you went.

Though, clearly, a man doesn't turn down a woman who wants to lie underneath him, whoever she is. Or one who, if you touch her with your finger, lies down on the ground and opens her legs.'

'Don't talk like that.'

'Very well, I won't, neither one way or the other. Do you really love her?'

I looked at him without replying.

'Ah ... but she's told her father she won't marry you, nor the other fellow. She won't marry you because the other one has made her unworthy of you; and she won't marry the other one because she can't stand the sight of him. In any case he's under no obligation whatsoever now to marry her. Nor are you.'

'Nobody's thinking of getting married.'

'And I think it's far too early for you to get married; in any case it would be a silly thing to do. But I want you and her to realise one thing: if you want, my house is at your disposal. She can stay here; you can get a transfer to Coimbra; I'll fix you up with some classes at the College. You can keep yourselves going until you've sorted out your life without having to ask your parents. I want you to know that, if you don't get married it's because you know you don't have to, and for no other reason.'

'Thank you.'

'I'm not telling you this for you to thank me.'

'I know,' I said, while our conversation somehow seemed vague and far away, like some hypothetical discussion of remote matters. An oblong form had distanced it from us and from everything. But suddenly it was as if this form were that dead dog whose stench had filled my nostrils.

My uncle was silent. Then, still without a word he sat down on the parapet, half turned towards the distance, his back half turned to me. And it was like that that he spoke, in a very casual fashion, as if he were talking about people and matters which were really remote, or as if the events, in taking their place, had become so. It was as if he accepted or, more than accepted, embraced it, because it suited him, the game of evasion in which I had trapped myself.

'It seems almost as if we were meant to be here,' he said, leaning out over the wall as if his eyes were following someone who was passing by the corner. 'For me, everything began and ended in this belvedere. If I had a son, a son who was already a young man, like you, I can't know if I would let him have the run of my house as I've let you have it. Perhaps not at all. And that wouldn't be right.

We're always more generous when we don't have anyone to give to. Who knows... Perhaps I might even throw him out of the house... Do you really not want to marry her?'

'It's not possible; and it doesn't matter. We could never be more married than we are,' I said and I realised that I could talk like that because the oblong shape had shrunk, and was now an indistinct mixture of a child's body and that of a dog. 'Do you want me to leave?' I heard myself ask, in response to his earlier remarks.

He got up and came over to me. Perplexed, he ran his fingers through his hair. Then he rested his hand on my shoulder. 'No, not at all. This house is yours.'

We stayed like that for some long time; I felt that such things would never be possible between me and my father, and that on certain occasions − if not always − we briefly came across parents such as ours, by virtue of being eternally our parents in fact, who could never be, or were prevented from being by this very fact. The thing lasted a few seconds and subsequently I felt it had been possible, because I had not been I (or that succession of successive or recurrent 'Is' which I was), but precisely for those few moments I had been other people, more virtual than real. And I had the terrible feeling − which suddenly identified itself and me with the emptiness that I felt within me − that, contrary to what was commonly supposed, our reality is composed of the virtual existence we all have in others and in ourselves, and only of this. It was something which made me shake with panic and gave me the immediate awareness of a terrifying freedom: human liberty was exactly this hypothetical condition, this virtuality which, in others and in ourselves, saves us from facing up to our being what we are. Mercedes' body as it had appeared stretched out on the floor of the belvedere, like a softly breathing corpse. I saw it. It was that splendid thing which we had made, beyond any kind of existence. And if freedom were this, then that is what it was: an absolute body which became, more than human, a thing which was more then a thing; or the total virtuality of our not being anything except that which, in the virtuality of others, gave us reality from an absolute irreality also.

We were ourselves by being always others, others who were not just badly deciphered images of ourselves, but *others*, the others who were virtually the windows in which other people declared themselves, through this virtual identification, some to other people and to us. We are ourselves insofar as we are the others *of other people*. And it is this which stops us, being us in ourselves, from being completely free. The absolute body is not, however, exempt from its own destruction. Neither is absolute virtuality, by which we may survive in the others. But the relationship between these two extremes had been exemplified there for me by my uncle's hand on my shoulder, and, even more, in the quasi-abandonment with which I had almost leaned against him. Neither was I myself for him, nor was he himself for me. But at that moment, the fact of our not being us, had constituted the reality of what we could be, much more profoundly, than what, in moment or two, we would be capable of being again.

The brevity of the time during which such things could occur or persist became evident even in the reluctance which I felt in his hand, which he already wanted to withdraw and in my unease which was fuelled by my wanting him to withdraw it. Yet neither of us had the courage to break the spell, to take on the responsibility of returning and of making the other return to less than himself in someone else. However, he remembered that he had something in his pocket to show me; and his hands, with his cane dangling from his arm, went hurriedly to a newspaper which he held out to me and which I grabbed avidly, though without the slightest curiosity.

It was a Lisbon paper, early evening edition; it was full of great paeons of praise for the 'nationalist' victories in Spain, with pictures of the heroes and of the supposed victims of the 'red' terror, together with a tiny item from Oporto saying that some prisoners, helping the police with their inquiries, had escaped from police custody in circumstances which suggested an extensive Communist conspiracy and that among them were two Spaniards suspected of being agents, in Portugal, of the Comintern. The paper added, in a short but outraged commentary, that the escapees, according to all the signs, had set off for the south in order to embark secretly from some port or other; furthermore, the audacity of this *coup de main* was more than enough evidence of the urgency with which the Portuguese Government should publicly declare its willingness, which had been, nevertheless, plain from the very start, to play its part in the triumph of a decisive struggle, in which was involved not only the whole of Christian civilisation, but also the very independence of the country, menaced by the butchers of Moscow, types to whom neither God, nor Country, nor Family meant anything. The Chief of Police, who was the one who according to the reporter had given him some kind of short interview, assured him that the redoubled vigilance of the forces of Law and Order would foil this attempt which had provocation written all over it, and which would duly receive its come-uppance.

I looked at my uncle.

'The east?' he asked. 'Two agents, two agents of the Comintern in Portugal,' he continued, 'spending summer at this of all times, in Figueira da Foz…'

'In Figueira?' I repeated, reading the item again. It had escaped me that it had been put about that those two dangerous agents had been discovered in Figueira some days before, thanks to the dedicated actions of their countrymen who had recognised them. They must have been those poor devils who had been captured during the rowdy scenes on the day I had arrived; it was comical. But by virtue of the very fact that they were preparing such a spectacular flight, perhaps they weren't such poor devils after all. Or were they? Because, after all, the two whom we had added to the group seemed and were poor devils, consumed by fear.

My uncle's train of thought must have paralleled my own. 'There were only five of the Spaniards,' he said, 'our two, the two from Oporto, and the other who was also holed up here in Figueira.'

'Were they really so important that they did all this for them?' I wondered.

My uncle picked up the paper and ran his eyes over the news again. 'Or was it that everybody was caught up in a 'provocation' which the Government had wanted to happen?' he said. 'Or did they make capital out of what really was a provocation? Do you remember all that about the coup in Sarajevo which, because it made Austria declare war on Serbia, then saved as a pretext for the World War; there are those who say it was all Germany's doing… Or perhaps even France's, too…'

'Will they get across and into Spain, to somewhere safe?' I asked.

'It depends; this news has only been printed because the censor allowed it to be, or because he ordered it to be … it depends on what the Government wants to get out of it. Either they'll hunt them down, to make them confess and cause a great public outcry; or they'll let them get there because that will be the decisive proof of that interference which they want to expose.'

'Either way they'll achieve what they set out to.'

'Who'll achieve what?' demanded my uncle ironically.

'Whoever set the whole thing up,' I replied, without restraining the memory of *who* had been behind that 'who', inasmuch as behind that 'who' could have been many others of whom I was unaware, whom the pronoun could not identify.

'The one who set it up was Ramos, there's no doubt about that at all. But who put him up to it, that's what I'd like to know. But who that is, even when someone comes out with it, we'll never know for sure. That's the way it is with politics.'

The name had been uttered. But for me it didn't really relate to any one individual, contrary to what I had feared. I was even shocked by my own unexpected indifference. I decided to put myself to the test.

'Whoever set this whole thing up won't be around to see the outcome,' I said.

'Well, what a great discovery that is!' exclaimed my uncle. 'Does anyone ever live to see the outcome of anything? And when we do see some outcome, can we be sure that we are seeing the outcome we've been expecting, or that it's the outcome of our own actions?'

'We'll see in due course. But when one packs it in beforehand there's no doubt one won't get to see anything.'

'It's all the same,' he said; there was a pause while he stared at me very intently. 'Who's packed it in beforehand?' he demanded.

I lowered my gaze. 'Ramos is dead,' I replied in a low voice. 'He was washed up on the beach in Buarcos, drowned.'

'How do you know?'

'I saw him; Mercedes and I went down to the beach and there were people standing round a big fish, and he was the fish.'

'Did she cry or call out? Did anyone notice that you'd recognised him?'

'She didn't cry till later; I don't think anyone noticed.'

'Did she go home?'

'Yes; but she won't say anything. Uncle … he killed himself or let himself be killed for us.'

'Oh, come on now…'

'Or because we meant more to him than all this, or because it was his revenge over us.'

'Or because he found out that he was mixed up in some adventure which had given rise to just the opposite effect to the one he intended. Who knows?'

'What now?'

'Now we're not going to talk about this any more. His death changes nothing, does it?'

'No. We had already decided we wouldn't get married.'

'So you're going to spend your whole life meeting when you can manage to fit it in, is that it?'

'She's going to write to me.'

'Of course she is. And you'll write back. And she'll write two weeks from now, and you'll write back a month later. And then you'll send each other Christmas cards while neither of you has sorted out your lives.'

'Sorted out; what do you mean?'

'Sorted out or not sorted out.'

'Or that too.'

My uncle put the paper back in his pocket and shook me by the shoulder, his stick hitting my legs. 'Are you going to make a profession out of being unhappy?' he asked.

'No, uncle.'

'That's how it seems. When you're together, you two, are you happy?'

'Oh uncle! It's much more than that.'

He let go my shoulder and moved a few paces away. 'That's so,' he said as if talking to himself. 'Happiness is a terrible thing; it's quite frightening, perhaps the most frightening thing there is. It's a lot easier to be unhappy... Come on, it's lunchtime.'

He set off through the thickets towards the house. I slowly set off after him, now almost savouring, in bittersweet fashion, the fetid odour which had been following me for some time, still lingering in my nostrils well after I had passed it. Death made no sense, couldn't make sense, however much those who had survived some strange death wanted to give it one, or however much someone wished to give some sense to his own death. Ramos was dead; I had seen him and it was horrible. He who was the very soul of cleanliness, so meticulous, so strict with himself, I had seen him, putrifying, disgusting. Him. For he did not exist except in the very thing which no longer existed, that heap of putrid flesh.

'We need to get that stinking thing out of there,' said my uncle, turning round and stopping by the side of the dining room door. 'We'd better dig a hole somewhere, or right there, and bury it,' he said, going in and bawling for his lunch as was his habit.

Ramiro hadn't returned so there were just the three of us at table, my aunt, uncle and me. There was an intimacy which was not even broken by the antics of Maria, showing off her hindquarters more than she had ever done, and her breasts slipping out of her low cut blouse as she bent over the serving dishes; nor was I upset by the fact that it was the product of my aunt and uncle's new conjugal arrangement, repellent as this was to me. On the contrary it helped me to see it all as commonplace, trivial, ordinary, banal, everyday, nugatory, this collapse of all the values and all the meanings which had reached their apogee in me. And it helped me even further in that I did not feel the pain of the enormous calamity of no longer feeling the pain. Eating with the ones who had been responsible, like me, for so much that had happened (responsible at least to the extent that there were things we had done or not done), it was as if we were eating on the moon, and the moon was the most earthbound place there was. I even wanted to laugh before the rice and steak which, as if drunk, I ate without relish. Laugh about what? About nothing? About nothingness? About the fact there was nothing to laugh at. That really was very comical, the very absence of anything funny.

But there was one thing I could laugh at: at my being there, when I myself was utterly posthumous, much more posthumous than any corpse. My role as agent and lover was over. To want to know things, see people ... that was to be posthumous. To want to carry on there as if nothing had happened ... that was impossible for me. My aunt and uncle lived in that house; it was theirs. All the others had their houses; there, living in them, they could forget what had happened. But living in a house which wasn't mine, in a town where I didn't live, how could I forget what had happened? What about those who had left like Mercedes? And those who remained, who didn't have houses, like Rodrigues? But I couldn't leave – at least not just yet. And my uncle had told me that his house was mine! In truth I didn't have a house. I realised that I hadn't. My parents' house was foreign to me, and would be even more so after everything that had happened, even if I were to forget everything and become utterly indifferent to what I recalled, even to the people whose paths I had crossed. For they would come back to me, and the facts, too, sooner or later. And even if neither they nor the facts should come back to me, in person or in my memory or through some analogous happening, I would not be any the less changed. Or instead of being changed, I would be reduced or magnified to a deeper or more shallow existence, depending on the possible nature of there being an existence which was not the everyday version of being. Reduced or magnified to the deepest level; reduced or magnified to the most superficial level. It was completely useless to me to know which of these four possibilities would be the correct one. This truth no longer depended on me, nor, properly speaking, on the others. In winning Mercedes I had lost her, or vice-versa. In freeing Rodrigues I had betrayed him, or the opposite. I was implicated – and how – in the death of Ramos. In the end I even had a part in the repercussions of the events, as if politics might be made up of successive, convergent parts of things which are not politics. Or was everything, after all, just politics, even the deaths of other people? Or above all was it what we made of the lives and deaths of others, so that we might have our own life?

All this was going through my head as I talked gently with my aunt and uncle; I was calmly finishing my lunch when Ramiro came in with the face and gait of someone hurrying along the last steps of his way, to make it clear just how precious was the news of which he was the bearer.

'José Ramos is dead on the beach,' he announced, his voice wavering dramatically and wearing an incongruous, triumphant smile. 'Everybody went down to Buarcos this morning to see him. He was washed up on the coast, having drowned at some point. It must have been after his night out with the other fellows. It's said they're looking for Carvalho and Matos to tell them what has happened.'

My uncle, scraping up the crumbs and nibbling at them with his lips, shot a fierce glance at the panic he could see on my aunt's face.

'And you? Did you talk to anyone?' he demanded.

'To a whole load of people.'

'You don't know anything, though; you didn't see anything.'

'I didn't see anything?'

'That's right; I'm not having snoopers in my house. Go and get your bag and get on the afternoon train to Lisbon,' he said, looking at his watch. 'Eat your lunch quickly and get cracking. You've ten minutes to have your lunch,' he added.

'But what have I done wrong? Oh uncle...' and his face was full of embarrassed supplication.

'Don't even ask me. Get yourself out of here. I'll write to your father later to tell him why I sent you packing.'

'But...'

'Shut up and eat. No ifs nor buts. Go with your cousin to the station,' he ordered, turning to me.

'But when this train gets to Alfarelos there isn't even a connection,' said Ramiro.

'What's that to do with me? Will it harm you if you have to mooch around in Alfarelos, waiting for the other train? Will it? Have you got money for the tickets?'

'I have,' he said, not lifting his face from the plate.

'And now a warning. Pay attention. If here or on the journey or in Lisbon you open your gob even once, to talk about Figueira, I'll go to Lisbon, or to hell, if I have to and cut your balls off.'

'Oh Justino,' said my aunt, automatically.

'Cut them off, I said. And I'll drop you in such shit there with your friends that you'll be thrown in prison to rot, not running loose and helping them save the country. They'd never come looking for your help again. And you had such a promising career lined up. Come on, eat, stop wasting your time gawping at me with that half-wit's face of yours.'

Ramiro put down his fork. 'But I was one of those who identified Ramos,' he said slowly.

'How did you identify him?'

'When I saw him I said it was him.'

'Don't bother your head about that; there'll be others who recognise him. If you think that you're so important that they'll miss you, you're very much mistaken. Before you get to be important I'm running you out of here and warning you about your future. Jorge! You be good enough to put him on the train and only leave the station once the train has disappeared over the horizon.'

'You're really sending me away, uncle...' said Ramiro.

'Of course I am; do you think I'm joking? I only joke about serious matters but with clowns like you, your aunt's nephew, I don't mess about. Go, and I mean go. Have you finished eating? Have you had enough or do you want more? No, no more. Well, go and pack your suitcase. Jorge, go and help him pack.'

We both got up from the table and went up to our rooms. Ramiro went ahead of me, his head bent. 'One of these things ... he's crazy,' was all he said. He began to put his things into his case, very deliberately.

'Don't waste time,' I said. 'Get a move on.'

He straightened himself up and gave me a look full of hate. 'You and he and all the rest, you'll pay for this.'

'Let us have the bill later then. But, look, he really will cut your balls off...'

'Cut them off be damned. Really he's afraid of me; he'll see.'

'We'll all see. But the one who won't see anything is you. Have you finished packing?'

'Yes,' he said, fuming. As we went out of the room I turned back; he had left some things in the cupboard. We put the case on the bed to open it and stuffed them in, furiously. We went down the stairs. We stopped in front of my aunt and uncle by the dining room door.

'Ramiro here says we're all going to have to pay for this,' I informed them, with particular pleasure.

My uncle's face dissolved into a wide, sweet smile. 'Of course we will. Everything has to be paid for in this world. Isn't that true, woman, we have to pay for everything?' he said, embracing Ramiro who was overwhelmed by this sudden sweetness. 'Remember me especially to everybody, have a good journey and you can say my house is always open to all my nephews; explain why, now, with your aunt being not too well, you can't stay here any longer, and that even your cousin for the same reason isn't sleeping in the house,' he said, embracing him again and smiling happily at his own joke.

We set off running as quickly as the heavy case would allow. From time to time, after changing the case from one hand to the other, putting it down, and blowing on his hands and rubbing them together, I would pick it up, with him trotting alongside me, terribly red-faced with fatigue and fury. We didn't say a word to each other the whole way to the station.

As I went into the station forecourt I felt something odd about the atmosphere, as if everybody was keeping an eye on everybody else, and they were all being watched by some invisible eye, whose presence they suspected somewhere. It might have been my own trepidation, which had nothing to do with my cousin, or the fear that he might say something out loud which would compromise me, or that I had in effect begun to feel an uncomfortable sensation of being watched (uncomfortable because I had not known that it existed previously, or because it had existed without my realising it, or because it had become more intense, or because all these things were coming together at that very moment), which hovered over all those who were bustling around in the hall. There was a great deal of to-ing and fro-in, highly unusual it seemed to me, such as one experienced at the end of the holiday period. And the hubbub of Spanish voices marked this bustle as part of the exodus. These were the ones who had awaited the unfolding of events, to see which way the wind was blowing, or those who thought it better to return to a country at war, before they were summoned, or before they might be suspected of disloyal delay. When my cousin got to the head of the queue for the ticket office he bought his ticket.

'Get me a platform ticket,' I said, standing at his elbow.

He bought one and pushed it towards me across the booking office counter. We went through the gate to the platform, I helped him get on the train and he sat down. I climbed down from the train.

'You can go now,' he said.

I said nothing and stayed on the platform, opposite where he was sitting, sharing the glances between him and the people passing by to take their seats or getting on then off the train and on again. My cousin leaned out to look at the station clock.

'It's time; you can go,' he said.

'The train might be late leaving,' I replied.

He sat down again and muttered some angry, less than complimentary, words. Finally when I could no longer bear to stay, feeling that all those prying eyes directed at me were deliberate, the engine gave a whistle and the train started to move.

'You bastards, you'll all pay for this,' said my cousin, suddenly leaning out of the window. I remained on the platform waving goodbye, though my gesture only made him go back inside as soon as he saw me raise my hand.

I left the station, looking behind me every ten paces, very pleased with the smooth banishment of my cousin. Expelled to Lisbon, the harm that he could do would be curbed, would have nothing to do with Figueira. Not that he would do us any. At the most he would tell his parents about the terrible life I was leading in Figueira and they would pass this on to my parents. And they wouldn't do anything, nor could they; I had reached my majority. And in any case what could they hold against me? Moreover, however terrible were the things that had happened, and however much they might grow in the telling and re-telling, they wouldn't make any impression on my mother who would only be so astounded that, as usual, she wouldn't be able to grasp their enormity. And my father, should I return, would tell me solemnly, 'hard truths', in his haste to get back to his usual routine. And if it didn't turn out like that, than let them go to hell. The expression amazed me. What harm had they ever done me? None. Nor any good. I had no feelings about them either way. And now wasn't the time for me to be letting them into my life through the back door. If they started getting on my nerves I'd be off, in short order. And Luís? What had I to do with him? And I saw Carlos Macedo, on a boat, lost in the Atlantic, between the Spaniards, strangers to him, and the venal crew (among whom I saw, swaying his hips as he went, the old woman's nephew), but no Almeida, who hadn't gone with them, nor Ramos, who had died.

Under what circumstances had he died? I could think about them because I wasn't doing so in relation to me, but insofar as the effect they would be having or had had on Macedo and which, in retrospect, had made his request that I should look after his brother so much more urgent and painful. I saw his features bending over the waves, so alone that he knew not how he could escape it, certainly not with that ready gift of the gab he had when there were others around to stimulate him. The tight, pained features of a man completely lost, who had seen his friend die (how?), the one who was his leader and whose word was law. With an odd, even unpleasant sensation, I realised that if Ramos had taken Mercedes from my arms (or had insisted that she leave them) he had thrust Luís into them. Could I, for reasons of friendship, accept as my inheritance the very thing from which I had wanted to run away? In what way was it that, posthumously, the actions or the destiny of others could influence things themselves with which they had no direct, intentional relationship? Abandoned by the others, Carlos Macedo had acquired, retrospectively, a more pleading voice, the one with which he had begged me to look after his brother. This new accent in his voice did not, it is clear, stem from some refrain which José Ramos and he had put together, but one which, now that Ramos was dead, his own isolation made more urgent, at the same time as it gave him responsibilities he hadn't had before, and in so doing, made the transfer of other responsibilities, like the one he had demanded of me, more pressing.

But if this appeared to be the case, wouldn't it finally depend on how and in what circumstances Ramos had died? An accident? Suicide? Murdered? In any case death – in a very different way from that of the eventual fading away of a relative – had abruptly entered our lives, my life. Ramos was, through his sister and through whatever I had contributed to the whole thing, profoundly wrapped up in my life. His death, however contingent it might have been, did not have the randomness of a death we could call routine, one for which we could no more be held responsible than for the sun or the rain. However little it was linked to the facts, it had nevertheless happened in their unfolding. If he had fallen into the sea and drowned, he had nevertheless drowned on account of the fact that he had set off on that boat. And for this to have been possible, if it meant that someone had intervened decisively to make it so, that someone was me. How then could my relations with Mercedes give way to a merely protective and masculine relation with the brother of another man who had not played a decisive part in linking my person with that of Ramos? At that moment various images – some of which I had lived through, others which had been brought to life by the words of others – and various phrases collided with others in my memory, showing me that the link between everything and everybody, through me, was much deeper and more terrible than what I or the rest of them had ever consciously put into words: the Macedos, the Ramos brother and sister, Rodrigues, my aunt and uncle, Rufininho, they all made up, together with me, a knot of interchangeable parts, which the unexpected death of José Ramos had crystalised with terrible clarity: one always being sold to the other, in the place of that one he had himself sold. For dreadful reasons – which should never figure in a relationship between men – Carlos Macedo had handed Rufininho over to Rodrigues. The latter had defended himself, worshipping my aunt, in the place of the mother he hated, and hating my uncle in the place of the father he despised. I had replaced the image of my aunt for him with that of my uncle's mother-in-law, so that I could continue to have Mercedes, for whom I had taken Almeida's place. Ramos had given me his sister, in exchange for the chance to realise his own venture. And so that Rodrigues should not see in Luís and Carlos what he had not had, the latter had handed over his brother to me.

When Mercedes' love had become something unattainable for me, by being too deep in me and in her, and when José Ramos had died, and Carlos Macedo was forever (or as though for ever) far away, I remained, with the others, in the same situation as that of a group of castaways huddled on a narrow raft, and compelled by circumstances to exercise openly the spiritual cannibalism which, secretly, everybody had practised. I felt that this spiritual cannibalism (whose carnality I could understand, although what one absorbed was only symbolic) was also one of the meanings of life, from the moment in which we became aware of it. Children devour in cannibal fashion the things around them, in order to take control of the world into which they are about to enter; men, though, devour each other, just to remain in it. And not only the lives of each one: above all, too, the very being of each one. When somebody is changed as the result of our actions, it is as if these actions were a ritual banquet of all that he had been up to then. Therefore we only take on as our responsibility, in reality, that which we have seized by cannibalism, and we all live by devouring the innocence of others. Innocence was only the condition of anyone's existence until the moment when others helped themselves to his body or his thoughts; or of our own existence until the moment when, even if only through our thought, we helped ourselves to others or to our own selves.

Was there such a thing as innocence in fact? Could one live without losing it? Or could one, from the moment he was born, hang onto it? Or, in living, did we go along losing *another* innocence at each new part we played? These questions already presupposed an answer which was buried in the heart of what 'substitution' was. As I had already thought, this substitution would destroy us, insofar as it gave us an *instead of*, insofar as, with it, we ran away from the very relations which obliged us to be. But wasn't it the case that destruction (even to the extent of physical death, as was now the case with Ramos) constituted a substitution, too? If we did not exist but through others and in them, who could tell me that we weren't free precisely insofar as we were devoured by that which stopped us being the others? What kind of freedom was this, though, which consisted in our not being free except in unreality and in death, when freedom no longer really had any sense whatever? Suddenly, in confusion, the whole thread of my thoughts broke off, as if I was overcome by vertigo while looking into the abyss. Other, earlier, thoughts, other strands, tumbled over them and were in turn swallowed up. There was one thing I was still not sure of: were they tumbling over themselves, or was it me, fearful and tormented, who was causing them to be swallowed up? Wasn't I just giving up the ghost? I was. I was not letting myself think. It had all finished, or it was all just about to begin. To think – but what for – if I didn't know what was going to happen, or even how? I turned towards Rodrigues' boarding house.

XXXII

He was in, according to the man in reception, and I went up and knocked on the door of his room. He half opened it to see who it was and then went back to his bed, leaving me to close the door behind me. As usual he was completely naked.

'I've been waiting for you to show up,' he said, his belly upwards and his legs crossed, as if he were seated in a chair.

'Why?'

'Didn't you know that Ramos...'

'Yes, I think everybody knows. I was one of the first to see him on the beach.'

'You were having a private dawn stroll, were you?'

'Yes.'

He looked at me, dividing his gaze between me and the fingernails he was cleaning. 'How far are you to blame for all this?' he demanded.

'That's something I'd like to know for sure.'

'You don't know then? You don't happen to know about the scene that Almeida created in the casino? Where is she by the way?'

'She'll have left for Oporto this morning with her parents.'

'Because of the scene.'

'Partly.'

'And partly because of Zé's death?'

'No; they left without knowing about it.'

'Did she not know either?'

It was my turn to stare at him intently. 'She knew. We both saw him dead on the beach,' I replied.

'And now?'

'And now? What?'

'Do you mean that it's all over as far as you're concerned? It's certainly all over for him. And who's going to bury him?'

'His stepfather will have to come back, won't he? I am obliged, as much as you, to bury him. Do you think it's only because I was his sister's lover, and Almeida seems to have made some scene about it, that he killed himself? Is that what you're thinking?'

'That and other things. What's all this story about a boat, hired to go off somewhere I've no idea where, nor with whom?'

'Who told you that?'

'My sources of information.'

'There's one thing they haven't told you, though.'

'What's that?'

'That it was you who paid for the boat. And that what could have happened was that he fell into the water from that boat.'

He sat down on the bed, wide-eyed, his mouth half open, his whole body shaking. 'Me?... You ... but that's even worse... You sold me in order to pay for the boat?'

'Yes,' I said, my eyes lowered so that I could only just make him out at the edge of my vision.

He bent over, his head almost resting on his knees; he looked insignificant, shrunken, unkempt, trembling with cold and fear.

'It was all lies, then?' he asked in a barely audible voice. 'All lies?'

'Yes.'

He raised his tear-stained face to me, his hands tugging at his hair. 'And the boat? What about the boat? Was Almeida mixed up in this? And who else?'

'If I tell you who else was in the boat, you'll be even more hurt.'

'Tell me.'

Without mentioning the Spaniards I explained the plans of Ramos, Macedo and Almeida, waiting all the while for him to unleash his anti-Spanish sentiment. But it didn't come.

'Did Ramos know that you were Mercedes' lover?' he said instead.

'Yes.'

He fell backwards in the bed, momentarily silent; he began to shake violently, his body twisted by the tremors. It seemed as if he was having an epileptic fit. I got up and bent over him to lend him some succour, at the same time fearful of the fury which he couldn't but help feel towards me. But it was laughter which had convulsed him, laughter which moved him, turned him, rocked him, which moved through him, mechanically, in waves, as if he were at the height of some long drawn-out, immensely pleasurable, sexual spasm. I stepped back, puzzled, shocked, scandalised, and uneasy, too. It lasted ages, or at least it seemed like it did. I remained leaning against the wall, waiting, sickened by the nakedness which shook obscenely with laughter, which, little by little, calmed down, until he lay face down, now along instead of across the bed.

Then he turned over, looked at me absently and then sat up. 'And then at the end of it all the geezer topped himself,' he said and once again unleashed successive waves of mirth. I lost my temper and began to hit him, to put a stop to his hysteria. That only made it worse; he laughed even more. And at every blow he would laugh more, glorying in the defiance, relishing it while my hands rained blows upon him. Until, all of a sudden he grabbed my fists.

'No, you're not getting away with it like that,' he said through clenched teeth. 'Either you or I, one of us, will finish what you started.' And he got up, menacingly.

I struggled to free myself. 'Let me go,' I demanded.

'No. What did you come for? Was it like the criminal returning to the scene of his crime? You killed Ramos, you killed something in me, twice over, you killed Mercedes, you killed Macedo, how many have you killed? How many? How much more do you want? Do you want me to give you my arse? Do you want me...'

I managed to free myself. 'Are you crazy?' I said, but he got between me and the door, covering it with his body.

'You're not getting out of here without choosing, you're not. Not even if I have to kill you,' and suddenly he picked up and opened a penknife which was on the dressing table.

'Put it down,' I said.

'I'll kill you,' he said brandishing the penknife, 'I'll poke your eyes out.'

'Put it down.'

'Aren't you afraid of me? Aren't you ashamed of what you've done to me?'

'No. I've already told you to put it down.'

'I'll kill you, though.'

'If you could you would have already killed me. Put it down.'

He came towards me, in one bound, the knife shining in a sudden lunge which ripped open the sleeve of my jacket and caused the knife to go flying. We both scrambled to pick it up and, ridiculously, our heads clashed, and we were left sitting on the ground on our side of the room. We sat there, motionless, with the knife between us. With great care I put my hand out towards and grasped it. He didn't move. I got up; he stayed seated. But when I made to walk away he grabbed me round the legs and I fell, still holding out my arm to keep the knife out of his reach. However, he didn't try to take it off me. I tried to free myself from his grasp and gave him a kick in the face with my heel. In putting his hands instinctively to his face he let go my legs and I got up, closed the penknife and put it in my pocket. He remained sitting on the ground and drew his

legs together to rest his head on the points of his knees. I didn't
know whether to leave or wait for some response from him; I stayed
for it seemed to me that the scene was not yet over and I hadn't
the right to go before he had finished.

'You stuck your heel in my face,' he murmured, without lifting
his head.

'I did; I'm sorry.'

'You sold me to your aunt and uncle, and the three of you sold
me to that dirty old woman, you watched while your uncle treated
me like some dog, and now you kick me in the face.'

I said nothing.

'I should have killed you, but I couldn't.'

Once again I did not reply.

'I'm stronger than you; I could kill you if I wanted to.'

I still said nothing.

'But at bottom I didn't want to.'

Silence.

'If I were to kill you I would be killing the only witness of who
I truly am,' he said before looking up at me. 'It's as if you were me
myself. If I were to kill you, after all you've done to me, it would
be like killing what you've left me, after all that has happened.'

'Change the subject. You can't kill anyone with a penknife.'

'So what would be enough to kill someone?' he said, smiling.
'Come on, out with it, you're the specialist in these matters.'

'I don't know. I suppose it depends on the people and the
situation.'

He got up, rubbing his face and sat on the edge of the bed.
'Everybody always used me, always in exchange for another. What
harm have I done? Why is it always me they use to have and to do
what they want with?'

'Have you never done what you wanted to do?'

'No, I've never done what I wanted. I've never had what I
wanted. I've never...' He was silent before continuing: 'And I've
paid, with my cock and with the only love I've ever had, for these
idiots to go off and fight in Spain, in Spain! The land whence they
came to cuckold my father. You wouldn't believe if you hadn't
seen it. And you, my one friend, the only man I've always trusted,
you were the one who sold me. What a farce.'

'But if it seemed to you that you were free,' I said. 'Aren't you
even freer now?'

'I am ... but it's a base kind of freedom, like when you have a shit. Remember that you are shit, that you will return to shit, isn't that what is written on the gates of the cemetery?'

'No; there they talk about dust and ashes.'

'That's just a posh way of saying the same thing. Now, what about Ramos, what's going to become of him?'

'I don't know and I don't really care. Anyway, I've already lost Mercedes. What I don't understand, I'm sorry, is how futile everything is. All this so that the expedition could take place and so that I could keep Mercedes; and I've lost Mercedes, and José Ramos is dead. And the trip's gone ahead all the same.'

'With the money I earned.' He looked at me with a malevolent gleam in his eye. 'There's one more thing though that you don't know... Something just for you, like what you did to me was just for me... She gave herself to Almeida as well.'

'That's supposed to be news?' I said, through gritted teeth.

'Oh, but it is – to you. She gave herself to him again after you'd had her.'

'That's a lie.'

'It's not a lie. I saw it.'

'It's not possible. Even if she had wanted to she just didn't have the time.'

'She did. Do you know when? The night before last.'

'I slept with her all last night.'

'And he all the previous night.'

'Where?'

'In her boarding house. I saw it. It must have been to shut them up, mustn't it? He already suspected something was going on, for sure.'

'But how did you see it? Where were you, to be able to see it?'

'You believe me, don't you?' he said, with a bitter, relieved laugh. 'Sure I saw it because ... it's not true, I swear I saw nothing, that I don't know anything.'

'You know something, though.'

A ferocious smile crossed his face; sitting on the edge of the bed he seized his cock and waving it around began to speak with it. 'We know, don't we? Shall we tell you what we know? No? Don't you want to tell? Do you?'

'That's the only thing you know how to speak with,' I replied, filled with rage and revulsion.

'Of course it is. Isn't it the language of men, the language everybody understands? Even those who are afraid to use it? Aren't you my tongue?' he went on in the same vein. 'He says that I only talk to you. Is it true I only talk to you? Is it?'

'Goodbye. I think we've already said all we have to say. You've already done whatever damage you wanted to.'

'Already, eh? Well then, we're quits again. And we can still be friends,' he said, waving his cock again. 'Hang on, don't go just yet because he wants to tell you a secret.'

I stopped by the door, my hand on the handle.

'Do you know what the secret is? I'll tell you on his behalf. This piece of meat here won't rest until it's been inside her. It and her hole were made for each other, by the whole lot of you. It's just like hunger: it's a good sauce when you want to eat.'

I turned towards him and spoke, emphasising each word: 'It's all the same to me. If she wants to be yours, then it doesn't matter to me because she'll never be anything other than mine.'

'Are you so sure about that? Even with Almeida there in between?'

'I'm absolutely sure. And truly I don't give a damn, whoever might have been there between the times I was with her.'

'Is that how you made her really yours?'

'Yes.'

Now standing, he took hold of his cock once again and lifted it towards him to whisper to it intimately. 'You see? It's really going to be a good sauce when you want to eat. But you're going to work as much as you can, aren't you? So we can get shut of that guy once and for all and all the other guys, eh?'

The end of his cock nodded back in agreement and I went out, slamming the door. Still in the corridor I felt a terrible urge to kill Almeida. He needed to be taught a lesson, but how? Without thinking, I turned round and, without knocking, went back into Rodrigues' room. He was laid out on his bed, gazing at the roof and masturbating. Startled, he turned round.

'What is it?'

'I've got an idea for you.'

He covered himself with the pillow.

'What?'

'We'll get rid of Almeida. If we get rid of him I'll do everything in my power to make Mercedes yours.'

'Get rid of Almeida? Are you serious? No, we won't kill him,' he said, entering into the spirit of the thing. 'We'll cut his balls off, that's it,' he said and then suddenly changed the subject. 'Look, if the trip really went ahead, like you said, did Carlos Macedo go alone? That unsullied purity, lost on the high seas, in the middle of a gang of smugglers ... all of whom he already knew since he was a kid, there on the beach. That's a good one, that is! And one more reason to cut Almeida's balls off. Damned Communist rabble! They're all scum.' And then it came out: 'To protect some Spanish riff-raff, that's why they ruined me and everything else, the bastards!'

'Have you read today's paper? Macedo can't have been alone. Some Spaniards who escaped from Oporto must have gone with him.'

'Escaped from Oporto? Would they be the ones involved in that brawl the day you arrived?'

'That's what it says in the paper. It says they escaped and the police believe they tried to embark from some port south of Oporto. But it doesn't mention Macedo's boat.'

'And Almeida then wanted Mercedes in exchange for going, and he couldn't have her because she was yours, was that it? And then he was up there shouting it all about that she was a whore, after he had made her one by sleeping with her, after she was yours, pretending that was the price of his silence and for going, eh?'

'That must have been how it was. But did she really sleep with him then?'

'She did. I'm telling you the truth. She did. After they had all left in the cars, I saw him go into the boarding house and I slipped the nightwatchman some money to see whether he would come out again and he didn't. And then at dawn he gave him some money to say that he hadn't seen him. I really wanted to tell you but you wouldn't let me.'

'I don't even know why I asked you; just a bad habit. Mercedes is mine, even if she sleeps with the lot of you, even with you. She belongs to me so completely that if you need to sleep with her to feel that you are a real man, I'll lend her to you. Just one condition: that when I want her, she sleeps with me. And the others can only have her when I don't want her, while I don't want her.'

'Aagh ... she'll be just like Rufininho with me.'

'I'd rather you didn't make such distasteful comparisons. I'm telling you something I've never told you before: I don't believe this story with Rufininho. If it were true you wouldn't talk about these things to anybody; you'd be terrified of someone finding out. But since there at the school everybody knew about it, you could boast about it to try and make a joke of your fame.'

'Fame, and advantage.'

'But the fame was greater than the advantage. I saw you, the other day, on the beach, with those chaps. You're just a kid who grew up slower than that big dick of yours and you never lost the thrill of waving it about in front of people, making them jealous, the sort who think it's something special. When you've got it in your fist, like you had it just now when I came in, I reckon you can't think of anything else.'

'You're wrong. Just a few days ago I was thinking about your aunt. Now that I've nobody else to think about, I was thinking whether she would ...'

'Shut up.'

'It was you who wheedled it out of me... Gang of bastards ... just to smuggle some Spanish riff-raff... maybe some shitty Galicians like my father... Shall we cut Almeida's tongue off?'

'How?'

'Leave it with me. Cutting his balls off will be like cutting them off the whole lot of you, bastards,' he said, his eyes burning with rage. 'I'll get everything ready and let you know when the show can start.'

He was like a devil let off the leash. And as he got up to close the door behind me I saw at a glance that he was about to come although I didn't know whether it was because he was still excited from his previous efforts which I had interrupted, or whether he was aroused anew by the thought of the bloody revenge to come.

In the street, almost empty of people, a peaceful evening reigned and I remembered that my uncle would be uneasy until he knew for sure whether I had got Ramiro off safely to Lisbon. If, until the previous day, reality has been like some mad children's game, that calm evening showed me even more that reality, as far as my life was concerned, and just at the moment when I thought that everything had finished and that I might be reborn, had merely got the bit between its teeth. It was no longer just a madness; it was beginning to be a massacre. Ramos had died. Rodrigues was lusting after Mercedes. And what were we going to do to Almeida? Why had I gone to Rodrigues' boarding house? To hand him over to Mercedes in exchange for Almeida? But if Mercedes was lost to me – and now I understood what had happened between us the day before – if, lost, she was my greatest love, and if I would never have had her if things had not happened as they did, with her brother, with Almeida, with the devil, why on earth was I going back to the beginning, and heaping on Almeida the blame which was attached to all of us? And all of a sudden I felt that I didn't want to know the reason for anything else, that I would prefer to be carried from one eddy to the next, until this unreal violence itself, which was what reality had become, should let me go and the others, too, whenever and wherever it suited it. It was as if the frenzy within which the others had been whirled around had also seized me. And in the despair which seemed to me like an abyss, at once smoking and frozen, this frenzy acted as a kind of liberation, and, yet more than a liberation, as a paradoxical serenity: to launch ourselves upon each other in some kind of civil war.

And the comparison pierced me with such enormous clarity that I stopped in my tracks. When life and things acquire an unbearable tension it is necessary to kill someone, even if we do it by proxy. When things have reached such a pitch that we felt we had been robbed, when we have discovered that, before knowing that we had already been robbed, we no longer possessed what should be ours, and when someone was like a race of lords born to rob, and even though we too were robbing others, without being able to restore our own crumbling heritage by that means, a civil war would break out, even though it was a latent, surreptitious war, merely the reflex of a conflict in which others were dying for us. The world in which I was living had erupted. Or the façade had cracked open. The tumultuous events in Spain had opened great fissures in our lives, at first only as an earthquake opens them far from the epicentre. But now, even though guns were not being waved about, even though political positions were not yet clear, it was no longer just a distant tremor, but a civil war which had split from top to bottom that world which was as spuriously calm as the evening which surrounded me.

We would all be on one side or the other and even our own private problems, our bitterness, our betrayals, they would all cease to mean anything, in the narrow sense which they had before, and only have meaning in relation to this event. And, in return, we felt the civil war as though it were a personal problem: a Mercedes lost, a Ramos who died, a Rodrigues betrayed, an Almeida who couldn't bear to be a cuckold at my hands. Within my now lucid spirit one shadow still lingered stubbornly, while I laughed to myself at all the things piling up and forming around it. And this shadow was rather like a discreet warning whose meaning I was figuring out: the truth was still not that, but, for the time being, could not but be other than one which I, and all the others with me, were still unaware of. Meanwhile Almeida would pay. And one day, when it was no longer worth knowing, we would know why. Was it true that Ramos, he of such strong political convictions, knew, or not? Let them explain themselves to each other in another world; unless, for them, or some of them, there was not any other world in which they could explain themselves. And there wasn't, of this I was utterly convinced. And that was what made it at the same time so important and so useless that we should know the whys and wherefores of things. And so lacking in meaning that we should be interested in other people's whys and wherefores. As far as these people were concerned it was only their actions which mattered: we enjoyed these actions or suffered them or made others suffer. Or, whether we wanted to or not, we killed them. Or we bundled them onto a train bound for Lisbon. Or we made them come down, down to the filthy, rubbish-strewn ground, from the top of the tree of life.

XXXIII

My aunt was sitting with her sewing at the dining room table. Coming through the window, the light reflected off the garden and bestowed a golden sheen on the polished furniture and on her hair, which, as if in contrast, had acquired a sombre, brooding, dullness. She lifted her smiling face.

'Your uncle had to go out. Did you see Ramiro off?' she asked.

At the very moment I said it I felt that even the reference to Ramiro's banishment, which had been so contingent on everything else that had occurred, could not disturb the domestic peace now prevailing there; it was a peace so much like that of other times, now long gone, but which through a refusal to face up to things or through some kind of delirium could somehow be rekindled.

She shook out and stretched her sewing in order to look at it more closely (and where she had sewn and all that she still had to sew struck me, suddenly, as the veil behind which she would rebuild that domestic peace – or perhaps just her own).

'Your uncle thought it would be a good idea if you and Maria were to bury the dog; we won't be able to stand the smell much longer,' she said.

Not even the mention of the dead dog changed the expression on her calm, vaguely smiling face, nor did anything flicker over it; the smell though, irrespective of anything else, was reason enough for any discomfort. For me, however, the dead dog was the last straw.

'It was Rodrigues who killed it, that night,' I said.

'It must have been,' she agreed, imperturbable.

'Did you know he's still going to Coimbra?'

'I don't doubt it, but it won't be for long. Does he think it'll last much longer?'

'I haven't asked him.'

'Nor should you. We don't have anything to do with that kind of life.'

'Don't you think so? But we were the ones who connived at it, weren't we?'

She stared at me with her pale, very clear eyes. 'But we weren't

the ones who went to Coimbra, were we? Nor carried on going
there, nor wanted him to go. From that moment on, that's what I
mean by that kind of life,' she added, turning to look closely at the
piece of cloth.

'But what we did made a difference to people, to the way they
behaved.'

'But they were the ones who behaved like that, weren't they?'

'Auntie, don't you think we were responsible?'

'Responsible? Look, my lad, in a tricky game like this the one
responsible is the one who keeps the score, like the one who believes
it all. People only believe what they want to.'

'And regret, auntie, don't you regret it?'

'Regret what?'

'What happened to Rodrigues, for example. What happened
here,' I said, looking at her in open defiance.

'No. Why should I? He always seemed to me a bit of a wag, and
I thought him rather amusing.'

'And has he lost it, his charm?'

'Men neither have nor don't have charm. They are either men
or they're not.'

'So he isn't a man?'

'Maybe he is. Though that is something which, except in very
obvious cases, we're not in a position to know. Only the man
himself knows.'

'And what if the man himself needs someone to help him know
for sure?'

'When somebody doesn't know for sure nobody can help him.
He either knows or he doesn't.'

'But nobody can ever be completely sure of anything; that's why
we need other people – whether they like it or not.'

'And that makes things surer?' she said with a gentle chuckle
while giving me a mischievous look, as if we were just talking about
everyday, light-hearted matters, the sort that confirm our conviction
that life is really a matter of the superficial, the grotesque and the
ridiculous.

I had been sitting down while we talked; I got up.

'I'll go and bury the dog. When all is said and done we spend
our lives burying other people's dogs,' I said.

My aunt frowned, like someone concentrating on the next stitch;
she added one more and then turned to me.

'Do you know something? Dogs are like people, they're always a bit shiftless. To bury the dead, even dead dogs, is an act of charity.'

At the door I turned round. 'Charity is everything, isn't it?' I asked ironically.

'Much more than you think.'

'I feel that, as far as the present matters are concerned, I'm not at all sure it is.'

'It seems to me, too, that you're not sure. But you'll learn one day.'

'I'll go and bury the dog.'

'You'll be doing your uncle and me a great favour.'

I went to the kitchen where I found only Micaela, stirring the pots on the stove. Maria must have been cleaning upstairs. Micaela herself put down her wooden spoon and went to the bottom of the garden to get a spade and a rake. 'Bury the dog deeply,' she said, giving them to me. 'Dogs should be buried deeply.'

'Why?' I asked, whereupon she just shrugged, as if it were something I should know. Then she want to the foot of the stairs and shouted for Maria.

Maria, swinging her hips and in a net blouse which her breasts threatened to burst out of, came down and stood next to us with a half-expectant, half-foolish expression on her face. She laughed when I told her we were going to bury the dog.

In the middle of the long grass, close by the dog, around which green horseflies were buzzing, and whose carcass seemed at the same time both dried up and yet sticky, sickening, and with a pungent sweetish smell which felt like it could poison one's saliva, I picked out, in an opening where the weeds where lower and thinner and the earth showed through, a spot where I thought the ground was not so hard. I handed the spade to Maria and told her to dig.

'You want me to dig?'

'Yes.'

'I didn't become a maid to start digging. If that's what you want, do it yourself.'

'It was your employer who said you should.'

'That's as maybe, but I'm not digging anything,' she said, standing her ground and leaning on the spade with an air of stubborn defiance. 'I'd rather see if you're man enough for this,' she added, swaying provocatively.

In my anger I dug furiously, stopping only to remove the coat I had forgotten to take off. The sweat poured down my face.

'Ah, look how exhausted he is,' she mocked. 'Digging's not for him.'

I continued digging until I was knee-deep in the hole. She stood on the edge, glanced at the dog and then at the hole again, and then at me, wiping the sweat away. 'That's enough,' she said.

I climbed out of the hole and together we dragged the dog to the edge and rolled it over in a flurry of flies, as its belly burst open and its blackened guts spilled out. We covered it up, I with the rake and she with the spade. Finally we stood side by side, with the tools in our hands. The foul smell lingered in my nose and the flies would not leave us alone, alighting on us and where the dog had lain. The smell of our own sweat mingled with the lingering stench. She let go of the spade and it fell, disturbing a swarm of horseflies; lunging swiftly she put her hands over my cock. I pushed her over and she pulled up her skirt to show she was naked underneath it.

'Dig here a while, but when you come, leave your seed outside,' she said.

When we had finished we both got up; while she was shaking off the dirt and straightening out her dress, she moved around the earth where we had lain with her foot and muttered some prayers.

'What is it? Why did you do that?'

She held out her hand to me with an animal tenderness. 'I must; otherwise the earth will suck you dry and you'll only be able to do it this way. It's God's punishment.'

I laughed. 'In that case he'll have to punish every young lad, long before they get their hands on a woman,' I said.

She didn't laugh. 'It's a punishment just the same,' she said seriously.

We made our way to the dining room door where I waited for Maria, following behind with the spade and rake. My aunt lifted her head and looked me up and down. 'Have you finished?' she asked.

'Yes,' I said, going in.

'The best thing you can do is have a bath and change your clothes. You've brought that awful smell with you.'

'That's just what I was about to do.'

As I was climbing the stairs Maria came and blocked my way and put her arms round my neck, trying to kiss me. I averted my mouth as she struggled to press her lips against mine. 'Tonight I'll come and sleep with you,' she whispered. 'After all, you always wanted me.'

As she moved away from me Micaela appeared behind her. 'You're like dogs; you don't even bother to hide.'

'Your problem is you're jealous,' said Maria as she passed her.

'Jealous, me? Slut. What I don't understand is how a nice clean boy like him could go with a filthy slut like you.'

Maria turned round and lifted her skirt up above her belly. 'Come on, then, old crone, come and smell it; don't miss your chance, it's what a man smells like.'

'Shameless slut,' hissed Micaela.

'Fine, call me a slut, but sooner a slut on the end of a man than a slut on the end of my own finger,' retorted Maria as the other was already trying to throttle her.

'What's going on there?' said my aunt, her voice ringing clearly from within the dining room.

None of us replied and they disappeared into the shadows of the stairwell while I went off upstairs.

After I had had my bath I went to lie down on my bed, looking through the open window at the sky which was turning a shade of green as the sun sank below it. I felt utterly miserable. That half-finished business with some foul-mouthed woman, over the grave of a putrifying, murdered dog was truly an image of my life. More than that, the perfect image was of that woman's foot covering over my sperm with soil and scratching away at it, as it lay spilled on the ground. Just so that in the future, as the superstition had it, I could pour into others the same thing I had now spilled outside, just as she had asked and I was careful to do. All I needed now was to have a Rufininho kneeling before me; in the degradation to which everything had come it would not be difficult and I shuddered at the thought, almost, that Rodrigues, this very day, had seemed to want just that, and that subsequently, in order to punish Almeida and to get my and others' revenge on him, I had offered Mercedes to Rodrigues when he had demanded her.

I covered my eyes with my hands and tried to forget it all. However, I was already beginning to forget it all in that I no longer remembered anything or anyone clearly. But it was all the same, whether I remembered or not. If I forgot I knew that the anguish I felt was memory, a memory which did not live in the memory itself, but throughout my whole body, viscerally, in the beating of my heart, in the rumblings of my guts, breathing, in the movements of my hands, and not only in my cock, but in whatever it felt and in the intoxication it brought me. Even, as had just happened, in an act which had been a sudden urge, in which there had been no love, nor any sense of myself, but just a furious animal abandon at which I had been present, had seen myself, felt myself, indulged myself, as if it had been someone else who was doing all that for my satisfaction. Even more: it wasn't another, it was *others*, all the actors in my life and in whose lives I had played a part. And, because all my love had made the body of Mercedes, and everybody had made it with me, I understood the unbelievable reason why I had *said* to Rodrigues that I would let him have Mercedes. But nobody would possess anybody. Everybody belonged to all the others, and above all that we loved the most. In desperation I turned upon myself, revolted by that final dissolution of possession. Everything within me rose up against the deadly promiscuity into which my life had been plunged and at the same time I felt a perverse pleasure in imagining Mercedes, her legs wide open, taking into her, one after the other, a series of erect cocks, one after the other. It was as if she alone was wholly mine, that absolute body which was more than mine, after they had all raped her, left her exhausted and bleeding, insensible to the pleasure that *anyone else* might give her. Only then would our love, our possession of each other, be possible; it would still be so, even if she were dead. I would never be at peace, I would never be myself, if she weren't dead. Happily, with a feeling of relief, I did not fight the idea and inside my room, as well as at the open window, night fell abruptly all around me.

It was a moment which seemed terribly long-drawn-out to me, or perhaps, on the contrary, a lengthy interval of time which I grasped but as a moment. It was like death, though, and I could bear it no longer. Either my life was a nightmare from which I wanted to escape – and, once the horror of a nightmare ceases, whatever it might have been, it still seems horrible to us – and there was no other way to escape it; or death seemed to me a nightmare which covered everything with its putrefaction, everybody, and me too, and it wasn't death I wanted, but to be free of death, mine and everybody else's, even if, for this to happen I had to die. Maybe there were those who were born mad, those who were born stupid, those who became, little by little, immune to all that was sordid and evil. But I was neither one nor the other, or things had happened so precipitately, at such dizzying speed, that one person alone could not find the time to acquire such an immunity. The jab would only take effect once it was no longer needed. Or the vaccine was a collective matter, like I remembered it at school, when we all lined up and the doctor made a scratch on all of us with the same sharp spatula. But they could not vaccinate us collectively against individual anguish, such as I felt and which nobody could share with me. We had all shared everything, more or less, or we would share still more; but that anguished isolation I felt – for isolation it was – seemed as though it would only grow if I ever shared it. In growing it would set us even more one onto the others, and one against the others – and against the others, I no longer knew whether it would be to love, or whether to wound fatally. And thus, in some inextricable heap, like a knot of worms or vipers, each one of us was his own, terrifying isolation, the more terrifying the more of us there were.

It was another world which had emerged. A world which it would undoubtedly take many years to make its outlines clear; and one which would no longer be the same once it was fully defined. I must be, poor creature, on the threshold of horrors. I was still in the position of not knowing the slightest thing except that I was horrified, of not yet knowing whether I was horrified by the world into which the world – or I – had fallen, or whether all this was merely the horror of one who still remembered living in another world. And for how long would everything remind us of a rank quietude, as rank as the commotions of the present? People had been themselves, confident in their grasp of good and evil, serenely shutting out their own selves, only feeling alone when there was nobody around to keep them company. Now it wasn't a matter of lacking company, and it wasn't within me that I felt alone, but in the others. How long – sharing such an ardent fury, all feeling that we could not save ourselves alone without the others, nor that that company existed for those empty hours, but for other, busier hours – how long would this emptiness last, this being alone in the midst of unbridled disorder of a reality which consisted of all of us and none of us, since, rent from top to bottom, it had ceased to be the same for everybody? How could anything else but death help me to bear all this? I could stand it no longer. And distraught with rage, I took the bolster in my arms, to throttle it and to possess Mercedes within it, as if she were me myself.

There was a knocking at the door and I heard Maria's voice: 'Come down to dinner; your uncle's calling for you.'

I switched on the light. My head reeling at its brightness and at the unbearable material reality of the bedroom furniture, I got dressed. I went down the stairs as if drunk, stumbling, to the dining room where the light dazzled me. Still in a daze, as though I were part of it, I heard my uncle's voice saying that everything had been tidied up. '... did you hear me? Sit down, man, you look like a ghost!'

I sat down and he repeated what he had just said. He had spoken to Captain Macedo, they had gone to the chap in the harbour, the one who supervised the beaches; they'd called Ramos' stepfather on the phone; Ramos was with the family in Oporto; the lads had told them how in the end Ramos had parted from them that night and hadn't gone along with them out on the town, and the girls had said that he had slept with them and it was true; and nobody recognised the corpse, which must have been that of some foreign sailor who had fallen into the sea from some passing boat. The autopsy has shown that the body had undoubtedly been many days in the water before it was washed up on the shore.

'But it was him,' I stammered, 'it was him, I saw him.'

'Come on ... come on,' said my uncle, staring at me, full of scorn.

'She saw him, too, it was him,' I carried on, managing to sort out my thoughts.

'She didn't see anything. She saw a dead body on the beach, and in her distress thought it was her brother.'

'But he can't be in Oporto; he's dead. Everybody knows he's dead.'

'And what the devil does it matter what people think? What matters is what they say.'

'But if he's dead he can't be there in Oporto.'

'If his stepfather thinks he is, then what has it to do with you?'

'But a person can't just disappear like that,' I said, remembering other disappearances. 'And what about Carlos Macedo? And the Spaniards?'

'Carlos really did vanish from his house. Captain Macedo even asked us to look for him in Lisbon.'

'He isn't in Lisbon; he took the boat.'

'Are you sure?' And to repeat the question more effectively, he kept his fork in the air.

'I'm not sure about anything at all,' I said in low voice, feeling something I could not name rise in my gorge against everything that was happening.

'Eat up; your dinner's in front of you,' said my uncle and I saw that I had drunk my soup and that my aunt was holding out to me the plate which she had filled. I took the plate, sensing Maria at my side as she took away the empty bowl. I looked at my aunt anxiously, as if I was expecting her to make some sign which would break the spell I felt in the air around me and which had transfixed me. My uncle, wiping his mouth with his napkin, looked at me and her surreptitiously, but my aunt, with a slight smile playing over her lips, moved naturally through what was for me an enchanted atmosphere, peeling an apple which she ate quarter by quarter. I was the one who was enchanted, only me and she was part of the spell. I had a sudden urge to get up and run away, but all I could do was to carry on eating distractedly I knew not what. When I had finished my uncle rolled and licked his cigarette, and then lit it, drawing deeply on it and running his fingers through his hair.

'I'm enjoying having you in the house,' he said, 'but, if I were you, I'd reckon my holidays were over and get back to Lisbon.'

I looked at him in astonishment, not really understanding what he was saying. 'Ahh, while we're on the subject,' he want on, 'I suppose you put Ramiro on the train?'

I nodded.

'Fine, fine. You can go tomorrow morning; Captain Macedo asked if Luís could go with you.'

So that was it. It was all arranged. They hadn't wasted any time. 'We all have to go; nobody's exempt,' I said.

My uncle replied philosophically, between two extremely deep drags on his cigarette: 'That's what happens, sooner or later, to everybody in this world. Your time has come to change planets. Have you got enough money for the train?'

'No,' I replied, and in my mixed-up memories of those days, if I'd had time to count my money, I wouldn't have had enough.

'That's the least of things; we still have money for your ticket.'

How that 'we still had money' made me shudder. And much more than the fact that my ticket might be bought with it. However, the shudder was soon followed by a feeling of relief that my uncle had given me a shove in that direction. In truth I wanted to be off, I wanted to vanish from circulation, forget everything, I couldn't even put into words what I wanted. I got up from the table and headed for the door. Once there I turned round. Seeing them – my aunt was getting up as well – a terrible anger made me realise what it was I wanted: a machine gun to mow down the whole world.

'Are you going out?' asked my uncle, while Maria, in the doorway, looked at me.

'Yes.'

My aunt's hair, as she stood at his side, shone lustrously.

'Don't go before it's time,' said my uncle. 'Remember, it's tomorrow morning.'

And it seemed to me that there was a catch in his voice, at once affectionate and cold, which continued to ring in my ears once I had turned my back and left.

XXXIV

There was nowhere I wanted to go, nor had I anybody or anything in mind, the only thing I really wanted to do was gun down the whole world. A massacre which would be more real than all the reality in which people were and were not themselves, died and did not die, were and were not corpses, disappeared and didn't disappear, loved and didn't love, gave themselves to you and didn't give themselves, were everybody's and nobody's, were and were not themselves. And, by being and not being themselves, they lost their own identity after all. In a world in which everything was up for sale or could be stolen, this identity was the only good, the only personal possession we could claim for ourselves. In death we were stuck with this identity which was our guarantee in life. Nor was even this identity safe: we could have it snatched from us, not even exchanged for another one, but purely and simply withdrawn, or denied even. It was as if, in a nightmare, we cried out that we were who we were – although we were, while being ourselves, everyone else, and we were only ourselves when with them – and all around us all these through whom we were, drowned out our desperate voice with cries that we were not, that we did not exist, never had existed. And if in effect we were only what we were through all the others, then our identity depended on these others, and they were free not to acknowledge it, to dispute it, change it for another one, or even deny us it absolutely. Identity was like a provisional passport for our being, which could be valid for our whole life and even beyond death, as long – and only as long – as it suited the others.

And as I told myself over again that it was only this and no more, I found myself in front of the old woman's little house, in the empty street, while a dog I vaguely recalled sniffed around my trousers. I gave it a sharp kick on the nose; it howled and ran to the corner from where it barked at me furiously. I went down the street and on as far as the avenue which ran alongside the beach. I stopped. There, it must have been in the direction of those two boats, that's where he had appeared, where he was. I had seen him; this very morning. Or was it yesterday, or the day before? No; not even a day had passed since I had seen him, he couldn't even be buried yet, and it wasn't even him. Incredible – but as incredible as his being dead. There, on the beach, in the clarity of dawn, in the midst of a group of dark shadowy figures bending over him. More or less in the direction of those two boats, where now flowed the white, keening foam, in the dim light of the streetlamps. The coming and going, now roaring and surging, now sucking back and soughing, of the waves tumbling over each other, was like a sound which was alternately black and white over the whole beach. From a distance it was not so much a sound as sonorous clarity covering the sands stretching out before it. Nothing remained there, nor anywhere else. And that was so because the fact that people might have died was no longer any guarantee that they might have been killed, or of the occasion on which and by which they had died. I had seen him lying there dead; he wasn't in Oporto. It was impossible.

He must be somewhere – where? Perhaps in the chapel at the cemetery, or in the one at the hospital, left abandoned, naked and still more decayed; and it wasn't him but the body of a pale, blond sailor who had fallen into the sea and drowned – an Englishman, a Norwegian, perhaps even a German, which he was in part. It could have happened like that, some sailor had fallen overboard, and some family, somewhere in Germany one day might claim that unrecognisable body as their own. And he who detested all that Germany represented, perhaps even hated it within himself! Mercedes had talked about something of the sort with me; somebody had – or not? I couldn't recall it dearly. And then a terrible pain tightened my chest, so that I could hardly breathe, making me unsteady on my feet; it seized my head, my guts and even annihilated the first stirrings of desire that I felt in my cock. Things and people could all be replaced, their identity and meaning transferred, suppressed, anything. But the events in which they figured couldn't be recreated. Because, whoever we were, whatever we chose to do and say, the events *had happened*. This was more important than life or death; neither memory nor forgetting had any power against this fact, that they 'had happened', against their not having happened at another time, or their not having been different from what had been. Even when this 'what had happened' had been the cause of the greatest bitterness, had brought betrayals and deaths, and to recall them only brought us regret – which was what I also felt – not for what had been but for what might have been, in other circumstances, or for what could have been, if we had known what we would know later – and precisely because we hadn't known then – *had happened*. It was horrifying, dreadful, unbelievable, but it had happened. It had left us with a guilty, frustrated feeling, to the very marrow, but it had nevertheless happened; and against that everything else was powerless. That was the certainty, the safety. And it was also the greatest pain which made itself known to me violently, as if I should, from then on, not so much feel it as remember that I *had felt it*. Or, whenever I felt it, feel also the memory of having discovered it.

I continued along the avenue, feeling the sea beside me. There were shapes sitting by the side of the avenue, turned towards the beach, some leaning against the lamp-posts, or in the shadows of the walls of the houses, and at the corners. Alone, or in small groups, other figures strolled around in the sea air. I could hear vaguely distant voices and among them the crackling of a radio – or perhaps of more than one. It was in a tavern, where a whole crowd had gathered to listen to it since it was the closest. Absently, I turned towards the door; the voice, hoarse and overwrought, addressed with great vehemence the enemies of Christian civilisation, urging them to lay down their arms before they were wiped out by the combined forces of Nazi-Fascism, inveighed against France and England and, increasingly hoarse, mocked their apathy and the duplicity of their actions, hamstrung as they were by the betrayals of Judeo-Communist democracy; the voice trilled, still hoarse and strident but now more tremulous, as it informed the heroic defenders of the Alcázar in Toledo that they could be sure that the world fought in spirit alongside them, since, that very afternoon – although the news was not yet officially confirmed – the Portuguese Government had offered, in response to the provocations directed against it, its unconditional support to General Mola, one of the glorious leaders of the free revolution. The political prescience of the head of the Government, a Portuguese of the same spirit as Constable Nuno Álvares Pereira and the Infante D. Henrique, for, just as the first had saved the country in its hour of danger, and the second had planted it on the path of its highest destiny – the one which its ships had followed when they boldly sailed into the Dark Sea of decadence, the domain of those nations embroiled in the Red menace – so this same prescience, this wisdom, drawn from the deepest wellsprings of nationhood had not needed to attend upon some formal word from the Spanish Government, to declare itself, before the whole world, given that, in the holy war, the Government was nothing short of indestructible, it concluded triumphantly, within the union of hearts and guns. Almost choked by coughing, croaking, the voice concluded:

'Heroic cadets of the Alcázar, flower of Spanish youth, you may sleep in peace, your heads resting on your devoted guns. Like those sentinels of yours, who were there, their eyes staring, at the barbarous destruction of your cathedral wherein lay a King of Portugal, but who kept watch, Salazar is with you. He watches, he watches. Death to the enemies of our country!'

I wandered away, my ears still ringing with his concluding exhortations and the military chords of the anthems. What kind of Portugal was he talking about? A country common to us and to those cadets. His country? Mine? That of my friends? Which? But in the weariness of my sorrow, an exhaustion made up of everything which had affected me physically and had been consuming me these last few hours, this country was, for me, a body which I saw delivering itself to me, laid out on a bed on which was spread the weeping putrefaction of a corpse, sucked up by the sheets as though they were sand. Was that what the fellow coveted? I carried on towards the end of the beach, where the shadows thickened in the already distant lights. At my side a shadow materialised into a lanky shape.

'What a terrible, terrible thing it was, wasn't it?' said a soft voice. I looked sideways, thinking now he's going to fall on his knees, with his mouth open and his hands reaching out for my flies, and I couldn't hold back a laugh which, in the giggles which followed, almost choked me. He stepped back, fearful and scandalised at the same time.

'What are you laughing about? What happened was no laughing matter... I'm sorry if I disturbed you,' he said, and just as elusively as he had appeared, he merged again into the shadows which were not so dark as the figure which had recently emerged.

'No,' I called after him, 'come back; I wasn't sending you packing.'

He re-emerged at my side, moving easily. But he was still shocked; or, now that he was more at ease, only this remained to cast a shadow over his satisfaction at being with me, for I could see that he was still anxious by the furtive glances he kept casting around him.

'Why did you laugh? What's so funny about such a terrible thing, my God? Don't you think it's terrible?'

'What?'

'You mean you don't know? Of course you do, don't tell me

you don't,' he said, and even in such a dramatic question there was coquetry in his voice.

I remembered that I had never talked to him as I was talking now and that I had never even seen him so closely as now. But it was as if I had known him for ages, so deeply was he involved in the lives of those who were mixed up in mine. More: his presence there at my side truly had something of a 'materialisation' about it; that had been my first impression, for not only was he deeply involved, but he had been 'others' at the roots of others who had been or had run away from being, in a series of events which had led to me. However, my fear of being seen with him was no less; but in heading for the darker streets I felt that the suspicion would be confirmed by appearances and so I turned towards the better lit, busier streets of the Bairro Novo. He was lamenting Ramos' death as we went along, punctuated with silences which were redolent of the fascination of his person; he mentioned the boat, the old woman's nephew, the house, the contacts he still kept with Rodrigues.

Happy at strolling around in public with a man, and forgetful of the designs on me which perhaps he hadn't even had, he spoke volubly, not noticing that I said nothing in return. But curiously his gestures, his little affectations, the swaying of his body, had acquired a certain masculine strength; even his voice was less honeyed and had acquired some depth, and so as not to lapse into those exclamations of his of affected surprise, had become almost hoarse. I felt that, deep within him, even within his body, there was a yearning to be a man, a naturalness, which made him more composed; only the sudden movements of the head as he turned to cast, almost automatically, long glances at the shapes of men denied it, more from a habit which he wanted, without knowing it, to suppress at that moment, than as a means of not missing any opportunity which he would not welcome while he was by my side. That was when I noticed the difference, not exactly between him and Rodrigues, but between the ways in which we behaved towards them both.

'Why are you like this?' I asked him all of a sudden.

Intoxicated by the present pleasure, notwithstanding the expressions of deep sorrow at the events which punctuated his discourse, he didn't hear my question. I repeated it.

'Like what?' thinking that I had asked him to explain the transcendence of things.

'You.'

'Me?'

'Yes, you. What pleasure do you get from mincing around like this. Would you rather be a woman?'

The shock halted him in his tracks and was followed immediately by a look of rage which, like some unctuous bath, swiftly and brazenly drained away all his strength.

'If I were a woman,' he said, his hand on his waist, 'men wouldn't like me the way they do. Do you understand? It was my choice.'

'But who are they that like you anyway? And what have you chosen? To be a figure of fun? To call attention to yourself? You only attract the attention of those who find you disgusting.'

'Heavens above, what sort of question is that? Would you credit such a curious little mind?'

His heavy mockery of my curiosity was intended to hurt me, and to turn on its head, by way of revenge, the normality of the relationship which my questions had shattered. I had asked, though, not to hurt him but because it shocked me to see him display a feminine core which I had realised was not entirely his. But in fact my curiosity was very great indeed, as if the explanation of so many things depended on satisfying it, if not the reason for them. I didn't want him to go on feeling hurt.

'I am curious, yes, I would like to know,' I said.

He leant against the wall, while his eyes followed the boys who were passing by; and it was with the air of someone who was being pestered by an unwelcome admirer who was trying to insinuate his own desires between him and other, more appealing figures and their cocks, that, with a shrug, he agreed.

'And what is it exactly that you want to know?' he said. 'Ask, and I'll tell you.'

It might have been an impression but the situation was beginning to look decidedly suspicious to any keen-eyed passer-by. I felt that people were staring at us, wondering what was going on, and heads turned to see exactly who I was. I grabbed his arm. 'Let's get out of here,' I said.

'Where to?' he asked, letting me lead him away though.

Two boys who crossed our paths as we were turning a corner, backtracked, sniggering, and one of them spent a few moments shouting abuse at us.

'One of the best ones I ever had was like that,' said Rufininho. 'Every time he went with me the more he enjoyed it, and me, too, the more he called me names.'

'Shut up and keep going,' I said, tightening my grip on his arm.

'But where do you think you're taking me? What kind of person do you think I am? Do you think I go along with the first person who grabs my arm like this?' he protested, still letting himself be led along.

Where was I taking him? I had no idea. But I wanted to ask him how it was that Rodrigues, getting him as part of some bargain, could have made him what he was. What he was was at the root of all this, although it wasn't really the beginning of all of it. And like some kind of 'moment', throughout the holidays he was pursued by guffaws or by jeers, among those for whom he was the scapegoat: the very transformation which he was undergoing, by accentuating what he was on the outside, made up for the extent to which, as time went by, he might become just a vague memory of acts which were utterly forgettable in their grubby and infantile irresponsibility. But he had 'chosen'; hadn't he said just that?

I stopped and made him stop too.

'Let me go,' he said, looking at me. 'I'm not going to run away.'

'You said you had chosen.'

'I did. When it all started I didn't like it much. But I liked the fellows who were doing it, so I did everything they wanted, let them do anything. Then I was sorry that I wasn't like the rest of them – not thinking about girls all the time – and I didn't want to go on, but they made me, never left me alone, looking for me at all hours, grabbing me… Later on, though you might not believe it, I even went with girls, on my own, in secret, because those fellows wouldn't have believed that I had, and they would have wanted to see me at it, and if they had then I'm sure I wouldn't ever have managed it,' he said and then paused; in that pause there lingered a kind of melancholy, or so it seemed to me, a reflex of the sympathy which he assumed my question contained, though it was only from curiosity which did not primarily concern him, but rather had flowed through him, almost in the same way that others had entered him while thinking of another's body. The pause gave me a chance for a further question.

'If it was as you say it was, how could you carry on with them, or with Rodrigues, especially?'

'He claimed to be the first, didn't he? And that Carlos Macedo had had a bet with him?'

'Macedo told me the same thing, as well.'

'He wasn't, though; he wanted to be, but he wasn't.'

'Wasn't he?'

'No; they didn't know that there'd been someone else, the first one. And I did everything to make Rodrigues notice me; I dreamed of him, day and night. I hadn't enjoyed it up till then, I wasn't enjoying it, but it was all going to be different with Rodrigues.'

'And was it?'

'How wrong you are! He's not all he cracks himself up to be nor what he goes round telling everybody. He's all gong and no dinner. But, from time to time, when the last time was no great shakes, he wants to show me that this time it'll be better. Everybody reckons he's not much cop, but it's they who are wrong. They get an eyeful but it's all a delusion. He's missed his real calling, you know?'

'But you found yours, through him, in spite of everything, didn't you?'

'No. I chose,' and he pronounced the word with an especial relish. 'But only later. I think I was looking for what he couldn't give me.'

My fury at his having been much more, and much less, too, in the beginning of everything, showed me, shockingly, what we had not dared name in our conversation. Abruptly, I started away from him, breaking once more, this time in the opposite sense, any intimacy with him. But my action had another effect.

'I chose, yes, indeed, I chose; and do you know what it was I chose? To appear to be the very thing that all the others thought I should be. That's what your friend Rodrigues gave me. Whenever he insults me or points me out in the street, he has no idea of the pleasure I get from mincing around like this.'

'If you did that in Lisbon or Oporto you'd have the police after you.'

'Me?' he said, laughing cynically. 'If I didn't do it, it would be the same thing. That way everybody already knows that it's not worth trying anything on with me because I'm not afraid to be seen to be what I am. And ... I have enough money to pay for what I need, or whoever I need,' he said, walking along beside me, talking once again in his hoarse voice, and striding firmly along. 'And I'll tell you one more thing, oh yes. Everybody has his price, everybody.'

'Get out of my sight before I break your neck!'

'If there are those I haven't bought yet it's because so far I haven't wanted to...'

I turned towards him but he slipped from my hands.

'If you hit me,' he hissed, 'it's because you want me.'

In the confusion which overwhelmed me I lost sight of him; instead I saw, in the deserted, remote street where we had been walking, two or three shapes watching us, motionless also, waiting for something to happen. I set off hurriedly in the opposite direction to Rufininho. Who could they be? At the corner I shot a glance behind me, but the shapes had gone. Were they following him? Offering themselves to him? Fixing a price? Haggling over with him over who was the cheapest? Beating him up? And was what he had said true? What had led him to tell me? Was he trying to attract me with some version of things which he imagined was more plausible, more acceptable to me? Or were they just lies which he was quite aware of, too? Or had he felt less himself, or a deeper, truer version of himself, once I had given him the chance to talk to me? He, too, had betrayed people; and in betraying himself – towards himself and towards others – had he in the end got what he wanted? Or just the opposite? There had been someone there first... before those who were obsessed with the idea that it was they who had ruined him. And meanwhile he was transforming himself to conform to what they wanted and to the prejudices of the rest. Did I have a price, too? The horror which had gripped me made me want to crush him underfoot like a cockroach, but almost gently, so as not to make it burst open and so that that disgusting white stuff, the guts of the thing, wouldn't squirt out all over my foot. Was that my price? But I had never been one to persecute him nor had I had any particular animosity towards him, nor tried to stop him being what he was. I never had any strong feelings towards him, unlike the rest; it was only now, in my fury, that I thought of crushing him underfoot.

And I recalled that, in allowing him to feel, perhaps even without wanting it, that he was a man alongside me, I had instinctively grasped the difference between the way I had put up with Rodrigues while never being able to bear having Rufininho too close to me. It wasn't so much the too flagrant virility of the one which made me tolerate him but rather that he lacked the effeminate insolence of the other, which kept him at a distance which he himself had chosen to ignore, in the company of men, in his perverse relations with them. Nor was it either the fact of the effeminacy of the one which was inextricably bound up with his passive role as a pederast, while the other exhibited a masculine availability which, in his need to impress himself, to impose himself on others, was his revenge on people like Rufininho, not through the fact that they were or pretended to be like women, but because they were still, in spite of and because of this, men. It was exactly that which would attract a Rodrigues, and which ensured that he was still a man (in a relationship which, really, as I saw it, was utterly perverse, in as much as he didn't accept, or even seek, a Rufininho through whom he would have something completely different, in effect, or at least experience it like that); it was what Rufininho only allowed others to glimpse when he forgot about, through some kind of mimicry of nature, the inversion which he had adopted as his way of being. Was Rodrigues, in giving in to his desires (or foisting his own onto him), less of an invert than Rufininho? Of course not. But Rodrigues wanted others to be like that, or he forced them to be like that, with the fascination that he had over them (and, in these terms, could he have ensnared a Rufininho, still a child, who was not yet, in a way, the Rufininho of the future?); and Rufininho only wanted what was his own. Rodrigues, Rufininho had said out of spite, has missed his calling; and this 'mistake', which put him at the disposal of whoever cared to approach him, available in a way not so much unscrupulous as compliant (since some scruples merely served to increase the perverse pleasure which informed Rodrigues' despair), was exactly what had given him and had taken the spell which Rufininho had seen in him, and which had allowed him, involved with Rufininho at several levels, to escape being treated, although with a compulsion which he delighted in exacerbating, as one of us.

For his part, Rufininho wanted nothing more than that a man be a man, and with him, without being one himself, except insofar as he needed to be in order to attract a man like Rodrigues. And this same thing, by which he betrayed what he was, made him as much ridiculous as sinister, and set him apart from a world in which he had no place. But, if it did set him apart, it gave him the freedom of his choice; while Rodrigues struggled not to be set apart, by the way in which he showed himself to be constantly drawn to that which was only sought by those who let themselves be drawn to it. When I had told Rodrigues that he was a mere exhibitionist, and Rufininho that, in other circumstances, he would not be able to make a spectacle of himself as he did there in Figueira, I had touched a nerve in each of them. Hidden in our world, a man who preferred men, he would be denounced and persecuted unless he were to hide behind a more or less admitted professionalism; setting himself apart in public, Rufininho was not a professional rent-boy, even when he did sell himself, and, in the contempt in which he found his freedom, he had acquired an inconceivable respectability – inconceivable, not because it had been won by a creature like him, but because he had done it by assuming, on the outside, a highly conventional effeminacy who, probably, Rodrigues would never acquire, even if he were to slip, or fall, into a complete identification with Rufininho, and start procuring, who knows, even men like Rufininho in order to be, surreptitiously, the Rufininho of those moments in which they felt they were Rodrigues.

As I wandered along the streets I had almost reached the terraces which marked the end of the beach; and there in the dark I saw before me, hovering in the air, diaphanous and opaque at the same time, in my desire, Mercedes' body. Those men who among themselves desire other men ... yes, I was beginning to understand now, still more deeply, my love for her. They were looking, some of them, for what there is of femininity in a man and which we lack; while others sought what was excessively masculine within them, in their obsession to eradicate any sign of femininity. And the old fellow and the boy at the church? Suddenly, it was they who came between my discovery and Mercedes' body. I raised my hands to brush away what soon emerged as the sight of the old man kneeling in front of us all. I shuddered and shut out Mercedes, who had knelt down, too. But I wanted her so intensely, as much for the past as the future, that they both seemed fantastic, the product of my imagination, that I began to understand even more. Although vicious, these men were not aping our love: they were sex before or after love, when through sex we do not seek another, but the would-be or despairing completion of our very selves. The love of two different beings, different even in their bodies, is not the completion of anything we lack; nor is it the twin soul... No: they were seeking what was missing in another of the same sex.

My love for Mercedes was not born out of what I lacked, or of the other part of me that I had finally found and lost in her but then won back in me. If I saw her body so complete, so suspended in time and space; if our love had made it like that; if in all certainty I was for her a body fixed forever; if I was so indifferent, in the fearful sorrow that I might not possess her, that I didn't possess her, that I had lost her, when I had won her in the creation of herself; if the idea that she had constantly betrayed me filled me with horror, and did so precisely because betrayal was, paradoxically, the confirmation of a love which I could not doubt; if, going as far as the point where everything came together in that complete absence of identity, which she had achieved in that glowing reality of a body which was more than just an object and was the incarnation of herself and of me – that was because she had not been that which had made me complete, nor I her, but because, from our being different, a love which had been sexual, had created a sexuality which lived in us, independently. That old man, kneeling down, and who was the inversion of everything – a respectable father gone hoary by being the mother of the son who was not his lover, a man whose old age is what preceded us, by being a Rufininho who worshipped in us sex freely bestowed – and he was too (and like the betrayals of Rodrigues and Rufininho, not so much of sex as of their own lives) an image of the world, which, for me, even though I wasn't aware of it, nor the others in this with me, had degraded itself in front of me as far as hierarchy was concerned so that the body of Mercedes might be, beyond all else, this terrible passion which I felt. And it was a passion which no order, however routinely or conventionally imposed, could ever, either in my conscience, or even in the skin which covered my cock, or in the convulsions of emptying myself into the body of the one I loved, allow me to feel.

Everything had happened to make such an enormous transfiguration possible (and I felt that it was both enormous and transcendent, without it having about it that which would make it specifically ours, something exclusively meant for us, which could only happen to us and not to anybody else), but it was necessary, too, that everything should be destroyed and brought tumbling down around us. This love had not been created out of death and infamy, in spite of everything. Without either death or infamy, ours and those of others, however, our love would be but a love which would never discover that it was stronger and more powerful than everything that surrounded it and was destroying it. And it would not be the necessary freedom, the inescapable freedom, freedom like a curse which could not be reduced to mere reasons, whether those of others or of the world itself.

XXXV

My possession of Mercedes was tranquil, overflowing, a desire which desired more than desire. But … the repleteness which I now felt, was perhaps not the repleteness of having been with her a whole night – not that there were many of them, nor did we have much time together – but that which we had the previous evening, and was it not the case that, after the exhaustion of that night and of everything that had happened subsequently, I had still had Maria because she had refused me earlier. I was just tired, exhausted, way beyond the normal limits; and the indifference and absence of restraint into which I had plunged – more than I knew – were they not only for me to lay on Mercedes the impossibility of all love, so that I might be free? For I had given her up to Rodrigues, in exchange for Almeida, in the same way that I had pushed her away from me, like an impossible, futile dream which I could dispose of, as if it were some object.

How could it have been possible for him to ask for her and me to hand her over, first of all in a show of indifference, and then suggesting an exchange? And it didn't even hurt me to have done it like that. Why? Because I hadn't really given her, and it would depend on our love that she accepted it as love – and she would not accept it. And because, even if she did accept the idea and betrayed me at the deepest level with him, she was, through a chain of people being eliminated and replaced, the image – now degraded – of what he needed as a guarantee his very self. If he desired women, they could only be women who belonged to others, deflowered and possessed by these others; it wasn't they, the women, who aroused him, but the memory, buried deep down, identifying it with them, of the male organ which had possessed them. This memory had the effect of making these women, their legs open under him – and they could only be women haunted by a similar memory – as if they had their backs turned to him, while he sensed their cocks on the other side. When he wasn't being a pederast he would be running after whores or those who belonged to someone else.

And Mercedes was someone else's, she had sold herself, and through a series of subtle interactions she had become the supreme image of femininity, though at the opposite pole of degradation, of the double nature which, more than anything infantile or juvenile, was staunchly her own. Before achieving the degree which I had attained we were all living, or were able to remain in or between the vertices of that triangle of promiscuity. Mercedes had been the price all of us had paid, the terrible incarnation within which innocence and virginity, instead of being identical or parallel were contradictory. When I had ended up, on impulse, proposing to Rodrigues to exchange her for Almeida, and when he had accepted, having earlier said that he wanted her and my having said that I didn't give a damn, so sure was I of my absolute possession of her, I had forcibly made the link of her loss of virginity, for which Almeida had been responsible, with her loss of innocence, too, in which we were all implicated; and in this link, made in the person of Rodrigues, I gave her back her innocence, paradoxically, just as my love had given her back her virginity. But it was all just a madness; I felt this above all, or the madness, in having been shared by so many, made itself felt in me.

Where would Rodrigues go to find Almeida? What could he do to him? Nothing could be more speculative, more a matter of what might be. And the next morning I would be off, everything would peter out, everything withdrawing into a fantastical past, in which all the actors would be almost anonymous, featureless, just as they were now: Mercedes in Oporto, Ramos dead, my aunt and uncle calm and untroubled, Carlos Macedo on a boat making for Spain, Almeida getting on with chasing skirt, Rufininho running after men, Rodrigues sharing himself out between men, in a degraded version of maleness, and old women, in a debased version of motherhood. And the relations between one and the other had been merely fortuitous, so fortuitous that the same things could have happened to someone else if they hadn't happened to them and to me.

It was late and getting cold and I had been going round in circles in the town. The casino lights drew me towards them like a kind of yearning for that straightforward holiday I could have had. I went in with a strange feeling that I was taking my leave, not of those days during which I had aged years, but of the holidays I hadn't had; my farewell was in a way, though, as if I had had them. The bustle was greatly reduced, and the casino, perhaps because it was already so late, appeared empty. The emptiness, though, was not like that after a party, with the kind of disorder which marks, whether in a room or in a bed, the passage of people. It was the emptiness before a party, when everything is neatly arranged, coldly set out, awaiting everyone's arrival; or the emptiness of some doomed feast, when everything is prepared, ready for use, in gaudy anticipation, only to remain so, sadly, as the dust begins imperceptibly to settle on it. The music from the bar sounded mechanical, listless; only two couples were dancing. The waiters, in a huddle by the bar, gazed at the half dozen customers, who in the deserted hall, looked as though they were keeping vigil over some dead friend, muttering low, and replacing their glasses and bottles silently. When I appeared at the door the waiters began to move, their solicitude professional and automatic; but, since I didn't go in, they soon resumed their bored poses, looking at me disdainfully even. I went up to the doors of the hall which were half in shadow and thence to the gaming room, where there were barely any people round the roulette wheel, fewer still around the card table; there was more activity by the bacarrat, where my uncle, surrounded by some onlookers, was breaking the bank.

His chips were scattered in a heap before him, while the movements of his body, expansive and self-absorbed, only scattered them more. With his hair wild, his no longer lit cigarette at the corner of his mouth, his gaze fixed on the cards, he continued playing and winning, methodically, as if his luck rested on some complex, abstruse calculations, or, as if, too, he was receiving invisible, critical, messages from the gods, by means of which his calculations came out right every time. He placed his bets by pushing contemptuously at the heaps of chips, which he didn't deign to count; these in turn came back to him in greater numbers, piling up into a heap which divided him from the croupier who, surrounded by other croupiers, dealt him his cards and doled out his winnings. The checker, standing, and with his hands on the table, watched the game, fascinated, while even the fellows who staffed the ticket counters had joined the throng, like members of the public among the croupiers. Behind my uncle other players and onlookers, their faces tense with envy, made up a silent claque. And, at the corner of the table, an old woman, her hair snowy white, carried on playing, aware of nobody, and nobody aware of her.

One of the directors came and made his way through to my uncle, bending to say something in the ear of my uncle who barely moved his head. The claque was silent, as if they wished by their silence to banish him, so that the man hesitated behind my uncle, next to the 'gofer' who had gone to fetch him.

'The casino is not obliged to continue this game,' said the checker from the other side of the table.

My uncle shoved the whole pile into the middle of the table except for a few chips which lay scattered on the table like random droplets.

'There is a limit on bets,' said the croupier.

A low murmur of dissent came from my uncle's claque. The croupier did not move and, without taking out any cards, kept his eyes fixed on the pile of chips. Extremely slowly, my uncle picked up his stick and, holding it by the end, hooked the curve of the handle round the croupier's neck; he tugged on the stick a little across the table.

'Come on then, half-wit, play,' he ordered.

Everybody was about to spring to their feet, on one side or other of the table; it was as if the stick were, in spite of appearances, a prop preventing the two opposing sides falling in on each other.

The croupier leant forward slightly, in obedience to my uncle's tug, and almost automatically restarted the game. There was a gasp of relief, followed at once by smiles, and then immediately a low wave of laughter in which everyone shared. My uncle won again. The claque applauded, the croupier got up, taking off his green eyeshade and wiping his face, while the other croupiers hesitated and the checker talked animatedly to one of them; the director made his way through to my uncle again who, still seated, was resting his chin pensively on his stick. I could still see it hooked around the croupier's neck though this was no longer the case.

'We could let you have a cheque, sir,' he said, 'but you must never set foot in here again.'

My uncle got up, leaning on the stick, took a box of matches from his pocket, lit the cigarette which had gone out, and with his stick over his arm, flicked the spent match at the director, who, startled, tried to shake it off the front of the starched shirt which he wore under his dinner jacket.

'A cheque? Pay me with a cheque? Cash, the exact sum. And if you can't manage that than take up a collection here for charity so that you can. I'm not leaving without my money.'

The claque echoed his words, demanding immediate payment and in cash. The cashiers hurriedly made for the till, the director disappeared, followed by some of the onlookers and the croupiers. Still by the table were my uncle, the checker, the old lady, still in the same place, and I. It was then that he saw me, once the noisy crowd had moved away. He laughed, satisfied by his triumph. 'Now, look, you ...' he said, as a slight shadow crossed his face. 'If I had won all this money a few days ago, how many others would I not have fleeced!' he said, while his eyes, at the same time, contemplated the empty space and watched the checker who was sorting out the chips so that he count them up.

From the till and from the director's safe, followed by an excited troop of his henchman, came bundles of notes. Everyone there – it seemed that even more people had crept out from the far corners of the casino – joined in the counting of the chips, exchanging them for the bundles which the director was handing over to my uncle. There was something solemn about the whole proceeding, in spite of the shining eyes, the nervous movements of the hands, the interrupted conversations. When it was all over, my uncle, munificently, pushed bundles of notes to the croupiers, who dissolved into smiles. Between the chuckles of those watching he proceeded to stuff the bundles into his various pockets, with grand gestures, making a great show of his efforts to cram them into the pockets he now found and which he pretended he did not know he had. Then he stuffed two bundles into my pocket. He picked up another and just when we realised that the old lady was still sitting in the same place, he put it down in front of her. She remained impassive. Two bundles still remained. My uncle plucked a note from one of them and held it out to the director.

'Take it; it's your tip,' he said and the director, still in shock, put it absent-mindedly into his pocket.

Then he undid the remaining bundles and, moving his hand in a wide arc, he threw the notes up in the air.

'For anyone who can catch them,' he said.

We set off together, with him holding onto my arm, and waving his stick like some dandy from another time, picking our way among the jutting backsides of those who, on all fours, were scrambling after the scattered notes.

At the main door my uncle handed a note to the porter. 'Go and call a taxi,' he said.

'With all this money,' he added as we waited, 'you could even get married...'

His remark made my heart thump; I felt only a dull pain. When the taxi drew up the porter got out and stood by the car to open and close the door. My uncle stooped to get in and then started to straighten up and rummage in his pockets for something he couldn't find among all the bundles of notes. He handed me a few of them and then pulled out a folded envelope.

'Put them back in the same place,' he said, raising his arms. 'Just before you got there they brought me this letter to give to you.' And after I had duly crammed the bundles back in his coat pockets he gave it to me.

'Are you coming or staying here?' he asked, getting into the taxi.

I had the letter in my hand; I hesitated. 'I'll stay,' I replied eventually.

'OK, then, I'll see you tomorrow. Don't forget the time.'

The car set off and I opened the letter.

It was a note from Rodrigues, hastily signed. 'If you don't want to miss the fun and you get this in time, be at the old woman's house at midnight.' I glanced at my watch; it was well past midnight. However I turned to the porter and with the same air of authority as my uncle I ordered him to get me a taxi. I told the driver I wanted to go to Buarcos and I would tell him where exactly it was. I got out by the corner of the street, paid the driver and waited until the car had gone. What was it I was after, when all was said and done? What had I come for? To be present at what undoubtedly was or would be Almeida's come-uppance, or to stop the further deadly unfolding of this madness where the blame always belonged to somebody else? I didn't know. I knocked on the door, feeling that I had arrived too late and had missed the fun, or that I was free to break in on it.

The door opened cautiously; it was Rodrigues. 'So you've got here at last,' he said. 'We couldn't have waited any longer.'

I went in and I had the feeling that the house was full of people I didn't know, as happens at somebody's wake. The impression was confirmed by Rodrigues. 'The man's over there,' he said.

He was, too. As in a dream of vengeance he was stretched out on the bed on which I had so many times possessed Mercedes; he who had violated her and deluded her. Now he was naked, gagged, bound hand and foot, helpless. How had they got hold of him? And who? How had they got him there? Who were they all? Then, looking around, I recognised some of them: Carvalho, Matos, Oliveira, some other lads. And in their midst, Luís. How had they all got together like this?

Rodrigues, the master of ceremonies, a guide to the national heritage, explained that Almeida had confessed to all his sins, had already been found guilty and now had only to choose one of the following condign punishments: to be castrated – and he gleefully showed me the knife; or to kill himself, having left behind a letter disowning all he had done and said; or to sign the letter (which had already been written for him) and then be raped in front of everybody.

'Kill himself? How?' I asked.

'That's the problem. In this case I've advised him to choose' – the word made me shudder – 'one of the other two possibilities. But, foolishly, he's trying to gain some time. You're the one who's benefited from the delay.'

I looked around at the others to see if they were taking this seriously, if they were prepared to go along with such a monstrous thing. They were, though, all serious of mien, impassive, set on the man's destruction. Then Rodrigues showed me the letter: it said that he was a pervert, and had never had or raped any woman because he couldn't; that it was only to show off, and to take revenge on Ramos for having rejected him when he propositioned him, that he had gone round saying that he was Mercedes' lover and that she was a whore. The confession had been demanded of him by a group of friends – neither my name nor Rodrigues' figured among them – who had come across him unexpectedly in some low dive in the company of a man. He ended by begging the pardon of Mercedes, José Ramos and their family.

'But this isn't true,' I protested.

'Of course not,' agreed Rodrigues. 'But if he prefers the truth it will cost him, according to his wishes, his arse or his balls.'

Almeida moved on the bed.

'It looks like he wants to say something,' said a voice.

'Do you want to say something?' asked Rodrigues, going over to the bed.

Almeida nodded his head.

'But if he knows we're going to take the gag off he'll be quite free to start shouting and bawling,' said another voice.

Rodrigues went a bit closer to him. 'Do you want to sign the paper?'

Almeida nodded his assent.

A scornful murmur ran through the room.

'Very well,' said Rodrigues. 'Is there anything more?'

Almeida did not move.

'He wants to sign the paper first,' said a voice.

They grasped him firmly and untied his hands so that he could sign. He struggled a little, but then took the pen they held out to him. He signed and they tied his hands together again.

'And now?' several voices demanded.

Would he choose death?

No. He turned face down in silent answer.

'You are all witness to the fact that he has chosen freely,' said Rodrigues, who then turned to Almeida. 'If tomorrow morning, you go to the newspaper to state that you were drunk and that it was all a lie, then this piece of paper will not be made public. But we're not going to tear it up and it will be always hanging over your head. In any case, you are ruined, since you have chosen in front of all of us and everyone's a witness... And you must know that nobody would kill you. You knew that nobody would kill you. Turn over for I wouldn't even soil myself in you. I am already filthy enough on your account. I wouldn't touch you with a bargepole.'

They untied him, removed the gag, handed him some torn, unwearable clothes – they must have undressed him when he was already bound, it was clear. He put them on as best he could, his head hanging, and when he had done he just sat on the bed.

'You can go,' said a voice; it was Matos. 'And not a word either about anything, or the declaration will come into effect,' he said in a low voice as Almeida passed him.

Someone opened the door for him and he vanished.

'Now, let's leave, one by one,' said Rodrigues.

I made to go, but he held me back. The others filed out in silence. 'See you tomorrow,' said Luís, his voice barely audible.

I grabbed Matos who had stayed back.

'Wait; tell me what happened.' I said. The three of us went out.

'Now you already know,' said Rodrigues to me; this was a quid pro quo to Matos, who thought that I already knew what I wanted him to tell me (and which he did not want to divulge in front of Rodrigues). Matos' car was standing at the end of the street. We climbed in, me in front, Rodrigues behind. The car set off; Matos was silent and absorbed by my side.

'Now the three of us are off to find some whores,' bellowed Rodrigues. 'It's the least you owe me.'

I turned round. 'Where was the old woman?' I asked. 'Who closed the door behind us?'

'She wasn't there; she's off somewhere. I've got a key, though.'

We went from place to place but nobody wanted to let us in, saying that it was much too late and telling us to go to hell.

'To hell...' mused Rodrigues. 'How can we go to hell when that's where we are already?'

In the end one place opened its doors to us and the 'girls' appeared, still sleepy, wearing dressing gowns over their nightshirts.

Then all of a sudden I remembered the money I was carrying. I took out one of the bundles. 'I want a party that will last until tomorrow morning,' I yelled.

On seeing the notes the distaste vanished from the madam's face and the girls awoke as if by magic.

Bottles of beer appeared, glasses, someone switched on the radio and began to fill the silence. Then a gramophone and some records. There were five girls and they pulled us into their dance. The radio crackled.

'Stop this shit before some bastard starts making a fuss,' I said, and then I told Matos what I had heard. He already knew.

'It's just the five of them dancing,' I said, flinging myself on the sofa while Rodrigues cavorted in the middle of them and each one begged him to dance with her. Matos came and sat down beside me. The record finished and the same girl, blonde and stout, ran over to change it or put it on again and then sat on a small bench at the side, away from the dance.

'Two by two, clap your hands,' called out Rodrigues, as if he was directing a quadrille. Two by two they tucked up their skirts, rubbing against each other in time to the music.

'How did Ramos die?' I asked.

'It's not him.'

'I know very well it's not him. But how did he die?'

'Kiss the holy relics,' said Rodrigues as the girls passed in front of us, one by one.

'When the cars got to the beach it was still early and the car from Oporto hadn't arrived, though the boat was already in the offing and the rowing boat was waiting on the beach.'

'And now a preliminary visit to the catacombs,' said Rodrigues, though they didn't understand what he was getting at, which was for them to show us their backsides, bending over in front of us. Matos and I got up and bumped into their backsides, one by one.

'The Spaniards had a row with Ramos and Macedo and with the other Spaniard, too; they didn't want to embark. Almost forcibly Ramos and the two sailors who had brought the rowing boat, bundled them into it and put them on board. Then it came back and Ramos ordered them to sit at their oars, ready to make off at once, should it be necessary. By that time it was getting late and the car from Oporto still hadn't arrived. The only ones on the beach were me and Ramos and Macedo, because the other Spaniards had gone on board too and Carvalho, who wasn't needed, had left.'

'Now, the waterfall of beer.'

One of them, dark and stocky, got up on the table and we drank the beer which the others were pouring over her breasts, licking it up as it ran down her legs. Two of them came and sat on the sofa with Matos and me; we rolled around with them as they grabbed our cocks, crying out and complaining that we were scratching them with our nails. The other two undressed Rodrigues who had his arms around the legs where the stream of beer was running, and he put his head between her legs, saying that up there was a sponge which was soaking up all the beer belonging to him. Then the madam, who had been invisible since the arrival of the beer, butted in.

'No, it's one thing for the girls to be going around naked, but a customer, no, that's beyond the bounds of decency,' she protested.

I gave her a note. 'Be off with you, and don't bother looking. I'll pay.'

And off she went, leaving the girls behind, taunting her, saying that she should go and sleep with the dog and that the dog was waiting for her in bed.

'And then?' I asked Matos, as I squeezed the breasts of the one who had returned to me, and the other undid my trousers.

'It was when we heard the car coming, with the Spaniards from Oporto, and with them – he was driving – a fellow whom Ramos knew.'

'I want five, all five of them,' said Rodrigues.

'I've had enough of being on this table,' cried the dark girl.

'One in my mouth, one in each hand, one in front of me, one behind me. Keep quiet; he's paying.'

But the one who had been left to the last protested. No, she'd never done that, and she wouldn't either.

'He's paying!'

'The chap and the Spaniards were very angry when they got to know that they – the other two, I mean – had already gone aboard, and against their will, too.'

'Come on, let's make a pyramid; get your clothes off, everyone behind the finger.'

We got undressed and all that pile of bodies was squirming and wriggling, bumping into each other, which got in the way sometimes of Rodrigues' efforts. The dark girl on top of the table started to howl. Then the group seemed to melt away as Rodrigues shuddered hugely. I was still holding on to the shoulders of my girl, my pleasure at its height and with my hands underneath her arms when I saw that he had lifted the kneeling girl up in front of him and was kissing her avidly on the mouth.

I wiped myself down with a shirt which was lying on the floor and went back to the sofa with Matos and with the dark girl who, unsteady, had fallen down from the table on top of Rodrigues... She lay panting between us. Rodrigues, sitting on the ground, demanded that the other four, one by one, give him the holy relic to kiss. He was going to satisfy them all; and the one who had licked him in the catacombs would get a special treat.

Lying back on the sofa, his eyes half closed, Matos began to speak, looking over the breasts of the dark girl round whose waist I had wrapped my arm.

'The other then said that there was no time to lose, that the roads were all being watched, and that Ramos should go with them to the south,' he said, as a movement from the dark girl made him pause. He pushed her off the sofa. 'Go on, go and get him all worked up; he deserves paying back in the same coin.' She went off to join the crowd around Rodrigues.

'Ramos said he wasn't going, that he couldn't, that it was his duty to be on board, that he was responsible for the whole thing. He wasn't responsible for anything at all, said the other, but he soon would be if he didn't obey. Ramos retorted that he wouldn't obey, that he wanted to go with the boat, that he was responsible to the people whom he had brought this far. Macedo said nothing, nor the two Spaniards, and much less I. The other fellow than came to the boat, and I too, and the others as well. The Spaniards embarked and I realised that Macedo didn't know what to do. Anyway, the fellow ordered him to embark, saying to Ramos that he was to hand over to Macedo all the money he had brought, and the papers – what papers I don't know, everything. And that if he did embark, and didn't come with him, then he was the agent provocateur that he had always suspected him to be. There were the three of them on the beach and the men on the boat were saying that they couldn't delay any longer or the tide would turn. The fellow ordered the boat to set sail, which it did. "Let's go," he said and he turned to me and said: "You've played your part, thank you very much, and it's up to us now." But I felt that I shouldn't leave Ramos behind, because he didn't want to go with them, and so I said I wasn't going, seeing that Ramos was completely within his rights to want to come home with me if he didn't fancy going with him.'

'They've all been served,' said Rodrigues, getting hold now of the dark girl, and pulling her towards him so that she could climb on him and telling the others that, if they took her by the arms and legs, they could be all around her as he put his haunches under her while the others were like donkeys on a waterwheel, stepping on him as they passed.

'And Ramos told me that he was very grateful, but it had nothing to do with me and that it was a matter for the two of them. And that I should be very well aware that he was not an agent provocateur. And as sure proof that he wasn't he asked me to leave.'

'And did you?'

'No. I didn't go too far away, and I came back the moment I heard them quarrelling violently.'

'Not like that,' Rodrigues cried out. 'Go round properly or you'll break my dick.'

'When I got back I saw that the fellow had a coat in his hands and I stumbled over Ramos' shoes. I demanded to know where the devil he was, whereupon the fellow held out the coat to me and fled to his car and made off.'

'That's it, that's it, stop, stop, now, let her go.'

'And then?'

'I came back to the car and went home.'

'What about the coat?'

'I took it with me.'

They had fallen in a heap on Rodrigues and were laughing their heads off.

'Where is it?'

'I burnt it.'

'What about the shoes, where are they?'

'They're still there. What I did was go to the water's edge, the waves breaking all up my legs, and I called out, I kept calling to him. He didn't answer.'

Rodrigues, wrapped up in the middle of the girls, was smiling beatifically. 'And what are you two doing on your own over there?' he asked after a while, raising his head. 'Falling in love? Keeping a vigil over the dead?'

They all laughed. 'But he was a good swimmer,' I said.

'Yes, he was. I don't think he managed to reach the boat.'

At first I didn't reply. 'I don't think it mattered to him whether he reached it or not,' I murmured eventually.

Matos got up and put on his shirt. I got up too. 'Wait ... and now it wasn't him.'

'It was the least I could do, wasn't it, get into the spirit of the thing?'

I put on my shirt. 'But if he were still alive, hidden somewhere,' I said, 'it wouldn't prove what he wanted to prove.'

'But he's alive in Oporto and the fellow knows that he's laid out dead on a slab in the morgue in Figueira.'

'How can the family put up with something like this?'

'So you want to leave me behind at the mercy of these girls, just when we're all going to bed together?' asked Rodrigues, from the knot he made with the girls.

'The family doesn't know, though; they think he set off with the boat. Nobody warned them, or at least nobody went to tell them.'

I put my hand on his shoulder. 'Mercedes knows,' I said without looking at him. 'She saw him when she was with me, that dawn.'

'Look at them, just look, with their paws on their shoulders; and I'm supposed to be the one who prefers men, eh?' and the girls roared with laughter and mimicked his girlish little 'eh'.

'Do you want to stay, or would you rather go home?' asked Matos.

'We could stay.'

'With this devil?'

'With this devil,' I echoed.

He shrugged and went up to the group. 'Let's go to bed, then,' he said.

'I've done my stint,' said the dark girl. 'I'll go to bed all right – alone.'

'That's four for the three of us,' I said. 'Does anyone still want two?'

One of the others said that, if we didn't mind, she'd like to go to bed alone. The others insinuated that what she really wanted was to sleep with the dark girl, but the two of them, making lewd gestures, left the room together, after they had each received their due.

'Let's just have one more go,' said Matos. 'Get up off there.'

Rodrigues got up; he seemed pale with exhaustion. In the corridor between the rooms he stopped next to me. 'I swear I don't know how I stopped myself cutting it off,' he said, 'just so that I could let you have his dick on a plate.'

It was said in a voice so expressionless that I stared at him intently, in so far as I could; the weariness which assailed me meant that I couldn't even see straight. I was alone with him because in the meantime the girls had gone to their rooms and Matos was already holed up with one of them. Naked, our clothes over our arms, we stood before each other, while there was a lacerating, steady chill in his gaze. Gently, he pushed me down the corridor a little and then crouched down before me. I closed my eyes and felt the cold sweat all over me. I heard his voice speak. 'Was it with this that you made her yours then?'

I didn't reply; even if I had wanted to I could not have. Nothing happened. It was with relief that I heard his voice in my ear and I opened my eyes. 'It's full of shit. Wash yourself first,' said the voice.

He went into one room, I into another.

XXXVI

I washed myself before lying down beside the woman, the one who had been running her tongue up and down Rodrigues' body. It was impossible to feel any desire for her, and equally impossible to sleep, such was my weariness and disgust. Moreover, if I had let myself fall asleep I wouldn't have woken up again. She played around with my cock a while, out of a sense of duty, but her endearments were more addressed to it than to me. Then she got fed up, but hiding her feelings she settled down in the sheets.

'It's time for bye-byes. Sleep and don't piss in the bed,' she said.

I just leaned back on the smooth, soft pillows, smoking, the smoke only making me feel even worse. There was a knock at the door; I leapt up and Rodrigues came in. 'I want to swap, this one here is mine,' he said, and he had his clothes over his arm.

Without saying a word I picked up my clothes, took a few notes out of my pocket, gave them to him and then went to the other room. The new one was energetic and adept at her job and she managed to suck out of me, perhaps even mixed with blood, the last vestige of life, of feeling. Exhausted, I collapsed into a deep sleep still stroking her head in gratitude.

There were noises: of bells, shrill sounds and a clock ticking somewhere and then the whistle of a train, wheels outside, the tinny echo of an alarm clock. I opened my eyes and peered at my watch. It was half past seven. I got dressed and went looking for my shoes which I couldn't remember taking off. I left a note on the bedside table and tiptoed out. I don't know how I got home. In the kitchen I caught a glimpse of Maria's head; when she saw me she got up and went out and I went through to the dining room where I found my uncle sitting at the table, having his breakfast.

'You're just in time to have something before you go. I thought you weren't coming. Your aunt's still in bed; she's recovering from last night's binge.'

'Binge?'

'Of course! What do you think we did when I got home with all that lolly? We opened some champagne. Sit down and eat.'

I did as I was told.

'It's a good thing you're going,' he said as though it had been my decision and not his. 'If you were to stay here any longer I'd end up sending you home in a coffin to your parents.'

The bread was a hard lump; I couldn't swallow it.

'It's not worth choking yourself for.'

'I know how he died.'

'Do you? Who told you?'

'Matos.'

'Ah, so he's still around, is he?'

'He virtually saw what happened; it was as if he were there.'

He didn't reply, wiping his lips with his napkin. 'Now, I'm in the money for a bit,' he said, lighting a cigarette. 'I think I'm going to send my mother-in-law a present.'

'Last night we gave Almeida what he had coming to him.'

'Almeida? Why? Do you know what I'm going to do?'

'She knows, only she knows. The godfather didn't come in the end.'

'The beans – I'm going to let those idiots off.'

'I sold her.'

'You're a witness; I'm going to tear up the IOUs.'

He took his wallet from his pocket and extracted the pieces of paper which he then methodically tore into little squares. Neither of us said a word.

'Go and pack. By now Captain Macedo will already be at the station, worrying that you're not coming.'

'Where am I supposed to take Luís?'

'Home, or to a boarding house you know somewhere, anywhere.'

'Haven't you written?'

'Written? Why? Everything can be sorted out. Go and pack.'

I went up to my room; while I was packing Maria entered. 'Well, it's a good job you came back, isn't it? And now you're off again.'

I shut my suitcase without replying.

'If I have a baby, you'll hear about it.'

'A baby? How? From what? Only if it comes from where the dog's buried.'

'You can laugh… You'll see whether it comes from where the dog's buried or not.'

I picked up my case and set off down the stairs. She followed behind me. 'First of all you didn't want me and sent me away, then you did and look what happened, and last night you were off with God knows who rather than with me. And now you're going.'

'Get yourself another father for the kid.'

'Get a move on; the car must be here by now,' said my uncle, as I entered the dining room.

'The car?'

'Yes, the car. I ordered a taxi yesterday.'

We left the house and he came with me along the avenue of palms, our feet scraping on the gravel. Maria followed behind like a dog.

The car was waiting just down from the gate. My uncle turned to Maria.

'What's that smell?' he demanded. 'Go back to the house.'

She stopped, bewildered.

'Go on back, can't you hear me? Or do you think you're going to Lisbon as well?'

She made her way slowly back, her hands in her apron.

'Women,' he said, 'where you're concerned they're like dogs and you're the lamp-post. They go sniffing round where they've pissed.'

'Not all of them.'

'It must only be the ones you've pissed on.'

With an elaborate bow the driver opened the door.

'Aren't you coming with me, uncle?'

'Me? You only want me to pay for the taxi. No, I'm not coming; I'm not very good at saying goodbye,' he said, chuckling.

The moment had arrived for him to perform the ritual farewell; I stood waiting for him to embrace me, send his best wishes to the family, some show of feeling. But there was nothing; quite the contrary.

'What are you waiting for? Get cracking,' he said drily, leaning on his stick.

I got in the car and as it set off I turned to see him. But he had turned on his heel and disappeared through the gate.

There weren't many people at the station; I bought my ticket and made my way to the platform where I saw Captain Macedo standing stiffly by the train. And Luís? What had become of him?

The Captain, stroking his moustaches, offered me an apology; that was the very word he used.

'I have come here only to offer an apology; I'm very grateful for what you were ready to do for my son, but he isn't coming. At least for the time being. It's better that way. It's already enough...' and he was surely about to add 'to lose a son' when he changed tack. 'I have not been able to dedicate myself sufficiently to my sons, what with all the things I have had to do, don't you think? I wish you a pleasant journey.'

'Thank you very much.'

He didn't go, though. 'If you only knew, sir…' he said, instead.

'I'm in no state to know anything, if that's what you think.'

'Yes, but sometimes, as chance would have it…'

'Only by chance.'

'A pleasant journey,' he said, finally moving off. I stayed there watching him, his back slightly bent as he inclined gallantly towards the ladies to whom he gave his arm. I climbed into a carriage, put my case on the luggage rack, sat down, my head against the side and closed my eyes. At that very moment the door was wrenched open and Luís, breathless and panting, hurled himself onto the seat across from me.

'He was at the door, keeping a look out; I only had time to sneak out the other side of the house and set off running. My aunt raised hell but it didn't stop me.'

'I can see that,' I murmured.

'You've got some money, haven't you? Can you lend me some for a ticket?'

'Yes.'

Amid whistles and slamming doors the train groaned into motion. He squinted out of the window and then settled back with a great sigh. 'At last we're off. I'm free.'

'From what? Has your father been mistreating you?'

'No, but I'd rather it were that. Now I'm going to grab some sleep. I didn't sleep a wink all night, waiting for the dawn.'

He lay out on the seat, made himself comfortable, took off his coat, rolled it up and stuck it under his head. Then he took a deep breath and stretched happily.

'Didn't you bring any luggage?' I asked.

He opened his eyes to look at me. 'I was going to bring a small case but my aunt grabbed it as I was leaving. It was worth it, though, so I could get away,' he added, smiling.

He settled down again and closed his eyes.

I could see his lanky figure stretched in front of me, motionless and breathing peacefully; he had no luggage, only the coat folded under his head, while his hair was ruffled by the breeze coming from the window. I got up and closed it. But a chill ran through the compartment, as if it was blowing on the open shirt over which his hands were crossed. I took down my case, took out another coat, put the case back on the rack and laid the coat out over him.

The train whistled as it passed a small halt. From the other side of the track the road ran, nearer or further away, but always slightly higher up the slope on which a steep path suddenly opened up before disappearing from sight. The track followed now the line of the higher ground, now the lower, damp plains on which the river could occasionally be seen, among the high grasses, in patches of silver. Leaning over a little I could see through the window of the carriage door, as the train went round a curve, white walls on a hill and a tower, which seem to rotate and then disappear.

I sat up straight, my head on one side, my eyes cast down, contemplating from head to foot, that boy, who was sound asleep, such was his confidence in me. He was nothing to me, I barely knew him, I didn't know what to do with him. But it was as though he was my son, a son whom all of them, men and women, had created in the deepest part of me. And he had instinctively recognised this. He had emerged, a fully grown adolescent, from the grave in which I had buried a dead dog. I didn't know him. But I wouldn't have known him any better had he been my real son, and had grown up beside me, if there was such a thing, without my knowing exactly when, he had ceased to be a child and become a man.

I woke with a start; somebody was calling me. I had nodded off, too. But it was him speaking to me.

'Do you know what I'm going to do?'

'No.'

'I'm going to run away to Spain to find my brother.'

'You won't because I won't let you.'

'You won't let me? You swear?'

'Yes.'

He was silent. Then he spoke again. 'Do you mind giving me your hand?'

I leant forward and held out my hand to him; he took it and held it tight. 'It's as if I have nobody else but you; but I don't need anyone else.'

'You'll soon see you don't even need me.'

He held my hand even tighter and then immediately slackened his grip. 'Do you forgive me all this?'

'There's nothing to forgive.'

He sighed, closed his eyes and left his arm outstretched, keeping my hand in his.

'Luís...' I said, gently.

'What?'

'Men don't usually hold hands for so long.'

But I didn't let him suddenly let go my hand. 'Listen, Dona Micaela, it's only frightened little boys who do that,' I added, just as gently.

He looked at me with wide open, smiling eyes, withdrew his hand and put it underneath his coat. He gave a little shudder of pleasure. 'I'm not afraid of anything,' he said.

'I know you aren't. But you have to learn to beware of everything, except yourself, the only sure thing. Now leave me in peace; I didn't sleep a wink all night either.'

'What?' he asked, full of curiosity. 'After all that you still went off somewhere?'

'We went off whoring.'

'You and who else?' he asked but when I didn't reply he changed it to an 'Oh that'.

'It was something else, wasn't it? The guy shot out of there like a scalded cat.'

'We all did. And now we two are running away, as well.'

'But...'

'Be quiet and go to sleep,' I said, stretching out on my seat, with my hands behind my head.

The train stopped with a great clanging of carriages and someone opened the door, looked in and then closed it again. The train set off once more. I felt myself falling asleep, but sleep didn't come.

'Jorge...' Luís called.

'What do you want now?' I demanded turning my head towards him.

'Nothing,' and he smiled, hugging himself.

XXXVII

Later, laid out on the bed, I felt a burning sensation. I didn't recognise anybody from among the shapes I could see all around me; it was hard but I tried my best not to put names to any of them or, more accurately, since they were all mixed up with many other shapes, it was as though I wanted to call them all together and they somehow eluded me. The walls of the room turned slowly around, briefly stopping now and then, which caused me to shiver. From time to time little bumps appeared on the walls; the bumps rippled, moved apart, came back together again, shrinking into tiny, almost imperceptible bubbles which then began to grow again in some other spot until they were bumps again. Sometimes holes appeared in the bumps so that they were like faces without a face which I, by closing my eyes, could make disappear. The bed shook as if it were on a moving train, which, however, ran close to the waves on the sea. And, at my back, stuck close to the narrow, lengthways strips of the bench on which I was lying, there was the uncomfortable prickling of sand. Meanwhile, though, the itching on my back was gently enjoyable: it made me feel I existed and gave me a peace which I could not find in anything else, either without or within me. My mouth, along whose lips I ran my tongue all the time to moisten them, seemed to be covered by invisible kisses which I tried to push away with my hand because I wanted to breathe deeply and that ardent embrace made my breast and gums burn. The kisses, though, belonged to nobody, nor did I want them to. It was intensely hot, and the sweat poured down all over me, and from time to time I threw off the bedclothes which seemed to weigh a ton. Someone covered me up again with a sheet of such dazzling white that I did not know whether it came from the little bedside light, or from the window with its open shutters.

At times I dozed off and it was as if I had remained in such a vivid state of wakefulness that night and day seemed fused interminably into one; at others I was awake and everything around me was steeped in a somnolence so deep it wiped out all shapes, all contrasts. The most curious thing of all, I thought, was that the voices were silent: there were no voices in the room, not even in my memory, not even in my own speech. When, distractedly, I noticed this and felt curious enough to test that odd silence, it was as if I had unlearned the art of listening, of speaking, of remembering words, even as sounds and as shapes. At that moment, with a huge effort, I tried to focus my sight on some object or other. They were shapeless, fluctuating, much larger than me, and even had a brightness that one could reach out to with one's hand. But they didn't amount to anything I recognised, even though I touched them. But in any case, to raise an arm and reach out one's fingers to them felt as if one's arm had detached itself and was stuck fast to the object without sending me back any information about what it was. To try to make it go back to its proper place was extremely difficult, while at such moments the room grew immeasurably in size. The way this happened was not always the same: now the walls, or only the two before me, stretched away from me, now the roof would rise up high, now, though not so often, my bed would fall away beneath me while the weight of my body tried hard to fall along with it.

All this made me dizzy, though I could control it, screwing up my eyes more or less tightly, to the point where I felt I was on my feet and wandering around in some dark corridor. There was always a tree at the end of the corridor, or rather, not so much a tree but the place where a tree would be, somewhere in the space, in the shape of a tree, which I didn't know was a tree, though I knew it was where a tree should be. Stretching out my hands to the place there were things which my hands caught hold of, slipping from one to the other, nameless and shapeless. It was impossible to know which was the heat and which my shivering: my shivers ran hot, like the spasms of the tepid water which was my skin; and the heat, a burning cloud of steam which enveloped me, was, on the contrary, fresh and streaked with ice. Without words or shape, only feeling that I existed through my sense of touch, though what I felt was neither things nor persons, like the sand on which I was lying, and in the middle of a room whose middle was, for most of the time, in one of the corners, and whose vastness was polygonal, on all its doorless sides; where only the brightness from the shutters, half-open – though they were in any case not really shutters at all, but a kind of fluid opening through which there came now darkness, now light – while I, without being myself, not knowing myself, was like someone before I became me, before I had learnt of the distances which govern the shapes of things, and the words which define them, before being born, or before coming back from death to life.

I didn't feel sick, though, nor did I know whether I was dead or alive, or whether it was important. Even saying that I 'was' is not quite right, for, in that suspension of being which was my condition then, to speak of 'being' made no sense. In truth, *I was not being, I was not*, for I had put myself (without being the *one* who had done whatever it was to put *me* there) beyond space and time. However, this beyond was not *beyond*; it would be better to say *within* – within space and time. A within from which I emerged, not so much through any effort of mine than through the fact that it withdrew of its own accord; or a beyond into which I had gone more because of the way it had changed its own qualities than through anything I had done to change it. And, in the process, their changing had changed me, without anything changing in the whole emptiness which surrounded me, or which was projected out from me, to the interior of a consciousness I had, or to the exterior of another which I had abandoned. All this, together with a feeling of total anguish, gave me – or I gave to it – a sense of delightful well-being; not the well-being of someone who feels relaxed and happy, nor that of someone who feels he has escaped from some nightmare. A nightmare it had been, as well as a counter-nightmare against some bigger one. And I did not feel relaxed and happy. As it happened I did not feel, either, un-relaxed nor un-happy. It was as if the nightmare were not so dreadful because some real nightmare was being gradually absorbed and effaced within it.

Suddenly I became aware of myself on the bed.

'Mercedes!' I called out.

There was a voice at my side. 'You've slept for two whole days,' it said.

I turned towards the voice and I saw Luís, sitting on a bed alongside my own.

'What did I just cry out?'

'Nothing. You just woke up.'

I recognised my own room in which another bed had been erected – the one on which he was sitting. But the room seemed different, and not only because a space had been made for the other bed.

I stretched underneath the sheet. 'Did I sleep two whole days? What time is it?'

He spread himself out on the bed, with his hands behind his head, gazing at the ceiling.

'Your uncle sent a telegram to your mother, asking if I could stay until I had got my life sorted out. He said she had talked to my father and that everything had been dealt with.'

I didn't reply.

'The telegram ... the money ... your uncle,' he spluttered.

I couldn't help laughing to myself. 'You didn't have to be gazing at the ceiling just to tell me that,' I said. 'Nor did it need a telegram from my uncle.'

He pulled himself up and sat on the edge of the bed again. 'Lisbon's a terrific city, isn't it? Houses on every street... And so many people, just like Figueira in the summer,' he said.

'From what I can see you didn't sleep for two days like me.'

'I don't think it would look too good, me sleeping like that in a house which doesn't belong to me.'

'Where's my mother?'

'In the house somewhere; she came and peeped in just a few moments ago. Do you want me to go and call her?' he asked, already by the door. But he stopped. 'Jorge ... excuse me ... but don't you want to use the familiar form of address with me? You always did before.'

'When didn't I use the familiar form?' I asked, using the more formal mode.

He pointed an outstretched finger at me. 'Right now.' And I heard my own inconsistent form of address, at the same time as I felt a thudding within me, like that of a door blown open by the wind. But nobody came in through the door.

'Don't...' I said, tripping over my own tongue, 'don't bother about it.'

The cloud lifted from his face and he went out, closing the door behind him.

Before long the door opened and my mother came in, followed by two maids, one of whom I had never seen, and Luís.

'Son, what a terrible fright! I was even thinking of calling a doctor, my God, but Luís said it wasn't necessary and that there was nothing wrong with you apart from the fact that you were tired after your journey. And who doesn't know that awful train on the west coast line, the one that never seems to be going anywhere? And then, what with all the delays ... and all the trains running late because of the war! Anyway, how are you? Do you want some lunch? Bring the boy's lunch,' she ordered the two maids who, turning round to look again at that man under the sheet, who used to be just a boy, and who had slept for two whole days.

'I don't want to eat here,' I said. 'I'll get up,' and, throwing the sheet off, I stood up and then fell back, sitting on the bed.

'You see, Luís, you see? He really isn't well. We were wrong not to call the doctor. I'm going to send for one now.'

'Don't call anyone or anything. There's nothing wrong with me. What I need is a bath and some food.'

'But you could have your lunch first in bed and then get up. You must still be weak... It's true, isn't it, Luís, he's still weak?'

There was no doubt he had won her over, which would help me to escape her over-protectiveness. But the promotion of Luís to the role of court counsellor got on my nerves. I was going to tell them both to leave when her attentions, which for so long had tried my patience, suddenly seemed more comical than anything – and at that moment I realised I had slept so long in order to forget everything, and that nothing would ever be as before.

'And to think I needed a younger son who wouldn't be such a handful as you were...' said my mother, almost as if she had some inkling of what I was thinking.

'Now you've got one. Look after him and leave me alone,' I said, but my words came with a smile which embraced them, too, and had a soothing effect. The door opened so that the steaming trays could be brought in.

'Take them away,' I said, but as my mother shooed them away, with Luís, so lanky and delicate, behind her, returning my smile with one which was already shading into anxiety, I felt I was jealous of both of them: of him because he belonged to me, it was me in whom he had placed his trust; and of her because she had so readily accepted the intrusion of another world into what was really, through forgetfulness and contrast, more mine, or, one which, abruptly, not wanting to have any more, I claimed as mine. I didn't open my mouth, though, to say what I wanted; I didn't even know what it was. The same detachment from things, which I had dreamt of or had felt, held my tongue, unlike what had occurred earlier, not being used to it, and with the difference of the smile. Unthinkingly, I thought that, between the hell which I had visited and the land to which I had returned, I had no possible choice as far as the reality of both these worlds was concerned; to deny one was not to make the other more real. My mother and Luís seemed to be hanging on my word, awaiting some kind of revelation, standing side by side, in a relationship which was only possible through me, through what had happened and I had seen happen or knew had happened. Looking at them I was utterly indifferent as to whether what had happened had been real or not, whether completely or only partially.

Together, they were points of reference for me: she had given birth to me; he was like a souvenir left to us by someone whom we would not choose to remember. But – either they were not real, or I wasn't. And actually I didn't remember. That time during which I had slept, that sleep which had nothing to do with sleep, had done its work. And Luís, next to my mother, was in exactly the same situation as her. The indifference between me and my parents – I felt it then – was much greater than I had imagined, and so great that that boy (the awkward witness of events we wanted to suppress) was no further from me than she was. But also revealing was the extent of what had happened aside from my parents, and of which Luís was the result, so that this indifference was lit by the counterfeit tenderness which I, now completely awakened from my daydreams, found in me through him. It was not the affection I had felt on the train, when, really, I had been telling myself apparently similar things, borne by the emotions of the final flight from everything. It was, on the contrary, an indifference within which I felt responsible for him, at the same time as I felt powerless to guide his steps. Just as if a guardian angel – the image flitted through my head and I smiled to myself – had no other powers than that of suffering, silently wringing his hands, shrugging his shoulders, too, at the edge of some precipice which his charge was uncertainly negotiating and into which he would surely fall. He wouldn't fall from any dereliction of mine, but I could never prevent him falling if it was his own fault. By the side of my mother who was pursing her lips and raising her eyebrows expectantly, in that most elegant and conventional of maternal gestures, it was as if he had suddenly become invisible. Guilt, no. Certainly not. Guilt, how? I wasn't going to let him interfere with my life.

I got up slowly, feeling, in truth, terribly feeble; and then I pushed them both together out of the door.

Leaning against the foot of the bed I sighed with relief. I needed to be alone, completely alone, just to think. About what? About nothing. Once again the room seemed strange to me, not only as if I hadn't lived in it for many years, but even more as if everything in it, all those little things which I had kept throughout my life, were but the junk of some attic or lumber room, like when someone moves house and leaves behind him a heap of broken chairs, suitcases that won't close, rags, torn papers, nothing with any sort of memory attached to it, or worthy of any curiosity. I went to the window and opened the shutters. I drew back the curtains and gazed out at the building across the road whose yellowing white tiles shone in the sun like a vertical beach which the sky gently touched. I felt painfully dizzy and had to put my head against the window pane; and at the same moment I heard a silent voice whisper, like thunder, something to me which I had already heard. They were not words though I heard them as such. It was like being assaulted by a cadence of sounds, one after the other, abstract, something like words, multiform, like the ghosts of words. Sometimes the assault was made up of longer-lasting sounds, while others were suddenly cut off and only the memory of the cadences hung in the air, inaudible, meaningless. On these occasions my pain increased, a vague shiver, full of expectant anxiety, as if I were begging for the thing not to stop. It could be said that not only existence but also the value of everything depended on its continuing, unintelligible as it was. An everything that had nothing to do with things, neither with memories, nor feelings, nor guilt, nor bitterness, nor life, nor death, nor the world, nor love, nor longing, nor the frustration of everything that had taken place or not taken place; nor was it the idea of things, or the notion of memory, through which memory recognises itself, or the mental image of feelings or of blame or bitterness, or the feeling of being alive, or of having seen or felt death, or the idea of longing, or the loss of non-things. An everything which, being nothing, was itself the value on which everything else depended.

Little by little, like chemical precipitates which, assuming colour and fluid shape, go on depositing solids at the bottom of a test tube (or, in contrast, like the undulating shapes of fish which emerge from the shadowy waters, so that, once on the surface, their scales glitter in sudden but precise flashes, which are multiplied by the water which surrounds them), the abstract sounds and the assault began to acquire mass, opacity, edges, while the silent voice carried on retreating to its tranquil limbo. As these things began to coalesce my anxiety was becoming more febrile, more demanding, surer of itself; it was as if I, not knowing myself, not wanting anything, not thinking of anything, had never felt so lucid. It was then I read the words which I felt I hadn't written, on paper I didn't know I had fetched: 'Signs of fire, the men take their farewell,/weary and calm, of these cold ashes,/launching the boats of other life onto the seas.' I remained staring at the paper where the lines, so precipitately written, wavered. But I didn't waste my time re-reading them, trying to understand them. They were perfectly understandable to me, irrespective of what they said. What was strange about them was that my understanding of them, even if it did not strictly depend on their being clear and logical, equally did not depend on what I understood in them, because everything to which they alluded seemed transformed by another system of relations situated, not in the plane of memory or of any fantasy concerning memory, or the plane of memory suppressed, but in another, where memory, whether it was accepted or denied, was but a contributory element to what was written there. Meanwhile it was as if everything to which the words alluded was strictly contained within them, at the same time as, by some paradox which must have been that of the diverse system of relations, these words were less than that and were, themselves, contained within that which contained them, although the two areas, however, were not the same: each one of them, contained in the other, was yet great and wider than the other.

They were verses, more or less the same as those which had previously come to me, although, without remembering them now, it seemed to me that they were not exactly the same. In any case – and I froze with terror at this – things had happened later and those sequences of words (since there were three sequences in juxtaposition), although slightly modified (if indeed they were), could not possibly mean what they had meant before. And, therefore, it was either lucky guesswork, or there was an inescapable correlation between the events which could be divined, or the verses were an attempt to give sense to something which had no sense, or they were, quite simply, just a 'flatus vocis', consisting of words and sentiments, which the facts, by the merest chance, had fused together and which lingered in my verbal memory even when it was left empty by events. But by what reason should any of these possibilities occur in that way, in successive lines which one could call verses? And, if I knew nothing of that art, nor even had any special feeling for 'poetry', why had it happened to me like that? It didn't give me any pleasure at all to have written them; on the contrary, it had aroused in me a feeling of perplexity, as if some new responsibility which I had not looked for in myself were forming in my conscience: that of writing whenever I felt that pregnant anxiety forming in a void, and that of supposing – or urging the supposition – that that meant something to me and to the rest of them.

At that moment the door opened and Luís came in; I quickly stuffed the paper into my pyjama pocket.

'Well, has something happened? Are you coming to have lunch or not?'

'Nothing's happened,' I replied and immediately I thought that, in lying, I hadn't lied at all, because what had happened meant nothing, or amounted to nothing.

'Do you know what your father told me he was going to fix up, which would be the best thing for me?'

'What?'

'First, I'd go to sea, as an apprentice; then I'd do the course. I always knew it could be done that way and he's said he'll fix it up for me.'

'How come?'

'He knows somebody in one of the companies; he has a friend who's a commander in one.'

I recalled Commander Abreu, with his haughty, curled moustaches towering above me, and who sometimes, though very rarely, visited us when he was in Lisbon; on these occasions he seemed shy, in odd contrast to his imposing elegance.

'It seems a good idea.'

'I think so; don't you?'

'Yes, I do.'

'Whenever I come back I'll come here, if that's all right with you,' he said after a short silence.

'Of course it is.'

'That way I'll start to earn money at once.'

'That's good.'

'You don't seem to think much of the idea.'

'Don't I? Why?'

'Because you're not saying anything.'

'But what should I say? Didn't you come down here to join the merchant navy? Well, then, join it. But you could have joined in Figueira, too.'

'Fishing for cod, is that it? Six months at sea, cooped up in some hole, without a glimpse of land, like Almeida?'

'Like whom?' I demanded drily, and the violence of my question made us both feel as if he had bitten me.

'That's just what I don't want to be,' he explained, lowering his gaze.

'No ... you only want to be something similar ... and in addition to which you want to get out of the house,' I added, smiling, 'and mooch around Lisbon a bit, don't you?'

'That too.'

XXXVIII

In the next few days I showed him a Lisbon even I had never seen before, climbing up to places where I had never been or lingered before, from these high places expertly pointing out to him buildings I had never noticed; we went to Outra Banda, and systematically cut a swathe through all the brothels I knew and yet others where I had never set foot. None of my other friends were in town and these days were holidays such as I had never had, being accustomed to spending long holidays away from home. Then we had money to throw around, because my parents, heeding my uncle's request, did not want anything from Luís. We were like some newly rich bumpkins in the dance halls, we saw all the films in the cinemas twice, and we arrived back home in the early hours, tired and happy. In the mornings, late, when we got up, Luís started a courtship, standing just inside the window of the bedroom, with much play with signals and athletic contortions of his skinny, naked body, with a small blonde girl who had appeared one day in the building across the way. Then the courtship took to the street, and he was so carried away he could not think of anything else, and spent his days like some sentry, waiting for a sign, and running to the grocer's to buy things for my mother, not vegetables and such like, but things such as the girl went to buy and which my mother didn't need. The maids mocked him mercilessly, somewhat put out because the excessive amount of parsley deprived them of any pretext for doing the same when they felt like a stroll. He was extremely popular with them, though I, in my role of elder brother, felt inhibited from showing them too much attention, although one of them certainly merited it and showed every sign of welcoming it. Sometimes, at night, Luís, after pretending to believe that I was not pretending to be already asleep, slipped away towards their room. When he returned later he laid out on top of the bed and stretched himself at length, with the sighs of a satisfied male, one or another of which were intended, with discreet exhibitionism, to relieve the frenetic, unrestrained way of life he had now adopted. The days, still hot and bright, rolled by in much the same way. And once, over lunch, my mother asked, her spoonful of fruit salad halfway to her mouth, why we didn't go off to the beach, to one of the beaches which we could get to on the Cascais train.

We were sitting on either side of her in the dining room, in whose dark corners glittered the crystal and silver which my mother had polished every day (so that my father was moved to comment that the silver was bound to lose weight with so much rubbing). It was as if a bomb had gone off in the middle of the table; once the initial shock had passed Luís and I exchanged glances.

Beaches, boats, deaths and disappearances – we had a tacit agreement not to mention any of these things. Posters, maps like my father had pinned up on the study wall, full of little flags, the racket of phone calls everywhere and at all hours (I had heard them distinctly as I was leaning over the Miradouro of Santa Luzia, showing Luís the view over the Alfama and the Tagus), the impassioned discussions of visitors or relatives, filled with the justified conviction that, in so speaking, they were making their contribution to the salvation of a civilisation menaced by anarchy, the bold type of the newspapers which my mother scattered over all the tables and chairs in the house, and in which now, beyond the death notices and crime reports, she slowly read the main headlines, none of this had managed to make any impression on us. We had not seen, nor heard anything, since our arrival in Lisbon – or rather, since I had awoken. We had slipped between the interstices of all these things. And then suddenly, the suggestion over lunch, that we should go off to the beach, made by someone who had not the least idea of the special significance that all that held for us, brought tumbling down upon us, on top of the white, embroidered tablecloth, the rancid stench of a body, of betrayal, of all that was sordid and vile, of what even at that moment had no savour of any worth.

'Obviously Luís has had enough of the beach,' my mother continued. 'Those who live on a beach never think much of it, and he's enjoying Lisbon so much. But in summer, and what with this heat, it looks odd not to go. In summer boys always go to the beach; it's vital for your health. If you go to the beach in summer you don't have so many problems with colds in winter,' she added, sucking the little bits of fruit off the spoon and chewing them with relish.

'What about you, madam?' asked Luís. 'Don't you ever go to the beach?'

'When I was a girl, I used to go a lot, you know,' replied my mother, smiling indulgently at what she supposed were his attempts at mockery. 'We would go to Espinho. Oh, if I were to go back now I wouldn't recognise anything. Espinho must have moved back from the coast; in the winter the sea always encroached a little bit more, taking houses and everything with it. On the beach in those days each wave... The attendant would take us in his arms into the water, and I and my sisters, in the attendant's arms, we'd raise such a hullabaloo, kicking and wriggling, making out that we were afraid. But here, on these Lisbon beaches, there aren't any waves to speak of, except at the spring tides. But it's not the season for them yet. You should go to the beach. Get the early train, take a snack with you, or have something there, and come back in the afternoon. You could even go in twice, once in the morning when you get there and then in the afternoon. In my day nobody took a dip in the afternoon; only in the morning, quite early, and everything according to the clock, ten minutes the first time, twelve the second and so on until you could stay in half an hour.'

'And then it was twenty-five minutes again and you went back in reverse to nothing, didn't you?' enquired Luís.

My mother, coquettishly, slapped him lightly on the arm. 'Trying to be funny, eh? You should know then that there are those who recommend just that way of doing it and it is actually called ... yes ... the regressive method. Now, I think you could go tomorrow.'

'Where to?' I asked.

'Hmm ... let me see ... as far as Cruz Quebrada it's all rather dirty and a bit common, so they tell me. The beach at Caxias is too small. Paço de Arcos is an old beach.'

'Old?' said Luís in surprise.

'Yes, it's an old-established beach, like the one in Cascais, where people used to go formerly, in the time of the kings.'

'What about Estoril? We could go to Estoril. I've never been to Estoril,' added Luís.

'Oh, Estoril, no, that's a very expensive beach; and there's a casino, a terrible place,' said my mother, while Luís and I exchanged a mocking glance. 'Before Estoril there's Parede, which is frightful, what with the sanatorium and the beach full of people with tuberculosis, all skin and bone. Nobody goes there. I think you should go to Santo Amaro d'Oeiras or to Carcavelos. Oh, but in Santo Amaro you've got your aunt and uncle, your uncle Sarzedas,' she said by way of explanation, 'what am I thinking of, they always go there. And it's the best beach. If I were you I'd go to Santo

Amaro. And you, Jorge, could introduce Luís to your cousins, that would be much nicer. There's no other beach like it on that line. I'll phone your uncle at his office to tell him you'll be coming tomorrow,' she said, getting up from the table and going out.

Facing each other we contemplated our lunch plates, in the midst of which were all sorts of scraps and leftovers, though not the same on each plate. 'Why don't we go,' said Luís.

'You're right, we should – but I'm not going to look up my aunt and uncle and cousins.'

'You've had enough of your relations and beaches, or a beach full of relations, I suppose.'

'Never again,' I said, thinking he didn't know the half of it.

That afternoon I stayed alone in my room; Luís having gone out on his own. I searched among my papers, in the drawer to which I had moved everything, for the scrap on which I had written the verses. I read them without much enthusiasm; they didn't rhyme, nor did I know whether they scanned or not, but scanning or not that was the way they had come out. But what importance did they have for me? Some, for I had kept them. I got up and looked in the bookcase for an old grammar book with an appendix that I somehow remembered; I leafed through the section which dealt with metre. Each line could have from one to twelve syllables, with accents on given syllables, as I, in theory, was aware; rhymes were coupled and crossed and a whole lot more; there was alliteration, too, and the lines should be grouped in stanzas or strophes, to make poems. In essence, poetry was this, exactly this and no more. And the pages, with their examples highlighted (quotations which seemed to me to be pretty poor and said nothing to me), which I read and re-read, did not explain to me what, in my deluded way, I had hoped to find in them. It showed how to write verses but it only meant something to someone who didn't need to know these things.

Did I need to know? Why and what for? Because everything had lost its meaning for me and I needed to invent it or discover it again? Because I felt completely alone and needed silence, and, as a consequence, needed words which could say that without saying it? But in any case what reason did those words have for pursuing me, always the same words – or virtually the same? And, if I had never been much interested in such things as verses, if I was just a man like all the others, if I had suffered like the others did, why had I begun to write verses? But what had happened to me was perhaps somewhat unusual, so maybe I wasn't just like the rest (who was?). And if someone was interested in verses he had to start somewhere. I wanted to laugh at this argument raging within me. The laughter changed in an instant to an almost physical pain, gnawing at my body with rage, filling it completely, from my head to my feet. A fury, a despair, an urge to smash the world, a wish to die but to carry on living, a desire to bawl out at the top of my voice that nothing was nothing, a curse on everything that had been heaped on me, together they hurled me onto the bed, huddled and twisted. No, it couldn't be. Everything that had transpired was impossible, insane, ridiculous, absurd, a conspiracy of madmen to rob me of my life. I had nothing to do with all that; it was only because for half a dozen days I had been the lover of a girl who was implicated in events which did not concern me. Just because I had fucked her didn't give life itself nor anyone in it the right to fuck me up. If she had deceived me, used me, well, I had used her, too, and how. My pain grew to the point where I started to shake with the fear of going crazy. I rolled around on the bed, my eyes shut tight, my fists clenched, my knees drawn up to my stomach, crying out, almost choking, and then howling out loud.

My mother rushed in, panic stricken. 'What's the matter? What's the matter with you?' she cried, as the maids peered through the door.

Just to be seen in that state, in that inconceivable grief, was some relief, a certain assurance that, if it was a consolation to me to know I had been observed in that state, it was because I was not entirely alone with less than me, myself, the very self that they had stolen, at the very moment just when I had discovered that there could be an *I*.

'Nothing, there's nothing the matter. Leave me alone.'

'Have you got a tummy ache?'

And as I continued to roll around from one side to the other, hunched up, I heard the diagnosis. 'It's appendicitis, my God, I'm sure it is. Call the doctor at once.'

I sat up on the bed. 'Appendicitis? Don't be so silly! Do you know what's the matter with me, don't you? It's the pain of knowing you have been deceived, knowing you're a poor cuckold, that's what's the matter.'

'Is that any way to talk? Is that any way to talk … to … your mother? How old do you think you are?'

'Old enough to be a cuckold, or to talk about being a cuckold.'

My mother slammed the door as she left the room.

I laid out on the bed, utterly weary, my pain in no way lessened, except that it had become keener and more deep-seated, closer to me, more familiar, a paradoxical pleasure, almost, which called to me from afar, with an irresistible fascination, though I felt it extremely close, leaning up against the walls, making them almost visible to me, from a desire which had closed them. In the doleful way it rubbed up against these walls there was an almost sexual voluptuousness which throbbed, in little spasms, in my head, in my lower belly, in my cock. It was however very different from that pleasure when one starts to desire a body that one fancies or has already made contact with, or of imagining oneself possessing a body one already desires. It was at once the voluptuousness of desire and consummated pleasure, received and returned. But, even in this, it nevertheless conveyed an impulse to leave me, to leave the room, the street, the city, the world, a departure which was not flight, but a kind of passing over these places, slowly, deliberately, like someone who, in the midst of a group of people, or in the street, or on some public transport, puts his hand in his pocket to finger a piece of paper on which is written an address, or a ticket to somewhere, a small souvenir once given him, something which has no other value than that it is a secret, unknown to anyone, even something perhaps utterly worthless to anyone else.

I got myself ready and left the room. When I had gone down the stairs my mother appeared on the landing above.

'Where are you going? Are you feeling better?' she asked.

I paused and looked at her; she was leaning over the banister, putting on in all sincerity the requisite expression of maternal concern, which did not allow her, in all conscience, to hear her son going out without some enquiry – her son who might be suffering from appendicitis, for all that it was caused by grief. But that air, which was one of the things about her that most infuriated me, and by means of which she concealed not only from me but also from everybody in everything she did, and even I believe from herself, a remoteness, an indifference, neither hurt nor shocked me. All at once I had something like an epiphany: I saw that that indifference, hidden under a cloak of concern was her defence against the fact that, in her life, nothing had ever happened to her, the fact that her life had been and still was, for her, less than she had hoped for. It was a kind of provisional affair, such as that of some petty functionary who zealously fulfils some higher duty in the interim, knowing that he will never be offered the job.

My mother was still on the landing, waiting for my reply, which amounted to no more than a moment's lifting of my abstracted gaze.

'I think I'm better,' I said, smiling at her like a 'dutiful son'. 'And I feel like going out; it'll do me good.'

'What if you feel ill again in the street?' Don't you want an aspirin? Or some fruit salts?'

'No thanks. I won't hang around... Goodbye for now.'

Down in the street I wasn't aware of the pain, but in the calm clarity which presaged the end of the afternoon and which, as it fell from a blue sky dotted with straggling white clouds, settled pale and tepid over the houses and the air and the few slow passers-by, I was aware of something else: the knowledge that I needed to live, though not as I had been in those days during which I had pretended that the recent past had not been so terrible. I could not recall, but I could not forget either, and if it was not possible for life and things to have the same meaning without meaning which they had had, more or less undisturbed since I was born and which had been mine ever since I had been able to conceive the idea that I was a person, it nevertheless behoved me to accept that the meaningless might now have some provisional meaning, in which the continuity of being someone had ceased to be independent of what happened or didn't happen, and might depend instead just on the fact that the events could only be partly ours. The provisional was not necessarily an insecurity which replaced the false security of someone who had never been involved in the lives of others: it could be a state of mind, an expectant acceptance, an openness to the pieces of a 'puzzle' (without believing that the 'puzzle' had to be personal and intransmissable, except where what cannot be transmitted nor communicated is not so much the incommunicable as the unverifiable). Whatever I knew and what still stayed with me concerning myself and others was precisely equivalent to whatever I did not know of them and of myself. And that part of each one which another could never know, is exactly that part of each which one is not given to know, either because communication is impossible, or because between those two there is nothing except a common denominator, or because the incommunicable is precisely the way of existence common to these two, in the brief instant in which one person's passage through time crosses that of the other.

It was as if I had discovered that we are parallel rivers (had I not already thought of this?) which sometimes come together only to flow apart at once in currents which, though the waters are mixed and common, do not flow along the same bed. Whatever words might try to say about all this they would say much less the more they thought to put it analytically, because the rational awareness is made up of words and phrases, but the representation of what comes *before them* can only be a form of awareness, when words, in not saying anything, would speak, and in speaking would be saying nothing. Therefore, no treatise on metre, however high-flown, could tell me what poetry might be or what appeared from experimenting with verses. Those sorts of treatise start from the principle that there are forms prior to any experience (and that is true when we live in a world which preserves its imposed formulas as if they were modes of valid experience), and that the experience of composing verses is not necessarily congruent with the intimate reasons we have for composing them. Only other verses would say something to me, or books which told of lives, even imaginary ones. The fact that the lives were imaginary would not change the value of what they said, rather the opposite; how could I envisage reality, if I were not capable of imagining it? Any non-imagined reality would always be less than reality. Everything that had happened to me or had involved me had, though, been beyond the realms of the imaginable – yes, but only in appearance. The horror of it was in my constant surprise at the unimaginability of a catastrophe which had been unleashed on a scale I wasn't accustomed to. The astonishing and the monstrous cannot, however, be something we can grow used to, nor can life's experience be made up of uncommon experiences. But the fact that experiences might give us the knowledge that the limits of the possible are not those of the probable or the predictable – this is what would make us realise that life itself is, or can be, at any moment, a whirlwind which drags in its wake the innocent and the unwary, which dispenses, indifferently, corpses and detritus all laid out side by side, thunderstruck at finding themselves thus thrown together.

Sitting in the tram from where I was watching the street glide by, stopping occasionally, I still asked myself: what purpose did it all serve, to write it down? For what? Yes, for what? What use was that bit of paper with words scrawled on it which I was carrying in my pocket? Had it any use for me? For the others? If the others don't know that someone has started to write, nor have ever asked him to, what possible interest could it hold for them? And if I too, had not wanted to write them, what possible use could they be to me? Weren't they just a form which I, somewhere within me, had discovered just so I could escape from the concrete memory and the tortured awareness of thinking unblinkingly about what could not be? Were they not, instead of valuable symbols of truth, slippery formulas, a kind of exorcism, like that practised by someone who burns hates on Fridays to drive away witches? Or who says novenas to help him find something he's lost? Undoubtedly they were that too; but in addition they were a way of giving an external and concrete presence to what might be an anguish or a complex, barely apprehended grief, too deep-seated and wide ever to reach the level of logical thought, or too obsessive and stifling to find an outlet in feelings, in a flurry of action, in a few tears of relief. However, was not what I had started to do, on the contrary, going to add just one more kind of anguish? If I hadn't written easily, if I hadn't found a way out for what I had started to write, if I had not finished it, would I not now be going to go on to suffer yet another affliction which would be that of managing, at each step, to say what I did not even know how to say? That scrap of paper in my pocket was already burning a hole, was weighing heavy, without my knowing how to expand on what I had written. And, if I were to force it, if I set to work on it, coaxing more words from those written, what certainty could I have, from any given time onwards, that I wasn't just making it up, if only to finish off, falsely, what, within me, was perhaps something completely different? And what guarantee would there be, within me, that *which was* couldn't be construed differently, exactly because, existing on another plane, it was not, nor ceased to be, that which was? And in that way, what significance and what worth could the transformation of the *that which* was not, *into that* which it came to be, have?

I got up from my seat and stepped down from the tram. At the very moment I was answering my own questions, pausing at the sign saying bus stop, I saw Almeida at my side; he had jumped off the cross platform of the same tram. He seized my arm as I tried to free myself by shoving him away. But amid our jostling, and as the people around turned to stop and stare, he managed to speak: 'Don't make a scene; it won't help things.'

I stopped and we crossed the street and he hailed a passing taxi. 'Let's go.'

In the taxi he gave an address in Graça and leant back in his seat.

'I've been following you around for days to see if I could get you alone.'

'What do you want?'

Motioning with his chin to the back and the neck of the driver, he half-closed his eyes to tell me to be quiet. And while the car was going up to Graça, out of the corner of my eye I glimpsed Almeida's profile, fleetingly, and I felt that not only was it not worth ordering the car to stop so that I could jump out and run away, but that between him and me there was an attraction which was no less powerful even as I shuddered with repulsion and rage. It was an odd feeling, in which there was no sort of curiosity about what he wanted with me, nor any fear of what he might want. But at the same time, along with the disgust and the distastefulness of having him almost rubbing his leg against mine (vaguely leaning the leg closer to me as he braced against a curve as the road climbed upwards, which made me pull my legs together), I felt a compliant identification with him, as if my having been there at his humiliation, at the humiliation of the man who had preceded me and had used the same vagina as me in those periods when I wasn't using it (and I shuddered with horror at the explicitly anatomical picture) had in the end created between us more than a camaraderie and a complicity; it was disagreeable, to be sure, but immediately real from the moment in which one of us might appeal to the other. The very fact of the appeal, whatever the reasons, good or bad, aggressive or otherwise, was enough to give such a relationship a firm foundation.

When the car stopped in one of those streets running down towards the Caminhos-de-Ferro, and he leant forward with his purse in his hand, and put his hand out by the shoulder of the driver who had half turned, I let my eyes rest even longer on his profile as he busied himself more than was necessary, I felt, in the act of paying, perhaps because of the odd fact that I was looking at him without the slightest sign of hostility. Getting out (and I was on the same side as the pavement) I wondered whether that studied restraint of his, coming round the back of the car as it drove away, and smoothly taking hold of my arm, to guide me towards a door which he opened in front of me with his other hand, not looking at me the while, was not in truth hiding, not so much a singularity itself as the singularity of having realised that I was feeling about him the same thing that he, just as anxiously, sensed that he was feeling about me, in the strange circumstance of having been following me around, and of bringing me here, and of my really coming here.

'It's on the second floor,' he said as I climbed stairs mechanically from the vestibule. 'I live here, in my own room.'

Suddenly the situation made me want to laugh out loud, what with the room he had, with the door to the stairs, which, just as one might say in those days, had something fishy about it. And then, immediately after, I shivered with fear – fear that it might be some kind of ambush, that he was going to have his revenge, helped by a bunch of thugs, just as we had done to him. This fear did not abate as he slipped a key into the lock and opened the door to the room. But before I could see that the room was empty (and devoid of furniture, too), I thought that it would be too much of a coincidence if there were somebody waiting for me here, since he had not had any guarantee of finding me. Meanwhile, the best thing was to spend as little time hanging around there as possible.

'I don't wish you any harm at all,' he said, after closing the door, as if he had guessed what I was thinking, or because my apprehension was more evident than I had imagined. 'Don't think I brought you here for revenge,' he added and sat down on the narrow bed which was, along with a chair on which he had hung some clothes, and a case on the ground – apart from an incongruous, exaggeratedly blue reproduction of Our Lady hanging on the wall – the only furniture. The sight of that bright emptiness which I had glimpsed from the landing was certainly no illusion, but I had not noticed just how dirty the room was and that the bed on which he was sitting had not been made. Without getting up he picked the clothes up off the chair and put them on the bed, motioning me to sit down. I sat down and, feeling uncomfortably close to him, dragged back the chair instinctively.

'What do want with me?' I asked, and the question came out as just too obvious, as though it didn't matter to me, or I already knew what he wanted.

'Since I arrived I've been walking around your house, following you around everywhere (I can tell you exactly where you've been with that boy), just waiting for the chance to talk to you. My intention wasn't to bring you here, just to speak to you. But when you resisted I thought then it might be better here and that there wasn't any other way, really. But now you're here, I don't know what I want to say to you,' and he looked up at me with a bitter smile on his face, his gaze uncomfortably frank.

'And what am I supposed to make of this?'

'What happened doesn't matter; it was just boys fooling around,' he said, lowering his gaze just long enough for me to wonder whether that event or those events had really been just some boys' prank.

'What?'

'What they did to me.'

'So why did you come to Lisbon then? Just to follow me around and talk to me?'

'I could have written to you but I'm no writer, and in any case it would have been dangerous. You have to understand...'

'Understand what? What explanation do you feel you have to give me?'

'I had to come to Lisbon; it wasn't anything to do with you.'

'And then?'

'I want you to know that it was they who involved me in all this business.'

'What's that to do with me? And who are "they"?'

'Those two.'

'Ever since you rubbed your knee against hers in the dark, in the cinema?' I said, and it was he who now stared, though his stare was hard and mocking.

'No, later, in Figueira. But now I have to finish what I'm saying. He really did die. That's why I came to Lisbon.'

'Are you going to set sail from here for Spain?'

He got up and went to the window, whose filthy curtains cut out too much of the afternoon light. 'There are more important things than a woman,' he murmured.

'That depends on the occasion and the people involved,' I suddenly heard myself say. 'As far as we are concerned it seems there aren't.'

He turned around. 'You are mistaken; I can hardly say how much. She means not the slightest thing to me.'

'Then,' I said, and my voice could not conceal my surprise, 'what do I matter to you? If I don't have anything to do with the other things?' I felt like a liar.

'But you have; don't you understand that?'

'In what way?'

He sat down again. 'You were an important part of it all. You are one of the people who know everything, perhaps even the one person who knows everything.'

'But I don't know anything; what I know is exactly nothing.'

'I don't believe you; that wasn't what I was told.'

'Well, you've been had. And let me tell you that I thought it was you who knew everything.'

'That's not true; is that what they told you?'

'Nobody told me anything.'

It was as if the thickening twilight were bringing with it a dark mantle of absurdity which covered us and made us stick to each other.

'Maybe there's nothing more to be known,' I murmured wearily, 'and nobody knows nothing about anything.'

'No, they were playing with us like someone playing with a ball. The difference is that they flung you out and flung me in.'

'In what?' I demanded and immediately regretted the question, feeling that he wanted to pull me 'in'.

But he didn't reply, getting ready the net in which he would catch me. And, suddenly, it was as if some cry had made him jerk his head round and let the net slip out of his hands. 'Did you love her very much?' he asked, lowering his voice.

'And you?'

'To tell the truth, I don't know,' he said smiling readily. 'A man like me has all the women he wants, when he wants, returns to one he's had before, or has two on the go at the same time, but it's all so perfunctory, all like I don't know... If I had got engaged to her properly... But, like that, it was the same old thing at the same time, and I was the one who was old enough to have some sense, to get married... It's clear that, if I had married her, or someone else, it would be to get married to the right one, someone who loved one, belonged to me and nobody else and who...'

'Would do as a bit of a breather when you weren't busy with all the others?' I asked bitterly.

'Do you think a man can be satisfied with only one woman?'

Our conversation was turning academic and abstract, as if we were two friends mulling philosophically over our lives. I got up; I could take no more.

He got up, too, and stood almost leaning against me. I took a few steps towards the door. He followed and when I opened the door he held it for a moment. 'Tell me ... did you love her?'

'This has nothing to do with you.'

'It has; you know it has. I want to know.'

'I didn't only love her. I do love her.'

Notwithstanding the dark I could see his eyes glittering. 'She's terrific in bed, though, isn't she? Do anything. What a good fuck, eh?'

My blows were so violent that he fell backwards into the room and I dived on top of him. We rolled on the floor, grappling with each other, in a hail of blows and getting entangled with the chair which trapped us on the bed. He was a lot stronger than me, his arms and legs were unyielding, his teeth were white in his mouth like the fangs of a wolf. He turned me around and then was on top of me, and as he raised himself so that he could grab me more tightly by the throat the iron bedstead came apart and collapsed beneath us.

To my surprise he let go my throat and we were both there like two shipwrecked sailors, sympathetic to each other's plight, trying to extricate ourselves from the broken bed. There was a knock at the door. 'Mr Almeida, Mr Almeida! What's going on?' asked a woman's anxious voice.

He crawled from under the bed and dusted himself down and smoothed his hair. 'It's nothing, don't worry, it was just the bed; it collapsed.'

I got up, too, and made towards the exit. He, with his face at the door which led into the inside of the house was reassuring the woman. 'No, no, don't worry, that's not necessary. I'll sort it out.'

I sped down to the street but he came running after me. I turned round by an already lit street lamp and grabbed for support while I delivered a kick. He dodged it.

'Listen, listen … I'm sorry.'

'Let me go or I'll start shouting for help. Go away.'

He retreated a few paces and then stopped, his hair lit by the street lamp, in an awful mess, lustreless; he stretched out his open hands. 'Listen, I swear that wasn't what I wanted to tell you.'

'Just go away.'

'You'll still be hearing about me.'

I turned my back on him and went down the street. I heard his steps behind me but I didn't turn round.

'I'm not what you think I am. You'll see.'

At this a shape emerged from a doorway and from the shadow of a woman who was right at my side, and must have grabbed him. 'What the devil do you want with this fellow?' it said. ' Let go of him and be off with you.'

He must have done as he was bidden because when I turned

round by the corner at the end of the street I couldn't see anyone; the only thing in the street was the feeble glow of the lamp.

From the corner the street curved steeply back on itself, opening into a wide, shadowy thoroughfare, at the bottom of which passed the yellow lights of an electric tram, crowded with people. Down there I stood perplexed on the other corner, unable to sort out my thoughts clearly in my head, uncertain what to do. The light of the street lamp reminded me that I must have cut a sorry figure and indeed I did: my shirt hanging out, minus the button on my shirt collar, which was the least of it, and the shirt itself torn across the front. I tucked my shirt in and tried to fasten my coat but the button was missing and so I fastened it with another button in quite the wrong place. The back of my neck was hurting and I could still feel his fingers on it. A great feeling of peace came over me, though, so great that I had to screw up my eyes against the brightness which now lit up the street. I rummaged in my pocket for the piece of paper but couldn't find it. I wanted to write, had to write, but when I slipped my hand into the pocket where I kept my pen I felt something damp. It was broken and my hands were stained with ink. It didn't seem to matter: torn, ink-stained as I was I still had to find something to write with. I found a pencil, and a piece of paper in my wallet. Until I started to write I didn't know what to write and so I couldn't write the words in my mind. I rested the paper against my wallet and despite the fact that my pencil made holes in it I began to write:

Signs of fire, the men bid farewell,
weary and placid, to these cold ashes.
And the wind which blows these ashes away from us
is not ours, but is the one who relights
other signs burning in the distance,
a brief moment, gestures and words,
anxious embers which soon die out.

I stopped and read again what I had written. There was something missing; I couldn't remember what. Then I saw a paper waving between two waters, I saw waters shimmering with reflections, and I saw some ships gliding over them. Ships from another life. Which other life? Which ships? Those ships didn't make sense, there, at this time. I had withheld the ships from the whole sense of what I had written, although, reading it yet again there was some clear sense which eluded me. I put the paper in my pocket, and I hailed a passing taxi. In the taxi, with the driver staring most suspiciously at me as he pulled up beside me, I leant back, enjoying the restful movement of the car. 'I didn't just love her. I do love her.' No, I wasn't going to think about that any more. What for?

Once home I opened the door and went into my darkened room. I picked out the outline of Luís against the window and he turned towards me. The window across the way was lit up and the girl disappeared inside as soon as I switched on the light.

'Look at the state of you; what happened?' said Luís, coming over to me.

I took off my coat and lay down on the bed. I stretched and took a deep breath. 'Nothing. I met ... guess who I met?'

'Who?'

'Almeida.'

'Almeida's in Lisbon?'

'Yes. We had a bit of a scrap.'

'And now?'

'Now? Nothing. I guess it was something we both needed.'

'Who won?'

His face, as it bent over me, was so lit by curiosity that I could feel the immense distance, in terms of our experience of life, that separated us. 'I don't know,' I said, smiling. 'We both won.'

He sat down on the edge of the bed, lost for words. Then he spoke: 'He won as well?'

I looked at him. 'OK, then,' I offered, 'maybe I won.'

'But he's very strong.'

'Not as strong as he looks.'

He got up, observing himself admiringly. 'Hmm ... others are strong though they don't look it.'

I laughed. '...while others don't look it but are extremely strong,' I said finishing the sentence for him. I didn't know exactly why I had laughed. It wasn't on his account, as I looked at him, but on account of the pocket of my coat, stained blue with ink.

XXXIX

From then on the days followed one after the other as if reality was some pleasant dream. My mother's enthusiasm, as she got everything ready for Luís' departure for the high seas – my father had fixed him up with a boat – was contagious and involved everybody in the house. Luís' interview one evening with Commander Abreu had also contributed to the overall atmosphere; he had said to my father that first of all he wanted to meet the boy *en famille*, as a kind of initial examination, an idea which my father didn't think made much sense, but which my mother thought was perfectly reasonable and a good omen. In fact it had been a triumph, comically so even.

Abreu had come in haughtily, like some great big popinjay, stroking his shiny moustaches, and following my mother to the sitting room, sidling crabwise, as if, walking behind her, he was still ushering her reverently past. In the sitting room, installed on the sofa, with my father in one armchair, my mother in another, and me in a chair further away (there was a hierarchy in the way the chairs were arranged), he had hesitated, as usual, before lighting the inevitable cigar which shook between his fingers, notwithstanding my mother's assurance that he could smoke whenever he felt like it. Waiting for some even more forceful assurance from my mother (whom he listened to, trembling and respectful), he was about to burn his fingers on the lit match. Then, between puffs which seemed to settle him down, he brightened up a bit, and treated us for the hundredth time to little vignettes from an extremely uneventful trip which my father had made to Angola in the ship under his command. My father, who had known him since they were at school together, smiled patiently and even helped him out in some details. For the rest those conversations always seemed to me like some sort of game between them – one pretending he couldn't remember, the other pretending that he hadn't twigged that the other was only pretending he had forgotten, so that their memory became some kind of mutual ritual. My mother served at this mass, with the knowledge she picked up in his various visits: and she did it so well that it was that famous voyage which always came up, as if they were recalling some trifling events from their days together in the same school, a school she had not attended.

After these initial skirmishes the drama of the cigar was repeated, but this time involving a glass of port wine, which my mother insisted he drank – a glass, just a little glass – and which he always ended up accepting – a drop, madam, just a drop. Once the bell was rung (and it was always my father who got up to ring the bell, responding to some discreet sign from my mother when she judged that their exchanges had fulfilled the degree of ceremony expected by Abreu), the maid entered with the salver with the port wine, the tall slender glasses, which they had already got out in the dining room when it was known that it was the Commander who was knocking at the door. My mother poured out the port (for some years now I had been included among the drinkers), the maid put the salver on the table and withdrew, and after we had briefly tasted the wine, we all held our glasses in our hands, waiting for the considered, definitive judgement of Commander Abreu. Sniffing the 'bouquet', feigning appreciation (I always felt that in truth he couldn't stand the stuff), he would declare that it was an exceptional wine, he would study the clarity, take another sip, sigh deeply, replace the glass on the table and, as he put it down, his fingers would disturb the cigar, dropping a little ash on the table, to his great confusion so that once again mistaking the glass for the cigar, he would take out a handkerchief of white silk which was sticking out from the top pocket of his layered coat, to brush it lightly over the tablecloth, helped by my father who had got up in case the former should knock his glass over.

Sometimes it wasn't the ashes which fell but the glass which splashed its contents and then my father would pick up the cigar, and the handkerchief would flutter over the tablecloth while my mother responded to Abreu's abject apologies with a soothing 'think nothing of it'. Once all this had been done the real conversation began which would range over current matters or some subject which Commander Abreu had expressly come to broach, as was the case on this occasion. Although my father had already put him in the picture he preferred to hear the whole thing from the beginning. At the end of the story there was a long, pregnant silence, and then the Commander, wreathed in smoke, at length and with his eyes half-closed, pondered his reply.

'Very well then,' was all he said this time, 'let's have the boy in.'

Luís, who had been waiting inside the house for the summons, came in, not in response to a bell (bells, except the doorbell, were just for the maids), but because it was my father who had got up and opened the door to the sitting room. His entry was marked by an ominous silence. The Commander, puffing away even more on his cigar, looked him closely up and down, his eyes half-closed, as though he were buying a slave in some Arabian marketplace. As for the rest, the moustache, the smoke from the hookah, the stiff bearing, all gave the Commander the air of a sheikh fully versed in the business of buying slaves. It was my mother who roused him from his studied, judicious contemplation.

'Well,' she said, getting up, 'I shall withdraw; you men need to talk together.'

At which Luís half turned, with a tight little smile, which followed her retreating figure to the door.

'Sit down, boy, sit down,' said the Commander, at which we all laughingly echoed his words. A new silence fell. He put his hand on his thigh and leaned over towards my father. 'I think we have the man, yes indeed, sir.'

The sigh which Luís now let out and which he had been holding back throughout that silence, could be heard throughout the room. And the Commander began to talk thirteen to the dozen, something I had never known him do before, not even on those occasions when, following my mother's withdrawal, their men's talk had touched on themes somewhat beyond those which would have permissible in her presence. Luís had done well to choose a career in the Merchant Navy, there was no better career for a young fellow who wasn't married, and if he should marry (he himself had never married) that was even better because every time he returned his wife would be waiting for him like a newly wed bride, while the time ashore in Lisbon never exceeded that of a decent honeymoon anyway (laughter), and then a fellow turned his back on the land, his ship left the bar behind and it was as if the world was no longer there to spoil things for anyone, nor anyone to spoil things for the world. Not that there weren't serious problems on one voyage or another, or people who got fed up with things. But they weren't the same things as on land: they were different and had to be dealt with according to the laws of the sea. The Commander was at pains to emphasise the complete difference in quality and in kind between terrestrial and maritime law, which, moreover, had the great advantage of being international and did not change from country to country. In any case, what was a country? A country was a port, a quay when there was one – which many ports didn't have.

There was a silence, which gave us, and especially Luís, the time to let this truth sink in; meanwhile the Commander was happily wreathed in clouds of smoke before going on to stress just how hard life was a sea, which made it a school of character and decent living – above all in the Merchant Navy. And he repeated: 'In the Merchant Navy', with its implied criticism of the other Navy. And his criticism now took the form of historical speculation. When had Portugal been great? When? When it had had a strong navy. But which navy was that? Indeed, which navy? – and the question was directed straight at Luís. The Commander, though, did not let him reply. He stroked the ends of his moustaches, methodically, one after the other, before he spoke.

'The Merchant Navy, the Merchant Navy, yes indeed sir,' he declared. 'It had cannons, it certainly had, for the seas were infested with pirates. But in the hold, what did it have in the hold? Pepper. Pepper. And more pepper. Those were the great days,' he concluded, as though his own personal testimony was sufficient guarantee.

As he was leaving the Commander allowed himself to place his hand on Luís' shoulder, and as the conversation had grown more lively we had recounted the story of Luís running away from home so that he could go to sea, something which was no secret any longer. The Commander was clearly impressed: 'Look here, my lad,' he confided, 'here we have another one who ran away from home to go to sea.'

My mother came out to say goodbye, while he descended the stairs like someone solemnly coming down from the bridge to the afterdeck, and then vanished beneath the landing.

'What's all this now?' exclaimed my father after the door had closed. 'When did he ever run away to sea?'

We exchanged glances, not knowing what to say.

'What are you talking about?' asked my mother. My father told her.

'Well, how on earth are we to know?' she said. 'Sometimes someone runs away and nobody knows about it.'

'But I've known him since he was a boy,' insisted my father. 'He never ran away from home; it's just a story.'

But my mother didn't give in. 'Now, now, there you are, keeping on about it. Were you living in the same house as him? Is that how you know? If he says he ran away then it's because he did.' And she called the maid to come and take away the port and wash the glasses.

Then the preparations began in earnest. My mother worked out exactly how many socks, vests and underpants he would need for a voyage of two and a half months, there and back. And I stayed there while she made all these endless preparations; Luís joined in, jocular but comforted, too. Between him and me I sometimes glimpsed the figure of Abreu, puffing out great clouds of smoke and stroking his moustache, and wondered how many trips of two and a half months it would take for Luís, however different he might be, to become like him, or like Almeida – and curiously I felt Almeida's fingers tightening round my throat. But I didn't let it bother me, even though it seemed somehow menacing.

On the day that Luís' uniforms came back from the tailor's it was like a carnival. He tried them on, one after the other, turning round to show himself off, front and back, to my mother (for whom not even uniforms were enough to rid her of the idea that this new life of his was not just one long holiday on the beach); he went to the kitchen to nuzzle up to the maids who uttered little cries as if a uniform were some kind of erect phallus; several times he ran to his bedroom window to show himself off to his girl, who, for some reason or other, was not at home, or had been ordered, from that day on, not to go to the window. He was all for going down to the street, but among the first-aid instructions concerning the behaviour of an officer of the Merchant Navy while ashore, which Commander Abreu had given him on his visit, was one which said that apprentice officers who had not reached their majority, and were therefore no more than officers-in-waiting, were not to wear uniform in the street, except later when overseas, so that they were not mistaken for the others, those of the Navy proper, who moreover, unlike the Army, also rarely walked about the street in uniform. Uniform was, in this case, something strictly linked to the sea, so it seemed, or perhaps more: a ritual dress which the officer refrained from wearing ashore, like some prince who chose to remain incognito.

In obeying these little lessons of Abreu Luís showed no reproach, no resentment of the fact that he had perforce to go around ashore in mufti; quite the contrary, since it might be said that the jostling of the landlubbers could only soil the virginal marine purity of the sacred vestment. That night when my father returned home – he had had to dine out – the uniforms, at my mother's instigation, were donned once more. Luís hesitated and it was as if there was already an unbridgeable distance between him and my mother (only temporarily overcome by mooring ropes and gangways between the ship and the quay): my father had already begun to be just another landlubber. Women, as in the case of my mother and the maids, had, however, a special status which, without them ceasing to be essentially of the land (as was the case with the priesthood, women could not be officers in the navy), made them, through their sex, intermediaries between the land and the sea. But this state lacked dignity and merely put them all on the same level as the girls in the port whose destiny was, in a transaction lacking real intimacy, but to be the recipients of all that male seed accumulated during the days of lonely voyaging.

The fact that I didn't feel shut out, and that Luís maintained, in the midst of all his showing off, the same intimacy with me (and, discovering the different shades of his behaviour, already taking shape, I had feared to lose him, jealous, like a father or a mother who suddenly realise their son is a man, well equipped with his own cock, belonging to a world apart, a world capable of poisoning relations between them), was surely accounted for by the fact that I was partly a father to him, partly a brother, though if I had really been that, in truth, then those would have been precisely the root causes of his shutting me out. However, although I had wondered (jokingly, hiding my deep disquiet) how long it would take before he became like Commander Abreu, I realised that it was the very ambiguity and unreality of the relationship, which had so quickly grown up between us, which perhaps permitted me an intimacy which could not now ever be restored with his family. Even more, brother and father that I was, he too was my companion in those sexual exploits which, when we recalled them at a later date, would not open between us a gulf of pain and shame, as would have been the case with his real brother.

This comparison made me wonder what would become of Carlos, and then I was shocked to realise that in all the time he had been in Lisbon Luís had not once mentioned his brother. It was beyond belief that he had forgotten or tried to forget all that had taken place; after all he didn't have such pressing reasons for doing so as I had. In truth he had always remained somewhat outside the events – and, until these had been unleashed, his relationship with his brother had been that of a boy who enters adolescence (or the others believe that he was entering, although he had already entered it long before) alongside someone who is already a man. This had not lasted longer, it could be said, than his relationship with me. And I was still there, the brother had vanished, while Luís did not have, either with his father or his aunt, the kind of relationship which might replace, clinch or consolidate a recent link which fate had cut off so abruptly. Besides, I had been his path to Lisbon and to the open sea, his new life whose white skin, already donned, he paraded before me, for the benefit of the other onlookers. His brother had disappeared before any of this, before, in the train in which he made his escape, Luís had placed his trust in me.

At that moment, in the turmoil of mixed feelings, I felt that I did not want to be the repository of anyone's trust; I did not accept that circumstances (the same ones which had changed me) had any right to land me with the responsibility for someone whom in truth I had not chosen, but, at the same time, I feared lest I was not guardian enough, lest Luís escape from me, even though I was no sort of guard or ceased to be one for him. We were in the bedroom and he, once more scanning the closed windows of the building across the way, hesitated before he finally took off his uniform. Without her, and in a less imposing outfit, he was once again just that uncertain, skinny, abandoned boy. But I had to ask myself to what extent he was really so, whether he wasn't putting on an act for me, through me and even for himself. The hesitant belief that I was strong (a strength which had depended on my having discovered it in my struggle with Almeida) perhaps concealed a real strength which he hadn't yet had the chance to discover for himself, or perhaps it was that kind of strength which is more the enduring, deep-rooted resistance of a reed in the wind, and is not however the strength of the weaklings who abase themselves, surrender, fawn and get up, kicking out slyly at the first opportunity. Not that strength, although sometimes both kinds are confused, but the strength of someone who is flexible, exactly because he has, at the same time, a fragile stem and a strong root. What he had done, in running away, might be some infantile irresponsibility, of a part with the ease with which he had settled in my house, as if he had always lived there. But, on the other hand, this ease was also the assurance of someone who feels at home anywhere, because truly he doesn't need any place to survive. A ship, with its solid deck swaying, suspended over the depths which might at any moment open up and swallow all that solid mass, was perhaps after all his true habitat, so to speak.

To the extent that I was pondering all this, I vaguely responded to what he was telling me about the life he was about to embark on, his duties, all that was demanded of an apprentice. But, notwithstanding the interest he deserved from me, and not just because I was preoccupied with my own train of thought, I did not manage to take at all seriously those details which were so important for him. It was as if everything was even more insignificant than it really was, and utterly devoid of value as far as our relationship was concerned. The daily details of that life of his, the career which he was starting – in truth they meant nothing to me. I felt that, at the same time as I feared exclusion from a relationship which was more than fraternal, which was dear to me, I had no desire to take part in it indirectly in the way that is common in such relationships, to be really part of life, this one, which did mean something to me. I understood then that what I had gone through had put, or could yet put, all my capacity to feel on another level, a deeper level, or a more superficial one (or perhaps an awareness that the depths and the surface are the same), than that of the old, acquired ways of feeling and thinking about human relationships. I could genuinely be interested in someone without having the slightest interest in that person's life. Or even more: the life of those people who might have interested me was precisely what had ceased to interest me, this lack of interest being by way of compensation the distinctive sign of that interest. But then how was I to distinguish in life, in my own life, between the people who meant something to me and those, the very same ones, who left me completely cold? Wouldn't it be the case that none of them, all alike, would mean anything at all to me? And that my interest in that boy, for whom I was some kind of protector, only served as a cloak for what could only be termed indifference? Could it be the case that I had lost the knack of communicating with others, in the worst sense, which is that of giving them, or allowing them, the illusion that some kind of communication did exist? Or was it only that I had, because of the rebuffs I had suffered, been awakened to the lucid knowledge that communication does not exist?

Or – perhaps more simply – was my lack of interest merely, in the present case, a generalisation, a rationalisation of the fact that Almeida was an officer in the Merchant Navy? A navy devoted to trade or to fishing, it was still the Merchant Navy. And all this air of detachment, to which I had responded in the same coin, merely stemmed from the fact that I had seen in the fellow, above all after he had provoked me to blows, someone who had shown a lack of respect towards a woman for whom I had more and less than respect; nor had he known or wanted, on account of the way of life he had got used, to make her more than except when the circumstances arose. It was as if I was condemning him precisely for the love which he hadn't given her, though he had made the opening into which my love had penetrated. That expression – which had passed fleetingly through my mind, though not with the same clarity – made me shudder: the physical analogies which it awakened pained me terribly. And in the pain, I started to hear more clearly what Luís was saying.

'I think I'll be an apprentice for two years before I return to land to attend the Nautical School. But I'll have to make sure I get a change of ships, so that I can go off on other routes and see the whole world. To begin with it's the best thing [*it was as if the open emptiness in Mercedes' belly was within me, like some cavern in deep shadow in which I was kept prisoner, peering through the narrow gap, unable to do anything, at the up and down movements of the cocks as they were having her*].

'I'm bound to go to Brazil and across the whole of Europe, and then to the East and to America. Afterwards I'll tell you all about it, what the ports and cities are like, and all the women I'll enjoy, the differences between them [*my terror, what brought me out in a cold sweat, was that the orgasm would be unleashed, swamping me, dirtying me, drowning me, but the cocks kept coming, some slowly, others forcing their way in, never the same ones, or it was still the same one but it never reached a climax*], some wide, some tight, some longer, others shorter, some – I know it's like that, I read it in a book – which are better, and which the girls enjoy more, from behind, others are better if they close their legs, however wide they are [*and then, in my terror, I saw that the entrance was closed and the atmosphere was becoming heavier, reeking of blood and rotten meat, and a sticky mass was growing alongside me, squeezing me up against the moist walls*] I'll have to put it all in my diary.'

'To read again, when you're an old man? [*the mass was choking me, pressing down on me painfully, until the walls began to contract in periodic spasms which grew ever stronger*] Or for a comparative study which you'll never ever finish? [*suddenly the entrance was torn open and the huge suffocating mass dragged me out with it*] It's not worth writing all that down.'

'It's not for the sake of writing, not at all, it's just a record of everything,' and he laughed, and with his hand on his cock, added: 'Because this little chap has no memory at all.'

[*In a wave of dirty water and blood a child and I were side by side on a sandy beach*] 'That's what you think. You're still very young and he hasn't got a lot to remember yet. When you're older and if you love someone, you'll see whether he doesn't remember, every time, all the other times, even if you don't.'

He glanced at the uniform on the bed [*and I felt drained by the waking nightmare; I could not recall it with any clarity, but there was something within me, some sense, rather than a feeling, of relief, as if I had just thrown up*]: 'Well, we've got to celebrate today. Let's be off to the girls [*but it was as though the sand had absorbed all the filth and all the blood, and I felt clean and free*]: I'm going to fuck the same one.'

'Do you want to go with the same one after, or before?' [*did I understand what he was thinking?*]

'No, that's not what I mean. Why don't the three of us go to the room together and...' but he broke off, embarrassed, unable to go on, or because he didn't really know what he wanted, or because he feared my reaction.

[*I remembered the idea of one in front and one behind, 'but not like that'*] 'Look, stuff like that, in cold blood, it doesn't work.'

'In cold blood? But if I'm thinking about it how can it be in cold blood?'

I got up. 'Let's go,' I said. 'As far as these things are concerned, if you think about it first it's always going to be in cold blood,' I replied as we were already leaving the house.

At the door the hot air and the darkness (in spite of the street lights) made me shiver. It was as though he was with me, growing alongside me, in the cavern.

XL

But in the tram going down to the Baixa, with the breeze in my face, my unease vanished, or rather, it became no more than some tiny, calm knot which could just be felt under all the high spirits which gripped us. It was a kind of disquiet, a nervous tension, like that which, years earlier, I had felt, going like this in a tram to visit a brothel for the first time. Talking excitedly with Luís I had to smile gently at myself – it might be said for the first time – although the smile did not dispel my apprehension, which did not change at all. In addition there was some kind of agitation in the air which, little by little, was becoming apparent to me. The glances which Luís shot around, tracking some odd thing from time to time were, as much as my own, proof to me that something unusual was happening. The tram was virtually empty but on the streets (though they were no more crowded than any other summer night) there was evidently some sort of unusual coming and going, in which the air of keen expectation of those who were merely standing around contrasted with that of the other groups, or some of them, who were moving along the streets.

'What's going on out there today' I asked, as much to myself as Luís.

'I don't know, but...' and he turned round, following everything with his eyes, his head raised, so that he could see better out of each side of the tram.

When we got to the Baixa, and the few passengers got up to get off, I halted next to the conductor who had got up onto the platform to have a word with the brakeman.

'What's going on?'

They looked at each other and then at us, guardedly. 'The rally in the Campo Pequeno,' replied the brakeman. 'It's just begun.'

The word 'rally' was one which was hardly used in those days and so associated was it with the pre-historic disturbances that I repeated the word like a question.

The brakeman was a swarthy fellow, stocky and short, middle-aged, while the conductor was tall and thin and younger. 'A rally, yes indeed,' replied the brakeman. 'Didn't you see it in the papers, didn't anybody ring you to tell you about it? Yes, there's a rally today in support of the revolution in Spain.'

'We haven't gone along,' added the conductor with an uncertain smile, 'because we're still working.'

'In the Campo Pequeno? Where exactly?' asked Luís.

'In the bullring,' explained the conductor. 'Aren't you gentlemen from Lisbon? Have you come up from somewhere else?' he asked.

'Yes, that's right,' I answered.

'So you haven't come for the bullfight,' said the conductor with a furious smile in his eyes.

'Oh, number 273 ...' said the brakeman, 'be careful what you say.'

'It's already too late to go there now,' continued the conductor.

'We don't want to,' said Luís. 'We're off to see the girls.'

'At least they aren't such big cunts,' said the conductor. 'But this is going to blow up, isn't it, number 1460?'

'Now?... But you'd better shut up.'

'You can trust us,' I said. 'Good night,' and we got off.

The conductor leant out in friendly fashion from his platform. 'Are you really off to see the girls? And I've still three hours more work to do... Be careful, make sure you use a noddy bag: there's a nasty dose of clap going around which is no laughing matter.'

We went into the Rossio and crossed the square towards the Restauradores. Groups of ordinary people, some just curious, others bawling out uninhibitedly, blocked the pavements. Loudhailers enveloped us with noise and one voice in particular, which could barely speak in its patriotic fervour, added to the general clamour. Some people were selling little flags, though without much success for almost nobody was actually waving them. Certainly, the ones who were committed – if there were any – had already made their way there, or were all gathered there, where they would have been provided with the badges of their enthusiasm. For the rest, just like some of those who were milling around in the square, the flag sellers must already be at the entrance to the bullring. The people there formed groups which soon dispersed; evidently from the way in which they were hanging around, they seemed to me to be of two distinct species. Some were the usual denizens of that place at that time, though there were more of them than usual: nocturnal creatures, without a settled – or with an uncertain – way of life, and those who came out at night, as part of their regular way of life, to stroll around alongside them. The others, who didn't know their way around there so well, walking, then stopping, stood out as strangers, and would be those who had been brought in from other parts of the country for the demonstration in the bullring, and had gone along with it as a way of seeing the capital city by invitation or on the cheap. They probably didn't have much money and so wouldn't be up to going on to the red-light district in the Bairro Alto; and, attracted and fascinated, they weren't ready to withdraw or had nowhere to go to. It was certainly this part of the crowd among whom some lads were moving and handing out the pamphlets which were littering the pavements and the street. Between the tumult of the square and the bawling of the loudhailers there was no real communication. Up to a certain point the excuse for both lots of noise was the same, but this simple coincidence was like a neutral zone of silence, which separated them and where, at the same time, the fluttering flags that nobody was buying and pamphlets which nobody had read were trodden underfoot.

One of the flag sellers, taking us for recent arrivals, came up to us, offering them to us for what he said was half the price, 'to get rid of them'. We told him to be off, with an obvious hostility which he sensed but which, paradoxically, made him all the more determined to cling to us. He followed along at our side, four flags in his fist, holding them out in front of us, the four of them for the price of one. The flags weren't flags as such, but instead a composite of them: the Portuguese flag, the Italian, the German and a flag with the Cross of Avis, all round the Spanish flag. And there were various mottoes above them. The seller was thin, very dark, and in his bearded, hungry face his eyes were bright with anger. He was in shirtsleeves, his white shirt filthy, and was wearing tattered, cheap sandals; he trotted along at our side, now demanding that we help him to live, that we rescue him from the ill-fortune of failing to sell all his flags. And then he turned to threats for it was only communists who wouldn't buy those flags.

We stopped on the corner by the lift in Glória. 'So then all these people here are communists if nobody buys your flags.'

'Have you no shame,' he shouted, furious with us. 'On top of everything else you look down on someone who's poor... Heaven help the poor if this rabble win... Uncharitable sods... Rascals, murderers...'

Little by little a circle of people gathered, detaching themselves from the larger groups. The awareness of having an audience encouraged the man, who had already stopped threatening us and trying to make us buy his flags and had begun to address those around him: in his role of advocate now he was attracted by the spectacle and the chance of revenge. I tried to get away from him, making use of the circle of people around as a curtain which would conceal us from him and hold him back. But neither did the circle open up easily (the people sensing that, if we did escape, then the spectacle would vanish into thin air), nor did he let go of Luís who was pulling at his shirtsleeve and telling him to keep quiet.

'Rascals, rogues ... these kids here are the worst of all... Look, gentlemen ... a man goes about earning his living, offering his flags at half-price, less than half-price, at cost, just to get rid of them, and they still look down on you... But it's all going to change, from today it's all going to change. We're going to put all these rascals in prison. My mother is at home, paralysed, waiting for me to bring her a few pennies and I can't take her anything because of these rascals. And she, poor thing, praying every day to Our Lady of Fatima to give life and health to our President so that he can save us all from this pack of thieves. It's not right.'

The people standing around did not move, nor did they speak. And it didn't much look as though any of them were inclined to buy his flags. But there was no sympathy on their faces for us either. We were fine lads, fine fellows, well dressed, redolent of the city and of a prosperous way of life; we hadn't come up to the city from the sticks, nor from the far-flung suburbs, and all the hostile weight of social destinctions was being held against us. Nor was it a matter of sympathy towards the flag seller, far too lacking in any sort of 'class' for anyone to identify with him; it was, though, an opportunity to witness the humiliation of someone who was 'well brought up', 'well dressed', and who 'didn't need to work'. I managed to drag Luís away from the fellow and half burrow through the circle; at once the crowd divided into two circles, one surrounding the man waving his arms about and brandishing the flags, and the other which demanded that we tell them what had happened. The very fact that the groups had split (and seeing that both circles were now closed it was hard for anyone to move from one to the other without being left on the outside of both) began immediately to act upon the members of the respective groups, with those around us commiserating with us, though from the outset their hostility had simply changed to a scornful curiosity.

I explained that there was really nothing to it, that the fellow was a bit crazy and was just trying it on. He'd been badgering us to buy his flags and we hadn't bought any; that was all. Some didn't believe us: there was more to it than that. After all, they weren't all there in that circle just for nothing and there was a feeling, arising from their new-found sense of solidarity, that somehow they'd been robbed. In the other circle feelings were running high, fanned by the flag seller's eloquence, so that angry faces were turned towards us. One of the lads who'd been handing out pamphlets went up to the more incensed of the two groups and the vendor moved automatically on to another plane: in his voice could be heard the bitterness of the tribune who had lost his admirers to another star. The lad stared menacingly at us, from above the circle which had now become an uneven elipse concentrated on one focus alone, which was he. His height meant that his stares passed over the heads of the other poor boobies. And it wasn't long before he capitalised on the power of his stares, forcing the two groups to come together into one again. His hair shone brilliantly, his face was dominated by his elongated nose extended inordinately from his arched eyebrows to his nostrils and even seemed to continue as far as his mouth and bony chin only to peter out around his Adam's apple, its final mutation. And his hands which he raised to demand silence so that he could question us, were, with their long, knobbly fingers, the equivalent of his nose.

Our circle, though, heaved with resentment against this interruption and against the fact that he had reduced it to nothing more than some shapeless gathering which had, now that it was no longer its own master, lost any common reason for its existence. The argument became more general, some voices becoming more vehement, so that two more of the lads with the pamphlets bored their way through the mass to help their colleague whom they saw surrounded without knowing the reason why. The force which they used to break through the ring upset some of those in it (irrespective of whether they were part our group). There were some who demanded spitefully why they were there and not in the Campo Pequeno, and what they had to do with what was going on and so on. One evil-looking chap demanded sharply that they apologise for the elbows they had shoved in his ribs. This disturbance made it easier for Luís and me, in the confusion (which perhaps had not been entirely haphazard) to see our way out of the assembly where arms were now raised to the accompaniment of curses. At the same moment some middle-aged chap, with a wide-brimmed hat and an expensive foreign tie, grabbed hold of us, one in each hand and dragged us out to the pavement. His grip was like iron on my arm and Luís was almost crawling. We struggled, we

complained, but he only let us go once we were alongside a car
whose uniformed driver came running from the other side to open
the door, his cap in his hand, as if we were important people who
had hailed his car, calmly and with the utmost gravity, at the entrance
to a grand reception.

'Get in here,' he said, flinging us inside one after the other, forcing
us to sit merely with the thrust of his large frame following us inside.
Once in the car, slipping on the grey gloves of another era, he
ordered the driver ('António, let's be going') with a voice of smooth
authority, and with which he now began to sermonise. Were we
crazy? To go around provoking people there, in the Restauradores,
on that very night, when the dictator's mob wanted only some
pretext to justify the bullfight which was the creation of a
'Portuguese Legion' to fight communism?

Luís and I, squeezed in the car, did not even bother to look at
each other, such was our perplexity. The gallant gentleman (that
old-fashioned term was the best way we could think of to place
him) mocked us: were we – this was the other possibility – just
agents provocateurs? We weren't? No? We didn't look it; and he
laughed and lit a cigar. To tell what we were going to do seemed
to me even more absurd than this strange salvation. Luís' submissive
silence surely meant that he had read the situation in the same way.
After returning the shining lighter to the pocket of his waistcoat,
across which gleamed a watch chain, our saviour took up the thread
of his sermon again: we should be careful, very careful, not to expose
ourselves in such stupid fashion, sorry, in such juvenile fashion, oh
that fiery courage of youth, and instead conserve our energies for
the right moment, which was not right now. Or had someone led
us to believe that it was? Yes, he knew there were groups who
thought that way, who wanted action, to stir up the people. The
worst thing was that the people had been lulled by years of
propaganda and censorship, terrorised by the police, fearful of losing
their daily bread. And whoever was not an ordinary citizen was a
civil servant, who could be sacked at any moment. The truth is that
only the old republicans were resisting and it was essential that
nobody should let the republican cause get caught up in the Spanish
question, however much one's sympathies were with the Spanish
Republican Government, against the military who, in cahoots with
the clergy and the powerful, were now doing in Spain, amid
bloodshed, what had been done on the sly ten years ago in Portugal.
To help the Spanish Republicans was one thing, was the duty, even,

of every democrat, certainly, most certainly. But a direct involvement in counter-demonstrations was to play the game of the dictatorship, which needed no other pretext to accuse everybody of being communists.

Now, the republic, the old, glorious republic, could have been everything ... a little disordered, even, which he admitted, ah yes. And brought down by lamentable splits, mean-spirited jostling for power, betrayals by many who were now ministers in the dictatorship, or were getting ready to be (the car had stopped at the door of a mansion in Graça). But communist or anything like that, no, he had never been that; to say that was a slander. Liberal, liberal and democratic, that's what he had been, wasn't that true now? (We both nodded our heads.) And he thought that the Republic should be even more liberal than it had been, when it was restored. More liberal towards the left, towards the modern, for the other time it had been too liberal towards the right and this was the outcome, indeed, this was the outcome, what with the death of the institutions, with the monarchists governing a mere simulacrum of the republic. Here he stopped to address the driver:

'António, tomorrow,' he said, 'remind me so that I don't forget, a simulacrum of the republic.'

What was needed, now more than ever, was caution, great caution. Resist, always resist, but nothing reckless.

'But without doing anything, how can we resist?' demanded Luís, much to my surprise.

'António, these gentlemen are coming in for a cup of coffee and a glass of port. Oh, you can't refuse, you need to recover from your ordeal. Then, António,' he said to the driver who had got out of the car and who had, his cap in hand, opened the gate against which he stood outlined, 'take them home. It's not every day that an old Republican establishes relations with two fellow believers of the new generation.'

Hesitant and embarrassed, Luís and I got out and the illustrious gentleman, still half seated and in the midst of trying finally to heave himself out of the car (he had been seated on the opposite side) looked at us with paternal superiority, condescendingly, sardonically, a gesture which turned into the delicate strength with which his gloved hands, resting lightly on our shoulders, pushed us towards the wide door which opened in front of us and where an extremely old, bent, liveried janitor, put out his hand for the hats which we did not have. In front of us rose an enormous stone staircase, with a red carpet which was too narrow for the wide steps. Lamps like those on old carriages, but electrified, added some lustre to the middle of the entrance, lending some light to that space. But neither the lustre nor the lamps could dispel the sombre atmosphere, musty, echoing (our footsteps now resounded, now fell silent) of the grandiose, dimly lit entrance.

'Go up, do please go up,' said our host.

And his movement up the stairs, notwithstanding its deliberation, like that of someone savouring each upward step, obliged us to go up ahead of him. At the top another, younger, servant, in shirtsleeves, and wearing a striped black and white waistcoat, led us and his master through a heavy curtain which opened on to a long narrow room; this room gave the impression, on both sides, of a row of similar curtains. In between each pair of yellowed curtains there were consoles covered with knick-knacks, and gilded chairs and, on the wall, a mirror with a gilt frame.

'João,' said the master of the house behind us, who had been following the servant, 'serve the coffee in the library.'

João pulled up one of the curtains on the right so that we could go into the library; it was a round room, not very large, in blue and gilt, the walls lined by shelves which were filled with bound volumes, some bigger, others smaller, but almost all of them with very slim spines. There were gilded chairs as well, their legs, arms and backs covered in rococo swirls and with shiny flowers on the material which covered the seats and the backs. In one corner there was a desk which had a ceramic inkwell in which were duck's quills. The owner of the place sat down at the desk in a modern, revolving, chair which was quite out of keeping with the rest of the setting. When he sat, gesturing to us to sit, too, in the nearest chairs, I felt that he, just like the chair, didn't quite go with the setting either. Without his gloves and his wide-brimmed hat – which he had handed to the butler at the entrance – he didn't have the same imposing air which had earlier cowed us. His chubby, extremely white hands also seemed not to be the same ones which had gripped us like iron. His shiny, black hair, which he had plastered stiffly from one side of his head to the other to cover his bald pate made his head seem from the front like that of a baby with a black shako. In silence, with his smiling eyes blinking at us, he observed us at length while Luís and I waited, without looking at each other, until he opened his mouth – which was narrow and delicate, with pale lips – to speak.

'I don't propose to keep you. Make yourselves comfortable,' he said (our version of comfortable meant that we cast our eyes over the room and the spines of the books).

'After coffee and a glass of port – you'll no doubt have a coffee and port? – I only want to show you something from my collections, just to take your mind off things. I'm not asking for your thanks' (we hadn't thanked him in any way) 'for something which was no more than my duty on a day like this, to get you out of a fix. You'll have to forgive my intrusion' – and the way in which he emphasised the word showed that he wasn't entirely convinced that we weren't agents provocateurs, in the pay of Moscow, whose tricks he had thwarted as part of his plans to fight the dictatorship – 'but you must agree with me that the moment was inopportune and that you could have got into a terrible scrape. Even if it had all happened merely by chance, if the police had come along and carted you back to the barracks you could have been caught up in some plot, being made to change sides on some pretext or other, who knows what. Those lads in the Vanguard could have kicked up a great fuss. What they're after is to get the Government to accept them as shock troops, and since they know the Government won't fall for that, because it only wants what it can organise or nothing at all, they are desperate. Today the creation of the Portuguese Legion is certainly just robbery and jobbery' – he repeated the words with gusto, savouring the rhyme: robbery and jobbery – 'as far as their ambitions are concerned. Tomorrow the creation of a youth movement, which will happen – oh I know exactly what's going on – will be the end of them. They'll be forced to disband, so that, for those who are manipulating them, it's a matter of now or never.' The servant came in carrying a huge tray, laden with a silver coffee-pot, a silver sugar bowl, small cups, fine glasses, an even finer crystal decanter, which he set down on a table with cocks' feet in the corner. 'And now let's have our coffee,' (which the servant began to pour, first us then the master of the house), 'and a little glass of port, don't stand on ceremony, but this port is rather special.' The servant poured it for us.

'I hope you appreciate this wine; you won't find it anywhere else. It's my own produce, we don't sell it.'

Luís asked, when the servant had withdrawn, whether he had a villa in the Douro.

'Oh no, don't get the idea that I'm a landowner, oh no, just a little farm in Tua, which yields a couple of pipes a year, hardly enough to give to my friends. I go up there every year for the vintage, with my family.' (I looked at him in surprise, for he seemed to be someone above the ordinary contingencies of having a family, of which there was not the least sign in the house.)

'My young friend is surprised? Do you imagine that there would not be a family in a house like this? But there is. But the great thing about a spacious house — I wouldn't say large, because I don't want you think I could call this shack a palace — is that we can all live together without being on top of each other. Anyway ... where are you gentlemen from? Lisbon? Ah, one of you gentlemen is from Figueira, the other from Lisbon. Very good. Figueira, a lovely place. There was a time when I sometimes, in summer would spend a few days there. You too, sir? One of my sons, who is studying in Coimbra — I never studied there, it was always one of my dreams, ah, the Choupal park, the serenades, the view from the Penedo da Saudade, the old Cathedral, the little taverns, the student houses — we call them 'republics', wonderful name, republic, and appropriate, too, because it refers to the democratic organisation of those places — but the worst of it is that Coimbra has always been, the centre of reaction, with those law professors, who now are the ones who are all-powerful in this country, my son is a law student, actually, yes he is, do you like the wine? Kindly help yourselves to some more, don't stand on ceremony, treat this house as your own, my son — I have two — more or less your age, yes, about your age, this one is the older and he goes to Figueira a lot. Oh, I know what young lads are, I was one once, and let me tell you, in my time boys were boys.'

Luís and I glanced at each other, not sure whether the boys of his day were more or less innocent than those in ours.

'In those days we got up to all sorts of crazy things, though we didn't have much money. My son isn't like that; he can't imagine a night out without spending money. He was brought up differently, didn't want for anything. I've had to work hard, with these hands,' and he raised them, white and fat, quite unfitted for any manual work.

'My other son, who lives in Lisbon with me, is very different, a very quiet lad, studious, sometimes I have to tell him he should get out a bit, have some fun, but he doesn't want to. But you two gentlemen, I don't suppose you need your parents to tell you to go out, do you? But you will surely know my son, the one who is studying in Coimbra.'

'Perhaps,' I replied. 'What's he called?'

'I'm always telling him: study and enjoy your life, my lad, politics will come later. Politics means you have no life, it's for after you've lived a bit. What I've sacrificed for politics, what I could have been!' and he looked around the room imploringly, as if in sympathy for his wasted life…

'Now, there are lads who are interested in politics, but they're being manipulated, ah but they are,' and he shot us a probing look.

'I won't say they all are; many of them have the fire, the magnanimity, the enthusiasm, the ardour,' he said, pausing after every word, searching for the next one, 'the altruism which belong to youth. But politics is a very different matter, if you want me to put it like that it's skulduggery. You need a spirit of sacrifice, for the cause, a great deal of patience, and I would even say the stomach for it, to be able to swallow one fellow's dirty little machinations, another's meanness, the pettiness of almost everybody. There's nobody any more like we had in the Republic and those of us who've survived, we've suffered a great deal: persecution, splits, betrayals, it's never-ending. But we're not giving in; it's important not to give in. So you gentlemen know my son, eh? He's in Figueira now. He's got exams in October at the University so he didn't come to Lisbon this summer. He's called Alberto, like me, Alberto Coelho, junior.'

('No, no, we don't know each other, but some of our friends certainly will.')

'Ah, that's a pity. My son is also very interested in politics, though he's very faithful to the Republic. Do you really not know him? That's a real shame, he's pretty well known, I feel sure that if you gentlemen were from Coimbra or were students in Coimbra, you'd know him. And he's my son, we have the same names. As for me, who knows me? Indeed, who knows me? Do you gentlemen? No, don't be embarrassed, I can see you don't know me. There's no reason why you should. In any case I am a modest fellow, keep myself to myself, my name only appears at the top of a newspaper. Twenty years ago it was different: in politics, in literary matters, everybody knew who I was. But what does this matter to me? For years my only resistance has been at the head of a newspaper loyal to the Republic; for years I haven't published any of my poetry – not that I want to. Why should I? So that these modernist chaps whom I taught to write and who copy me can say that I'm past it? And then discovered that one can't be a republican and a modernist at the same time, or else one's fellow believers would suspect – and they'd be right – that one was a fascist. It's very sad, very sad. But I have the paper. Which paper? *The Democrat*, what else could it be? And my books, and my birds, yes, my birds, a collection which I shall donate to the Zoological Gardens. After we've looked at my books I'll show you the birds, or, speaking in zoological terms, the "avis", since I have many more than just the passerine birds, which you know are only one family of avis. First editions and rare birds are my downfall, and what I spend my money on. But the two things are complementary, they go well together. I only collect that which sings, or what is decorative, striking, elegant. Shall we say I collect whatever flies, either with real wings or with the wings of the spirit? All this stuff around us is all the books of poetry which have been published, or are being published in Portugal, good or bad, all bound the same, since, good or bad, they are all poets. But my birds are all exotic, all of them, just as poetry is exotic, even in one's own language. Do you understand how the two collections go together? The Republic, the poetry, the rare birds? The Republic and the poetry they're Portuguese only; the birds are from other worlds. And there are ugly birds, very ugly birds, very odd things, odd like bad poetry, and today it doesn't seem to matter whether poetry is odd or not. In my time when we wrote something odd it was for a reason, but today it's not even like that when someone writes something odd. How can you write something odd if you don't know what's right in the first place? Do you gentlemen like poetry? You don't know whether you do, do you? You can't be taught to like poetry... But how can you be taught what can't be learnt? Poetry is the creation of the dream, the beauty which we can't find in the world. The poet is the one who feels and sees what the other can't, someone who lives in a different world, one of delicacy, intelligence and sensitivity, from where he sends us news, no, not news, messages of enchantment. The language of the poet... But what am I doing, talking about things nobody's interested in? In today's world, with all its brutality and grossness, poetry is dead, it has no place. Could you imagine a Rosalía de Castro today? And poor Florbela killed herself. And I neither write nor publish my own unpublished verses. What on earth for, indeed what on earth for?'

And he remained lost in thought, gazing at the spines of the books above our heads, in a long silence, while Luís got up and plucked a book from the shelves behind him. He motioned me to come over. I got up to see what he wanted to show me: the book was closed, the pages had never been opened within its binding.

There was a voice beside us: 'There are some poets it's better not to open... Come and see the birds.'

We followed him down a long corridor, not unlike the large room, except that it was cluttered with furniture along the walls where the wide curtains hung, to a glass-enclosed veranda; he switched on the light. At once the veranda, which ran along all the length of the house, was filled with a great squawking; a flock of birds of all hues was flitting around in huge birdcages and on dozens of perches: macaws, parrots, including some from the far east, and buzzards shook their wings and opened their curved beaks for our benefit. The whiff of the hen run wafted through the air. Looking from one side to the other, we went along behind the man as he made friendly gestures to the creatures he was fondest of, whispered tender words to the cages and stopped at the end of the gallery, next to a cage where a huge bird was dozing without paying the slightest attention to the clamour of the rest. He asked us if we knew what it was. An eagle, said Luís. No, it wasn't an eagle, it was much more than that. Could we not guess? Oh, it was an Andean condor, the noble bird of the inaccessible peaks, the symbol of height and freedom, the one of which Rubén Darío, the great Rubén Darío, had sung. I had no idea who Rubén Darío was, and Luís even less. But we gazed upon that ruler of the birds, whose sleepy and detached air, curling feathers, and large, dishevelled body, did not suggest the magnificent cordilleras from whose heights he would look down disdainfully, with the bleary eye which he half opened on us.

'The condor is to the Andes,' commented our host, 'what the albatross is to the seas. Do you know that poem by Baudelaire?' (I recalled my French lessons.) '"His giant wings prevent him from walking". Sailors had captured the albatross and the bird, poor thing, used to flying freely over the waves, and did not know how to walk on the deck of the ship and stumbled over its wings. It's what happens to all of us, those of whose who ever fly. We spend the rest of our lives falling over our wings and beating our head against the cage; nor do you need to be a condor or an albatross' (and he turned towards the other cages). 'Look, even the little sparrows, those to whom St Francis of Assisi spoke, suffer in the same way. They too think that once without the cage they would be free. A terrible mistake, a terrible mistake my friends' (and he looked around him like a demiurge who would restore freedom to the winged world). 'It's a fine collection, isn't it? Some of these birds have cost me much more than many a first edition of poetry. But I don't want to keep them confined any longer. I don't want you to think that I'm going to keep them in a golden cage, like the ones that Salome had in her garden.'

He passed between the two of us and retraced his steps to the library. There he opened a drawer at the bottom of one of the bookcases and took out two oblong, yellowed-looking books, with garishly coloured covers. Oh, they were a couple of books he had published years ago, remaindered now, and which he was going to give us as a souvenir of our auspicious meeting. One of the books (and he asked our names so that he could write the dedication) was called *The Dead Hours of the Distant Princess* and on the red and black of the cover one could just make a princess coiled among peacocks. The other, which he gave to Luís, was called *Golden Dream of the Bronze Infinite*, on the cover of which was a figure sitting among narrow towers, illuminated by a huge, dying sun. No, we mustn't look through them, not even open them. His books were not to be opened, unless one day we might feel the desire to commune aesthetically with the poetic fantasy, the healthy vision, in short all those things, of some minor poet, an insignificant poet who had given up writing poetry. We could even, if we wished, leave the books somewhere, hurl them into the street, where, who knows some beggar, some pauper of the stars might even pick them up... And he rang a bell.

The servant appeared and was ordered to accompany us to the door. In vain did we say we didn't need transport. On the landing the poet bade us farewell effusively, suggesting that we visit him again, and that it would always be his pleasure. But by the time we got to the door and turned for a last bow, he had already disappeared from the top of the stairs. The driver, his cap in hand, put his hand on the car door; we got in and the door to the mansion was closed. The driver turned round in his seat to ask us where he should take us.

'Drop us down in town, in the Avenue Almirante Reis, anywhere,' I said, and the car proceeded silently round the various bends before coming to a stop in the Avenue. By now used to the ceremony, we instinctively waited for the driver to get out and open the door. He didn't even get up, nor bother to turn round when he asked if here was fine. We said it was and got out. The car set off.

We remained silent by the side of the pavement, each of us carrying his book in his hand.

'Where do they get people like that from?' asked Luís finally.

'Like what?'

'Like everything ... the house, the books, the parrots, his way of speaking... He seemed a bit crazy. And he must have money to burn.'

'He's no more crazy that any of us. He just lives in a different world.'

'In a different world? Oh ... I wouldn't mind a house like that, with all those servants.'

'Why?'

'Do you know what I'd do if that house were mine, out of the blue? I'd let all the birds go, the whole flock of them, all over Lisbon, the macaws in the Avenida da Liberdade. Then I'd sell all the books, and then ... and then ... and then I'd have parties in there, the doors open to whoever wanted to come in, and we'd make such a night of it until nothing remained in one piece.'

'And then?'

'I'd leave the place open and hop it.'

'Where to?'

'Where to? Where should I go?'

I said nothing; after a while I broke the silence. 'Where shall we go now?' I wondered.

'Ah, not home, at any rate.'

'It's late; we can't go anywhere at this time.'

'It's never too late. Let's go off somewhere. Give me the book and I'll put it in my pocket with the other one. If we lose them maybe someone, how did he put it?...'

'A pauper of the stars.'

'Yes, maybe one of those chaps will see a firefly glowing in the street and find it. Let's go this way.'

We set off down the deserted avenue.

'What's this pauper of the stars business supposed to mean?' demanded Luís.

'I don't know; probably someone who begs from something which doesn't exist.'

'But that's just a lot of ridiculous nonsense.'

'I think so, too, but perhaps in his day it wasn't.'

'Let's see when he published this stuff.'

We stopped under a street lamp to look for the date. It wasn't difficult to find, for it was somewhere there in the design on the cover. One book was dated 1912, the other 1915.

'Hmm…' said Luís. 'I was still just a twinkle in my father's eye, as my aunt puts it. That's more than twenty years ago. These books are pretty old.'

'There are lots older,' I said, 'centuries old.'

'But that's different; they aren't in anyone's drawer.'

'They might be in the bookshelves, like the ones he had.'

'Do you think he's read all of them? Or are they all unopened like the one I picked up?'

'He'll have read the ones he's interested in.'

'So what does he want the others for?'

'Didn't you see that he's a collector? It's one thing to collect them, another to read them.'

'Me, if I had any books, I'd read them all.'

'But you don't read anything.'

'I've never had time. When I have time I'll read.'

'On the ship now, you'll have plenty of time.'

'Who said I'll have plenty of time? I won't. What about the time to look at the sea, when I've nothing to do? Just looking at the sea takes up a lot of time.'

We were already in the backstreets into which the avenue had petered out. On the corners were shapes, and the smell of garbage and drains assailed our nostrils sharply, together with the scent of the sea when the tide is out (though that could have been the fish rotting in the gutter. We continued on as far as a tavern, where some women were leaning against the door, talking to some shabbily dressed youths who were joking with them. One of the youths peeled away from the group and followed along behind us.

'At this hour nowhere's going to open up for you,' he said, coming alongside us. 'But if you'll come along with me we can fix something up.'

'We can do that ourselves,' I said.

'You can? How? With your fist?' he said, giving a coarse laugh.

'Where is this place?' asked Luís, pretending he hadn't heard the other's remark.

'How much will you pay me?'

'You?' I queried.

'Sure, my commission. If the tart opens the door to you it's because she knows I've brought you. And then I'll bring you another one; there to the same house.'

'Where is it?' demanded Luís.

'Near enough; just round the corner.'

'How much do you want for yourself?' I asked him.

He stopped in the middle of the street, his hands in the pockets of his tight trousers. 'Twenty escudos, OK? There are two of you, aren't there? And, if you give me fifty,' he whispered with a smile, coming closer to us so that we could smell the wine on his breath, 'I'll join the dance, too, and then you'll see things you've never seen before. I get a hard on just...'

'We've already seen everything,' I said.

'You've never seen the likes of me with this tart; she's a real artist. She shouldn't be here, she should be in some classy house somewhere, where she'd be more appreciated.'

'Will she do anything we want?' asked Luís.

'The lot. You don't even have to ask her; I'll have a word with her first, though. Now, do you want the girls for the whole night?'

'No,' I said.

'But if you like them you could stay all night with them, and only pay for the room because they'd have to pay for that anyway.'

'We'll pay for the room,' declared Luís.

'Right, let's go then.'

I hung back at the door of the building; the stairway was lit by a dirty bulb hanging from the high ceiling. Luís might, if ... but was I going to let him go alone? What if they attacked him and robbed him? Well, he was old enough to look after himself... He, though, didn't give me time to make up my mind for he was off up the stairs behind the youth. I followed. On the second floor our guide knocked on a door; it was opened by a scrawny old woman.

'No rooms, we're full,' she said, trying to close the door, (but not before I heard the old woman whisper to him that she didn't want two at the same time, and that Sr Agostinho had been waiting for him for hours).

'But they've come for Suzete,' said the youth.

The old woman opened the door and held out her hand. 'That's twenty escudos.'

'But it's only one room,' protested Luís.

The old woman stared at him a moment. 'It's all the same,' she said.

Luís took out his wallet and paid her; the youth stepped between them: 'What about me?'

Luís gave him another twenty escudo note and he slipped off

down the long corridor and knocked slowly and deliberately at a door, meanwhile motioning us to come closer. The door opened while he exchanged a few words out of sight behind it. We peered round it to take a look at her: she was still very young, with dyed hair and was certainly very beautiful. She stuck her head through the door to look at us.

'Two of them? At this time of night? Go to hell. Call Rosa; she's just along the way.'

The youth smacked her lightly across the mouth. 'Go to hell yourself. They've already paid me so you do what I tell you, you whore.'

'Anybody who gets mixed up with ponces like you who have it off with anybody, anyway, they're the ones who ...' she retorted.

He smacked her again and grabbed her arm.

'Let the woman go; if she doesn't want to, we'll be off.'

'No, sir, you've paid, you're entitled to some service,' he said and shoved her into the room. 'And you'll pay me what you said you would.'

'And if I wasn't telling the truth,' she hissed. 'Be off with you, the old chap's waiting for you.'

The youth's manner suddenly changed, and he put his hands over his cock, smiling at us and winking. 'When you've got one like this, everybody wants a bit,' he said. 'Now, behave yourself, and do everything they ask you to, eh? No messing, or you don't eat here again,' he added, already by the door.

There we were, three of us in the room, just as Luís had wanted.

She sat on the edge of the bed and stretched. 'What a life; what a shit,' she said, swearing under her breath. Then she smiled at us. 'Each of you has to pay twenty escudos,' she announced, taking off the lace blouse she was wearing and throwing it behind her onto the bed. Since I did not move and Luís seemed torn between fascination and remorse she opened her legs, drawing back the lips of her sex with her fingers. 'So you only want to look, do you? Well, have a good look then.'

It was really quite delicate and beautiful, pink and tight, the lips soft and shiny, not at all like that of a woman who had surely been had by hundreds of men of all shapes and sizes; it seemed intimate and virginal in a way which was at odds with the coarseness of the gesture with which she showed it. Luís must have felt the same way because he got down on his knees to look at it and run his fingers over it. She rolled over, smiled and sprang up so that she was once again sitting on the edge of the bed. She grabbed Luís by the ears.

'Get undressed and come here,' she said.

Luís, without taking his eyes off her, slowly took his clothes off and stood in front of her, holding his erect cock in his hands. She looked over at me.

'What about you? Don't you want to get undressed? Take your clothes off and come here.'

Not to get undressed would have been even more absurd than to keep my clothes on, but I merely felt a deep seated pain, a desire to go away, to run out into the street, alone, in spite of the fact that I felt myself already caught inside that delicate, easeful sex of hers. I got undressed and went up to her and she took hold of my cock, whose state reflected my own confusion.

It was to my cock that she spoke, as though to a child: 'Don't you know what you want, my little darling? Go on, go on, I know what you want. Come on, now, up you get, like this young fellow here... Come on, head up, don't be shy ... what is there to be shy of? Aren't you a bigger boy than he is? It's only your head that's not so big, eh?' And then she pulled us over onto the bed with her.

With our arms around her, we were a tangle of arms and legs, in the midst of which I felt my cock go soft against her leg. She noticed it, too, and put her hand down to check. Her professional pride was wounded and she pushed Luís away so that she could concentrate on me, trying out a few things but in vain. I got up off the bed.

'Let him have a go,' I said. 'I'll come another time.'

'No, no, let him go first,' panted Luís, still clinging to her. I had started to get dressed and he took my hands in his.

'No, no, come on,' he begged, and dragged me onto the bed where, in a rage, I grabbed the woman and finally managed to enter her. When I had done and climbed off the top of her Luís was on his knees on the bed at my side. She made as if to get up but he, diving on top of her, did not give her the time to and entered her forcibly. I went to wash myself, averting my eyes from his rhythmic movements, and trying not to hear his wild grunting, in which his excitement did not seem to be borne out by his interminable delay in coming. But now his movements were more controlled than in the beginning; horrified, I realised that, in spite of his excitement, he was putting off the climax so that he could all the more enjoy the sensation of splashing about in what I had left in there. Without formulating it clearly I now understood what, since the start of the evening, I had in reality understood: that was what he had wanted, what he had not stopped thinking about, and that the opportunity had been granted to him in princely fashion. I let the money fall on top of the dresser, opened the door and went out. He could go to the devil.

There was nobody in the unlit corridor, nor on the stairs. On the street I carried on walking until I heard a taxi; I hailed it. I went into my house; in my bedroom I took off my clothes, climbed into my pyjamas, went to the bathroom and immersed myself in a long bath. I returned to my room and lay on top of the bed. All I felt was an immense weariness, a disgust with everything and with myself, a desire to sleep forever under murmuring waters which would wash me and block out every noise. But I wasn't at all sleepy, the light of dawn was streaming in through the half-closed window when the door opened and Luís quietly entered.

I didn't move, my eyes almost closed, watching his movements anxiously. I was full of anguish, fury at having given in; I just wanted him to disappear once and for all. And fear, too, an unease at what he would do now. But what could he do, in fact? Attack me? I had never felt any kind of foreboding which might make me suspect he had any such intention. What had happened was some childishness which didn't mean anything. Meanwhile Luís got undressed and went out. Meaningless, no; but it didn't mean what I thought it did; that was what appalled me because I had finally given in to his suggestion, I had lent myself to his fantasies and it had been my sperm in which he had dipped his own cock until he had come. I understood yet did not understand what had been going through his head during the night, like some *idée fixe*, of which my cock was part, and so strong and obsessive, that the circumstances had bent before it – the circumstances and me, too. Luís came back in, closing the door slowly, and sat down on the edge of his bed. He looked over at me and finally called me, in a very low voice, asking if I was asleep. I didn't reply, but kept quite still, my eyes closed now, but quiveringly alert. A cold sweat covered me, just as it had when Rodrigues had crouched in front of me and I had imagined heaven knows what.

'I know you're not asleep,' he said, calling me again. 'I need to talk to you. I don't want you to be angry with me, to think ill of me.'

I opened my eyes and moved slightly, gazing at the ceiling in the now pale shadows; I didn't turn my head towards him (though he was within my field of vision). And I said nothing. If such a thing had happened by chance, during some orgy in which more than one man had climbed onto the same woman, one after the other, that would have been different. But this was no a matter of chance, quite the opposite: the woman had not mattered, it was me whom he had chosen, in one way or another; and he felt it weigh so heavily on his conscience that he just had to explain himself. Explain what? It was better not to try, to keep quiet, to sleep and let me sleep. Tomorrow I would find some answer to the matter.

'You don't want to talk to me,' he persisted, 'and you left me there alone; when the door closed I didn't see you any more. Why on earth did you leave? Because of what I did? What's the harm in it? What on earth do you think of me? Was it because I wanted you to go first? If I had gone first wouldn't you have minded?'

'Shut up.'

'But I don't want you to carry on being mad at me; you're the last person in the world I would want to be angry with me. I don't have anybody except you.'

'Shut up.'

'Let me speak,' he said, haltingly. 'It was on account of being such a close friend that I wanted it to happen like this one day. It's true, I only wanted it to happen just the once. The worst thing was that I hadn't told you earlier that was what I wanted and why.'

'Shut up and get out.'

'Don't send me away, it's only a few days before I leave. And then, if that's what you want, I won't come back again, ever, you'll never ever see me again. But don't kick me out, it's only a few days. If you want you can be angry with me on the day I leave. But not just yet.'

'Shut up.'

'Let me explain what I want.'

'You've already had what you wanted; there's nothing to explain.'

'But it's not what you think – I swear it isn't. How can you think something like that, knowing me the way you do?'

'Nobody really knows anybody; until something happens one day...'

'Let me explain.'

'If there's no harm in it, then what is there to explain?'

'The harm is in what you're thinking; that's why I need to explain.'

He didn't say any more. He got down on his knees by the side of my bed, sobbing. I sat up with a start, as if he had put his hand on me, too close for comfort. I couldn't contain myself.

'What's all this about? And now, on top of everything else, you're blubbing just like some big soft tart. They had you weighed up at school when they all called you Dona whatever it was.'

He sobbed even more. 'Don't ever tell anyone,' he said, between tears. 'You'll never believe this… If you'd known you'd never have let me go with you… You know I'm a man, a real man, and I've proved it more than once.'

'When you've got the rest of them there, to help you.'

He raised a tear-stained face to me. 'That's true. That's quite true. But it's because I was terrified I wouldn't be able to do it, I always was. With everything they did to me, said to me, if you knew how much nastiness they were capable of, I was afraid, so afraid that, if I couldn't do it, then I really wouldn't be a man, just as they had said. And you believed in me, accepted me, and not because I was my brother's brother, it was for me, I know it was. In the train I was sure. That's why I wanted … wanted … it was like your blessing. After doing what I did I could go out into the world on my own.'

'And you needed that, before you could go to the maids' rooms here in this house? You need to be anointed by me?'

He gazed at me, wide-eyed, astonished. 'But they're your maids!'

'I've never fucked them.'

'But you can, whenever you want.'

I looked at him some more until he smiled at me. 'Have I explained everything? You're not angry with me now, are you?'

'That's all right; we won't mention this again.'

He sat down on the edge of the bed and I pulled the bedclothes over me, ready to sleep. All I could think about now was sleep. He, though, didn't lie down; he still had something on his mind. 'Jorge,' he whispered before long, 'can I ask you one more thing?'

'What?'

'Swear you won't think ill of me.'

'That depends.'

'Swear, and I swear I won't ask for anything bad.'

'What is it you want?'

'Get out of bed, please.'

I got up, and stood next to him.

'Now,' he said in a very low voice, 'hold me as tight as you can.'

'Eh?'

'Hold me; don't be afraid.'

I held him, and I felt him close to me, all over, embracing me tightly. Puzzled I went along with it until he relaxed his hold. He smiled triumphantly and then dropped the pants of his pyjamas. He shook his soft cock.

'There,' he said, 'if the friendship I have for you, great, great as it is, were what you thought it was then this thing wouldn't be like this. I'm absolutely sure of it.'

I lay down again and he threw himself, naked, on top of his bed, already visible in the light from the window. Still gazing at the ceiling he continued to wave his cock around.

'What's all this about?' I exclaimed.

'Nothing. I can't even get the thing up.'

'Piss off, once and for all.'

I pulled the sheets up to my shoulders and turned my back on him.

'Jorge...'

'What now?'

'Nothing ... thank you.

XLI

It was already after midday when we awoke to the sound of one of the maids knocking on the door.

'You can come in,' said Luís to her; it was the maid he'd been sleeping with.

'My mistress sent me to say it's time to get up for lunch.'

'Come here,' said Luís.

She looked at him distrustfully and took a few steps into the room.

'Come and look at this in the light of day!' he said and threw back the sheet, revealing his erection.

'For shame!' she cried out and ran out of the room.

I sat on the side of my bed 'Don't you think we've had enough of this childishness?'

'Childishness be damned. She's well acquainted with him; she's even got the rubber johnnies to slip over him.'

'Rubber johnnies?'

'Yes, sir. She says she found them in the street...'

'Used ones, I suppose?'

'No, brand new ones. And now she comes over all ashamed. I didn't buy a ubber johnnie to use with her, she's the one who buys them, which is fine by me, so we won't ever forget.'

He went to the bathroom and when he came out he seemed worried. 'I suppose that was a daft thing to do. She'll have gone and complained to your mother. What do you think she told her?'

'Wait a minute,' I said, going to the bathroom.

My mother came from the kitchen to meet me.

'I'm not having this. That boy is crazy. I can't even believe it's happening here,' she said, looking up at me, her face burning. 'It's not something I want to talk about; I'll leave it for your father to deal with when he comes home.'

'Isn't it something I can sort out?'

'You were there ... you must have seen... Was it true what she said?'

'Which one? What happened?'

'Go to the kitchen and speak to her yourself,' she said and slipped into her room.

In the kitchen the object of the outrage was sitting on a bench, weeping, while the other one stirred the pots on the stove.

'What's all this? What did you say to my mother?'

'Sir ... the boy ... you were there, you saw what he did.'

'I didn't see anything.'

'You didn't see... They're all the same,' she complained bitterly to the other through her tears of rage.

'They just cover up for each other.'

The other one buried her nose in the pots, tasting each one with her wooden spoon.

'OK, then, I did see. And then?'

'What does he think I am? Some slut? Some dirty whore?'

'So you've never seen one before? You don't know what it is? Is it only whores who get a glimpse of what you've just seen?'

The other maid choked with laughter on a spoonful she was tasting, to the fury of her colleague.

'That's it, now make fun of me, on top of everything else,' she exclaimed.

'But who's making fun of you? You came in as he was getting up. It was an accident, that's all; it's all over now.'

'An accident?' she demanded, not understanding.

'An accident. Go and tell my mother it was an accident, that you came into the bedroom just as he was getting up.'

She began to sob softly. 'But he has no right to be so disrespectful to me. I've always been so kind to him.'

'We all know that... Go and tell my mother that it was an accident, and that'll be the end of it.'

She remained quite still, red with indecision and frustration. I was afraid, though, lest the greater scandal should be revealed.

'The best thing would be for you to leave this very day.'

She looked at me with her eyes blazing. 'Are you dismissing me?'

'No; I'm just saying it would be better for you to go. Go and tell my mother that there was no harm in it, but that you've been thinking of moving for some time.'

'So I'm the one who has to leave? And he stays here, laughing, is that it?'

'Laughing at what? Aren't you free to go wherever you wish, whenever you wish? And what's he got to laugh at, any more than any of the others?'

'The others? Who do you think I am?'

'A woman who has the right to do what she wants, without

anybody else poking their noses in. But, if she complains about it, she loses the right.'

It was too hard for her to take; she became even more still and withdrawn. The other one was struck dumb, gazing at me. I took advantage of the moment to call my mother; she came to the kitchen door but she did not enter, as if what was going on in the kitchen was not something fitting for a lady just at that moment. The maid got up without looking at her.

'Madam,' she said, 'what happened was an accident ... I went into the room...' and she burst out crying. 'I want to leave, though; I can't stay here another day.'

My mother realised that there was more to the situation than met the eye (had she not guessed already?) but pretended not to understand. 'What is this? What have they done to you? You seemed so happy here ... and I've been so happy with your work. But, never mind ... you want to leave, and so you shall. I'll work out your wages. You can go after you've served lunch.'

She served lunch for the three of us.

Delighted by the news in that day's paper, which carried the resolutions passed at the previous evening's rally in large headlines, my mother no longer paid any heed to the embarrassment of just a few minutes earlier; she was so determined not to think about it that she paid no attention at all to the story we were telling her of what we had got up to. While the maid was serving lunch, she refused even to acknowledge our presence, beyond the usual conventions of being seated there at the same table. Only when we were alone, stirring our coffee, did she condescend to hear the story of our adventures, even though they just seemed absurd to her, compared to the unanimous decision of the rally to approve, by acclamation, a request asking the Government to create a Portuguese Legion. The man and his parrots seemed to her the perfect image of the legendary corruption of the Republic. What was needed was for everybody to join the army, prepared and determined, to form a front against the threats which hung over the country.

'Do you think my father will join?' I asked.

'The very idea, indeed! Your father's too old for that sort of thing. He isn't the right age. This thing's for young people.'

'No, that's where you're wrong, it's for everybody, as much as for him as for me.'

'For you? That's all I need.'

'Mother, you want everybody to join up to save the country, but you don't want father and me to enlist? If all the ladies in the country thought like you, who would there be to join up?'

'You've put your finger on it,' she said, and convinced of her case, she tried to formulate clearly the ideas which her reactions had awakened. 'All those who have mothers who aren't ladies can enlist, as well as anyone who's mixed up in politics because he ought to. Things like this are always a bit of a hodgepodge.'

'What you're afraid of is that those who enlist would be sent to Spain.'

'Not at all. I can read the paper. This has nothing to do with Spain; it's to fight communism here.'

'And to take note of those who don't join up. You'll see; that's what they're after.'

'Them? Who do you mean? What sort of a way to speak is that, in my house?'

'Those involved in politics; you mentioned them yourself.'

'I did?'

'Yes.'

She looked at me and then at Luís (who had tried to make himself invisible throughout the lunch, only taking part in the story of the incident in the Restauradores and of our forced visit to the house of the collector of poets and birds in so far as he quietly echoed everything I said); she frowned.

'These controversies, this business of who said what and who didn't, this way of criticising everything just to put people's backs up, confuse them, that's what the communists do. Everybody knows. It's a lack of respect for everything, anarchy…' and after wondering whether she should come out with it, she made up her mind, and added emphatically, 'immorality, free love, shamelessness in everything. I don't want such things in my house; it's a real danger,' she added, her tone of voice changing suddenly, 'a real danger. These are troubled times. At the least thing a person could find his house full of policemen,' she said, starting to get carried away by the notion, 'has that ever occurred to you? The police. All we need is for some respectable family to get in some altercation with the police. Yesterday, for instance, if that chap hadn't plucked you out of that ruckus, where do you think you'd be right now? In the slammer, yes sir, in the slammer, like any old vagrant. And the shock? The shock I'd have, not even knowing where you were? That's why…' The flow of her words had led her to a collision between a 'liberal attitude', according to which boys should be allowed their escapades, and her domestic 'authoritarianism', according to which boys were to be protected from all sorts of dangers; these were the two opposing poles of her 'philosophy' of life, which was a much more a matter of the refined art of ignoring anything which might disturb the benign unfolding of her existence... 'That's why every precaution is barely enough. There's no way of avoiding it. People help, or they don't, but from outside; let the others deal with it. The best thing is to get home early and not go out at night, because all the worst things happen at night,' – the night of the family, of non-involvement, of 'letting the others deal with it', was prior to the invention of electricity and street lighting, the era of 'all cats are grey at night'. 'The times are troubled, it's best not to go out at night,' – which went strongly against the grain of such ideas of manliness as the right to go out at night, to 'have the key of the door'. 'And you shouldn't be going across the Restauradores so early,' she concluded.

'But the flag seller isn't still there selling his little flags,' I said.

'He won't be there selling flags but he could be there selling something else. And the others could be knocking around there, too.'

'Now,' I said, 'they've all got other things to do. The flag seller, at this time, will be selling pencils in Estrela or heavens knows where, and the others going about their own business.'

My mother got up from the table. 'You're just that way out today, you just want to pick an argument. Go your own way then if that's what you want. I've other things to do. I've got to see the girl off, pay her wages. And where am I going to get another now, at such short notice?'

Luís still had his head down, embarrassed, as if he had forgotten that the maid was going on his account, while my mother was talking as if, rather than the other maid having to work twice as hard, the burden would fall on her; she took advantage of the situation to scold him. 'And just at this time, getting everything ready for your departure... And that means there are only a few days...'

Luís leapt up from his chair, frightening my mother who had not expected such a violent reaction. 'What date is it today?'

'Today? Why?' my mother and I exclaimed together.

'What time is it?' he said, snatching up the paper which was open at the far end of the table.

We all bent over the paper. The twenty-ninth. The 29th of August. The dining room clock showed three o'clock.

'I've got to go and get that paper from the Captain today,' he said, dashing out into the corridor.

My mother's gaze followed him out. 'That boy is crazy; he's not normal. Just as well it's only for a few days more, and then we'll have some peace in this house. And a bit of common decency.'

'Let's not say any more about that. It's over and done with.'

'Over and done with?... And very well, too... But what sort of a person gets it in his head to do something like that?'

'Everybody gets it in his head but we don't do it because it's not the sort of thing one does.'

My mother closed her eyes. 'It's astonishing what's gone on in this house. What impertinence.'

'What do you mean, impertinence?'

She opened her eyes and fixed me with them, severe and prominent. 'You, talking like that, in front of me, as if I was one of those women you hang around with.'

'I don't knock around with any woman.'

'You know very well what I'm talking about. Look, what sort of time do you call it when you got home last night. You didn't even both come in at the same time.'

'But I wasn't knocking around with anyone; the only knocking around I did was by tram or taxi...'

'Just so, spending money you haven't earned. When it's all gone, then we'll see. You don't know what work is; Luís will find out, and soon enough.'

'Are you going to tell me about work then?'

'That's enough from you. Go on, be off to the street with you. Men weren't made to hang around at home.'

'During the day.'

'Why during the day? Who said anything about that?'

'Because it's dangerous to be out in the streets at night.'

'You've changed since you went to Figueira. And I still don't know why you came back. You didn't need to come back with him as well.'

'I'd had enough of Figueira. And I didn't follow him here, he followed me. He wanted to come to Lisbon, didn't he, and since I was coming back he came as well.'

I got up from the table. 'I think I'll go out for a bit.'

The maid appeared at the door. 'Do you mind, madam? ... when you're ready, madam, we can work out my wages.'

My mother went off to the kitchen and I went out.

I took the tram as far as Belém where I changed onto one for Algés; it was stopped, waiting for the departure time, with two or three people inside, and the brakeman and the conductor sitting on a bench in front, chatting and smoking. The white mass of the Monastery of the Jerónimos made me think that I had never seen the inside of the Tower of Belém, but only glimpsed it behind the heaps of coat along with the gasometers, from the Estoril train. I didn't even know how to get there, or where to get off the tram. I went to ask the conductor; he and the brakeman had to think about it. Neither of them knew for sure, but they both agreed that the way must be the same as the way to the Fort. The best thing was to get off in the Largo da Princesa. Didn't I know where that was? A square alongside the tram line, with a public fountain, just up ahead? They would tell me when we got there; I went and sat down. One of the passengers turned round in his seat: was it the Tower I wanted? There was a guard – he knew the chap – who lived nearby, but the poor fellow had got fed up with looking after somewhere where nobody ever went, and where one was always frozen stiff, even in the height of summer, so he wasn't always there. If he wasn't I should ask at the Fort, alongside the Tower; the guard would usually leave the keys with one of the sentries. But why did I want to see inside the Tower? There was nothing in there, he'd been in himself. And he looked at me enquiringly. He was middle-aged, had gone very grey, and looked like a cobbler or something of the sort. He was wearing a modest suit, a bit threadbare and faded, which might once have brown or grey. He was wearing a tie, though, fraying at the ends and stained. And he wanted to talk.

I wasn't from Lisbon, was I? I was? Who'd have thought it? But, yes, I could be from Lisbon, yes, now that he knew. But this notion of visiting the Tower... I was a student, wasn't I? Of course I was. You could tell at once. He'd been a student, too... The tram set off, he sat up in his seat, interrupting the talk which had been going on softly, in that flat voice of his, a little hoarse. After a few short moments he turned round again to warn me to get off at the stop after his, and then discontinued the conversation, as if it was something he only felt like while the tram was stopped. When he had got off and the tram had set off again I got up and rang the bell, so that the conductor ran to get my fare. He didn't bother the old chap, perhaps because he knew he had a pass. I got off and stood there in front of the square. I had often passed by on the tram and I recognised vaguely the square though I had never really noticed it. Crossing the tramlines, I stepped into the square; it was paved unevenly with round stones whose irregularities time had not smoothed out, some of them bluish, others white, all higgledy-piggledy, which did not make a pavement alongside the street but instead formed a shallow gutter. I noticed too that the square was enclosed on three sides by stone railings, up against which were some old stone benches, the type which has a large slab with worked edges, supported by two huge legs with spirals carved into them, similar to the benches one finds spaced out along the street. The fountain rose up elegantly in the middle of that space from whose pavement grew, as if from invisible roots, a few sparse trees, some slender, others sturdier. From one side and another of the square narrow paths led down, while there was another path behind it. The houses – modest and old like the square – emerged on the other side of the paths, their windows on a level with the railings, which made them seem both far away and close by at the same time. The benches along the street seemed to mark the point where two worlds divided: one in which there were trams passing between the old walls, and the other, gathered there, in which time had been frozen two centuries ago and where the only sound was that of the soft gurgling of the waters flowing from one of the taps on the fountain. The square was deserted, there was no movement from the houses, the breeze gently stirred the leaves and the shadows across the blue and white stones of the pavement all added to the whole effect, giving it not exactly a dream-like air, but of lost reality, of a space vacated by the time which encircled it.

I sat down on one of the benches drinking in that peace, that solitariness, that clear light which from time to time the yellow streak of a tram would fleetingly cross. Sometimes, while wandering absently through certain parts of Lisbon I had found around me or slipping by, at my side, the same sort of atmosphere. At other times, in some street which was being widened or otherwise altered, which unfinished demolition work had filled with debris and rubble, or in which half knocked down walls, to which signs of life still clung, on one side of the street, I had felt that on the other side – the one that had not been touched by the changes – an old mansion, or a row of modest houses, had something of the same air about them, similar to this one, so far marked only by the ravages of time. Yet other times – for example in Graça, Estrela, Amoreiras or in the Costa do Castelo going to Alfama – the atmosphere persisted, but more urgently: as when, in the silence broken by footsteps, the echoing of voices, far away cries, the hubbub of the bustle in many different streets lay, one on top of the other. But even though in more venerable, more picturesque places, more encrusted with the past, I could have felt such an atmosphere more strongly or more suggestively, perhaps never before had it got through to me so much, and in such a soothing way, as in the almost mean simplicity of that square now, an awareness of what the past might be, stripped of history and memory, with neither bitterness nor longing, shorn of blame and turmoil, a space in which to linger, not so much to return to it than to be there in it with no thought of return. A space which does not seek any end or to impose itself in any way, but a space in which one finds oneself and which does not have anything in common with us beyond the fact, the coincidence, of its being there.

All of a sudden I was seized by the need to say this very thing. I got ready to write; slowly I wrote. But what emerged was something utterly different, at least on first reading, which filled me with surprise and astonishment. Then it seemed to me that it needed a title and I read it again, doubting whether, if it did need a title, it would be able to express what the title suggested. Then I read it again, with its title:

Glass Cage

Like walls through which
We see the world through others' being,
Who we come to know surrounds us,
Multiplying the faces of the cage
Around which is woven our life.

In the space within (but which does not depend
On the number of faces or the distance between them)
We are who we are: only distinct
From each one of the rest, for whom
We are only a face among many,
In view of which becomes in us, beyond space,
A vision of transparent windows.

But what marks it out to us does not exist.

Trying to analyse it, it didn't seem to me to have any direct relation to what I had wanted to say. It was something else, something which had come before this, or something I had felt before the feeling or impression that had driven me to write. I had wanted to talk about a suspension of time, of a being in a space in which we found ourselves face to face with a past without memory. But, contrarily, I had spoken of life as being like a glass birdcage, a prism with as many facets, all around us, as the people whose lives we crossed. I had spoken, above all – even though indirectly, none the less above all, (though in different fashion) – of memory. Was it because that other being was known from before, like a mirror in which the others look at themselves repeatedly, in spite of seeing the rest of the world through us? But in truth, just as the square had suggested to me, I had stripped memory of any temporal correlation, of anything precisely memorised And, in all probability, when I had wanted to speak of the square, I had only wanted to write just what I had written (or something which had become that, once the words had been set out in the correct sequence), and the square had been the ideal image of those walls within which I felt that I was hopelessly trapped, as a living, thinking being; but it was still a sufficiently abstract image to enable the memories which I did not wish to recall – all those all too physical memories of anguish and confusion – to be transformed neatly into a meditation in which, as the people became anonymous objects, lacking human form and voice, life was a concrete, permanent presence, stripped of personal relationships – something with a more interior sense than an inconvenience, and more exterior than the need to live together. Meanwhile, the word 'birdcage' had kept, in the context, an allusion to the freedom which, increasingly, I saw did not exist and which, paradoxically, no amount of solitude could grant me.

I got up to go to the Tower, but when I had already gone down one of the paths and reached the street at the bottom, in which the houses, rooted in the ground, asserting their reality, in front of the supporting wall of the square, I had to stop so that I could write some more:

> In the vast deeps measured by the rowers' stroke,
> The night is asleep, peacefully.
> The boat slides by, all unaware
> That space or time exist in another life.

After writing these lines there was a great void within me. Subsequently I wrote:

> Or in that, in which breathing in the night
> Is the whisper of waters against the hull

lines which I instinctively rejected and put a line through so that I could continue thus:

> In which ships are wrecked and on the beaches
> There are the ruins of hulls, going rotten,
> And falling apart in the sun, the wind, the rain,
> Their names no longer to be discerned.

All that was lacking was an ending. What could it consist of? The parallel between the name which the weather had erased and that which the night obscures. Like what had happened, however, in the previous poem, the ending was a separate matter, though a continuation of the same theme, of the same guiding idea.

I began to write – 'Just as the night' – and once again rubbed it out. The ending that I wrote did not please me, and seemed restricted compared with the one I had used earlier.

> Of which, ploughing through the seas, the night hides the
> name.

But then, as I wrote the words I looked up from the paper and saw a man, gazing at me in astonishment; he was leaning against the wall on one of the corners, in the sun. Obviously he was surprised to see someone there in the street who had stopped to write something down, and either he had been there in the first place, watching me as I wrote, or he had stopped precisely because he wanted to be there at such an unusual – for him – scene. It was possible that my dissatisfaction with the ending (which seemed too hasty, something tacked on just for the sake of an ending) was the result of that intrusion, of which I hadn't been aware, the fact of somebody's gaze fixed on me. I crammed the paper hastily into my pocket and quickened my steps, just like the chap who, in some empty corner, squats down in response to an urgent need and then when he is discovered by some unexpected passer-by, fumbles to wipe his backside, shamefacedly pulling up his trousers and making off without a backward glance. That was exactly how I felt and it annoyed me intensely, like some filthy insult that I had directed at myself. Then, as a reaction, I pondered how everything that I was writing has something of the same private and shameful act about it, and that the difference between the waste products of the body and of the spirit obtained merely in the fact that the former were the physical, reeking tyranny of our day to day existence, something which in itself made no sense, while those of the spirit were the sublimation of the faeces of the mind, by which we transform what we cannot absorb through the experience of the soul, refining the experience to another plane. What I had written was the result of my life, of that in my life which had been unacceptable and intolerable – so intolerable and unacceptable that, in order to carry on living and know that I was living, it was necessary for words divorced from reality (a reality which was only real as a memory, like some dark, woeful stain) to create a generic experience on another spiritual plane; on this plane the ineffable experience would be reduced or blown up to a vision of things or relations on a human scale, and the words would produce a new form which was at once foreign to me and to the others, without ceasing to be, for me, the same amorphous, suffocating presence from which this shape had emerged.

Probably it was not the same for everybody, seeing that there were other people who would relish being observed in the act of writing, in the same way that plenty of people could only enjoy sexual pleasure if they imagined that they were watching themselves, or were being watched, or it was actually so. And what would happen to other people – those who didn't write, those to whom nothing like what had happened to me would ever happen: write? Would they suffer more or less in the same way as I did? If in a different way, how? These questions made me shudder, no less on account of the distasteful comparison which had given rise to these thoughts. Was I different from the rest? Had I, from the start been destined to be so? Or had some combination of circumstances wrought enough of a change for it to happen? But, if circumstances had conspired towards that end, was it not because I was already marked out as different, should such a combination ever come to bear on me, which might or might not happen? I didn't want to be different from the rest in any aspect and I certainly didn't feel I was different. On the contrary, what I had discovered, was still discovering was that *everyone was different*, from the moment they emerged. However, if not everybody wrote, why was I writing? And writing compulsively, artlessly, knowing nothing of composition, of prior planning, of accomplishing something which was worthwhile in itself as an autonomous creation?

There I was with three poems on scraps of paper at the bottom of my pocket. I began to feel rather ridiculous, a bit childish, stupid, since I had never thought of myself as a poet, while in my mind I had never regarded myself a literary type. A poet, as far as I and my family were concerned, and my friends too, was someone a little grotesque, cut off from everyday life, and who adopted a romantic pose in order to speak on his own behalf, or on that of others, as if what he said belonged to some higher, extraordinary level of transcendence, though not really so, except on very special occasions. One of my uncles wrote verses sometimes, for his own amusement and that of the family on birthdays. But was just a joke, for the sake of it, which nobody assumed meant anything more than the laughter he provoked with his puns, which in truth I never thought were all that funny. Could it have been that when I didn't find them funny I was already getting ready, deep within me, to recognise that poetry was something intimate, private, profoundly wrapped up in our own lives, and thus incompatible with the tomfoolery of a few limping feet which happened to rhyme, over dessert?

I was by now close to the Tower; the sight of it distracted me. I couldn't see it as a whole because the wall which carried on from the ramparts of the Fort obscured its lower part. As for the rest, there in front of me, as I followed along the tarmacadamed road was the gate of the Fort, which would have opened in the sloping wall, if it had not been, as was the case, only half open and with no sentry to be seen. Standing in front of it I then made my way to the left between the rampart and a red wall on top of which glittered heaps of coal. Once over the ridge of the rampart there was a smallish open space which extended to the edge of the wall and on which were dotted about a few tall weeds and little mounds of rubbish and other debris. I went across it towards the Tower, so that I followed the rough paths and, without even seeing it, I found myself on the road leading to the Fort. Near the Tower, walking around it on the side from which I had come and still some way from it, the wall went down a half paved slope to a tiny, filthy, beach. A few boys were running and leaping around near the water's edge, some in ragged underpants, others completely naked; little heaps of their clothing were scattered around colourfully at the base of the Tower. When they saw me coming down to the beach a few of them hurried to hide behind the wall which jutted from the Fort; others dashed towards their clothes. Without doubt they had taken me for some guard bent on stopping them swimming there, or who sometimes came along to tell the naked ones to get dressed. Seeing, though, that I was heading for the Tower and not for their clothing (which in all probability the guard used to confiscate in order to make them come and get it), they stopped looking at me secretly and one or two of them started to return in carefree fashion to their games in the water. Some of them were no longer boys but adolescents already.

One of them, slipping on his underpants, came running towards me; as he drew near, holding out a fag end and asking me for a light, I realised what he had been looking for among the rags, as he bent over the pile of clothes. I gave him a light. It was some time before the fag end caught light, but I felt there was something deliberate in the delay which could not be explained merely by the size of the cigarette butt, nor by the well-versed way in which he bent his head towards me so that he could light his cigarette from mine. The fag end was already lit but he continued to pretend to be pulling on it, his cigarette still against mine. And his eyes, looking at me sidelong, were what drew my attention to what, secretly, his other hand was doing: he was scratching his cock through the fly of his underpants, in such a way that everything was both visible and covered up at the same time.

'Hey,' I said, stepping back and frowning, 'your fag's already lit. Now be off with you.'

He stood up straight and looked at me defiantly. 'Strolling round here, then? There are better beaches up over there.'

'I've only come to see the Tower.'

'The Tower?' he said, shrugging in its direction, without turning towards it. 'The Tower's closed,' he added.

I walked away and continued round the monument, looking for the entrance on the other side. In the shade, by the steps which were partly buried in the sand, were two women with two men, who ceased rolling around on top of them when I appeared round the corner. The gate was indeed closed. The four of them, shaking the sand off, remained seated and eyed me up suspiciously. The two men were evil-looking characters and seemed to be weighing up how much my wallet might be worth; the two women weren't exactly whores: in the foolish smiles which dulled their features there was the mark of those who hung around the neighbourhood, dispensing their favours for a few coppers behind some hedge or fence, lying on a mound of rubbish. To show that the Tower was my goal, I climbed the steps and banged on the gate.

'There's nobody there,' said one of the men behind me. 'Just now some gentlemen came by and then they went off again, in a car at that.'

I thanked him and went back to the beach, remembering that the key was in the Fort, according to what I had been told by the man on the tram. The lad who had asked me for a light was peeping at me from the corner and ran to sit down by his clothes. He must have found my behaviour implausible, perhaps being more used to some ritual of prior, careful refusals which he had to overcome (a flashback to the beach at Figueira passed across my inner eye, with Rodrigues exposing himself to the fellows who were lying on the sand some distance away), and he whistled shrilly. I carried on to the Fort; when I got there the sentry came out from inside the gate.

'Who goes there?' he demanded.

I asked him for the key to the Tower and if I could visit it. The soldier, who was squat and very small, looked me up and down, knitting his brows in concentration so that his head seemed even shorter.

'The key? Only if by asking the officer of the day.'

'Well, go and ask him then.'

He shouted through the gate and another soldier appeared. The latter knew, yes indeed, that the key was kept in the guard's house, when the usual chap who showed people around the Tower had gone off during the normal hours; he went to call the sergeant. The sergeant arrived; he was fat, with a very thick, black beard, and thin legs which seemed even thinner in black leather gaiters: he looked like some little bluish bird. What did I want? What was I doing there? Visiting the Tower? But the Tower was closed; I couldn't visit it. Why not? Well now! Orders, yes sir, and would I be good enough not to linger by the Fort since nobody was permitted in the vicinity. Why not? Well now! Orders, yes sir, the Fort was there under guard. And he looked at me, bristling, to impress on me the gravity of the fact. As soon as I repeated the word questioningly he came to his senses again, with a great fuss. Not to put too fine a point on it he had already spoken far too much: guarding things was a sort of state secret which he had let me in on, though I wasn't family or even a neighbour.

'Being under guard,' he stuttered, 'is just a way of speaking. Exercises, they're exercises,' and retreated solemnly back inside. The soldiers remained on the gate as if they were preparing to repel any assault of mine. It wasn't worth making a fuss in such a ridiculous situation so I wandered off.

When I reached the way I had come to the Fort I remembered
that my initial idea had not been to visit the Tower at all but to go
on foot to Algés. I hesitated. Maybe it was possible to follow the
railway line. Yes, of course it was, since I remembered seeing people
on the beaches which extended uninterrupted as far as Algés, when
one time or another during the season I had passed by on the train
to Oeiras or Estoril. I turned back, resolved to follow the road which
went along by the Fort. When I got to the little crossroads in front
of the gate the same small soldier come forth from between the
gates.

'Where are you going, sir? Don't you know it's forbidden for
anyone to be on the military roads? You can't go that way.'

The road was, as far as I could make out, only a bare dozen metres
along the ramparts, which petered out into piles of debris. In the
past it would have continued since the tarmac, with its stones
scattered around, disappeared abruptly under the heaps of rubbish;
further on, though, there were now just clumps of weeds and planks
which must have been the huts where some people lived. I explained
that I merely wished to go to the beach, pointing out to him that
if those things yonder were huts then the people who lived there
had to pass that way. He started to lose his temper with my refusal
to take no for an answer and took refuge in saying that those people,
since they lived on the land could go that way, but since I didn't I
couldn't.

'Yes, those people,' he argued, with great lucidity, 'but they're
not even people, they're less than human, and so they can pass, just
like the dogs and cats with nothing to do.' He laughed with glee
at his own logic, revealing twisted, filthy teeth. But he finally let
me pass, persuaded by what he thought was my joke that he should
make believe I was a dog or a cat, and, peering out of the corner
of his eye at the gate, he hastily grabbed the cigarette I proffered
him.

As I crossed the open space I was thinking about him and about
the lad who had cadged a light off me. Perhaps he had grown up
among pigs and chickens, in some village in the mountains, with
the winter cold cutting in through the gaps in the door, and the
mud from the stony ground crusted on his feet and legs. Those
people who moved around among the huts like shadows also had
hens (which ran around among the weeds). The filth, the lack of
even the least comfort, the level of poverty and ignorance couldn't
have been very different. But on coming down to the city, his

uniform, the sordid contacts in the dark streets, had given the soldier boy a would-be awareness of his superiority over those who, in the great metropolis in which he would often himself feel lost, lived in it, too, like the rubbish which was swept much further away from the door of life. He would feel that he was part of something which 'those people' could never be part of. Of course the way in which this was all impressed on him, by shouting or through the orders, whose reasons – if any – he would not know, his role – the glorious flag under which he served, the invincible army to which he belonged, etc. – this way would not be silent within him, except in the way he felt more of a man, arrogantly so, as if the uniform were an aphrodisiac guaranteed by the mere fact of all the others in uniform. But this would be enough, in the security of the soldiers' mess and his own bed, for him to feel, in obedience to the pressure which sustained the society which he saved and which didn't give a fig for him, an unbridgeable distance in terms of quality between his own person and those almost wholly degraded beings who had to cower beneath him before they could return to their squalid dumps of tin and planks.

When he returned to his village he would at first feel dispossessed or even get to feel acutely the lack of the baths he had never known there. Gradually, however, the effort he had made or which had been forced on him to accustom himself to a way of life which he knew to be provisional (and which he wished to be provisional in those hours when he felt a longing for his little plot of earth), would reveal itself to him imperceptibly as what in truth it had been (a temporary artificiality), and, greatly relieved, he would once again return to wearing no shoes and the filth, without though altogether losing his contempt for 'those people' who, in Lisbon, were less than human (affording him the illusion, which I would give him too, of being something more than them). The other one, the young lad who had begged a light, was different. This one (who would also find a soldier's life to his taste, if in the meantime an early experience of vice and misery did not unfit him for such a great honour) would not feel that he was more or less part of something within which he had been born and had grown up, and which was none of his doing. His way of looking, his gestures, showed that he realised that he was an outsider, and that only his cunning, although on a modest, mean scale, would guarantee him the desultory contacts he needed to survive. Detritus of the neighbourhood (and so perhaps not even believing, unlike the other, that those who dwelled in the huts were his inferiors) or of some far-flung suburb, his position was however superior, in truth, to that of the mere parasite which persisted in its survival, managing only because nobody could be bothered to spray it with insecticide. Superior, because his marginal status was, reciprocally, a social necessity which he could exercise through the act of selling himself.

The conversations I had heard, the gestures I had observed, the figures I had known in those Figueira days (and I saw Rodrigues again, jumping up and down on the bed, showing his backside in despair, or I don't know who, whose names escape me, mincing along the street), were only the one, horrifying face of yet another side, sadder still, which had ended up being revealed to me in various malevolent eyes and in a hand I knew. Their obsessions, their promiscuity, the mixed-up feelings of my friends in those terrible days (which drew themselves out at such length) were some adolescent game, even though prostitution was a part of it (and Rodrigues' fame was not innocent of this), on a par with what I had divined in that naked teenage body, one of whose sidelines was to be a hidden, available underworld. A chill ran down my spine on realising how much he was like Luís. But was he really? Or was it only their slender youthfulness which linked them, being more marked by the similarity of their ambiguous situations? A retrospective disgust filled me utterly when I recalled Luís' body against mine, in that ridiculous demonstration of his, which he had been so anxious to stage. What was it trying to prove to us, trying to prove to me? Was it some sort of test? What kind of uncertain, wavering frontier had separated Luís from me and from some catastrophe? Between the boy who wanted to put his arms around me to demonstrate that he didn't want me and the boy who exposed himself to see whether I wanted him – what fundamental difference was there? An erection? Neither of them showed any sign of one. Could it be that the difference was only the fact that one of them had grown up used to the idea of prostitution? Or was there, as I had always been sure there was, an innate difference: some are like that, others aren't? But does anyone who sells himself have to be like that? And anyone who doesn't, or is horrified by the idea, or the idea of anyone selling himself – or herself – on his behalf, couldn't be like that? Love, for sure. But had I ever even thought of loving a whore? What had love to do with it? Had Luís loved the maid, the one whom I had, with my mother's connivance, eased out of the house with that wretched, cunning, stroke of mine?

Bitterly, I reckoned that we had treated her without the slightest respect, like some cat which one took in a basket to the waste land on the outskirts of town where one left her just because she had got on one's nerves by pissing on the carpet (at least that's what we did with cats in my house). Where did one draw the line in human relations? I was already a long way from the Fort, having walked the length of the wall; in the distance I could see the beach at Cruz Quebrada, with its huts, towards the setting sun which covered it with the misty light of the late afternoon and the haze at the water's edge.

I paused and sat down on the wall while a train passed close behind me. Love, sex, friendship, family relationships, chance relationships, daily routines, politics, everything – none of this made up any sort of harmonious whole whose balance was disturbed from time to time. They were just like a whole lot of moving surfaces, one on top of the other, which sometimes coincided, crossed, or faded away, according to a huge host of chance events in such a variety of possible combinations of the people involved, even though at random, that the notion of some law, some order, some norm, of a fixed line between good and evil, would not be valid even for some lost village in the mountains, cut off from the world, where a scant half dozen people repeated the same gestures, the same steps, even, from generation to generation. In a life, in my view of life, in which everything depended on everything else, and everything echoed everything else, where it might be said that the rule was the accumulated quintessence of a whole lot of experiences, what happened was just that the rule became fluid, or false, or something imposed on one group of people by another group, in the name of something which, in truth, was not directly applicable to everyone. For, in the slippery, diverse surfaces by which at every moment we changed our own surface without ceasing to belong to all of them, not everybody was in the same situation. Some were freer than others, not by doing what they felt like, when they felt like it, or by the fact that they could do so (they were thus slaves of a freedom built on the lack of freedom of the majority), but because they either had enough strength to refuse, or they didn't have the desire in the first place (by the fact that they didn't have these tendencies) to use themselves or other people in the plane on which they met. Was the fact that one didn't feel that desire the same as being able to resist it? What were the conditions which enabled one to resist? Resist what? What was? What would be?

What must be? Who could pronounce on all this with authority? My conscience? Which conscience – psychological, moral, political, who knows which one? The authority of the majority? Dictatorship? The churches? Habits, prejudices, selfishness, envy and ambition?

The idea of some transcendent guarantee, of some ideal order involving the whole world, at the same time permitting the existence of evil and injustice, degradation and betrayal, filth and infamy, or more than permitting them, feeding off them, made me dizzy and sick. No – anything except an emptiness made up of the stupidity of death; anything except that mirage which was the result of our panic in the face of loneliness and uncertainty. But could it have been the case that in other times, loneliness and uncertainty were less complicated and mixed up than I imagined and felt inside? If, then, men believed in another world, to the extent of mortifying their own flesh so that they might get there more quickly, in the agony of their own lives and of life itself, would they suffer with little, if any, hope that life could somehow be better, or could be at least accepted in all its uniqueness and the fact that nothing could ever take its place, no matter what? No; that wasn't the question. All the evil of life had been present in their lives, perhaps much more than in mine; for some of them, just as for many others today, a great deal more, without doubt. Suffering, however, was measured by one's sensitivity towards it, by one's ability – innate or acquired – to feel in different ways, on diverse levels at the same time, the injustice of the world. This injustice, though, could not be measured or would not justice be its opposite, through the greater or lesser awareness of behaving unjustly or of being the victim of some injustice? If it were thus, and even though it were, wouldn't that be a greater injustice? But what was injustice? Doing to others what we didn't want doing to us? Not thinking of a person as somebody different in his own right at all times, in every different situation? It was that too, but not just that.

I jumped down from the wall onto the beach; it was a tongue of sand with boats scattered over it. I went down to the water's edge where tiny waves lapped gently, almost without spume, gurgling round the bits and pieces of every kind of rubbish. I sat down on the side of one of the boats.

To accept an order, defend it, carry it out, was to recognise that, even though it might be provisional, justice was inevitable. But a complete lack of order would mean the reign of the strongest, the most ruthless, the most violent, not the possibility of harmony and justice. Out of this had emerged humanity. Emerged? Or had violence been progressively replaced by indifference to violence, injustice by insensitivity to injustice, selfishness by a lack of awareness, fear of death by fear of life?

Lifting my gaze towards the sunset I realised that an enormous shadow had come between me and the light. A tall, oblong, precisely defined black shadow which I hadn't seen earlier in spite of its size. I headed for it; feeling the sand in my shoes; I went closer to the water so that I could run on the damp sand. It attracted me; it wasn't a violent attraction, based on curiosity and excitement but an odd kind of fellow feeling, as if that black thing were someone I had been wanting to meet and which was waiting for me now, calmly enough, at the end of some deserted street, where the smile implicit in the attraction could not be meant for anyone but me. When I went into the shadows made by those shapes, coming out of the other light by which I had first seen them, they began to take on definite outlines and colours, between black, brown and a reddish tone. What had at first seemed to me to be some huge thing was changing into some higgledy-piggledy building of some sort, tall, to be sure, but no more than three or so times my own height, and on which its irregular, uneven contours were nevertheless hard and sharp, while its surfaces seemed to glisten damply with some oily sheen. When I got close up to the shapes they seemed not so much to be rooted in the sand as to have been born out of the beach (as though shown by the fineness of the line between the wet sand and them, traced by a shallow thread of water), my eyes did not at first recognise in what they saw two iron ships, high and dry, dismantled, leaning against each other.

I was able to pass between them, as though I was in some shadowy nave which the dying sun splashed with colours from a stained glass window. But just as I had been reluctant to identify the two boats so also was the comparison with a nave negated by the enchantment of that black, brown, red, golden atmosphere, redolent of the sea, rust, sun and those places where the sun never shone except by way of a reflection from outside, never resting on anything. I walked round the boats. From the side lit by the sun, which lingered on something I could not at first make out (and which was, with the other, the shape which had been picked out for me by the water's edge), this atmosphere became less intense in the air which, on this side, smelt more of earth, of weeds and rotting rubbish. I sat down in the sand, close to what had been the prows of both boats which stuck out above me at the same time sharp and blunt... What sort of boats could they have been? How had they got washed up there? Who had decided they should lie together? And for what reason? Useless, almost invisible until one was on top of them, how much longer would they be there? And their position, one supported by the other, and one of them seeming to be sliding down the other which however served to support it (or was it the other way round?), how long could they last like that?

A slight sense of unease began to creep up on me: a mixture of nausea, giddiness, chill, occasional palpitations. I lay down behind them in the sand. The blue tinge of the sky and the few pale clouds were filled with white dots which followed one another. I closed my eyes. The white dots, now on a red background, continued to follow each other, but there weren't so many of them and they were grouped in quietly swirling convoys. A heavy sleepy feeling made everything seem softer, though without dulling the sounds around me – quite the contrary. The sigh of the wavelets, the sand shifting around beside my head, the motion of the weeds, stirred by the evening breeze, and far-off voices (some on the beaches, others inland) were all delicately orchestrated. A bugle sounded, perhaps in the Fort. A cadenced shudder of sound turned out to be the roar of a train passing by and that in turn became the vibration from out of which there came another train going in the opposite direction. Then, all of a sudden there was a complete silence, a total absence of movement – or I had stopped listening – for a few moments. The movement of the lights, which I saw inside my own head, stopped too, leaving me only the vision of an irregular penumbra. This lasted but an instant and half opening my eyes gingerly I had the impression that the prows of the two ships had slipped one against the other, about to topple down on me. Against the sky, as the colour drained from it, the silhouetted shapes left a white wake of their outlines; and it was as if the courses of the ships had crossed each other, in some static movement of which I was the path.

I got up, weary as though from a long journey. And then suddenly in the twilight which came on like black pools of water joined up by a light, whitish mist, a huge body, white and naked, started to emerge, hanging in the air, drifting towards me, with its legs open, its pink sex opening up damply, throbbing, in its little nest of black hair. The stomach was heaving, its breasts swinging and its legs hung down as if over the edge of a bed. It was her, yes, her, coming like some giant figure to meet me, holding and releasing her breasts so that they shook. It was what I wanted, it was what she was: that sex whose lips opened so rosy and gleaming. Dozens could have had her, dozens of stiff cocks have entered her, and have rubbed damply along the walls of her sex, violently, so that in the clash of pubic bones, they would have filled her full one after the other. That sex was mine, it was open for me; and all those that might open up for me would always be that same one, huge and gleaming and damp, which attracted and repelled, dripping from everyone who'd had her, the filth of all of them upon it. With my hands on my cock I entered it, feeling myself plunging deeply into the heat, ablaze all over. Her hips rippled around me, and in thrusts which gripped me with agony, rage, fury, that body began to melt away until it was just a few drops of semen on the sand, at which I gazed, crazy and beside myself with astonishment and grief.

A strange feeling of satiety, like some piercing longing which could be fended off easily enough, though never less than sharply physical, made me reconciled to the humiliating frustration. I wiped myself down with a handkerchief and looked around, anguished, feeling that before there hadn't been those thousands of scornful eyes to witness my shame. But there was nobody. I went to the wall by the railway embankment, looking for a hole in the wire fence which ran alongside the line. I found one further along. As if in some waking dream I walked on until I got to a track at the end of which I could see some telegraph poles. It was then that a choking wave of well-being, an ironic sort of well-being, sardonic, mocking, erupted in me in a silent cry which echoed in my eardrums, from the walls, in the already sombre atmosphere of the track. 'How much of you, love, did possess me in our embrace...'

Feverishly, yet at the same time with the serenity of one who is sure that the voices are with him and won't fail him (I could already hear the cadences rolling on), I wrote:

> How much of you, love, did possess me in our embrace
> In which in entering you I felt myself lost
> In having you for ever –
> How much of having you I possessed me in everything
> Which I should desire or see not thinking of you
> In the embrace to which I give myself –
> How much of giving is like an open face,

Minus eyes and mouth, only the doleful expression
Of one who is like death –
How much of death I got from you,
In the pure loss of possessing you in vain
Of love which betrayed us –
How much betrayal there is in possessing people
Without knowing that the body does not know
More than to feel itself in the other –
How much feeling you and you feeling me was nothing
But the eternal encounter which no image
Will ever separate –
How much of separation we will live in others
This moment which kills in us for
One who is not us and alone –
How much solitude is this being in everything
As in the indestructible absence which
Makes us be one in the other –
How much of being or not being the other
Is forever the only certainty
Which holds us to life –
How much pure life we devour
In the horror and misery of, while possessing, being
The earth on which others walk –
Oh my love, from you, through you and for you,
I receive freely as is received
Not death or life, but the discovery
Of the nothing wherever one of us be not.

I had the feeling of having written it all in seconds, but on trying to re-read it I could hardly make out the letters in the darkness which already surrounded me. And I found myself thinking curiously that, even if I did not really love that woman, forgot her, detested her even, I don't know, it was as if love remained with me in future words forever. The world might collapse around me, I might suffer beyond all imagination, but the liberating eventuality, that extravagant nausea, that would remain with me, indestructible, like a destiny revealed. Not a destiny like a life borne from day to day, a sad succession of cause and effect from some gesture whose consequences one never knew. No. Another destiny (which was not a destiny) which was beyond time and space and life, because it was the express essence of the other common destiny: the essential gratuitousness of the thought which is laid bare with its feet buried in the destiny which is life, but its head in the clouds of pure nothingness. Not in another world beyond the world, another life beyond life. A being in itself, though, in life as out of it, a being outside of it, as only in it. I shuddered as I realised that, in winning the right to see and to free myself I had lost for ever the security of living. I would live as securely as never before, whatever might happen, that was for sure, but between me and the innocence of being with others, there would be from then on not a wall of sentimental, soothing words like the poetry which I used not to like, but a chill vacuum, consisting of the eventuality that they created a meaning and a relation in everything if I allowed this to happen. It was as if it were a final virginity, which only a few lose, had been taken from me and I was alone, paradoxically and irremediably stained by my essential purity, by everything and everyone.

Neither life, nor I myself, would ever be what life and I, eventually, might be, in the experience of self-knowledge. The more I suffered and the rest of them, too, it would never be more, than an absurd, meaningless experience, to which, suddenly, in a silent scream, a certain arrangement of words would come to give reality. And the most terrible thing was that, knowing that sort of thing might happen to me at any time, no moment of my life in future would be insignificant; but rather something which could be replaced unexpectedly by any *other thing* which, being only in the mind, was an absolute reality which would steal the possible reality from everything else. Vaguely remembering (since the words would not come back to my mind) all that I had written, I felt that I had been seeking only the reality, the other, which is considered reality. It was not the other other, or another other which I had been trying to grasp in the anguished disorder of my life. And with a certain sad pride I felt that at last reality was within me; only I could see it and hear it. Yes, that was it. And perhaps that was why poets publish their verses (for the opposite reason that false poets publish theirs). If the reality was within me, in those occasional arrangements of words which, transposed, represented my life, publishing poetry was an attempt to build bridges between the people who, in life, would not understand us nor would fill for us the chill emptiness between us, and who, because they did not understand clearly what was not clear to me either, would be transported momentarily to live there where reality was like a given experience, decanted and transposed. But no. How could I think of ever publishing something which I had felt so deeply, so intimately, so nakedly expressed? And what knowledge given to others could compensate me for that fearful – and at the same time (I felt it now) proud and cynical – loss of final innocence? None. Probably there was not the slightest altruism in writing about it; on the contrary, it was the desire, like in life, to deflower everything. And to give them to drink not sorrow, nor words about sorrow, but the dreadful fact that sorrow hurts all the more the greater the emptiness.

Leaning against the bus stop I had been watching the now lighted trams passing by without flagging one of them down. Yes, from unhappiness one could manufacture the happiness of criticising unhappiness without ceasing to be unhappy. Or vice versa. I laughed; after all it was not something to be wondered at. Everything that had happened to me or to the rest of them – life and death – ended up in sybilline words in which there were not the least dregs of sordidness or ridicule, nor pettiness, nor betrayal, not even of the chance by which people betray each other much more than they even dream of doing. Words, an orderly way of thinking, though not exactly logical, where sometimes there was not even thought, merely a hapless or successful impulse. There I was, to all intents and purposes a poet, through the intervention of... To hell with it. For that walk neither time nor words would be enough; I would spend it all wandering around with papers in my pocket, in the permanent expectation that, as in the alchemist's basement, holder of the philosopher's stone (a philosopher's stone which, instead of making gold from base metal, would conjure words from life's excrement) the refined quintessence of events and experiences – mediocre or otherwise – would penetrate my awareness, changing my skin like a chasuble. Besides, I didn't even know whether that stuff was worth anything at all. But since it had emerged in the way it had, would I ever accept that it wasn't worth anything? And, not accepting it, was it not precisely a poet that I would remain?

XLII

In the following days, with that bundle of papers all covered in writing in my pocket I felt detached from everything, scornful of things. Nobody knew of the existence of those poems; probably nobody even noticed my detachment which was not evident on the outside, at least not in the way I behaved towards my mother and father at home and towards Luís. Perhaps it seemed to them that I had finally got back into my usual calm routine, and Luís, too, as he made a point of showing. As far as he was concerned this was undoubtedly a consequence of the approach of the date of his departure, now only days away; to the feverish excitement of starting a new life there was added the need to feel that he was part of a family which, although it was something very recent and in a certain sense superficial, had an enormous attraction for him through the complete novelty of there not being family intimacy to make things more complicated. Therefore the awkwardness which he still had (and which, uncomfortably, I felt too) from his experience with me and which he would feel on my behalf was dissolved in the fictitious pleasure with which he gave himself over to the anticipated nostalgia for a home which had never been his.

The distance I felt was reflected too in what was happening politically: the outcry from the papers, all fired up with enthusiasm for the Government, the spate of words from hysterical radio reports, the weighty assessments of military strategy destined to save our Christian civilisation, which had my parents and any visiting aunts and uncles poring heatedly and minutely over the map of Spain, merely seemed to me some gratuitous, absurd commotion; it was just a means by which various people endeavoured to fill the quiet peace of their lives – they did not really want to know anything about what might be happening in the world beyond their own daily round – with far away dead and wounded. A corpse and a boat which, curiously, for I hadn't seen it, was the image which memory brought to mind rather than the body I had seen; I imagined the boat battling with the wild sea in an attempt to reach somewhere on the coast of Spain. But if, for the ones who were talking about all those things in my house, the unreal became a reality, made up of news and maps (having been previously a reality which was

perhaps very different from the twisted version which the papers
put about), as far as I was concerned the small events which I had,
directly or indirectly witnessed, and in which I had been an agent,
were more and more taking on the opposing character of a cold
imagination, wholly unreal, which I had no means of making
symbolically objective with flags of conquest on a piece of paper.
And in that daily routine from which I felt, in my superior fashion,
I was so distant, that very smile of irony which I could not help but
cast on what seemed to me an infantile vanity, helped to remove
the virulence from everything, above all from that which had
changed me, perhaps for ever.

It was in that mood that I greeted the day on which I would go
with Luís to see him on board, his luggage having gone there on
the previous evening. Lunch was a funereal affair, with my mother
in tears. Luís was – or appeared to be for her benefit – more
expansive, in a certain shy fashion, youthful and a little indecorous,
attentively high-spirited, as if in answer to some permanently
unsatisfied maternal impulses which, in that way, I had never
satisfied, nor even ever allowed to come close to me. Watching
them, and without envy or rancour, I had to laugh at it all enjoying
more than them the paradoxical pleasure which both derived from
their sorrows. It was as if I were the detached spectator of what
would be a painful nostalgia which my mother might feel for me
or I for my house: a feeling somewhat novel and which, in diverting
me, nevertheless projected onto another plane the sadness I felt at
Luís' departure for another life; I had no doubt he would never
wholly return from that life to the same kind of intimacy with me,
the intimacy of one who had discovered in me a kind of 'alter ego'.
Through him I had lately tasted a delight in the family which I had
never been aware of before. And the terrible, equivocal, proximity
which he had assumed in relation to me had revealed to me depths
of the human being which I had experienced in those days in
Figueira, glancingly or without warning, but without that
connection to my childish past which had happened when Luís had
momentarily and provisionally occupied a place in my domestic
affections which I had always left empty. This made me understand
the extent to which I had been living in a dream, without even
seeing – almost – that my parents had given me life and had kept
me and also how so far they had kept themselves in the background,
an invisible place from which my father had still not emerged, not
even with Luís around. And, in the car taking us to the Cais da

Fundição, to the Caminhos-de Ferro, where Luís' boat was waiting, I realised suddenly, with astonishment and a strange kind of sorrow, that I didn't really know my father.

I had grown up in peaceful circumstances, an only son, not that you would know it since my parents didn't make too great a fuss of me. They had been like some kind of machine, modestly efficient in that they provided everything I needed; one of the things they had certainly given me was their ability to be there, discreetly, so that, while I lacked nothing, I had not felt the lack of them either. My mother, of necessity closer to me, had always come across as rather superficial, a figure of fun, someone who did not ask to be taken too seriously as she went about her daily business. Within that daily life my father hardly showed his face; but since he was nonetheless there everyday the little that he stood for personally did not arouse in me the hunger for any greater intimacy. I had become a man without them worrying about it and I had not felt any anxiety about being a man in their eyes. But this tepid water of my childhood and youth was in truth what had given me that fierce passion which had been unleashed within me: so great, so violent, so proud of itself that in the various guises it assumed it centred on itself to the selfish exclusion of everything else. Was it really selfish? If it were, would I concern myself so much with the others who were mixed up in my life? Or was it just that freedom which I had had to be myself, without even thinking about it, without having to struggle for it, which had amassed such a tremendous frenzy of love and friendship as that which, I now saw, I felt?

I shot a sideways glance at Luís, sitting next to me; he sensed my gaze upon him and returned it. The excitement of starting the trip, however, shone in his eyes, to the exclusion of anything else. They were bright but uncommunicative and he had a kind of juvenile vanity, glorying in his great event.

'Three months from now I'll be back,' he said.

'The three months will fly by.'

He didn't reply until we reached the quayside. 'Three months'll fly by, sure enough,' he said. 'The worst thing is not knowing what we'll find when we get back.'

We got out of the taxi and I paid (it was curious how Luís always let me pay, as if he were my son). 'Well, much the same as before,' I replied.

He stood without moving on the edge of the pavement, by the gate; he didn't go onto the quay.

'Come on,' I said, 'it's time.'

'What if I don't go?'

'Don't be daft. You can't not go now.'

'I don't know. I don't think I want to go.'

'Of course you're going. You should have thought of this earlier. Let's be off.'

'It looks like you want to be rid of me.'

I looked at him and he lowered his gaze. 'Me? I didn't have a thing to do with any of this.'

'No, you didn't. But you didn't do anything either to make me stay.'

'Don't be a fool. What the devil do you want me to do?'

'I don't know'

'Well then, if you don't know, don't talk rubbish. Let's go.'

'I want you to say goodbye to me here.'

That was when I realised that I felt a great sadness at his going and that I hadn't noticed any of the people and cars and luggage all mixed up around us, among which we were lost.

I held out my hand to him. '*Bon voyage*, Luís, and all the best. See you when you get back.'

He gripped my hand and then embraced me, in tears.

I clapped him on the shoulder. 'What's all this?' I asked. 'You're not going to be deported to the ends of the earth; you'll be back again in three months, so what's all this about?' And I pushed him away gently.

He wiped his eyes swiftly, looking around to check whether anybody had seen him. Everybody was caught up in the rush to get on board and they only paid any attention to us in so far as we were two fellows blocking their way; the cases barging against us were proof enough of that. Embarrassed, Luís paused for a moment before me, motionless; then he was carried away on the wave of bearers and passengers which swept him up and on through the gate. His arm rose fleetingly above the crowd to wave goodbye.

I went off along the street in the naked clarity which, in its white emptiness, contrasted sharply with the commotion around the gate to the quay. My feelings were mixed: great relief at Luís' departure, though somewhat disgusted with myself for feeling that way; and a bitter grief, too, which made me think that all the people to whom I was not at bottom indifferent, or who were not indifferent to me, were exactly those who passed through me so intensely before vanishing in some anonymous convulsion. Was it, as he had said, that I had done nothing to keep them, or was what I had done precisely what would not keep them, in themselves or because it was pitifully inadequate under the circumstances? Which people were they and what were they like, those whom we hung onto: those who wanted us, or those we wanted? And didn't it seem that the ones who ran away were precisely the ones we didn't want to lose, or those who paradoxically disturbed us by their very presence? Mercedes – I had lost her (and the sound of her name in my head made me shudder); Luís who was like a brother and a son – it was as if he had already gone. She, whom I had desired with an anguish which was more than just physical, I would not bring myself to see her nor have her again. He, whom I was deeply fond of, I had seen disappear with relief. At bottom what I wanted was to return to a state of innocence which both of them had robbed me of, and although I felt that such a return was impossible, to find myself in the soothing complacency of myself and of a life like everybody else's (like that which, apparently, everybody lives until we find out that one, or another, and another, do not …), even though I would carry with me the disquieting conviction that no other woman could be any more to me than a distant memory of what I had lost, and that no friend could ever touch me without my suspecting even his unconscious intentions.

Perhaps time was little by little wiping all this out, and I might come to smile as I remembered the past, or even be fortunate enough to forget it. Dreams or nightmares or interminable circles of hell which had one after the other had shown me the roots of life – might I forget them, would I once at least regain the unconsciousness which I had until that tragic involvement, in which circumstances had given me and taken from me the love of my life, and had led me to be the agent of the destruction and death of people who did not mean much to me or with whose purposes I was not directly involved? Had I not launched Rodrigues into an awareness of betrayal (which would launch him into all the filthy adventures to which he had given himself over merely in the spirit of youthful rebellion)? And to what extent was I responsible for the death of José Ramos, or for Carlos Macedo of whose whereabouts I had not the least idea? Hadn't Almeida showed me, too, just how much he depended on me?

I halted in the street, a little horrified by the fact that I had managed to think about all of them without a feeling of terror. Were they already consigned to the past, from the moment that Luís had crossed the gate to the quay? Or was it the case that, on the contrary, and unlike what had happened throughout these days since my return to Lisbon, they were now fixed permanently in my consciousness? A furious sense of unease brought back that vision I had seen on the beach, my imagined possession of Mercedes. But at the same time as I felt keenly the frustration of that virtual possession (which hadn't been the case before) and a kind of shame at that juvenile gesture which I – being now a man had let slip, it was as if what had happened on the beach had released me, had reduced Mercedes and my passion for her to the level of some adolescent desire which I had satisfied in the customary solitary fashion. The odd thing was, though, that I once again felt a terrible hunger for her, to which my hand, moving around in my trouser pocket, had already responded. I checked to see if I had enough money in my wallet and I hailed a taxi to take me to one of the houses I knew. Being the beginning of the evening there were no customers around and the ante-room was empty. The madam called three women and I went up the narrow stairs with one of them to the rooms above. We both undressed and I embraced her furiously on the bed, covering her with kisses and winding my legs round hers. She panted dutifully, urging me on professionally, whispering her feigned satisfaction at such a display of desire. It wasn't too long though before I realised that in spite of my intense, anguished desire my cock was limp. And how: it was as if I felt some cold lump there. There was no chance of the woman arousing it, nor could my own hands do the trick.

Worn out by our vain efforts, we lay stretched out on the bed, silent, side by side. The desire I had felt had not abated; it was still there somewhere in me, wrapped up in some sort of indifference which did not even allow me to feel clearly the shame of my failure.

She stroked my breast. 'You're married, aren't you?'

'Why?'

'Because this sometimes happens with married men. They come here to see the girls for a change but they can't get it up.'

'No, I'm not married.'

'Well, you must have something else on your mind.'

'No, not that either.'

'You have, I can feel it. We've learnt to know when there's something worrying a chap. Has your woman been putting it about a bit?'

'I've already told you I'm not married.'

There was a long silence.

'Don't I know you?' she said. 'I've seen you here before but you've never come up with me.'

There was a kind of gentle, dutiful sadness in her voice: I had never chosen her and now that I had chosen her I couldn't manage it with her. Truly I couldn't remember seeing her before.

I turned towards her touching her sex with my hand. 'There's always a first time.'

She sat on top of me, facing away from me and began to rub my cock against her sex and her backside. In vain. I sat up on the edge of the bed, ready to leave.

'Do you want me to call another girl?' she asked.

'No.'

'You won't have to pay; I'll see to it.'

'No, I don't want to.'

'We'll do it together for it and then you can...'

'No.'

'What if I call the lad to suck me off, would you like that?'

'The lad?'

'Yes, we have a young fellow here. You're the customer; I'll call him. And the way he goes at it, it's a sight to see.' There was a strained silence; her eyes gleamed. 'He won't mind if you want his arse,' she added.

'Who the hell do you think I am?'

'I don't know, who cares who you are; you're just a punter who can't get it up with me.'

'Haven't you ever had that before?'

'God, loads of them,' and she rubbed herself against me. 'It's just that none of them were as handsome as you... I don't want you to go before...'

'I'll pay anyway.'

'How do you think I'd feel being paid for something I haven't done?'

I almost burst out laughing at her professional concern. 'I'll just pay for wasting your time, it's all right,' was all I said though.

'It's all right?' she demanded. 'I'm not a taxi, I don't live on a meter. I live off this...' she said, opening the lips of her vagina with her hands.

As I began to get dressed she came and got hold of me. 'Don't go away all fed up like this; come back to bed with me.'

I let myself be dragged to the bed where she took off my shirt and the underpants I had already put on. Once again we rolled around on the bed but now it was me and not my cock which stiffened slightly, for I felt not the slightest desire. I wanted nothing more than to go, to be done with it all. She, in a pretended mixture of rage and tenderness (or perhaps it was no longer pretended), hissed through her teeth all kinds of filthy words, obscenities, sweet nothings. The anguish I felt at listening to her, the touch of her body on mine, was unbearable though.

'No, I don't want this,' I said and struggled out of her embrace and began again to get dressed.

On the edge of the bed she sat dumbfounded, not moving a muscle. I held out the money to her. 'Now when you get a hard-on,' she said, 'you can go and have a wank at home.'

I went out to the street, and on down the Rua do Alecrim to the Cais do Sodré. I sat down in one of the cafés with tables round the door, and I had such a feeling of serenity that I was not even troubled by the thought of what had just happened or indeed about anything, whatever it might be. Two shoeblacks, carrying their little boxes and bench, started to squabble over my shoes, each one maintaining that I had called him over first. I hadn't called either of them and well they knew it. Smiling, I told them as much and suggested they settle the matter between them or they would each get a kick on the head. One of them looked at me askance, hitched up his trousers, snatched up his box and made off. Without saying a word the other sat down in front of me, put my foot on the box and set about polishing my shoe assiduously, his tongue between his teeth, while from time to time looking up at me blankly, like a dog which scratches itself while gazing at us. One time he stopped rubbing and burst out laughing, gesturing at me with his chin.

'What is it?'

'It's all in full view, sir...'

It was quite true; I had forgotten to do up my trousers. I put down my foot and laughing silently, buttoned myself up discreetly. When I had finished and replaced my foot the boy started vigorously to buff up my shoe, only pausing to spit on his rag.

At the very moment that he finished one shoe and I was putting my other foot on the box a prow began to emerge from some nook of the river between the last corner at the water's edge and the statue, and a grey hull glided by in those few moments, with the prow appearing beyond the statue. I stood up to see it more clearly. The lad was none too pleased and turned round on his little bench. 'What are you looking at then?' he demanded.

'That ship.'

'Well, there's an awful lot of them come past here.'

'But I'm looking at that one.'

The lad got up and stood by my side looking too. 'You got family on her?'

'No.'

'I'll tell you, if I was here just watching the boats go by I'd starve.'

The ship had just passed by the statue and was disappearing. I sat down and the boy began to polish my other shoe, upon which the waiter came towards us looking disapproving.

'You lot, you idlers,' he said, 'you know very well you can't polish shoes here. The café has its own chap to do this.'

The lad retorted that he had almost finished, that it was I who had called him over (while his eyes implored me not to gainsay him). The waiter went off again, uttering threats that he'd better not tarry there again.

'See how it is, sir? I pay for a licence, I pay my boss, I pay the rascal who controls this square, the police don't let me stop anywhere when there's nobody around and now this bastard comes along pushing me around just because the other chap that works here gives half of what he earns to the owner. Have you ever known anything like it, tell me, have you ever?' he said, looking up at me with his thin face and his lank hair shaking with indignation.

I agreed with him and said that I felt sorry for him.

'I'm sorry, sir, I don't know what you must think of me,' he muttered, looking around him. 'But this can't go on like this, can it? We've all got a right to work, haven't we?'

'Of course.'

He looked at me doubtfully, and then his features broke into a smile. 'You're one of the smart ones, aren't you, sir; I bet you've got a job, eh?'

I smiled at him so that, in the moment's solidarity which he thought he'd found, I didn't have to disappoint him – and shame myself – with a no. He took my smile for a yes and redoubled his attack on my shoe. Finally he looked at his reflection in my shoe and concluded that one was rather less shiny than the other one (on which he'd worked before discovering our mutual solidarity).

'Give me the other one again and I'll just buff it up a bit more.'

He got up when he'd finished, accepting the money I gave him. 'I bet you don't have your shoes polished like that too often,' he said, his box in his hand. He lingered alongside the tables in defiance of the waiter who had returned to shoo him off the premises; he hurled insults at the waiter and moved off slowly and pointedly, secure in the knowledge that the waiter wouldn't risk a scene or damage the dignity of the place by chasing him.

I paid and crossed the square to get a tram at the Corpo Santo. I hopped on board the first one which came past; it was chock-a-block. Little by little I worked my way onto the platform, squeezing between the end of the tram and crush of people in front of me. There was a fat, perfumed backside pressed against me; it belonged to a blonde lady whose face I couldn't see. At every jerk of the tram her buttocks rubbed against me urgently; then there was a hand reaching round and pressing against my trousers. Curling round and stretching out, it started imperceptibly to work on my cock which, damn it, began to respond to the touch. Two fingers slipped into my flies and undid a couple of buttons, enough to reach inside and try to get inside my underpants. The opening wasn't big enough so the fingers retreated and undid another couple of buttons and then returned, the whole hand, to grasp my cock and caress it smoothly from the head to the softness of the shaft. And then the fingers began to move rhythmically up and down. That was enough; with an effort I stuck my hand in my pocket and got hold of my cock, stopping the movement. The fingers struggled with mine through my pocket and when they did not prevail the woman started to create a fuss, wailing that she had been terribly offended, trying to attract attention.

'You impertinent creature ... you wretch ... abusing a lady ... who on earth do you think I am ... let me pass ... let me get out of here.'

The crowd on the platform, unable to budge, could only turn their furious, shocked gaze on me. How the devil was I going to get out of that one? There were already voices in support of the woman and people craned their necks to see through the crush, sensing a scandal. The conductor pushed his way through as far as the door.

'What's going on?' he demanded.

'This man...' stuttered the woman, 'this man ... swine ... shameless creature...'

The tram halted, the tumult overflowed onto the street and I took advantage of the situation to button myself up partially. A policeman mounted the platform and made his way towards the middle of the group which encircled the conductor, the woman and me. How was I going to get away from there? One lady offered to go with the woman to the police station, for that was where they should go. At that a tall badly dressed boy made his way through as well.

'To hell with the police station!' he said. 'I know this woman, she's made this kind of scene time and time again when someone doesn't let her get away with it ... she tried it on with me once. And I'd swear that there are other chaps on this tram she's done the same to. If this gentleman has to go to the police station I'm going too.'

There was laughter from several quarters. 'Ah, so that's it then; the woman's been rubbing herself...' said one of them.

The policeman tried to restore some sort of order. 'Now then we'll sort all this out down at the station.'

The tall boy seized the woman's arm. 'Come on, then, to the police station and I'll tell them about the time I let you finish me off and nothing happened except I came; and then the other time when I didn't let her she burst out shrieking and making a scene.'

The woman was weeping, begging the policeman to take her away from these wretches who were in cahoots against her. Things, though, had calmed down somewhat by now and the lady who had gone to her aid had crept discreetly back onto the tram. A well-dressed gentleman leant out from a window of the tram.

'If the ladies here will excuse me,' he said, 'I can testify that this woman is quite used to behaving in exactly the way that this young fellow has described. I always wanted to see whether she would swear that I was just like him and the other chap she's accusing.'

'Off to the station, then,' cried the policeman, 'off to the station.'

But the woman did not want to go, saying she felt ill, that, who knows, she might have been mistaken, it was all a mistake, and she leant against the brake wheel.

'That settled her hash, didn't it?' said the boy who had spoken out for me. There was a ripple of laughter and even the policeman found it hard to keep a straight face. From within the tram there came cries: 'That's enough of this, let's get a move on.' There was another tram stuck behind us and people were getting down, curious to see what had happened. The woman, weeping and sighing, implored the policeman to let her go home, she lived close by and could go on foot. The conductor got on again and the passengers, too, and she got on the one behind. Neither the boy nor me got on again and the policeman stood in the street next to us. 'I catch queers doing this sort of thing, but a woman...' he said.

'That's true enough,' said the boy, 'but they don't complain if we don't let them...'

'Are you getting on or not?' shouted the conductor from the tram.

The policeman ran towards the front platform. We both looked at each other and laughed.

'Come and have a drink,' said the boy.

'It's me who owes you a drink,' I replied. 'If you hadn't...'

'True enough,' he said, 'there's a little place down there. But do you want me to tell you something? She never actually did to me what I said she did. But I already know her tricks, and she must have done it so many times, jerking fellows off or getting them hauled off to the station, that she doesn't know one from another. And besides, you see, she doesn't know what anybody looks like; only her hand knows your balls. So when I spoke she didn't know what to say. It's a lesson: if you want something and you haven't got it you end up paying for it, isn't that so? But she, the bitch, she's one of those, I bet even the cats in her house have their balls cut off.'

We went into the bar and bought each other some wine. Holding his glass in his hand he turned half towards the row of tables along the wall and half towards the landlord who was serving us. And, enjoying himself hugely, he recounted what had happened. The men and lads who filled the place laughed and began to tell other, similar, stories. The landlord, on hearing of our victory over the woman and relishing the policeman's discomfiture, served the next round free, including all those who were standing around with us at the bar. I left with the boy, saying that he should come and dine with us before going back to work that evening. In the street he bade me an effusive farewell.

'But,' he added, 'yet again the best thing is not to let her do anything, since I might not be on the tram next time.' He jabbed his finger into my chest. 'There are some geezers who'd give everything for a wank in a crowd.'

'I'm not one of those.'

'You mean so far, don't you? Your fly's still half unbuttoned,' he added and then at once put his hands in the air. 'OK, don't take it bad... Friends, uh? We've got to take advantage of anything we can get. Well, be seeing you,' and he set off quickly up the street.

I wandered slowly back home. Life was really doing its best to put me on the spot: there was no train of tragic or grotesque events so absurd, equivocal or pure, meaningless or incapable of any meaningful interpretation, which it had not inflicted on me or put in my way. It was as if one day, thanks to some innocent or gratuitous gesture (or one whose un-gratuitousness I hadn't suspected, or whose non-innocence I hadn't heeded), had irrevocably opened the gates to whatever was virtual, contingent or irrational. Or, on the other hand, in my heedless way, I had stumbled irretrievably into some super-reality which was reality, sure enough, but something barely suspected by anyone who had not lived through it. But really – who could be said to have lived through it? The one who proceeded calmly from one damned thing to the next, and from day to day, year by year, on to the end, without ever more than dimly understanding what was happening to him, or the one who threw himself into the maelstrom of events? Between these extremes there was no doubt that the verdict tended towards the latter. But was I one of those? Had I hurled myself into the maelstrom, or seen myself in the middle of it, barely able to understand what connection there was between the different events which seemed to comprise it? Suddenly everything in my life appeared to me to be stripped of sense and purpose, a gratuitous mix of the horrible and the grotesque, in which, uncertainly, some lights of love and friendship – odd, inconsistent, and misleading like will o' the wisps – had glimmered and flickered, as if I had been born to an awareness of life as an empty turbulence. Or not that exactly, but … yes … it was as if the life of others had suddenly assumed the air of a huge collective conspiracy whose deepest motives, whose unspoken reasons and whose essential logic I did not understand. Was that my fault or was there simply nothing to understand? Probably for both reasons, since both would be valid for everybody: it was just that some would be aware (either willingly enough, or bowing to the force of circumstance) and others had not been aware or had refused to be, or had been content with the explanation offered them. One thing was sure: I was completely alone, cut off utterly and lacking all contact with my conspirators in life. And the worst of it was that, feeling more what it seemed to me I should feel I was one of them.

What I had allowed myself to write would be proof that I was: while some acted I composed riddling messages. About what? Perhaps about the greatest secret: at the very moment that life had seemed to me most terrible, a network of fraught, catastrophic responsibilities which one could never predict, and from which one could never extricate oneself I was discovering that unpredictability was nothing but a sign that the greatest horror of responsibility lay in the fact that there was no such thing as responsibility. People existed just to delude themselves and others, too, to torture themselves and everybody else, to destroy themselves for love, for friendship or as a way of amusing themselves. All this comprised the colossal conspiracy, aimless, random except in its triumphant ability to survive not so much death as life itself.

When I got home my mother and father were finishing the dinner prepared for them by our cook, There was an odd somnolence in the air, or was it just my impression? One might say that the lights shone right through things and people, without illuminating them, like a halo vaguely around them, fluid colours of the rainbow, a misty far-offness. I wished them good evening; they said nothing in return, and I went and had a wash and sorted myself out. When I sat down at the table the same silence reigned and I, wrapped in the same train of thoughts with which I had walked home, wondered as I eyed my soup whether I was responsible for that silence which had accompanied me into the room or whether, on the contrary, it was already awaiting me, on account of some specific reason of which I was as yet unaware. But these doubts did not in truth bother me: within me there was an acceptance of everything, a bitter emptiness, an ironic enchantment. Truly, whatever happened or didn't happen, I would no longer be surprised. The blow might fall, I might suffer some awful shock, but surprise – no. Nothing could be unexpected as far as I was concerned: only that I would not know what was unexpected and what wasn't.

Without lifting his eyes from the peach which he was so carefully peeling so that the peel came off in one piece (he loved to show off the unbroken helix when he'd finished) my father addressed me.

'Did the boy get off then?'

'I think so,' I replied, helping myself to the stew which the maid held out to me.

'You think so? You only think so?' he said, paying particular attention to the last part of the delicate operation with the peach.

'I said goodbye to him at the gate to the quay; that's where he wanted to say goodbye and then later I saw the boat leave. So I suppose he was on board.'

'He would have flunked it if you hadn't gone with him,' commented my mother. 'A bad lot, shameless, bad companion,' she added after a pause. My father sent the fine ribbon of peel spinning and said nothing.

'It happens to all of us,' continued my mother. 'Some chap comes crashing into your house out of the blue.'

'It was your brother who recommended him, wasn't it?' said my father, now carving the peach into slices with his knife and fork as though it was not him who had spoken.

'No. He fetched up here first followed by my brother's recommendation.'

'It doesn't matter,' said my father, his fork in mid-air. 'I can't see much point in going on about it any more. He came, stayed here, got himself the job he wanted, went to sea and that's the end of it.'

'In three months he'll be here knocking on the door again.'

'He doesn't have anyone else in Lisbon.'

'So anyone who doesn't have a place in Lisbon can come and put themselves up in our house then?'

'If you feel sorry for the lad,' said my father, smiling, without looking at her, 'and you don't know whether you should feel sorry for him or not that's no reason why we should have to put up with it, least of all me.'

My mother seemed baffled; this always happened when she was confronted by one of his calmly ironic ripostes. Tears welled up in her eyes. 'How can you talk so coldly about these things? It gives me the willies. Some poor creature can just disappear and you don't even bat an eyelid.'

He finished eating his peach and the carefully arranged his knife and fork on the plate, pushing the peel to one side. 'In this world of ours thousands of people disappear every day, one way or another.'

It was my turn to feel a shiver down my spine. 'That's something different,' sniffed my mother. 'We don't know them; it doesn't make any difference to us.'

My father continued with his little game, playing with her feelings. 'And a voyage makes even less difference; and even less so when a voyage ... that is, when going on voyages is a way of life.'

'When you're in this mood nothing matters to you at all...' she said, wiping her eyes with the handkerchief she'd plucked from her sleeve.

He smacked her hand gently and affectionately and got up. I got up as well and went to my room. Switching on the light I realised that the changes which Luís had wrought in it had vanished. Everything was as it had been previously. I sat down on the edge of the bed; sorting out my room seemed the most attractive option of all. It gave me a light agony which, in contrast, made me realise just how terribly weary I was, though this was entirely a reaction to the day's events, even though I couldn't recall them clearly, or couldn't make the effort to recall them. Thus the pain and the weariness evened themselves out in a kind of precarious balance which, little by little, making my weariness pleasant, empty, void of intentions, reasons and causes. Words passed indistinctly, slowly, joining and unjoining, through my head. Leaning back on the bed I felt myself smile pleasurably, letting the words escape, dissolve uncertainly, returning in whispers like the rough motions and counter motions on the surface of some dark, silent waters which then become still and the oily surface is like a placid mirror.

XLIII

When I awoke a clear light was coming through the window; I had forgotten to close the shutters. It wasn't the light which woke me but the hubbub coming from within the house, commotion, the sound of voices throughout the whole house. It was still early, only eight o'clock. I felt rested, full of beans and my curiosity was aroused. What could it be? I got up; I had to see what it was. My mother was going up and down the corridor telling the maid to get down to the grocer's, no, right now, before it closed – if indeed it was open – and to bring back potatoes, salt cod, rice, and salt, not to forget the salt. The maid hurried off and then came back to add one more thing to her shopping, one more item on the list. My father merely said that we should keep calm, that he'd heard nothing, it might be just a rumour, we needed to know first of all what had happened. Which was my question. It was my mother who supplied the answer: the baker had brought the news that there had been a revolution. My father commented that if there had been, it hadn't happened yet, seeing that everything was so calm. The maid seemed terrified at the idea of a revolution, yet anxious to get out onto the street, ostensibly to get the groceries, to see what they were talking about.

'You mean to say you don't remember what a revolution is?' said my mother in response to my father's words. 'Don't you remember how everything was closed because of the attacks on the shops? That time it was days before we could buy anything.'

He replied that, 'Well, would you believe it, but this time, even with the shooting and everything else in the streets, the grocer had still sent his assistant out, poor chap, to find out whether we needed anything and to bring them round.'

'But what exactly did the baker say?'

'That there was a revolution last night.'

'Where?'

'Here in Lisbon. I was actually waiting for something like this to happen one day,' she added. 'They've already had enough of peace and quiet, that's what it is. Now it's going to be the same inferno as before.'

'We don't really know what's happened, though; everything's

quite calm, we haven't heard anything and it could be just a rumour. Or it's nothing serious,' said my father.

'Of course it's something serious! These things are always terribly serious. Nobody's leaving this house,' said my mother, staring at my father and me. 'I don't want to be stuck here, worried and on my own, without a man in the house, Heaven help me.'

'Are you crazy? You mean I won't be able to go to work?'

At the door the maid hesitated. 'Go on,' ordered my mother peremptorily, 'off you go to the grocer's, and on the way find out what's been going on.' The maid set off.

'I'd better phone the office to see what's happened, what's going on,' said my father.

The telephone in those days, in most houses was an imposing ornament which nobody used except in extreme emergencies. It only rang, it was only ever lifted off its hook, when something truly momentous was happening.

'That's it, phone, ask them,' agreed my mother, and we followed in procession behind him towards the object itself, at the end of the corridor, in the corner by the dining room, on a stand from which hung a white cloth which served to highlight the dignity and nobility of the little black monstrosity.

As my father spoke it was clear that everything was running normally at the office, notwithstanding the air of excitement which seemed to come from the telephone and which my father punctuated with nods of his head and various 'ahs'. Putting the receiver back on the hook my father waited a few moments, savouring our solemn expectancy. Then he began his summary of events.

'It seems that the navy has rebelled and that some ships have gone down the river and were sunk by guns from the forts. But that was all; the Government is in control of the situation and it's all over.'

'Well,' said my mother, 'that's what governments always say. The best thing is to wait until tomorrow and if there's no shooting in the meantime then it's true.'

'But there's just been some shooting,' I said unable to contain myself, 'and we heard nothing in the house.'

My mother was about to slap me down with a sharp retort when the maid returned overflowing with news.

'Oh, madam, in the grocer's, there was a crowd of people' ('You see?' said my mother triumphantly to my father) 'and they said there'd been a revolution and that it was over already but they didn't really know if it was or not because it could break out again and that some of the warships' ('Ships of war,' corrected my mother) 'let fly some shots and killed all the officers and then they were sunk because the Government ordered them to be and it was the forts who sank them and now we don't know anything else and it looks as if everything is quiet now. Madam, potatoes have gone up and salt cod and rice, too, and Sr Joaquim – the grocer – said there might not be enough and that's why they're more expensive.'

'It's just like it was before,' said my mother, 'once he smells a revolution that fellow puts up the price of everything. It's a bad sign.'

'I'm off to the office anyway,' said my father. 'I'm already late.'

'No, don't go; I don't want to be left here alone, not knowing what's going on.'

'The boy's here.'

'When did he ever stay at home? As soon as he's dressed he'll be off out the door and there's nobody to stop him.'

'Well, I'll see you soon. I'll phone later,' said my father, going out the door and leaving my mother on the landing crying out that he hadn't any sense or prudence and that he was leaving her in distress.

As soon as the door was shut my mother turned to me. 'Have you anything to do with this? Are you mixed up in all this?' The maid meanwhile stared at me in amazement.

'Me?' I exclaimed, laughing at such an absurd question; I felt that I could neither laugh nor answer her, and that it was as if I were involved in that thing, in it up to my neck. Beaches, people, snatches of conversation, a huge, powerful prow, all swirling around me, drowning, in a mist, slipping slowly by and leaving a trail of thin threads of blood which dissolved into the water.

My mother sent the maid off to the kitchen and dragged me off to the dining room, closing the door behind us.

'Heaven help us! I knew it in my heart of hearts. What now?'

'What now? What do you mean? You don't understand, mother: I'm not mixed up in *this*, not in any revolution. It's something else.'

'What other thing? I knew from the start that this idleness of yours would get you into trouble.'

'Don't go getting things all mixed up,' I said, though I felt that everything inside me was all mixed up, 'it's not a novel. I've already told you that I've nothing to do with any of this. And don't you think,' I added, in a moment of inspiration, 'if I had been I would have spent last night at home?'

Clearly this impressed her. 'I don't know ... maybe not... Do you swear you're not in any danger, knocking around with a bad crowd?'

'I swear it,' I said, at the same time wondering who was and who wasn't dangerous.

'Be careful, though; don't bring disgrace on yourself or on us.'

I went to the bathroom thinking of that philosophy of hers: 'don't disgrace yourself or us', as if to disgrace others, voluntarily or inadvertently, or through some unforeseen train of events, were merely secondary. I shuddered, recognising therein the worst kind of selfishness, without doubt: the selfishness of innocence, of ignorance, of conformism, the dreadful selfishness of those who prefer themselves and others to be innocent, ignorant, conformist, each one shut away, untroubled, left in peace, defending – which was worse than ferociously – with goodwill, honestly and even good-naturedly the inviolable frontiers of his first, second or even third floor, not to mention the silver and the children, against any sign of distress. Stretched out in the bath, surrendering to the intoxication of the hot, soapy water, I still didn't feel clean or rested; even floating half-submerged in the tub gave me a feeling of horror. But I refused to remember whatever it was, to make any connections between events and people. All of a sudden I got up – or it was an idea which made me get up: if the fort – one of the forts from which they had sunk the ships – had been on alert the previous evening it was because the Government had known what was going to happen – or, not knowing the extent of what was going to happen, was awaiting the outbreak of the revolution so as to be able to act then. Or it had known perfectly well how big it would be and had let it happen because they served its purposes even better. And the ships were sunk, people were killed, according to a cold calculation of political advantage. But was I innocent of such calculations myself? And had I even the excuse of a plan of action which, through idealism or through some shabby calculation, or even through obedience to those sordid interests which I might have been detailed to defend, might justify my actions? In the end, though, was justification the same as being on the side of justice and reason? But what justice and what reason would not serve to justify everything?

I put my pyjamas on again and went down for breakfast, where my mother was sitting at the table reading the paper with great concentration. I leant over her shoulder to read it, too.

'Sit down and eat something first; it's already late,' she said, put out that somebody should be reading the paper over her shoulder, unwilling to make allowances even under the present exceptional circumstances.

As I ate she read out to me bits of news from the paper; I disliked intensely this piecemeal way of hearing the news.

'Just read it,' I said, 'I'll read it later.'

But my mother ploughed on regardless: 'An uprising on board the "Afonso de Albuquerque" and the anti-torpedo boat the "Dão"... and what about this: several dozen commanders and sailors took control of the boats ... what kind of people are they?... Sailors, oh real scum ... ah! wait ... sailors, representing a small part of the crews of those boats, took control of the ships ... there weren't many of them, that's obvious ... they arrested the duty officers ... arresting officers, what dreadful lack of respect ... and attempted to sail out to join the Spanish Marxist squadron... Where did they think they were going?'

'To join the Spanish fleet, the one supporting the Government.'

'What Government, I don't call that a Government, you see what damage a bad example can do? Listen, wait... Heavy and accurate fire from the batteries of the Almada and the Alto do Duque rendered the rebels helpless... Serves them right, about time, too... Within a matter of minutes... It didn't last long, so that's why we couldn't hear anything ... forcing them to raise the white flag by which time the boats were already shipping water... Shipping water?' (Sinking, I explained) 'Apart from these two boats the whole fleet maintained its discipline absolutely. In the end it was just two boats. And they didn't kill the officers' (there was something in my mother's voice of an unconscious self-deception which caused her to skim the paper so hurriedly and carelessly). 'No, it doesn't say anything about them killing officers.'

'They could only kill two, one from each ship.'

'Don't be daft. Doesn't each boat have lots of officers?'

'Yes, but they stay at home. It's like in the barracks; and that's just what they say there, isn't it? "They arrested the duty officers"; in other words, they were the only ones there.'

'And ... they didn't kill the duty officers... But it doesn't say whether the ships were sunk ... there were only two of them because it says here that "of the twenty-one boats which were at anchor in the Tagus only two joined the revolt, captained by small committees". Here it is... "bringing the dead, the wounded and the captured ashore". See? Some were killed or wounded.'

'The sailors and their leaders.'

'Ah, wait ... the Government knew beforehand.' (I shuddered.) '"The Government, which was already aware of the insurgents' intentions, had taken the necessary steps to bring them back into line immediately." Look, and they're going to punish "those officers and sergeants who did not do everything in their power to control the uprising".'

'Why are they doing that?'

'Why? It's obvious that they have to be punished.'

'But if they weren't on board – given that only the duty officers were there – it's because they didn't know anything about it, nor the Government. Or the Government did and they didn't, and so why are they paying for something they didn't know about?'

'Don't ask me. But why are you trying to baffle me like this? Look, do you want to know something else. If you're the boss, you give the orders. The Government has its reasons. Oh, my God... It says here that there were some copies of the *Red Sailor* on the ship. How awful!'

'Why? Have you ever read it?'

'I don't need to; the name is sufficient. Sailors are drunks and murderers, full of all sorts of vice and now Reds as well. Where are you going?'

'I'm going to look at the ships.'

'You're not leaving this house. It's quite enough that your father has had to go out. Who ordered him to call his office? Obviously they were going to say at once there was nothing going on; those people wouldn't stop even for a revolution. But you don't have to do anything; your duty is to stay at home and make sure your mother is safe.'

'Safe from what?'

The argument went on and on, my mother arguing this and that, going round in circles, now at the door to the street, her arms flung wide, dramatically, while the maid followed along behind me, imploring me not to go out, because her mistress was so upset and why didn't I take any notice?

I stormed out of the room, slamming the door behind me; my mother immediately opened it, weeping and shouting imprecations after me, interspersed with dreadful warnings about the risk I was running; and from the landing her cries followed me down to the street. In the street I had nowhere else to go so I set off down to the Baixa.

I didn't feel any change at all in the people or things around me. Perhaps there was an air of something going on around us, some movement around the doors of the grocers' and other shops, people stopping in the street and opening their newspapers ostentatiously (to augment the atmosphere which they sensed or wanted to sense) and then looking to meet the gaze of other passers-by for the reassurance of some tacit agreement. But – and it might just have been my impression – others averted their gaze. It was as if two pairs of eyes looked up from the paper, or met to exchange some silent agreement or the start of a conversation and then retreated back to their usual wary reserve. Suddenly I felt that that solitude of mine, that of knowing what I knew and not knowing how much I knew, was no more than a particular example of that other, greater solitude which falls surreptitiously on everything and everybody, and to which everybody surreptitiously submits. It was not that people were the conspirators of a failed revolution, a rebellion, some 'wild scheme', as I'd heard people say when I was small, and feared lest they betray it with just a word or a gesture. Some of them, of course, were reading the paper with the same fearful pleasure and hope that order and discipline would be upheld as I had heard in my mother's voice. And, in any case, these same people felt that they were alone and cut off because they had accepted that order and discipline were things outside of them, maintained by others, in the name of a Government which had taken upon itself the task of defining them and believed in its own omniscience, even over any revolution which might break out and bring death and injury in its wake. And even as they egged each other on it would always be something terribly sad, as if driven by the need to make up for what they would never know they had lost or abandoned.